THE COLLECTED STORIES OF RAY BRADBURY

Volume 3: 1944–1945

# Dead Men Rise Up Never

## By
## RAY BRADBURY

They're in the choir
loft. . . .

"They say some of the first padres built it, but the land settled slowly and the little cathedral sank. On clear days you can see it lying there in the water, very quiet." Bradbury submitted this noir tale of unrequited love and gangland rivalries as "The Sea Cure," but his editors published it as "Dead Men Rise Up Never." Fourteen of the stories that Bradbury wrote during the volume 3 period were crime tales, and seven of them appeared in the detective pulps during 1944 and 1945. The uncredited title illustration is from the July 1945 issue of *Dime Mystery*; copyright 1945 by Popular Publications, Inc. Image from *Dime Mystery* courtesy of Steeger Properties, LLC. Copyright © 2016 Steeger Properties, LLC. All rights reserved.

# THE COLLECTED STORIES OF RAY BRADBURY

## A CRITICAL EDITION

## VOLUME 3: 1944–1945

Jonathan R. Eller, General Editor and Textual Editor

The Kent State University Press    Kent, Ohio

An Approved Edition
Committee on Scholarly Editions

© 2017 by The Kent State University Press, Kent, Ohio 44242
All rights reserved
Library of Congress Catalog Card Number 2010023893
ISBN 978-1-60635-302-8
Manufactured in the United States of America

V. 3 1944–1945.

LIBRARY OF CONGRESS CATALOGING-IN-PUBLICATION DATA
Bradbury, Ray, 1920–
  [Short stories. Selections]
  The collected stories of Ray Bradbury : a critical edition / volume editors, Jonathan R. Eller and William F. Touponce ; general editor, William F. Touponce.
     v.   cm.
A three-volume edition of Bradbury's stories, presented chronologically, 1938–1968.
Includes bibliographical references and index.
Contents: v. 1. 1938–1943
ISBN 978-1-60635-071-3 (v. 1 : hardcover : alk. paper) 1. Science fiction, American.
2. Fantasy fiction, American. 3. Horror tales, American. I. Eller, Jonathan R., 1952–
II. Touponce, William F. III. Title.
  PS3503.R167A6 2010
  813'.54—dc22
                    2010023893

21  20  19  18  17     5  4  3  2  1

To **Karl Zimmer Jr.,** and **Barbara Zimmer,** in memoriam,

who together made it possible to publish this series.

With gratitude for their part in recovering these glimpses

of the young writer who became Ray Bradbury.


To **Ray Bradbury,** in memoriam,

who created miracles of rare device,


and


**Michelle, Elizabeth,** and **Donn Albright,**

who preserved these miracles for generations to come.

THE COLLECTED STORIES OF RAY BRADBURY
A CRITICAL EDITION
*is edited by*

The Center for Ray Bradbury Studies

Institute for American Thought

Indiana University School of Liberal Arts (IUPUI)

Jonathan R. Eller, General Editor and Textual Editor

Robin L. Condon, Associate Editor

Joseph D. Kaposta, Associate Editor

Diana Dial Reynolds, Assistant Editor

Mattie Hensley, Editorial Associate

Austen Hurt, Editorial Associate

Jeffrey B. McCambridge, Editorial Associate

David E. Spiech, Production Editor


Consulting Editors:

Donn Albright, Pratt Institute

Phil Nichols, University of Wolverhampton (U.K.)

# CONTENTS

# ACKNOWLEDGMENTS

"I have been so busy humanizing the science fiction story the last few years that I have forgotten the stars, and that's a hell of a thing to forget." In this May 1950 comment to Arkham House publisher August Derleth, Ray Bradbury confessed his diminishing ability to keep up with the recent work of his friends and mentors in the science fiction field. But even when he didn't have time to read, Bradbury would always remember to acknowledge those who helped him achieve his dreams.

The Center for Ray Bradbury Studies endeavors to follow his example as we recognize those who have made it possible to document and recover the earliest stories of a rapidly maturing storyteller through successive volumes of *The Collected Stories of Ray Bradbury.* For volume 3, we continue to be indebted to the Indiana University School of Liberal Arts (IUPUI) for founding and sustaining the Bradbury Center within the Institute for American Thought. I'm grateful to School of Liberal Arts leaders like Dean William Blomquist and his successor, Dean Thomas Davis, for continuing the tradition of assigning research faculty and professional staff to the Institute's resident scholarly editions. Institute cofounder and Chancellor's Professor of History Marianne S. Wokeck (director of the Institute for American Thought since 2013) has provided wise counsel and strong encouragement during the preparation of *Collected Stories* volume 3. My thanks go as well to Professor Martin Coleman, general editor of the *Works of George Santayana,* for allowing two of his staff editors to support volume production.

David Spiech, a full-time textual and technical editor with the Santayana edition, continued as our production editor, providing valuable liaison support as the volume moved through the various stages of design and layout conducted by The Kent State University Press. I'm also grateful to Kristine Frost, associate editor of the Santayana edition, for supporting the very demanding pre-editing stages of proofreading required to ensure that our transcribed texts accurately reflect the early versions of Bradbury's stories chosen as copy-text for the present edition. Their long years of experience in scholarly editing endeavors fulfilled key needs in the early and late stages of volume production.

The editorial staff members directly assigned to the Center for Ray Bradbury Studies were simply indispensable to volume production. Associate editor Robin Condon, who is also the Bradbury Center's director of operations, contributed significant story content annotations for the tales published in this volume, as well as summaries of the unpublished Bradbury stories that form a largely unknown underlayment to the volume period. She also established fully articulated procedures for the research and preparation of the massive but very accessible editorial apparatus prepared for each volume of *The Collected Stories of Ray Bradbury*. Joseph D. Kaposta, who moved up from assistant to associate editor for this volume, established all aspects of transcription and stabilization of the story texts all the way through editorial emendation and submission to press; he also contributed in significant ways to the volume's annotations and the record of the stories from this period that Bradbury composed but never published.

I'm deeply indebted as well to Diana Dial Reynolds, originally the first transcription editor of the *Collected Stories* series, who came out of retirement to serve as assistant editor for this volume. She worked with our graduate editorial assistants to complete the extensive variant collation records for the Bradbury stories, and used that large database to create the initial draft lists for volume 3's intricate textual apparatus. Her work built on the tireless efforts of editorial associates Mattie Hensley and Jeffrey B. McCambridge, who worked long days and countless hours comparing all the published forms of the stories and recording thousands of variants in the historical collations. During his unprecedented two-year stint as a graduate fellow and intern with the Bradbury Center, Jeffrey also researched and prepared selected content annotations and reorganized the genre magazine collections (the author's own copies) that are so essential to preparing the original story texts for this volume. During the final stages of volume preparation, graduate interns Amy M. Demien and Adelea I. Willman provided bibliographical verifications. The talents of this extended editorial team made it possible for us to navigate the complex textual variants of Bradbury's creative history as we worked to recover and document his earliest intentions for the stories he composed during the final year of World War II.

We continue the series tradition of opening with a period illustration from the first publication of a story featured in the current volume. Robert Weinberg, vice president of Argosy Communications and a noted scholar of genre history, graciously granted permission to use the frontispiece image facing the title page. As always, I am deeply indebted to Will Underwood, former director of The Kent State University Press, for his vision and guidance in publishing the *Collected Stories of Ray Bradbury* critical edition series. His leadership, as well as the dedication and professionalism of Managing Editor Mary D. Young and Design and Production Manager Christine Brooks, have made it possible to bring a significant aspect of Ray Bradbury's legacy home to his midwestern roots.

Although they live oceans apart, two long-term Bradbury scholars deserve special recognition for volume 3 and for the entire *Collected Stories* series. Consulting editors Donn Albright (Pratt Institute) and Phil Nichols (University of Wolverhampton, U.K.) have advised on every stage of research. Phil has advised on our biographical references and is the primary source of information for Bradbury's media adaptations. Donn Albright's legacy is woven deeply into the life and career of Ray Bradbury; he has been the principal Bradbury bibliographer and archivist for nearly forty years, and his legendary collection of elusive magazine printings (including Canadian issues) provided the archival proofreading artifacts for many of the stories. His advice and guidance has helped to shape all aspects of the Center for Ray Bradbury Studies and its publications, as has the counsel of Professor Emeritus William F. Touponce, founding general editor of the *Collected Stories* series. I continue to be grateful for the advice of all three of these friends.

Publication of the *Collected Stories* series would not be possible without the vision and support of the late Karl Zimmer Jr., who passed away in 2014. Karl and his late wife Barbara Zimmer provided the permissions funding for the volume 1 stories. In subsequent years, Karl made it possible to extend the series into multiple volumes through a generous gift of long-term support. Karl played a pivotal role in the postwar expansion of American publishing overseas, but before embarking on those adventures he had been part of Ian Ballantine's original marketing staff during the 1953 Ballantine release of Ray Bradbury's now-classic title *Fahrenheit 451*. Karl and Barbara, a dedicated educator in her own right, maintained an abiding appreciation of Bradbury's vision and shared in our work with enthusiasm to the end of their remarkable lives—and beyond.

Ray Bradbury's 1950 acknowledgment of his friends and mentors came just as *The Martian Chronicles* began to establish his enduring reputation beyond the genre fields where he began. He never forgot his roots, and I hope that the Center for Ray Bradbury Studies will continue to acknowledge and honor those who initially seeded the *Collected Stories* concept. Ray Bradbury's decision to allow us to shine a light on his creative origins made the series possible, and I will always be grateful for his friendship and encouragement through the years. I continue to be indebted to his daughter Zana, who has supported this series as both her father's representative and as my friend. A special note of thanks goes as well to Bradbury estate trustee Marsha R. Lumetta of Los Angeles, and to Michael Congdon and Cristina Concepcion of Donn Congdon Associates in New York, who work tirelessly to maintain a standard for publication and recognition of Ray Bradbury's works in ways that preserve the Bradbury passion for reading in an increasingly technological age.

Jonathan R. Eller

Winter 2016

• • •

Reprinted by permission of Ray Bradbury Literary Works LLC

This compilation of stories is copyright 2017 by Ray Bradbury Literary Works, LLC

YESTERDAY I LIVED! © 1944 by Popular Publications, renewed 1971 by Ray Bradbury

IF PATHS MUST CROSS AGAIN © 2009 by Ray Bradbury

THE MIRACLES OF JAMIE © 1946 by *Charm Magazine,* renewed 1975 by Ray Bradbury

THE LONG WAY HOME © 1945 by Popular Publications, renewed 1973 by Ray Bradbury

FOUR-WAY FUNERAL © 1944 by Popular Publications

THE REINCARNATE © 2005 by Ray Bradbury

CHRYSALIS (story first published in *The Cat's Pajamas*) © 2004 by Ray Bradbury

THE POEMS © 1945 by *Weird Tales,* renewed 1972 by Ray Bradbury

DEFENSE MECH © 1945 by Love Romances, Inc.

HELL'S HALF HOUR © 1944 by Fictioneers, Inc., renewed 1972 by Ray Bradbury

I'M NOT SO DUMB! © 1944 by Popular Publications, renewed 1972 by Ray Bradbury

INVISIBLE BOY © 1945 by Street and Smith Publications, renewed 1972 by Ray Bradbury

YLLA © 1949, renewed 1977 by Ray Bradbury

THE TOMBSTONE © 1944 by *Weird Tales,* renewed 1972 by Ray Bradbury

THE WATCHERS © 1945 by Street and Smith Publications, renewed 1972 by Ray Bradbury

LORELEI OF THE RED MIST (with Leigh Brackett) © 1946 by Love Romances, Inc.

CORPSE CARNIVAL © 1945 by Popular Publications, renewed 1972 by Ray Bradbury

DEAD MEN RISE UP NEVER © 1945 by Popular Publications, renewed 1972 by Ray Bradbury

SKELETON © 1945 by *Weird Tales,* renewed 1972 by Ray Bradbury

AND SO DIED RIABOUCHINSKA © 1953 by Street and Smith Publications, renewed 1981 by Ray Bradbury

SKELETON © 1945 by *Script,* renewed 1972 by Ray Bradbury

THE BLACK FERRIS © 1948 by *Weird Tales,* renewed 1975 by Ray Bradbury

Professor Andrew Jewell of the University of Nebraska (Lincoln) vetted the texts and apparatus of this volume for the Modern Language Association's Approved Edition seal.

# INTRODUCTION
# THE TYRANNY OF WORDS
## Bradbury's Stories, 1944–1945

> Where's your next WEIRD yarn—and don't forget *horror,*
> not arty or child stuff.
> —Bradbury's agent, Julius Schwartz, October 12, 1944

By the spring of 1944, Ray Bradbury's rapidly rising reputation balanced on the threshold of a dream.

The dream itself was well formed in his conscious mind: a vision of achieving an enduring legacy as a master storyteller who had transcended genre boundaries. What he did not yet know was how close he was to the realization—or the denial—of this dream; the way forward was clouded by pulp publishers who measured his value at a penny a word, and editors who appreciated his talents but demanded adherence to genre rules and genre subjects with every submission. He could count on the friendship and counsel of Julius Schwartz, a pioneering pulp agent with easy access to all the genre magazine houses in New York City. But Schwartz also had to remind Bradbury of the realities of that market and constantly encouraged him to slant his writing toward formula plots and characters.

The pressure was enormous and ran counter to nearly every story idea that welled up from Bradbury's subconscious. He was beginning to realize that the quality stories he had so far produced were formed around the world he understood best—the focused emotional experiences of childhood, and the often traumatic challenges of carrying these experiences into the adult world. Schwartz was able to pitch such off-trail stories in ways that secured reluctant publication in *Weird Tales,* but in return he had to relay constant editorial impatience. Bradbury's rejoinders have not survived, but his stress surfaced in his late September 1944 letter to Arkham House founder August Derleth, who was already considering publication of a collection of Bradbury's horror tales: "*Weird* warns me not to write any more child fantasies, and this saddens me because I have ten or more of them finished or half-finished. And I hate to write about vampires, darn it."[1]

Bradbury was still a bit in awe of Derleth, whose reputation as a genre publisher, fiction writer and anthologist was at its peak, and the "gee whiz" tone of his letter buried the intense frustration he felt. He was living off a penny a word from *Weird Tales* and gained little satisfaction from the one and a quarter to one and a half cents a word he could expect through his more recent success with the detective pulps. But during 1944 he read a book that would provide the motivation to believe in himself—Ayn Rand's recent bestseller, *The Fountainhead*. More than sixty years later, he would remember the significance of this moment in a private interview: "It was the right age. I was twenty-four, and I needed to believe in my own character, to hold still in spite of people doubting me . . . So when I read *The Fountainhead,* it gave me courage to just stand and say to people, 'Go away and leave me alone.'"[2]

He was not interested in Rand's philosophy, but the character of Howard Roark, her iconoclastic architect who would go his own way no matter what the cost, became an abiding inspiration. *The Fountainhead* was also emblematic of the most significant year in his entire reading life. As he wrote on through 1944 and into 1945, Bradbury embarked on an intense and largely self-guided reading plan through contemporary literature. This adventure of the mind would begin to shape his approach to fiction writing and pave the way for his breakthrough into the major market magazines.

This single year of writing is representative of a full decade of creative development. Revised versions of the stories that Bradbury published during the 1940s eventually radiated out into the major collections and novelized story cycles that established his reputation at home and abroad during the 1950s and 1960s: *The Martian Chronicles, The Illustrated Man, The Golden Apples of the Sun, The October Country, Dandelion Wine, A Medicine for Melancholy, Something Wicked This Way Comes, The Machineries of Joy,* and *I Sing the Body Electric!* Still other tales were refashioned for nearly twenty story collections and novels that he assembled during the final four decades of his life.

His own inner world of creativity emerged through the various fictional masks he fashioned during the earliest years of his career: delusional gangsters, neurotics, hypochondriacs, wisecracking detectives, hypnotized spacemen, strange savants, backwoods witches, and peculiar children. The original versions of his 1940s stories recovered for *The Collected Stories of Ray Bradbury* series, presented in the order in which they were written and first sent off to find life in the magazine market, suggest that his masks didn't always appeal to his editors. The volume 3 stories were all written between March 1944 and March 1945, and the surviving letters of this period reveal the private conflict raging between Bradbury's efforts to define a distinct style and creative vision at home in Los Angeles and the tyranny of genre requirements more or less imposed by the distant pulp publishing world in New York.

Most of the twenty-two stories composed during this pivotal year in his development reflected the impact of these creative pressures. Five made it into the pages of *Weird Tales,* and seven appeared in the various detective magazines issued by Popular Publications, but only two of the weirds—heavily rewritten versions of "Skeleton" and "The Black Ferris"—found an enduring place in Bradbury's later collections and novels. He never thought of his detective stories as mature work at all; only the lack of copyright control forced Bradbury to allow the seven detective tales from this period to reach print again. Rewritten versions of "Riabouchinska" took more than eight years to reach print, and three long-deferred tales—"If Paths Must Cross Again," "The Reincarnate," and "Chrysalis," a condemnation of racism that was well ahead of its time—failed to sell at all; they remained unpublished until Bradbury placed them in twenty-first century collections and anthologies. His writing was still uneven at times, and there was always the temptation to go for effect over careful plotting; he could still count on some degree of genre writing advice, but his remaining weaknesses were aggravated by the lack of guidance or mentorship aimed at developing the kind of restraint and originality he would need for the leap into major market prominence.

Nevertheless, the volume 3 period also produced important markers in his maturing creativity. "Lorelei of the Red Mist," a *Planet Stories* novella in the interplanetary romance tradition that he took over when his friend and mentor Leigh Brackett stopped at mid-story to script *The Big Sleep* for Warner Brothers, demonstrated an ability to produce effective traditional genre work when the situation required it. And three of these 1944–45 stories—"The Miracles of Jamie" (1945), "Invisible Boy" (1946), and "Ylla" (1950)—were among the first wave of Bradbury tales to reach the mainstream markets. The early versions recovered for volume 3, some emerging from his surviving typescripts and several restoring lost text preserved only in the Canadian serial versions, provide an unprecedented snapshot of his writing and his inspirations during the final year of World War II. Underlying this year of creativity was the new world of reading that would prove to be a crucial factor in his development.

.  .  .

His paradigmatic leap in reading during 1944 and 1945 was nonetheless part of a lifetime continuum that had very little to do with formal education. From 1938 to 1942, when many of his Los Angeles High School classmates were entering college or trade schools, he sold newspapers at the corner of Olympic and Norton every weekday afternoon. Many evenings he attended films, professional ballet performances, and concerts, and for two years he ushered symphony nights at the Hollywood Bowl. He lived between two worlds, writing in a day office he kept in a tenement owned by the mother of his friend Grant Beach at the corner of Temple and Figueroa, and, after his downtown newspapers were sold, returning home in the evenings (by way of the Red Line streetcars) to Venice Beach to write in the garage of his parents' home on Venice Boulevard, a tiny house owned by his father's employer, the Bureau of Power and Light.[3]

He could retreat into these sanctuaries to explore what he would later call "the hidden theatre of the mind,"[4] escaping from the often demanding friendship of the hypochondriac Grant Beach during the day, and at night from the tiny four-room house and the bed he still shared, in his mid-twenties, with his older brother Skip. In the day office, he could observe the comings and goings of humanity in the crowded multi-ethnic neighborhood around the downtown Figueroa Street tenement. Through the window of his walled-off garage office at home, he could watch the glowing machinery and feel the vibrations of the adjacent power substation, where the invisible power grid of the utility company fed his imagination as the voltages were stepped down to residential levels. And both day and night, he read to feed his almost instinctive love of literature.

It was a love not born of any formal education beyond high school. It had begun in the mid-1920s, with the Edgar Alan Poe tales and the L. Frank Baum Oz novels that his aunt Neva, almost young enough to be a sister, read to him in his boyhood home of Waukegan, Illinois. During high school in Los Angeles, he benefitted from the guidance of his fiction teacher, an accomplished Stanford graduate named Jennet Johnson. His reading life accelerated in the fall of 1937, during his senior year, when he joined the Los Angeles chapter of the Science Fiction League, a fan-based correspondence network founded by *Wonder Stories* publisher Hugo Gernsback. As the national infrastructure faded away, this chapter continued to attract fans and local professional writers after 1939 as the L. A. Science Fantasy Society. He drifted away from regular attendance during the mid-war years, but the early connections made there would have a lasting impact on his nascent creativity.

From the beginning of his LASFL days, his naïve but intense desire to become a writer was rewarded when such professionals as Henry Kuttner, Leigh Brackett, and Robert A. Heinlein critiqued his stories and recommended readings. This group of advisers expanded from time to time to include older professionals like Ross Rocklynne and the long-established genre writers Jack Williamson and Edmond Hamilton. Bradbury's occasional hijinks and loudness were usually forgiven, and as he matured he supplemented his usual public library fare and bookstore browsing by tracking down or borrowing the books his mentors recommended.

Prior to 1944, the most significant reading recommendations came from Leigh Brackett and Henry Kuttner.[5] Both were versatile writers who easily navigated the pulp genre boundaries with their science fiction and fantasy tales. Kuttner was also popular in horror, and Brackett had broken into crime fiction. Bradbury was always surprised that Kuttner, a quiet man with a fascination for pseudonyms that masked public recognition of his full talents, bothered with him at all. Nevertheless, Kuttner led him to the short stories of Eudora Welty, Katherine Anne Porter, William Faulkner, and Willa Cather, as well as Sherwood Anderson's novelized story cycle *Winesburg, Ohio*. In genre work, Kuttner recommended the often humorous "who-done-its" of Thorne Smith and the dark fantasy tales of John Collier. Most of these recommendations were intended as short-fiction models and inspirations for Bradbury, but Kuttner also persuaded him to read the crime novels of Dashiell Hammett and James M. Cain.

Brackett extended Bradbury's reach into noir fiction and its sources, including the novels of Raymond Chandler. The protagonists of Hammett, but more so Cain and Chandler, held Bradbury's interest and complemented his earlier readings about neuroses by Sigmund Freud and Karen Horney. Brackett also lent him her copy of the police "primer" *New Horizons in Criminology* by Barnes and Teeters. She was interested in the same issues in semantics that attracted other science fiction writers of the time, and recommended S. I. Hayakawa's *Language in Action* as well as *The Tyranny of Words,* an earlier study by Stuart Chase. That Bradbury followed Brackett, Heinlein, and others into these readings (and into the General Semantics of Alfred Korzybski) is evident from the ways that he brought semantics into four of the stories that he wrote between January and June 1943, most extensively in "Referent" (volume 2, selection 7).

These core readings in semantics focused on the need for more precise linguistic structures if science and technology were to lead us to the stars; the ideas were interesting to explore, but idea generation was already one of Bradbury's core strengths as a writer; what he needed was more discipline in *shaping* his stories. *The Tyranny of Words,* in which Stuart Chase explored the limitations of traditional metaphors in conveying abstract ideas for an increasingly technological age, provided an ironic metaphor for Bradbury's real-world dilemma: how to refine his ability to explore universal truths and compelling emotional situations under the word-by-word tyranny of genre conventions.

To be sure, his mentors were showing him how to find an accommodation with the various genre magazine editors without betraying too much of his talent. He could visit Ross Rocklynne or Jack Williamson and listen as they critiqued his story drafts. Many Sundays during the war, he would trade and discuss works-in-progress with Leigh Brackett on Santa Monica Beach. By 1944, however, the war and various job opportunities had depleted his network of mentors. Kuttner had entered the Army in early 1942 and was assigned to Medical Corps duties in New Jersey. That same year Jack Williamson left for duty with the Army Air Corps weather service. Edmond Hamilton, too old for the draft, was back East during most of the war. In 1944 Ross Rocklynne began a four-year assignment as a story analyst for Warner Brothers, and by the summer of 1944 Leigh Brackett was scripting *The Vampire's Ghost* for Republic pictures.

On one level, Bradbury was worried that he might simply peak in the pulps, at best becoming the kind of major influence that Brackett, Hamilton, the versatile husband-wife team of Kuttner and C. L. Moore, and Jack Williamson would share as a legacy across several of the Golden Age genres. In 1944 he even consulted the prominent Los Angeles psychiatrist J. M. Nielson about his anxieties before he realized, during his only consult with Nielson, that time had been the key for most mainstream authors. Almost immediately, he became proactive in the only way he knew: to launch his own reading plan from the momentum provided by his mentors in earlier years.

He had been a systematic reader before, when he explored the sensate world in ways that brought a compelling sense of texture to his works. In earlier years he had devoured "Books on the olfactory sense, books on the construction of the eye and the phenomena of seeing, books on the ear, books on the tactile sense," he recalled in a late-life private interview. "So I educated myself to all of my senses, and that's one of the reasons why my books are memorable, because I make you reach out with your hand, and with your nose, and with your ears, and with your eye, and with your tongue."[6] He now began to plan a much broader education through reading, and it would begin with a systematic survey of contemporary writers.

During the summer of 1944 he extended his earlier reading of John Steinbeck and Thomas Wolfe, authors he had grown to love during his final years of high school. He read new collections by Eudora Welty and Katherine Anne Porter, the latest novels of James M. Cain, and began an extensive reading of Hemingway's short fiction. He had long been a reader of Aldous Huxley and now read his essays as well as the novels that Huxley had written since becoming one of Britain's many Hollywood expatriates. Oddly, a minor work of Huxley's would have a transformative impact on the *way* that Bradbury read and contemplated art.

*The Art of Seeing* emerged from Huxley's quest to moderate the chronic inflammation of the cornea that had severely impaired his sight since his teenage years. In this book he gave testament to the greatly debated Bates method of eye exercises, which involved a form of self-hypnosis designed to address both the physical impairment and the state of mind that Bates believed to be inextricably linked to vision. Bradbury had an abiding fear that the near-sightedness he had lived with since grade school, initially misdiagnosed as leading to blindness, would end his writing career almost before it began. Intellectually he knew that his myopia would always be correctable, but the gradual increase in his near-sightedness—a common progression for myopics—kept that nightmare at play in his overactive imagination. By the summer of 1944 this fear, and his natural susceptibility to the power of suggestion, resulted in a successful screening with Huxley's own Bates consultant and a year of counseling with a Bates practitioner.

The Bates method was never accepted for general clinical practice, but Bradbury always maintained that his nearsightedness stabilized from that point on. Yet there's no doubt that his exercises became a sheltered environment for his new reading regimen. The regimen (at least as adapted by Bradbury) included hours of sunning on the nearby Venice Beach and further relaxation contemplating—and creating—art. In his surviving letters to Kuttner and August Derleth, we find Bradbury coming to appreciate the hallmarks of artists he had dismissed or merely glanced at before, including Matisse, Dali, Van Gogh, and Picasso. Most would find places, and even a degree of homage, in his later stories and poems. Bradbury's high school experience with ceramic art now resurfaced as a form of creative therapy directed at Grant Beach, who found some distraction from his hypochondria (and fear of premature death) through the ceramics studio that the two men built in Mrs. Beach's house, adjacent to the tenement on Figueroa Street. Here Bradbury crafted ceramic figurines that survive today in the Albright Collection, and transformed his love of cartooning and caricatures into a habit of painting that continued throughout much of his life.

As his discrimination in the visual arts matured, so too did his ability to discriminate between the works of his various reading passions. He was never really able to separate a work of literature from the author, and this of course put him at odds with the High Modernist objective of masking the author entirely. It also affected his reading of the more mainstream moderns; during the summer of 1944, his first pass through some of Hemingway's stories left him off balance, wondering how to penetrate the author's masks and make sense of the darker suggestions that lurked between the lines. By the end of the summer, though, he could tell Derleth that he had come to appreciate the understated Hemingway style; very soon "Ylla," his Martian tale of a marriage gone cold, would show this influence through the unspoken tensions that are discernible beneath the brief intervals of dialog. Within a year Bradbury would begin to experiment more extensively with this style in writing about the death and poverty he saw as he journeyed through Mexico.

It's not always clear if his other literary judgments were emerging directly from his reading, or from the comments dropped in letters from Derleth or Kuttner; for instance, he may have simply followed Derleth's lead by agreeing, in his next letter, that *The Wide Net*, Eudora Welty's second collection of stories, represented a decline from her promising first collection, *A Curtain of Green*. But he had worked his way through most of Steinbeck's novels on his own, from *To a God Unknown* through *The Grapes of Wrath*, and considered Steinbeck his favorite author of the interwar generation. Once again he tried to look through the text to glimpse the author, and could not escape the impression that Steinbeck's newer titles—*Cannery Row, The Moon Is Down,* and *The Pearl*—manifested the effects of a failed marriage and alcoholism. And there were other markers of his growing critical ability; in spite of his high regard for Huxley, he picked up on the plot flaws of his latest novel, *Time Must Have a Stop.* Bradbury still had his blind spots, however; his unconditional love for the emotional intensities of Thomas Wolfe remained high, and in October 1944 he purchased *The Face of the Nation,* a compilation of passages from the late author's works. He seemed to know that finding a consistently reasoned critical path through mainstream literature was still just beyond his grasp; as he remarked to August Derleth just a month earlier, "what a hell of a long way I've got to go yet."[7]

So far this broader reading plan rose on the foundation of earlier recommendations from his mentors. In his letters, Kuttner occasionally introduced him to works that struck a chord with Bradbury, including Charles Jackson's riveting and tightly focused treatment of alcoholism in *The Lost Weekend.* But as the summer of 1944 progressed, Bradbury began to leave the trail of his earlier reading behind; from there on, his most significant guide into contemporary fiction and criticism came through the annual prize anthologies and the *Saturday Review of Literature,* where he could read about the latest best-sellers as well as critically acclaimed books and stories that fell just outside the best-selling spotlight. In the *Review* and other literary magazines he could also follow the full-blown debates that raged concerning new writers as well as those whose works had become prominent during the the interwar decades.

His firsthand encounters with contemporary fiction came through Doubleday's annual *Best American Short Stories* volumes, edited by Martha Foley. His favorite selections from the 1944 *BASS* annual, noted in a letter to August Derleth, included Lionel Trilling, Jessamyn West, Edita Morris, and Dorothy Canfield. Foley's showcasing of contemporary women authors complemented Bradbury's foundational readings in their more established predecessors and solidified his long-lasting regard for their trials and triumphs. If he had a prejudice concerning mainstream literature, it would eventually stand against the celebration of dark realism and resignation that denied any life-affirming futures.[8] But that was a battle for later years; he found little of this in the *BASS* volumes or in the *O. Henry Prize Stories* annuals of 1944 and 1945. He could not know that he would place stories in both of these highly regarded venues within the next two years.[9]

Bradbury did, however, have reservations about some of the more prominent titles of the day. His growing anxiety about the postwar world led him to reject certain melodramas and historical novels as simply wrong for the times; in this way such best-sellers as *Mildred Pierce,* Kathleen Windsor's *Forever Amber,*

Lloyd C. Douglas's *The Robe,* and Franz Werfel's *Song of Bernadette,* all eventually destined for popular motion picture adaptations, were dismissed out of hand. Kuttner's expressed opinions on some of these titles may have influenced him, but it's more likely that Bradbury's enthusiastic reading of certain cultural studies and political tracts may have played into these rejections; he was greatly taken by Phillip Wylie's *Generation of Vipers,* a jeremiad against American isolationism and cultural complacencies that contributed to the rise of totalitarianism and a second round of world war. Along these lines, his 1944–45 reading included Lewis Mumford's *The Condition of Man* and Thomas Dewey's *The Case Against the New Deal,* titles that may also have influenced his critical judgment.

Back in the genre world, he retained his interest in fiction that explored isolation and the fear of otherness that reflected the nightmares just beneath the surface of everyday lives. Bradbury was fascinated by the noir of Cornell Woolrich, in which sudden unexpected events destroy the routine lives of everyday people. He further extended his reading plan to include Walter Van Tilburg Clark's western classic *The Oxbow Incident,* not as a gateway to the genre of the western, but because of its inversion of the genre's formula. Clark's novel was an authoritarian tragedy that had a universal significance for a war-torn world that transcended genre boundaries, and thereby reinforced Bradbury's instinctive desire to go his own way. These darker readings no doubt influenced his detective tales of the period, but he was more suited to respond in prose to the kind of light horror produced by John Collier. Kuttner had led him to Collier's *Fancies and Goodnights* collection a few years earlier, but during his summer 1944 blaze of reading, he discovered Collier's more wide-ranging collection, *A Touch of Nutmeg and Other Unlikely Stories.* Once again, Bradbury was learning from a writer who shook off conventions and reminded readers not to take literature (or themselves) too seriously.

Almost inevitably, his extended reading program came at the cost of an increased anxiety about genre influence; other than Collier and a few new talents, he would reduce his reading in the horror tradition where he had first found success. Bradbury did collect Derleth's recent horror genre anthologies, perhaps because he was scheduled to appear in a subsequent one. But he read little of such traditional influences as Arthur Machen, Algernon Blackwood, A. E. Coppard, or Robert W. Chambers. Among the more contemporary pulp practitioners of the genre, he narrowed his reading to Kuttner, Fritz Leiber, and Jack Williamson's occasional dark fantasies.

Given his broader reading of the science fiction and fantasy pulps, his break away from reading in those genres was even more extreme. He still read the work of his friends Brackett and Hamilton, as well as the blended and often pseudonymous work of the Kuttner-Moore marriage. He read Theodore Sturgeon and Nelson Bond but little else, even as he continued to collect broader runs of the magazines that his stories had appeared in. His dislike for William J. Delaney and what he later described as "the money men at the head of *Weird*" led him to stop reading *Weird Tales* altogether; he kept his 1930s collections of issues from the Farnsworth Wright days, but during the 1940s he only kept author's copies from the issues in which his work appeared. His growing anxiety of influence within the pulp genres, and his parallel explosion of reading through contemporary mainstream literature, fairly shouted out his desire to broaden his market and be free of what he perceived as genre tyranny.

He soon found, if he didn't know already, that a similar form of tyranny governed the major market slicks. Bradbury had no representation in the mainstream magazine market at all, and his occasional submissions to the slicks were based on his intuitive feeling that some of the stories he had already produced—tales such as "The Lake" and "The Man Upstairs"—had major market potential. Ironically, "The Man Upstairs," rejected by *Weird Tales* as another one of the child perspective stories, would eventually reach print in *Harper's*. But this and other slick successes remained beyond the horizon of 1944. That spring, he acted on an earlier recommendation from Kuttner to check out New York agent Ed Bodin and sent Bodin four stories he had just knocked out.[10]

The titles and dates are documented in Bradbury's surviving composition and submission log sheets; Bodin failed to sell any of them, but the two surviving stories of this group, "If Paths Must Cross Again" and "The Miracles of Jamie," were clearly intended for the mainstream magazines. It would take another year for Bradbury to sell "Jamie" to *Charm* on his own, but in the meantime—with Bodin out of the picture—Bradbury had hoped that one of the major market editors might take him under his wing; by July 1944 he settled on *Story* editor Whit Burnett, former husband of *BASS* editor Martha Foley, but soon found that Burnett had no time to advise a new author.[11] Acting without counsel, Bradbury would continue to submit his stories scattershot through the editorial offices of various mainstream magazines but would have no success for the better part of another year.

His reading program and his occasional submissions in the mainstream market went on beneath the surface of his ongoing "dramedy" within the pulp world. On the positive side, he still had the experienced support of Julius Schwartz, who continued to represent Bradbury in the pulp world even after becoming an editor within the All American comic subsidiaries in February 1944. An unexpected corporate merger would soon propel Schwartz into the larger world of DC Comics,[12] where he would be a mainstay for the next half century. But he probably knew the inner workings of the various pulp world magazine syndicates better than any other agent in New York and gave Bradbury every opportunity to succeed with his nontraditional submissions. Schwartz had no pretensions to represent Bradbury's work to the more lucrative slick magazines, and his continuing focus on the pulp market ensured that nothing would fall through the cracks. On the agency side, Schwartz did reduce his clientele to only a few authors as he also worked—often with established pulp authors like Edmond Hamilton, Otto Binder, and Alfred Bester—on storyboards for a wide range of established comic book series.

The comic book writers, including all the pulp crossover authors, were required to live within commuting distance of New York to ensure minimal turnaround time on storyboard revisions, leaving Bradbury out of consideration. Schwartz would have liked to bring him aboard—comic strip writing paid significantly more than pulp writing—but such a temptation would have diverted Bradbury's attention from writing fiction at a crucial time in his career. Instead, he focused on his weekly story submissions to Schwartz amidst a constantly changing tableau of magazine titles and publishing schedules.

The various pulp magazine syndicates sometimes offered an absurd reflection of a world at war. Paper shortages began with America's entry into World War II, forcing publishers to choose from a variety of undesirable options.[13] Many magazines reduced the page run for each issue or reduced the frequency of publication or both. Some publishers, in concert with their chief editors, made more draconian cuts, which weren't always based on literary merit. Popular Publications chief editor Alden Norton, who oversaw Popular's stable of five detective magazines as well as *Famous Fantastic Mysteries*, reluctantly suspended publication of *Flynn's Detective* so that his publishers could continue their love romance titles. Popular's prewar subsidiary, Fictioneers, Inc., was also hit hard. Norton had to suspend both of the subsidiary's titles, *Astonishing Stories* and *Super Science Stories;* the return of *Super Science* was delayed until 1949, and *Astonishing* never returned at all.

Norton's Fictioneers subsidiary represented a second-tier market, paying less than a penny a word for stories, but the war impacted top-line magazines as well. Over at Street & Smith, John Campbell began the war as editor of *Astounding*, leader among the science fiction pulps, and a significant fantasy and *Weird Tales* companion, *Unknown Worlds*. After October 1943 Campbell had suspended *Unknown*, and was never able to bring it back at all. Campbell was able to maintain monthly publication of *Astounding*, but many of the monthly pulps became bimonthlies or quarterlies.

The impact of these unexpected wartime changes was magnified by an unprecedented prewar expansion of titles that seemed, for a time, to favor new talent. Unfortunately, Bradbury broke in as a published pulp professional in November 1941—literally days before the attack on Pearl Harbor—and the contraction of the field had an unmistakable effect on his early successes. "The Emissary" would have been his first appearance in *Unknown*, which was beginning to eclipse *Weird Tales* as a top-tier outlet for dark fantasy tales, but the wartime suspension left him without the prestige or a publisher. His first two pulp sales had appeared in *Super Science Stories* and *Astonishing Stories,* but this market suddenly dried up when Norton had to close them both down. The effect continued on into the volume 3 story period. "No Phones, Private Coffin," published in the August 1944 issue of *Flynn's Detective* as "Yesterday I Lived," represented his breakthrough into one of the oldest and most popular magazines in the genre, but it would be *Flynn's* final issue. With the narrowing of the pulp field, Bradbury's refusal to write formula prose left him at even more of a disadvantage.

The three remaining Popular Publications detective magazines represented Bradbury's biggest market through most of 1944 and into 1945. Bradbury's focus on this market was strongly encouraged by Julius Schwartz, who was finally rewarded when the syndicate's editor-in-chief, Alden Norton, published the retitled "No Phones, Private Coffin" in the venerable but doomed *Flynn's Detective.* Even Henry Kuttner agreed that it was one of Bradbury's best-constructed noirs, meeting Schwartz's expressed challenge that Bradbury "plot a story with all the necessary trimmings for Norton." Eventually Norton accepted "Mr. Priory Meets Mr. Caldwell" for *New Detective,* retitling it "Hell's Half Hour."

Norton's associate Mike Tilden, who by this time was eager to purchase Bradbury submissions for both *Detective Tales* and the more horrific appetites of *Dime Mystery* readers, secured two Bradbury stories for the former: "'I'm Not So Dumb!'" and "The Very Bewildered Corpses" (published as "Four-Way Funeral"), a sequel to his hard-boiled detective parody "Enter—The Douser" ("Half-Pint Homicide"). But Tilden asked for a rewrite on "The Very Bewildered Corpses," and rejected "Long Live the Douser," Bradbury's third story in this series. "The Long Way Around," the gruesome "One Minus One," and the weakly plotted "The Sea Cure"—retitled by Tilden as "The Long Way Home," "Corpse Carnival," and "Dead Men Rise Up Never," respectively—were less substantial tales that slotted nicely into *Dime Mystery.* Nothing here reached the quality of Bradbury's tightly controlled Hollywood murder mystery "No Phones, Private Coffin." Kuttner would later bring him up short for "One Minus One," a Siamese twin circus murder caper published under a pseudonym: "Your *Dime Mystery* yarn under the name of D. R. Banat was a misprint for banal, as you should have realized. Let us have no more of this self-deception."

As usual, things were a bit more difficult over at *Weird Tales.* Lamont Buchanan was more likely to tolerate what Schwartz called Bradbury's "arty or child stuff" than editor-in-chief Dorothy McIlwraith, but even Monty balked at "The Reincarnate." He accepted "The Poems" but warned that this would be the last "arty" story they would take. Bradbury redeemed himself with the Lovecraftian horror of "The Watchers" but would always single it out as his most embarrassing lapse into slanting. The chilling and graphic "Skeleton" was a surprisingly easy sale (perhaps because he at least gave *Weird*'s editors a traditional horror title motif), but "The Black Ferris" would not be ready for submission for another two years.

Bradbury's focus on detective "yarns" and his continuous struggle to slip anything off-trail past his editors at *Weird Tales* left little time for science fiction throughout most of this period. He did manage to write "Defense Mech," an interesting study in hypnosis that fascinated Schwartz: a crewman on the first Martian expedition, terrified by the alien landscape and the vast distance from Earth, is hypnotized by the ship's doctor to believe he's still on Earth; he improbably translates an attack by hostile Martians into a football game, and saves the entire crew. The terror of Otherness would emerge again in some of Bradbury's finest Martian stories, but this outlandish first effort became another one of the apprentice tales that Schwartz would sell to *Planet Stories* sub-editor Wilbur Peacock during the war years.

"Defense Mech" had initially followed a parade of Bradbury submissions across the desk of *Astounding*'s John W. Campbell. He had never had much luck with Campbell, placing only one story ("Doodad," or "Everything Instead of Something") and two "Liars Tale" column pieces in early wartime issues of *Astounding*. Yet his continuing failure to land a second sale in this specialized hard science fiction magazine was, in some ways, a blessing; as Kuttner told him, more or less off the record, "One disadvantage of writing much for Campbell is that it's apt to spoil you for other markets; you specialize too much."[14]

During the late fall of 1944, Bradbury wrote few stories at all as he composed the second half of Leigh Brackett's *Planet Stories* novella "Red Sea of Venus," a gamble that paid off through his demonstrated ability to master a form of interplanetary romance that he would rarely write again. Bradbury enthusiast Wilbur Peacock had departed from *Planet*'s staff by the time Schwartz submitted it under Brackett's original commitment, but Malcolm Reiss's new sub-editor Chester Whitehorn quickly accepted it for a postwar issue of the backlogged quarterly as "Lorelei of the Red Mist," a title almost certainly supplied by Bradbury with the blessing of Brackett.

Other stories anchored in the volume 3 period would take years to fully form as circulating tales. "Riabouchinska," his first and most psychologically compelling step toward his so-called "marionette" stories, was more famous for its radio (CBS, *Suspense*, 1946) and television (CBS, *Alfred Hitchcock Presents*, 1956) adaptations than it would be as a 1953 crime digest story in *The Saint Detective Magazine;* Bradbury finally brought it into his 1964 story collection, *The Machineries of Joy.* He would have to wait to publish "The Reincarnate," "If Paths Must Cross Again," and "Chrysalis" on his own, when he turned back in the twenty-first century to rescue lost gems. There are only the faintest echoes of his work on "Ylla" and "The Black Ferris" from the 1944–1945 period, but

both of these tales would go on to anchor two of his most enduring books—
*The Martian Chronicles* and *Something Wicked This Way Comes*. A full history
of every story in this volume appears in the individual headnote essays of the
textual apparatus; the stories that remain unpublished from this period are
summarized in Appendix B.

    . . .

One by one, Bradbury's mentors conveyed a sense that his pulp career was
secure. Brackett knew he was up to the task of writing the second half of one of
her best-conceived planetary romances, and "Lorelei of the Red Mist" became
a model of seamless collaboration in the field. Her future husband, Edmond
Hamilton, offered Bradbury a similar vote of confidence on the final day of
1944: "You always did have the 'knack' of writing—I don't know just what to
call it, but a person either has it or doesn't, and you do. . . . But you've added to
the ability to pour it out, the ability to shape a story and make it flow smoothly
to a satisfying conclusion, and that's what you needed most, so you are all set
now."[15] These comments and opportunities meant the world to him, but as
1945 opened out, he had no idea if he had a future in the broader markets that
his mentors never sought for themselves.

Fortunately, his long-distance correspondence with Henry Kuttner remained
as an avenue to further development. Kuttner had received his discharge from
the army medical corps in July 1944 and was back to full-time writing with his
wife, "Kat," who had been doing double duty as both halves of the Kuttner-
Moore writing team. Kuttner wrote letters more often now, and on Christmas
day 1944 Bradbury offered an update that his reading plan had broadened out
into "a liberal education in politics, psychology and art." The discoveries that
he reported to Kuttner were still very elementary and scattered, but there was
a real excitement in his discovery of the literary and artistic transitions from
Romanticism to Realism, or his discovery of a new book on dramatic writing.
For his part, Kuttner just wanted Bradbury to cut through all the excitement
and focus on the essentials.

By early March 1945, Bradbury was beginning to think about polishing or
even rewriting the representative weird tales he was collecting for his Arkham
House collection. Over the next eighteen months, his commitment to moderat-
ing the more florid carnival elements of his new *Dark Carnival* collection would
be more than just a headache for August Derleth, who ended up spending more
on Bradbury's press corrections than he had on all of his previous Arkham House
books. But at this moment in the late winter of 1945, Bradbury's careful rewrites
also represented a first tentative step toward major market recognition. He asked
Kuttner about even broader options and received back an idea that moved one
step beyond the representative selections planned for *Dark Carnival*—why not

gather the weirds and murder mysteries told from a child's perspective? Kuttner had already intuited that these were the tales that Bradbury knew best and felt that the next big break might come through such stories.

Bradbury had indeed produced three child-centered tales destined for major market success—"The Man Upstairs," "The Miracles of Jamie," and "Invisible Boy." They were indeed well-plotted stories, told with restraint and centered on characters that emerged as real people rather than genre types. This was the manner in which Kuttner had always advised him to write. But Kuttner had not seen these stories, and Bradbury remained unaware that he was ready to cross the threshold of the major market dream. There was one key element lacking, and that involved style. Bradbury had not truly found his own style yet, and at times he still became excessively self-indulgent. "From Now On," one of his latest story submissions, suffered from just this sin, and through a series of circumstances it soon landed in Kuttner's hands.

John Campbell had reviewed (and declined) many of Bradbury's stories for *Astounding,* and once before Julius Schwartz had brought Kuttner in for advice. Kuttner was now living in nearby Hastings-on-Hudson, and Schwartz didn't hesitate to bring him in again. In March 1945 Schwartz sent Kuttner "From Now On" to see if this long new story could be salvaged from Campbell's initial rejection. Kuttner's response was swift and harsh, for he knew that Bradbury was better than this story indicated.

"From Now On" was a story about a close brush with a comet that renders everyone on Earth invisible; the family at the center of the story, everyone they interact with, and by extension everyone in the world, must come to grips with this traumatic change, both practically and psychologically. As even Campbell noted, there were good elements in the story. Old prejudices disappear; people are no longer judged by their appearance. "From Now On" touches on the sensitive themes of equality that Bradbury explored throughout his early career. But it had no plot and only a pretentious "given" that invisibility had simply "happened" with the passing of the comet. It was humorous at times, stylistically self-indulgent, and on March 26, 1945, Kuttner targeted the style issue in his no-holds-barred response: "Readers aren't interested in your style. They're interested in the people and things you create, and what they do. Style helps, but not great gobs of it slathered on like whipped cream. You and your malted milks."

Kuttner's pointed reference to his younger friend's legendary love of malts extended into analogy as he drove home the point that none of the pulp editors would ever buy this story: "It's simply an example of Bradburyism, and it cannot stand on pure style. Can you drink twelve malted milks? Well, I hope they make you sick, then." Kuttner hit hard at the temptation of self-indulgence, which he saw as far more destructive than genre slanting could ever be. Beyond this slap in the face, however, were extensive and patient reminders that style transcended the simple sequence and selection of words on a page: "If you will remember, your best stories were the simplest, clearest, and—important—the ones founded on basic human emotions, usually the ones you know."

Here was crucial advice indeed, offered at just the right time. Bradbury's wide-ranging gift for rich story ideas often overwhelmed the writing process itself; he needed the kind of focus and narrative restraint that Kuttner relentlessly demanded in letter after letter. As the spring of 1945 drew near, Bradbury began to focus on stories that embodied the core emotions he knew best, told through the life situations he knew best, already cast in the poetic, metaphor-rich language that would soon become a hallmark of his work. What he needed in order to cross the threshold of his dream was the realization that *style is truth;* more than twenty years later, he would reflect on this realization and how it established the defining consistency of his writing: "Style isn't worthwhile unless it's absolute truth. They're synonymous. If you tell the truth you automatically have a style. What you're trying to do is bring out all your truths at various levels. Your fear of the dark, your dread of violence, your hostility of one thing, your love of another."[16]

The volume 3 period reveals some advances—and some relapses—in his genre market fiction, but the potential for his coming leap into the mainstream is apparent in such stories as "The Miracles of Jamie" and "Invisible Boy." In the months ahead, he would write two more stories from a child's point of view and fire all four of them off to the slick magazines; together they would become his first four sales to the major market magazines, landing in the pages of *The American Mercury, Charm, Colliers,* and *Mademoiselle.* His occasionally wayward yet ever-maturing path through the pulp world continued as well, resulting in many enduring tales that stretched beyond genre boundaries, often indistinguishable in tone and impact from his parallel major market successes.

Henry Kuttner died much too soon, succumbing to heart failure barely more than a dozen years later at the age of 42. Bradbury kept Kuttner's letters close at hand for the rest of his long life, for they had illuminated the unknown future at a crucial time in his career, pushing him firmly toward the subjects he knew best—the fundamental emotional truths found in the province of the heart.

Jonathan R. Eller
Chancellor's Professor of English

# Notes

1. Bradbury to Derleth, Sept. 21, 1944 (Wisconsin Historical Society).

2. Ray Bradbury, interview with the author, Oct. 8, 2006.

3. Eller, "Living in Two Worlds," chap. 8 in *Becoming Ray Bradbury* (Urbana: Univ. of Illinois Press, 2011), 53–58.

4. Bradbury, "Introduction," *Timeless Stories for Today and Tomorrow* (New York: Bantam, 1952).

5. An extended account of his reading life during the early 1940s is documented in *Becoming Ray Bradbury,* chapters 9 through 17.

6. Bradbury, interview with the author, Mar. 14, 2002.

7. Bradbury to Derleth, Sept. 21, 1944 (Wisconsin Historical Society); this letter also contains his summary of readings in the Martha Foley *Best American Short Stories* anthology of 1944.

8. Eller, *Ray Bradbury Unbound,* 232–33.

9. His *O. Henry Prize Stories* anthology appearances included "Homecoming" (1947) and "Powerhouse" (third place, 1947). Martha Foley selected a total of four Bradbury tales for the *Best American Short Story* annuals, including "The Big Black and White Game" (1946), "I See You Never" (1948), "The Other Foot" (1952), and "The Day It Rained Forever" (1958). The dates refer to volume publication of stories selected from the previous year.

10. See this volume's Chronological Catalog for the dates of the Bodin submissions, which included "These Are the Good Old Days," "A Dress for Janie," "If Paths Must Cross Again," and "The Miracles of Jamie."

11. Bradbury to Derleth, July 5, 1944.

12. Schwartz to Bradbury, Feb. 26, Mar. 10, July 4, and Oct. 21, 1944 (Albright Collection).

13. Tymn and Ashley's *Science Fiction, Fantasy, and Weird Fiction Magazines* (Westport, CT: Greenwood Press, 1985) offers a comprehensive summary of the consequences of wartime austerity on the pulps.

14. Kuttner to Bradbury, Mar. 5, 1945 (Albright Collection).

15. Hamilton to Bradbury, Dec. 31, 1944 (Albright Collection).

16. Bradbury, television interview with John Stanley, 1968.

# BRADBURY CHRONOLOGY

1920    Ray Douglas Bradbury born August 22, 1920, in Waukegan, Illinois, the third child of Esther Moberg Bradbury and Leonard Bradbury. Twin boys were born four years earlier, but one, Samuel, died at age two. Leonard Jr. (known as "Skip") survived. Ray retains memories of his own birth.

1924    In February (age three), taken by mother to see Lon Chaney in *The Hunchback of Notre Dame*. Learns about radio from his paternal grandfather.

1925    Given first book of fairy tales, *Once Upon a Time*, by his aunt Neva Bradbury for Christmas. Parents help him learn to read from the newspaper comics. Grandfather shows him pictures of the 1892 and 1903 world's fairs.

1926    Sees Lon Chaney's *Phantom of the Opera* with his mother and again with his brother, Skip. Grandfather Bradbury dies, and Aunt Neva starts reading Ray the Oz books by L. Frank Baum. Begins first grade in Waukegan, but father moves family to Roswell, New Mexico, then to Tucson, Arizona, looking for work.

1927    Ray's sister, Elizabeth Jane Bradbury, is born in Tucson. Family moves back to Waukegan in May. A young cousin almost drowns in Lake Michigan; he uses this incident much later in "The Lake."

1928    Ray's baby sister, Elizabeth, dies of pneumonia in February. Sick in bed with whooping cough, Ray misses three months of school during the fall term. Aunt Neva reads him Edgar Allan Poe's works. Discovers *Amazing Stories Quarterly,* one of the earliest science fiction pulps. Is terrified of crossing local ravine and uses this fear later in "The Night" and "The Whole Town's Sleeping," stories later novelized within *Dandelion Wine.*

1929    Discovers the romances of Edgar Rice Burroughs and begins to read Burroughs's John Carter of Mars series.

1931    Given a book on magic for his eleventh birthday; attends local perfor-
        mances by Blackstone the Magician several times between 1928 and 1931.
        Performs his own magic act for various service clubs and lodges and on
        Christmas Eve at the Veterans of Foreign Wars Hall.

1932    Begins to read Jules Verne. Father loses his job with the telephone com-
        pany and moves family back to Tucson. Receives toy dial typewriter
        for Christmas. Attempts a sequel to a John Carter of Mars novel. Reads
        Sunday comics to kids on a local radio station in Tucson.

1933    Father moves family back to Waukegan in the spring. Ray reads bor-
        rowed copies of *Wonder Stories* and *Amazing Stories*. Attends the Cen-
        tury of Progress Exposition (the Chicago World's Fair) that summer
        with his parents and again with his aunt Neva; he is fascinated by "The
        City of the Future" and the dinosaurs of the "Sinclair Prehistoric Exhibit."

1934    Favorite uncle Inar Moberg moves to California. Years later Ray would
        write a story in which he gave his uncle wings and makes him a vampire.
        His father, again out of work, drives family to Los Angeles. Ray attends
        Berendo Junior High.

1935    Ray roller-skates to Paramount Studios and collects autographs. Re-
        sumes his grade-school compilation of Flash Gordon and Buck Rog-
        ers comic strips. Starts sending stories to the *Saturday Evening Post* and
        other quality magazines. In September, enters Los Angeles High School.

1936    Joins drama club and determines to be an actor. Starts—but never fin-
        ishes—his first novel. Poem "In Memory of Will Rogers" printed in
        Waukegan *News-Sun*. Two teachers, Jennet Johnson and Snow Longley
        Housh, encourage his creative development. He would later acknowl-
        edge their influence in his dedication to *Something Wicked This Way
        Comes* (1962).

1937    Discovers the novels of Thomas Wolfe. Has poem "Death's Voice" pub-
        lished in *Anthology of Student Verse* in March. Scripts annual high school
        talent show, the *1937 Roman Review*. Buys first real typewriter for $10. In
        early October, joins the Los Angeles Science Fiction League (LASFL).

1938    In January, his first amateur story, "Hollerbochen's Dilemma," is printed
        in the LASFL chapter's fan magazine (fanzine), *Imagination!* Poem
        "Truck Driver After Midnight" appears in citywide anthology *Morning
        Song*. Contributes reviews and commentary to *Blue and White Daily*, the
        Los Angeles High School student newspaper. Graduates in June; starts
        selling newspapers in September from a street corner newsstand.

1939    Launches his own fanzine, *Futuria Fantasia*, which will run for four is-
        sues. Attends the first World Science Fiction Convention in New York.

Takes Hannes Bok's art portfolio with him and wins Bok his first commission from *Weird Tales*. Reads Hemingway, Steinbeck, Wolfe, and other American novelists.

1940   Sees Disney's *Fantasia* multiple times. Moves with family to downtown Los Angeles. Receives advice from Robert A. Heinlein. Publishes "It's Not the Heat, It's the Hu—" in the November 2 issue of the nonpaying but professional *Script* magazine; this is his first professional story publication. Active in amateur productions of Laraine Day's Wilshire Players Guild.

1941   First professional story sale, "The Pendulum," written with Henry Hasse, appears in the November issue of *Super Science Stories*. His first agent, Julius Schwartz, negotiates this sale and two more before the end of the year.

1942   Spends many Sundays at Muscle Beach with Leigh Brackett, critiquing and revising stories. Publishes "The Candle" in *Weird Tales*. Moves with family to Venice Beach. Quits selling newspapers.

1943   Poor vision keeps him out of military service. Three major stories appear: "The Wind" and "The Crowd" in *Weird Tales* and "King of the Gray Spaces" in *Famous Fantastic Mysteries*.

1944   Places detective stories in *Detective Tales, New Detective*, and *Dime Mystery*. Writes second half of Leigh Brackett's novella "Lorelei of the Red Mist" while she coauthors screenplay of *The Big Sleep* for director Howard Hawks. Undertakes extensive readings of contemporary American and British fiction writers.

1945   First anthology sale, "The Lake," appears in *Who Knocks*. Sells "The Big Black and White Game" to *American Mercury*. Three major market magazine sales enable him to travel in Mexico with close friend Grant Beach. This trip results in the classic story "The Next in Line."

1946   Meets future wife Marguerite "Maggie" McClure at Fowler's Book Shop, where she clerks. First *Martian Chronicles* story, "The Million Year Picnic," appears in *Planet Stories*. "The Big Black and White Game" selected for *Best American Short Stories 1946*. Meets future agent Don Congdon.

1947   Bradbury's radio play "The Meadow" broadcast on *World Security Workshop* and selected for *Best One-Act Plays 1947–48*. His as-yet-unpublished story "Riabouchinska" adapted and broadcast on the CBS radio dramatic series *Suspense*. Marries Maggie McClure. His story "Homecoming" is selected for *O. Henry Award: Prize Stories 1947*. First story collection, *Dark Carnival*, published. Don Congdon becomes his agent.

1948    Wins third place in *O. Henry Award: Prize Stories 1948* with "Power House." "I See You Never" in *Best American Short Stories 1948*. *Dark Carnival* reprinted (abridged) in Great Britain.

1949    Trip to New York. Meets Walter Bradbury at Doubleday. They conceive the idea for *The Martian Chronicles*. Applies (unsuccessfully) for Guggenheim grant with a novel concept, *The Masks*. First daughter Susan born. Named Best Author of Science Fiction 1949 by the National Fantasy Fan Federation.

1950    *The Martian Chronicles* published in May. Now publishing regularly in major market magazines. Receives significant review from Christopher Isherwood in *Tomorrow* for *The Martian Chronicles*.

1951    "The Fireman" published as a novella in February issue of *Galaxy*; he will later revise and expand it into *Fahrenheit 451*. *The Illustrated Man* is published, his second book from Doubleday. Second daughter, Ramona, born. Major interview for *New York Times Book Review* published in August.

1952    First book on Ray Bradbury, *The Ray Bradbury Review*, edited by William F. Nolan. Guest of honor at Westercon 5 in San Diego; becomes president of the newly formed Science Fantasy Writers of America. "The Other Foot" published in *Best American Short Stories 1952*. Edits *Timeless Stories for Today and Tomorrow* for Bantam. *The Illustrated Man* is runner-up for the International Fantasy Award.

1953    In March *The Golden Apples of the Sun* published by Doubleday. Writes a critical piece on science fiction for *The Nation*. John Huston asks Bradbury to write the *Moby Dick* screenplay in late August; they spend the next eight months in Ireland and London as Bradbury prepares the script. His first novel, *Fahrenheit 451*, is published by Ballantine Books. "The Beast From 20,000 Fathoms" and an original screen treatment, *It Came From Outer Space*, made into films.

1954    Wins annual gold medal from Commonwealth Club of California for *Fahrenheit 451*. Wins Benjamin Franklin magazine award for best short story, "Sun and Shadow." Wins National Institute of Arts and Letters literature award for *Fahrenheit 451*. Bradbury and his family return from Europe in June.

1955    Pantheon publishes *Switch on the Night*, his first children's book, in March. First textbook appearance in *The Informal Reader* with "There Will Come Soft Rains." Third daughter, Bettina, born. *The October Country* released in October from Ballantine Books. "Shopping for Death" picked for *Best Detective Stories of the Year*.

1956    Wins Boys Club of America Award for *Switch on the Night*. Edits the Bantam anthology *The Circus of Dr. Lao and Other Improbable Stories*. Writes "Happy Birthday 2115 A.D.," an unproduced operetta, for Elsa Lanchester and Charles Laughton. John Huston's production of *Moby Dick*, filmed from Bradbury's screenplay, released as a feature film by Warner Brothers.

1957    In London for the summer. Writes screenplay of "And the Rock Cried Out" for Carol Reed. September sees release of *Dandelion Wine* from Doubleday. His father dies at age sixty-six in October.

1958    In April, receives a 1957 Society of Midland Authors award for *Dandelion Wine* as runner-up to Jessamyn West's *To See the Dreams*. Represented in *Best American Short Stories* with "The Day It Rained Forever." Fourth daughter, Alexandra, born. The Bradburys move on Thanksgiving Day to Cheviot Hills.

1959    *A Medicine for Melancholy* released in February by Doubleday. The British edition published with modified contents as *The Day It Rained Forever*.

1960    First professional stage play, *The Meadow*, produced at the Huntington Hartford Theater in Hollywood. *Life* article published in October, "A Serious Search for Weird Worlds."

1961    In January wins appellate court ruling against CBS television for a 1957 *Playhouse 90* plagiarism of *Fahrenheit 451*. Cofounds the Writer's Guild Film Society with Arthur Knight. Writes the voice-over narrative for MGM's *King of Kings* (uncredited).

1962    Major teleplay, "The Jail," appears on *Alcoa Premier* in February. His script for "The Jail" is nominated by the Writer's Guild of America for the Television and Radio Writers Award in the category of Television Anthology Drama. In the fall, *Life* publishes his article "Cry the Cosmos." Simon & Schuster publishes Bradbury's long-awaited novel, *Something Wicked This Way Comes*. *R Is for Rocket*, a compilation of Bradbury stories for young readers, published by Doubleday.

1963    Receives Academy Award nomination for the 1962 animated short film, *Icarus Montgolfier Wright*, adapted from his story; George Clayton Johnson and illustrator Joseph Mugnaini share the nomination. Film wins Golden Eagle Award from the Council on International Non-Theatrical Events (CINE). In October, Dial publishes Bradbury's dramatic adaptations of his own Irish stories as *The Anthem Sprinters and Other Antics*.

1964    His "American Journey" narrative opens at the U.S. Pavilion of the World's Fair in New York. Produces his own plays in Los Angeles as *The World of Ray Bradbury*. Receives the Peter Pan Award from the

Department of Pediatrics, Cedars-Sinai Hospital. Simon & Schuster publishes Bradbury's short story collection *The Machineries of Joy*.

1965    *Life* publishes his fictional tribute to Hemingway in January. He produces his play *The Wonderful Ice Cream Suit* in Los Angeles. "The Other Foot" selected for *Best American Short Stories 1915–1965*. *The Vintage Bradbury* released by Vintage Books, Random House. Ballantine publishes *The Autumn People*, the first of two mass-market paperbacks featuring the early 1950s EC Comics graphic adaptations of Bradbury stories. Receives the first of two Ann Radcliffe Awards for contributions to Gothic Literature from the Count Dracula Society, precursor to the Academy of Science Fiction, Fantasy, and Horror Films. *The World of Ray Bradbury* has a short New York run at the Orpheum Theatre.

1966    François Truffaut's *Fahrenheit 451* distributed by Universal as a major film. *S Is for Space*, a companion collection to *R Is for Rocket*, published by Doubleday. Ballantine publishes *Tomorrow Midnight*, the second of two mass-market paperbacks featuring the early 1950s EC Comics graphic adaptations of Bradbury stories. Bradbury's mother dies at age seventy-eight in Los Angeles in November.

1967    Musical production of *Dandelion Wine* opens at Lincoln Center in April. *Life* publishes "An Impatient Gulliver above Our Roofs."

1968    Wins Aviation Space Writers Association's Robert Ball Memorial Award for "An Impatient Gulliver above Our Roofs." *Leviathan '99* produced and broadcast as a radio play by the BBC in London. Named president of the Chamber Symphony Society of California in June. August sees his final essay for *Life*, "Any Friend of Trains Is a Friend of Mine."

1969    *The Illustrated Man* distributed as a major film by Warner Brothers / Seven Arts. *I Sing the Body Electric!* released by Knopf in October. His *Christus Apollo* performed at UCLA with Charlton Heston as narrator.

1970    Works as part of WED (Disney Imagineering think tank) on Robot Factory exhibits. "Mars Is Heaven!" ("The Third Expedition," 1948) selected for the first volume of Doubleday's *Science Fiction Hall of Fame* anthology.

1971    Apollo 15 crew names a lunar impact feature Dandelion Crater in honor of Bradbury. Participates in a panel discussion, "Mars and the Mind of Man," at California Institute of Technology. "The Poems" (1945) receives the Seiun Award for best foreign short story at the Japanese Science Fiction Convention. Receives his second Ann Radcliffe Award for contributions to Gothic Literature from the Count Dracula Society.

1972    *The Wonderful Ice Cream Suit and Other Plays* published by Bantam. Feature film *Picasso Summer*, based on his story "In a Season of Calm

Weather," released by Warner Brothers / Seven Arts. "The Blue Bottle" ("Death Wish," 1950) receives the Seiun Award for best foreign short story at the Japanese Science Fiction Convention. *The Halloween Tree,* a novel for young adults, published by Knopf.

1973    First poetry book, *When Elephants Last in the Dooryard Bloomed,* released by Knopf. "The Black Ferris" (1948) receives the Seiun Award for best foreign short story at the Japanese Science Fiction Convention.

1974    Receives Valentine Davies Career Award from the Writer's Guild of America, West, for contributions to motion picture screenwriting. Records *Bradbury Reads Bradbury* with the Listening Library for high school use.

1975    *Pillar of Fire and Other Plays* published by Bantam in October.

1976    *Fahrenheit 451* (as read by Bradbury) nominated for Best Spoken Word Recording by the National Academy of Recording Arts and Sciences. *Long After Midnight* published by Knopf (his first collection in seven years). Receives first Life Achievement nomination (for 1975) from the jurors of the World Fantasy Awards.

1977    Selected as the Life Achievement Award winner (for 1976) by jurors of the World Fantasy Awards. Receives California Association of Teachers of English Writer of the Year Award. Knopf publishes second book of verse, *Where Robot Mice and Robot Men Run Round in Robot Towns.*

1978    First nomination for the Gandalf Grand Master of Fantasy Award (for 1977), an honor sponsored by the annual Hugo Awards competition. Abrams publishes *The Mummies of Guanajuato,* a book of photos built around Bradbury's classic story "The Next in Line."

1979    Second nomination for the Gandalf Grand Master of Fantasy Award (for 1978). Receives an honorary doctorate from Whittier College. Hosts the ABC hour-long special broadcast *Infinite Space: Beyond Apollo.*

1980    Selected as the Gandalf Grand Master of Fantasy Award winner (for 1979) on his third nomination. Receives Space Medicine Award for "Medicine for the Twenty-first Century" from NASA. Knopf releases the hundred-story collection *The Stories of Ray Bradbury* in October.

1981    Receives performance award from the Mental Health Association of Los Angeles for his contributions. His third collection of verse, *The Haunted Computer and the Android Ape,* published by Knopf.

1982    Perfection Form releases a series of his short stories in booklet format for schools.

1983    *Dinosaur Tales* published by Bantam. *Something Wicked This Way Comes* released by Disney. Bradbury's screenplay receives the Saturn Award for Writing from the Academy of Science Fiction, Fantasy, and Horror Films.

1984     Receives "Key to the City" from Waukegan, Illinois. *Novels of Ray Bradbury* published by Granada in Great Britain. Dell releases a collection of Bradbury's early detective stories as *A Memory of Murder*. *Fahrenheit 451* receives Prometheus Award for best Hall of Fame Classic Fiction from the Libertarian Futurist Society; co-winner is George Orwell's *1984*.

1985     In its first season, *The Ray Bradbury Theater* receives an ACE (Award for Cable Excellence); by its final season (1993) the series would earn a total of ten ACE nominations and net six wins, as well as two Emmy nominations. First mystery novel, *Death Is a Lonely Business*, published by Knopf in October. Receives the Body of Work Award for lifetime achievement from the writer's group PEN USA.

1986     Guest of honor at World Science Fiction Convention. Dramatic Publishing releases a series of Bradbury's plays for theatrical use.

1987     St. Martin's publishes Bradbury's story *Fever Dream* as a children's glow-in-the-dark edition.

1988     Knopf releases his first story collection in nine years, *The Toynbee Convector*.

1989     Named a Grand Master by the Science Fiction and Fantasy Writers of America for his lifetime achievement in these fields. Joshua Odell Editions publishes *Zen in the Art of Writing* in March. *The Toynbee Convector* nominated for a 1988 Bram Stoker Award by the Horror Writer's Association.

1990     Portion of the Yeoman Creek ravine near Bradbury's childhood home in Waukegan, Illinois, named the Ray Bradbury section of Powell Park. Receives the Turner Tomorrow Award. Knopf publishes his second mystery novel, *A Graveyard for Lunatics*.

1991     *Ray Bradbury on Stage*, a compilation of his published stage plays, released by Donald I. Fine. *Yestermorrow!* (an essay collection) published by Joshua Odell Editions.

1992     *Green Shadows, White Whale*, a novelization of his Irish stories and his 1953 to 1954 experiences in Ireland writing the screenplay for *Moby Dick* under John Huston's direction, published by Knopf. Society for the Study of Midwestern Literature presents the Mark Twain Award to Bradbury for his distinguished contributions to midwestern literature. The Science Fiction and Fantasy Writers of America establish The Ray Bradbury Award for excellence in screenwriting. Spacewatch project astronomers at Kit Peak observatory name a newly discovered asteroid, 9766 Bradbury, in honor of the author. Television documentary *Ray Bradbury: An American Icon* airs, with narration by Academy Award–winning actor and Bradbury friend Rod Steiger.

1993    Bradbury's feature-length animated teleplay of his 1972 novel, *The Halloween Tree,* is aired October 20, 1993, on the Turner Broadcasting Channel; subsequently released by Hanna-Barbera on video. Bradbury shares a CableACE award for *The Ray Bradbury Theater* as Best Dramatic Series; this is the last of ten ACE nominations (and six wins) for the Bradbury series.

1994    Wins an Emmy for his animated screenplay adaptation of *The Halloween Tree.*

1995    Named Los Angeles Citizen of the Year for his contributions to city planning.

1996    Receives honorary doctorate of Humane Letters from California Lutheran University. Nominated for the First Fandom Hall of Fame Award, a Hugo ceremony honor recognizing original fans from the days of the first World Science Fiction Convention of 1939. Avon Books releases *Quicker Than the Eye* (a story collection) in November. Los Angeles names a room in its main library for Ray Bradbury.

1997    *Driving Blind* (story collection) released in September by Avon.

1998    His second children's picture book, *Ahmed and the Oblivion Machines,* published by Avon. *Driving Blind* is nominated for a World Fantasy Award.

1999    Bradbury receives the George Pal Memorial Award from the Academy of Science Fiction, Fantasy, and Horror Films. The British edition of *Driving Blind* (published in 1998) nominated for a British Fantasy Award. Bradbury inducted (along with Robert Silverberg and posthumous inductees A. Merritt and Jules Verne) into the Science Fiction Hall of Fame.

2000    Awarded the National Book Foundation Medal for Distinguished Contribution to American Letters on November 15. In honor of this award, Morrow, now publisher of Avon Books, publishes *A Celebration of Ray Bradbury.*

2001    The World Horror Convention names Bradbury a Grand Master. July sees publication of *A Chapbook for Burnt-Out Priests, Rabbis, and Ministers* (Cemetery Dance), a collection of Bradbury's speculative writings on the cosmos and faith. *From the Dust Returned,* a novelized story cycle started more than fifty years earlier, published by Morrow. *Ray Bradbury, His Life and Work* printed by Book-of-the-Month Club in conjunction with its rerelease of four major Bradbury classics. Mayor James Hahn of Los Angeles proclaims Ray Bradbury Day for Friday, December 14.

2002    *From the Dust Returned* nominated for a Bram Stoker Award for best
        Horror novel; it is also nominated for a World Fantasy Award. *One
        More for the Road* (a story collection) published in March by Morrow.
        *Fahrenheit 451* becomes the "One Book, One City" selection for Los
        Angeles; other cities eventually select *Fahrenheit 451* for subsequent
        reading programs. Recognized for his contributions to film with the
        2,193rd star on the Hollywood Walk of Fame in April.

2003    *One More for the Road* receives the Bram Stoker Award for best fiction
        collection. *Bradbury Stories,* his second hundred-story compilation, pub-
        lished by Morrow. Maggie Bradbury passes away in November. His third
        mystery novel, *Let's All Kill Constance!* published by Morrow in December.

2004    *It Came From Outer Space,* a documentary edition of his four screen
        treatments for this film, published by Gauntlet Press. The 62nd World
        Science Fiction Convention awards *Fahrenheit 451* the Retro-Hugo as
        best novel fifty years after its 1953 publication; other nominations in this
        category include period novels by Arthur C. Clarke, Isaac Asimov, and
        Theodore Sturgeon. *The Cat's Pajamas,* a story collection with a cover
        illustration by Bradbury, published by Morrow. Receives the National
        Medal of Arts from President Bush on November 17.

2005    Ray's older brother, Skip, passes away in March. *Bradbury Speaks,* a col-
        lection of articles and essays, published in July by Morrow. *Maggie Re-
        membered,* a tribute from Bradbury to his late wife, published by Hill
        House. A four-text archival edition of *The Halloween Tree* published by
        Gauntlet Press.

2006    The National Endowment for the Arts selects *Fahrenheit 451* for "The
        Big Read" national reading program. *The Homecoming* published as a
        children's book, illustrated by Dave McKean for Collins Design. *Fare-
        well Summer,* the original novel from which *Dandelion Wine* was ex-
        tracted, published by Morrow.

2007    *Match to Flame,* the historical collection of Bradbury's *Fahrenheit 451*
        precursors and related stories, published by Gauntlet Press. Bradbury
        receives the French Ordre des Arts et des Lettres (Commandeur) Medal.
        *Now and Forever,* a pairing of the short novels *Somewhere a Band Is
        Playing* and *Leviathan '99,* published by Morrow. The Center for Ray
        Bradbury Studies opens at Indiana University, Indianapolis. On April
        16, Bradbury is awarded a Pulitzer Prize special citation for his "prolific
        and deeply influential" career.

2008    Bradbury named Grand Master Poet at the Rhysling Awards for sci-
        ence fiction and fantasy verse. Receives the first J. Lloyd Eaton Award
        for Lifetime Achievement in Science Fiction, from the University of

California, Riverside. *Masks,* a gathering of materials from an unpublished novel of the late 1940s, published by Gauntlet Press. *Moby Dick: A Screenplay* published by Subterranean Press from his submitted 1954 script of the John Huston film. The Center for Ray Bradbury Studies begins publication of *The New Ray Bradbury Review.* Story collection *We'll Always Have Paris* published by Morrow in December.

2009   Hill & Wang releases a graphic novel adaptation of *Fahrenheit 451.* Bradbury receives an honorary doctorate from Columbia College, Chicago.

2010   Receives ComicCon Icon Award during the Scream Awards, celebrating the history of horror, science fiction, and fantasy feature films; ceremonies aired October 19 on SPIKE TV. Bradbury's ninetieth birthday celebrated in and around Los Angeles through various events coordinated by writer Steven Paul Leiva; Los Angeles City Council passes a resolution declaring August 22–28 to be Ray Bradbury Week.

2011   Hill & Wang releases a graphic novel adaptation of *Something Wicked This Way Comes.*

2012   William Morrow publishes the Bradbury tribute volume *Shadow Show,* with stories by a wide range of contemporary writers. "Take Me Home," a short essay, published in a special science fiction issue of the *New Yorker.* Bradbury dies on June 5 at Cedars Sinai Hospital in Los Angeles. The Jet Propulsion Laboratory and NASA name the Mars rover Curiosity's landing zone after Bradbury on what would have been his ninety-second birthday, August 22. A Los Angeles City Council resolution renames the land across from the Los Angeles Central Library (at 5th Street and Flower Avenue) as Ray Bradbury Square.

2013   Publication of *Nolan on Bradbury,* a collection of writer and friend William F. Nolan's publications on Bradbury spanning six decades. Dedication of the Palms-Rancho Park Branch of the Los Angeles Public Library to Ray Bradbury, September 23, hosted by Steven Paul Leiva. Dedicatory speakers included Harlan Ellison, George Clayton Johnson, and Susan Bradbury Nixon.

2014   Nominated posthumously on the April shortlist by World Science Fiction Convention voters for the 1939 Retro-Hugo Awards in the categories of Best Short Story for 1938 ("Hollerbochen's Dilemma") and Best Fan Writer; announced as the winner in the Best Fan Writer category, August 14, in London. Accepted on behalf of the Bradbury family and Don Congdon Associates by Anna Carmichael, Abner Stein Agency.

2015   Founding of the Ray Bradbury Waukegan Carnegie Library, Inc., in Waukegan, Illinois, an initiative dedicated to restoring Bradbury's childhood hometown Carnegie library building in his honor; articles of incorporation filed April 20.

2016    Nominated posthumously on the April shortlist by World Science Fiction Convention voters for the 1941 Retro-Hugo Awards in the categories of Best Fanzine and Best Fan Writer for 1940; announced as the winner in both categories; August 18, in Kansas City. Accepted on behalf of the Bradbury Family and Don Congdon Associates by the Center for Ray Bradbury Studies director.

## Sources

Donn Albright, principal Bradbury bibliographer; Jonathan R. Eller, Bradbury interviews, 1998–2012, and *Becoming Ray Bradbury* and *Ray Bradbury Unbound* (Champagne, IL: University of Illinois Press, 2011 and 2014); Jonathan R. Eller and William F. Touponce, *Ray Bradbury: The Life of Fiction* (Kent, OH: Kent State University Press, 2004); The Locus Index to SF Awards (www.locusmag.com/SFAwards/Db/Locus.html); Phil Nichols, Ray Bradbury (www.bradburymedia.co.uk); William F. Nolan, *The Ray Bradbury Companion* (Detroit: Gale, 1975); David Mogen, *Ray Bradbury* (Boston: Twayne, 1986); Harry Warner, Jr., *A Wealth of Fable,* expanded edition (Van Nuys, CA: SCIFI Press, 1992); Sam Weller, *The Bradbury Chronicles* (New York: Morrow, 2005).

THE COLLECTED STORIES OF RAY BRADBURY

Volume 3: 1944–1945

# ONE

# NO PHONES, PRIVATE COFFIN (YESTERDAY I LIVED!)

Years went by and after all the years of raining and cold and fog going and coming through Hollywood Cemetery over a stone with the name Diana Coyle on it, Cleve Morris walked into the studio projection room out of the storm and looked up at the screen.

She was there. The long, lazy body of hers, the shining red hair and bright complementary green eyes.

And Cleve thought, *Is it cold out there, Diana? Is it cold out there tonight? Is the rain to you yet? Have the years pierced the bronze walls of your resting place and are you still—beautiful?*

He watched her glide across the screen, heard her laughter, and his wet eyes shimmered her into bright quivering color streaks.

*It's so warm in here tonight, Diana. You're here, all the warmth of you, and yet it's only so much illusion. They buried you three years ago, and now the autograph hunters are crazy over some new actress here at the studio.*

He choked on that. No reason for this feeling, but everyone felt that way about her. Everyone loved her, hated her for being so lovely. But maybe *you* loved her more than the others.

Who in hell are you? She hardly ever saw you. Cleve Morris, a desk-sergeant spending two hours a day at the front desk buzzing people through locked doors, and six hours strolling around dim sound stages, checking things. She hardly knew you. It was always, "Hello, Diana," and "Hi, sarge!" and "Good night, Diana," when her long evening gown rustled from the stages, and over her smooth shoulder, one eye winking, "Night, sarge; be a good boy!"

Three years ago. Cleve slid down in his projection room loge. The watch on his wrist ticked eight o'clock. The studio was dead, lights fading one by one. Tomorrow, action, lots of it; but now, tonight, he was alone in this room looking over the old films of Diana Coyle. In the projection booth behind him, checking the compact spools of film, Jamie Winters, the studio's A-1 cameraman, did the honors of projection.

So here you are, the two of you, late at night. The film flickers, marring her lovely face. It flickers again, and you're irritated. It flickers twice more, a long

1

time, then smooths out. Bad print. Cleve sank lower in his seat, thinking back three years ago, along about this same hour of night, just about the same day of the month . . . three years ago . . . same hour . . . rain in the dark sky . . . three years ago. . . .

.  .  .

Cleve was at his desk that night. People strode through doors, rain-spangled, never seeing him. He felt like a mummy in a museum where the attendants had long ago tired of noticing him. Just a fixture to buzz doors open for them.

"Good evening, Mr. Guilding."

R. J. Guilding thought it over and vetoed the suggestion with a jerk of one grey-gloved hand. His white head jerked, too. "Is it?" he wanted to know. You get that way being a producer.

*Buzz.* Door open. *Slam.*

"Good evening, Diana!"

"What?" She walked from the rainy night with it shining in little clear gems on her white oval face. He'd like to kiss them away. She looked lost and alone. "Oh, hello, Cleve. Working late. The darn picture's almost finished. Gosh, I'm tired."

*Buzz.* Door open. *Slam.*

He looked after her and kept her perfume as long as he could.

"Ah, flatfoot," somebody said. Leaning over the desk, smiling ironically, was a pretty man named Robert Denim. "Open the door for me, country boy. They never should've put you on this job. You're glamor-struck. Poor kid."

Cleve looked at him, strangely. "She doesn't belong to you any more, does she?"

Denim's face was suddenly not pretty. He didn't say anything for a moment, but by the look in his eyes Cleve's doubts were removed. Denim grabbed the door and jerked it viciously.

Cleve purposely left the buzzer untouched. Denim swore and turned around, one gloved hand balled into a fist. Cleve buzzed the buzzer, smiling. It was the kind of smile that drained Denim's hesitation, made him decide to pull the knob again and stride off down away into the halls, into the studio.

A few minutes later Jamie Winters entered, shaking off rain, but holding onto a man-sized peeve. "That Diana Coyle woman; I tell you, Cleve. She stays up late at night and expects me to photograph her like a twelve-year-old kid! What a job I got! Fooey."

Behind Jamie Winters came Georgie Kroll, and Tally Durham hanging onto him, so that Diana couldn't get him. But it was too late. By Georgie's face he was already got; and by Tally's she knew it but couldn't believe it.

*Slam.*

Cleve checked his name-chart, found that everybody who was working to-night was already in. He relaxed. This was a dark hive, and Diana was the queen bee with all the other bees humming around her. The studio worked late to-night, just for her, all the lights, sound, color, activity. Cleve smoked a cigarette quietly, leaning back, smiling over his thoughts. *Diana, let's just you and me buy a little home in San Fernando where the flood washes you out every year, and the wild-flowers spring up when the flood is gone. Nice paddling in a canoe with you, Diana, even in a flood. We got flowers, hay, sunlight, and peace in the valley, Diana.*

The only sound to Cleve was the rain beating at the windows, an occasional flare of thunder and his watch ticking like a termite boring a hole in the structure of silence.

*Tictictictictictic.* . . .

The scream pulled him out of his chair and half across the reception room, echoed through the building. A script girl burst into view, shambling with dead kind of feet, babbling. Cleve grabbed her and held her still.

"She's dead! She's dead!"

The watch went *tic, tic, tic* all over again.

Lightning blew up all around the place, and a cold wind hit Cleve's neck. His stomach turned over and he was afraid to ask the simple question he would eventually have to ask. Instead he stalled the inevitable, locking the bronze front doors, and making secure any windows that were open. When he turned, the script girl was leaning against his desk, a tremble in her like something shattered in a finely integrated machine, shaking it to pieces.

"On stage twelve. Just now," she gasped. "Diana Coyle."

Cleve ran through the dim alleys of the studio, the sound of his running lonely in the big empty spaces. Ahead of him brilliant lights poured from opened stage doors; people stood framed in the vast square, shocked, not moving.

He ran onto the set and stopped, his heart pounding, to look down.

She was the most beautiful person who ever died.

Her silver evening gown was a small lake around her. Her fingernails were five scarlet beetles dead and shining on either side of her slumped body.

All the hot lights looked down, trying to keep her warm when she was fast cooling. My blood, too, thought Cleve. Keep me warm, lights!

The shock of it held everybody as in a still photo.

Denim, fumbling with a cigarette, spoke first:

"We were in the middle of a scene. She just fell down and that was all."

Tally Durham, about the size of a salt-shaker, wandered blindly about the stage telling everybody, "We thought she fainted, that's all! I got the smelling salts!"

Denim sucked, deeply nervous, on his smoke. "The smelling salts didn't work . . ."

For the first time in his life, Cleve touched Diana Coyle.

But it was too late now. What good to touch cold clay that didn't laugh back at you using green eyes and curved lips?

He touched her and said, "She's been poisoned."

The word 'poison' spread out through the dim sound stage behind the glaring lights. Echoes came back with it.

Georgie Kroll stuttered. "She—she got a drink—from the soft drinks—box—a couple minutes ago. Maybe—"

Cleve found the soft drinks dispenser blindly. He smelled one bottle and tucked it aside carefully, using a handkerchief, into a lunch box that was studio property. "Nobody touch that."

The floor was rubbery to walk on. "Anybody see anybody else touch that bottle before Diana drank out of it?"

Way up in the glaring electrical heaven, a guy looked down like a short-circuited god and called, "Hey, Cleve, just before the last scene we had light-trouble. Somebody conked a main-switch. The lights were doused for about a minute and a half. Plenty time for someone to fix that bottle!"

"Thanks." Cleve turned to Jamie Winters, the cameraman. "You got film in your camera? Got a picture of—her—dying?"

"I guess so. Sure!"

"How soon can you have it developed?"

"Two, three hours. Got to call Juke Davis and have him come to the studio, though."

"Phone him, then. Take two watchmen with you to guard that film. Beat it!"

Far away the sirens were singing and Hollywood was going to sleep. Somebody onstage suddenly realized Diana was dead and started sobbing.

*I wish I could do that,* thought Cleve. *I wish I could cry. What am I supposed to do now, act tough, be a Sherlock? Question everyone, when my heart isn't working?* Cleve heard his voice going on alone:

"We'll be working late tonight, everybody. We'll be working until we get this scene right. And if we don't get it right, I guess we don't go home. Before the homicide squad gets here, everyone to their places. We'll do the scene over. Places, everybody."

They did the scene over.

. . .

The homicide squad arrived. There was one detective named Foley and another named Sadlowe. One was small, the other big. One talked a lot, and the other listened. Foley did the talking and it gave Cleve a sick headache.

R. J. Guilding, the director and producer of the film, slumped in his canvas chair, wiping his face and trying to tell Foley that he wanted this whole mess kept out of the papers and quiet.

Foley told him to shut up. Foley glared at Cleve as if he were also a suspect. "What've you found out, son?"

"There was film in the camera. Film of Diana—Miss Coyle's death."

Foley's eyebrows went like that. "Well, hell, let's see it!"

They walked over into the film laboratory to get the film. Cleve was frankly afraid of the place. Always was. It was a huge dark mortuary building with dead-end passages and labyrinths of black walls to cut the light. You stumbled through pitch dark, touching the walls, careening, turning, cursing, twisting around cut-outs, walked south, east, west, south again and suddenly found yourself in a green-freckled space as big as the universe. Nothing to see but green welts and splashes of light, dim snakes of film climbing, winding over spools from floor to high ceiling and back down. The one brilliant light was a printing light that shot from a projector and printed negative to positive as they slid by in parallel slots. The positive then coiled over and down into a long series of developing baths. The place was a whining morgue. Juke Davis moved around in it with ghoul-like movements.

"There's no sound-track. I'll develop it and splice it in later," said Davis. "Here you are, Mr. Foley. Here's your film."

They took the film and retreated back through the labyrinth.

In the projection room, Cleve, the detectives Foley and Sadlowe, with Jamie Winters operating the projector in the booth, watched the death scene printed on the screen for them. Stage twelve had been slammed shut, and other officers were back there, talking, grilling everyone in alphabetical order.

On the screen, Diana laughed. Robert Denim laughed back. It was very silent. They opened mouths but no sounds came out. People danced behind them. Diana and Robert Denim danced now, gracefully, quietly, leisurely. When they stopped dancing, they talked seriously with—Tally Durham and Georgie Kroll.

Foley spoke, "You say that this fellow Kroll loved Diana, too?"

Cleve nodded. "Who didn't?"

Foley said, "Yeah. Who didn't. Well—" He stared with suspicion at the screen. "How about this Tally Durham woman. Was she jealous?"

Was there any woman in Hollywood who didn't hate Diana because she was perfect? Cleve spoke of Tally's love for Georgie Kroll.

"It never fails," replied Foley with a shake of his head.

Cleve said, "Tally may have killed Diana. Who knows. Georgie'd have a motive, too. Diana treated him like a rag-doll. He wanted her and couldn't have her. That happened to a lot of men in Diana's life. If she ever loved anybody, it was Robert Denim, and that didn't last. Denim is a little too—tough, I guess that's how you'd put it."

Foley snorted. "Good going. We got three suspects in one scene. Any one of them could have dosed that pop bottle with nicotine. The lights were out for a minute and a half. In that time any guy who ever bought Black Leaf Forty nico-tine sulfate at the corner garden store, could have tossed twenty drops of it in her drink and gone back playing innocent when the lights bloomed again. Nuts."

Sadlowe spoke for the first time that evening, "There ought to be some way to splice out the innocents from this film." A brilliant observation.

Cleve caught his breath. *She* was dying.

She died like she had done everything in her life. You had to admire the way she did it, with the grace, fire and control of a fine cat-animal. In the middle of the scene she forgot her lines. Her fingers crawled slowly to her throat and she turned. Her face changed. She looked straight out at you from the screen as if she knew this was her biggest and, to a cynic, her best scene.

Then she fell, like a silken canopy from which the supports had been in-stantly withdrawn.

Denim crouched over her, mouthing the word, "Diana!"

And Tally Durham screamed a silent scream, as the film shivered and flut-tered into blackness, numbers, amber colors, and then nothing but glaring light.

Oh, God, press a button somewhere! Run the reel backward and bring her back to life! Press a button as you see in the comic newsreels; in which smashed trains are reintegrated, fallen emperors are enthroned, the sun rises in the west and—Diana Coyle rises from the dead!

From the booth, Jamie Winters's voice said, "That's it. That's all of it. You want to see it again?"

Foley said, "Yeah. Show it to us half a dozen times."

"Excuse me," gasped Cleve.

"Where are you going?"

He went out into the rain. It beat cold on him. Behind him, inside, Diana was dying again and again and again, like a trained puppet. Cleve clenched his jaw and looked straight up at the sky and let the night cry on him, all over him, soaking him through and through; in perfect harmony, the night and he and the crying dark. . . .

•  •  •

The storm lasted until morning, both inside and outside the studio. Foley yelled at everybody. Everybody answered back calmly that they weren't guilty; yes they had hated Diana, but at the same time loved her, yes they were jealous of her, but she was a good girl, too.

Foley evolved a colossal idea, invited all suspects to the projection room and scared hell out of everyone, proving nothing, by showing them Diana's last scene. R. J. Guilding broke down and sobbed, Georgie squeaked, and Tally screamed. Cleve got sick to his stomach, and the night went on and on.

Georgie said yes, yes, he'd loved Diana; Tally said yes, yes, she'd hated her; Guilding reaffirmed the fact that Diana had stalled production, causing trouble; and Robert Denim admitted to an attempted reconciliation between himself and his former wife. Jamie Winters told how Diana had stayed up late nights, ruining her face for proper photography. And R. J. Guilding snapped:

"Diana told me you were photographing her poorly, on purpose!"

Jamie Winters was calm. "That's not true. She was trying to shove the blame for her complexion off on someone else, me."

Foley said, "You were in love with her, too?"

Winters replied, "Why do you think I became her photographer?"

So when dawn came Diana was still as dead as the night before. Big stage doors thundered aside and the suspects wearily shambled out to climb in their cars and start home.

Cleve watched them through aching eyes. Silently he walked around the studio, checking everything when it didn't need checking. He smelled the sweet green odor of the cemetery over the wall.

Funny Hollywood. It builds a studio next door to a graveyard. Right over that wall there. Sometimes it seemed everyone in movietown tried to scale that wall. Some poured themselves over in a whiskey tide, some smoked themselves over; all of them looked forward to an office in Hollywood Cemetery—with no phones. Well, Diana didn't have to climb that wall.

Someone had pushed her over. . . .

Cleve held onto the steering wheel, tight, hard, wanting to break it, telling the world to get out of the way, dammit! He was beginning to get mad!

They buried her on a bright California day with a stiff wind blowing and too many red and yellow and blue flowers and the wrong kind of tears.

That was the first day Cleve ever drank enough to get drunk. He would always remember that day.

The studio phoned three days later:

"Say, Morris, what's eating you? Where you been?"

"In my apartment," said Cleve dully.

He kept the radio off, he didn't walk the streets like he used to at night, dreaming. He neglected the newspapers; they had big pictures of her in them. The radio talked about her, so he almost wrecked the thing. When the week was over she was safely in the earth, and the newspapers had tapered off the black ink wreathes, were telling her life story on page two the following Wednesday; page four Thursday; page five Friday; page ten Saturday; and by the following Monday they wrote the concluding chapter and slipped it in among the stock market reports on page twenty-nine.

*You're slipping, Diana! Slipping! You used to make page one!*

Cleve went back to work.

By Friday there was nothing left but that new stone in Hollywood Cemetery. Papers rotted in the flooded gutters, washing away the ink of her name; the radio blatted war, and Cleve worked with his eyes looking funny and changed.

He buzzed doors all day, and people went in and out. He watched Tally dance in every morning, smaller and chipper, and happy now that Diana was gone, holding onto Georgie who was all hers now, except his mind and soul. He watched Robert Denim walk in, and they never spoke to one another. He waved hello to Jamie Winters and was courteous to R. J. Guilding.

But he watched them all, like a dialogue director waiting for one muffed line or miscue.

And finally the papers announced casually that her death had been attributed to suicide, and it was a closed chapter.

.   .   .

A couple of weeks later Cleve was still sticking to his apartment, reading and thinking, when the phone rang.

"Cleve? This is Jamie Winters. Look, cop-man, come out of it. You're wanted at a party, now, tonight. I got some film clips from Gable's last picture."

There was argument. In the end, Cleve gave in and went to the party. They sat in Jamie Winters's parlor facing a small sized screen. Winters showed them scenes from pictures that never reached the theatre. Garbo tripping over a light cord and falling on her platform. Spencer Tracy blowing his lines and swearing. William Powell sticking his tongue out at the camera when he forgot his next cue. Cleve laughed for the first time in a million years.

Jamie Winters had an endless collection of film clips of famous stars blowing up and saying censorable things.

And when Diana Coyle showed up, it was like a kick in the stomach. Like being shot with two barrels of a shot-gun! Cleve jerked and gasped, and shut his eyes, clenching the chair.

Then, suddenly, he was very cool. He had an idea. Looking at the screen, it came to him, like cold rain on his cheeks.

"Jamie!" he said.

In the sprocketing darkness, Jamie replied, "Yes?"

"I've got to see you in the kitchen, Jamie."

"Why?"

"Never mind why. Let the camera run itself and come on."

In the kitchen, Cleve held onto Jamie, "It's about those films you're showing us. The mistakes. The censored clips. Have you any clips from Diana's last picture? Spoiled scenes, blow-ups, I mean?"

"Yeah. At the studio. I collect them. It's a hobby. That stuff usually goes in the trash can. I keep them for laughs."

Cleve sucked in his breath. "Can you get that film for me; all of it; bring it here tomorrow night and go over it with me?"

"Sure, if you want me to. I don't see,— "

"Never mind, Jamie. Just do like I say, huh? Bring me all the cut-outs, the scenes that were bad. I want to see who spoiled the scenes, who caused the most trouble, and why! Will you do it, Jamie?"

"Sure. Sure I will, Cleve. Take it easy. Here, sit down. Have a drink."

Cleve didn't eat much the next day. The hours went too slowly. At night he ate a little supper and swallowed four aspirins. Then he drove in a mechanical nightmare to Jamie Winters's house.

Jamie was waiting with drinks and film in the camera.

"Thanks, Jamie." Cleve sat down and drank nervously. "All right. Shall we see them?"

"Action!" said Jamie.

Light on the screen. "Take one, scene seven, *The Gilded Virgin:* Diana Coyle, Robert Denim."

*Clack!*

The scene faded in. There was a terrace by an ocean scene in moonlight. Diana was talking:

"It's a lovely night. So lovely I can't believe in it."

Robert Denim, holding her hands in his, looked at her and said, "I think I can make you believe in it. I'll—damn it!"

"Cut!" cried Guilding's voice off-screen.

The film ran on. Denim's face was ugly, getting dark and lined.

"There you go, hogging the camera again!"

"Me?" Diana wasn't beautiful any more. Not *this* way. She shook the gilt off her wings in an angry powder. "Me, you two-bit Thespian, you loud-mouthed, dirty—"

*Flick.* Dark. End of film.

Cleve sat there, staring. After a while he said, "They didn't get along, did they?" And then, to himself, almost, "I'm glad."

"Here's another one," said Winters. The camera ticked rapidly.

Another scene. A party scene. Laughter and music and cutting across it, dark, snapping, bitter and accusative:

"—damn you!"

"—if you fed me the wrong cue on purpose! Of all the cheap, common little—"

Diana and Robert Denim, at it again!

Another scene, and another, and another. Six, seven, eight!

Here was one of Denim saying:

"Honest to God, someone ought to shut you up for good, lady!"

"Who?" cried Diana, eyes flashing like little green stones. "You? You snivel-nosed ham!"

And Denim, glaring back, saying quietly, "Yes. Maybe me. Why not? It's an idea."

There were some bristling hot scenes with Tally Durham, too. And one in which Diana browbeat little George Kroll until he was nervous and sweating out an apology. All on film; all good evidence. But the ratio was seven of Denim's blow-ups to one of Tally's or Georgie's. On and on and on and on!

"Stop it, stop it!" Cleve got up from his chair. His figure cut the light, threw a shadow on the screen, swaying.

"Thanks for the trouble, Jamie. I'm tired, too. Can—can I have these film clips of Denim?"

"Sure."

"I'm going downtown to Police Headquarters tonight and turn in Robert Denim for the murder of Diana Coyle. Thanks again, Jamie. You been a great help. 'Night."

Five, ten, fifteen, twenty hours. Count 'em by twos, by fours, by sixes. Rush the hours by. Argue with the cops and go home and flop in bed.

*Toddle off to your gas-chamber, Robert Denim; that's a good little killer!*

And then in the middle of deep slumber, your phone rings.

"Hullo."

And a voice said over the phone in the night, "Cleve?"

"Yeah?"

And the voice said, "This is Juke Davis at the film laboratory. Come quick, Cleve. I been hurt, I been hurt, oh, I been hurt . . ." A body fell at the other end of the line.

Silence.

.   .   .

He found Juke lying in a chemical bath. Red chemical from his own body where a knife had dug out his dreams and his living and his talking forever and spread it around in a scarlet lake.

A phone receiver hung dangling on one greenish wall. It was dark in the laboratory. Someone had shuffled in through the dim tunnels, come out of the dark, and now, standing there, Cleve heard nothing but the film moving forever on its trellises, like some vine going up up through the midnight room trying to find the sun. Numbly, Cleve knelt beside Juke. The man lay half-propped against the film machinery, where the printing light shot out and imprinted negative to positive. He had crawled there, across the room.

In one clenched fist, Cleve found a frame of film; the faces of Tally, Georgie, Diana and Robert Denim on it. Juke had found out something, something about this film, something about a killer; and his reward had come swiftly to him through the studio dark.

Cleve used the phone:

"This is Cleve Morris. Is Robert Denim still being held at Central Jail?"

"He's in his cell, and he won't talk. I tell you, Morris, you gave us a bum steer with them film clips . . ."

"Thanks." Cleve hung up. He looked at Juke lying there by the machinery. "Well, who was it, Juke? It wasn't Denim. That leaves Georgie and Tally? Well?"

Juke said nothing and the machinery sang a low sad song.

One year went by. Another year followed. And then a third.

Robert Denim contracted out to another studio. Tally married Georgie, Guilding died at a New Years party of overdrinking and a bad heart, time went on, everybody forgot. Well, almost everybody . . .

*Diana, child, is it cold out there, tonight—?*

Cleve rose in his seat. Three years ago. He blinked his eyes. Same kind of night as this, cold and raining.

The screen flickered.

Cleve paid little attention. It kept on flickering strangely. Cleve stiffened. His heart beat with the sprocketing noise of the machine. He bent forward.

"Jamie, will you run that last one hundred feet over again?"

"Sure thing, Cleve."

Flickers on film. Imperfections. Long blotches, short blobs. Cleve spelled it out. W . . . i . . . n. . . .

.  .  .

Cleve opened the door of the projection room so softly Jamie Winters didn't hear him. Winters was glaring out at the film on the screen, and there was a strange, happy look on his face. The look of a saint seeing a new miracle.

"Enjoying yourself, Jamie boy?"

Jamie Winters shook himself and turned, and smiled, uneasily.

Cleve locked the door. He gave a little soft lecture:

"It's been a long time. I haven't slept well many nights. Three years, Jamie. And tonight you had nothing to do so you ran off some film so you could gloat over it. Gloat over Diana and think how clever you were. Maybe it was fun to see me suffer, too, you knew how much I liked her. Have you come here often in the past three years to gloat over her, Jamie?" he asked softly.

Winters laughed good-naturedly.

Cleve said, "She didn't love you, did she? You were her photographer. So, to even things up, you began photographing her badly. It fits in. Her last two films were poor. She looked tired. It wasn't her fault; you did things with your camera. So Diana threatened to tell on you. You would've been black-balled at every studio. You couldn't have her love, and she threatened your career, so what did you do, Jamie Winters? You killed her."

"This is a poor idea of a joke," said Winters, hardening.

Cleve went on, "Diana looked at the camera when she died. She looked at you. We never thought of that. In a theatre you always feel as if she were looking at the audience, not the man behind the camera. She died. You took a picture of her dying. Then, later, you invited me to a party, fed me the bait, with those film clips showing Denim in a suspicious light. I fell for it. You destroyed all the other film that put Denim in a good position. Juke Davis found out what you were doing. He worked with film all the time, he knew you were juggling clips. You wanted to frame Denim because there had to be a fall guy and you'd be clear. Juke questioned you, you stabbed him. You stole and destroyed the few extra clips Juke had discovered. Juke couldn't talk over the phone, but he shoved his in the printing light of the developing machine and printed your name W-i-n-t-e-r-s in black splotches as the film moved. He happened to be printing the negative of Diana's last film that night! And you began running it off to me ten minutes ago, thinking it was only a damaged film!"

Jamie Winters moved quickly, like a cat. He ripped open the projector and tore the film out in one vicious animal movement.

Cleve hit him. He pulled way back and blasted loose.

The case was really over now. But he wasn't happy or glad or anything but blind red angry, flooded with hot fury.

All he could think of now while he hit the face of Winters again and again and again, holding him tight with one hand, beating him over and over with the other, all he could think of was—

A stone in the yard of the cemetery just over the wall from the studio; a stone sweating blue rain over her bronzed name. All he could say in a hoarse, choked whisper was:

"Is it cold out there tonight, Diana; is it cold, little girl?"

And Cleve hit him again and again and again!

# TWO

# IF PATHS MUST CROSS AGAIN

They sat together in their own little world within the Zebra Room and she looked at his captain's bars and he looked at the scintillas caught in her dark hair.

She thought it was nice here at the Zebra, wasn't it?

Yes, he thought so, but he was wordless and held her hand in the semi-dark. The music beat around them in a slow, quiet rhythm. People murmured at the other tables. He wanted to know why he hadn't met her sooner? Six days. It appeared to him that it was no use trying to dress those six brief days up to make them seem like six years. She tried. He tried. But the fact remained they'd only met last Friday noon at tennis, and before that there was a long nothingness in all those other years.

She wondered how many times he'd wished they'd met sooner.

He counted them for her, and ran out of slender, sun-tanned fingers. He said that he'd traveled the United States for twenty-seven years and Good Lord wasn't it hellish luck that a week before he was due in Hawaii, he met her?

Over and over again she assured him that there would be time ahead for themselves.

He shrugged his maybe, hopelessly. Just maybe. But a man needs time to look back on. A man needs time forward and time in back of him to give his dreams shape and substance.

She reminded him that they had had a week anyway; but she knew instinctively it was far short of being enough.

They sat another ten full minutes sipping tasteless cocktails, when it occured to him to ask her about her home town. He knew her life down to its finest detail, but somehow in the week's tumult her home town had been folded under. What was its name?

She set her cocktail down. Her home town was Brentwood, Illinois.

Brentwood, Illinois! He was shocked. He sat there. No, it couldn't be! He looked at her. He dropped his mouth open. He spoke slowly and with frank astonishment. It just couldn't be Brentwood, Illinois, population 34,901! Because — well — because he had visited Brentwood in 1934, he swore it! and roomed in the YMCA right across the street from Central School all during the rainy spring and the hot summer. He had been seventeen years old, and his father had sent him up there from Chicago! What did she think of that?

Oh Lord, she didn't know WHAT to think! She had gone to Central School; it had been her sophomore year! What floor had he lived on at the Y? Her eyes were wide and unbelieving.

They both got excited. A door had been flung wide in them and sunshine poured down!

Why, he had lived right there on the fourth floor! He laughed delightedly.

It burst out of her. And *she* had been in teacher Griswald's room studying math. Right across from him! They laughed together!

God Bless Mr. Griswald!

God Bless the Young Men's Christian Association! Oh, darling, darling!

He had tripped on a hole in the sidewalk in front of the Y.

Why, she'd fallen over that hole a million times on her roller skates!

And there had been wooden bannisters on the school front, he remembered. She'd *slid* down them, slivers and all!

And Mick's! he cried.

Lord, yes, Mick's! where they had served those beautiful cheese hamburgers! She was laughing full and easy and free now. Mick's, her mother had said, was a horrid truck-driver's den, but she had eaten there anyway. Oh, gosh, all those years ago and they hadn't even known it!

He gentled his laughter down and held her hands tight. Nodding gently over the good memories. Every noon he had sat at one end of Mick's counter watching the school girls idle by in bright blouses and skirts.

And here they were in Los Angeles two thousand miles away and ten years removed from Mick's, and she was twenty-five and he was twenty-seven, she said, and it had taken all these years to meet.

He shook his head uncomprehendingly. Why couldn't he have found her then?

Maybe she hadn't been pretty enough.

Maybe *he* had been scared, he came back at her. That was probably it. He had been a frightened sort; girls had had to trip him, waylay him. He'd worn hornrims, carried thick books under his arm instead of muscles. Lord, Lord, darling, he had eaten more darn hamburgers at Mick's.

With large hunks of onion, she amended. And the hotcakes with syrup. Did he recall? She began thinking and it was hard, looking at him. She didn't remember him. She sent her mind back, searching frantically over the years, and she had never seen him before. At least not the way he was now.

Perhaps she had snubbed him, he volunteered.

She had if he had flirted.

He remembered only looking at a pretty dark-haired girl.

A dark-haired girl in Brentwood in the year 1934 in the springtime, she said. In Mick's, at twelve o'clock noon on a spring day. She thought back. How had this dark-haired girl been dressed?

He remembered a blue ribbon through her black, shining hair, tied in a large bow, and he had an impression of a blue polka dot dress and young breasts just beginning to fill. Oh, she had been pretty.

She asked him if he remembered the girl's face?

He remembered only that the girl had been beautiful. One doesn't recall single faces out of a crowd after so much time has gone. Think of all the people one meets on the street each day.

She closed her eyes. She told him that if she'd only known then that she'd meet him later in life, she'd have looked for him.

He smiled ironically. You never knew those things. You saw so many people every week, every year, every day, and most of them were destined for obscurity. All one could do, later, was look back at the dim movements of the years and try to see where one's life briefly touched or flickered against another's. The same town, the same restaurant, the same food, the same atmosphere, but two different paths and ways of living, each oblivious of the other. He kissed her fingers. He should have kept his eyes open for her, too. But the only girl he had noticed had been that dark-haired girl with the ribboned hair.

It irritated her that he and she had rubbed elbows, passed on the street, even. On summer nights, she even bet he had been down at the carnival by the lake!

Yes, he'd been down. He'd looked at the colored lights streaking the water, heard the merry-go-round jangling to the stars.

She remembered, she remembered! Eagerly she said it. And some nights maybe he'd gone to the Academy Theatre?

He nodded. Harold Lloyd's picture WELCOME DANGER had played there that summer!

Yes, yes, she'd seen that, too. Maybe they'd been seated only a few people apart! A short feature of Ruth Etting singing Shine On Harvest Moon was with it. Follow the bouncing ball! Did he realize how near and yet how far they'd been apart? Did he realize they'd practically knocked one another down going by for five months? It was terrible! Those brief months — together — and then ten years until last Friday! It happened all the time that way for people. You live a block from people in New York, never see them, go to Milwaukee and — boom — meet them at a party! And tomorrow night—she caught her breath and sobered. Never mind tomorrow night. Back now to that spring day in 1934, in Mick's, back to that dark-haired girl. She paused and spoke his name softly and said darling. Then, she made her confession.

That girl with the dark hair and the gay blue ribbon, she said quietly, well, that was herself.

He bent and kissed her, hard, on the lips. He had known it, known it all the time. It just *had* to be! He could hardly breathe, and he looked immortally bright and happy, as if this were the moment he had waited for. Now there was a past to give his dreams shape and substance.

He ordered another drink in celebration and just sat wondering and looking at her. He talked softly and earnestly and joyfully. He had loved her all these years. He had *known* her all this time. They had a mutual past, Praise the Lord. He murmured. Oh Praise the good sweet gentle Lord which had given him a miracle before his going away.

They sat another hour, smiling, talking of those days, the town, the theatres, the trees, the creek, the summer. Then he saw the hands of the clock on the dim Zebra wall. They had to go, it was late.

She leaned back, closing her eyes, touching his arm, his captain's bars. Just one more moment for her, please, she asked.

He closed his eyes, too, opened them, looked around and saw all the other people's faces. She followed his gaze. Perhaps they both thought the same strange thought.

He told her to look around. He told her to remember these faces. She must be warned and ready *this* time. She had forgotten to look for *him* ten years ago. But she must remember *these* faces. Maybe, if he didn't come back, she might some day meet someone else and she'd perhaps go with this someone else for six months and suddenly discover that their paths had crossed before — on an April night in 1945 at the Zebra Room in L.A. And, oh yeah, she'd been with a young army captain that night, what ever happened to him? Oh, he went off to war and never returned. And well, by gosh, she'd discover that one of these faces in the Zebra Room right now might be that somebody else in the future; right here and now looking at him and her, seeing this, seeing him talking to her now, noting her beauty and saying I love you, I love you, over and over. She must remember these faces and maybe they'd remember the young army captain and his beautiful lady . . .

Her fingers on his lips stopped his other words. She was crying and she saw the many faces of people turned her way, and she thought of all the paths and patterns of life, and did not *want* to remember these faces. She had not looked for him ten years ago, there was no need to look for anyone else now.

She lifted her head. That wasn't important, she said. What *was* important was the carnival, Brentwood, Central School, the Y, Mick's, he and she and the summer, their past . . .

And she with her dark hair and her blue ribbon, he said, smiling again. It was good for him, thinking of it.

They arose and she kissed him insistently, and his sunburnt hands went through her tumbling dark hair, holding her, and she was happy that he'd never never know that as a girl in 1934 she had never owned a blue ribbon for her hair, and had *never* worn one in all her life.

They exited, laughing.

# THREE

# THE MIRACLES OF JAMIE

Jamie Winters worked his first miracle in the morning. The second, third, and various other miracles came later in the day. But the first miracle was always the most important.

It was always the same: "Make Mother well. Put color in her cheeks. Don't let Mom be sick too much longer."

It was Mom's illness that had first made him think about himself and miracles. And because of her he kept on, learning how to be good at them so that he could keep her well and could make life jump through a hoop.

It was not the first day that he had worked miracles. He had done them in the past, but always hesitantly, since sometimes he did not say them right, or Ma and Pa interrupted, or the other kids in the Seventh Grade at school made noise. They spoiled things.

But in the past month he had felt his power flow over him like cool, certain water; he bathed in it, gloried in it, had come from the shower of it beaded with glory water and with a halo of wonder about his dark-haired head.

Five days ago he'd taken down the family Bible, with real color pictures of Jesus as a boy in it, and had compared them with his own face in the bathroom mirror, gasping. He shook all over. There it *was*.

And wasn't Ma getting better every day now? Well—*there!*

Now, on Monday morning, following the first miracle at home, he worked a second one at school. He wanted to lead the Arizona State Day parade as head of his class battalion. And the principal, naturally, selected Jamie to lead. Jamie felt fine. The girls looked up to him, bumping him with their soft, thin little elbows, especially one named Ingrid, whose golden hair rustled in Jamie's face as they all hurried out of the cloakroom.

Jamie Winters held his head so high, and when he drank from the chromium fountain he bent so carefully and twisted the shining handle so exactly, so precisely—so godlike and indomitable.

Jamie knew it would be useless to tell his friends. They'd laugh. After all, Jesus was pounded nail through palm and ankle to a Calvary Hill cross because he told on himself. This time, it would be wise to wait. At least until he was sixteen and grew a beard, thus establishing once and for all the incredible proof of his identity!

Sixteen was somewhat young for a beard, but Jamie felt that he could exert the effort to force one if the time came and necessity demanded.

The children poured from the schoolhouse into the hot spring light. In the distance were the mountains, the foothills spread green with cactus, and overhead was a vast Arizona sky of very fine blue. The children donned paper hats and crepe-paper Sam Browne belts in blue and red. Flags burst open upon the wind; everybody yelled and formed into groups, glad to escape the schoolrooms for one day.

Jamie stood at the head of the line, very calm and quiet. Someone said something, and Jamie realized that it was young Huff who was talking.

"I hope we win the parade prize," said Huff worriedly.

Jamie looked at him. "Oh, we'll win all right. I know we'll win. I'll guarantee it! Heck, yes!"

Huff was brightened by such steadfast faith. "You think so?"

"I *know* so! Leave it to me!"

"What do you mean, Jamie?"

"Nothing. Just watch and see, that's all. Just watch!"

"Now, children!" Mr. Palmborg, the principal, clapped hands; the sun shone on his glasses. Silence came quickly. "Now, children," he said, nodding, "remember what we taught you yesterday about marching. Remember how you pivot to turn a corner, and remember those special routines we practiced, will you?"

"Sure!" everybody said at once.

The principal concluded his brief address and the parade began, Jamie heading it with his hundreds of following disciples.

The feet bent up and straightened down, and the street went under them. The yellow sun warmed Jamie and he, in turn, bade it shine the whole day to make things perfect.

When the parade edged onto Main Street, and the High School band began pulsing its brass heart and rattling its wooden bones on the drums, Jamie wished they would play "The Stars and Stripes Forever."

. . .

Later, when they played "Columbia, Gem of the Ocean," Jamie thought quickly, oh yeah, that's what he'd meant—"Columbia," not "Stars and Stripes Forever"—and was satisfied that his wish had been obeyed.

The street was lined with people, as it was on the Arizona rodeo days in February. People sweated in intent layers, five deep for over a mile; the rhythm of feet came back in reflected cadence from two-story frame fronts. There were occasional glimpses of mirrored armies marching in the tall windows of the J.C.

Penney Store or of the Morble Company. Each cadence was like a whip thud on the dusty asphalt, sharp and true, and the band music shot blood through Jamie's miraculous veins.

He concentrated, scowling fiercely. Let us win, he thought. Let everyone march perfectly: chins up, shoulders back, knees high, down, high again, sun upon denimed knees rising in a blue tide, sun upon tanned girl-knees like small, round faces upping and falling. Perfect, perfect, perfect. Perfection surged confidently through Jamie, extending into an encompassing aura that held his own group intact. As he moved, so moved the nation. As his fingers snapped in a brisk pendulum at his sides, so did their fingers, their arms cutting an orbit. And as his shoes trod asphalt, so theirs followed in obedient imitation.

As they reached the reviewing stand, Jamie cued them; they coiled back upon their own lines like bright garlands twining to return again, marching in the original direction, without chaos.

Oh, so darn perfect! cried Jamie to himself.

It was hot. Holy sweat poured out of Jamie, and the world sagged from side to side. Presently the drums were exhausted and the children melted away. Lapping an ice-cream cone, Jamie was relieved that it was all over.

Mr. Palmborg came rushing up, all heated and sweating.

"Children, children, I have an announcement to make!" he cried.

Jamie looked at young Huff, who stood beside him, also with an ice-cream cone. The children shrilled, and Mr. Palmborg patted the noise into a ball which he made vanish like a magician.

"We've won the competition! Our school marched finest of all the schools!"

In the clamor and noise and jumping up and down and hitting one another on the arm muscles in celebration, Jamie nodded quietly over his ice-cream cone, looked at young Huff, and said, "See? I told you so. Now, will you believe in me!"

Jamie continued licking his cold cone with a great, golden peace in him.

.  .  .

Jamie did not immediately tell his friends why they had won the marching competition. He had observed a tendency in them to be suspicious and to ridicule anyone who told them that they were not as good as they thought they were, that their talent had been derived from an outside source.

No, it was enough for Jamie to savor his minor and major victories; he enjoyed his little secret, he enjoyed the things that happened. Such things as getting high marks in arithmetic or winning a basketball game were ample reward. There was always some by-product of his miracles to satisfy his as yet small hunger.

He paid attention to blond young Ingrid with the placid grey-blue eyes. She, in turn, favored him with her attentions, and he knew then that his ability was well-rooted, established.

Aside from Ingrid, there were other good things. Friendships with several boys came about in wondrous fashion. One case, though, required some little thought and care. The boy's name was Cunningham. He was big and fat and bald because some fever had necessitated shaving his skull. The kids called him Billiard; he thanked them by kicking them in the shins, knocking them down and sitting on them while he performed quick dentistry with his knuckles.

It was upon this Billiard Cunningham that Jamie hoped to apply his greatest ecclesiastical power. Walking through the rough paths of the desert toward his home, Jamie often conjured up visions of himself picking up Billiard by his left foot and cracking him like a whip so as to shock him senseless. Dad had once done that to a rattlesnake. Of course, Billiard was too heavy for this neat trick. Beside, it might hurt him, and Jamie didn't really want him killed or anything, just dusted off a little to show him where he belonged in the world.

But when he chinned up to Billiard, Jamie got cold feet and decided to wait a day or two longer for meditation. There was no use rushing things, so he let Billiard go free. Boy, Billiard didn't know how lucky he was at such times, Jamie clucked to himself.

One Tuesday, Jamie carried Ingrid's books home. She lived in a small cottage not far from the Santa Catalina foothills. Together they walked in peaceful content, needing no words. They even held hands for a while.

Turning about a clump of prickly pears, they came face to face with Billiard Cunningham.

He stood with his big feet planted across the path, plump fists on his hips, staring at Ingrid with appreciative eyes. Everybody stood still, and Billiard said:

"I'll carry your books, Ingrid. Here."

He reached to take them from Jamie.

Jamie fell back a step. "Oh, no, you don't," he said.

"Oh, yes, I do," retorted Billiard.

"Like heck you do," said Jamie.

"Like heck I don't," exclaimed Billiard, and snatched again, knocking the books into the dust.

Ingrid yelled, then said, "Look here, you can both carry my books. Half and half. That'll settle it."

Billiard shook his head.

"All or nothing," he leered.

Jamie looked back at him.

"Nothing, then!" he shouted.

He summoned up his powers like wrathful storm clouds; lightning crackled hot in each fist. What matter if Billiard loomed four inches taller and some several broader? The fury-wrath lived in Jamie; he would knock Billiard senseless with one clean bolt—maybe two.

There was no room for stuttering fear now; Jamie was cauterized clean of it by a great rage. He pulled away back and let Billiard have it on the chin.

"Jamie!" screamed Ingrid.

The only miracle after that was how Jamie got out of it with his life.

.  .  .

Dad poured Epsom salts into a dishpan of hot water, stirred it firmly, and said, "You oughta known better, darn your hide. Your mother sick an' you comin' home all banged up this way."

Dad made a leathery motion of one brown hand. His eyes were bedded in crinkles and lines, and his moustache was pepper-gray and sparse, as was his hair.

"I didn't know Ma was very sick any more," said Jamie.

"Women don't talk much," said Dad, dryly. He soaked a towel in steaming Epsom salts and wrung it out. He held Jamie's beaten profile and swabbed it. Jamie whimpered. "Hold still," said Dad. "How you expect me to fix that cut if you don't hold still, darn it."

"What's going on out there?" Mother's voice asked from the bedroom, real tired and soft.

"Nothing," said Dad, wringing out the towel again. "Don't you fret. Jamie just fell and cut his lip, that's all."

"Oh, Jamie," said Mother.

"I'm okay, Ma," said Jamie. The warm towel helped to normalize things. He tried not to think of the fight. It made bad thinking. There were memories of flailing arms, himself pinned down, Billiard whooping with delight and beating downward while Ingrid, crying real tears, threw her books, screaming, at his back.

And then Jamie staggered home alone, sobbing bitterly.

"Oh, Dad," he said now. "It didn't work." He meant his physical miracle on Billiard. "It didn't work."

"What didn't work?" said Dad, applying liniment to bruises.

"Oh, nothing. Nothing." Jamie licked his swollen lip and began to calm down. After all, you can't have a perfect batting average. Even the Lord made mistakes. And—Jamie grinned suddenly—yes, yes, he had *meant* to lose the fight! Yes, he had. Wouldn't Ingrid love him all the more for having fought and lost just for her?

Sure. That was the answer. It was just a reversed miracle, that was all!

"Jamie," Mother called him.

He went in to see her.

.  .  .

With one thing and another, including Epsom salts and a great resurgence of faith in himself because Ingrid loved him now more than ever, Jamie went through the rest of the week without much pain.

He walked Ingrid home, and Billiard didn't bother him again. Billiard played after-school baseball, which was a greater attraction than Ingrid—the sudden sport interest being induced indirectly by telepathy via Jamie, Jamie decided.

Thursday, Ma looked worse. She bleached out to a pallid trembling and a pale coughing. Dad looked scared. Jamie spent less time trying to make things come out wonderful in school and thought more and more of curing Ma.

Friday night, walking alone from Ingrid's house, Jamie watched telegraph poles swing by him very slowly. He thought, if I get to the next telegraph pole before that car behind me reaches me, Mama will be all well.

Jamie walked casually, not looking back, ears itching, legs wanting to run to make the wish come true.

The telegraph pole approached. So did the car behind.

Jamie whistled cautiously. The car was coming too fast!

Jamie jumped past the pole just in time; the car roared by.

There now. Mama would be all well again.

He walked along some more.

Forget about her. Forget about wishes and things, he told himself. But it was tempting, like a hot pie on a window sill. He had to touch it. He couldn't leave it be, oh, no. He looked ahead on the road and behind on the road.

I bet I can get down to Schabold's ranch gate before another car comes and do it walking easy, he declared to the sky. And that will make Mama well all the quicker.

At this moment, in a traitorous, mechanical action, a car jumped over the low hill behind and roared forward.

Jamie walked fast, then began to run.

I bet I can get down to Schabold's gate, I bet I can—

Feet up, feet down.

.  .  .

He stumbled.

He fell into the ditch, his books fluttering about like dry, white birds. When he got up, sucking his lips, the gate was only twenty yards further on.

The car motored by him in a large cloud of dust.

"I take it back, I take it back," cried Jamie. "I take it back, what I said, I didn't mean it."

With a sudden bleat of terror, he ran for home. It was all his fault, *all* his fault!

The doctor's car stood in front of the house.

Through the window, Mama looked sicker. The doctor closed up his little black bag and looked at Dad a long time with strange lights in his little black eyes.

Jamie ran out onto the desert to walk alone. He did not cry. He was paralyzed, and he walked like an iron child, hating himself, blundering into the dry river bed, kicking at prickly pears and stumbling again and again.

Hours later, with the first stars, he came home to find Dad standing beside Mama's bed and Mama not saying much—just lying there like fallen snow, so quiet. Dad tightened his jaw, screwed up his eyes, caved in his chest and put his head down.

Jamie took up a station at the end of the bed and stared at Mama, shouting instructions in his mind to her.

Get well, get well, Ma, get well, you'll be all right, sure you'll be fine, I command it, you'll be fine, you'll be swell, you just get up and dance around, we need you, Dad and I do, it wouldn't be good without you, get well, Ma, get well, Ma. Get well!

The fierce energy lashed out from him silently, wrapping, cuddling her and beating into her sickness, tendering her heart. Jamie felt glorified in his warm power.

She *would* get well. She *must!* Why, it was silly to think any other way. Ma just wasn't the dying sort.

Dad moved suddenly. It was a stiff movement with a jerking of breath. He held Mama's wrists so hard he might have broken them. He lay against her breasts sounding the heart and Jamie screamed inside.

Ma, don't, Ma, don't, oh Ma, please don't give up.

Dad got up, swaying.

She was dead.

Inside the walls of Jericho that was Jamie's mind, a thought went screaming about in one last drive of power: yes, she's dead, all right, so she is dead, so what if she is dead? Bring her back to life again, yes, make her live again, Lazarus, come forth, Lazarus, Lazarus, come forth from the tomb, Lazarus, come forth.

He must have been babbling aloud, for Dad turned and glared at him in old, ancient horror and struck him bluntly across the mouth to shut him up.

Jamie sank against the bed, mouthing into the cold blankets, and the walls of Jericho crumbled and fell down about him.

. . .

Jamie returned to school a week later. He did not stride into the school yard with his old assurance; he did not bend imperiously at the fountain; nor did he pass his tests with anything more than a grade of seventy-five.

The children wondered what had happened to him. He was never quite the same.

They did not know that Jamie had given up his role. He could not tell them. They did not know what they had lost.

# FOUR

# THE LONG WAY AROUND
# (THE LONG WAY HOME)

Charlie Guidney's heart was shaking inside him as he made the top of the stairs. He wore a hunted look as he leaned against the bannister and thought, well, another day's over. The office is behind me; the comptometers are behind me. I have a nice evening to look forward to. He winced. Inside, his heart sounded like a broken comptometer, off-rhythm, totaling up a colossal No Sale. What had his doctor said?

"That heart of yours needs a rest. Take it on a vacation."

Small and pale, Charlie Guidney moved slowly along the fourth floor hall. He dreaded telling his wife about his health, his heart—

He blinked sweat from his tired eyes. Through the long hot day the comptometers had sung like a million metal crickets in all the long, echoing office rooms. Mr. Sternwell had yelled at him. He'd like to kill Sternwell. Couldn't he understand that Charlie was a sick man?

Charlie stopped at his own apartment door. Inside waited the red-haired, half-alive woman he had once loved. Would she approve of his going away for a rest? No. Her mouth would bang shut like a trap when he spoke of his illness. Her eyes would hold sharp amusement, while her lips said he was all right, he just needed more sleep nights.

He put his shaking hand on the knob. Either he got away on a long vacation or some day, in a righteous fury, he'd push Mr. Sternwell out the tenth story window.

Oh, the monotony of coming-going on streetcars, work, the endlessly dull conversations with Lydia over half-fried foods! He feared for his sanity. Sometimes he even entertained ideas of killing Lydia. The way she stared fixedly, feverishly, at all the younger men in the apartment house—as if they were toys to be played with.

The door opened from the inside. A young man appeared, bobbing his blond head at Charlie Guidney in surprised welcome. "Oh, hi, Mr. Guidney. Just been fixing your radio."

Charlie watched Travis go down the hall, then entered. His wife sat spread out on a grey sofa, with a brilliant magazine for a head. Behind slowly fluttered pages Lydia's voice said coolly, "You're late!"

She had him off balance, as always. "It's only five after six," he said.

"And tomorrow night'll be ten after, the next night twenty after," she said sharply behind her reading. "And later and later and *later!*"

He fidgeted around so he could see her large white nose, wide jaw, her eyes, as shiny as two bits of blue glass. "My heart, the doctor—" he began. "Your heart," she scoffed. "Your damned heart again is it? I don't see you dead, much the worse for me, God save me," she muttered.

"Oh," he cried helplessly, "you're trying to cover up, confuse me. That young radio man, Travis, has been up here visiting again." She simpered and scanned her magazine, not reading it. This so infuriated him. He looked wildly about the drab room as if seeking some means of getting back at her.

"Look," he cried. "A mouse!"

"Ah, where!" she shrieked. She seized her huge feet from the floor, paling under her blazing wig of red hair, eyes searching, frightened.

There was no mouse. He had used the old trick again. Her eyes glittered straight at him. "Just for that," she pronounced slowly. "I'll take an extra ten dollars from your paycheck this week. Ten dollars or you fix your own suppers for a week, like you did last month!"

He stood wordlessly gesturing toward her, wanting to speak simply and say, "We've let marriage make us mean and small. Let's get out of Los Angeles, Lydia. Maybe if we got away we'd start living again. Maybe you'd be like you used to—"

He knew it was useless. Lydia was the kind of woman who viciously creamed your coffee if you loved it black, played the radio at a thunder if your head ached. How could he confess his illness and spiritual want to her? She'd say they couldn't afford travel for his health. She'd sit watching him die. His head swam. Sternwell. Office. Doctor. Lydia. Murder. He hesitated. *Murder.* Hold on! He lifted his head, laughing inwardly.

"Close the door, and hang up that dirty hat of yours," she snapped.

.  .  .

He said dully, "No, that won't do any good," frantically searching for something to say, "I just killed a man!"

Lydia didn't seem to understand. *"Really?* What's his name?"

Charlie flushed. "I said I *killed* a man!" he cried. "K-i-l-l-e-d! Killed. Murdered!"

"Killed!" she screamed, on her feet now. Charlie leaned his head against the door, shut his eyes. He was in for it now. He had to go through with it. There was no backing out. Make it good, he told himself frantically, make it good. Tell her. Go *on.* "I shot him right through his heart," he said in awed wonder. "Very pretty."

"Oh, Charlie—"

"I couldn't help it," said Charlie. "I didn't like his face. He was one of those people with no chin . . ."

"Oh, now, Charlie!"

"Yes," he laughed gently, slowly. "Oh, now, Charlie. That won't help. I blew his heart back through his spinal cord. He looked surprised."

It was almost as if he *had* killed some one. He imagined the explosion, the blood, the excitement. His heart pounded. His voice was high, shrill as the ring of alarm clocks in dreams.

He liked what it was doing to Lydia. She had forgotten her Mr. Travis and her radio and her scornful cruelty. She watched him as if he were a mechanical man for whom she'd lost the key. He sat down. His feet tracked mud across the green carpet.

She wanted to complain about the mud. It was easier to understand a dirty floor than a Charlie Guidney who had killed a human being.

He looked at the mud and then at her in strange triumph. "Everything's shot to hell," he said. "He folded over my gun like a marionette. God, it was exciting!" Lydia stared at him like a blind woman, her hands twisting, the blood gone from her face. Heaven help him *now* if he slipped!

"I got the idea today in the office. Mr. Sternwell yelled at me, and I thought to myself 'He shouldn't yell so loud, I don't like it.' And then I thought, 'He's no good to the world, he's getting old and somebody should stop him from shouting—' " He leaned forward, "Somebody. Who? All of a sudden I—"

He pointed at himself then, smiling. "Me. Mr. Charles Guidney, white collar worker, tidy, meek and pale, Charles C. Guidney. Blood all over the place." Lydia shivered, so he very carefully repeated, "Blood all over the place!"

Lydia's face was as it hadn't been in ten years. Everything bad was gone out of it in this moment. She was worrying. It was suddenly the greatest thing in the world to lie.

"I left work early," he said. "On Main Street you can't buy a gun without a permit, so I stole one. When the dealer went into the backroom for a moment I got one. Then I went back to the office and I followed Mr. Sternwell downstairs and in the alley I killed him!"

Lydia sat down unsteadily.

"So now I'm a fugitive," said Charlie, simply. "We'll have to leave town, take a trip—"

"We can't afford—" Lydia caught herself. Perhaps the vision of the five-thousand dollars at the bank, under her name, stopped her. Perhaps, too, she'd often wanted to get away, but never admitted it. She was not one to come out and agree on other people's plans.

This might be the turning point. They could go off, start again together, if she stuck by him now. But if she really hated him, she'd turn him over to the

police now, instantly. This was a test of her love for him, thought Charlie, as-
tounded at the implications he had not considered when starting his lie. The
embarrassment if she *did* turn him over to the cops. He'd have to tell the truth
in front of her and she'd glower and simper, hate him even more.

Lydia was very calm. "What do you want me to do?" she asked.

"You mean you'll help me? You love me enough to go with me?"

She examined him quietly. Maybe she knew he lied. Maybe she saw new pos-
sibilities in him because he showed enough imagination to frame a story such
as this. Perhaps her pride prevented her accepting the plan on just its vacation
merits. Perhaps she liked playing this game, too. She was a gun-moll now. He
almost laughed.

She repeated, "What do you want me to do?"

"I'll pack suitcases. You reserve tickets on tonight's San Diego bus!" He hurried around the room. "We'll forget the whole thing in Mexico for six months.
Oh, it'll be good with you, Lydia!"

Her expression was thoughtful as she put on her hat and coat. "And hurry," he
said, giving her the bus-ticket money. She walked out the door, shut it. Laughing, singing, Charlie stuffed clothes into suitcases. "She loves me!" he whispered,
amazed. "There *is* something to live for, then. She's actually helping *me*, going
with *me*. She doesn't care about any one but *me!*"

While shaving, he deliberately left the top off the cream tube. He did not dry
the brush nor rinse the bowl nor hang the towel straight.

Lydia stood stiff and calm in the bathroom door. "Here are the tickets,
Charlie," she announced.

"You're late," he said.

"I'm sorry," she said.

"Don't do it again," he said, "There's no excuse."

"There was a crowd," she explained, looking straight at him in the mirror,
taking off her hat. "I was lucky to get these. The bus leaves at nine sharp."

"Lydia," he said. He hesitated. He looked down at the bowl, at his wet hands,
then at her level eyes. "Lydia, you don't know what this means to me. To have
you backing me up—"

"Yes, Charlie, yes," she said, without tone.

A siren sounded below in the darkening street. For a moment Charlie did
not comprehend it. Then he jerked his hands up and let out a mock cry of
despair, hurled himself from the bathroom. "They'll surround the house!" He
thrashed into his coat, crammed his hat on, seized the two suitcases, put them
down, took the tickets from Lydia, stuck them dangling in his lapel pocket and
whispered swiftly. "Quick. Down the back way into the alley!"

Lydia stood very straight, her eyes to one side, her head tilted. "The police
car went on by, Charles," she told him.

"Well, we'd better go down the front way then, huh? I guess it'd look funny for us running down the alley. Go on ahead, Lydia!"

She marched out. He walked around the room, laughing at the walls and the ceiling. He wiped his shoes on the sofa they'd bought on an installment plan. He smashed two gaudy pictures on the wall. Nodding to the shattered frames, he was ready for the world. He went out and slammed the door hard.

.   .   .

A fat man waited below the steps outside as Charlie closed the front door cautiously and glanced around. Lydia gripped Charlie's elbow and croaked, "Mr. Kelly!"

Officer Kelly, mistaking this for a salutation, saluted them. "Ah, and hello to the two of you, Mr. and Mrs. Guidney!" he said cheerily.

Lydia stumbled and weaved and blinked many times, jerking her head first toward Charlie, then the policeman. "Oh, Mr. Kelly, please, Charlie didn't mean to kill that man!"

Charlie dumbfounded, balanced on the top step. He caught his wife and propelled her backward. "No, no, no," he hissed frantically. "Control yourself!"

Lydia, over Charlie's shoulder, pleaded with the cop. "He didn't know what he was doing. Don't shoot him, oh, please."

Kelly said from a great distance, "He didn't know he was doing what to who?"

"Nothing, nothing." Charlie smiled at the officer. "You don't understand."

Lydia cringed against Charlie. "He'll shoot us!" she screamed.

Charlie's heart began to kick up; it got the familiar pains.

"Hold on, hold on." Officer Kelly came up the steps with long slow movements of big heavy feet. Charlie groaned to his wife. "Go inside, go inside, Lydia. Nothing's wrong, Lydia. Oh God!"

"What," Mr. Kelly wanted to know, "are you two talking about?"

"It's Mr. Sternwell, he was old and mean and somebody should have shot him and Charlie did!" sobbed Mrs. Guidney in a wild torrent. Charlie managed to pump her through the door, slam it and stand against it facing officer Kelly.

"Well?" asked Kelly, scowling darkly.

"My wife's nervous. She—she thinks I—I shot a man. I didn't. No, sir, I didn't. All a joke. Just a joke."

"All a joke," said Kelly. "Ha ha." He thumped the suitcases with one foot. "And of course you're taking them clothes on over to the laundry to be rough-dried?"

Charlie made a surprised face. "Clothes?" Charlie discovered the baggage at his feet and his shoulders sagged.

"And," said Kelly as he very delicately plucked a paper from Charlie's lapel. "And this little piece of green tissue," he said politely. "This wouldn't be a bus ticket for San Diego?"

"I tell you my wife has the whole thing messed up."

"Suppose *you* tell me," said Kelly earnestly.

Charlie got indignant. "Call precinct headquarters! Ask them if any old men've been killed in the past three hours!"

"I am not that dense," said Kelly. "Maybe you hid the remains."

"Aw, now, Kelly, do I look like a fiend? Come here." And he led Kelly down a couple of steps and whispered the whole set up into one of Kelly's hairy ears. "You see?" he finished off. "And if she finds out it's a frame-up, I'll never lift my head again! She'll peel the hide off me."

Kelly's eyes flashed a squinting, understanding blue glance at him. Kelly put his hand on Charlie's shoulder, patting him. "That's different, now. I won't let the cat out. I know just how you feel. Sometimes *my* wife—but that's a long story better saved. I hope you will not mind if I make a phone call anyways, Mr. Guidney?"

Charlie laughed. "Sure, sure." He slapped Kelly's broad back. They went across the street. Now I'll have to tell Lydia I fooled Kelly, or she won't leave town.

Kelly talked into the round metal mouthpiece of the phone, feeling good. "This is Kelly. Yeah." Kelly listened. Charlie whistled and rocked on his heels. Mexico. Peace. Easy living. A dream coming true. "Yeah?" said Kelly. "Well, this is what I'm inquiring about. Listen—" and he told them. And he smiled. Charlie watched him. Kelly's smile faded, like smoke in a cold wind. "Yeah?"

Charlie shifted his feet. "What's up, Kelly?" Kelly listened again and said, "Oh, he *did*, did he?" Charlie swallowed hard. He hung onto Kelly's elbow. "There isn't anything wrong—is there?" Kelly listened. "Oh, it did, did it? I will."

"Will what, Kelly?" asked Charlie.

Kelly looked at him and talked in the phone. "He's standing right here beside me." Mr. Kelly hung up.

Charlie said, "No. No. Don't look at me that way. No!" Kelly replied, "Oh, yes, Mr. Guidney, it *can* be. Mr. Guidney, I hereby arrest you for the murder of one John Pastor, found bleeding to death from a gun wound half an hour ago. Shot dead with a .22 caliber pistol, he was, in an alley behind some trash bins, over on Temple Street. That's just eight blocks from here, close enough to make me think— "

Charlie kicked Mr. Kelly's shins just as Mr. Kelly was taking out his hand-cuffs. Kelly grunted. Charlie hit him with his fist. Kelly fell down and lay motionless on the sidewalk. His head had struck the pole on the way down.

Lydia lay against the wall inside the door as Charlie yanked it open. She was like ice. "Charlie, we can't escape—we can't escape. We were fools to try."

His jaw hung down. "But this is different. Something's happened. Wait for me, Lydia! I'll come back!"

"But what about the bus tickets?"

"We can't use them now!" he cried. "Good-bye, Lydia!"

"Charlie, come back! Where are you going?"

"I don't know!" The door slammed. His footsteps died out down the alley.

. . .

It was dark. Charlie grieved to himself, walking along in the shadows. How had he gotten into this? A lifetime of sturdy mediocrity and now—boom-crash-bang—Jack the Ripper! He shivered. Talk about the chill hand of Fate—

He looked around. This was the drab shopping district where he and Lydia often walked to pick up some Chinese chop suey, or some Russian rye bread or kosher corned beef. Liquor stores, gun stores, little cafes. Empty lots and dark alleys. Drunken men roaming, drunken men in the lots and in the alleys.

Thousands of people in Los Angeles. Any one of them could be a murderer brushing by him as he walked, watching for prowl cars. How could you tell which one: the man with the limping foot over there; the woman with the shopping bag?

You fool, he told himself. The cops will never believe your story now. How can you explain the bus-ticket, the packed bags, the running way—except as fleeing from a crime you just committed?

You're looking for an old man you never saw before and someone who killed him. You've got to find the real murderer. Out of a population of a million and a half that should be simple!

In the darkness most shops were shuttered and padlocked. A few hardware and credit shops were still lit, their proprietors living in the doorways to catch a breeze from the warm summer night.

Charlie paused in one door. "I hear there was some excitement around here?" The man to whom Charlie spoke folded his arms. He seemed unaware of any crisis. "Yeah. In the alley down there."

"An old man, wasn't it? Who was he? Who killed him?"

"I don't know. An old wino, that's all. Am *I* worried?"

"Did you see anything?"

"Nothing. I saw blue serge, and badges, and sirens I heard."

Charlie thanked him and walked away and the night came in to get him. He felt like stopping people and looking into their faces and saying, "You didn't happen to kill someone an hour ago, did you? No? Thanks, anyhow." On a few steps. Stop again. "Mister, are you a killer?" He haunted every open shop. Nobody had seen from nothing. It was a real hot night, wasn't it? Rain tomorrow, maybe? Would you like to buy a real piece of goods, mister? Step in, have a look!

The popcorn vendor stood at the corner of Temple Street and Boylston. Blue-yellow flame danced in the glass cube and popcorn was trembling within a metal-grid cage. The little dark vendor took Charlie's nickel, and they talked.

"The dead man? Johnny? He drank a lot. He prowled around the alleys here all the time; slept in them at night. Still, there was no reason for nobody to kill him. He didn't have no money." The vendor looked at Charlie with his trembling-flame eyes. "You know him?"

"I'm—very closely related to him."

A trolley car roared down the asphalt hill behind him in a mechanical cataclysm. In that riot of wheels on hard tracks, Charlie rushed with thoughts, saw himself in his drab office totaling up numbers for years, jangling up accounts, fingering reports, Sundays off, half a day Saturday, coming home on loud street cars through the monotonous streets, meeting Lydia in their forty-a-month coffin where they argued coffee-cocoa-tea, switched radio on-off, conflicted over double features, swore about the heat, damned the cold.

So one night, while thinking about killing Mr. Sternwell, his boss, on the way home Charlie Guidney changed his life. With the shot of a gun he propels himself and wife out of a workaday world into change, movement, chaos.

But he hadn't killed anybody. He was disgusted with his imagination. Well, then, smart guy, his mind replied, if you aren't insane and not the murderer— *who* is?

. . .

He began to walk. He wandered into gunsmiths and hardware stores and swap shops. He asked the only question he could:

"Mister, did anyone buy a gun from you today?" he said. "A twenty-two?"

And the answers came back:

"You kidding?" said one. "No," said another. "Hell, no," said a third. "I don't sell guns," said a fourth.

"Don't bother me," said the last one. "It takes a permit to buy a gun. People don't buy guns every day."

"Did anyone ask to *see* your guns? Anyone at all?" pleaded Charlie.

"One or two people. I don't remember."

"Are any of your guns missing?"

The man looked annoyed. "No."

He went back to the other dealers, one by one. He was getting tired. "Are any of your guns missing?" he asked.

"Hold on just a minute," said the proprietor of the first shop he'd started with. "I don't think so, but—" He counted the clutter of guns in his glass case. "Only eight. There should be nine. I'll count again. One, two, three—" He choked and his eyes bulged. "I'll be damned, one's gone!"

"Do you remember who was in here today to look at them?"

"Sure, sure! Only one person. They didn't have a permit. So they couldn't buy the gun. I went back into the little room there and when I came out they were gone. They needed the gun so they swiped it! Just wait! I'll tell the cops!"

"Can you describe the person?" asked Charlie.

The proprietor then proceeded into a wealth of detail concerning the person responsible for the disappearance of a .22 caliber pistol.

Charlie slapped his hand to his face. His knees gave out from under him. The shop dissolved around him. Finally he got the proprietor back in focus. "Do you read the papers?"

"What's that got to do with it?"

"A murderer could steal your gun, shoot someone a few blocks from here, and bring the gun back before you noticed it was missing, couldn't he?"

"Sure, sure, I guess so. But they didn't bring it back. It's still gone."

Charlie was trying to think, a fog in his eyes. "That way a person could get a gun, use it; the police would never trace it; the gun-seller would never suspect, either. The police wouldn't think to check the guns you've had here for years; they might ask if any were missing, or if you'd sold any .22's, but that's all." He rose unsteadily from the chair. "The murderer didn't plan on my checking with you, or anyone checking with you, for that matter. . . ."

"Hey, come back here—" said the shopkeeper.

Very paralyzed, not feeling anything, Charlie headed toward home.

On the way he saw a little store lighted up and there were things in the window—certain kinds of weapons for which you needed no license. He went in and laid some money on the counter and when he emerged his hand cuddled the weapon in his right coat pocket. . . .

. . .

It was about ten o'clock. Officer Kelly was looking up at those stars over the city, cursing to himself, when he heard footsteps behind him. He turned and almost bumped into Charlie Guidney.

"I guess you'll have your killer this evening, Kelly," Charlie said amiably.

"So there you are!" Kelly grabbed him. "It's a good thing for you, me lad, you came back under your own power!"

"Can I say good-bye to my wife first?"

Kelly hemmed and hawed. "I guess I can let you say good-bye. Go along."

They climbed the dim interior of the house. Charlie put his hand on that very familiar door knob. "Could you wait outside, Kelly?"

Kelly could. Charlie shut the door. Lydia snapped off the radio, turned to him. "Charlie!"

"Hello, Lydia."

"Oh, Charlie, you're all right. I was afraid they'd shoot—"

"They almost did. They might yet."

She sank upon the couch. "We'll never escape. Charlie, why did you do it?"

"I didn't."

"What?" Her eyes widened.

"I lied. Didn't you guess I was lying from the very first, Lydia? Didn't you guess I was in a mental rut, going berserk, wanting to leave town forever? Didn't you?"

"Why, no, I didn't," she said.

"And didn't you have a nice set-up, my dear wife?"

"I don't understand, Charlie."

"I sent you to buy tickets. All you had to do was stop in a shop that sold guns, ask for some article that would get the owner out of the room for a moment, steal the gun, walk down Temple Street, find any one of the dozens of winos and stumble-bums that sleep in the alleys there, in the dark, shoot the man, then go on down to the bus-depot, buy the tickets and come home."

"Charlie, what *are* you saying?"

"Then when you saw the policeman you pretended hysteria to give me away. A good frame! Except you didn't think I'd escape to check the gun sellers. You planned to return the gun probably tomorrow. Your testimony against me would be devastating. I came home, you would say, and I told you I'd killed someone. Exactly what I *did* say, even though I lied. You hoped the police might even shoot me in a struggle. The bus tickets, our packed baggage, my employers not even notified, our friends unaware of our plans—all that was damning evidence against me!"

"Oh, now, Charlie!"

"Me in prison for years, or executed maybe, and you—*free!* Free with your bus-tickets anytime you wanted to travel, taking along your friend, Mr. Travis—taking that five-thousand dollars from the bank with which to coax him? No more boredom, Lydia?"

He shut his eyes, tight. "I'm sorry it worked this way. We could've been happy, trying again. Even when you guessed I lied about the murder, you should've played along. It would have been good, exciting. Have you hated me this much in all these years? Didn't you see a change was what we needed to make us over? I was only trying to get us out, and you—"

"You're insane!" she cried.

He felt the weapon in his pocket. "Tell the truth!"

"You're a murderer!" she screamed. "And you're trying to blame me! Get out, you hateful, horrible little man!"

"First," he said, "Lydia, take a look at *this!*"

Yanking the weapon from his pocket he pointed it, advanced on her swiftly. She stared, unbelieving, at it, fell back against the couch, screaming, clawing to escape him.

"Charlie, Charlie, Charlie!" It was like a high whistle shrieking. Something broke, exploded in her. He shoved the weapon closer. "I did it, I did it, I killed him! But take that thing away, take it away!" she sobbed.

The door burst open. Kelly ran in, gun leveled. "Okay, Mr. Guidney, I heard her! Leave her alone. I'll take care of her now. Hand over your weapon!"

Charlie turned, his eyes shut. He held out his hand and dropped the weapon into Kelly's amazed fingers.

The white rat with the shiny pink eyes scampered inside Kelly's hand.

# FIVE

# THE VERY BEWILDERED CORPSES (FOUR-WAY FUNERAL)

"Pardon me," said the Douser, "but you look like a criminal."

The well-dressed gentleman looked down upon his neat gloves, his shining shoes, his seventy-dollar overcoat draped over one casual arm. Then the well-dressed gentleman stared at Douser Mulligan and sidled away somewhat.

"The intellectual criminal type, of course," added Douser, hastening not to offend the man. "The better species, I'll allow." Douser studied the man's tailoring. "Fine, fine." His manicure. "Good, good." His haircut. "Nice long grey hair, cut and combed. A clean collar. So."

"Go," said the gentleman, "away."

"I don't want to," said Douser.

"If you don't go," said the gentleman, "I shall summon the police."

"You are not the kind," observed the Douser. "Your use of the word *summon* indicates that you would call in a tidy, soft voice that no decent policeman would pay any attention to. You have to *yell* for cops. You, sir, are not the yelling kind. You hate publicity, shun notoriety, detest causing a scene. No, no."

The gentleman's narrow green eyes were amused. About fifty years' worth. One gloved hand flexed upon a cane's handle; he seemed to be deliberating whether to ride Douser out of the Square upon it, but he laughed a small laugh. "Go away, little man."

"Not," persisted the Douser, "until you admit you're a criminal."

"All right, if it'll satisfy you, I'm a criminal. Glad?"

Douser blinked. "Not very. It's not much fun this way. All the other people I ever met wouldn't admit it. Then I had to kick their shins or bite their ankle. I tell you it's a lot of work. But you, now. This is something new. A guy who admits he is a manicured louse. I'll hate putting you in jail."

"Are you going to do that?" wondered the white-haired man, putting a grey, neat hat upon that grey, neat hair.

Douser shrugged. "Can't see my way out of it. You're bad. Now, if you'd make up your mind to reform, we might work out a deal!"

The gentleman stood there, not much taller than Douser, who was very short. Behind him were the twilight trees of the park, the bushes, the peopled benches, the knots of arguing sidewalk politicians, the yellow cab traffic, the pedestrians. Beyond that the red and yellow theatre neons and the square light fronts of stores. The gentleman tilted his head. "You're a peculiar little man. I sort of like you."

"That's funny; most people learn to loathe me."

"Will you have coffee with me," invited the gentleman. "My name is Earl Lajos, the lawyer. I'd like to see what makes you tick."

"Vice-versa, and I do mean vice," said Douser. "We can talk awhile and I'll decide whether to jail you or not. Okay?"

"Fine, fine," said Lajos. They walked from the park, in step.

. . .

Shrimps lay upon the plate looking at Douser. Douser looked back at his delicious relatives. Lajos brandished cutlery delicately, slicing, forking, chewing deftly and quietly, nodding at Douser, who popped his like popcorn into a midget incinerator.

"Have you a detective badge?" asked the lawyer.

"I have only my heart beneath my vest," said Douser, sadly. "The D.A. framed and hung me in the Museum of Extinct Mammalia, Sub-Category: Private Detective, a couple of years back."

"That makes me feel better," said Lajos. He speared another shrimp with cold precision and heartlessly vanquished it molecule by molecule. "I've heard of you, Mr.—Douser, is it not? Yes, the Douser, they call you. You—irritate people. Having no legal authority any longer you—bother criminals. I remember the case. Seems your brother, a policeman, was slain in San Francisco some years back and it kind of hurt your mind. A delightful little chap, but an unbelievable mania for wrongdoers." Lajos crossed knife and fork on his vacuumed plate, leaning forward earnestly. "Well, how would you like to catch *three* criminals? Not one. Not two. But *three*. Count them." He held up fingers in a manicured trio.

"Three," breathed the Douser. "Speak on, MacDuff!"

Lajos toyed with his water glass. "Naturally, you can not have three unless you let me go scot-free, unleashed, unharmed, unhampered."

"I was afraid of that," winced Douser. "Three for one. A good deal. I'd rather have four, but I won't even get those three unless I play ball with you." He bit his lip. "It's a deal, but with a time limit." The man scowled, Douser hurried on. "I'd only guarantee not to molest you for three—well, make it four years." Lajos smiled agreeably. "But first," said Douser, "name the criminals. I don't want any second-rate winos or snow-hounds!"

"I will guarantee," said Lajos, "that these fellows are A-1, bonafide, gilt-edge criminals of the first water. Their names are as follows: Calvin Drum, Hollywood's great actor; William Maxil, who is running for District Attorney next spring, and Joey Marsons, the horse-racing and bookie specialist."

"My God!" cried the Douser. "I can't believe it. Shake, Mr. Lajos, shake!"

. . .

They drove into Beverly Hills in Lajos' big roadster. Lajos gave a few details, showing how the three afore-mentioned were connected each to help the other, each to protect the other. But it seemed that—"these gentlemen are in my way. Their removal would give me room to live in. I will help you gather evidence against them, Mr. Mulligan."

"Funny thing," mused Douser. "I been thinking of them three birds a long time. Been doing some research on them, fact is."

"Really?" said Mr. Lajos, as if he hadn't known this.

Lajos' house was a big white cliff among dark trees. They parked on the brick drive and walked inside, down a hall and into a room. It all worked very smoothly and Douser was prepared for anything.

A door slammed, the lock clicked and Douser said to himself, "Goodie, goodie, a trap. I might have known. Gee, this is exciting."

The Messrs. Drum, Maxil and Marsons glanced up grimly from a game of blackjack and saw Douser standing there. The way they looked he was a dead pigeon all ready. Mr. Lajos, behind Douser, drew out a clean, neat little revolver and pressed it oh so delicately into Douser's spinal cord. Drum, the actor, shouted gaily, *"Surprise!"*

Drum, the actor, crushed out a king-size cigarette that had been burnt down to a commoner. "You're late."

"That is because," said Douser, "we stopped by to see your woman on the way."

Drum's dark black brows went like that. "What?"

Lajos laughed. "Don't listen to him, Drum. We didn't."

"Quite a pretty woman, too," said Douser.

Drum said, very low, "If you've bothered Elice—"

"Yes, Elice!" said Douser, now equipped with a name to use if he needed a wedge. His small bright black button eyes took in the square, foggy room, quickly measuring distances between chairs, windows, the door, the people at the round table. Clickety-clickety-click. *Spung.* Fourteen by seventeen by six inches by three by—

Douser walked away from the gun in his back as if it fired rubber-bands. He sat down in an empty chair, leaning back cozily. "Do we do it now, Lajos, or wait until we lull them into ignorance?"

Maxil was at Douser's right, in a baggy business suit, with one double-chin and one belly, but not much fat anywhere else. His eyeballs popped white, like little pale stomachs in his tired face. He had pouting lips and looked un-washed. To Douser's left was the nervous, flickering, horse-like Marsons, who kept twitching cards out on the table. Across the table sat the collar-ad hero, Drum. "Boy," said Douser, "have we got plans for you, people." He smacked his lips. "Lajos and I are running for D.A. and City Council, aren't we, Grandma?"

Lajos walked primly up to Douser. "Please, keep quiet."

Douser ignored this minor interruption. "First, we eliminate you big frogs, then we muscle in and—well, you see, Lajos hates playing second fiddle to you guys and—"

The pretty little gun touched Douser's right ear. "Yes, sir," said Douser, shut-ting up.

Lajos looked down upon him, his aristocratic face a little on edge as he talked to his friends. "Don't believe a word he says. He's lying. I met him in the park, as we planned. I walked back and forth until he noticed. He fell for the bait. I promised him three criminals—and here we are. Simple."

Douser laughed a little. "Oh, you poor suckers."

Maxil chewed a cigar. "Cut it, Douser. We're wise to you. We heard about how you cause trouble, bother people. You can't split us among ourselves. We're good pals, ain't we, boys?"

"Yes, certainly, of course, yeah, unh-hunh," said everybody with dim fervor.

"You can't break us up," said Maxil, reinforcing his convictions.

"That's right," said everybody, doing the same.

"You can't fool us," said Maxil.

"You can't," said everybody.

. . .

Douser drew his chair close, laid small hands like little springy spiders on the table top. The spiders walked around with his words. "My friends, do you think for one moment that I'd walk into an obvious trap like this? Think I'd believe Grandma Lajos' trumped up yarn? Me, Douser? You know me better than that, boys. Maybe I don't give a damn about living, sure, but I wouldn't come to a thing like this on roller skates. Think it over."

He let them think it over. Lajos swallowed some saliva down his Hart, Schaff-ner and Marx trachea. Drum, the actor, burnt the royal jools off a king-size. Mar-son clicked his deck of cards. Maxil felt of his stomach with curious big hands.

Douser continued. "The only reason I walked into this lion's den, kiddies, is because Uncle Lajos laid out the long green."

The 'kiddies' paid attention. Douser added, quickly, "And if he shoots me now, it'll prove he's guilty, trying to shut me up!"

Lajos' eyes narrowed into small green gems. His manicure tightened upon the gun impatiently.

Douser drew out cigarette papers and a tobacco bag. He began making a cigarette, quietly. He got half through rolling, fixing it into a rut to pour to-bacco in when he said, "Some damn guy in some damn detective novel did this all the time. Every time there was a lull in the conversation he did this. I can't for the hell of it figure why. Called the guy Sam Spade, I think."

The square room held them in a smoke web, waiting.

Lajos snorted delicately, arching his cute nostrils. "Here go our plans. I warned you, Maxil, if we ever got hold of Douser it would be like battling fly paper. We never should have bothered. He's in the room two minutes and look—*look*—by the Holy Mary, he's turning one against the other, methodically. You see—*you see?*"

Maxil said, eyes lidded sleepily, "I'm lookin'."

Marsons gritted the cards with a fingernail. "Let's get it over with. This guy messes in everyone's business for years now. We say we kill him before he starts on us, okay, let's kill him. We don't want him bolixing our election plans next spring, do we?"

Drum swore and looked so handsome doing it, too, kid. "Yes, that's what I say. We want him killed, so let's you kill him!"

"What is there about a mouse that makes the elephants scream?" wondered Douser, half aloud. He threw away the half-made smoke. "Some day I'll learn to do that, dammit." He glanced at Maxil. "You're running for D.A. As D.A. you'll assist the gambling interests, especially in the studios. Marsons is your right hand man, all around bookie president. Drum, better known as Drum-Tiddie-Um-Tum, will be the main contact among the actors and actresses. A nice business, you got planned. And in case of trouble we have our Chanel Number Five and Shiny Fingernails Mr. Lajos." Douser rubbed hands together and leaned back. "*But—*" he cried. "Mr. Lajos had plans for himself. He would fain be D.A.! So tonight, on the way here, he gives me one thousand bucks on account, with nine more to come!"

Maxil said, sleepy-eyed, "Why're you telling us this? Why didn't you go ahead? Why you blabbing?"

"I happen to hate Mr. Lajos' guts. I don't like double-crossers. I figure he deserves to be double-crossed himself."

"But this way," said Maxil, "you get killed for your trouble."

"I take my chances. I should've died a long time ago. I figure we can work a deal where you guys can tip me off to other criminals who you don't like and let me have at them. I keep the road clear for you and you let me alone and I let you alone. I'm bargaining. All you got to do is let me have Lajos, who is a slimy knifer-in-the-back, I assure you."

Drum said, "It sounds like a good proposition. Doesn't it, Maxil?"

"Maybe," said Maxil, slow to be impressed, but waking up. "You'll do any-thing to get criminals won't you, Douser?"

"Anything. Even if it means giving protection to a few so I can nab a dozen others. You got to play the game, I see that."

. . .

All during this palaver Lajos was getting taller and paler and more indignant, and trying to think of words, but not having any good ones right on hand. Everybody began thinking too much.

"He's lying!" shrilled Lajos.

Douser said, "Call Rochester 7611 and ask for Bert. Bert will tell all."

Maxil looked lovingly at the phone. Lajos, catching this look, stalked back and forth around the table, piping. "We won't call anybody for anything! We won't call anybody!"

Maxil tapped about half an inch of rosy-grey ash off his cigar and said to Marsons, "Call Rochester 7611—"

"If he touches the phone," declared Lajos, towering tall, "I quit! I'll be through, finished! We can't trust one another any longer!"

"It's just a precautionary routine call," said Maxil.

Lajos opened his jaw, snapped it shut, shook his head. "All right! Call! Phone! Go on!"

Marsons dialed alphabeticals and numerals and listened to the electric bee buzzing at the other end. Somebody killed the bee by unpronging it. Douser sat calmly small. Drum leaned forward like that scene in *Love, It's Nice*. Maxil listened with his fat eyes. Marsons said, nervously, "Bert?"

The receiver hung out in the silence, in Marsons' fist, so that Bert's voice could be heard, small and tiny and high in the smoke, far away. "Yeah?" said Bert.

Marsons blinked rapidly. "I'm calling about something that happened tonight, Bert," he said.

"You mean about the thousand dollars?" said Bert.

Lajos swallowed, paling out in his cheeks and in small lines around his mouth. Maxil mashed out his cigar. Marsons almost dropped the phone. Drum swore. Douser smiled.

"I'll keep it here for Douser," said Bert, "until he wants to pick it up. That sure is easy money."

Marsons cradled the phone in a long silence.

"It's not true," said Lajos, looking from Maxil to Drum, to Marsons. "Douser's lying!"

Maxil said, "Take his gun away from him, Drum."

Drum got up, walked around the table.

Lajos said, "Stay away from me. This is a frame. You've got to listen to me, give me a decent break, be democratic!"

Drum kept coming. He didn't think Lajos would shoot. Lajos didn't think so, either. It seemed instinctive. The gun went off with a loud sharp bark and a short finger of blue-red flame.

"Unh," said Drum. It was the best line he ever delivered. He stood there with a bullet in his stomach.

Marsons threw away his deck of cards like so many pigeons, numbered, taking flight in a fluttering. Maxil sat fat and frozen. Douser moved a little, just to be out of harm's way.

Lajos looked at the bullet-hole, not believing. "I didn't mean to do that," he said, amazed. "Here," he recoiled in horror. "Here, take it." He threw the gun and Marsons caught it. "I didn't mean to do that! I'm not guilty! It was an accident!" sobbed Lajos.

Drum stood there and Death stood below, cutting away his fibers, his roots of being. Death ran out of the way, cried, "Timber!" and Drum crashed down like a giant redwood, to lie silent.

*One away!* thought Douser, satisfied. *Two, really. One dead, the other guilty of homicide! Oh, joy!*

.  .  .

Everybody trembled now. Even Maxil. Marsons looked like the flank of a nervous palamino horse, shivering. Lajos now lay upon the sofa in one corner of the room, wrinkling his tailored suit and getting his ten-dollar tie all wet, sobbing like a woman. Douser was very excited and thrilled, like at a circus.

"Shut up!" Marsons said to the crying Lajos.

Maxil said, "Snap out of it, Lajos. Hey, old man." When the sobbing did not stop, Maxil turned to Douser, whose heart leaped in a hot pink dance. "Why'd you really come here, Douser?"

"To get in with you guys and meet more criminals."

Maxil lit his cigar, like warming over old thoughts and theories. "You'd risk your life for that?"

"I've risked it before, for less. This way I work from the inside out. I was on the outside before. This is better."

"Your story," said Maxil, balancing the idea with great slow dexterity upon the glowing tip of his cigar, "does not glue together. If Lajos planned on framing us, why did the two of you come here easy? Why didn't you run in shooting?"

Douser's heart moved in four directions. This was a good time to roll a cigarette. He produced tobacco and papers and began twitching the stuff together, thinking very fast, getting nowhere. Douser said, "We planned to come in and talk you off guard, first. That's how Lajos wanted it. He'd shoot you and Marsons and put the gun in Drum's hand and shoot Drum with your gun, then call the cops and scram. He needed my help in case he got scared. He figured I could kick people and yell and hit and jump on backs."

Maxil chewed on that. Lajos stopped sobbing long enough to say, "He's—he's lying—"

Douser laughed. "Trying to save your own skin. Drum, the great profile of Studio Films is dead, and look who killed him. Not me. Not you, Maxil. But *him*. Boy, what a smell. Try and bury *that*, peoples."

Maxil nodded heavily. "There's one big thing wrong, though—" Maxil sat up in his chair and looked at his stomach. "Why didn't Lajos keep on shooting after he shot Drum, shoot me and Marsons?"

Douser fumbled with his cigarette and had to admit, "You have a point there. You have a point."

Maxil thought it was a good point too, and said so. "Lajos dropped the gun, immediately. He didn't mean to shoot Drum. It was accidental. I think the truth is, Douser, that he only wanted *you* dead, all along. As we planned. He brought you here to kill you, and you got to talking. We got a keg of cement downstairs and a boat at Santa Monica so we could feed you to the fishes—"

"Accident, hell!" cried Douser. "The old guy lost his nerve. All the way up he kept whispering 'I hope I can do it, I hope I don't lose my nerve!' He's a double-crosser, and you can't prove he's not. Look, from now on, Maxil, I'm in with you. You're in a mess now, you have to admit—up to your chins. How'll you cover up Drum's murder?"

"I'll shoot you and put my gun in Drum's hand, Lajos' gun in yours," said Maxil.

"I never carry a gun," said Douser.

"You carried one tonight."

"I hate guns. The cops know that. They find me with one and they'll know something smells. They'll drag you in, work you over—first thing you know Lajos over there will sob out the whole works and then where will you be?"

Maxil looked worried. "I'm open to suggestions."

"Kill Lajos. Frame him for the murder. He's no good any more. You can't trust him." Lajos burst out with renewed hysteria.

"That's a good idea," said Maxil. "Thanks."

"You're welcome."

"No," screamed Lajos.

Things went fast. Clickety-clickety—the old hot blood, the old wild shouting of excitement. The room burst with emotion. Maxil shifted in his chair. "No," screamed Lajos. Douser suggested that he be shot before he got too hysterical and Maxil nodded, drawing a gun, and thinking along its bright blue barrel. Thinking, thinking, thinking. He pointed it at Lajos. "No," said Lajos, in a hoarse, raw voice. "Who's boss around here," said Douser, "you or him. Go ahead, Maxil, shoot him!"

Maxil shot him.

. . .

Douser arose in the spinning, sick universe and said, "Marsons, have you a gun?"

"Yeah." Marsons patted his arm holster.

"Point it at me, while I talk, Marsons. Go ahead. Take it out, point it. That's a good boy." Douser measured distances and timing and took in short, hot breaths. "Listen to me, Marsons, doesn't it look funny the way things have worked out, so many people shot?"

Maxil said, "Sit down, Douser!"

Everybody looked confused, irritated, unsure. Drum, lying at great length upon the carpet, did not believe for a minute that he was dead. Oh, no, not the great, the one and only Calvin Drum!

Neither did Lajos accept the reality of dissolution. His face was ridiculously angry and indignant, attached to the cooling thing that was his body! Both he and Drum had died incredulous and not understanding how in hell it could have happened this way. It wasn't fair!

"Marsons, take a look around," snapped the Douser eloquently. His black bright eyes darted from object to object. "Drum's dead. And why? Lajos shot him dead! Well, who told Drum to grab the gun away from Lajos? *Maxil* did! Maxil knew Lajos was edgy, nervous as a sick cat, and might shoot. But he told Drum to grab that gun anyhow. It was a death sentence! Look at Drum! Dead! Then, to even it up, Maxil shoots Lajos. My God, man, it's plain as the nose on your face! All your pals are dead! Peculiar, huh?"

"Douser!" shouted Maxil, lifting himself.

"Watch it, Marsons!" cried Douser, running, ferret-like now, measuring snap distances, shouting, ducking, skirting. "Shoot Maxil! Shoot Maxil before he rods you!"

Douser vanished behind Marsons, twisting him as Maxil fired his pistol. The bullet, planned for Douser's quick-moving body, pierced Marsons' hip.

"Oh, you dirty bum, Maxil!" groaned the confused, pained Marsons, realizing his position. He pressed the trigger in pain. Marsons gun fired three times, quickly. Three bullets hit Maxil and rammed him back into his chair. Maxil examined his new stomach with curious, unbelieving fingers. His eyes popped and froze. My God, he must have been thinking as death came, I used to only have one navel, now, *look! I got four! Three more just added!*

Douser grunted, hooked fingers into Marson's elbows, pulled back, kicked the knees out from under the gent and fell, rolling to one side. He heard the gun scutter on the floor by itself and Marsons swore bitterly. Douser got to his feet first and kicked Marsons in his very strange face as Marsons tried to grope back to reality. Marsons rolled over and played sleeping dog. A great quiet pervaded the battlefield. Standing there, Douser realized that it was the first time in his life he had ever seen so many bewildered corpses in one room.

Whistling like some detective from some detective story, but a little off-key, Douser withdrew from the scene.

. . .

The drug-store phone took Douser's nickel as he dialed a number. "Hello, Bert? You did a swell job tonight, Bert, swell—"

"That's okay, Douser. Any time, any time. A janitor like me gets sick of spending all night sweeping and washing by himself, alone. Did I remember my speech like you told me?"

"Exactly. And, don't forget, Bert—every night from now on, the same speech."

Bert cleared his throat. "Is it about the thousand dollars? I'll keep it here until Douser calls for it."

"Fine, Bert, fine. Goodnight, Bert." Douser hung up, beaming. Outside the drug-store he took out cigarette papers and tobacco. He tried to make another cigarette. Finally he threw it down and stepped on it, hard. "The hell with it! I'll learn—some day!"

A man walked by who looked like a bank robber. Douser stared.

"Hey, mister!" Douser said, falling quickly in beside the stranger. "Got a cigarette?"

# SIX

# THE REINCARNATE

After awhile you will get over the inferiority complex. Maybe. There's nothing you can do about it. Just be careful to walk around at night. The hot sun is certainly difficult on you. And summer nights aren't particularly helpful. So the best thing for you to do is wait for chilly weather. The first six months are your prime. The seventh month the water will seep through and the maggots will begin. By the end of the eighth month your usefulness will dwindle. By the tenth month you'll lie exhausted and weeping the sorrow without tears, and you will know then that you will never move again.

But before that happens there is so much to be thought about, and finished. Many thoughts to be renewed, many old likes and dislikes to be turned in your mind before the sides of your skull fall away.

It is new to you. You are born again. And your womb is silk-lined and fine smelling of tuberoses and linens, and there is no sound before your birth except the beating of the earth's billion insect hearts. Your womb is wood and metal and satin, offering no sustenance, but only an implacable slot of close air, a pocket within the mother soil. And there is only one way you can live, now. There must be an emotional hand to slap you on the back to make you move. A desire, a want, an emotion. Then the first thing you know you quiver and rise and strike your brow against silk-skinned wood. That emotion surges through you, calling you. If it is not strong enough, you will settle down wearily, and will not wake again. But if you grow with it, somehow, if you claw upward, if you work tediously, slowly, many days, you find ways of displacing earth an inch at a time, and one night you crumble the darkness, the exit is completed, and you wriggle forth to see the stars.

Now you stand, letting the emotion lead you as a slender antenna shivers, led by radio waves. You bring your shoulders to a line, you make a step, like a new born babe, stagger, clutch for support — and find a marble slab to lean against. Beneath your trembling fingers the carved brief story of your life is all too tersely told: Born — Died.

You are a stick of wood. Learning to unbend, to walk naturally again, is not easy. But you don't worry about it. The pull of this emotion is too strong in you, and you go on, outward from the land of monuments, into twilight streets, alone on the pale sidewalks, past brick walls, down stony paths.

You feel there is something left undone. Some flower yet unseen somewhere you would like to see, some pool waiting for you to dive into, some fish uncaught, some lip unkissed, some star unnoticed. You are going back, somewhere, to finish whatever there is undone.

All the streets have grown strange. You walk in a town you have never seen, a sort of dream town on the rim of a lake. You become more certain of your walking now, and can go quite swiftly. Memory returns.

You know every cobble of this street, you know every place where asphalt bubbled from mouths of cement in the hot oven summer. You know where the horses were tethered sweating in the green spring at these iron tying posts so long ago it is a feeble maggot in your brain. This cross street, where a light hangs high like a bright spider spinning light web across this one solitudinous spot. You soon escape its web, going on to sycamore gloom. A picket fence dances woodenly beneath probing fingers. Here, as a child, you rushed by with a stick in hand manufacturing a machine-gun racket, laughing.

These houses, with the people and memories of people in them. The lemon odor of old Mrs. Hanlon who lived there, remember? a withered lady with withered hands and gums withered when her teeth gleamed upon the cupboard shelf smiling all to their porcelain selves. She gave you a withered lecture every day about cutting across her petunias. Now she is completely withered like a page of ancient paper burned. Remember how a book looks burning? That's how she is in her grave now, curling, layer upon layer, twisting into black rotted and mute agony.

The street is quiet except for the walking of a man's feet on it. The man turns a corner and you unexpectedly collide with one another.

You both stand back. For a moment, examining one another, you understand something about one another.

The stranger's eyes are deep-seated fires in worn receptacles. He is a tall, slender man in a very neat dark suit, blonde and with a fiery whiteness to his protruding cheekbones. After a moment, he bows slightly, smiling. "You're a new one," he says. "Never saw you before."

And you know then *what* he is. He is dead, too. He is walking, too. He is 'different' just like yourself. You sense his differentness.

"Where are you going in such a hurry?" he asks, politely.

"I have no time to talk," you say, your throat dry and shrunken. "I am going somewhere, that is all. Please, step aside."

He holds onto your elbow firmly. "Do you know *what* I am?" He bends closer. "Do you not realize we are of the same legion? The dead who walk. We are as brothers."

You fidget impatiently. "I — I have no time."

"No," he agrees, "and neither have I, to waste."

You brush past, but cannot lose him, for he walks with you. "I know where you're going."

"Do you?"

"Yes," he says, casually. "To some child-hood haunt. To some river. To some house or some memory. To some woman, perhaps. To some old friend's cottage. Oh, I know, all right, I know everything about our kind. I know," he says, nodding in the passing light and dark.

"You know, do you?"

"That is always why the dead walk. I have discovered that. Strange, when you think of all the books ever written about the dead, about vampires and walking cadavers and such, and never once did the authors of those most worthy volumes hit upon the true secret of why the dead walk. Always it is for the same reason — a memory, a friend, a woman, a river, a piece of pie, a house, a drink of wine, everything and anything connected with life and — LIVING!" He made a fist to hold the words tight. "Living! REAL living!"

Wordless, you increase your stride, but his whisper paces you:

"You must join me later this evening, my friend. We will meet with the others, tonight, tomorrow night and all the nights until we have our victory."

Hastily. "Who are the others?"

"The other dead." He speaks grimly. "We are banding together against intolerance."

"Intolerance?"

"We are a minority. We newly dead and newly embalmed and newly interred, we are a minority in the world, a persecuted minority. We are legislated against. We have no rights!" he declares heatedly.

The concrete slows under your heels. "Minority?"

"Yes." He takes your arm confidentially, grasping it tighter with each new declaration. "Are we wanted? No! Are we liked? No! We are feared! We are driven like sheep into a marble quarry, screamed at, stoned and persecuted like the Jews of Germany! People hate us from their fear. It's wrong, I tell you, and it's unfair!" He groans. He lifts his hands in a fury and strikes down. You are standing still now, held by his suffering and he flings it at you, bodily, with impact. "Fair, fair, is it fair? No. I ask you. Fair that we, a minority, rot in our graves while the rest of the continent sings, laughs, dances, plays, rotates and whirls and gets drunk! Fair, is it fair, I ask you that they love while our lips shrivel cold, that they caress while our fingers manifest to stone, that they tickle one another while maggots entertain us! No! I shout it! It is ungodly unfair! I say down with them, down with them for torturing our minority! We deserve the same rights!" he cries. "Why should we be dead, why not the others?"

"Perhaps you are right."

"They throw us down and slam the earth in our white faces and load a carven stone over our bosom to weigh us with, and shove flowers into an old tin can and bury it in a small spaded hole once a year. Once a year? Sometimes not even that! Oh, how I hate them, oh how it rises in me, this full blossoming hatred for the living. The fools. The damn fools! Dancing all night and loving, while we lie recumbent and full of disintegrating and helpless passion! Is that right?"

"I hadn't thought about it," you say, vaguely.

"Well," he snorts, "well, we'll fix them."

"What will you do?"

"There are thousands of us gathering tonight in the Elysian Park and I am the leader! We will destroy humanity!" he shouts, throwing back his shoulders, lifting his head in rigid defiance. "They have neglected us too long, and we shall kill them. It's only right. If we can't live, then they have no rights to live, either! And you will come, won't you, my friend?" he says, hopefully. "I have coerced many, I have spoken with scores. You will come and help. You yourself are bitter with this embalming and this suppression, are you not, else you would not be out tonight. Join us. The graveyards of the continent will explode like overripened apples, and the dead will pour out to overflow the villages! You will come?"

"I don't know. Yes. Perhaps I will," you say. "But I must go now. I have some place ahead of me to find. I will come."

"Good," he says, as you walk off, leaving him in shadow. "Good, good, good."

.  .  .

Up the hill now, as quick as you can. Thank God there is a coolness upon the earth tonight. If it was a hot night it would be terrible to be above the ground in your condition.

You gasp happily. There, in all its rococo magnificence, is the house where Grandma sheltered her boarders. Where you as a child sat on the porch Fourth of July, watching sky rockets climb in fiery froth, the pinwheels cursing, sputtering sparks, the fire-crackers beating at your ears from the metal cannon of uncle Bion who loved noise and bought fifty dollars worth of crackers just to explode them with his hand-rolled cigarette.

Now, standing, trembling with this emotion of recapturence, you know why the dead walk. To see again things like this. Here, on nights when dew invaded the grass, you crushed the wet petals and grass-blades and leaves as your boy bodies wrestled, and you knew the sweetness of now, now, TONIGHT! who cares for tomorrow, tomorrow is nothing, yesterday is over and done, tonight live, tonight!

Inside that grand old tall house the incredible Saturday nights took place, the Boston-baked beans in hordes saturated with thick juices, panoplied with platforms of bacon. Oh, yes, all of that. And the huge black piano that cried out at you when you performed musical dentistry upon its teeth. . . .

And here, here, man, remember? This is Kim's house. That yellow light, around the back, that's her room. Do you realize that she might be in it now, painting her pictures or reading her books? In one moment, glance over that house, the porch, the swing before the door where you sat on August evenings. Think of it. Kim, your wife. In a moment you will see her again!

You bang the gate wide and hurry up the walk. You think to call, but instead slip quietly around the side. Her mother and father would go crazy if they saw you. Bad enough, the shock to Kim.

Here is her room. Glowing and square and soft and empty. Feed upon it. Is it not good to see again?

Your breath forms upon the window a symbol of your anxiety; the cold glass films with fog and blurs the exact and wonderful details of her existence there.

As the fog vanishes the form of her room emerges. The pink spread upon the low soft bed, the cherry-wood flooring, brilliantly waxed; throw-rugs like bright heavily-furred dogs slumbering acenter it. The mirror. The small cosmetic table, where her sorcery is enacted in an easy pantomime. You wait.

She comes into the room.

Her hair is a lamp burning, bound behind her ears by her moving. She looks tired, her eyes are half-lidded, but even in this uncertain light, blue. Her dress is short and firm to her figure.

Breathlessly, you listen against the cold shell of glass, and as from deep under a sea you hear a song. She sings so softly it is already an echo before it leaves her mouth. You wonder what she thinks as she sings and combs out her hair at the mirror.

The cold brine of you stirs and beats. Certainly she must hear your heart's cold thunder!

Thoughtless, you tap upon the window.

She goes on stroking her hair gently, thinking that you are only the autumn wind outside the glass.

You tap again, anxiously, a bit afraid.

This time she sets down the comb and brush and rises to investigate, calm and certain.

At first she sees nothing. You are shadowed. Her eyes, as she walks toward the window, are focused on the gleaming squares of glass. Then, she looks *through*. She sees a dim figure beyond the light. She still does not recognize.

"Kim!" You cannot help yourself. "It is I! I am here!"

Your eager face pushes to the light, as a submerged body must surge upon some black tide, suddenly floating, triumphant, with shimmering dark eyes!

The color drops from her cheeks. Her hands open to release sanity which flies away on strange wings. Her hands clasp again, to recapture some last sane thought. She does not scream. Only her eyes are wide as windows seen on a white house amidst a terrific lightning-shaft in a sudden summer squall, shadeless, empty and silvered with that terrific bolt of power!

"Kim!" you cry. "It is I!"

She says your name. She forms it with a numb mouth. Neither of you can hear it. She wants to run, but instead, at your insistence, she pulls up the window and, sobbing, you climb upward into the light. You slam the window and stand swaying there, only to find her far across the room, crucified by fear against the wall.

You sob raggedly. Your hands rise clean toward her in a gesture of old hunger and want. "Oh, Kim, it's been so long———"

. . .

Time is non-existent. For full five minutes you remember nothing. You come out of it. You find yourself upon the soft rim of bed, staring at the floor.

In your ears is her crying.

She sits before the mirror, her shoulders moving like wings trying to fly with some agony as she makes the sounds.

"I know I am dead. I know I am. But what can I try to do to this cold? I want to be near your warmness, like at a fire in a long cold forest, Kim. . . ."

"Six months," she breathes, not believing it. "You've been gone that long. I saw the lid close over your face. I saw the earth fall on the lid like a kind of sounding of drums. I cried. I cried until only a vacuum remained. You can't be here now—"

"I *am* here!"

"What can we do?" she wonders, holding her body with her hands.

"I don't know. Now that I've seen you, I don't want to walk back and get into that box. It's a horrible wooden chrysalis, Kim, I don't want its kind of metamorphosis—"

"Why, why, why did you come?"

"I was lost in the dark, Kim, and I dreamed a deep earth dream of you. Like a seventeen year locust I writhed in my dream. I had to find my way back, somehow."

"But you can't stay."

"Until daybreak."

"Paul, don't take of my blood. I want to live."

"You're wrong, Kim. I'm not that kind. I'm only myself."

"You're different."

"I'm the same. I still love you."

"You're jealous of me."

"No, I'm not, Kim. I'm not jealous."

"We're enemies now, Paul. We can't love any more. I'm the quick, you're the dead. We're opposed by our very natures. We're natural enemies. I'm the thing you most desire, you represent the thing I least desire, death. It's just the opposite of love."

"But I love YOU, Kim!"

"You love my life and what life means, don't you see?"

"I *don't* see! What are we like, the two of us sitting here, talking philosophically, scientifically, at a time when we both should be laughing and glad to see one another."

"Not with jealousy and fear between us like a net. I loved you, Paul. I loved the things we did together. The processes, the dynamics of our relationship. The things you said, the thoughts you thought. Those things, I still love. But, but—"

"I still think those thoughts and think them over and over, Kim!"

"But we are apart."

"Don't be merciless, Kim. Have pity!"

Her face softens. She builds a cage around her face with convulsive fingers. Words escape the cage:

"Is pity love? Is it, Paul?"

There is a bitter tiredness in her breathing.

You stand upright. "I'll go crazy if this goes on!"

Wearily, her voice replies, "Can dead people go insane?"

You go to her, quickly, take her hands, lift her face, laugh at her with all the false gaiety you can summon:

"Kim, listen to me! Listen! Darling, I could come every night! We could talk the old talk, do the old things! It would be like a year ago, playing, having fun! Long walks in the moonlight, the merry-go-round at White City, the hot-dogs at Coral Beach, the boats on the river—anything and everything you say, darling, if only—"

She cuts across your rapid, pitiable gaiety:

"It's no use."

"Kim! One hour every evening. Just one. Or half an hour. Any time you say. Fifteen minutes. Five minutes. One minute to see you, that's all. That's all."

You bury your head in her limp, dead hands, and you feel the involuntary quiver shoot through her at your rapid contact. After a moment, she dares to move, slightly. She leans back, her eyes tightly closed, and says, simply:

"I am afraid."

"Why?"

"I have been taught to be afraid, that's all."

"Damn the people and their customs and their old-wives tales!"

"Talking won't stop the fear."

You want to grasp, hold, stop her, shake sense into her, to clasp her trembling and comfort it as you would a wild bird trying to escape your fingers. "Stop it, stop it, Kim!"

Her trembling gradually passes like movements on a disturbed water pool calming and relaxing. She sinks down upon the bed and her voice is old in a young throat. "All right, darling." A pause. "Anything you say." Swallowing. "Anything you wish. If — it makes you happy."

You try to be happy. You try to burst with joy. You try to smile. You look down upon her as she continues talking vaguely:

"What ever you say. Anything, my darling."

You venture to say, "You won't be afraid."

"Oh, no." Her breath flutters in. "I won't be."

You excuse yourself. "I just had to see you, you understand? I just had to!"

Her eyes are bright and focused now on you. "I know, Paul, how it must feel. I'll meet you outside the house in a few minutes. I'll have to make an excuse to mother and dad to get out past them."

You raise the window and put one leg out and then turn to look back up at her before vanishing. "Kim, I love you."

She says nothing, but stares blankly, and shuts the window when you are outside, and she goes away, dimming lights. Held by the dark, you weep with something not quite sorrow, not quite joy. You walk to the corner to wait out the time.

Across the street, past a lilac shrub, a man walks stiffly. There is something familiar about him. You remember. He is the man who accosted you earlier. He is dead, too, and walking through a world that is alien only because it is alive. He goes on along the street, as if in search of something.

Kim is beside you now.

.  .  .

An ice-cream sundae is a most wonderful thing. Resting cool, a small white mountain capped by a frock of chocolate and contained in glass, it is something you stare at with spoon poised.

You put some of the ice-cream in your mouth, sucking the cold. You pause. The light in your eyes embers down. You sit back, removed.

"What's wrong?" the old man behind the ancient fountain looks at you, concerned.

"Nothing."

"Ice cream taste funny?"

"No. It's fine."

"Fly in it?" He bends forward.

"No."

"You tain't eating it?" he says.

"I don't want to." You push it away from you and your lump of heart lowers itself precariously between the lonely bleak walls of your lungs. "I am sick. I am not hungry. I can't eat."

Kim is at your left, eating slowly. At your sign, she lays aside her spoon, also, and cannot eat.

You sit very straight, staring ahead into nothing. How can you tell them that your throat muscles will longer contract efficiently enough to swallow food? How can you speak of the frustrated hunger flaming in you as you watch Kim's dainty jaw muscles close and open, finishing the white coolness of the ice within her mouth, tasting and liking it?

How can you explain of the crumpled shape of your stomach lying like a dried apricot against your peritoneum? How to describe that desiccated rope of intestine that is yours now? that lies coiled neatly, as if you heaped it by hand at the bottom of a cold pit?

Rising, you have no coin in your hand, and Kim pays, and together you swing wide the door and walk out into the stars.

"Kim—"

"That's all right. I understand," she says. Taking your arm, she walks down toward the park. Wordless, you realize that her hand is very faintly against you. It is there, but your feeling of it is lost. Beneath your feet, the sidewalk loses its solid tread. It now moves without shock or bump below you, a dream.

Just to be talking, Kim says, "Isn't that a marvelous smell on the air tonight? Lilacs in bloom."

You test the air. You can smell nothing. Panic rises in you. You try again, but it is no use.

Two people pass you in the dark, and as they drift by, nodding to Kim and you, as they gain distance behind, one of them comments, fading,

"—Don't you smell something — funny? I wonder if a dog was killed in the street today . . ."

"I don't see anything—"

"—well—"

"KIM! COME BACK!"

You grasp her fleeing hand. It seems that it is this moment she has waited for in a tensed, apprehensive, and semi-gracious silence. The passing of the people and their few words, are a trigger to thrust her away, almost screaming from you.

You catch her arm. Wordless, you struggle against her. She beats at you. She twists, and strikes at your binding fingers. You cannot feel her. You cannot feel her doing this! "Kim! Don't, darling. Don't run away. Don't be afraid."

Her brooch falls to the cement like a beetle. Her heels scuff the hard stony surface. Her breath pants from her. Her eyes are wide. One hand escapes and stretches out behind her as she leans back, using her weight to pull free. The shadows enclose your struggle. Only your breath sounds. Her face glows taut and not soft any more, breaking apart in the light. There are no words. You pull back, your way. She pulls in her direction. You try to speak softly, soothingly, "Don't let people frighten you about me. Calm down—"

Her words are bitten out in whispers:

"Let go of me. Let go. Let go."

"No, I can't do that."

Again the wordless, dark movement of bodies and arms. She weakens and hangs limply sobbing against you. At your touch she trembles very deeply. You hold her close, teeth chattering. "I want you, Kim. Don't leave me. I had such plans. To go to Chicago some night. It only takes an hour on the train. Listen to me. Think of it. To eat the most elegant food across fine linen and silver from one another! To let wine lift us by our bootstraps. To stuff ourselves full. And now—" you declare harshly, eyes gleaming in the leaf-dark, "Now—" You hold your thinned stomach, pressing in that traitor thing lying dry and twisted as a paint tube there. "And now I can't taste the cool of ice-cream, or the ripeness of berries, or apple pie or or—or—"

Kim speaks.

You tilt your head. "What did you say?"

She speaks again.

"Speak louder," you ask of her, holding her close. "I can't hear you." She speaks and you cry out, bending near. And you hear absolutely nothing at first, and then, behind a thick cotton wall, her voice says,

"Paul, it's no use. You see? You understand now?"

You release her. "I wanted to see the neon lights. I wanted to find the flowers as they were, to touch your hand, your lips. But, Oh god, first my taste goes, then I cannot eat at all, and now my skin is like concrete. And now I cannot hear your voice, Kim. It's like an echo in a lost world."

A great wind shakes the universe, but you do not feel it.

"Paul, this is not the way. The things you desire can't be had this way. It takes more than desire to insure these things."

"I want to kiss you."

"Can your lips feel?"

"No."

"Love depends on more than thought, Paul, because thought itself is built upon the senses. If we cannot talk together, hear together, or feel, or smell the night, or taste the food, what is there left for us?"

You know it is no use, but with a broken voice you argue on: "I can still *see* you. And I remember what it WAS like!"

"Illusion. Memory is an illusion, nothing more. It is a fire that needs constant tending. And we have no way to tend it if you cannot use your senses."

"It's so unfair! I want life!"

"You will live, Paul, I promise that. But not THIS way, the impossible way. You've been dead over half a year, and I'll be going to the hospital in another month—"

You stop. You are very cold. Holding to her shoulders, you stare into her soft, moving face. "What?"

"Yes. The hospital. Our child. *Our* child. You see, you didn't have to come back. You are always with me, Paul. You are alive." She turns you around. "Now I'll ask you. Go back. Everything balances. Believe that. Leave me with a better memory than this of you, Paul. Everything will work for the best, eventually. Go back where you came from."

You cannot even cry. Your tear-ducts are shriveled. The thought of the baby comes upon you, and sounds almost correct. But the rebellion in you will not be so easily put down. You turn to shout again at Kim, and without a sign, she sinks slowly to the ground. Bending over her, you hear her few weak words:

"The shock. The hospital. Quick. The shock."

You walk down the street, she lies in your arms. A grey film forms over your left eye. "I can't see. The air does things to me! Soon, I'll be blind in both eyes, Kim, it's so unfair!"

"Faith," she whispers, close, you barely hear the word.

You begin to run, stumbling. A car passes. You shout at it. The car stops and a moment later you and Kim and the man in the car are roaring soundlessly toward the hospital.

In the middle of the tempest, her talking stands out. "Have faith, Paul. I believe in the future. You believe it too. Nature is not that cruel or unfair. There is compensation for you somewhere."

Your left eye is now completely blind. Your right eye blurs ominously.

Kim is gone!

The hospital attendants run her away from you. You did not even say goodbye to her, nor she to you! You stand outside, helpless, and then turn and walk away from the building. The outlines of the world blur. From the hospital a pulsing issues forth and turns your thoughts a pale red. Like a big red drum it beats in your head, with loud, soft, hard, easy rhythms.

You walk stupidly across streets, cars just miss striking you down. You watch people eat in gleaming glass windows. Watch hot dogs sizzling juices in a Greek restaurant. Watch people lift forks, knives. Everything glides by on noiseless lubricant of silence. You float. Your ears are solidly blocked. Your nose is clogged. The red drum beats louder, with an even tempo. You long and strive and strain to smell lilacs, taste bacon, or remember what a mockingbird sounded like cutting pieces from the sky with the trilling scissors of his beak. All those wonderful memorious things you try to capture.

Sour-sick, an earthquake of thought and confusion shaking you, you find yourself swaying down a ravine path in Elysian Park. The dead, the dead are walking tonight. They gather tonight. Remember the man who talked to you? Remember what he said? Yes, yes, you still have some fragments of memory. The dead are banding tonight, forming a unit to swarm over the homes of the warm living people, to kill and decimate them!

That means Kim, too. Kim and the baby.

Kim will die and have to grope and stumble and gabble like this, stinking and falling away from the bone and have dull ears and blind eyes and dry, eroded nostrils. Just like *you*.

"No!"

The ravine rushes on both sides and under you. You fall, pick yourself up, fall again.

The Leader stands alone as you grope your way to him by the silent creek. Sucking hoarse breaths you stand before him, doubling your fists, wondering where the horde of the undead are, you do not see them. And now the Leader talks to you, explaining, shrugging angrily:

"They did not come. Not one of those cold dead people showed up. You are the only recruit." He leans wearily against the tree, as if drunk. "The cowards, the persecuted swine."

"Good." Your breath, or the illusion of breath, slows. His words are like cold rain on you, bringing confidence and quiet. "I'm glad they didn't listen to you. There must be some reason why they didn't obey you. Perhaps—" you grope for the logic of it . . . "perhaps something happened to them that we can't understand, yet."

The Leader makes a bitter move of his lips, shaking his head back. "I had wild plans. But I am alone. And I see the futility of it now. Even if all the dead should rise, they are not strong enough. One blow and they fall in upon their members like a fire-gutted log. We grow tired so soon. Above the earth our discrepancies are hastened. The lift of an eyebrow is slow, painful toil. I am tired—"

You leave him behind you. His muttering passes away. The red pounding beats in your head again like horses hooves on soft turf. You walk from the ravine, down the street, and into the graveyard, with mute purpose.

Your name is on the grave-stone still. The cavity awaits you. You slide down the small tunnel into the waiting wooden cavity, no longer afraid, jealous or excited. The complete withdrawal of your various senses has left you little but memory, and that seems to dissolve as the boxed satin erodes and the hard square wood softens. The wood becomes malleable. You lie suspended in warm round darkness. You can actually shift your feet. You relax.

You are overwhelmed by a luxury of warm sustenance, of deep pink thoughts and easy idleness. You are like a great old yeast contracting, the outer perimeter of your old fetidness crumbling, being laved away by a whispering tide, a pulsation and a gentleness of moves.

The coffin is now a round dim shell, no longer square. You breathe sufficiently, not hungry, not worried, and are loved. You are deeply loved. You are secure. The place where you are dreaming shifts, contracts, moves.

Drowsy. Your huge body is washed down in movements until it is small, tiny, compact, certain. Drowsy, drowsy on a slumbrous singing tide. Slow. Quiet. Quiet.

Who are you trying to remember? A name plays at the rim of a sea. You run to get it, the waves pluck it away. Somebody beautiful you try to think of. Someone. A time, a place. Oh, so sleepy. Close round darkness, warmth, tiredness. Soundless shell. Dim tide pulsing. Quiet contraction.

A river of dark bears your feeble body on a series of loops and curves, faster, faster and yet faster.

You break into an open-ness and are suspended upside down in brilliant yellow light!

The world is immense as a new white mountain. The sun blazes and a huge red hand binds your two feet close as another hand strikes your naked spine to force a cry out of you.

A woman lies below, tired; sweet perspiration beads her face, and there is a wide singing and refreshened and sharpened wonder to this room and this world. You cry out into it with a newly formed voice. One moment upside-down, you are swung right side up, cuddled and nursed against a spiced-sweet breast.

Amid your fine hunger, you forget how to talk, to worry, to think of all things. Her voice, above you, gently tired, whispers over and over:

"My little new born baby. I will name you Paul, for him. For him . . ."

These words you do not comprehend. Once you feared something terrifying and black, but what it was you do not know now. It is forgotten in this flesh warmth and suckling content. For but a moment a name forms in your thimble-mouth, you try to say it, not knowing what it means, unable to pronounce it, only able to choke it happily with a fresh glowing that arises from unknown sources. The word vanishes swiftly, leaving a quickly fading, joyous soon-erased after-image of triumph and high laughter in the tiny busy roundness of your head: "*Kim!*" "*Kim! Oh, Kim!*"

# SEVEN
# CHRYSALIS

Walter looked like an exclamation mark against the summer sky. He was a tall colored boy whose big hands seemed to illustrate a rule of gravity enforced, for they seemed to be forever hanging at his sides. As he looked at the sea, his eyes moved in soft brown starts and stops and wonderings, and his thumbs and forefingers rubbed lightly together. His mouth worked and his head turned now this way, now that, to give himself the benefit of it all.

Walter sat down for awhile and looked at the white sand. He picked some of it up in his hand and saw how much of it there was and then let it drift down in the hot wind over his bare feet.

The old man inside the hot dog stand on the boardwalk stared out at two o'clock and spatted his sizzling weiners with a steel spatula and his sharp eyes looked up and down the negro boy. The old man in the hot dog stand glanced at the clock and pursed his thin lips. Then he banged the stove with the spatula and stood balancing the instrument and putting one hand on his hips, shaking his head up and down in a little nervous tremor.

Walter looked at a green wave coming in like a train on the shore. It made the sound of a train coming and falling off a trestle and landing in a river. The wave, perfect one moment, fell and broke. He imagined himself inside the wave, rushing in, turned and twisted as a rag twists in a washing machine. The salt worked on his dark body, bleaching. The wave slid him in, deposited him with a creaming whisper on the shore and slid back out, leaving him to bake and whiten and dry.

*They* would find him hours later. His mother and father would discover him like those desert skulls and bones, bleached and dry and chalky white. And they would dance and sing with exultation at his new color, slapping their black hands together and tilting their dark lean faces.

. . .

Now he stood on the rough boardwalk, thinking all of this scene down inside the even cabbage rows of his copper-wire hair.

He smelled the hot dog smell from the nearby grill. A smacking of a steel spatula and a sizzling of meat and the sound of a high, sharp man's voice continued through the next timeless half hour. Walter stooped, unlaced his shoes, eased out of them.

Quite suddenly a swing door banged, squealed. The owner of the hot dog stand—hadn't he been glaring out at Walter for a long while now?—made small tight little steps on the wooden planks. He stopped beside Walter. He held the steel spatula in one thin hand, waving it like a querulous magician to make Walter disappear.

"Okay, nigger, move on. This is the white place. The nigger place is four miles *that* way!"

Walter swallowed and blinked like a lizard.

"I never seen a beach before, mister," he said. "Just got here from Georgia. My father works in town, and my mother she cooks at that hotel up there on the Palisades."

"I don't give a goddamn," said the man, wiping greasy hands on a dirty apron. "Just don't loaf around my stand! You been here over an hour, now!" His voice was faintly southern in accent.

Walter stood there. "This is California," he said, at last, quietly. "This ain't South."

The man took a quick step. "You gettin' cock-heavy with me, nigger?"

"I was just saying," said Walter.

"Any place is south where I am," cried the man, red color in his thin cheeks. "And a li'l more snot outa you and I'll——!" He jerked his spatula, turned around and shoved himself back into his hot dog grill. Walter looked after him, the sun polishing his high cheek-bones, a salt wind threading his big white teeth. The man inside his stand laid weiners down and beat them angrily with his spatula, glaring out at Walter.

Walter turned his long easy body around and walked north. The wonder and curiosity of this beach-place returned to him in a tide of water and sifting sand. At the very end of the boardwalk he stopped and squinted down.

A white boy lay lazily curled into a quiet posture on the white sands.

A puzzled light shone in Walter's large eyes. All white boys were strange, but this one was all the strangeness of them all rolled into one. Walter lapped one dark foot over the other, watching. The white boy seemed to be waiting for something down there on the sand.

The white boy kept scowling at his own arms, stroking them, peering over his shoulder, staring down the incline of his back, peering at his belly and his firm clean legs.

About ten minutes later the white boy sprang to his feet. Walter watched him closely, anxiously. The white boy trotted to his car, parked up on the highway, jumped in, and stared at himself in the rear-view mirror, curious and attentive, fingering his cheeks, tugging the skin in little jerks and massages.

Walter wondered what the boy was looking for, what he'd been waiting for all day on the beach. He half guessed, but it was so odd he couldn't admit it aloud to himself.

The car rushed away down the highway, roaring. Walter blinked slowly, thoughtfully after it.

. . .

Walter walked down from the hotel the next day and the day after that. The white boy lay in the same groove of sand. Walter shook his head, slow.

On the third day, Walter let himself down off the boardwalk, uneasily. Very carefully he pedaled the sand and stood nervously, hopefully over the white boy, licking his lips, throwing a shadow down.

The white boy sprawled like a stringless puppet, relaxed. The long shadow crossed his hands and he glanced up at Walter leisurely, then looked away, then back again.

Walter smiled self-consciously, and stared around as if it was someone else the white boy was looking at.

The white boy grinned. "Hi."

Walter said, very quietly, "Hello there."

"Swell day," said the boy.

"It most certainly is," said Walter, smiling.

He did not move. He stood with his long delicate fingers at his sides, and he let the wind run down the dark economical rows of hair on his head, and finally the white boy said, "Flop down!"

"Thanks," said Walter, immediately obeying.

The white boy moved his eyes in all directions. "Not many guys down this week. Wait'll next week when school quits. I graduated myself, last February, that's why I'm here."

"Oh, is that why," said Walter, nodding. "I saw you here, I did, every day now. I wondered about that."

The white boy sighed, lazing his head on crossed arms. "Nothing like the beach. What's your name? Mine's Bill."

"I'm Walter. Hello, Bill."

"Hi, Walt."

A wave came in on the shore, soft and shining into a wide satin skirt with a foam ruffle that Walter liked. Bill watched it, too.

"Boy, I'm really gonna get me a tan this year," said Bill.

"You like that?" asked Walter.

"Sure. You shoulda seen me last summer!"

"I bet you got all burnt up," said Walter.

"Heck, I *never* burn. I just get blacker and blacker. I get black as a—" The white boy faltered, stopped. Color rose in his face, flushed. "I get plenty dark," he ended lamely, not looking at Walter, embarrassed.

To show that he didn't mind, Walter laughed softly, almost sadly, shaking his head.

Bill looked at him, queerly. "What's funny?"

"Nothing," said Walter, looking at the white boy's long pale arms and half-pale legs and white-washed stomach. "Nothing whatsoever."

Bill stretched out like a white cat to take in the sun, to let it strike through to every relaxed bone. "Take off your shirt, Walt. Get yourself some sun."

"No, I can't do that," said Walter.

"Why not?"

"I'd get sunburned," said Walter.

"Ho!" cried the white boy. Then he rolled swiftly over to hush himself with one hand cupping his mouth. He lowered his eyes, raised them again. "Sorry. I thought you were joking."

Walter bent his head, blinking his long beautiful lashes.

"That's all right," he said. "I know you thought that."

Bill seemed to see Walt for the first time. Acutely self-conscious, Walter tucked his feet under his hams, because it had suddenly struck him how much like rain-rubbers they looked. Rain-rubbers worn against some storm that never seemed to quite come.

Bill was confused. "I never thought of that. I didn't know colored people got sunburned."

"Why, we sure do. All I got to do," said Walter, "is peel off my shirt and *boom* I'm all blistered! *Sure* we sunburn."

"I'll be darned." Bill couldn't comprehend it. "I'll be gosh-darned. I'm a nut. I should *know* these things. I guess we never think much about things like that."

Walter sifted sand in the palm of one hand. "No," he said, slowly. "I don't guess you do." He got up, then. "Well, I better get on up to the hotel. Got to help my Mom in the kitchen."

"See you again, Walt."

"Sure thing. Tomorrow and the next day."

"Okay. So long."

Walter waved and walked swiftly up the hill. At the top he squinted back. Bill still lay on the sand, waiting for some thing.

Walter bit his lips, shook his fingers at the ground.

"Man," he said aloud, "that boy is *crazy!*"

. . .

When Walter was a very little dark boy he'd tried to reverse things. Teacher at school had pointed to a picture of a fish and said:

"Notice how colorless and bleached this fish is from swimming deep in Mammoth Cave for generations. It is blind and needs no seeing organs, and—"

That same afternoon, years ago, Walter had rushed home from school and hid himself upstairs in Mr. Hampden's, the caretaker's, attic. Outside, the hot Georgia sun beat down. In the mothball darkness, Walter crouched, heard his heart drum. A mouse rustled across the dirty plankings.

He had it all figured out. White man working in the sun turned black. Black boy hiding in the dark, turn white. Why, sure! It was reasonable, wasn't it? If one thing happened one way, then the other thing would happen its own way, wouldn't it?

He stayed in that attic until hunger brought him shaking down the stairs.

It was night. The stars shone.

He stared at his hands.

They were still black.

But just wait until morning! This didn't count! You couldn't see the change at night, no, sir! Just wait, just wait! Sucking in his breath, he ran the rest of the way down the steps of the grand old house and hurried to his mama's shack down in the grove and sneaked into bed, keeping his hands in his pockets, keeping his eyes shut. Thinking hard as he went to sleep.

In the morning he awoke and a cage of light from the one small window enclosed him.

His very dark arms and hands lay upon the tattered quilt, unchanged.

He let out a great cry, and turned upon his pillow, burying his face. . . .

▪ ▪ ▪

Walter was drawn back to the boardwalk each afternoon, always careful to give the hot dog proprietor and his grill a wide go-around.

A great thing was happening, thought Walter, a great change, a progression. He would watch the details of the passing summer, and it would give him much to think of. He would try to understand the summer all the way to the end of it. Summer rose in a tidal wave, poised over him, ready to drop, suspended.

Bill and Walter talked each day and afternoons passed and their two arms lying near each other began to resemble one another in an oddly pleasing way to Walter, who watched, fascinated with this thing occuring, this thing Bill had planned and so patiently bided his time for.

Bill traced sand patterns with one pale hand that day by day became a darker hand. Each finger was dyed by the sun.

More white boys appeared. The process started for them. Walter walked away, but Bill yelled for him to stay, what the heck, what the heck! And Walter joined them playing volley-ball.

Summer plunged them into sand-flame and green water-flame until they were rinsed and lacquered with darkness. For the first time in his life, Walter felt a part of people. They'd chosen to cloak themselves in his skin and they danced, growing dark, on each side of the high net, tossing the ball and their laughter back and forth, wrestling with Walter, joking with him, tossing him into the sea.

Finally, one day Bill clapped his hand to Walter's wrist bone and cried, "Look here, Walter!"

Walter looked.

"I'm darker than you are, Walt!" cried Bill, amazed.

"I'll be darned, I'll be gosh-darned," murmured Walter, moving his eyes from wrist to wrist. "Umnh-umnh. Yes, sir, you *are*, Bill. You *sure* are."

Bill left his fingers on Walter's wrist, a sudden stunned expression on his face, half-scowling, lower-lip loosened, and thoughts starting to shift places in his eyes. He jerked his hand away with a sharp laugh and looked out to sea.

"Tonight I'm wearing my white sport shirt. It sure looks snatzy. The white shirt and my tan—boy-oh-boy!"

"I bet that looks nice," said Walter, looking to see what Bill was gazing at. "Lots of colored folks wear *black* clothes and wine-colored shirts to make their faces seem whiter."

"Is that so, Walt? I didn't know that."

Bill seemed uneasy, as if he'd thought of something he couldn't handle. As if it was a brilliant idea he said to Walter, "Hey, here's some dough. Go buy us a coupla dogs."

Walter smiled his appreciation. "That hot dog man don't like me."

"Here, take the dough and go anyhow. To hell with him."

"All right," said Walter, reluctantly. "You want everything on yours?"

"The works!"

Walter loped across the hot sands. Leaping up to the walk he passed into the odorous shadow of the stand where he stood tall and dignified and flute-lipped. "Two hot dogs, with everything on them, to go out, please," he said.

The man behind the counter had his spatula in his hand. He just examined Walter inch by inch, in great detail, with that spatula twitching in his lean fingers. He didn't speak.

When Walter got tired of standing there, he turned and walked out.

Jingling the money on his big palm, Walter walked along pretending he didn't care. The jingle stopped when Bill caught hold of him.

"What happened, Walt?"

"That man just looked at me and looked at me, that's all."

Bill twisted him around. "Come on! We'll get some hot dogs or I'll know why in hell not!"

Walter held off. "No. I don't want no trouble."

Bill argued awhile, then quieted, with white lines around his hard mouth. "Okay, anything you say. Damn it. I'll get the dogs myself. You stay here."

Bill ran over and leaned against the counter.

Walter saw and heard plainly and vividly all that happened in the next ten seconds. It stood in his brain like a scarecrow against a hot blue summer sky for years after.

The hot dog man snapped his head up to glare at Bill. He shouted, bitterly:

"God-damn you, nigger! You back here again!"

There was a silence.

Bill leaned across the counter into the steam of the hot dogs.

The hot dog man laughed hastily. "Oh, well I'll be damned. Hello, *Bill!* Just sort of looked out the corner of my eyes. In the shadow—and there's a glare from the water—you looked just like that goddamn nigger. What'll you have?"

Bill leaned across the counter, siezed the man's arm. "I don't get it. I'm blacker than him. Why you kissing *my* big toe?"

The proprietor labored at his answer. "I tell you, Bill, you standing there in the glare—"

"God damn you to hell!" said Bill.

He came out into the bright light, pale under his suntan, took Walter's elbow and started walking.

"Come on, Walt. I'm not hungry."

"That's funny," said Walt. "Neither am I."

. . .

Where the summer vanished, Walter never knew. Autumn came and the two tides, the salt one and the human one, pulled back from one another, disengaged themselves from their contortions. The honk of horns faded. The wooden frontings of the hot dog palaces slammed down and were nailed fast, and a great lonely wind ran along the chilling shore.

One day Walter sat down beside Bill who was all alone once more on the empty beach.

"Well, I won't see you no more, Walt."

"How's that?"

"Moving to San Diego to work in the shipyard. It's the end of the beach season here, anyhow."

"It sure is," said Walter.

"It was a good year," said Bill.

Walter nodded. "It was a very *fine* year."

"I sure got tan."

"You sure did."

"It's beginning to come off now, though," said Bill, regretfully. Peering over his shoulder he gestured at his back. "See? This damn stuff's peeling off, and it itches. You mind taking off a coupla patches of it for me?"

"I don't mind," said Walter. "Turn around."

Bill turned silently and Walter, reaching out, eyes shining, gently pulled off a strip of skin.

Piece by piece, flake after flake he peeled the dark skin off Bill's shoulders, neck, spine, bringing out the pearly pink naked white underneath.

When he finished, Bill looked nude and lonely and small. Walter realized he had done something to Bill but Bill took it philosophically, didn't worry about it. A light blazed suddenly in Walter, out of the whole summer's time!

He had done something to Bill that was right and natural and there was no way of escaping or getting around it, that was the way it was and had to be. Bill had waited the summer through and thought he had something, but it really wasn't there all the time. They had both lain waiting for the opposite thing to happen to each of them.

The wind blew away the flakes of skin.

"You been here all June and July and August for this," said Walter, slowly. He tossed away a fragment. "And there it goes. And I been waiting *all my life* and I guess it goes to the same place." He turned his back proudly to Bill and then, half-sad, half-happy, but at peace with himself he said,

"Come on now, let's see you peel some offa me!"

# EIGHT
# THE POEMS

It started out to be just another poem. And then David began sweating over it, stalking the rooms, talking to himself more than ever before in the long, poorly-paid years. So intent was he upon the poem's facets that Lisa felt forgotten, left out, put away until such time as he finished writing and could notice her again.

Then, finally—the poem was completed.

With the ink still wet upon an old envelope's back, he gave it to her with trembling fingers, his eyes red-rimmed and shining with a hot, inspired light. And she read it.

"David—" she murmured. Her hand began to shake in sympathy with his.

"It's *good,* isn't it?" he cried. "Damn good!"

The cottage whirled around Lisa in a wooden torrent. Gazing at the paper she experienced sensations as if words were melting, flowing into animate things. The paper was a square, brilliantly sunlit casement through which one might lean into another and brighter amber land! Her mind swung pendulum-wise. She had to clutch, crying out fearfully, at the ledges of this incredible window to support herself from being flung headlong into a three-dimensional impossibility!

"David, how strange and wonderful and—*frightening.*"

It was as if she held a tube of light cupped in her hands, through which she could race into a vast space of singing and color and new sensation. Somehow, David had caught up, netted, skeined, imbedded reality, substance, atoms—mounting them upon paper with a simple imprisonment of ink!

He described the green, moist verdure of the dell, the eucalyptus trees and the birds flowing through their high, swaying branches. And the flowers cupping the propelled humming of bees.

"It *is* good, David. The very finest poem you've ever written!" She felt her heart beat swiftly with the idea and urge that came to her in the next moment. She felt that she must see the dell, to compare its quiet contents with those of this poem. She took David's arm. "Darling, let's walk down the road—now."

In high spirits, David agreed, and they set out together, from their lonely little house in the hills. Half down the road she changed her mind and wanted to retreat, but she brushed the thought aside with a move of her fine, thinly sculptured face. It seemed ominously dark for this time of day, down there toward the end of the path. She talked lightly to shield her apprehension:

"You've worked so hard, so long, to write the perfect poem. I knew you'd succeed some day. I guess this is it."

"Thanks to a patient wife," he said.

They rounded a bend of gigantic rock and twilight came as swiftly as a purple veil drawn down.

"David!"

In the unexpected dimness she clutched and found his arm and held to him. "What's happened? Is this the dell?"

"Yes, of course it is."

"But, it's so dark!"

"Well—yes—it is—" He sounded at a loss.

"The flowers are gone!"

"I saw them early this morning; they can't be gone!"

"You wrote about them in the poem. And where are the grape vines?"

"They *must* be here. It's only been an hour or more. It's too dark. Let's go back." He sounded afraid himself, peering into the uneven light.

"I can't find anything, David. The grass is gone, and the trees and bushes and vines, all gone!"

She cried it out, then stopped, and it fell upon them, the unnatural blank spaced silence, a vague timelessness, windlessness, a vacuumed sucked out feeling that oppressed and panicked them.

He swore softly and there was no echo. "It's too dark to tell now. It'll all be here tomorrow."

"But what if it *never* comes back?" She began to shiver.

"What are you raving about?"

She held the poem out. It glowed quietly with a steady pure yellow shining, like a small niche in which a candle steadily lived.

"You've written the perfect poem. Too perfect. That's what you've done." She heard herself talking, tonelessly, far away.

She read the poem again. And a coldness moved through her.

"The dell is here. Reading this is like opening a gate upon a path and walking knee-high in grass, smelling blue grapes, hearing bees in yellow transits on the air, and the wind carrying birds upon it. The paper dissolves into things, sun, water, colors and life. It's not symbols or reading any more, it's LIVING!"

"No," he said. "You're wrong. It's crazy."

. . .

They ran up the path together. A wind came to meet them after they were free of the lightless vacuum behind them.

In their small, meagerly furnished cottage they sat at the window, staring down at the dell. All around was the unchanged light of mid-afternoon. Not dimmed or diffused or silent as down in the cup of rocks.

"It's not true. Poems don't work that way," he said.

"Words are symbols. They conjure up images in the mind."

"Have I done more than that?" he demanded. "And how did I do it, I ask you?" He rattled the paper, scowling intently at each line. "Have I made more than symbols with a form of matter and energy. Have I compressed, concentrated, dehydrated life? Does matter pass into and through my mind, like light through a magnifying glass to be focused into one narrow, magnificent blazing apex of fire? Can I etch life, burn it onto paper, with that flame? Gods in heaven, I'm going mad with thought!"

A wind circled the house.

"If we are not crazy, the two of us," said Lisa, stiffening at the sound of the wind, "there is one way to prove our suspicions."

"How?"

"Cage the wind."

"Cage it? Bar it up? Build a mortar of ink around it?"

She nodded.

"No, I won't fool myself." He jerked his head. Wetting his lips, he sat for a long while. Then, cursing at his own curiosity, he walked to the table and fumbled self-consciously with pen and ink. He looked at her, then at the windy light outside. Dipping his pen, he flowed it out onto paper in regular dark miracles.

Instantly, the wind vanished.

"The wind," he said. "It's caged. The ink is dry."

. . .

Over his shoulder she read it, became immersed in its cool heady current, smelling far oceans tainted on it, odors of distant wheat acres and green corn and the sharp brick and cement smell of cities far away.

David stood up so quickly the chair fell back like an old thin woman. Like a blind man he walked down the hill toward the dell, not turning, even when Lisa called after him, frantically.

When he returned he was by turns hysterical and immensely calm. He collapsed in a chair. By night, he was smoking his pipe, eyes closed, talking on and on, as calmly as possible.

"I've got power now no man ever had. I don't know its extensions, its boundaries or its governing limits. Somewhere, the enchantment ends. Oh, my god, Lisa, you should see what I've done to that dell. It's gone, all gone, stripped to the very raw primordial bones of its former self. And the beauty is here!" He opened his eyes and stared at the poem, as at the Holy Grail. "Captured forever, a few bars of midnight ink on paper! I'll be the greatest poet in history! I've always dreamed of that."

"I'm afraid, David. Let's tear up the poems and get away from here!"

"Move away? Now?"

"It's dangerous. What if your power extends beyond the valley?"

His eyes shone fiercely. "Then I can destroy the universe and immortalize it at one and the same instant. It's in the power of a sonnet, if I choose to write it."

"But you *won't* write it, promise me, David?"

He seemed not to hear her. He seemed to be listening to a cosmic music, a movement of bird wings very high and clear. He seemed to be wondering how long this land had waited here, for centuries perhaps, waiting for a poet to come and drink of its power. This valley seemed like the center of the universe, now.

"It would be a magnificent poem," he said, thoughtfully. "The most magnificent poem ever written, shaming Keats and Shelley and Browning and all the rest. A poem about the universe. But no." He shook his head sadly. "I guess I won't ever write that poem."

Breathless, Lisa waited in the long silence.

Another wind came from across the world to replace the one newly imprisoned. She let out her breath, at ease.

"For a moment I was afraid you'd over-stepped the boundary and taken in all the winds of the earth. It's all right now."

"All right, hell," he cried, happily. "It's marvelous!"

And he caught hold of her, and kissed her again and again.

Fifty poems were written in fifty days. Poems about a rock, a stem, a blossom, a pebble, an ant, a dropped feather, a raindrop, an avalanche, a dried skull, a dropped key, a fingernail, a shattered light bulb.

Recognition came upon him like a rain shower. The poems were bought and read across the world. Critics referred to the masterpieces as "—chunks of amber in which are caught whole portions of life and living—" "—each poem a window looking out upon the world—"

He was suddenly a very famous man. It took him many days to believe it. When he saw his name on the printed books he didn't believe it, and said so. And when he read the critics' columns he didn't believe them either.

Then it began to make a flame inside him, growing up, climbing and consuming his body and legs and arms and face.

Amidst the sound and glory, she pressed her cheek to his and whispered:

"This is your perfect hour. When will there ever be a more perfect time than this? Never again."

He showed her the letters as they arrived.

"See? This letter. From New York." He blinked rapidly and couldn't sit still. "They want me to write more poems. Thousands more. Look at this letter. Here." He gave it to her. "That editor says that if I can write so fine and great about a pebble or a drop of water, think what I can do when I—well experiment with real life. Real life. Nothing big. An amoeba perhaps. Or, well, just this morning, I saw a bird—"

"A bird?" She stiffened and waited for him to answer.

"Yes, a hummingbird—hovering, settling, rising—"

"You didn't . . . ?"

"Why NOT? Only a bird. One bird out of a billion," he said self-consciously. "One little bird, one little poem. You can't deny me that."

"One amoeba," she repeated, tonelessly. "And then next it will be one dog, one man, one city, one continent, one universe!"

"Nonsense." His cheek twitched. He paced the room, fingering back his dark hair. "You dramatize things. Well, after all, what's one dog, even, or to go one step further, one man?"

She sighed. "It's the very thing you talked of with fear, the danger we spoke of that first time we knew your power. Remember, David, it's not really yours, it was only an accident our coming here to the valley house—"

He swore softly. "Who cares whether it was accident or Fate? The thing that counts is that I'm here, now, and they're—they're—" He paused, flushing.

"They're what?" she prompted.

"They're calling me the greatest poet who ever lived!"

"It'll ruin you."

"Let it ruin me, then! Let's have silence, now."

He stalked into his den and sat restlessly studying the dirt road. While in this mood, he saw a small brown dog come patting along the road, raising little dust-tufts behind.

"And a damn good poet I am," he whispered, angrily, taking out pen and paper. He scratched out four lines swiftly.

The dog's barking came in even shrill intervals upon the air as it circled a tree and bounded a green bush. Quite unexpectedly, half over one leap across a vine, the barking ceased, and the dog fell apart in the air, inch by inch, and vanished.

Locked in his den, he composed at a furious pace, counting pebbles in the garden and changing them to stars simply by giving them mention, immortalizing clouds, hornets, bees, lightning and thunder with a few pen flourishes.

It was inevitable that some of his more secret poems should be stumbled upon and read by his wife.

Coming home from a long afternoon walk he found her with the poems lying all unfolded upon her lap.

"David," she demanded. "What does this mean?" She was very cold and shaken by it. "This poem. First a dog. Then a cat, some sheep and—finally—a man!"

He seized the papers from her. "So what!" Sliding them in a drawer, he slammed it, violently. "He was just an old man, they were old sheep, and it was a microbe-infested terrier! The world breathes better without them!"

"But here, THIS poem, too." She held it straight out before her, eyes widened. "A woman. Three children from Charlottesville!"

"All right, so you don't like it!" he said, furiously. "An artist has to experiment. With everything! I can't just stand still and do the same thing over and over. I've got greater plans than you think. Yes, really good, fine plans. I've decided to write about everything. I'll dissect the heavens if I wish, rip down the worlds, toy with suns if I damn please!"

"David," she said, shocked.

"Well, I will! I will!"

"You're such a child, David. I should have known. If this goes on, I can't stay here with you."

"You'll have to stay," he said.

"What do you mean?"

He didn't know what he meant himself. He looked around, helplessly and then declared, "I mean. I mean—if you try to go all I have to do is sit at my desk and describe you in ink . . ."

"You . . ." she said, dazedly.

She began to cry. Very silently, with no noise, her shoulders moved, as she sank down on a chair.

"I'm sorry," he said, lamely, hating the scene. "I didn't mean to say that, Lisa. Forgive me." He came and laid a hand upon her quivering body.

"I won't leave you," she said, finally.

And closing her eyes, she began to think.

.  .  .

It was much later in the day when she returned from a shopping trip to town with bulging grocery sacks and a large gleaming bottle of champagne.

David looked at it and laughed aloud. "Celebrating, are we?"

"Yes," she said, giving him the bottle and an opener. "Celebrating you as the world's greatest poet!"

"I detect sarcasm, Lisa," he said, pouring drinks. "Here's a toast to the—the universe." He drank. "Good stuff." He pointed at hers. "Drink up. What's wrong?" Her eyes looked wet and sad about something.

She refilled his glass and lifted her own. "May we always be together. Always."

The room tilted. "It's hitting me," he observed very seriously, sitting down so as not to fall. "On an empty stomach I drank. Oh, Lord!"

He sat for ten minutes while she refilled his glass. She seemed very happy suddenly, for no reason. He sat scowling, thinking, looking at his pen and ink and paper, trying to make a decision. "Lisa?"

"Yes?" She was now preparing supper, singing.

"I feel in a mood. I have been considering all afternoon and—"

"And what, darling?"

"I am going to write the greatest poem in history—NOW!"

She felt her heart flutter.

"Will your poem be about the valley?"

He smirked. "No. No! Bigger than that. Much bigger!"

"I'm afraid I'm not much good at guessing," she confessed.

"Simple," he said, gulping another drink of champagne. Nice of her to think of buying it, it stimulated his thoughts. He held up his pen and dipped it in ink. "I shall write my poem about the universe! Let me see now . . ."

"David!"

He winced. "What?"

"Oh, nothing. Just, have some more champagne, darling."

"Eh?" He blinked fuzzily. "Don't mind if I do. Pour."

She sat beside him, trying to be casual.

"Tell me again. What is it you'll write?"

"About the universe, the stars, the epileptic shamblings of comets, the blind black seekings of meteors, the heated embraces and spawnings of giant suns, the cold, graceful excursions of polar planets, asteroids plummeting like paramecium under a gigantic microscope, all and everything and anything my mind lays claim to! Earth, sun, stars!" he exclaimed.

"No!" she said, but caught herself. "I mean, darling, don't do it all at once. One thing at a time—"

"One at a time." He made a face. "That's the way I've been doing things and I'm tied to dandelions and daisies."

He wrote upon the paper with the pen.

"What're you doing?" she demanded, catching his elbow.

"Let me alone!" He shook her off.

She saw the black words form:

"Illimitable universe, with stars and planets and suns—"

She must have screamed.

"No, David, cross it out, before it's too late. Stop it!"

He gazed at her as through a long dark tube, and her far away at the other end, echoing. "Cross it out?" he said. "Why, it's GOOD poetry! Not a line will I cross out. I want to be a GOOD poet!"

She fell across him, groping, finding the pen. With one instantaneous slash, she wiped out the words.

*"Before the ink dries, before it dries!"*

"Fool!" he shouted. "Let me alone!"

. . .

She ran to the window. The first evening stars were still there, and the crescent moon. She sobbed with relief. She swung about to face him and walked toward him. "I want to help you write your poem—"

"Don't need your help!"

"Are you blind? Do you realize the power of your pen!"

To distract him, she poured more champagne, which he welcomed and drank. "Ah," he sighed, dizzily. "My head spins."

But it didn't stop him from writing, and write he did, starting again on a new sheet of paper:

"UNIVERSE—VAST UNIVERSE—BILLION STARRED AND WIDE—"

She snatched frantically at shreds of things to say, things to stave off his writing.

"That's poor poetry," she said.

"What do you mean 'poor'?" he wanted to know, writing.

"You've got to start at the beginning and build up," she explained logically. "Like a watch spring being wound or the universe starting with a molecule building on up through stars into a stellar cartwheel—"

He slowed his writing and scowled with thought.

She hurried on, seeing this. "You see, darling, you've let emotion run off with you. You can't start with the big things. Put them at the end of your poem. Build to a climax!"

The ink was drying. She stared at it as it dried. In another sixty seconds—

He stopped writing. "Maybe you're right. Just maybe you are." He put aside the pen a moment.

"I know I'm right," she said, lightly, laughing. "Here. I'll just take the pen and—there—"

She had expected him to stop her, but he was holding his pale brow and looking pained with the ache in his eyes from the drink.

She drew a bold line through his poem. Her heart slowed.

"Now," she said, solicitously, "you take the pen, and I'll help you. Start out with small things and build, like an artist."

His eyes were gray-filmed. "Maybe you're right, maybe, maybe."

The wind howled outside.

"Catch the wind!" she cried, to give him a minor triumph to satisfy his ego. "Catch the wind!"

He stroked the pen. "Caught it!" he bellowed, drunkenly, weaving. "Caught the wind! Made a cage of ink!"

"Catch the flowers!" she commanded, excitedly. "Everyone in the valley! And the grass!"

"There! Caught the flowers!"

"The hill next!" she said.

"The hill!"

"The valley!"

"The valley!"

"The sunlight, the odors, the trees, the shadows, the house and the garden, and the things inside the house!"

"Yes, yes, yes," he cried, going on and on and on.

And while he wrote quickly she said, "David, I love you. Forgive me for what I do next, darling—"

"What?" he asked, not having heard her.

"Nothing at all. Except that we are never satisfied and want to go on beyond proper limits. You tried to do that, David, and it was wrong."

He nodded over his work. She kissed him on the cheek. He reached up and patted her chin. "Know what, lady?"

"What?"

"I think I like you, yes, sir, I think I like you."

She shook him. "Don't go to sleep, David, don't."

"Want to sleep. Want to sleep."

"Later, darling. When you've finished your poem, your last great poem, the very finest one, David. Listen to me—"

He fumbled with the pen. "What'll I say?"

She smoothed his hair, touched his cheek with her fingers and kissed him, tremblingly. Then, closing her eyes, she began to dictate:

"There lived a fine man named David and his wife's name was Lisa and—"

The pen moved slowly, achingly, tiredly forming words.

"Yes?" he prompted.

"—and they lived in a house in the garden of Eden—"

He wrote again, tediously. She watched.

He raised his eyes. "Well? What's next?"

She looked at the house, and the night outside, and the wind returned to sing in her ears and she held his hands and kissed his sleepy lips,

"That's all," she said, "the ink is drying."

.  .  .

The publishers from New York visited the valley months later and went back to New York with only three pieces of paper they had found blowing in the wind around and about the raw, scarred, empty valley.

The publishers stared at one another, blankly:

"Why, why, there was nothing left at all," they said. "Just bare rock, not a sign of vegetation or humanity. The home he lived in—gone! The road, everything! *He* was gone! His wife, *she* was gone, too! Not a word out of them. It was like a river flood had washed through, scraping away the whole countryside! Gone! Washed out! And only three last poems to show for the whole thing!"

No further word was ever received from the poet or his wife. The Agricultrural College experts traveled hundreds of miles to study the starkly denuded valley, and went away shaking their heads and looking pale.

But it is all simply found again.

You turn the pages of his last small thin book and read the three poems.

She is there, pale and beautiful and immortal; you smell the sweet warm flash of her, young forever, hair blowing golden upon the wind.

And next to her, upon the opposite page, he stands gaunt, smiling, firm, hair like raven's hair, hands on hips, face raised to look about him.

And on all sides of them, green with an immortal green, under a sapphire sky, with the odor of fat wine-grapes, with the grass knee-high and bending to touch exploring feet, with the trails waiting for any reader who takes them, one finds the valley, and the house, and the deep rich peace of sunlight and of moonlight and many stars, and the two of them, he and she, walking through it all, laughing together, forever and forever.

# NINE

# DEFENSE MECH

Oh, my God, do you realize how far from Earth we are? Do you really *think* about it? It's enough to scare the guts from a man. Hold me up. *Do* something. Give me sedatives or hold my hand or run call mama. A million cold miles up. See all the flickering stars? Look at my hands tremble. Feel my heart whirling like a hot pinwheel!

The captain comes toward me, a stunned expression on his small, tight face. He takes my arm, looking into my eyes. Hello, Captain. I'm sick, if that's what you want to know. I've a right to be scared—just look at all that space! Standing here a moment ago, I stared down at Earth so round and cloud-covered and asleep on a mat of stars, and my brain tore loose and screamed, man, man, how'd you get in a mess like this, in a rocket a million miles past the moon, shooting for Mars with a crew of fourteen others! I can hardly stand up, my knees, my hands, my heart, are shaking apart. Hold me up, sir.

What are hysterics like? The captain unprongs the inter-deck audio and speaks swiftly, scowling, into it. I hope he's phoning the psychiatrist. I need something. Oh, dammit, dammit!

The psychiatrist descends the ladder in immaculate salt-white uniform and walks toward me in a dream. Hello, doctor. You're the one for me. Please, sir, turn this damned rocket around and fly back to New York. I'll go crazy with all this space and distance!

The psychiatrist and the captain's voices murmur and blend, with here and there an emphasis, a toss of head, a gesture:

"Young Halloway here's on a fear-jag, doctor. Can you help him?"

"I'll try. Good man, Halloway is. Imagine you'll need him and his muscles when we land."

"With the crew as small as it is, every man's worth his weight in uranium. He's *got* to be cured."

The psychiatrist shakes his head.

"Might have to squirt him full of drugs to keep him quiet the rest of the expedition."

The captain explodes, saying that is impossible. Blood drums in my head. The doctor moves closer, smelling clean, sharp and white.

"Please, understand, Captain, this man is definitely psychotic about going home. His talk is almost a reversion to childhood. I can't refuse his demands, and his fear seems too deeply based for reasoning. However, I think I've an idea. Halloway?"

Yes, sir? Help me, doctor. I want to go home. I want to see popcorn exploding into a buttered avalanche inside a glass cube, I want to roller skate, I want to climb into the old cool wet ice-wagon and go *chikk-chikk-chikk* on the ice with a sharp pick, I want to take long sweating hikes in the country, see big brick buildings and bright-faced people, fight the old gang, anything but this—*awful!*

The psychiatrist rubs his chin.

"All right, son. You can go back to Earth, now, tonight."

Again the captain explodes.

"You can't tell him *that*. We're landing on Mars *today!*"

The psychiatrist pats down the captain patiently.

"Please, Captain. Well, Halloway, back to New York for you. How does it sound?"

I'm not so scared now. We're going down on the moving ladder and here is the psychiatrist's cubicle.

He's pouring lights into my eyes. They revolve like stars on a disc. Lots of strange machines around, attachments to my head, my ears. Sleepy. Oh, so sleepy. Like under warm water. Being pushed around. Laved. Washed. Quiet. Oh, gosh. Sleepy.

"—listen to me, Halloway—"

Sleepy. Doctor's talking. Very soft, like feathers. Soft, soft.

"—you're going to land on Earth. No matter what they tell you, you're landing on Earth . . . no matter what happens you'll be on Earth . . . everything you see and do will be like on Earth . . . remember that . . . remember that . . . you won't be afraid because you'll be on Earth . . . remember that . . . over and over . . . you'll land on Earth in an hour . . . home . . . home again . . . no matter what anyone says. . . ."

Oh, yes, sir, home again. Sleepy. Home again. Drifting, sleeping, oh thank you, sir, thank you from the bottom of my drowsy, sleepy soul. Yes, sir. Yes, sir. Sleepy. Drifting.

. . .

I'm awake!

Hey, everybody, come look! Here comes Earth! Right at us, like a green moss ball off a bat! Coming at us on a curve!

"Check stations! Mars landing!"

"Get into bulgers! Test atmosphere!"

Get into your *what* did he say?

"Your baseball uniform, Halloway. Your baseball uniform."

Yes, sir, it's over in that metal locker. I'll take it out. Head, arms, legs into it—I'm dressed. Baseball uniform. Ha! This is great! Pitch 'er in here, ole boy, ole boy! *Smack!* Yow!

"Adjust bulger helmets, check oxygen."

What?

"Put on your catcher's mask, Halloway."

Oh. The mask slides down over my face. Like that. The captain comes rushing up, eyes hot green and angry.

"Doctor, what's this infernal nonsense?"

"You wanted Halloway able to do his work, didn't you, captain?"

"Yes, but what in hell've you done to him?"

Strange. As they talk, I hear their words flow over my head like a wave dashed on a sea-stone, but the words drain off, leaving no imprint. As soon as some words invade my head, something eats and digests them and I think the words are something else entirely.

The psychiatrist nods at me.

"I couldn't change his basic desire. Given time, yes, a period of months, I could have. But you need him *now*. So, against all the known ethics of my profession, which say one must never lie to a patient, I've followed along in his own thought channel. I didn't dare frustrate him. He wanted to go home, so I *let* him. I've given him a fantasy. I've set up a protective defense mechanism in his mind that refuses to believe certain realities, that evaluates all things from its own desire for security and home. His mind will automatically block any thought or image that endangers that security."

The captain stares wildly.

"Then, then Halloway's insane!"

"Would you have him mad with fear, or able to work on Mars hindered by only a slight 'tetched' condition? Coddle him and he'll do fine. Just remember, we're landing on Earth, *not* Mars."

"Earth, Mars, you'll have *me* raving next."

The doctor and the captain certainly talk weirdly. Who cares? Here comes Earth! Green, expanding like a moist cabbage underfoot!

"Mars landing! Air-lock opened! Use bulger oxygen."

Here we go, gang! Last one out is a pink chimpanzee!

"Halloway, come back, you damn fool! You'll kill yourself!"

Feel the good sweet Earth! Home again! Praise the Lord! Let's dance, sing off-key, laugh! Ha! Oh, boy!

In the door of the house stands the captain, his face red and wrinkled, waving his fists.

"Halloway, come back! Look behind you, you fool!"

I whirl about and cry out, happily.

Shep! Shep, old dog! He comes running to meet me, long fur shining under amber in the sunshine. Barking. Shep, I haven't seen you in years. Good old pooch. Come 'ere, Shep. Let me pet you.

The captain shrieks:

"Don't pet it! It looks like a carnivorous Martian worm. Man, the jaws on that thing! Halloway, use your knife!"

Shep snarls and shows his teeth. Shep, what's wrong? That's no way to greet me. Come on, Shep. Hey! I pull back my fingers as his swift jaws snap. Shep circles me, swiftly. You haven't rabies, have you, Shep? He darts in, snatches my ankle with strong, locking white teeth! Lord, Shep, you're crazy! I can't let this go on. And you used to be such a fine, beautiful dog. Remember all the hikes we took into the lazy corn country, by the red barns and deep wells? Shep clenches tight my ankle. I'll give him one more chance. Shep, *let go!* Where did this long knife come from in my hand, like magic? Sorry to do this, Shep, but—*there!*

Shep screams, thrashing, screams again. My arm pumps up and down, my gloves are freckled with blood-flakes.

Don't scream, Shep. I *said* I was sorry, didn't I?

"Get out there, you men, and bury that beast immediately."

I glare at the captain. Don't talk that way about Shep.

The captain stares at my ankles.

"Sorry, Halloway. I meant, bury that 'dog,' you men. Give him full honors. You were lucky, son, another second and those knife-teeth'd bored through your ankle-cuff metal."

I don't know what he means. I'm wearing sneakers, sir.

"Oh, yeah, so you are. Yeah. Well, I'm sorry, Halloway. I know how you must feel about—Shep. He was a fine dog."

I think about it a moment and my eyes fill up, wet.

. . .

There'll be a picnic and a hike; the captain says. Three hours now the boys have carried luggage from the metal house. The way they talk, this'll be some picnic. Some seem afraid, but who worries about copperheads and water-moccasins and crawfish? Not me. No, sir. Not me.

Gus Bartz, sweating beside me on some apparatus, squints at me.

"What's eatin' you, Halloway?"

I smile. Me? Nothing. Why?

"You and that act with that Martian worm."

What're you talking about? What worm?

The captain interrupts, nervously.

"Bartz, lay off Halloway. The doctor'll explain why. Ask him."

Bartz goes away, scratching his head.

The captain pats my shoulder.

"You're our strong-arm man, Halloway. You've got muscles from working on the rocket engines. So keep alert today, eh, on your hike to look over the territory? Keep your—b.b. gun—ready."

Beavers, do you think, sir?

The captain swallows, hard, and blinks.

"Unh— oh, beavers, yeah, beavers. Sure. Beavers! Maybe. Mountain lions and Indians, too, I hear. Never can tell. Be careful."

Mountain lions and Indians in New York in this day and age? Aw, sir.

"Let it go. Keep alert, anyhow. Smoke?"

I don't smoke, sir. A strong mind in a healthy body, you know the old rule.

"The old rule. Oh, *yes*. The *old* rule. Only joking. I don't want a smoke anyway. Like hell."

What was that last, sir?

"Nothing, Halloway, carry on, carry on."

I help the others work, now. Are we taking the yellow streetcar to the edge of town, Gus?

"We're using propulsion belts, skimming low over the dead seas."

How's that again, Gus?

"I said, we're takin' the yellow streetcar to the end of the line, yeah."

We're ready. Everyone's packed and spreading out. We're going in groups of four. Down Main Street past the pie factory, over the bridge, through the tunnel, past the circus grounds and we'll rendezvous, says the captain, at a place he points to on a queer, disjointed map.

*Whoosh!* We're off! I forgot to pay my fare.

"That's okay, I paid it."

Thanks, Captain. We're really traveling. The cypresses and the maples flash by. *Kaawhoom!* I wouldn't admit this to anyone but you, sir, but momentarily there, I didn't see this streetcar. Suddenly we moved in empty space, nothing supporting us, and I didn't see any car. But *now* I see it, sir.

The captain gazed at me as at a nine-day miracle.

"You do, eh?"

Yes, sir. I clutch upward. Here's the strap. I'm holding it.

"You look pretty funny sliding through the air with your hand up like that, Halloway."

How's that, sir?

"Ha, ha, ha!"

Why are the others laughing at me, sir?

"Nothing, son, nothing. Just happy, that's all."

*Ding Ding. Ding Ding.* Canal Street and Washington. *Ding Ding. Whoosh.* This is real traveling. Funny, though, the captain and his men keep moving, changing seats, never stay seated. It's a long streetcar. I'm way in back now. They're up front.

By the large brown house on the next corner stands a popcorn wagon, yellow and red and blue. I can taste the popcorn in my mind. It's been a long time since I've eaten some . . . if I ask the captain's permission to stop and buy a bag, he'll refuse. I'll just sneak off the car at the next stop. I can get back on the next car and catch up with the gang later.

. . .

How do you stop this car? My fingers fumble with my baseball outfit, doing something I don't want to know about. The car is stopping! Why's that. Popcorn is more important.

I'm off the car, walking. Here's the popcorn machine with a man behind it, fussing with little silver metal knobs.

"—*murr—lokk—loc—cor—iz—*"

*Tony!* Tony, bambino! What are you doing here?

"*Click.*"

It can't be, but it is. Tony, who died ten long years ago, when I was a freckled kid! Alive and selling popcorn again. Oh, Tony, it's good to see you. His black moustache's so waxed, so shining, his dark hair like burnt oily shavings, his dark shining happy eyes, his smiling red cheeks! He shimmers in my eyes like a cold rain. Tony! Let me shake your hand! Gimme a bag of popcorn, senor!

*Click-click-click—sput-click—reeeeeeeeeeeeee—*

The captain didn't see you, Tony, you were hidden so well, only *I* saw you. Just a moment while I search for my nickel.

"*Reeeeeee.*"

Whew, I'm dizzy. It's very hot. My head spins like a leaf on a storm wind. Let me hold onto your wagon, Tony, quick, I'm shivering and I've got sharp needle head pains . . .

"*Reeeeeeee.*"

I'm running a temperature. I feel as if I have a torch hung flaming in my head.

Hotter. Pardon me for criticizing you, Tony, but I think it's your popper turned up too high. Your face looks afraid, contorted, and your hands move so rapidly, why? Can't you shut it off? I'm hot. Everything melts. My knees sag.

Warmer still. He'd better turn that thing off, I can't take any more. I can't find my nickel anyhow. Please, snap it off, Tony, I'm sick. My uniform glows orange. I'll take fire!

Here, I'll turn it off for you, Tony.

You *hit* me!

Stop hitting me, stop clicking those knobs! It's hot, I tell you. Stop, or I'll—

Tony. Where are you? Gone.

Where did that purple flame shoot from? That loud blast, what was it? The flame seemed to stream from my hand, out of my scout flashlight. Purple flame—eating!

I smell a sharp bitter odor.

Like hamburger fried overlong.

I feel better now. Cool as winter. But—

Like a fly buzzing in my ears, a voice comes, faint, far off,

"Halloway, damn it, Halloway, where are you?"

Captain! It's his voice, sizzling. I don't see you, sir!

"Halloway, we're on the dead sea bottom near an ancient Martian city and—oh, never mind, dammit, if you hear me, press your boyscout badge and yell!"

I press the badge intensely, sweating. Hey, Captain!

"Halloway! Glory. You're *not* dead. Where are you?"

I stopped for popcorn, sir. I can't see you. How do I hear you?

"It's an echo. Let it go. If you're okay, grab the next streetcar."

That's very opportune. Because here comes a big red streetcar now, around the corner of the drug store.

"*What!*"

Yes, sir, and it's chock full of people. I'll climb aboard.

"Wait a minute! Hold on! Murder! What *kind* of people, dammit?"

It's the West Side gang. Sure. The whole bunch of tough kids.

"West Side gang, hell, those are Martians, get the hell outa there! Transfer to another car—take the subway! Take the elevated!"

Too late. The car's stopped. I'll have to get on. The conductor looks impatient.

"Impatient," he says. "You'll be massacred!"

Oh, oh. Everybody's climbing from the streetcar, looking angry at me. Kelly and Grogan and Tompkins and the others. I guess there'll be a fight.

The captain's voice stabs my ears, but I don't see him anywhere:

"Use your r-gun, your blaster, your blaster. Hell, use your slingshot, or throw spitballs, or whatever the devil you imagine you got holstered there, but *use* it! Come on, men, about face and back!"

I'm outnumbered. I bet they'll gang me and give me the bumps, the bumps, the bumps. I bet they'll truss me to a maple tree, maple tree, maple tree and tickle me. I bet they'll ink-tattoo their initials on my forehead. Mother won't like this.

The captain's voice opens up louder, driving nearer:

"And Poppa ain't happy! Get outa there, Halloway!"

They're hitting me, sir! We're battling!

"Keep it up, Halloway!"

I knocked one down, sir, with an uppercut. I'm knocking another down now. Here goes a third! Someone's grabbed my ankle. I'll kick him! *There!* I'm stumbling, falling! Lights in my eyes, purple ones, big purple lightning bolts sizzling the air!

Three of them vanished, just like that!

I think they fell down a manhole.

I'm sorry. I didn't mean to hurt them bad.

They stole my flashlight.

"Get it back, Halloway! We're coming. Get your flash and use it!" That's silly. "Silly," he says. "Silly. Silly."

. . .

I got my flashlight back, broken, no good. We're wrestling. There are so many of them, I'm weak. They're climbing all over me, hitting. It's not fair, I'm falling down, kicking, screaming!

"Up speed, men, full power!"

They're binding me up. I can't move. They're rushing me into the streetcar now. Now I won't be able to go on that hike. And I planned on it so hard, too.

*"Here we are, Halloway! Blast 'em, men! Oh, my Lord, look at the horrible faces on those creatures! Guh!"*

Watch out, Captain! They'll get you, too, and the others! *Ahh!* Somebody struck me on the back of my head. Darkness. Dark. Dark.

Rockabye baby on the tree-top . . . when the wind blows . . .

"Okay, Halloway, *any* time. Just any old time you want to come to."

Dark. A voice talking. Dark as a whale's insides. Ouch, my head. I'm flat on my back, I can feel rocks under me.

"Good morning, *dear* Mr. Halloway."

That you, Captain, over in that dark corner?

"It ain't the president of the United States!"

Where is this cave?

"Suppose *you* tell us, you got us into this mess with your eternally blasted popcorn! Why'd you get off the streetcar?"

Did the West Side gang truss us up like this, captain?

"West Side gang, *goh!* Those faces, those inhuman, weird, unsavory and horrible faces. All loose-fleshed and—gangrenous. Aliens, the whole rotting clutch of 'em."

What a funny way to talk.

"Listen, you parboiled idiot, in about an hour we're going to be fried, gutted, iced, killed, slaughtered, murdered, we will be, ipso facto, dead. Your 'friends' arc whipping up a little blood-letting jamboree. Can't I shove it through your thick skull, we're on Mars, about to be sliced and hammered by a lousy bunch of Martians!"

"Captain, sir?"

"Yes, Berman?"

"The cave door is opening, sir. I think the Martians are ready to have at us again, sir. Some sort of test or other, no doubt."

"Let go a me, you one-eyed monster! I'm coming, don't push!"

We're outside the cave. They're cutting our bonds. See, captain, they aren't hurting us, after all. Here's the brick alley. There's Mrs. Haight's underwear waving on the clothes-line. See all the people from the beer hall—what're they waiting for?

"To see us die."

"Captain, what's wrong with Halloway, he's acting queer—"

"At least he's better off than us. He can't see these creatures' faces and bodies. It's enough to turn a man's stomach. This must be their amphitheatre. That looks like an obstacle course. I gather from their sign lingo that if we make it through the obstacles, we're free. Footnote: nobody's ever gotten through alive yet. Seems they want you to go first, Berman. Good luck, boy."

"So long, Captain. So long, Gus. So long, Halloway."

Berman's running down-alley with an easy, long-muscled stride. I hear him yelling high and clear, even though he's getting far away.

Here comes an automobile!

Berman! Ahh! It hit him! He's fallen!

Berman, get up, get up!

"Stay here, Halloway, it's not your turn yet."

My turn? What do you mean? Someone's gotta help Berman.

"Halloway, come back! Oh, man, I don't want to see this!"

. . .

Lift up my legs, put them down, breathe out, breathe in, swing arms, swing legs, chew my tongue, blink my eyes, Berman, here I come, gee, things are crazy-funny, here comes an ice-wagon trundling along, it's coming right at *me!* I can't see to get around it, it's coming so fast, I'll jump inside it, jump, jump, cool, ice, ice-pick, *chikk-chikk-chikk,* I hear the captain screaming off a million hot miles gone, *chikk-chikk-chikk* around the ice perimeter, the ice-wagon is thundering, rioting, jouncing, shaking, rolling on big rusty iron wheels, smelling of sour ammonia, bouncing on a corduroy dirt and brick alley-road, the rear end of it seems to be snapping shut with many ice-prongs, I feel intense pain in my left leg, *chikk-chikk-chikk-chikk!* piece of ice, cold square, cold cube, a shuddering and convulsing, a temblor, the wagon wheels stop rolling, I jump down and run away from the wrecked wagon, did the wagon roll over Berman, I hope not, a fence here, I'll jump over it, another popcorn machine, very warm, very hot, all flame and red fire and burning metal knobs . . .

Oops, I didn't mean to strike the popcorn man down, hello, Berman, what're you doing in my arms, how'd you get here, did I pick you up, and why? an obstacle race at the high-school? you're heavy, I'm tired, dogs nipping at my heels, how far am I supposed to carry you? I hear the captain screaming me on, for why, for why? here comes the big bad truant officer with a club in his hand to take me back to school, he looks mean and broad . . .

I kicked the truant officer's shins and kicked him in the face . . . Mama won't like that . . . yes, mommy . . . no mommy . . . that's unfair . . . that's not ethical fighting . . . something went squish . . . hmm . . . let's forget about it, shall we?

Breathing hard. Here comes the gang after me, all the rough, bristly Irishmen and scarred Norwegians and stubborn Italians . . . hit, kick, wrestle . . . here comes a swift car, fast, fast! I hope I can duck, with you, Berman . . . here comes another car from the opposite way! . . . if I work things right . . . uh . . . stop screaming, Berman!

The cars crashed into each other.

The cars still roll, tumbling, like two animals tearing at each other's throats.

Not far to go now, Berman, to the end of the alley. Just ahead. I'll sleep for forty years when this is over . . . where'd I get this flashlight in my hand? from one of those guys I knocked down? from the popcorn man? I'll poke it in front of me . . . people run away . . . maybe they don't like its light in their eyes . . . The end of the alley! There's the green valley and my house, and there's Mom and Pop waiting! Hey, let's sing, let's dance, we're going home!

"Halloway, you so-and-so, you did it!"

Dark. Sleep. Wake up slow. Listen.

"—and Halloway ran down that amphitheatre nonchalant as a high-school kid jumping hurdles. A big saffron Martian beast with a mouth so damn big it looked like the rear end of a delivery truck, lunged forward square at Halloway—"

"What'd Halloway do?"

"Halloway jumped right inside the monster's mouth—right inside!"

"What happened then?"

"The animal looked dumbfounded. It tried to spit out. Then, to top it all, what did Halloway do, I ask you, I ask you, what did he do? He drew forth his boy-scout blade and went *chikk-chikk-chikk* all around the bloody interior, pretending like he's holed up in an ice-wagon, chipping himself off pieces of ice."

"No?"

"On my honor! The monster, after taking a bit of this *chikk-chikk-chikk* business, leaped around, cavorting, floundering, rocking, tossing, and then, with a spout of blood, out popped Halloway, grinning like a kid, and on he ran, dodging spears and pretending they were pebbles, leaping a line of crouched warriors and saying they're a picket fence. Then he lifted Berman and trotted with him until he met a three hundred pound Martian wrestler. Halloway supposed it was the truant officer and promptly kicked him in the face. Then he knocked down another guy working furiously at the buttons of a paralysis machine which looked, to Halloway, like a popcorn wagon! After which two gigantic black Martian leopards attacked, resembling to him nothing more than two very bad drivers in black automobiles. Halloway sidestepped. The two 'cars' crashed and tore each other apart, fighting. Halloway pumped on, shooting people with his 'flashlight' which he retrieved from the 'popcorn' man. Pointing the flash at people, he was amazed when they vanished and—oh, oh, Halloway's waking up, I saw his eyelids flicker. Quiet, everyone. Halloway, you awake?"

Yeah. I been listening to you talk for five minutes. I still don't understand. Nothing happened at all. How long I been asleep?

"Two days. Nothing happened, eh? Nothing, except you got the Martians kowtowing, that's all, brother. Your spectacular performance impressed people. The enemy suddenly decided that if *one* earthman could do what you did, what would happen if a million more came?"

Everybody keeps on with this joking, this lying about Mars. Stop it. Where am I?

"Aboard the rocket, about to take off."

Leave Earth? No, no, I don't want to leave Earth, good green Earth! Let go! I'm afraid! Let go of me! Stop the ship!

"Halloway, *this* is Mars—we're going back *to* Earth."

Liars, all of you! I don't want to go to Mars, I want to stay here, on Earth!

"Holy cow, here we go again. Hold him down, Gus. Hey, doctor, on the double! Come help Halloway change his mind back, willya!"

*Liars! You can't do this! Liars! Liars!*

# TEN

# MR. PRIORY MEETS MR. CALDWELL (HELL'S HALF-HOUR)

The room was in a terrible state. The pictures were flung violently from the walls, the furniture was tumbled, overturned, there were deep gashes in the woodwork and wallpaper where Mr. Caldwell, the blind man, had dug, clutched, searched with his fingernails. The amount of damage was phenomenal.

Chris Priory, lieutenant of homicide for the town of Green Bay, California, stood beside me for a long while, just looking.

Caldwell, his dark glasses ground into powder, lay against the farthest wall, at its center, one hand struck up as if to claw through its frustrating thickness, the back of his skull caved in. He was a young, fine-looking, sensitively featured man, with dark, curly hair and a smooth complexion. Death had done things to his handsomeness.

"Lord, what a mess," I said.

Downstairs, on the first floor, we could hear the landlady weeping.

Priory looked at me and said, wonderingly, "Caldwell was blind."

"Yes," I said. "The landlady said he arrived here on October seventeenth, with his sight rapidly failing. Two weeks later he was stone blind, and he's been that way ever since. That was six weeks ago."

"Strange," muttered Priory. "It stands to reason that if someone came to murder Caldwell last night, he could have killed him right off, without all this muss. It must have taken a good twenty minutes to have done all this to the room. No need for it. A blind man's at the mercy of any killer. One good blow on his undefended and unsuspecting head—" Priory broke off, walking across to bend beside the corpse. "He was trying to get away, escape, trying to find the door in a wild, hysterical frenzy, when he died."

I glanced at the slashed furniture, the scarred walls. "Or else the place was wrecked to make it look like a fight?"

Priory shook his head. "Caldwell did most of it. Look. Under his fingernails: crescents of wallpaper, plaster, a sliver from the door, a thread of material from the couch. And here—his pants, at the knee, scuffed with violent rubbing. The tips of his shoes bruised with kicking at the locked door."

"Brutal," I said.

"Brutal, yes," admitted Priory. "And his forehead, too, you see. Those bruises came from colliding headlong with the wall, in flight. That cut on his cheek derives from shattering a picture and being cut by the falling glass. The death blows were delivered from the rear as he tried to scoop a hole through the wall with cut and bleeding raw fingernails . . ."

I swallowed uneasily. "Granted all that's true, what's the motive? Perhaps the killer searched afterwards for money, letters, other valuables."

Priory bent and pointed to the outer material of a chair. He showed me how it had been slashed by fingernails, but none of the stuffing pulled out, or disturbed. The same way with the davenport. The desk was gashed, but the drawers were all closed and the pens, pencils and writing paper neat inside them. Nowhere, either around or behind the pictures, were the scratches more than superficial. A man looking for something would have pounded gaping holes in plaster, and ripped the cotton guts from the furniture. I had to admit this was true. Everywhere the marks were simply those of a man who'd raked fingers swiftly over surfaces, in violent moves. The picture backs were not pried in any manner, nor were tacks lifted from the carpet at any spot.

I stood up. "That fixes that. Perhaps Caldwell carried something on his person?"

"Then the killer would have knocked him down and taken it, wouldn't he? But no, the killer was very methodical, cold blooded, took his time. Or maybe he *had* to take his time. Maybe—"

"Maybe what?"

Priory shrugged. "Let's go talk to the landlady."

.  .  .

The landlady lay in bed, her small, thin face so white it almost blended with the wrinkled pillow. She lifted a weak hand and began to talk:

"Mr. Caldwell came two months ago, exactly to the day. Almost hysterical he was. I was very sympathetic to him. He was going blind and two weeks after he took the room he was totally in the dark. I often heard him sobbing, upstairs. I'd knock on his door—that was before I took ill in bed—and he'd quiet down and come open the door with his cheeks all wet and when I'd try comforting him, he'd say, 'I've done a horrible thing, I've done a horrible thing. I know what it is now. Oh, my God, it's dark.'"

"Was Caldwell his real name?"

"I don't know. He seemed awfully jumpy, as if he were running from someone. When anyone came near he'd cry 'Who's there!' and I'd say 'No one but Miss Tarvey, sir,' or 'It's only the butcher's boy, bringing poultry.' An ordinary blind man would have asked politely. Not Mr. Caldwell. His face always paled out and his hands trembled and he cringed at people's footsteps."

The landlady paused to get her breath.

"I'm all alone here, and Mr. Caldwell was one of two roomers. My other roomer, Miss Tarvey, works nights, so she was gone. This man who came to visit Mr. Caldwell called earlier yesterday. Miss Tarvey answered the phone. The man asked where the blind man lived. He didn't ask by name, he just asked where the blind man lived. I thought that queer. And Miss Tarvey told him upstairs on the second floor and the voice on the phone asked which room, on which side of the hall, and Miss Tarvey said the first door on the right. Then the phone suddenly clicked, without so much as a thank you. And an hour later, at nine-o'clock, when Miss Tarvey had gone, this man came into the front hall."

"He didn't rap on the front door?" Priory asked.

"No. Just walked right in. I remember calling to see who it was. There was no answer, but I didn't worry much about it. He went upstairs and knocked on Mr. Caldwell's door. Then I heard the door open, Mr. Caldwell cry out, and the door slammed and locked."

"And then the noises began?"

The landlady sighed, closing her eyes, her voice weak, pale, far away. Her fingers twisted the bed quilt as she continued:

"The little noises began. And me lying here in bed, not able to do a thing. First of all, a man walking across the floor. It wasn't Mr. Caldwell, I could tell by his shoes. Then I heard a sharp thump. Mr. Caldwell cried out. I pushed myself up in bed. I called, 'Mr. Caldwell, you all right?' but he didn't hear me, I guess. Then I heard Mr. Caldwell, walking now, towards the door."

"Walking? At a regular, even pace?"

"Yes. Like you might stroll through the park. And then this other man began walking, too, and for three or four minutes they did nothing but walk around upstairs. I tensed myself, listening."

"They just walked around?"

The landlady lay listening to the memory of it; it was vivid and real to her still. "Yes. It sounded so—queer. Walking around—and talking. I couldn't figure out a word. Mr. Caldwell would say something and then this other man would say something," she remembered. "They began to walk a little faster. It kept speeding up, faster and faster. Mr. Caldwell would make a little run across the floor, then the man would make a little run after him. Then Mr. Caldwell would run some more, bump something, fall, get up, run on, and the man coming right after him, striding like."

I looked at the ceiling. The landlady flicked her tongue over her withered lips, stretched her eyes wider, staring, made wild, remembering movements with white eyeballs and focused pupils, dark, turned upward, at that room.

"Back and forth, back and forth, faster and faster, faster and faster. And they began to shout, things I can't remember, things I didn't understand. Walking,

walking, walking, the two of them. Running, now, quickly, like waltzing mice. Queer, odd. I kept lifting myself, calling, 'Mr. Caldwell, stop that, I can't sleep!' But they shouted louder and finally thumps and scratching sounded, like mice, rats in the walls. Pictures fell crashing. Furniture tipped back like tons of hard lumber, shaking the lights. I heard glass tinkle. I heard a table fall like a young tree cut. I heard a knob rattle, quick, quick; Mr. Caldwell started screaming. Then—then there was more scurrying—" she breathed it out, gasping, eyes fixed, immovable. "More shouting, blundering back and forth, back and forth, like a gigantic pendulum in that room; more rats in the wall. Mr. Caldwell collapsed down. I heard him fighting, scratching, digging right up there, *there*, you *see!* Digging like a dog at a gopher hole, sobbing wild! And then—"

The landlady stopped, stiffened her entire thin body.

"Then I heard the last sounds. The sounds of something striking Mr. Caldwell over and over again. Again and again!"

The landlady relaxed, sinking back on the bed, resting, perspiration on her brow, sighing to a finish.

"Right after that, the man came downstairs, silent, and went out the door. I tried screaming, but it was six hours before Miss Tarvey arrived to call the police."

I had sat down. Priory was scowling and nervous himself. "Of all the damnable things," he murmured. "You heard Mr. Caldwell's voice right up to the last?" The landlady nodded. "That proves it all occurred with Caldwell alive and moving, anyway. There was little time for the killer to search."

"No, sir. He came down immediately and went away."

I lighted a cigarette and looked at the match flame a while. "That killer must have enjoyed himself immensely. Immensely."

"Half an hour it was," said the landlady. "Thirty minutes they walked and ran around up there like nightmares on a treadmill."

"Thirty minutes to toy with his victim," I said.

Priory grunted. "It doesn't hold water." He turned to the door. "If you'll pardon me, I've some phone calls to make. Then I'm going out into the town for a few hours and see if I can't find myself a waltzing mouse. You stay here and watch the other homicide boys go over the room with a comb, eh? Good boy."

"Are you serious?" I asked, but Priory walked off.

. . .

Priory returned late in the afternoon, beaming. He talked excitedly and paced back and forth. "Douglas, suppose you were a killer. It wouldn't be hard tracing a blind man. A blind man can't run far with much secrecy. Or fast. And people remember him. So if you were the killer, how would you approach your victim if he lived in the next town, say?"

"I'd drive to where he was, kill him and leave town."

"Why?"

"If I took the train or bus or cab, people would remember me. A cabbie might describe me from memory."

"And if you had a scar on your face?"

"All the more reason for me to drive my own car and then get back home quickly as possible, preferably at night, so even my own neighbors wouldn't know I had gone away at all."

"And you wouldn't take half an hour to commit that murder?"

"No," I cried. "I'd get it over with."

"Ah, and that is exactly where our killer gave himself away. Remember it took him half an hour. Because of that, I know what he looks like! I've gone up and down the street asking people if they've seen the murderer, checked every yellow cab driver, every bus depot. No soap. The killer *must* have come by his own car."

"How could you describe the killer on such flimsy evidence!"

Priory looked at me sadly, as at a faithful but very ignorant puppy. "Simply on the basis of the half hour it took for the murder. Like to bet on it, Douglas, boy?"

"You're damn right I do. You can't tell me that's enough of a clue to catch a criminal on!" We shook hands.

Priory now drew a list from his pocket. "Here are three people, the only suspects in town, who might have, but didn't, kill Caldwell."

"What kind of people?"

"People who'd take half an hour to commit murder," he said, maddeningly. "But their alibis were all good. So, what have I done but turned up my main suspect over in Orange City. A young, fairly well to do gentleman by the name of John Melton who was attacked on the morning of October sixteenth—"

"And Caldwell arrived here on October seventeenth, the next day."

"Right. Caldwell was fleeing after what he'd done. This Orange City suspect fits in every way my mental picture of the killer. The police file is all too clear on that point. And I've discovered a very concise and horrible motive for this murder. This man Melton, after the attack, refused to name his assailant; therefore there's no mention of Caldwell, but the very nature of the attack leaves little doubt that it was he who attacked Melton. Shall we drive over and arrest Melton as our murderer?"

"You're that certain, are you?"

"Positively. I haven't one other clue to my name. Not a damn one. No one saw the killer. No positive corpse identity. Just the waltzing mice. If—I emphasize the 'if'—if the murder had occurred instantly I might never have guessed the solution. It was simply the fact that the murderer took half an hour. Think it over, Douglas, while you drive me over to Orange City to arrest our man."

We drove to Orange City. Myself, very irritated. Priory, very quiet and certain about the whole affair.

.  .  .

In Orange City, an elderly, kind-faced but tired looking, plump woman, Mrs. Melton, the mother of our suspect, answered the door when we rang. She listened to Priory explain that it was just a routine call, cautioned us to be quiet, because John was very tired, and then let us in, adding the fact that the last two months had been a severe shock to John. Priory said that he understood perfectly and, as we entered the hall of the medium-wealthy family, nodded me to a chair and went on ahead into a side room where I could hear Melton and him conversing. Mrs. Melton went away into another part of the house.

I had begun to fidget, when finally, through the door, I heard him say,

"Frankly, Mr. Melton, I'm investigating a friend of yours named Caldwell."

Melton's voice was very young, clear and self-assured. "I don't know any one by that name, Lieutenant."

Priory cleared his throat. "He was about your age, on the verge of blindness last October, when he suddenly moved from this town over to Green Bay. Does that help recall him?"

A long silence. "Oh, you mean Bill Calder."

"Calder—Caldwell, it's pretty nearly the same. He was going blind, was he not?"

"He was."

"And on the morning of October sixteenth, in a discussion concerned with his blindness, didn't this Calder—or Caldwell—attack you?"

After a much longer silence, Melton replied. "He did." And his voice was older, suddenly. "How could I ever forget that?"

"He was a friend?"

"We were never friends. We loved the same woman, if that means anything."

"It does. After attacking you, Calder-Caldwell moved to Green Bay in a highly emotional state, seeming to expect someone to follow and hurt him. Could you tell me more about your fight with him on that October morning? How did it begin?"

"It was all over Doris. She's a very beautiful woman. Calder was supposed to marry her at that time, but then his old eye ailment recurred. He discovered he was going progressively blind. It almost drove him crazy, I imagine."

"And then—"

"Doris broke off with him. She didn't want marriage to a blind man. She realized that in a matter of weeks he'd be totally helpless, with no hope for a cure." A pause. "Doris and I became engaged almost immediately."

Priory observed, "She doesn't sound like a very kindly person."

Melton laughed bitterly. "She isn't."

"You didn't marry her?"

Again, bitterness. "No. *It* happened."

"What do you mean by—*it?*"

Melton took a deep breath. I leaned forward on my chair in the hall. Melton explained:

"I was happy, triumphant, swell-headed. One morning, October sixteenth, I visited Calder, or Caldwell, as you know him. We'd always hated each other's guts, so I guess I talked too much. I said something I shouldn't have said. It crushed him down. I could see him wither under it. I shouldn't have said it. Christ, if I'd kept my mouth shut I'd be happy with Doris today—"

Melton seemed to have difficulty continuing. Priory asked him, "What did you say to Calder that made him attack you?"

"I looked at him, laughed and declared, 'Doris and I are getting married. She doesn't want to be married to a blind man!'"

"Good Lord," exclaimed Priory.

"Yes," said Melton, dully, "that's what I said. I was a fool. Calder screamed, 'I can still see enough to fix you!' and he leaped toward me!"

Silence.

"Next day, Calder left town. The police interviewed me, but I wouldn't prefer charges, or tell them who it was attacked me."

"And then Doris didn't marry you?"

"No. She went off with someone else."

Priory said, "Well, Calder's finally turned up again. He was murdered in Green Bay last night, Mr. Melton. You didn't happen to be in Green Bay last night, did you—after a tedious six weeks' search located Caldwell?"

"No. My mother will tell you I was here, resting."

"Your mother loves you; she'd say anything. She'd pay good money to your chauffeur who *had* to drive you there, too," retorted Priory. "Sorry; you're under arrest."

"Where's your proof?"

"Proof? First, your motive. A strong, terrible motive. But above all else, was the condition in which we found Caldwell's room and the *length of time it took to kill Caldwell.* There were other clues which would probably have tripped you up much later, but the one clue of the time length pointed right at you. I was able to locate you immediately."

"I don't understand!"

"The two of you, scrambling, falling, slashing walls, furniture, doors, rugs, smashing pictures, darting from wall to wall faster and faster, for thirty minutes until you finally got to him and crushed in his head with your cane!"

I rose from my chair, shaking.

I heard Melton's voice break and tremble and husk:

"All right, all right. I don't care! It was luck I got home! I intended giving myself up, anyway. There's not a damn thing worth living for. All I wanted was to find and kill him! Two blind men groping about a room, one dodging to escape, behind tables, chairs, sofas, the other going on and on and on trying to find and kill him! It took me quite half an hour's search until I got him, Mr. Priory."

"Douglas," Priory called to me through the door. "Come in."

I opened the hall door, stepped in. The case was over.

There sat Mr. Melton, looking at but not seeing me, a red and white striped cane with a heavy lead tip leaned across his knee; his eyes scarred and blinded from that October morning when he had joked at Caldwell's eye failure, and when Caldwell in a wild, screaming rage had attacked, thrown Melton down and gouged his eyes out with merciless fingernails!

# ELEVEN

# "I'M NOT SO DUMB"

Oh, I'm not so dumb. No, sir. When those men at Spaulding's Corner said there was a dead man hereabouts, you think I ran quick to the Sheriff's office to give in the news?

You got another think coming. I turned around and walked off from them men, looking over my shoulder every second or so, to see if they was smiling after me, their eyes shining with a prank, and I went to stare at the body first. It was Mr. Simmons's body in that empty-echoed farm house of his where the green weeds grew thick for years and there was larkspur, bluebird sprouts and morning fires fringing the path. I tromped up to the door, knocked, and when nobody said they was home, I squeaked the door open and looked in.

Then, and *only then,* did I get going for the Sheriff.

On the way, some kids threw rocks at me and laughed.

I met the Sheriff coming. When I told him he said yes, yes, he knew all about it, get outa the way! and I shied off, letting him and Mr. Crockwell smelling of farm dirt and Mr. Willis smelling of hardware hinges and Jamie MacHugh smelling of soap and scent and Mr. Duffy smelling of bar beer past.

When I got back to that lonely grey house they were inside bending around like an Italian labor crew working a ditch. Can I come in, I wondered, and they grumbled, no, no, you should go away, you would only be underfoot, Peter.

That's the way it is. People always shake me to one side, chortling at me. Those folks who told me about the body, you know what they expected? Expected me to call the Sheriff without stopping to see if they lied or not. Not me, any more. I realized what went on last spring when they sent me jogging for a skyhook and shore line for the twenty-seventh time in as many years; and when I sweated all the way down the shore curve to Wembley's Pier to fetch a pentagonal monkey-wrench which I never found in all my tries from the age of 17 on up to now.

So I fooled them this time by checking first and then running for help.

The Sheriff slouched out of the house half an hour later, shaking his dusty head. "Poor Mr. Simmons, his head is all rucked in like the skin of a rusted potbelly stove."

"Oh?" I asked.

The Sheriff flickered a mean yellow glance at me, switching his mustache around on his thin upper lip, balancing it. "You damn right it is."

"A murder mystery, hunh?" I asked.

"I won't say it's a mystery," said the Sheriff.

"You know who done it?" I asked.

"Not exactly, and shut up," snapped the Sheriff, thumb-rolling a cigarette; and sucked it into half-ash with his first flame. "I'm thinking."

"Can I help?" I asked.

"You," snorted the Sheriff, looking up at me on top of my mountain of bones and body, "help? Ha!"

Everybody laughed, holding rib-bones like bundles of breathing sticks and blowing out cheeks and glittering their sharp shiny eyes. Me, help, that was sure something to tickle.

Mr. Crockwell, he was the farmer man, he laughed, and Mr. Willis, he was the hardware-store man and tough as a rail-spike, he laughed like tapping a sledge on a beam-iron, and Mr. Duffy's Irish bartender laugh made his tongue jig around pink in his mouth; and Jamie MacHugh, who would run away if you yelled boo, he laughed, too.

"I been reading Sherlock Holmes," I said.

The Sheriff raked me over. "Since when you reading?"

"I can read, never mind," I said.

"Think you can solve mysteries, eh?" cried the Sheriff. "Get the hell away afore I boot the big rump off you!"

"Leave him be, Sheriff," laughed Jamie MacHugh, waving one hand. He clicked his tongue at me. "You're a first-rate sleuth, ain't you, Peter?"

I blinked at him six times.

"Sleuth, detective, Sherlock Holmes, I mean," said Jamie MacHugh.

"Oh," I said.

"Why, why-high," laughed Jamie MacHugh, "I'd bet my money on big Peter here any day, *ann-eee* day! Strong, strapping lad, Sheriff. He could solve this case with one shuffle of his big left shoe, couldn't he, men?"

Mr. Crockwell winked at Mr. Willis and Mr. Willis tonked a laugh out like cleaning your pipe on a flat stone, and everybody shot little sly glances at the Sheriff, nudging one another's ribs and chuckling. "Sure, I'd bet good money any autumn on Peter there. Here's fifty cents says Peter can solve the case afore the Sheriff!"

"Now, look here!" bellowed the Sheriff, standing stiff.

"Here's seventy cents says the same," drawled Mr. Willis.

And here came round money silver shining, and green money like little wings flapping on their hairy hands.

The Sheriff kicked a boot angrily. "Odd dammit. No feeble-minded giant can solve any murder case with me around!"

Jamie MacHugh tilted back and forth on his heels. "Scared?"

"Hell's gate, no! But you're all riding my goat!"

"We mean it. Here's our money, Sheriff; you meeting it?"

The Sheriff crackled he sure as hell would, and did. Everybody boomed out laughter like on bass drums and with brass trumpets. Somebody slapped me on the back but I didn't feel it. Someone yelled for me to go in there and show him, Peter, show him, but it was all underwater, far away. Blood pounded around on big red boots in my ears, kicking my brain back and forth like a wrinkled football.

The Sheriff looked at me. I looked at him with my heavy hands hanging. He laughed right out.

"God, I'll solve this case before Peter has time to open his mouth for spit!"

. . .

The Sheriff wouldn't let me be in the room with the corpse unless I stood on one leg and put both hands out in the air. I had to do it. The others said it was fair. I did it. I must have stood there during most the time we talked, on one leg, hands out to balance and them snickering when I toppled.

"Well," I said, over the corpse, "he's dead."

"Brilliant!" Jamie MacHugh had a bone of laughter caught in his throat, choking him.

"And he's been head-bashed," I said, "with a heavy thing."

"Colossal! Wonderful!" spluttered Jamie.

"And no woman done it," I said. "Because a woman couldn't have done it so heavy and hard."

Jamie laughed less. "True enough." He glanced at the others, eyebrows up a tremor. "That's true; we didn't think of that."

"That counts out all females," I said.

Mr. Crockwell teased the Sheriff. "You didn't say *that*, Sheriff."

The Sheriff's cigarette hissed sparks in a Fourth of July pinwheel. "I was *going* to say it! Damn, anyone can see a woman didn't do it! Peter, you go and stand in the corner and do your talking!"

I stood in the corner on one foot.

"And—" I said.

"Shut up," said the Sheriff. "You've had your say, let me have mine." He hitched up his trousers on his rump. Silence. The Sheriff scowled. "Well, like he says, the man's dead, head stove in, and a woman didn't do it and—"

"Ha-ha," said Mr. Crockwell.

The Sheriff shot him a blazing look. Mr. Crockwell covered his mouth with his hand.

"And the body's been dead twenty-four hours," I said, sniffing.

"Any dimwit knows that!" yelled the Sheriff.

"You didn't say that before," said James MacHugh.

"Do I have to say, can't I think a few?"

I looked around the empty room. Mr. Simmons was a strange man, living alone with no furniture in the house and only carpets here and there, and one cot upstairs. Didn't want to spend money on stuff. Saved it.

I said, "There wasn't much fuss or fight; nothing's upset. Must of been killed by someone he trusted."

The Sheriff started to swear but Jamie MacHugh said for him to let me talk, this was damn interesting. The others said so too. I smiled. I closed my eyes, grinning soft, and opened them again and everyone looked me for the first time in my life as if I was good enough to stand beside them. I stepped from the corner, slowly.

I crouched beside Mr. Simmons, looking. He was blood-ripe. The Sheriff quick followed, imitating me, on his knees. I peered close. The Sheriff peered close. I fussed with the rug. Sheriff fussed with the rug. I smoothed Mr. Simmons's right sleeve. Guess who smoothed Mr. Simmons's left sleeve? I made a humming sound like a comb and tissue in my throat. The Sheriff ground his teeth together. Everybody stood high and sweating sour in the summer-heated quiet.

"What was that about him being murdered by a friend?" Mr. Crockwell wanted to know.

"Sure," I said. "Someone he trusted, no commotion."

"That's right," said Mr. Willis, who didn't speak much.

Everybody said it was right, all right.

"Now," I said, "what people didn't like the cold man here?"

The Sheriff's voice was high and stringy with irritation. "Simmons wasn't liked by many. Always phitted with folks, tetchy-like."

.  .  .

I looked at the men, wondering which one I could detect to be the murderer. My eyes kept snapping in rubber-band moves to Jamie MacHugh. Jamie always was flighty. You lost your matchbox and stared at Jamie, he'd whine, guilty, "I didn't take it." If you dropped a nickel and it went away Jamie'd say, "I didn't do it!"

Funny. Something scared him as a kid, all the time he felt guilty, whether or not he was. So I couldn't help but see him now, and go up and down him with my eyes, him so nervous and losing his head over things. Just opposite of Hardware Willis who would stand rock-stiff while lightning bounced around him.

"I heard Jamie say Mr. Simmons should be killed," I said.

Jamie opened his eyes. "I never said that. And if I did, you know how you say things you never mean."

"I heard you say it, anyways."

"Now, now, now," said Jamie three times. "You, you, you are not Sheriff for this city, city. You just shut your trap."

The Sheriff fox-grinned. "What's the matter with you, Jamie? Second ago you was egging Peter on, all het up for his side."

"I don't want anybody accusing me, that's all, you big slob," said Jamie to me. "Go stand on one foot in the corner!"

I didn't blink my eyes. "I heard you say Mr. Simmons should be dead."

"You look sort of nervous, Jamie?" remarked the Sheriff.

"I remember," said Mr. Willis. "You did say that, Jamie. Say, Peter, you got a good memory." He nodded at me smartly.

"I bet fingerprints of Jamie are around here," I said.

"Sure," cried Jamie, pale. "Sure they're here. I was here early yesterday afternoon to try and get back my thirty dollars from that damn scoundrel lying limp on the floor, you elephant!"

"You see," I said. "He was here. His fingerprints all around like ants at a picnic." And I added, "I bet if we looked in his pocket we'd find Mr. Simmons's wallet full of money, I bet we would."

"Nobody looks though my pockets!"

"I'll do it," I said.

"No," said Jamie.

"Sheriff," I said.

The Sheriff looked at me, looked at Jamie. "Jamie," he said.

"Sheriff," said Jamie.

"Who was it picked me to solve this case?" I said. "Jamie did, Sheriff."

The Sheriff's cigarette hung cold on his lip, twitching. "That's right."

"Why'd he want me solving it, Sheriff?" I asked and answered, "Because he thought I'd only kick up mud in the creek, rile you so you wouldn't get nothing done."

"Well odd damn, imagine that," murmured the others, moving back.

The Sheriff squinted tight.

"Peter, I got to admit, you got something. Jamie was sure hot to bring you in to mess around. He started them goddamn bets. Irritate me with you until I can't see beans from breakfast!"

"Yes," I said.

"Well, now, I didn't kill nobody, I didn't sic Peter on you for that purpose, Sheriff, oh, no, I didn't," said Jamie MacHugh, sweat gobbering out his head like water from them fancy park sprinkling systems in the concrete skull of them pretty naked women statues.

The Sheriff said, "Let Peter search you."

Jamie said no, as I grabbed his wrists with one big hand and held them while I put my other hand in his rear pants pocket and pulled out the dead man's wallet.

"No," whispered Jamie like at a ghost.

I let him go. He swung around next thing, gibbering, and slammed out the door, crying, before anybody could stop him.

"Go get him, Peter!" everybody yelled.

"You really want me to?" I asked. "You're not kidding like with the skyhook and shore line?"

"No, no," they cried. "Get him!"

I thundered out the door and ran after Jamie in the hot sun over a green hill, through a little woods. What if Jamie gets away, I thought. No, he can't do that. I'll run fast.

Just near the edge of town I caught up with Jamie.

He never should have tried to fight me.

*Crunch.*

. . .

So now people sit around the Sheriff's office on summer evenings dangling their shoes in a little laced pattern and speaking with smoke blowing from their easy mouths about how the Sheriff let me solve the case. And the Sheriff says he don't care, he's just as pleased that I caught the criminal as if he'd done it himself; but the Sheriff winces when he says this.

Kids on the street don't kick my shins no more, or throw rocks at me. They come ask to hold my hands as we walk downtown. They ask me to tell how I did it. Even ladies in pretty blue or green dresses look over back fences and ask. And I shine up the battered silver star the Sheriff had left over from twenty years ago, catch it on my chest where it sparkles and I tell everybody again how I solved the Simmons case and caught the murderer Jamie MacHugh who broke his neck trying to get out of my hands.

Nobody ever tells me to run get a skyhook or shore line or a left-handed screwdriver no more. They think my silences are thinking ones. Men nod at me from cars and say hello Peter and they don't laugh so much, they sort of admire me and just this morning asked if I intended solving any more cases.

I'm very happy. Happier than in all my days. I'm certainly glad now that Mr. Simmons died and I had a chance to catch Jamie MacHugh that way. No telling how much longer these people might have pestered me.

And if you'll promise, cross you heart, hope to die, spit over your left shoulder, not to tell nobody, I'll let you in on a little secret.

I killed Mr. Simmons myself.

You understand why, don't you?

As I said, at the beginning—I'm not so dumb.

# TWELVE

# INVISIBLE BOY

Old Lady beat the dead frog into a powder with a long iron spoon, talking to it quickly and every now and then shifting her beady, gray bird eyes to the cabin. Each time she looked, a head in the small, thin window ducked as if she'd thrown a stone.

"Charlie!" cried Old Lady. "you come outa there! I'm fixing a magic to unlock that door; you come out now and I won't use it!"

The only sound was the warm mountain sun on the high green pine trees, a squirrel going around and around on a trunk, the ants moving in a fine brown line at Old Lady's bare, blue-veined feet.

"You been in there two days, darn you!" she panted, ringing the spoon against a flat rock, causing the plump gray miracle bag at her waist to swing. Sweating sour, she rose and marched at the cabin, bearing the pulverized flesh. "Come out, now!" She flicked a pinch of powder inside the lock. "All right, I'll come get you!" she wheezed.

She spun the knob with one spindly-fingered fist, first one way, then the other. "Fling this door wide, oh Lord!" she intoned.

When nothing flung, she added yet another pinch and waited. Her long blue untidy skirt rustled as she peered into her bag of wonders to see if she had any other charms there, like the frog which she'd killed months ago for such a crisis as this.

She heard Charlie breathing against the door. His folks had gone off into some Ozark town early this week, leaving him, and he'd run most six miles to Old Lady for company—she was by way of being an aunt or cousin or some such, and he didn't mind her fashions.

But then, two days ago, Old Lady, having gotten used to the boy around, decided to keep him for convenient company. She pricked her thin shoulder bone, drew out three blood pearls, spat wet over her right elbow, tromped on a crunch cricket and at the same instant clawed her left hand at Charlie, crying, "My son you are, you are my son, for all eternity!"

Charlie, bounding like a startled hare, had crashed off into the bush, heading home.

But Old Lady, skittering quick as a gingham lizard, cornered him in a dead end and Charlie holed up in this old hermit's cabin and wouldn't come out, no matter how she whammed door, window or knothole with amber-colored fist or trounced her ritual fires, explaining to him that he was certainly her son now, all right.

"Charlie, you there?" she asked, cutting holes in the door planks with her bright little slippery eyes.

"I'm all of me here," he replied finally, very tired.

Maybe he would fall out on the ground any moment. She wrestled the knob hopefully. Perhaps a pinch too much frog powder had grated the lock wrong? She always overdid or underdid her miracles, she mused angrily, never doing them just exact, Devil take it!

"Charlie, I only wants someone to night-prattle to, someone to warm hands with at the fire. Someone to fetch kindling for me mornings, and fight off the spunks that come creeping of early fogs! I ain't got no fetchings on you for yourself, son, just for your company!" She smackered her lips. "Tell you what, Charles, you come out and I *teach* you things!"

"What things?" he suspicioned.

"Teach you how to buy cheap, sell high. Catch a snow weasel, cut off its head, carry it warm in your hind pocket. There."

"Aw," said Charlie.

She made haste. "Teach you to make yourself shot-proof. So if anyone bangs at you with a gun, nothing happens."

When Charlie stayed silent, she gave him the secret in a high fluttering whisper. "Dig and stitch mouse-ear roots on Friday during full moon, and wear 'em around your neck in a white silk."

"You're crazy," Charlie said.

"Teach you how to stop blood or make animals stand frozen or make blind horses see, all them things I'll teach you! Teach you to cure a swelled-up cow and unbewitch a goat. Show you how to make yourself invisible!"

"Oh," said Charlie.

Old Lady's heart beat like a salvation tambourine.

The knob turned from the other side.

"You," said Charlie, "are funning me."

"No, I'm not," exclaimed Old Lady. "Oh, Charlie, why I'll make you like a window, see right through you. Why, child, you'll be surprised!"

"Real invisible?"

"Real invisible!"

"You won't fetch onto me if I walk out?"

"Won't touch a bristle of you, son."

"Well," he drawled reluctantly. "All right."

The door opened. Charlie stood in his bare feet, head down, chin against chest. "Make me invisible," he demanded.

"First we got to find us a bat," said Old Lady. "You find one!"

She watched him climb up a tree. It was certainly nice having him around after so many years alone with nothing to talk to but bird droppings and snail tracks.

Pretty soon a bat with a broken wing came fluttering down out of the tree. Old Lady picked it up beating warm and shrieking between its sharp white teeth, and Charlie dropped down after it, hand upon clenched hand, yelling.

. . .

That night, with the moon nibbling at the spiced pine needles, Old Lady extracted a long silver needle from under her wide blue dress. Gumming her excitement and secret anticipation, she sighted up the dead bat and held the needle steady-steady.

She had long ago realized that her miracles, despite all effort, failed. She always hoped that one day the miracles might start functioning, which would prove that God had forgiven her for her sinful life as a young lady. So far God had made no comment, but nobody knew this except Old Lady.

"Ready?" she asked of Charlie, who crouched cross-kneed, wrapping his pretty legs in long goose-pimpled arms, his mouth open, making teeth. "I'm ready," he said, shivering.

"There!" She plunged the needle deep in the bat's right eye. "So! Like that!"

"Oh!" cried Charlie, wadding up his face.

"Now I wrap it in gingham and here, you put it in your pocket, keep it there, bat and all. Go on."

He pocketed the charm.

"Charlie! Charlie!" she shrieked suddenly, in a shrill, fearful voice. "Where are you? I can't see you, child!"

"Here!" He jumped so the light ran in red streaks up his body. "I'm here, Old Lady!" He stared wildly at his arms, legs, chest and toes. "I'm here!"

Her eyes looked as if they watched many butterflies each crisscrossing the others in flight.

"You went *fast!* Quick as a hummingbird! Come back, Charlie!"

"But I'm here!" He looked scared.

"Where?"

"By the fire. And I can see myself. I'm *not* invisible!"

Old Lady rocked on her lean flanks. "Course you can see yourself. Every invisible person knows himself, otherwise, how could you eat, walk, or go around places? Charlie, touch me, so I know you."

Uneasily, he put out a hand.

She pretended to jerk at his touch and cried, "Ah!" as if startled.

"You mean to say you can't find me?" he asked. "Truly?"

"Not the least half rump of you!"

She found a tree to look at and looked at it with eyes shining, careful not to glance at him. "Why, I sure did a trick that time," she sighed with wonder. "Whoo-eee. Quickest invisible I ever did. How you feel, Charlie?"

"Like creek water all stirred."

"You'll settle."

Then she added, after a pause, "Well, what you going to do now, Charlie, since you're invisible?"

All sorts of things shot through his brain, she could tell. Adventures stood up and danced like hell-fire in his eyes, and his mouth, just hanging, told what it meant to be a boy who imagined himself like the mountain winds. In a cold dream he said, "I'll run across wheat fields, climb snow mountains, steal white chickens off'n farms. I'll kick pink pigs when they ain't looking. I'll pinch pretty girls' legs when they sleep, snap their garters in schoolrooms." Charlie looked at Old Lady, and from the shiny tips of her eyes, she saw something wicked shape his face. "And other things I'll do, I'll do, I will," he said.

"Don't try nothing on me," warned Old Lady. "I'm brittle as spring ice and I don't take handling." Then: "What about your folks?"

"My folks?"

"You can't fetch home looking like that. Scare the inside ribbons out of them. Your mother'd faint straight back like timber falling. Think they want you about the house to stumble over and your Ma have to call you every three minutes, even though you're in the room next her elbow?"

Charlie had not considered that. He sort of simmered down and whispered out a little "Gosh" and felt of his long bones carefully.

"You'll be mighty lonesome. People looking through you like a telescope, people knocking you aside because they didn't reckon you to be underfoot. And women, Charlie, women—"

He swallowed. "What about women?"

"No woman will be giving you a second stare. And no woman wants to be kissed by a boy's mouth they can't even find."

Charlie dug his bare foot in the soil, contemplatively. He pouted. "I'll stay invisible, anyway, a little while. I'll have a little fun. I'll be careful that's all. Stay out from front of wagons and horses and Pa. Pa shoots at the least sound." Charlie blinked. "Some day Pa'd fill me full of shot, thinkin' I was a squirrel in the dooryard. Oh."

She nodded at a tree. "That's likely."

"Well," he decided, "I'll be invisible for tonight and you can fix me back whole again tomorrow, Old Lady."

"If that ain't just like a boy, always wanting to be what he can't be," remarked Old Lady to a beetle on a log.

"What do you mean?" asked Charlie.

"Well, it was hard work," explained she, "fixing you up. It'll take a little time for it to wear off. Like a coat of paint wears off, boy."

"You!" he demanded. "You make me see-able! You did this!"

"Hush," she said. "It'll wear off a hand or a foot at a time."

"How'll it look, me around the hills with just one hand showing?"

"Like a five-winged bird hopping over the stones and brambles."

"Or a foot showing?"

"Like a small pink rabbit jumping thicket!"

"Or my head floating?"

"Like a hairy balloon at the Chautauqua!"

"How long before I'm all *whole?*" he asked.

She deliberated that it might pretty well be a year.

He groaned and sobbed and bit his lips and made fists. "You did this to me. You did this to me. I won't be able to go home."

She winked. "But you can stay here, child, with me, I'll keep you fed well."

He flung it at her. "You did this on purpose! You mean old hag, you want to keep me here!"

He ran off into the shrubs in an instant.

"Charlie, come back!"

No answer but the pattern of his feet on the soft dark turf, and his wet choking, passing swiftly off.

She kindled herself a fire. "He'll be back," she whispered. And thinking inward on herself, "I'll have company through spring into late summer. Then, when I'm tired of him and want silence, I'll send him home."

.   .   .

Charlie returned noiselessly with the first gray of dawn, gliding over rimed turf to where Old Lady sprawled like a bleached stick before scattered ashes.

He sat on pebbles and stared at her.

She didn't dare look at him or beyond. He had made no sound, so how could she know he was about? She couldn't.

He sat there, tear marks on his face.

Pretending to be just waking, but she had found no sleep all night, she stood up, grunting, yawning, and said to the dawn:

"Charlie?"

Her eyes passed from pines to soil, to sky, to hills. She called over and over, and she felt like staring plumb at him but she restrained herself. "Oh Charles?"

He sat, beginning to grin a bit, suddenly, knowing he was close to her, yet she must feel alone. He felt secret power, security, pleased with his invisibility.

She said, "Where can that boy be? If he made a noise so I could tell where he is, maybe I'd fix him breakfast."

She prepared breakfast, irritated at his continuous quiet. She fried bacon on a stick. "The smell of it will draw his nose."

While her back was turned, he swiped all the frying bacon and devoured it.

She whirled, crying out, "Lord, Lord!"

She eyed the clearing, suspiciously. "Charlie, that you?"

Charlie wiped clean his mouth on his wrists.

She trotted about the clearing, making like she was trying to locate him and finally, with a clever thought, acting blind, she headed straight for him, groping. "Charlie, where are you?"

A lightning streak, he evaded her, bobbling, ducking.

It took all her will power not to give chase; but you can't chase an invisible boy, so she sat down, pouting, and tried to fry more bacon, but every fresh strip she cut he would steal hot off the fire and run away far. Finally, cheeks burning, she cried, "I know where you are! Right over there! I hear you run!" She pointed to one side of him, not too accurate. He ran some more. "Now, you're there!" she said. "There and there!" pointing to all the places he was in the next five minutes. "I hear you snap a twig, press a grass blade. I got fine shell ears, delicate as rose flowers!"

Silently, he galloped off among the trees, his voice coming back. "Can't hear me when I'm set on a rock. I'll just set!"

All day he sat on an observatory rock in the wind, motionless and tongue-tied.

Old Lady gathered wood in the forest, feeling his eyes on her spine. She wanted to babble "Oh, I see you, I see you! I was only fooling about invisible boys! You're right there!" but she didn't.

The following morning he began springing from behind trees, making horrible faces at her, drawing down his lips with his fingers, popping eyes, pushing up his nose so you could look in and see his brain thinking.

Once she dropped her kindling. She made off as like it was a blue jay startled her.

He made a motion as if to strangle her.

She trembled a little.

He made another motion as if to kick her shins and spit on her cheek.

These motions she bore without a lid-flicker or mouth-twitch.

He stuck out his tongue, making strange bad noises. He wiggled his ears so she wanted to laugh, and finally she did laugh and explained it by saying, "Sat on a lizard. Whew, how it poked!"

But at high noon the whole affair reached its terrible climax.

It was at that time that Charlie raced down the valley stark naked!

Old Lady nearly fell flat with shock.

Charlie raced naked up one side of the valley and naked down the other, his feet shimmering in the manner of a humming-bird.

Old Lady's tongue locked her mouth. What could she say? Charlie, go dress? For shame? Stop that? Could she? Oh, Charlie, God Almighty! Could she say that now, *could* she?

Upon the big rock she witnessed him dancing up and down, naked as the day of birth, stomping bare feet, smacking his hands on stark knees and sucking in and out his white stomach like blowing and deflating a circus balloon.

She shut her eyes tight and prayed.

After three hours of this, she pleaded, "Charlie, Charlie, come here, I got something to tell you!"

Like a fallen leaf he came; dressed again, praise the Lord.

"Charlie," she said, looking at the pine trees, "I see your right toe. There it is."

"You do?" he said.

"Yes," she said, very sadly. "There it is like a horny toad on the grass. And there, up there's your left ear hanging on the air like a pink butterfly."

Charlie danced. "I'm forming in, I'm forming in!"

Old Lady nodded. "Here comes your ankle!"

"Gimme both my feet!" ordered Charlie.

"You got 'em."

"How about my hands?"

"I see one crawling on your knee like a daddy longlegs."

"How about the other one?"

"It's crawling, too."

"I got a body?"

"Shaping up fine."

"I'll need my head to go home, Old Lady."

To go home, she thought, wearily. "No!" she said, stubborn and angry. "No, you ain't got no head. No head, at all," she cried. She'd leave that to the very last. "No head, no head," she insisted.

"No head?" he wailed.

"Yes, oh my God, yes, yes, you got your blamed head!" she snapped, giving in. "Now, fetch me back my bat with the needle in his eye!"

He threw it at her. "Haaa-yoooo!" His yelling went all up the valley, and long after he had run toward home, she heard his echoes, racing.

Then she plucked up her kindling with a great dry weariness and started back toward her shack, sighing, talking. And Charlie followed her all the way, *really* invisible now, so she couldn't see him, just hear him, like a cone dropping or a deep underground stream trickling, or a squirrel clambering a bough; and over the fire at twilight she and Charlie sat, him invisible, and she fed him bacon he wouldn't take, so she ate it herself, and then she fixed some magic and fell asleep with Charlie, made out of sticks and rags and pebbles, but still warm and her very own son, slumbering and nice in her shaking mother arms . . . and they talked about golden things in drowsy voices until dawn made the fire slowly, slowly wither out. . . .

# THIRTEEN

# YLLA
# (I'LL NOT ASK FOR WINE)

They had a house of crystal pillars by the edge of the quiet sea, and every morning you could see Mrs. K in her cooking room, making a red cake or sweeping the floor with soft fluffs of spider web. In the afternoons, when the dead sea was hot and empty, and the trees were stiff and silent in the yard, and the little, distant Martian stone town was all enclosed and no one moved out the doors, you could see Mr. K himself sitting in his room reading from a metal book with raised heiroglyphs over which he brushed his fingers, as one might play a harp. And from the book, as his fingers stroked, a voice sang, a soft ancient voice, which told tales of when the sea was alive and fierce upon the shore and ancient men had carried shields and swords into battle.

Mr. and Mrs. K had lived by the dead sea for twenty years, and their ancestors had lived in the same house for ten centuries. They were not old. They had the fair, brownish skin of the true Martian, the yellow eyes, the soft musical voices. Once they had liked painting, swimming in the stone canals, and talking into the dawn together by a fire of blue phosphorous. They were not happy now.

This morning, Mrs. K stood between the pillars of her wine room, listening to the desert sands heat and melt into yellow wax and seemingly run on the horizon. Something was going to happen.

She waited.

She watched the blue sky as if it might at any moment grip in on itself, contract, and expel a shining miracle down upon the sand.

Nothing happened.

Tired of waiting, she walked through the misting pillars of the house. A gentle rain sprang from the fluted tops of the pillars, cooling the scorched air, falling gently on her as she moved. In the distance, she heard her husband playing his book steadily, his fingers never tired, his ears never numb with the old songs. Quietly, she wished he might one day again spend as much time holding and playing her like a little harp as he did his incredible books.

But no. She shook her head, an imperceptible, forgiving shrug, her eyelids closed softly down upon her golden eyes. Marriage made people old and familiar, even if the participants in the day to day attacks and counterattacks of ego were still young.

She lay back in a chair that moved to take her shape, even as she moved. She closed her eyes tightly and nervously.

The dream occurred.

Her brown fingers trembled, came up, grasped at the air. A moment later she sat up, startled, gasping.

She glanced about swiftly as if expecting someone there before her. She seemed disappointed the space between the pillars was empty.

Her husband appeared in a triangular door. "Did you call?" he asked, irritably.

"No!" she cried.

"I thought I heard you cry out."

"Did I? I was almost alseep and had a dream!"

"In the day time? You don't often do that."

She sat as if struck in the face by the dream. "How strange, how very strange," she said. "The dream."

"Oh?" He evidently wished to return to his book.

"I dreamed about a man," said Mrs. K.

"A man?"

"A tall man, six feet one inch tall."

"How absurd; a giant, a misshapen giant."

"Somehow—" she tried the words, "—he looked all right. In spite of being tall. And he had, oh I know you'll think it silly, he had *blue* eyes."

"Blue eyes! Gods!" cried Mr. K. "What'll you dream next? I suppose he had *black* hair?"

"How did you *guess?*" She was excited.

"I picked the most unlikely color," he replied, coldly.

"Well, black it was!" she cried. "And he had a very white skin, oh he was *most* unusual! He dressed in a strange uniform and he came down out of the sky and spoke pleasantly to me." She smiled.

"Out of the sky, what nonsense!"

"He came in a metal thing that glittered in the sun," she remembered. She closed her eyes to shape it again. "I dreamed there was the sky and something sparkled like a coin thrown into the air, and suddenly it grew large and fell down softly to land, a long silver craft, round and alien. And a door opened in the side of the silver object and this tall man stepped out."

"If you *worked* harder you wouldn't have these silly dreams."

"I rather enjoyed it," she said, lying back. "I never suspected myself of such an imagination. Black hair, blue eyes and white skin; what a strange man, and yet—quite handsome."

"Wishful thinking."

"You're unkind. I didn't think him up on purpose, he just came in my mind while I drowsed. It wasn't like a dream. It was so unexpected and different. He looked right at me and he said, 'I've come from the third planet in my ship. My name is Nathaniel York—'"

"A stupid name; it's no name at all," said the husband.

"Of course it's stupid, because it's a dream," she explained softly. "And he said, 'This is the first trip across space. There are only two of us in our ship, myself and my friend John.'"

"Another stupid name."

"And he said, 'We're from a city on *Earth,* that's the name of our planet,'" said Mrs. K. "That's what he said. 'Earth' was the name he spoke. I remember it was so peculiar. He spoke in another language."

"And you *understood* him?"

"Somehow, I did. With my mind. Telepathy, I suppose."

Mr. K turned away. She stopped him with a word. "Yll?" she called quietly.

"What is it?" He twitched his fingers.

"Do you ever think, I mean, do you ever wonder if there are people living on the third planet?"

"The third planet is incapable of supporting life," stated the husband patiently. "Our scientists have said there's far too much oxygen in their atmosphere. One hundred times more oxygen than we have."

"But wouldn't it be interesting if there *were* people?"

"I suppose."

"And they traveled through space in some sort of ship?"

"Really, Ylla, you know how I hate this emotional wailing."

. . .

It was late in the day when she began singing the song as she moved among the whispering pillars of rain. She sang it over and over again.

"What's that song you're singing?" snapped the husband at last, coming to sit down at the fire table.

"I don't *know,*" said the wife, softly, looking up, surprised at herself even. She put her hand to her mouth, unbelieving, as if to examine the words as they came out. The sun was setting. A small wind blew among the pillars and the fire table bubbled its pool of silver lava. The wind blew her hair behind her ears, stirring it. She stood looking out into the great distance, as if remembering something, her eyes soft and moist. "Drink to me only with thine eyes, and I will pledge with mine," she sang, softly, quietly, slowly. "Or leave a kiss within the cup, and I'll not ask for wine." She hummed now, moving her hand on the air ever so lightly, her eyes shut. She finished the song.

It was very beautiful.

"Never heard that song before, did you make it up?" he inquired, his eyes sharp.

"No. Yes. No, I don't know, really!" She hesitated. "I don't even know what the words are, they're another language!"

"What language?"

She dropped a piece of meat numbly into the bubbling fire lava of the table. "I don't know." She took the meat out, cooked, after a minute and gave it on a plate to him. "It's just a crazy thing I made up, I guess, I don't know why."

He said nothing but sat watching her dip vegetable and meats into the cooking pool of fire that was the table. The sun sank and slowly slowly the night came in to fill the room, swallowing the pillars and both of them, like a dark wine poured to the ceiling. Only the fire table's glow lit their faces. She hummed the strange song again and for some reason, instantly, he snapped up from his chair when she hummed it, and stalked out of the room.

.   .   .

He finished supper later, alone. When he arose, he stretched, looking at her and said, yawning. "Let's take the sand ship in to town tonight to see an entertainment."

"You don't *mean* it?" she said. "Are you *feeling* all right?"

"What's so strange about that?"

"But we haven't gone for an entertainment in six months!"

"I think it's a good idea."

"Suddenly you're so solicitous," she said.

"I wish you wouldn't talk that way," he said, angrily. "Do you or do you *not* want to go?"

She looked out at the desert. The twin moons were rising. The room was cool. She began to tremble just the least bit. She wanted very much to sit quietly here, soundless, not moving until this thing occurred, this thing she had been expecting all day, this thing that could not occur but *might*. A drift of song went through her mind.

"I—"

"Do you good," he urged. "Come along now."

"I'm tired," she said. "Some other night. Tomorrow night or the next."

"That's no way to be." He went and fetched her veil and laid it on the stone sill. "We haven't gone anywhere in months."

"Except you, twice a week to Xi City." She didn't look at him.

"Business," he said.

"Oh?" She whispered to herself.

.   .   .

The sand ship waited on the cooling smooth sands, its white webs of sail ballooning on the night wind, flapping softly. She sat forward in the prow as the anchorets were cast off and the sand slid under, whining, and the hills moved by, moved by, leaving their home behind, leaving the silent pillars, the waiting rooms, the caged flowers, the singing books. She did not look back at her husband. She heard his hand moving the tiller. There was a smell of evening and a sound of skimming sand.

She watched the sky.

The husband spoke.

The ship moved over the dry sea bottom.

"Did you hear what I *said?*"

"What?"

He exhaled. "You might pay attention."

"I was thinking. I'm sorry."

"I never thought you were a nature lover, but you're certainly interested in the sky tonight," he said.

"It's very beautiful."

"I was figuring," said the husband, slowly. "I think I'll call Hulle tomorrow. I'd like to talk to him about us spending some time, oh only a week or so, in the Blue Mountains. It's just an idea—"

"The Blue Mountains!" She held to the edge of the ship with one hand, turning swiftly toward him. She stared back at him.

"Oh, it's just a suggestion."

"When do you want to go?" she asked.

"I thought we might leave tomorrow morning. You know, an early start and all that," he said, very casual about it.

"But we *never* go this early in the year!"

"Just this once, I thought—" He smiled. "Do us good to get away, some peace and quiet, you know. You haven't anything else planned? We'll go, won't we?"

She took a breath, waited, and then said, "No."

"What?" He almost turned the ship over in surprise.

"No," she said, firmly. "It's settled. I won't go."

He looked at her. They did not speak after that. She turned away.

The ship slid on over the milky sands, whispering.

. . .

She wakened at dawn to find her husband standing by the side of her bed. He looked as if he had stood there for hours, watching her. She did not know why, but she could not look him in the face.

"You've been dreaming again," he said. "You moved all about the bed and kept me awake. I *really* think you should see a doctor."

"I'll be all right."

"You talked in your sleep," he said.

"Did I?" She started up.

Dawn was cold in the room. Fog from off the long canals drifted between the crystal pillars. A grey light filled her as she lay there.

"What was your dream?" he asked.

She had to think a moment to remember. "The ship," she said. "It came from the sky again, landed, and the tall man stepped out and talked with me, telling me little jokes, laughing, and it was pleasant."

Mr. K touched a crystal pillar. Clouds of flame arose in them, until the walls were suffused with a roseate fire. The room was a gentle whispering furnace, warming, now. Mr. K's face was impassive.

"And then," she said, "this man, who said his strange name was Nathaniel York, told me I was beautiful and—and kissed me."

"Ha!" cried the husband, turning violently from the bed, his jaw muscles working.

"It's only a dream." She was amused. "You act so weirdly."

"Keep your silly, feminine dreams to yourself!" he cried.

"You're acting like a child." She lapsed into her pillows. After a moment she laughed softly. "I thought of some *more* of the dream," she said.

"Well, what is it, what *is* it!" he shouted.

"Yll, you're *so* bad-tempered."

"Tell me!" he demanded. "You *can't* keep secrets from me!" His face was dark and rigid as he stood over her.

"I've never seen you this way!" she said, half shocked, half entertained with him. "All that happened was this Nathaniel York person told me, well, he told me that he'd take me away into his ship, into the sky with him, and take me back to his planet with him. It's really quite ridiculous."

"Ridiculous, is it!" he almost screamed. "You should have heard yourself, fawning on him, talking to him, singing with him. Oh God, all night, you should have *heard* yourself!"

"Yll!"

"When's he landing? Where's he coming down with his damned ship?" he cried.

"Yll, keep your voice down, please."

"Voice be damned!" He bent stiffly over her. "And *in* this dream—" he seized her wrist in his fingers. "Didn't the ship land over in Green Valley, *didn't* it? Answer me!"

"Why, yes—"

"And it landed this afternoon, *didn't* it?" he kept at her.

"Yes, yes, I think so, yes, but *only* in a dream!"

"Well." He flung her hand from him, stiffly. "It's good you told the truth. I heard every word you said in your sleep. You mentioned the valley and the time." He was breathing hard now as he walked between the pillars like a person blinded by a lightning bolt. Slowly, his breath returned. She watched him as if he were quite insane. She arose finally and went to him. "Yll," she whispered.

"I'm all right," he said, tiredly. "Let me alone."

"You're sick," she said.

"No." He forced a smile. "Just—childish. Forgive me, darling. Yes, forgive me." He gave her a rough pat. "Too much work lately. I'm sorry. I think I'll lie down awhile—"

"You were so *excited.*"

"I'm all right now. Fine." He still breathed with difficulty. "Let's forget it. Say, I heard a joke from Uel yesterday, I meant to tell you. What do you say you fix breakfast, I'll tell the joke, and let's not talk about it."

"It was only a dream," she said, holding his arm.

"Of course." He kissed her cheek mechanically. "Only a dream."

.   .   .

At noon, the fog cleared away to let the sun shimmer on the canal and touch the hills into light.

"Aren't you going to town?" asked Ylla of her husband.

"Town?" he raised his brows, faintly.

"This is the day you *always* go." She adjusted a cage of flowers on its pedestal. The flowers moved within, slowly and rhythmically, opening their small yellow mouths.

He closed his book. "No. With the fog and all, it's too late."

"Oh." She finished her task and took off the thin web that kept her clean in her housework. "Well," she said, gaily. "I thought that I might run over to Pao's this afternoon, she asked me over, I haven't seen her in a *long* time. Is that all right with you?"

"What? Pao's?" He looked at his hands, coughing. "Well, I'm sorry, I forgot to tell you, but I invited Dr. Nlle out this afternoon, and it *would* be nice if you were here to entertain him with me. You won't mind?"

"But Pao asked me—"

"Pao can wait, darling," he smiled. "Besides, it's a terribly long walk to Pao's. All the way over through Green Valley and then past the big canal and down, isn't it? And it'll be hot now the fog's gone. And Dr. Nlle would be *delighted* to see you. Well?"

She did not answer, but turned her fingers over, slowly, looking at them, expressionlessly.

"Ylla," he inquired. "You *will* be here, won't you?"

"Yes," she said, after a long time. "I'll be here."

"All afternoon?"

"All afternoon." Her voice was dull.

.   .   .

Late in the day, Dr. Nlle had not put in an appearance. Ylla's husband did not seem overly surprised. When it was quite late he murmured something, went to a closet in the wine room and drew out his hunting rifle.

"Where are you going?" she asked.

"What? Oh." He checked the load quietly, inserting fresh shells. "If Dr. Nlle insists on being late, I'll be damned if I'll wait for him. I'm going out to hunt for a bit. I'll be back. You be sure to stay right here now, won't you?" He did not look at her.

"Yes."

"And tell Dr. Nlle I'll be back. Just hunting."

The door closed. His footsteps faded down the hill.

She watched him walking through the sunlight, until he was gone. Then she returned to her work of blowing the light spider webs from a little machine in her hands. The web clung to everything, and when you drew it off, intact, dirt and dust came with it. She worked energetically, but on occasion a numbness came over her, and she caught herself singing the strange song and looking out beyond the crystal pillars at the sky.

She stood very still, waiting.

It was coming nearer. It might happen any moment. It was like those days when you heard a thunder storm coming and there was the waiting silence and then the faintest pressure of the atmosphere as the climate moved over the land in shifts and shadows and vapors. And the change pressed at your ears and you were suspended in the waiting time of the coming storm. You began to tremble. The sky was stained and colored; the clouds thickened, the mountains took on an iron taint. The caged flowers blew with soft sighs of warning. You felt your hair stir softly. Somewhere in the house, the voice-clock sang, 'Time, time, time, time—' ever so faintly, no more than water tapping on velvet.

And then the storm. The electric illumination, the engulfments of dark wash and sounding black fell down, shutting in, forever.

That's how it was now. A storm gathered, yet the sky was clear. Lightning was expected yet there was no cloud.

Ylla moved through the breathless summer house. Lightning would strike out of the sky at any instant, there would be a thunder clap, a boll of smoke, a silence, footsteps on the walk, a rap on the crystalline door and her *running* to answer!

Crazy Ylla! she scoffed. Why think these things with your idle mind?

And then, it happened.

There was a warmth as of a great fire passing in the air. A whirling rushing sound. A gleam in the sky.

Ylla cried out. Running through the house, she flung wide the door. She faced the hills, but by this time there was nothing.

She was about to run down the hill, when she stopped herself. She was supposed to stay here, go nowhere. The doctor was coming to visit, and her husband would be angry if she ran off.

She waited in the door, breathing rapidly, her hand out.

She strained to see but saw nothing.

Silly woman. She went inside. You and your imagination, she thought. That was nothing but a bird, a leaf, the wind, or a fish in the canal. Sit down. Rest.

She sat down.

A shot sounded.

Very clearly, sharply, the sound of the rifle.

Her body jerked with it.

It came from a long way off. One shot. And then a second shot, precise and cold and distant.

Her body winced again and for some reason she started up, screaming, and screaming, and never wanting to stop screaming. She ran violently through the house and once again threw wide the door.

The echoes were dying away, away.

Gone.

She waited in the yard two minutes, her face pale.

Finally, with slow steps, her head down, she wandered about the house, laying her hands to things, her lips trembling, until finally she sat alone, in the darkening wine room, waiting. She began to wipe an amber glass with the hem of her scarf.

And then, from far off, the sound of footsteps, crunching on the thin, small rocks.

She rose up to stand in the center of the quiet room. The glass fell from her fingers, crashing to bits.

The footsteps hesitated outside the door.

Should she speak, should she cry out, "Come in, oh, come in!"

She went forward a few paces.

The footsteps walked up the steps. A hand twisted the door-latch.

She smiled at the door.

The door opened. She stopped smiling.

It was her husband.

He entered the room and stopped and looked at her for only a minute. Then he snapped his rifle open, cracked out two empty, odorous shells, heard them spat on the floor as they fell, and placed the gun firmly in the corner of the room as she bent down and tried over and over, with no success, to pick up the pieces of the shattered glass. "What were you doing?" she asked.

"Nothing," he said, with his back turned.

"But, the gun, I heard you fire it. Twice."

"Just hunting. Once in a while you like to hunt. Did Dr. Nlle arrive?"

"No."

"Wait a minute." He snapped his fingers, disgustedly. "Why, I remember now. He was supposed to come visit *tomorrow* afternoon. How stupid of me."

They sat down to eat. She looked at her food and did not move her hands. "What's wrong?" he asked, not looking up from cutting his meat.

"I don't know. I'm not hungry," she said.

"Why not?"

"I don't know, I'm just not."

The wind was rising across the sky, the sun was going down. The room was small and suddenly cold.

"I've been trying to remember," she said, in the silent room, across from her cold, erect, golden-eyed husband.

"Remember what?" He sipped his wine.

"That song. That fine and beautiful song." She closed her eyes and hummed, but it was not the song. "I've forgotten it. And, some how, I don't want to forget it. It's something I want always to remember." She moved her hands as if the rhythm might help her to remember all of it. Then she lay back in her chair. "I can't remember." She began to cry.

"Why are you crying?" he said.

"I don't know, I don't know, but I can't help it. I'm sad and I don't know why, I cry, and I don't know why, but I'm crying."

Her head was in her hands, her shoulders moved again and again.

"You'll be all right tomorrow," he said.

She did not look up at him, she looked only at the empty desert and the very bright stars coming out now on the dark sky, and far away there was a sound of wind rising and canal waters stirring cold in the long canals. She shut her eyes, trembling.

"Yes," she said. "I'll be all right, tomorrow."

# FOURTEEN

# THE TOMBSTONE

Well, first of all there was the long trip, and the dust poking up inside her thin nostrils, and Walter, her Oklahoma husband, swaying his lean carcass in their model-T Ford, so sure of himself it made her want to spit; then they got into this big brick town that was strange as old sin, and hunted up a landlord. The landlord took them to a small room and unlocked the door.

There in the middle of the simple room sat the tombstone.

Leota's eyes got a wise look, and immediately she pretended to gasp, and thoughts skipped through her head in devilish quickness. Her superstitions were something Walter had never been able to touch or take away from her. She gasped, drew back, and Walter stared at her with his droopy eyelids hanging over his shiny gray eyes.

"No, no," cried Leota, definitely. "I'm not moving in any room with any dead man!"

"Leota!" said her husband.

"What do you mean?" wondered the landlord. "Madam, you don't—"

Leota smiled inwardly. Of course, she didn't really believe, but this was her only weapon against her Oklahoma man, so—"I mean that I won't sleep in no room with no corpse. Take him out of here!"

Walter gazed at the sagging bed wearily, and this gave Leota pleasure, to be able to frustrate him. Yes, indeed, superstitions were handy things. She heard the landlord saying, "This tombstone is the very finest gray marble. It belongs to Mr. Whetmore."

"The name carved on the stone is WHITE," observed Leota coldly.

"Certainly, that's the man's name for whom the stone was carved."

"And is he dead?" asked Leota, waiting.

The landlord nodded.

"There, you *see!*" cried Leota. Walter groaned; a groan which meant he was not stirring another inch, looking for a room. "It smells like a cemetery in here," said Leota, watching Walter's eyes get hot and flinty. The landlord explained:

"Mr. Whetmore, the former tenant of this room was an apprentice marble-cutter, this was his first job, he used to tap on it with a chisel every night from seven until ten."

"Well—" Leota glanced swiftly around to find Mr. Whetmore. "Where is he? Did he die, too?" She enjoyed this game.

"No, he discouraged himself and quit cutting this stone to work in a defense plant."

"Why?"

"Made a mistake." The landlord tapped the marble lettering. "WHITE's the name here. Spelled wrong. Should be WHYTE, with a Y instead of an I. Poor Mr. Whetmore. Inferiority complex. Gave up at the least little mistake and scuttled off."

"I'll be damned," said Walter, shuffling into the room and unpacking the rusty brown suitcases, his back to Leota. The landlord liked to tell the rest of the story:

"Yes, Mr. Whetmore gave up easily. To show you how touchy he was, he'd percolate coffee mornings, and if he spilled a teaspoonful it was a catastrophe— he'd throw it all away and not drink coffee for days! Think of that! He got very sad when he made errors. If he put his left shoe on first, instead of his right, he'd cease trying and walk barefooted for ten or twelve hours, on cold mornings, even. Or if someone spelled his name wrong on his letters, he'd replace them in the mail-box marked NO SUCH PERSON LIVING HERE. Oh, he was a great one, was Mr. Whetmore!"

"That don't paddle us no further up-crick," pursued Leota grimly. "Walter, what're you commencing?"

"Hanging your silk dress in this closet; the red one."

"Stop hanging, we're not staying."

The landlord blew out his breath, not understanding how a woman could grow so dumb. "I'll explain once more. Mr. Whetmore did his home work here; he hired a truck which carried this tombstone here one day while I was out shopping for a turkey at the grocery, and when I walked back—tap-tap-tap—I heard it all the way downstairs—Mr. Whetmore had started chipping the marble. And he was so proud I didn't dare complain. But he was so awful proud he made a spelling mistake and now he ran off without a word, his rent is paid all the way till Tuesday, but he didn't want a refund, and now I've got some truckers with a hoist who'll come up first thing in the morning. You won't mind sleeping here one night with it, now will you? Of course not."

The husband nodded. "You understand, Leota? Ain't no dead man under that rug." He sounded so superior, she wanted to kick him.

She didn't believe him, and she stiffened. She poked a finger at the landlord. "He wants his money, and you, Walter you want a bed to drop your bones on. Both of you are lying from the word 'go'!"

The Oklahoma man paid the landlord his money tiredly, with Leota chastising him, the landlord ignored her as if she were invisible, said good-night and she cried "Liar!" after him as he shut the door and left them alone. Her husband undressed and got in bed and said, "Don't stand there staring at the tombstone, turn out the lights. We been traveling four days and I'm bushed."

Her tight criss-crossed arms began to quiver over her thin breasts, "None of the three of us will get any sleep," she said.

Twenty minutes later, disturbed by various sounds and movements, the Oklahoma man unveiled his vulture's face from the bedsheets, blinking stupidly. "Leota, you still up! I said, a long time ago, for you to switch off the light and come sleep! What you doing there?"

It was quite evident what she was about. Crawling on rough hands and knees, she placed a jar of fresh-cut red, white and pink geraniums beside the headstone, and another tin-can of new-cut roses at the foot of the imagined grave. A pair of shears lay on the linoleum, dewy with having snipped flowers in the night outside a moment before.

Now she briskly whisked the colorful linoleum with a midget whisk broom, praying so her husband couldn't hear the words but just the murmur. When she rose up, she stepped across the grave carefully so as not to defile the buried one, and in crossing the room she skirted far around the spot, saying, "There, that's done," as she darkened the room and laid herself out on the whining spring which sang in tune with her husband who now asked, "What in the Lord's name!" and she replied, looking at the dark around her, "No man's going to rest easy with strangers sleeping right atop him. I made amends with him, flowered his bed so he won't stand around rubbing his bones together late tonight."

Her husband looked at the place she occupied in the dark, and couldn't think of anything good enough to say, so he just swore, groaned, and sank down into sleeping.

Not half an hour later, she grabbed his elbow and turned him so she could whisper swiftly, fearfully into one of his ears, like a person calling into a cave: "Walter!" she cried. "Wake up, wake up!" She intended doing this all night, if need be, to spoil his superior kind of slumber.

He struggled with her. "What's wrong?"

"Mr. White! Mr. White! He's beginning to haunt us!"

"Oh, go to sleep!"

"I'm not fibbing! Listen to him!"

The Oklahoma man listened. From under the linoleum, sounding about six feet or so down, muffled, came a man's sorrowful talking. Not a word came through clearly, just a sort of sad mourning.

The Oklahoma man sat up in bed. Feeling his movement, Leota hissed, "You heard, you heard?" excitedly. The Oklahoma man put his feet on the cold linoleum. The voice below changed into a falsetto. Leota began to sob. "Shut up, so I can hear," demanded her husband, angrily. Then, in the heart-beating quiet, he bent his ear to the floor and Leota said, "Don't tip over the flowers!" and he cried, "Shut up!" and again listened, tensed. Then he spat out an oath and rolled back under the covers, "It's only the man downstairs," he muttered.

"That's what I mean. Mr. White!"

"No, not Mr. White. We're on the second floor of an apartment house, and we got neighbors down under. Listen." The falsetto downstairs talked. "That's the man's wife. She's probably telling him not to look at another man's wife! Both of them probably drunk."

"You're lying!" insisted Leota. "Acting brave when you're really trembling fit to shake the bed down. It's a haunt, I tell you, and he's talking in voices, like Grandma Hanlon used to do, rising up in her church pew and making queer tongues all mixed, like a black man, an Irishman, two women and three frogs caught in her craw! That dead man, Mr. White, hates us for moving in with him tonight, I tell you! Listen!"

As if to back her up, the voices downstairs talked louder. The Oklahoma man lay on his elbows, shaking his head hopelessly, wanting to laugh, but too tired.

Something crashed.

"He's stirring in his coffin!" shrieked Leota. "He's mad! We got to move outa here, Walter, or we'll be found dead tomorrow!"

More crashes, more bangs, more voices. Then silence. Followed by a movement of feet in the air over their heads.

Leota whimpered. "He's free of his tomb! Forced his way out and he's tromping the air over our heads!"

By this time, the Oklahoma man had his clothing on beside the bed, and was putting on his boots. "This building's three stories high," he said, tucking in his shirt. "We got neighbors overhead who just come home." To Leota's weeping he had this to say, "Come on. I'm taking you upstairs to meet them people. That'll prove who they are. Then we'll walk downstairs to the first floor and talk to that drunkard and his wife. Get up, Leota."

Someone knocked on the door.

Leota squealed and rolled over and over making a quilted mummy of herself. "He's in his coffin again, rapping to get out!"

The Oklahoma man switched on the lights and unlocked the door. A very jubilant little man in a dark suit, with wild blue eyes, wrinkles, gray hair and thick glasses danced in.

"Sorry, sorry," declared the little man. "I'm Mr. Whetmore. I went away. Now I'm back. I've had the most astonishing stroke of luck. Yes, I have. Is my tombstone still here?" He looked at the stone a moment before he saw it. "Ah, yes, yes, it is! Oh, hello." He saw Leota peering from many layers of blanket. "I've some men with a roller-truck, and, if you don't mind, we'll move the tombstone out of here, this very moment. It'll only take a moment."

The husband laughed with gratitude. "Glad to get rid of the damned thing. Wheel her out!"

Mr. Whetmore directed two brawny workmen into the room. He was almost breathless with anticipation. "The most amazing thing. This morning I was lost, beaten, dejected—but a miracle happened." The tombstone was loaded onto a small coaster truck. "Just an hour ago, I heard, by chance, of a Mr. White who was dying of pneumonia. A Mr. White, mind you, who spells his name with an 'I' instead of a 'Y'. I have just contacted his wife, and she is delighted that the stone is all prepared. And Mr. White not cold more than sixty minutes, and spelling his name with an 'I', just think of it. Oh, I'm so happy!"

The tombstone, on its truck, rolled from the room, while Mr. Whetmore and the Oklahoma man laughed, shook hands, and Leota watched with suspicion as the commotion came to an end. "Well, that's now all over," grinned her husband as he closed the door on Mr. Whetmore and began throwing the canned flowers into the sink and dropping the tin cans into a waste-basket. In the dark, he climbed into bed again, oblivious to her deep and solemn silence. She said not a word for a long while, but just lay there, alone-feeling. She felt him adjust the blankets with a sigh, "Now we can sleep. The damn old thing's took away. It's only ten-thirty. Plenty of time left for sleep." How he enjoyed spoiling her fun.

Leota was about to speak when a rapping came from down below again. "There! There!" she cried, triumphantly, holding her husband. "There it is again, the noises, like I said! Hear them!"

Her husband knotted his fists and clenched his teeth. "How many times must I explain. Do I have to kick you in the head to make you understand, woman! Let me alone. There's nothing—"

"Listen, listen, oh, listen," she begged in a whisper.

They listened to the square darkness.

A rapping on a door came from downstairs.

A door opened. Muffled and distant and faint, a woman's voice said, sadly, "Oh, it's you, Mr. Whetmore."

And deep down in the darkness underneath the suddenly shivering bed of Leota and her Oklahoma husband, Mr. Whetmore's voice replied: "Good evening again, Mrs. White. Here. I brought the stone."

# FIFTEEN

# THE WATCHERS

In this room the sound of the tapping of the typewriter keys is like knuckles on wood, and my perspiration falls down upon the keys that are being punched unceasingly by my trembling fingers. And over and above the sound of my writing comes the ironical melody of a mosquito circling over my bent head, and a number of flies buzzing and colliding with the wire screen. And around the naked filament-skeleton of the yellow bulb in the ceiling a bit of torn white paper that is a moth flutters. An ant crawls up the wall; I watch it—I laugh with a steady, unceasing bitterness. How ironical the shining flies and the red ants and the armoured crickets. How mistaken we three were: Susan and I and William Tinsley.

Whoever you are, wherever you are, if you do happen upon this, do not ever again crush the ants upon the sidewalk, do not smash the bumblebee that thunders by your window, do not annihilate the cricket upon your hearth!

That's where Tinsley made his colossal error. You remember William Tinsley, certainly? The man who threw away a million dollars on fly-sprays and insecticides and ant-pastes?

There was never a spot for a fly or a mosquito in Tinsley's office. Not a white wall or green desk or any immaculate surface where a fly might land before Tinsley destroyed it with an instantaneous stroke of his magnificent flyswatter. I shall never forget that instrument of death. Tinsley, a monarch, ruled his industry with that flyswatter as a scepter.

I was Tinsley's secretary and right-hand man in his kitchenware industry; sometimes I advised him on his many investments.

Tinsley carried the flyswatter to work with him under his arm in July, 1944. By the week's end, if I happened to be in one of the filing alcoves out of sight when Tinsley arrived, I could always tell of his arrival when I heard the swicking, whistling passage of the flyswatter through the air as Tinsley killed his morning quota.

As the days passed, I noted Tinsley's preoccupied alertness. He'd dictate to me, but his eyes would be searching the north-south-east-west walls, the rug, the bookcases, even my clothing. Once I laughed and made some comment about Tinsley and Clyde Beatty being fearless animal trainers, and Tinsley froze and turned his back on me. I shut up. People have a right, I thought, to be as damned eccentric as they please.

"Hello, Steve." Tinsley waved his flyswatter one morning as I poised my pencil over my pad. "Before we start, would you mind cleaning away the corpses."

Spread in a rumpled trail over the thick sienna rug were the fallen conquered, the flies; silent, mashed, dewinged. I threw them one by one in the waste-bin, muttering.

"To S. H. Little, Philadelphia. Dear Little: Will invest money in your insect spray. Five thousand dollars—"

"Five thousand?" I complained. I stopped writing.

Tinsley ignored me. "Five thousand dollars. Advise immediate production as soon as war conditions permit. Sincerely." Tinsley twisted his flyswatter. "You think I'm crazy," he said.

"Is that a p.s., or are you talking to me?" I asked.

The phone rang and it was the Termite Control Company, to whom Tinsley told me to write a thousand-dollar check for having termite-proofed his house. Tinsley patted his metal chair. "One thing I like about my offices—all iron, cement, solid; not a chance for termites."

He leaped from his chair, the swatter shone swiftly in the air.

"Damn it, Steve, has THAT been here all this time!"

Something buzzed in a small arc somewhere, into silence. The four walls moved in around us in that silence, it seemed, the blank ceiling stared over us and Tinsley's breath ached through his nostrils. I couldn't see the infernal insect anywhere. Tinsley exploded. "Help me find it! Damn you, help me!"

"Now, hold on—" I retorted.

Somebody rapped on the door.

"Stay out!" Tinsley's yell was high, afraid. "Get away from the door, and stay away!" He flung himself headlong, bolted the door with a frantic gesture and lay against it, wildly searching the room. "Quickly now, Steve, systematically! Don't sit there!"

Desk, chairs, chandelier, walls. Like an insane animal, Tinsley searched, found the buzzing, struck at it. A bit of insensate glitter fell to the floor where he crushed it with his foot in a queerly triumphant sort of action.

He started to dress me down but I wouldn't have it. "Look here," I came back at him. "I'm a secretary and right-hand stooge, not a spotter for high-flying insects. I haven't got eyes in the back of my head!"

"Neither have They!" cried Tinsley. "So you know what They do?"

"They? Who in hell are They?"

He shut up. He went to his desk and sat down, wearily, and finally said, "Never mind. Forget it. Don't talk about this to anyone."

I softened up. "Bill, you should go see a psychiatrist about—"

Tinsley laughed bitterly. "And the psychiatrist would tell his wife, and she'd tell others, and then They'd find out. They're everywhere, They are. I don't want to be stopped with my campaign."

"If you mean the one hundred thousand bucks you've sunk in your insect sprays and ant pastes in the last four weeks," I said. "Someone should stop you. You'll break yourself, me, and the stockholders. Honest to God, Tinsley—"

"Shut up!" he said. "You don't understand."

I guess I didn't, then. I went back to my office and all day long I heard that damned flyswatter hissing in the air.

. . .

I had supper with Susan Miller that evening. I told her about Tinsley and she lent a sympathetically professional ear. Then she tapped her cigarette and lit it and said, "Steve, I may be a psychiatrist, but I wouldn't have a tinker's chance in hell, unless Tinsley came to see me. I couldn't help him unless he wanted help." She patted my arm. "I'll look him over for you, if you insist, though, for old time's sake. But half the fight's lost if the patient won't cooperate."

"You've got to help me, Susan," I said. "He'll be stark raving in another month. I think he has delusions of persecution—"

We drove to Tinsley's house.

The first date worked out well. We laughed, we danced, we dined late at the Brown Derby, and Tinsley didn't suspect for a moment that the slender, soft-voiced woman he held in his arms to a waltz was a psychiatrist picking his reactions apart. From the table, I watched them, together, and I shielded a small laugh with my hand, and heard Susan laughing at one of his jokes.

We drove along the road in a pleasant, relaxed silence, the silence that follows on the heels of a good, happy evening. The perfume of Susan was in the car, the radio played dimly, and the car wheels whirled with a slight whisper over the highway.

I looked at Susan and she at me, her brows going up to indicate that she'd found nothing so far this evening to show that Tinsley was in any way unbalanced. I shrugged.

At that very instant, a moth flew in the window, fluttering, flickering its velvety white wings upon the imprisoning glass.

Tinsley screamed, wrenched the car involuntarily, struck out a gloved hand at the moth, gabbling, his face pale. The tires wobbled. Susan seized the steering wheel firmly and held the car on the road until we slowed to a stop.

As we pulled up, Tinsley crushed the moth between tightened fingers and watched the odorous powder of it sift down upon Susan's arm. We sat there, the three of us, breathing rapidly.

Susan looked at me, and this time there was comprehension in her eyes. I nodded.

Tinsley looked straight ahead, then. In a dream he said, "Ninety-nine percent of all life in the world is insect life—"

He rolled up the windows without another word, and drove us home.

Susan phoned me an hour later. "Steve, he's built a terrific complex for himself. I'm having lunch with him tomorrow. He likes me. I might find out what we want to know. By the way, Steve, does he own any pets?"

Tinsley had never owned a cat or dog. He detested animals.

"I might have expected that," said Susan. "Well, good-night, Steve, see you tomorrow."

The flies were breeding thick and golden and buzzing like a million intricately fine electric machines in the pouring direct light of summer noon. In vortexes they whirled and curtained and fell upon refuse to inject their eggs, to mate, to flutter, to whirl again, as I watched them, and in their whirling my mind intermixed, I wondered why Tinsley should fear them so, should dread and kill them, and as I walked the streets, all about me, cutting arcs and spaces from the sky, omnipresent flies hummed and sizzled and beat their lucid wings. I counted darning needles, mud-daubers and hornets, yellow bees and brown ants. The world was suddenly much more alive to me than ever before, because Tinsley's apprehensive awareness had set me aware.

. . .

Before I knew my actions, brushing a small red ant from my coat that had fallen from a lilac bush as I passed, I turned in at a familiar white house and knew it to be Lawyer Remington's, who had been Tinsley's family representative for forty years, even before Tinsley was born. Remington was only a business acquaintance to me, but there I was, touching his gate and ringing his bell and in a few minutes looking at him over a sparkling good glass of his sherry.

"I remember," said Remington, remembering. "Poor Tinsley. He was only seventeen when it happened."

I leaned forward intently. "It happened?" The ant raced in wild frenzies upon the golden stubble on my fingers' backs, becoming entangled in the bramble of my wrist, turning back, hopelessly clenching its mandibles. I watched the ant. "Some unfortunate accident?"

Lawyer Remington nodded grimly and the memory lay raw and naked in his old brown eyes. He spread the memory out on the table and pinned it down so I could look at it, with a few accurate words:

"Tinsley's father took him hunting up in the Lake Arrowhead region in the autumn of the young lad's seventeenth year. Beautiful country, a lovely clear cold autumn day. I remember it because I was hunting not seventy miles from there on that selfsame afternoon. Game was plentiful. You could hear the sound of guns passing over and back across the lakes through the scent of pine trees. Tinsley's father leaned his gun against a bush to lace his shoe, when a flurry of quail arose, some of them, in their fright, straight at Tinsley senior and his son."

Remington looked into his glass to see what he was telling. "A quail knocked the gun down, it fired off, and the charge struck the elder Tinsley full in the face!"

"Good God!"

In my mind I saw the elder Tinsley stagger, grasp at his red mask of face, drop his hands now gloved with scarlet fabric, and fall, even as the young boy, struck numb and ashen, swayed and could not believe what he saw.

I drank my sherry hastily, and Remington continued:

"But that wasn't the least horrible of details. One might think it sufficient. But what followed later was something indescribable to the lad. He ran five miles for help, leaving his father behind, dead, but refusing to believe him dead. Screaming, panting, ripping his clothes from his body, young Tinsley made it to a road and back with a doctor and two other men in something like six hours. The sun was just going down when they hurried back through the pine forest to where the father lay." Remington paused and shook his head from side to side, eyes closed. "The entire body, the arms, the legs, and the shattered contour of what was once a strong, handsome face, was clustered over and covered with scuttling, twitching, insects, bugs, ants of every and all descriptions, drawn by the sweet odor of blood. It was impossible to see one square inch of the elder Tinsley's body!"

. . .

Mentally, I created the pine trees, and the three men towering over the small boy who stood before a body upon which a tide of small attentively hungry creatures ebbed and flowed, subsided and returned. Somewhere, a woodpecker knocked, a squirrel scampered, and the quail beat their small wings. And the three men held onto the small boy's arms and turned him away from the sight. . . .

Some of the boy's agony and terror must have escaped my lips, for when my mind returned to the library, I found Remington staring at me, and my sherry glass broken in half causing a bleeding cut which I did not feel.

"So that's why Tinsley has this fear of insects and animals," I breathed, several minutes later, settling back, my heart pounding. "And it's grown like a yeast over the years, to obsess him."

Remington expressed an interest in Tinsley's problem, but I allayed him and inquired, "What was his father's profession?"

"I thought you knew!" cried Remington in faint surprise. "Why the elder Tinsley was a very famous naturalist. Very famous indeed. Ironic, in a way, isn't it, that he should be killed by the very creatures which he studied, eh?"

"Yes." I rose up and shook Remington's hand. "Thanks, Lawyer. You've helped me very much. I must get going now."

"Good-by."

I stood in the open air before Remington's house and the ant still scrambled over my hand, wildly. I began to understand and sympathize deeply with Tinsley for the first time. I went to pick up Susan in my car.

Susan pushed the veil of her hat back from her eyes and looked off into the distance and said, "What you've told me pretty well puts the finger on Tinsley, all right. He's been brooding." She waved a hand. "Look around. See how easy it would be to believe that insects are really the horrors he makes them out to be. There's a Monarch butterfly pacing us." She flicked a fingernail. "Is it listening to our every word? Tinsley the elder was a naturalist. What happened? He interfered, busybodied where he wasn't wanted, so They, They who control the animals and insects, killed him. Night and day for the last ten years that thought has been on Tinsley's mind, and everywhere he looked he saw the numerous life of the world and the suspicions began to take shape, form and substance!"

"I can't say I blame him," I said. "If my father had been killed in a like fashion—"

"He refuses to talk when there's an insect in the room, isn't that it, Steve?"

"Yes, he's afraid They'll discover that he knows about Them."

"You can see how silly that is, yourself, can't you. He couldn't possibly keep it a secret, granting that butterflies and ants and houseflies are evil, for you and I have talked about it, and others too. But he persists in his delusion that as long as he himself says no word in Their presence . . . well, he's still alive, isn't he? They haven't destroyed him, have They? And if They were evil and feared his knowledge, wouldn't They have destroyed him long since?"

"Maybe They're playing with him?" I wondered. "You know it is strange. The Elder Tinsley was on the verge of some great discovery when he was killed. It sort of fits a pattern."

"I'd better get you out of this hot sun," laughed Susan, swerving the car into a shady lane.

.  .  .

The next Sunday morning, Bill Tinsley and Susan and I attended church and sat in the middle of the soft music and the vast muteness and quiet color. During the service, Bill began to laugh to himself until I shoved him in the ribs and asked him what was wrong.

"Look at the Reverend up there," replied Tinsley, fascinated. "There's a fly on his bald spot. A fly in church. They go everywhere, I tell you. Let the minister talk, it won't do a bit of good. Oh, gentle Lord."

After the service we drove for a picnic lunch in the country under a warm blue sky. A few times, Susan tried to get Bill on the subject of his fear, but Bill only pointed at the train of ants swarming across the picnic linen and shook his head, angrily. Later, he apologized and with a certain tenseness, asked us to come up to his house that evening, he couldn't go on much longer by himself, he was running low on funds, the business was liable to go on the rocks, and he needed us. Susan and I held onto his hands and understood. In a matter of forty minutes we were inside the locked study of his house, cocktails in our midst, with Tinsley pacing anxiously back and forth, dandling his familiar flyswatter, searching the room and killing two flies before he made his speech.

He tapped the wall. "Metal. No maggots, ticks, woodbeetles, termites. Metal chairs, metal everything. We're alone, aren't we?"

I looked around. "I think so."

"Good." Bill drew in a breath and exhaled. "Have you ever wondered about God and the Devil and the Universe, Susan, Steve? Have you ever realized how cruel the world is? How we try to get ahead, but are hit over the head every time we succeed a fraction?" I nodded silently, and Tinsley went on. "You sometimes wonder where God is, or where the Forces of Evil are. You wonder how these forces get around, if they are invisible angels. Well, the solution is simple and clever and scientific. We are being watched constantly. Is there ever a minute in our lives that passes without a fly buzzing in our room with us, or an ant crossing our path, or a flea on a dog, or a cat itself, or a beetle or moth rushing through the dark, or a mosquito skirting around a netting?"

Susan said nothing, but looked at Tinsley easily and without making him self-conscious. Tinsley sipped his drink.

"Small winged things we pay no heed to, that follow us every day of our lives, that listen to our prayers and our hopes and our desires and fears, that listen to us and then tell what there is to be told to Him or Her or It, or whatever Force sends them out into the world."

"Oh, come now," I said impulsively.

To my surprise, Susan hushed me. "Let him finish," she said. Then she looked at Tinsley. "Go on."

Tinsley said, "It sounds silly, but I've gone about this in a fairly scientific manner. First, I've never been able to figure out a reason for so many insects, for their varied profusion. They seem to be nothing but irritants to we mortals, at the very least. Well, a very simple explanation is as follows: the government of Them is a small body, it may be one person alone, and It or They can't be everywhere. Flies can be. So can ants and other insects. And since we mortals cannot tell one ant from another, all identity is impossible and one fly is as good as another, their set-up is perfect. There are so many of Them and there have been so many for years, that we pay no attention to Them. Like Hawthorne's 'Scarlet Letter,' They are right before our eyes and familiarity has blinded us to Them."

"I don't believe any of that," I said directly.

"Let me finish!" cried Tinsley, hurriedly. "Before you judge. There is a Force, and it must have a contactual system, a communicative set-up, so that life can be twisted and adjusted according to each individual. Think of it, billions of insects, checking, correlating and reporting on Their special subjects, controlling humanity!"

"Look here!" I burst out. "You've grown worse ever since that accident back when you were a kid! You've let it feed on your mind! You can't go on fooling yourself!" I got up.

"Steve!" Susan rose, too, her cheeks reddening. "You won't help with talk like that! Sit down." She pressed against my chest. Then she turned rapidly to Tinsley. "Bill, if what you say should be true, if all of your plans, your insect-proofing your house, your silence in the presence of Their small winged creatures, your campaign, your ant pastes and pitifully small insect sprays, should really mean something, why are you still alive?"

"Why?" shouted Tinsley. "Because, I've worked alone."

"But if there is a They, Bill, They have known of you for a month now, because Steve and I have told Them, haven't we Steve, and yet you live. Isn't that proof that you must be wrong?"

"You told Them? You told!" Tinsley's eyes showed white and furious. "No, you didn't, I made Steve promise!"

"Listen to me." Susan's voice shook him, as she might shake a small boy by the scruff of his neck. "Listen, before you scream. Will you agree to an experiment?"

"What kind of experiment?"

"From now on, all of your plans will be above-board, in the open. If nothing happens to you in the next eight weeks, then you'll have to agree that your fears are baseless."

"But They'll kill me!"

"Listen! Steve and I will stake our lives on it, Bill. If you die, Steve and I'll die with you. I value my life greatly, Bill, and Steve values his. We don't believe in your horrors, and we want to get you out of this."

Tinsley hung his head and looked at the floor. "I don't know. I don't know."

"Eight weeks, Bill. You can go on the rest of your life, if you wish, manufacturing insecticides, but for God's sake don't have a nervous breakdown over it. The very fact of your living should be some sort of proof that They bear you no ill-will, and have left you intact."

.  .  .

Tinsley had to admit to that. But he was reluctant to give in. He murmured almost to himself, "This is the beginning of the campaign. It might take a thousand years, but in the end we can liberate ourselves."

"You can be liberated in eight weeks, Bill, don't you see? If we can prove that insects are blameless? For the next eight weeks, carry on your campaign, advertise it in weekly magazines and papers, thrust it to the hilt, tell everyone, so that if you should die, the word will be left behind. Then, when the eight weeks are up, you'll be liberated and free, and won't that feel good to you, Bill, after all these years?"

Something happened then that startled us. Buzzing over our heads, a fly came by. It had been in the room with us all the time, and yet I had sworn that, earlier, I had seen none. Tinsley began to shiver. I didn't know what I was doing, I seemed to react mechanically to some inner drive. I grabbed at the air and caught the tight buzzing in a cupped hand. Then I crushed it hard, staring at Bill and Susan. Their faces were chalky.

"I got it," I said, crazily. "I got the damned thing, and I don't know why."

I opened my hand. The fly dropped to the floor. I stepped on it as I had seen Bill often step on them, and my body was cold for no reason. Susan stared at me as if she'd lost her last friend.

"What am I saying?" I cried. "I don't believe a damn word of all this filth!"

It was dark outside the thick-glassed window. Tinsley managed to light a cigarette and then, because all three of us were in a strange state of nerves, offered to let us have rooms in the house for the night. Susan said she would stay if: "you promise to give the eight-week trial a chance."

"You'd risk your life on it?" Bill couldn't make Susan out.

Susan nodded gravely. "We'll be joking about it next year."

Bill said, "All right. The eight-week trial it is."

My room, upstairs, had a fine view of the spreading country hills. Susan stayed in the room next to mine, and Bill slept across the hall. Lying in bed I heard the crickets chirping outside my window, and I could hardly bear the sound.

I closed the window.

Later in the night I got no sleep so I began imagining that a mosquito was soaring freely about in the dark of my room. Finally, I robed myself and fumbled down to the kitchen, not actually hungry, but wanting something to do to stop my nervousness. I found Susan bending over the refrigerator trays, selecting food.

We looked at one another. We handed plates of stuff to the table and sat stiffly down. The world was unreal to us. Somehow, being around Tinsley made the universe insecure and misty underfoot. Susan, for all her training and mind-culture, was still a woman, and deep under, women are superstitious.

To top it all, we were about to plunge our knives into the half-shattered carcass of a chicken when a fly landed upon it.

We sat looking at the fly for five minutes. The fly walked around on the chicken, flew up, circled, and came back to promenade a drumstick.

We put the chicken back in the ice-box, joking very quietly about it, talked uneasily for awhile, and returned upstairs, where we shut our doors and felt alone. I climbed into bed and began having bad dreams before I shut my eyes. My wrist-watch set up an abominable loud clicking in the blackness, and it had clicked several thousand times when I heard the scream.

. . .

I don't mind hearing a woman scream occasionally, but a man's scream is so strange, and is heard so rarely, that when it finally comes, it turns your blood into an arctic torrent. The screaming seemed to be borne all through the house and it seemed I heard some frantic words babbled that sounded like, "Now I know why They let me live!"

I pulled the door wide in time to see Tinsley running down the hall, his clothing drenched and soaked, his body wet from head to foot. He turned when he saw me, and cried out, "Stay away from me, oh God, Steve, don't touch me, or it'll happen to you, too! I was wrong! I was wrong, yes, but near the truth, too, so very near!"

Before I could prevent him, he had descended the stairs and slammed the door below. Susan suddenly stood beside me. "He's gone mad for certain this time, Steve, we've got to stop him."

A noise from the bathroom drew my attention. Peering in, I turned off the shower which was steaming hot, drumming insistently, scaldingly, on the yellow tiles.

Bill's car thundered into life, a jerking of gears, and the car careened down the road at an insane speed.

"We've got to follow him," insisted Susan. "He'll kill himself! He's trying to run away from something. Where's your car?"

We ran to my car through a cold wind, under very cold stars, climbed in, warmed the motor, and were off, bewildered and breathless. "Which way?" I shouted.

"He went east, I'm certain."

"East it is, then." I poked up the speed and muttered, "Oh, Bill, you idiot, you fool. Slow down. Come back. Wait for me, you nut." I felt Susan's arm creep through my elbow and hold tight. She whispered, "Faster!" and I said, "We're going sixty now, and there are some bad turns coming!"

The night had gotten into us; the talk of insects, the wind, the roaring of the tires over hard concrete, the beating of our frightened hearts. "There!" Susan pointed. I saw a gash of light cutting through the hills a mile away. "More speed, Steve!"

More speed. Aching foot pressing out the miles, motor thundering, stars wheeling crazily overhead, lights cutting the dark away into dismembered sections. And in my mind I saw Tinsley again, in the hall, drenched to the skin. He had been standing under the hot, scalding shower! Why? Why?

"Bill, stop, you idiot! Stop driving! Where are you going, what are you running away from, Bill?"

We were catching up with him now. We drew closer, yard by yard, bit by bit, around curves where gravity yanked at us and tried to smash us against huge granite bulwarks of earth, over hills and down into night-filled valleys, over streams and bridges, around curves again.

"He's only about six hundred yards ahead, now," said Susan.

"We'll get him." I twisted the wheel. "So help me God, we'll get to him!"

Then, quite unexpectedly, it happened.

.  .  .

Tinsley's car slowed down. It slowed and crept along the road. We were on a straight length of concrete that continued for a mile in a firm line, no curves or hills. His car slowed to a crawling, puttering pace. By the time we pulled up in back of him, Tinsley's roadster was going three miles an hour, just poking along at a pace like a man walking, its lights glaring.

"Steve—" Susan's fingernails cut my wrist, tight, hard. "Something's—wrong."

I knew it. I honked the horn. Silence. I honked again and it was a lonely, blatant sound in the darkness and the emptiness. I parked the car. Tinsley's car moved on like a metal snail ahead of us, its exhaust whispering to the night. I opened the door and slid out. "Stay here," I warned Susan. In the reflected glare her face was like snow and her lips were trembling.

I ran to the car, calling, "Bill, Bill—!"

Tinsley didn't answer. He couldn't.

He just lay there behind the wheel, quietly, and the car moved ahead, slowly, so very slowly.

I got sick to my stomach. I reached in and braked the car and cut the ignition, not looking at him, my mind working in a slow kind of new and frightened horror.

I looked once more at Bill where he slumped with his head back.

It didn't do any good to kill flies, kill moths, kill termites, kill mosquitoes. The Evil Ones were too clever for that.

Kill all the insects you find, destroy the dogs and the cats and the birds, the weasels and the chipmunks, and the termites, and all animals and insects in the world, it can be done, eventually by man, killing, killing, killing, and after you are finished, after that job is done you still have—microbes.

Bacteria. Microbes. Yes. Unicellular and bi-cellular and multi-cellular microscopic life!

Millions of them, billions of them on every pore, on every inch of flesh of your body. On your lips when you speak, inside your ears when you listen, on your skin when you feel, on your tongue when you taste, in your eyes when you see! You can't wash them off, you can't destroy all of them in the world! It would be an impossible task, impossible! You discovered that, didn't you, Bill. I stared at him. We almost convinced you, didn't we, Bill, that insects were not guilty, were not Watchers. We were right about that part of it. We convinced you and you got to thinking tonight, and you hit upon the real crux of the situation. Bacteria. That's why the shower was running at home just now! But you can't kill bacteria fast enough. They multiply and multiply, instantly!

I looked at Bill, slumped there. "The flyswatter, you thought the flyswatter was enough. That's a—laugh."

Bill, is that you lying there with your body changed by leprosy and gangrene and tuberculosis and malaria and bubonic all at once? Where is the skin of your face, Bill, and the flesh of your bones, your fingers lying clenched to the steering wheel. Oh, God, Tinsley, the color and smell of you—the rotting fetid combination of disease you are!

Microbes. Messengers. Millions of them. Billions of them.

God can't be everywhere at once. Maybe He invented flies, insects to watch His peoples.

But the Evil Ones were brilliant, too. They invented bacteria!

Bill, you look so *different.* . . .

You'll not tell your secret to the world now. I returned to Susan, looked in at her, not able to speak. I could only point for her to go home, without me. I had a job to do, to drive Bill's car into the ditch and set fire to him and it. Susan drove away, not looking back.

. . .

And now, tonight, a week later, I am typing this out for what it is worth, here and now, in the summer evening, with flies buzzing about my room. Now I realize why Bill Tinsley lived so long. While his efforts were directed against insects, ants, birds, animals, who were representatives of the Good Forces, the Evil Forces let him go ahead. Tinsley, unaware, was working for the Evil Ones. But when he comprehended that bacteria were the real enemy, and were more numerous and invisibly insidious, then the Evil Ones demolished him.

In my mind, I still remember the picture of the Elder Tinsley's death when he was shot as a result of the quail flying against his gun. On the face of it, it doesn't seem to fit into the picture. Why would the quail, representative of Good, kill the Elder Tinsley? The answer to this comes clear now. Quail, too, have disease, and disease disrupts their neural set-up, and disease, on that day long ago, caused the birds to strike down Tinsley's weapon, killing him, and thus, subtly, animals and insects.

And another thought in my mind is the picture of the Elder Tinsley as he lay covered with ants in a red, quivering blanket. And I wonder if perhaps they were not giving solace to him in his dying and decay, talking in some silent mandibled tongue none of us can hear until we die. Or perhaps they are all.

The game of chess continues, Good against Evil, I hope. And I am losing.

Tonight I sit here writing and waiting, and my skin itches and softens, and Susan is on the other side of town, unaware, safe from this knowledge which I must set on paper even if it kills me. I listen to the flies, as if to detect some good message in their uneven whirring, but I hear nothing.

Even as I write, the skin of my fingers loosens and changes color and my face feels partially dry and flaking, partially wet, slippery and released from its anchorage of softening bone, my eyes water with a kind of leprosy and my skin darkens with something akin to bubonic, my stomach gripes me with sickening gastric wrenches, my tongue tastes bitter and acid, my teeth loosen in my mouth, my ears ring, and in a few minutes the structure of my fingers, the muscles, the small thin fine bones will be enmeshed, entangled, so much fallen gelatin spread over and down between the black lettered keys of this typewriter, the flesh of me will slide like a decayed, diseased cloak from my skeleton, but I must write on and on and on until etaoin shrdlucmfwyp cmfwyp . . . cmfwaaaaa dddddddddddddddddddd. . . .

# SIXTEEN
# LORELEI OF THE RED MIST

The Company dicks were good. They were plenty good. Hugh Starke began to think maybe this time he wasn't going to get away with it.

His small stringy body hunched over the control bank, nursing the last ounce of power out of the Kallman. The hot night sky of Venus fled past the ports in tattered veils of indigo. Starke wasn't sure where he was any more. Venus was a frontier planet, and still mostly a big X, except to the Venusians—who weren't sending out any maps. He did know that he was getting dangerously close to the Mountains of White Cloud. The backbone of the planet, towering far into the stratosphere, magnetic trap, with God knew what beyond. Maybe even God wasn't sure.

But it looked like over the mountains or out. Death under the guns of the Terro-Venus Mines, Incorporated, Special Police, or back to the Luna cell blocks for life as an habitual felon.

Starke decided he would go over.

Whatever happened, he'd pulled off the biggest lone-wolf caper in history. The T-V Mines payroll ship, for close to a million credits. He cuddled the metal strongbox between his feet and grinned. It would be a long time before anybody equaled that. His mass indicators began to jitter. Vaguely, a dim purple shadow in the sky ahead, the Mountains of White Cloud stood like a wall against him. Starke checked the positions of the pursuing ships. There was no way through them. He said flatly, "All right, damn you," and sent the Kallman angling up into the thick blue sky.

He had no very clear memories after that. Crazy magnetic vagaries, always a hazard on Venus, made his instruments useless. He flew by the seat of his pants and he got over, and the T-V men didn't. He was free, with a million credits in his kick.

Far below in the virgin darkness he saw a sullen crimson smear on the night, as though someone had rubbed it with a bloody thumb. The Kallman dipped toward it. The control bank flickered with blue flame, the jet timers blew, and then there was just the screaming of air against the falling hull.

Hugh Starke sat still and waited . . .

He knew, before he opened his eyes, that he was dying. He didn't feel any pain, he didn't feel anything, but he knew just the same. Part of him was cut loose. He was still there, but not attached any more.

He raised his eyelids. There was a ceiling. It was a long way off. It was black stone veined with smoky reds and ambers. He had never seen it before.

His head was tilted toward the right. He let his gaze move down that way. There were dim tapestries, more of the black stone, and three tall archways giving onto a balcony. Beyond the balcony was a sky veiled and clouded with red mist. Under the mist, spreading away from a murky line of cliffs, was an ocean. It wasn't water and it didn't have any waves on it, but there was nothing else to call it. It burned, deep down inside itself, breathing up the red fog. Little angry bursts of flame coiled up under the flat surface, sending circles of sparks flaring out like ripples from a dropped stone.

He closed his eyes and frowned and moved his head restively. There was the texture of fur against his skin. Through the cracks of his eyelids he saw that he lay on a high bed piled with silks and soft tanned pelts. His body was covered. He was rather glad he couldn't see it. It didn't matter because he wouldn't be using it any more anyway, and it hadn't been such a hell of a body to begin with. But he was used to it, and he didn't want to see it now, the way he knew it would have to look.

He looked along over the foot of the bed, and he saw the woman.

She sat watching him from a massive carved chair softened with a single huge white pelt like a drift of snow. She smiled, and let him look. A pulse began to beat under his jaw, very feebly.

She was tall and sleek and insolently curved. She wore a sort of tabard of pale grey spider-silk, held to her body by a jeweled girdle, but it was just a nice piece of ornamentation. Her face was narrow, finely cut, secret, faintly amused. Her lips, her eyes, and her flowing silken hair were all the same pale cool shade of aquamarine.

Her skin was white, with no hint of rose. Her shoulders, her forearms, the long flat curve of her thighs, the pale-green tips of her breasts, were dusted with tiny particles that glistened like powdered diamond. She sparkled softly like a fairy thing against the snowy fur, a creature of foam and moonlight and clear shallow water. Her eyes never left his, and they were not human, but he knew that they would have done things to him if he had had any feeling below the neck.

. . .

He started to speak. He had no strength to move his tongue. The woman leaned forward, and as though her movement were a signal four men rose from the tapestried shadows by the wall. They were like her. Their eyes were pale and strange like hers.

She said, in liquid High Venusian, "You're dying, in this body. But *you* will not die. You will sleep now, and wake in a strange body, in a strange place. Don't be afraid. My mind will be with yours, I'll guide you, don't be afraid. I can't explain now, there isn't time, but don't be afraid."

He drew back his thin lips baring his teeth in what might have been a smile. If it was, it was wolfish and bitter, like his face.

The woman's eyes began to pour coolness into his skull. They were like two little rivers running through the channels of his own eyes, spreading in silver-green quiet across the tortured surface of his brain. His brain relaxed. It lay floating on the water, and then the twin streams became one broad flowing stream, and his mind, or ego, the thing that was intimately himself, vanished along it.

It took him a long, long time to regain consciousness. He felt as though he'd been shaken until pieces of him were scattered all over inside. Also, he had an instinctive premonition that the minute he woke up he would be sorry he had. He took it easy, putting himself together.

He remembered his name, Hugh Starke. He remembered the mining asteroid where he was born. He remembered the Luna cell blocks where he had once come near dying. There wasn't much to choose between them. He remembered his face decorating half the bulletin boards between Mercury and The Belt. He remembered hearing about himself over the telecasts, stuff to frighten babies with, and he thought of himself committing his first crime—a stunted scrawny kid of eighteen swinging a spanner on a grown man who was trying to steal his food.

The rest of it came fast, then. The T-V Mines job, the getaway that didn't get, the Mountains of White Cloud. The crash . . .

The woman.

That did it. His brain leaped shatteringly. Light, feeling, a naked sense of reality swept over him. He lay perfectly still with his eyes shut, and his mind clawed at the picture of the shining woman with sea-green hair and the sound of her voice saying, *You will not die, you will wake in a strange body, don't be afraid . . .*

He was afraid. His skin pricked and ran cold with it. His stomach knotted with it. His skin, his stomach, and yet somehow they didn't feel just right, like a new coat that hasn't shaped to you . . .

He opened his eyes, a cautious crack.

He saw a body sprawled on its side in dirty straw. The body belonged to him, because he could feel the straw pricking it, and the itch of little things that crawled and ate and crawled again.

It was a powerful body, rangy and flat-muscled, much bigger than his old one. It had obviously not been starved the first twenty-some years of its life. It was stark naked. Weather and violence had written history on it, wealed white marks on leathery bronze, but nothing seemed to be missing. There was black hair on its chest and thighs and forearms, and its hands were lean and sinewy for killing.

It was a human body. That was something. There were so many other things it might have been that his racial snobbery wouldn't call human. Like the nameless shimmering creature who smiled with strange pale lips.

Starke shut his eyes again.

He lay, the intangible self that was Hugh Starke, bellied down in the darkness of the alien shell, quiet, indrawn, waiting. Panic crept up on its soft black paws. It walked around the crouching ego and sniffed and patted and nuzzled, whining, and then struck with its raking claws. After a while it went away, empty.

The lips that were now Starke's lips twitched in a thin, cruel smile. He had done six months once in the Luna solitary crypts. If a man could do that, and come out sane and on his two feet, he could stand anything. Even this.

It came to him then, rather deflatingly, that the woman and her four companions had probably softened the shock by hypnotic suggestion. His subconscious understood and accepted the change. It was only his conscious mind that was superficially scared to death.

Hugh Starke cursed the woman with great thoroughness, in seven languages and some odd dialects. He became healthily enraged that any dame should play around with him like that. Then he thought, What the hell, I'm alive. And it looks like I got the best of the trade-in!

He opened his eyes again, secretly, on his new world.

. . .

He lay at one end of a square stone hall, good sized, with two straight lines of pillars cut from some dark Venusian wood. There were long crude benches and tables. Fires had been burning on round brick hearths spaced between the pillars. They were embers now. The smoke climbed up, tarnishing the gold and bronze of shields hung on the walls and pediments, dulling the blades of longswords, the spears, the tapestries and hides and trophies.

It was very quiet in the hall. Somewhere outside of it there was fighting going on. Heavy, vicious fighting. The noise of it didn't touch the silence, except to make it deeper.

There were two men besides Starke in the hall.

They were close to him, on a low dais. One of them sat in a carved high seat, not moving, his big scarred hands flat on the table in front of him. The other crouched on the floor by his feet. His head was bent forward so that his mop of lint-white hair hid his face and the harp between his thighs. He was a little man, a swamp-edger from his albino coloring. Starke looked back at the man in the chair.

The man spoke harshly. "Why doesn't she send word?"

The harp gave out a sudden bitter chord. That was all.

Starke hardly noticed. His whole attention was drawn to the speaker. His heart began to pound. His muscles coiled and lay ready. There was a bitter taste in his mouth. He recognized it. It was hate.

He had never seen the man before, but his hands twitched with the urge to kill.

He was big, nearly seven feet, and muscled like a draft horse. But his body, naked above a gold-bossed leather kilt, was lithe and quick as a greyhound in spite of its weight. His face was square, strong-boned, weathered, and still young. It was a face that had laughed a lot once, and liked wine and pretty girls. It had forgotten those things now, except maybe the wine. It was drawn and cruel with pain, a look as of something in a cage. Starke had seen that look before, in the Luna blocks. There was a thick white scar across the man's forehead. Under it his blue eyes were sunken and dark behind half-closed lids. The man was blind.

Outside, in the distance, men screamed and died.

Starke had been increasingly aware of a soreness and stricture around his neck. He raised a hand, careful not to rustle the straw. His fingers found a long tangled beard, felt under it, and touched a band of metal.

Starke's new body wore a collar, like a vicious dog.

There was a chain attached to the collar. Starke couldn't find any fastening. The business had been welded on for keeps. His body didn't seem to have liked it much. The neck was galled and chafed.

The blood began to crawl up hot into Starke's head. He'd worn chains before. He didn't like them. Especially around the neck.

A door opened suddenly at the far end of the hall. Fog and red daylight spilled in across the black stone floor. A man came in. He was big, half-naked, blond, and bloody. His long blade trailed harshly on the flags. His chest was laid open to the bone and he held the wound together with his free hand.

"Word from Beudag," he said. "They've driven us back into the city, but so far we're holding the Gate."

No one spoke. The little man nodded his white head. The man with the slashed chest turned and went out again, closing the door.

A peculiar change came over Starke at the mention of the name Beudag. He had never heard it before, but it hung in his mind like a spear point, barbed with strange emotion. He couldn't identify the feeling, but it brushed the blind man aside. The hot simple hatred cooled. Starke relaxed in a sort of icy quiet, deceptively calm as a sleeping cobra. He didn't question this. He waited, for Beudag.

The blind man struck his hands down suddenly on the table and stood up. "Romna," he said, "give me my sword."

The little man looked at him. He had milk-blue eyes and a face like a friendly bulldog. He said, "Don't be a fool, Faolan."

Faolan said softly, "Damn you. Give me my sword."

Men were dying outside the hall, and not dying silently. Faolan's skin was greasy with sweat. He made a sudden, daring grab toward Romna.

Romna dodged him. There were tears in his pale eyes. He said brutally, "You'd only be in the way. Sit down."

"I can find the point," Faolan said, "to fall on it."

Romna's voice went up to a harsh scream. "Shut up. Shut up and sit down."

Faolan caught the edge of the table and bent over it. He shivered and closed his eyes, and the tears ran out hot under the lids. The bard turned away, and his harp cried out like a woman.

Faolan drew a long sighing breath. He straightened slowly, came round the carved high seat, and walked steadily toward Starke.

"You're very quiet, Conan," he said. "What's the matter? You ought to be happy, Conan. You ought to laugh and rattle your chain. You're going to get what you wanted. Are you sad because you haven't a mind any more, to understand that with?"

He stopped and felt with one sandaled foot across the straw until he touched Starke's thigh. Starke lay motionless.

"Conan," said the blind man gently, pressing Starke's belly with his foot. "Conan the dog, the betrayer, the butcher, the knife in the back. Remember what you did at Falga, Conan? No, you don't remember now. I've been a little rough with you, and you don't remember any more. But I remember, Conan. As long as I live in darkness, I'll remember."

. . .

Romna stroked the harp strings and they wept, savage tears for strong men dead of treachery. Low music, distant but not soft. Faolan began to tremble, a shallow animal twitching of the muscles. The flesh of his face was drawn, iron shaping under the hammer. Quite suddenly he went down on his knees. His hands struck Starke's shoulders, slid inward to the throat, and locked there.

Outside, the sound of fighting had died away.

Starke moved, very quickly. As though he had seen it and knew it was there, his hand swept out and gathered in the slack of the heavy chain and swung it.

It started out to be a killing blow. Starke wanted with all his heart to beat Faolan's brains out. But at the last second he pulled it, slapping the big man with exquisite judgment across the back of the head. Faolan grunted and fell sideways, and by that time Romna had come up. He had dropped his harp and drawn a knife. His eyes were startled.

Starke sprang up. He backed off, swinging the slack of the chain warningly. His new body moved magnificently. Outside everything was fine, but inside his psycho-neural setup had exploded into civil war. He was furious with himself for not having killed Faolan. He was furious with himself for losing control enough to want to kill a man without reason. He hated Faolan. He did not hate Faolan because he didn't know him well enough. Starke's trained, calculating, unemotional brain was at grips with a tidal wave of baseless emotion.

He hadn't realized it was baseless until his mental monitor, conditioned through years of bitter control, had stopped him from killing. Now he remembered the woman's voice saying, *My mind will be with yours, I'll guide you . . .*

Catspaw, huh? Just a hired hand, paid off with a new body in return for two lives. Yeah, two. This Beudag, whoever he was. Starke knew now what that cold alien emotion had been leading up to.

"Hold it," said Starke hoarsely. "Hold everything. *Catspaw! You green-eyed she-devil! You picked the wrong guy this time.*"

Just for a fleeting instant he saw her again, leaning forward with her hair like running water across the soft foam-sparkle of her shoulders. Her sea-pale eyes were full of mocking laughter, and a direct, provocative admiration. Starke heard her quite plainly:

"You may not have any choice, Hugh Starke. They know Conan, even if you don't. Besides, it's of no great importance. The end will be the same for them—it's just a matter of time. You can save your new body or not, as you wish." She smiled. "I'd like it if you did. It's a good body. I knew it, before Conan's mind broke and left it empty."

A sudden thought came to Starke. "My box, the million credits."

"Come and get them." She was gone. Starke's mind was clear, with no alien will tramping around in it. Faolan crouched on the floor, holding his head. He said:

"Who spoke?"

Romna the bard stood staring. His lips moved, but no sound came out.

Starke said, "I spoke. Me, Hugh Starke. I'm not Conan, and I never heard of Falga, and I'll brain the first guy that comes near me."

Faolan stayed motionless, his face blank, his breath sobbing in his throat. Romna began to curse, very softly, not as though he were thinking about it. Starke watched them.

Down the hall the doors burst open. The heavy reddish mist coiled in with the daylight across the flags, and with them a press of bodies hot from battle, bringing a smell of blood.

Starke felt the heart contract in the hairy breast of the body named Conan, watching the single figure that led the pack.

Romna called out, "Beudag!"

She was tall. She was built and muscled like a lioness, and she walked with a flat-hipped arrogance, and her hair was like coiled flame. Her eyes were blue, hot and bright, as Faolan's might have been once. She looked like Faolan. She was dressed like him, in a leather kilt and sandals, her magnificent body bare above the waist. She carried a longsword slung across her back, the hilt standing above the left shoulder. She had been using it. Her skin was smeared with blood and grime. There was a long cut on her thigh and another across her flat belly, and bitter weariness lay on her like a burden in spite of her denial of it.

"We've stopped them, Faolan," she said. "They can't breach the Gate, and we can hold Crom Dhu as long as we have food. And the sea feeds us." She laughed, but there was a hollow sound to it. "Gods, I'm tired!"

She halted then, below the dais. Her flame-blue gaze swept across Faolan, across Romna, and rose to meet Hugh Starke's, and stayed there.

The pulse began to beat under Starke's jaw again, and this time his body was strong, and the pulse was like a drum throbbing.

Romna said, "His mind has come back."

. . .

There was a long, hard silence. No one in the hall moved. Then the men back of Beudag, big brawny kilted warriors, began to close in on the dais, talking in low snarling undertones that rose toward a mob howl. Faolan rose up and faced them, and bellowed them to quiet.

"He's mine to take! Let him alone."

Beudag sprang up onto the dais, one beautiful flowing movement. "It isn't possible," she said. "His mind broke under torture. He's been a drooling idiot with barely the sense to feed himself. And now, suddenly, you say he's normal again?"

Starke said, "You know I'm normal. You can see it in my eyes."

"Yes."

He didn't like the way she said that. "Listen, my name is Hugh Starke. I'm an Earthman. This isn't Conan's brain come back. This is a new deal. I got shoved into this body. What it did before I got it I don't know, and I'm not responsible."

Faolan said, "He doesn't remember Falga. He doesn't remember the long-ships at the bottom of the sea." Faolan laughed.

Romna said quietly, "He didn't kill you, though. He could have, easily. Would Conan have spared you?"

Beudag said, "Yes, if he had a better plan. Conan's mind was like a snake. It crawled in the dark, and you never knew where it was going to strike."

Starke began to tell them how it happened, the chain swinging idly in his hand. While he was talking he saw a face reflected in a polished shield hung on a pillar. Mostly it was just a tangled black mass of hair, mounted on a frame of long, harsh, jutting bone. The mouth was sensuous, with a dark sort of laughter on it. The eyes were yellow. The cruel, brilliant yellow of a killer hawk.

Stark realized with a shock that the face belonged to him.

"A woman with pale green hair," said Beudag softly. "Rann," said Faolan, and Romna's harp made a sound like a high-priest's curse.

"Her people have that power," Romna said. "They can think a man's soul into a spider, and step on it."

"They have many powers. Maybe Rann followed Conan's mind, wherever it went, and told it what to say, and brought it back again."

"Listen," said Starke angrily. "I didn't ask . . ."

Suddenly, without warning, Romna drew Beudag's sword and threw it at Starke.

Starke dodged it. He looked at Romna with ugly yellow eyes. "That's fine. Chain me up so I can't fight and kill me from a distance." He did not pick up the sword. He'd never used one. The chain felt better, not being too different from a heavy belt or a length of cable, or the other chains he'd swung on occasion.

Romna said, "Is that Conan?"

Faolan snarled, "What happened?"

"Romna threw my sword at Conan. He dodged it, and left it on the ground." Beudag's eyes were narrowed. "Conan could catch a flying sword by the hilt, and he was the best fighter on the Red Sea, barring you, Faolan."

"He's trying to trick us. Rann guides him."

"The hell with Rann!" Starke clashed his chain. "She wants me to kill the both of you, I still don't know why. All right. I could have killed Faolan, easy. But I'm not a killer. I never put down anyone except to save my own neck. So I didn't kill him in spite of Rann. And I don't want any part of you, or Rann either. All I want is to get the hell out of here!"

Beudag said, "His accent isn't Conan's. And the look in his eyes is different, too." Her voice had an odd note in it. Romna glanced at her. He fingered a few rippling chords on his harp, and said:

"There's one way you could tell for sure."

A sullen flush began to burn on Beudag's cheekbones. Romna slid unobtrusively out of reach. His eyes danced with malicious laughter.

Beudag smiled, the smile of an angry cat, all teeth and no humor. Suddenly she walked toward Starke, her head erect, her hands swinging loose and empty at her sides. Starke tensed warily, but the blood leaped pleasantly in his borrowed veins.

Beudag kissed him.

Starke dropped the chain. He had something better to do with his hands.

After a while he raised his head for breath, and she stepped back, and whispered wonderingly,

"It isn't Conan."

. . .

The hall had been cleared. Starke had washed and shaved himself. His new face wasn't bad. Not bad at all. In fact, it was pretty damn good. And it wasn't known around the System. It was a face that could own a million credits and no questions asked. It was a face that could have a lot of fun on a million credits.

All he had to figure out now was a way to save the neck the face was mounted on, and get his million credits back from that beautiful she-devil named Rann.

He was still chained, but the straw had been cleaned up and he wore a leather kilt and a pair of sandals. Faolan sat in his high seat nursing a flagon of wine. Beudag sprawled wearily on a fur rug beside him. Romna sat cross-legged, his eyes veiled sleepily, stroking soft wandering music out of his harp. He looked fey. Starke knew his swamp-edgers. He wasn't surprised.

"This man is telling the truth," Romna said. "But there's another mind touching his. Rann's, I think. Don't trust him."

Faolan growled, "I couldn't trust a god in Conan's body."

Starke said, "What's the setup? All the fighting out there, and this Rann dame trying to plant a killer on the inside. And what happened at Falga? I never heard of this whole damn ocean, let alone a place called Falga."

The bard swept his hand across the strings. "I'll tell you, Hugh Starke. And maybe you won't want to stay in that body any longer."

Starke grinned. He glanced at Beudag. She was watching him with a queer intensity from under lowered lids. Starke's grin changed. He began to sweat. Get rid of this body, hell! It was really a body. His own stringy little carcass had never felt like this.

The bard said, "In the beginning, in the Red Sea, was a race of people having still their fins and scales. They were amphibious, but after a while part of this race wanted to remain entirely on land. There was a quarrel, and a battle, and some of the people left the sea forever. They settled along the shore. They lost their fins and most of their scales. They had great mental powers and they loved ruling. They subjugated the human peoples and kept them almost in slavery. They hated their brothers who still lived in the sea, and their brothers hated them.

"After a time a third people came to the Red Sea. They were rovers from the North. They raided and reived and wore no man's collar. They made a settlement on Crom Dhu, the Black Rock, and built longships, and took toll of the coastal towns.

"But the slave people didn't want to fight against the rovers. They wanted to fight with them and destroy the sea-folk. The rovers were human, and blood calls to blood. And the rovers like to rule, too, and this is a rich country. Also, the time had come in their tribal development when they were ready to change from nomadic warriors to builders in their own country.

"So the rovers, and the sea-folk, and the slave-people who are caught between the two of them, began their struggle for the land."

The bard's fingers thrummed against the strings so that they beat like angry hearts. Starke saw that Beudag was still watching him, weighing every change of expression on his face. Romna went on:

"There was a woman named Rann, who had green hair and great beauty, and ruled the sea-folk. There was a man called Faolan of the Ships, and his sister Beudag, which means Dagger-in-the-Sheath, and they two ruled the outland rovers. And there was the man called Conan."

The harp crashed out like a sword-blade striking.

"Conan was a great fighter and a great lover. He was next under Faolan of the Ships, and Beudag loved him, and they were plighted. Then Conan was taken prisoner by the sea-folk during a skirmish, and Rann saw him—and Conan saw Rann."

Hugh Starke had a fleeting memory of Rann's face smiling, and her low voice saying, *It's a good body. I knew it, before . . .*

Beudag's eyes were two stones of blue vitriol under her narrow lids.

"Conan stayed a long time at Falga with Rann of the Red Sea. Then he came back to Crom Dhu, and said that he had escaped, and had discovered a way to take the longships into the harbor of Falga, at the back of Rann's fleet, and from there it would be easy to take the city, and Rann with it. And Conan and Beudag were married."

Starke's yellow hawk eyes slid over Beudag, sprawled like a young lioness in power and beauty. A muscle began to twitch under his cheekbone. Beudag flushed, a slow deep color. Her gaze did not waver.

"So the longships went out from Crom Dhu, across the Red Sea. And Conan led them into a trap at Falga, and more than half of them were sunk. Conan thought his ship was free, that he had Rann and all she'd promised him, but Faolan saw what had happened and went after him. They fought, and Conan laid his sword across Faolan's brow and blinded him; but Conan lost the fight. Beudag brought them home.

"Conan was chained naked in the market place. The people were careful not to kill him. From time to time other things were done to him. After a while his mind broke, and Faolan had him chained here in the hall, where he could hear him babble and play with his chain. It made the darkness easier to bear.

"But since Falga, things have gone badly for Crom Dhu. Too many men were lost, too many ships. Now Rann's people have us bottled up here. They can't break in, we can't break out. And so we stay, until . . ." The harp cried out a bitter question, and was still.

.  .  .

After a minute or two Starke said slowly, "Yeah, I get it. Stalemate for both of you. And Rann figured if I could kill off the leaders, your people might give up." He began to curse. "What a lousy, dirty, sneaking trick! And who told her she could use me . . ." He paused. After all, he'd be dead now. After all, a new body, and a cool million credits. Ah, the hell with Rann. He hadn't asked her to do it. And he was nobody's hired killer. Where did she get off, sneaking around his mind, trying to make him do things he didn't even know about? Especially to someone like Beudag.

Still, Rann herself was nobody's crud.

And just where was Hugh Starke supposed to cut in on this deal? Cut was right. Probably with a longsword, right through the belly. Swell spot he was in, and a good three strikes on him already.

He was beginning to wish he'd never seen the T-V Mines payroll ship, because then he might never have seen the Mountains of White Cloud.

He said, because everybody seemed to be waiting for him to say something, "Usually when there's a deadlock like this, somebody calls in a third party. Isn't there somebody you can yell for?"

Faolan shook his rough red head. "The slave people might rise, but they haven't arms and they're not used to fighting. They'd only get massacred, and it wouldn't help us any."

"What about those other—uh—people that live in the sea? And just what is that sea, anyhow? Some radiation from it wrecked my ship and got me into this bloody mess."

Beudag said lazily, "I don't know what it is. The seas our forefathers sailed on were water, but this is different. It will float a ship, if you know how to build the hull—very thin, of a white metal we mine from the foothills. But when you swim in it, it's like being in a cloud of bubbles. It tingles, and the farther down you go in it the stranger it gets, dark and full of fire. I stay down for hours sometimes, hunting the beasts that live there."

Starke said, "For hours? You have diving suits, then."

"What are they?" Starke told her. She shook her head, laughing. "Why weigh yourself down that way? There's no trouble to breathe in this ocean."

"For cripesake," said Starke. "Well I'll be damned. Must be a heavy gas, then, radioactive, surface tension under atmospheric pressure, enough to float a light hull, and high oxygen content without any dangerous mixture. Well, well. Okay, why doesn't somebody go down and see if the sea-people will help? They don't like Rann's branch of the family, you said."

"They don't like us, either," said Faolan. "We stay out of the southern part of the sea. They wreck our ships, sometimes." His bitter mouth twisted in a smile. "Did you want to go to them for help?"

Starke didn't quite like the way Faolan sounded. "It was just a suggestion," he said.

Beudag rose, stretching, wincing as the stiffened wounds pulled her flesh. "Come on, Faolan. Let's sleep."

He rose and laid his hand on her shoulder. Romna's harpstrings breathed a subtle little mockery of sound. The bard's eyes were veiled and sleepy. Beudag did not look at Starke, called Conan.

Starke said, "What about me?"

"You stay chained," said Faolan. "There's plenty of time to think. As long as we have food—and the sea feeds us."

He followed Beudag, through a curtained entrance to the left. Romna got up, slowly, slinging the harp over one white shoulder. He stood looking steadily into Starke's eyes in the dying light of the fires.

"I don't know," he murmured.

Starke waited, not speaking. His face was without expression.

"Conan we knew. Starke we don't know. Perhaps it would have been better if Conan had come back." He ran his thumb absently over the hilt of the knife in his girdle. "I don't know. Perhaps it would have been better for all of us if I'd cut your throat before Beudag came in."

Starke's mouth twitched. It was not exactly a smile.

"You see," said the bard seriously, "to you, from Outside, none of this is important, except as it touches you. But we live in this little world. We die in it. To us, it's important."

The knife was in his hand now. It leaped up glittering into the dregs of the firelight, and fell, and leaped again.

"You fight for yourself, Hugh Starke. Rann also fights through you. I don't know."

Starke's gaze did not waver.

Romna shrugged and put away the knife. "It is written by the gods," he said, sighing. "I hope they haven't done a bad job of the writing."

He went out. Starke began to shiver slightly. It was completely quiet in the hall. He examined his collar, the rivets, every separate link of the chain, the staple to which it was fixed. Then he sat down on the fur rug provided for him in place of the straw. He put his face in his hands and cursed, steadily, for several minutes, and then struck his fists down hard on the floor. After that he lay down and was quiet. He thought Rann would speak to him. She did not.

The silent black hours that walked across his heart were worse than any he had spent in the Luna crypts.

.  .  .

She came soft-shod, bearing a candle. Beudag, the Dagger-in-the-Sheath. Starke was not asleep. He rose and stood waiting. She set the candle on the table and came, not quite to him, and stopped. She wore a length of thin white cloth twisted loosely at the waist and dropping to her ankles. Her body rose out of it straight and lovely, touched mystically with shadows in the little wavering light.

"Who are you?" she whispered. "What are you?"

"A man. Not Conan. Maybe not Hugh Starke any more. Just a man."

"I loved the man called Conan, until . . ." She caught her breath, and moved closer. She put her hand on Starke's arm. The touch went through him like white fire. The warm clean healthy fragrance of her tasted sweet in his throat. Her eyes searched his.

"If Rann has such great powers, couldn't it be that Conan was forced to do what he did? Couldn't it be that Rann took away his mind and moulded it her way, perhaps without his knowing it?"

"It could be."

"Conan was hot-tempered and quarrelsome, but he . . ."

Starke said slowly, "I don't think you could have loved him if he hadn't been straight."

Her hand lay still on his forearm. She stood looking at him, and then her hand began to tremble, and in a moment she was crying, making no noise about it. Starke drew her gently to him. His eyes blazed yellowly in the candlelight.

"Woman's tears," she said impatiently, after a bit. She tried to draw away. "I've been fighting too long, and losing, and I'm tired."

He let her step back, not far. "Do all the women of Crom Dhu fight like men?"

"If they want to. There have always been shield-maidens. And since Falga, I would have had to fight anyway, to keep from thinking." She touched the collar on Starke's neck. "And from seeing."

He thought of Conan in the market square, and Conan shaking his chain and gibbering in Faolan's hall, and Beudag watching it. Starke's fingers tightened. He slid his palms upward along the smooth muscles of her arms, across the straight, broad planes of her shoulders, onto her neck, the proud strength of it pulsing under his hands. Her hair fell loose. He could feel the redness of it burning him.

She whispered, "You don't love me."

"No."

"You're an honest man, Hugh Starke."

"You want me to kiss you."

"Yes."

"You're an honest woman, Beudag."

Her lips were hungry, passionate, touched with the bitterness of tears. After a while Starke blew out the candle . . .

"I could love you, Beudag."

"Not the way I mean."

"The way you mean. I've never said that to any woman before. But you're not like any woman before. And—I'm a different man."

"Strange—so strange. Conan, and yet not Conan."

"I could love you, Beudag—if I lived."

Harpstrings gave a thrumming sigh in the darkness, the faintest whisper of sound. Beudag started, sighed, and rose from the fur rug. In a minute she had found flint and steel and got the candle lighted. Romna the bard stood in the curtained doorway, watching them.

Presently he said, "You're going to let him go."

Beudag said, "Yes."

Romna nodded. He did not seem surprised. He walked across the dais, laying his harp on the table, and went into another room. He came back almost at once with a hacksaw.

"Bend your neck," he said to Starke.

The metal of the collar was soft. When it was cut through Starke got his fingers under it and bent the ends outward, without trouble. His old body could never have done that. His old body could never have done a lot of things. He figured Rann hadn't cheated him. Not much.

He got up, looking at Beudag. Beudag's head was dropped forward, her face veiled behind shining hair.

"There's only one possible way out of Crom Dhu," she said. There was no emotion in her voice. "There's a passage leading down through the rock to a secret harbor, just large enough to moor a skiff or two. Perhaps, with the night and the fog, you can slip through Rann's blockade. Or you can go aboard one of her ships, for Falga." She picked up the candle. "I'll take you down."

"Wait," Starke said. "What about you?"

She glanced at him, surprised. "I'll stay, of course."

He looked into her eyes. "It's going to be hard to know each other that way."

"You can't stay here, Hugh Starke. The people would tear you to pieces the moment you went into the street. They may even storm the hall, to take you. Look here." She set the candle down and led him to a narrow window, drawing back the hide that covered it.

Starke saw narrow twisting streets dropping steeply toward the sullen sea. The longships were broken and sunk in the harbor. Out beyond, riding lights flickering in the red fog, were other ships. Rann's ships.

"Over there," said Beudag, "is the mainland. Crom Dhu is connected to it by a tongue of rock. The sea-folk hold the land beyond it, but we can hold the rock bridge as long as we live. We have enough water, enough food from the sea. But there's no soil nor game on Crom Dhu. We'll be naked after a while, without leather or flax, and we'll have scurvy without grain and fruit. We're beaten, unless the gods send us a miracle. And we're beaten because of what was done at Falga. You can see how the people feel."

Starke looked at the dark streets and the silent houses leaning on each other's shoulders, and the mocking lights out in the fog. "Yeah," he said. "I can see."

"Besides, there's Faolan. I don't know whether he believes your story. I don't know whether it would matter."

Starke nodded. "But you won't come with me?"

She turned away sharply and picked up the candle again. "Are you coming, Romna?"

The bard nodded. He slung his harp over his shoulder. Beudag held back the curtain of a small doorway far to the side. Starke went through it and Romna followed, and Beudag went ahead with the candle. No one spoke.

. . .

They went along a narrow passage, past store rooms and armories. They paused once while Starke chose a knife, and Romna whispered: "Wait!" He listened intently. Starke and Beudag strained their ears along with him. There was no sound in the sleeping dun. Romna shrugged. "I thought I heard sandals scraping stone," he said. They went on.

The passage lay behind a wooden door. It led downward steeply through the rock, a single narrow way without side galleries or branches. In some places there were winding steps. It ended, finally, in a flat ledge low to the surface of the cove, which was a small cavern closed in with the black rock. Beudag set the candle down.

There were two little skiffs built of some light metal moored to rings in the ledge. Two long sweeps leaned against the cave wall. They were of a different metal, oddly vaned. Beudag laid one across the thwarts of the nearest boat. Then she turned to Starke. Romna hung back in the shadows by the tunnel mouth.

Beudag said quietly, "Goodbye, man without a name."

"It has to be goodbye."

"I'm leader now, in Faolan's place. Besides, these are my people." Her fingers tightened on his wrists. "If you could . . ." Her eyes held a brief blaze of hope. Then she dropped her head and said, "I keep forgetting you're not one of us. Goodbye."

"Goodbye, Beudag."

Starke put his arms around her. He found her mouth, almost cruelly. Her arms were tight about him, her eyes half closed and dreaming. Starke's hands slip upward, toward her throat, and locked on it.

She bent back, her body like a steel bow. Her eyes got fire in them, looking into Starke's but only for a moment. His fingers pressed expertly on the nerve centers. Beudag's head fell forward limply, and then Romna was on Starke's back and his knife was pricking Starke's throat.

Starke caught his wrist and turned the blade away. Blood ran onto his chest, but the cut was not into the artery. He threw himself backward onto the stone. Romna couldn't get clear in time. The breath went out of him in a rushing gasp. He didn't let go of the knife. Starke rolled over. The little man didn't have a chance with him. He was tough and quick, but Starke's sheer size smothered him. Starke could remember when Romna would not have seemed small to him. He hit the bard's jaw with his fist. Romna's head cracked hard against the stone. He let go of the knife. He seemed to be through fighting. Starke got up. He was sweating, breathing heavily, not because of his exertion. His mouth was glistening and eager, like a dog's. His muscles twitched, his belly was hot and knotted with excitement. His yellow eyes had a strange look.

He went back to Beudag.

She lay on the black rock, on her back. Candlelight ran pale gold across her brown skin, skirting the sharp strong hollows between her breasts and under the arching rim of her rib-case. Starke knelt, across her body, his weight pressed down against her harsh breathing. He stared at her. Sweat stood out on his face. He took her throat between his hands again.

He watched the blood grow dark in her cheeks. He watched the veins coil on her forehead. He watched the redness blacken in her lips. She fought a little, very vaguely, like someone moving in a dream. Starke breathed hoarsely, animal-like, through an open mouth.

Then, gradually his body became rigid. His hands froze, not releasing pressure, but not adding any. His yellow eyes widened. It was as though he were trying to see Beudag's face and it was hidden in dense clouds.

Back of him, back in the tunnel, was the soft, faint whisper of sandals on uneven rock. Sandals, walking slowly. Starke did not hear. Beudag's face glimmered deep in a heavy mist below him, a blasphemy of a face, distorted, blackened.

Starke's hands began to open.

They opened slowly. Muscles stood like coiled ropes in his arms and shoulders, as though he moved them against heavy weights. His lips peeled back from his teeth. He bent his neck, and sweat dropped from his face and glittered on Beudag's breast.

Starke was now barely touching Beudag's neck. She began to breathe again, painfully.

Starke began to laugh. It was not nice laughter. "Rann," he whispered. "Rann, you she-devil." He half fell away from Beudag and stood up, holding himself against the wall. He was shaking violently. "I wouldn't use your hate for killing, so you tried to use my passion." He cursed her in a flat sibilant whisper. He had never in his profane life really cursed anyone before.

He heard an echo of laughter dancing in his brain.

Starke turned. Faolan of the Ships stood in the tunnel mouth. His head was bent, listening, his blind dark eyes fixed on Starke as though he saw him.

.  .  .

Faolan said softly, "I hear you, Starke. I hear the other breathing, but they don't speak."

"They're all right. I didn't mean to do . . ."

Faolan smiled. He stepped out on the narrow ledge. He knew where he was going, and his smile was not pleasant.

"I heard your steps in the passage beyond my room. I knew Beudag was leading you, and where, and why. I would have been here sooner, but it's a slow way in the dark."

The candle lay in his path. He felt the heat of it close to his leg, and stopped and felt for it, and ground it out. It was dark, then. Very dark, except for a faint smudgy glow from the scrap of ocean that lay along the cave floor.

"It doesn't matter," Faolan said, "as long as I came in time."

Starke shifted his weight warily. "Faolan . . ."

"I wanted you alone. On this night of all nights I wanted you alone. Beudag fights in my place now, Conan. My manhood needs proving."

Starke strained his eyes in the gloom, measuring the ledge, measuring the place where the skiff was moored. He didn't want to fight Faolan. In Faolan's place he would have felt the same. Starke understood perfectly. He didn't hate Faolan, he didn't want to kill him, and he was afraid of Rann's power over him when his emotions got control. You couldn't keep a determined man from killing you and still be uninvolved emotionally. Starke would be damned if he'd kill anyone to suit Rann.

He moved, silently, trying to slip past Faolan on the outside and get into the skiff. Faolan gave no sign of hearing him. Starke did not breathe. His sandals came down lighter than snowflakes. Faolan did not swerve. He would pass Starke with a foot to spare. They came abreast.

Faolan's hand shot out and caught in Starke's long black hair. The blind man laughed softly and closed in.

Starke swung one from the floor. Do it the quickest way and get clear. But Faolan was fast. He came in so swiftly that Starke's fist jarred harmlessly along his ribs. He was bigger than Starke, and heavier, and the darkness didn't bother him.

Starke bared his teeth. Do it quick, brother, and clear out! Or that green-eyed she-cat. . . . Faolan's brute bulk weighed him down. Faolan's arm crushed his neck. Faolan's fist was knocking his guts loose. Starke got moving.

He'd fought in a lot of places. He'd learned from stokers and tramps, Martian Low-Canalers, red-eyed Nahali in the running gutters of Lhi. He didn't use his knife. He used his knees and feet and elbows and his hands, fist and flat. It was a good fight. Faolan was a good fighter, but Starke knew more tricks.

One more, Starke thought. One more and he's out. He drew back for it, and his heel struck Romna, lying on the rock. He staggered, and Faolan caught him with a clean swinging blow. Starke fell backward against the cave wall. His head cracked the rock. Light flooded crimson across his brain and then paled and grew cooler, a wash of clear silver-green like water. He sank under it . . .

He was tired, desperately tired. His head ached. He wanted to rest, but he could feel that he was sitting up, doing something that had to be done. He opened his eyes.

He sat in the stern of a skiff. The long sweep was laid into its crutch, held like a tiller bar against his body. The blade of the sweep trailed astern in the red sea, and where the metal touched there was a spurt of silver fire and a swirling of brilliant motes. The skid moved rapidly through the sullen fog, through a mist of blood in the hot Venusian night.

Beudag crouched in the bow, facing Starke. She was bound securely with strips of the white cloth she had worn. Bruises showed dark on her throat. She was watching Starke with the intent, un-winking, perfectly expressionless gaze of a tigress.

Starke looked away, down at himself. There was blood on his kilt, a brown smear of it across his chest. It was not his blood. He drew the knife slowly out of its sheath. The blade was dull and crusted, still a little wet.

Starke looked at Beudag. His lips were stiff, swollen. He moistened them and said hoarsely, "What happened?"

She shook her head, slowly, not speaking. Her eyes did not waver.

A black, cold rage took hold of Starke and shook him. Rann! He rose and went forward, letting the sweep go where it would. He began to untie Beudag's wrists.

A shape swam toward them out of the red mist. A longship with two heavy sweeps bursting fire astern and a slender figurehead shaped like a woman. A woman with hair and eyes of aquamarine. It came alongside the skiff.

A rope ladder snaked down. Men lined the low rail. Slender men with skin that glistened white like powdered snow, and hair the color of distant shallows.

One of them said, "Come aboard, Hugh Starke."

Starke went back to the sweep. It bit into the sea, sending the skiff in a swift arc away from Rann's ship.

Grapnels flew, hooking the skiff at thwart and gunwale. Bows appeared in the hands of the men, wicked curving things with barbed metal shafts on the string. The man said again, politely, "Come aboard."

Hugh Starke finished untying Beudag. He didn't speak. There seemed to be nothing to say. He stood back while she climbed the ladder and then followed. The skiff was cast loose. The longship veered away, gathering speed.

Starke said, "Where are we going?"

The man smiled. "To Falga."

Starke nodded. He went below with Beudag into a cabin with soft couches covered with spider-silk and panels of dark wood beautifully painted, dim fantastic scenes from the past of Rann's people. They sat opposite each other. They still did not speak.

. . .

They raised Falga in the opal dawn—a citadel of basalt cliffs rising sheer from the burning sea, with a long arm holding a harbor full of ships. There were green fields inland, and beyond, cloaked in the eternal mists of Venus, the Mountains of White Cloud lifted spaceward. Starke wished that he had never seen the Mountains of White Cloud. Then, looking at his hands, lean and strong on his long thighs, he wasn't so sure. He thought of Rann waiting for him. Anger, excitement, a confused violence of emotion set him pacing nervously.

Beudag sat quietly, withdrawn, waiting.

The longship threaded the crowded moorings and slid into place alongside a stone quay. Men rushed to make fast. They were human men, as Starke judged humans, like Beudag and himself. They had the shimmering silver hair and fair skin of the plateau peoples, the fine-cut faces and straight bodies. They wore leather collars with metal tags and they went naked like beasts, and they were gaunt and bowed with labor. Here and there a man with pale blue-green hair and resplendent harness stood godlike above the swarming masses.

Starke and Beudag went ashore. They might have been prisoners or honored guests, surrounded by their escort from the ship. Streets ran back from the harbor, twisting and climbing crazily up the cliffs. Houses climbed on each others' backs. It had begun to rain, the heavy steaming downpour of Venus, and the moist heat brought out the choking stench of people, too many people.

They climbed, ankle deep in water sweeping down the streets that were half stairway. Thin naked children peered out of the houses, out of narrow alleys. Twice they passed through market squares where women with the blank faces of defeat drew back from stalls of coarse food to let the party through.

There was something wrong. After a while Starke realized it was the silence. In all that horde of humanity no one laughed, or sang, or shouted. Even the children never spoke above a whisper. Starke began to feel a little sick. Their eyes had a look in them . . .

He glanced at Beudag, and away again.

The waterfront streets ended in a sheer basalt face honeycombed with galleries. Starke's party entered them, still climbing. They passed level after level of huge caverns, open to the sea. There was the same crowding, the same stench, the same silence. Eyes glinted in the half-light, bare feet moved furtively on stone. Somewhere a baby cried thinly, and was hushed at once.

They came out on the cliff top, into the clean high air. There was a city here. Broad streets, lined with trees, low rambling villas of the black rock set in walled gardens, drowned in brilliant vines and giant ferns and flowers. Naked men and women worked in the gardens, or hauled carts of rubbish through the alleys, or hurried on errands, slipping furtively across the main streets where they intersected the mews.

The party turned away from the sea, heading toward an ebon palace that sat like a crown above the city. The steaming rain beat on Starke's bare body, and up here you could get the smell of the rain, even through the heavy perfume of the flowers. You could smell Venus in the rain—musky and primitive and savagely alive, a fecund giantess with passion flowers in her outstretched hands. Starke set his feet down like a panther and his eyes burned a smoky amber.

They entered the palace of Rann. . . .

She received them in the same apartment where Starke had come to after the crash. Through a broad archway he could see the high bed where his old body had lain before the life went out of it. The red sea steamed under the rain outside, the rusty fog coiling languidly through the open arches of the gallery. Rann watched them lazily from a raised couch set massively into the wall. Her long sparkling legs sprawled arrogantly across the black spider-silk draperies. This time her tabard was a pale yellow. Her eyes were still the color of shoal-water, still amused, still secret, still dangerous.

Starke said, "So you made me do it after all."

"And you're angry." She laughed, her teeth showing white and pointed as bone needles. Her gaze held Starke's. There was nothing casual about it. Starke's hawk eyes turned molten yellow, like hot gold, and did not waver.

Beudag stood like a bronze spear, her forearms crossed beneath her bare sharp breasts. Two of Rann's palace guards stood behind her.

Starke began to walk toward Rann.

She watched him come. She let him get close enough to reach out and touch her, and then she said slyly, "It's a good body, isn't it?"

.  .  .

Starke looked at her for a moment. Then he laughed. He threw back his head and roared, and struck the great corded muscles of his belly with his fist. Presently he looked straight into Rann's eyes and said:

"I know you."

She nodded. "We know each other. Sit down, Hugh Starke." She swung her long legs over to make room, half erect now, looking at Beudag. Starke sat down. He did not look at Beudag.

Rann said, "Will your people surrender now?"

Beudag did not move, not even her eyelids. "If Faolan is dead—yes."

"And if he's not?"

Beudag stiffened. Starke did too.

"Then," said Beudag quietly, "they'll wait."

"Until he is?"

"Or until they must surrender."

Rann nodded. To the guards she said, "See that this woman is well fed and well treated."

Beudag and her escort had turned to go when Starke said, "Wait." The guards looked at Rann, who nodded, and glanced quizzically at Starke. Starke said:

"Is Faolan dead?"

Rann hesitated. Then she smiled. "No. You have the most damnably tough mind, Starke. You struck deep, but not deep enough. He may still die, but . . . No, he'd not dead." She turned to Beudag and said with easy mockery, "You needn't hold anger against Starke. I'm the one who should be angry." Her eyes came back to Starke. They didn't look angry.

Starke said, "There's something else. Conan—the Conan that used to be, before Falga."

"Beudag's Conan."

"Yeah. Why did he betray his people?"

Rann studied him. Her strange pale lips curved, her sharp white teeth glistening wickedly with barbed humor. Then she turned to Beudag. Beudag was still standing like a carved image, but her smooth muscles were ridged with tension, and her eyes were not the eyes of an image.

"Conan or Starke," said Rann, "she's still Beudag, isn't she? All right, I'll tell you. Conan betrayed his people because I put it into his mind to do it. He fought me. He made a good fight of it. But he wasn't quite as tough as you are, Starke."

There was a silence. For the first time since entering the room, Hugh Starke looked at Beudag. After a moment she sighed and lifted her chin and smiled, a deep, faint smile. The guards walked out beside her, but she was more erect and lighter of step than either of them.

"Well," said Rann, when they were gone, "and what about you, Hugh-Starke-Called-Conan."

"Have I any choice?"

"I always keep my bargains."

"Then give me my dough and let me clear the hell out of here."

"Sure that's what you want?"

"That's what I want."

"You could stay a little while, you know."

"With you."

Rann lifted her frosty-white shoulders. "I'm not promising half my kingdom, or even part of it. But you might be amused."

"I got no sense of humor."

"Don't you even want to see what happens to Crom Dhu?"

Starke got up. He said savagely, "The hell with Crom Dhu."

"And Beudag."

"And Beudag." He stopped, then fixed Rann with uncompromising yellow eyes. "No. Not Beudag. What are you going to do to her?"

"Nothing."

"Don't give me that."

"I say again, nothing. Whatever is done, her own people will do."

"What do you mean?"

"I mean that little Dagger-in-the-Sheath will be rested, cared for, and fattened, for a few days. Then I shall take her aboard my own ship and join the fleet before Crom Dhu. Beudag will be made quite comfortable at the masthead, where her people can see her plainly. She will stay there until the Rock surrenders. It depends on her own people how long she stays. She'll be given water. Not much, but enough."

Starke stared at her. He stared at her a long time. Then he spat deliberately on the floor and said in a perfectly flat voice: "How soon can I get out of here?"

Rann laughed, a small casual chuckle. "Humans," she said, "are so damned queer. I don't think I'll ever understand them." She reached out and struck a gong that stood in a carved frame beside the couch. The soft deep shimmering note had a sad quality of nostalgia. Rann lay back against the silken cushions and sighed.

"Goodbye, Hugh Starke."

A pause. Then, regretfully:

"Goodbye—Conan!"

.  .  .

They had made good time along the rim of the Red Sea. One of Rann's galleys had taken them to the edge of the Southern Ocean and left them on a narrow shingle beach under the cliffs. From there they had climbed to the rimrock and gone on foot—Hugh-Starke-Called-Conan and four of Rann's arrogant shining men. They were supposed to be guide and escort. They were courteous, and they kept pace uncomplainingly though Starke marched as though the devil were pricking his heels. But they were armed, and Starke was not.

Sometimes, very faintly, Starke was aware of Rann's mind touching his with the velvet delicacy of a cat's paw. Sometimes he started out of his sleep with her image sharp in his mind, her lips touched with the mocking, secret smile. He didn't like that. He didn't like it at all.

But he liked even less the picture that stayed with him waking or sleeping. The picture he wouldn't look at. The picture of a tall woman with hair like loose fire on her neck, walking on light proud feet between her guards.

She'll be given water, Rann said. Not much, but enough.

Starke gripped the solid squareness of the box that held his million credits and set the miles reeling backward from under his sandals.

On the fifth night one of Rann's men spoke quietly across the campfire. "Tomorrow," he said, "we'll reach the pass."

Starke got up and went away by himself, to the edge of the rimrock that fell sheer to the burning sea. He sat down. The red fog wrapped him like a mist of blood. He thought of the blood on Beudag's breast the first time he saw her. He thought of the blood on his knife, crusted and dried. He thought of the blood poured rank and smoking into the gutters of Crom Dhu. The fog has to be red, he thought. Of all the goddam colors in the universe, it has to be red. Red like Beudag's hair.

He held out his hands and looked at them, because he could still feel the silken warmth of that hair against his skin. There was nothing there now but the old white scars of another man's battles.

He set his fists against his temples and wished for his old body back again—the little stunted abortion that had clawed and scratched its way to survival through sheer force of mind. A most damnably tough mind, Rann had said. Yeah. It had had to be tough. But a mind was a mind. It didn't have emotions. It just figured out something coldly and then went ahead and never questioned, and it controlled the body utterly, because the body was only the worthless machinery that carried the mind around. Worthless. Yeah. The few women he'd ever looked at had told him that—and he hadn't minded much. The old body hadn't given him any trouble.

He was having trouble now.

Starke got up and walked.

Tomorrow we reach the pass.

Tomorrow we go away from the Red Sea. There are nine planets and the whole damn Belt. There are women on all of them. All shapes, colors, and sizes, human, semi-human, and God knows what. With a million credits a guy could buy half of them, and with Conan's body he could buy the rest. What's a woman, anyway? Only a . . .

*Water. She'll be given water. Not much, but enough.*

Conan reached out and took hold of a spire of rock, and his muscles stood out like knotted ropes. "Oh God," he whispered, "what's the matter with me?"

*"Love."*

It wasn't God who answered. It was Rann. He saw her plainly in his mind, heard her voice like a silver bell.

"Conan was a man, Hugh Starke. He was whole, body and heart and brain. He knew how to love, and with him it wasn't women, but one woman—and her name was Beudag. I broke him, but it wasn't easy. I can't break you."

Starke stood for a long, long time. He did not move, except that he trembled. Then he took from his belt the box containing his million credits and threw it out as far as he could over the cliff edge. The red mist swallowed it up. He did not hear it strike the surface of the sea. Perhaps in that sea there was no splashing. He did not wait to find out.

He turned back along the rimrock, toward a place where he remembered a cleft, or chimney, leading down. And the four shining men who wore Rann's harness came silently out of the heavy luminous night and ringed him in. Their sword-points caught sharp red glimmers from the sky.

Starke had nothing on him but a kilt and sandals, and a cloak of tight-woven spider-silk that shed the rain.

"Rann sent you?" he said.

The men nodded.

"To kill me?"

Again they nodded. The blood drained out of Starke's face, leaving it grey and stony under the bronze. His hand went to his throat, over the gold fastening of his cloak.

The four men closed in like dancers.

. . .

Starke loosed his cloak and swung it like a whip across their faces. It confused them for a second, for a heart-beat—no more, but long enough. Starke left two of them to tangle their blades in the heavy fabric and leaped aside. A sharp edge slipped and turned along his ribs, and then he had reached in low and caught a man around the ankles, and used the thrashing body for a flail.

The body was strangely light, as though the bones in it were no more than rigid membrane, like a fish.

If he had stayed to fight, they would have finished him in seconds. They were fighting men, and quick. But Starke didn't stay. He gained his moment's grace and used it. They were hard on his heels, their points all but pricking his back as he ran, but he made it. Along the rimrock, out along a narrow tongue that jutted over the sea, and then outward, far outward, into red fog and dim fire that rolled around his plummeting body.

Oh God, he thought, if I guessed wrong and there *is* a beach . . .

The breath tore out of his lungs. His ears cracked, went dead. He held his arms out beyond his head, the thumbs locked together, his neck braced forward against the terrific upward push. He struck the surface of the sea.

There was no splash.

Dim coiling fire that drifted with infinite laziness around him, caressing his body with slow, tingling sparks. A feeling of lightness, as though his flesh had become one with the drifting fire. A sense of suffocation that had no basis in fact and gave way gradually to a strange exhilaration. There was no shock of impact, no crushing pressure. Merely a cushioning softness, like dropping into a bed of compressed air. Starke felt himself turning end over end, pinwheel fashion, and then that stopped, so that he sank quietly and without haste to the bottom.

Or rather, into the crystalline upper reaches of what seemed to be a forest.

He could see it spreading away along the downward-sloping floor of the ocean, into the vague red shadows of distance. Slender fantastic trunks upholding a maze of delicate shining branches, without leaves or fruit. They were like trees exquisitely molded from ice, transparent, holding the lambent shifting fire of the strange sea. Starke didn't think they were, or ever had been, alive. More like coral, he thought, or some vagary of mineral deposit. Beautiful, though. Like something you'd see in a dream. Beautiful, silent, and somehow deadly.

He couldn't explain that feeling of deadliness. Nothing moved in the red drifts between the trunks. It was nothing about the trees themselves. It was just something he sensed.

He began to move among the upper branches, following the downward drop of the slope.

He found that he could swim quite easily. Or perhaps it was more like flying. The dense gas buoyed him up, almost balancing the weight of his body, so that it was easy to swoop along, catching a crystal branch and using it as a lever to throw himself forward to the next one.

He went deeper and deeper into the heart of the forbidden Southern Ocean. Nothing stirred. The fairy forest stretched limitless ahead. And Starke was afraid.

Rann came into his mind abruptly. Her face, clearly outlined, was full of mockery.

"I'm going to watch you die, Hugh-Starke-Called-Conan. But before you die, I'll show you something. Look."

Her face dimmed, and in its place was Crom Dhu rising bleak into the red fog, the longships broken and sunk in the harbor, and Rann's fleet around it in a shining circle.

One ship in particular. The flagship. The vision in Starke's mind rushed toward it, narrowed down to the masthead platform. To the woman who stood there, naked, erect, her body lashed tight with thin cruel cords.

A woman with red hair blowing in the slow wind, and blue eyes that looked straight ahead like a falcon's, at Crom Dhu.

Beudag.

Rann's laughter ran across the picture and blurred it like a ripple of ice-cold water.

"You'd have done better," she said, "to take the clean steel when I offered it to you."

She was gone, and Starke's mind was as empty and cold as the mind of a corpse. He found that he was standing still, clinging to a branch, his face upturned as though by some blind instinct, his sight blurred.

He had never cried before in all his life, nor prayed.

There was no such thing as time, down there in the smoky shadows of the sea bottom. It might have been minutes or hours later that Hugh Starke discovered he was being hunted.

.  .  .

There were three of them, slipping easily among the shining branches. They were pale golden, almost phosphorescent, about the size of large hounds. Their eyes were huge, jewel-like in their slim sharp faces. They possessed four members that might have been legs and arms, retracted now against their arrowing bodies. Golden membranes spread wing-like from head to flank, and they moved like wings, balancing expertly the thrust of the flat, powerful tails.

They could have closed in on him easily, but they didn't seem to be in any hurry. Starke had sense enough not to wear himself out trying to get away. He kept on going, watching them. He discovered that the crystal branches could be broken, and he selected himself one with a sharp forked tip, shoving it swordwise under his belt. He didn't suppose it would do much good, but it made him feel better.

He wondered why the things didn't jump him and get it over with. They looked hungry enough, the way they were showing him their teeth. But they kept about the same distance away, in a sort of crescent formation, and every so often the ones on the outside would make a tentative dart at him, then fall back as he swerved away. It wasn't like being hunted so much as . . .

Starke's eyes narrowed. He began suddenly to feel much more afraid than he had before, and he wouldn't have believed that possible.

The things weren't hunting him at all. They were herding him.

There was nothing he could do about it. He tried stopping, and they swooped in and snapped at him, working expertly together so that while he was trying to stab one of them with his clumsy weapon, the others were worrying his heels like sheep-dogs at a recalcitrant wether.

Starke, like the wether, bowed to the inevitable and went where he was driven. The golden hounds showed their teeth in animal laughter and sniffed hungrily at the thread of blood he left behind him in the slow red coils of fire.

After a while he heard the music.

It seemed to be some sort of a harp, with a strange quality of vibration in the notes. It wasn't like anything he'd ever heard before. Perhaps the gas of which the sea was composed was an extraordinarily good conductor of sound, with a property of diffusion that made the music seem to come from everywhere at once—softly at first, like something touched upon in a dream, and then, as he drew closer to the source, swelling into a racing, rippling flood of melody that wrapped itself around his nerves with a demoniac shiver of ecstasy.

The golden hounds began to fret with excitement, spreading their shining wings, driving him impatiently faster through the crystal branches.

Starke could feel the vibration growing in him—the very fibres of his muscles shuddering in sympathy with the unearthly harp. He guessed there was a lot of the music he couldn't hear. Too high, too low for his ears to register. But he could feel it.

He began to go faster, not because of the hounds, but because he wanted to. The deep quivering in his flesh excited him. He began to breathe harder, partly because of increased exertion, and some chemical quality of the mixture he breathed made him slightly drunk.

The thrumming harp-song stroked and stung him, waking a deeper, darker music, and suddenly he saw Beudag clearly—half-veiled and mystic in the candle light at Faolan's dun; smooth curving bronze, her hair loose fire about her throat. A great stab of agony went through him. He called her name, once, and the harp-song swept it up and away, and then suddenly there was no music any more, and no forest, and nothing but cold embers in Starke's heart.

He could see everything quite clearly in the time it took him to float from the top of the last tree to the floor of the plain. He had no idea how long a time that was. It didn't matter. It was one of those moments when time doesn't have any meaning.

The rim of the forest fell away in a long curve that melted glistening into the spark-shot sea. From it the plain stretched out, a level glassy floor of black obsidian, the spew of some long-dead volcano. Or was it dead? It seemed to Starke that the light here was redder, more vital, as though he were close to the source from which it sprang.

As he looked farther over the plain, the light seemed to coalesce into a shimmering curtain that wavered like the heat veils that dance along the Mercurian Twilight Belt at high noon. For one brief instant he glimpsed a picture on the curtain—a city, black, shining, fantastically turreted, the gigantic reflection of a Titan's dream. Then it was gone, and the immediate menace of the foreground took all of Starke's attention.

. . .

He saw the flock, herded by more of the golden hounds. And he saw the shepherd, with the harp held silent between his hands.

The flock moved sluggishly, phosphorescently.

One hundred, two hundred silent, limply floating warriors drifting down the red dimness. In pairs, singly, or in pallid clusters they came. The golden hounds winged silently, leisurely around them, channeling them in tides that sluiced toward the fantastic ebon city.

The shepherd stood, a crop of obsidian turning his shark-pale face. His sharp, aquamarine eyes found Starke. His silvery hand leapt beckoning over harp-threads, striking them a blow. Reverberations ran out, seized Starke, shook him. He dropped his crystal dagger.

Hot screens of fire exploded in his eyes, bubbles whirled and danced in his eardrums. He lost all muscular control. His dark head fell forward against the thick blackness of hair on his chest; his golden eyes dissolved into weak, inane yellow, and his mouth loosened. He wanted to fight, but it was useless. This shepherd was one of the sea-people he had come to see, and one way or another he would see him.

Dark blood filled his aching eyes. He felt himself led, nudged, forced first this way, then that. A golden hound slipped by, gave him a pressure which roiled him over into a current of sea-blood. It ran down past where the shepherd stood with only a harp for a weapon.

Starke wondered dimly whether these other warriors in the flock, drifting, were dead or alive like himself. He had another surprise coming.

They were all Rann's men. Men of Falga. Silver men with burning green hair. Rann's men. One of them, a huge warrior colored like powdered salt, wandered aimlessly by on another tide, his green eyes dull. He looked dead.

What business had the sea-people with the dead warriors of Falga? Why the hounds and the shepherd's harp? Questions eddied like lifted silt in Starke's tired, hanging head. Eddied and settled flat.

Starke joined the pilgrimage.

The hounds with deft flickerings of wings, ushered him into the midst of the flock. Bodies brushed against him. *Cold* bodies. He wanted to cry out. The cords of his neck constricted. In his mind the cry went forward:

"Are you alive, men of Falga?"

No answer; but the drift of scarred, pale bodies. The eyes in them knew nothing. They had forgotten Falga. They had forgotten Rann for whom they had lifted blade. Their tongues lolling in mouths asked nothing but sleep. They were getting it.

A hundred, two hundred strong they made a strange human river slipping toward the gigantic city wall. Starke-Called-Conan and his bitter enemies going together. From the corners of his eyes, Starke saw the shepherd move. The shepherd was like Rann and her people who had years ago abandoned the sea to live on land. The shepherd seemed colder, more fish-like, though. There were small translucent webs between the thin fingers and spanning the long-toed feet. Thin, scar-like gills in the shadow of his tapered chin, lifted and sealed in the current, eating, taking sustenance from the blood-colored sea.

The harp spoke and the golden hounds obeyed. The harp spoke and the bodies twisted uneasily, as in a troubled sleep. A triple chord of it came straight at Starke. His fingers clenched.

"—and the dead shall walk again—"

Another ironic ripple of music.

"—and Rann's men will rise again, this time against her—"

Starke had time to feel a brief, bewildered shivering, before the current hurled him forward. Clamoring drunkenly, witlessly, all about him, the dead, muscleless warriors of Falga, tried to crush past him, all of them at once . . .

Long ago some vast sea Titan had dreamed of avenues struck from black stone. Each stone the size of three men tall. There had been a dream of walls going up and up until they dissolved into scarlet mist. There had been another dream of sea-gardens in which fish hung like erotic flowers, on tendrils of sensitive film-tissue. Whole beds of fish clung to garden base, like colonies of flowers aglow with sun-light. And on occasion a black amoebic presence filtered by, playing the gardener, weeding out an amber flower here, an amythystine bloom there.

And the sea Titan had dreamed of endless balustrades and battlements, of windowless turrets where creatures swayed like radium-skinned phantoms, carrying their green plumes of hair in their lifted palms and looked down with curious, insolent eyes from on high. Women with shimmering bodies like some incredible coral harvested and kept high over these black stone streets, each in its archway.

Starke was alone. Falga's warriors had gone off along a dim subterannean vent, vanished. Now the faint beckoning of harp and the golden hounds behind him, turned him down a passage that opened out into a large circular stone room, one end of which opened out into a hall. Around the ebon ceiling, slender schools of fish swam. It was their bright effulgence that gave light to the room. They had been there, breeding, eating, dying, a thousand years, giving light to the place, and they would be there, breeding and dying, a thousand more.

The harp faded until it was only a murmur.

Starke found his feet. Strength returned to him. He was able to see the man in the center of the room well. Too well.

The man hung in the fire tide. Chains of wrought bronze held his thin flesh-less ankles so he couldn't escape. His body desired it. It floated up.

It had been dead a long time. It was gaseous with decomposition and it wanted to rise to the surface of the Red Sea. The chains prevented this. Its arms weaved like white scarves before a sunken white face. Black hair trembled on end.

. . .

He was one of Faolan's men. One of the Rovers. One of those who had gone down at Falga because of Conan.

His name was Geil.

Starke remembered.

The part of him that was Conan remembered the name.

The dead lips moved.

"Conan. What luck is this! Conan. I make you welcome."

The words were cruel, the lips around them loose and dead. It seemed to Starke an anger and embittered wrath lay deep in those hollow eyes. The lips twitched again.

"I went down at Falga for you and Rann, Conan. Remember?"

Part of Starke remembered and twisted in agony.

"We're all here, Conan. All of us. Clev and Mannt and Bron and Aesur. Remember Aesur, who could shape metal over his spine, prying it with his fingers? Aesur is here, big as a sea-monster, waiting in a niche, cold and loose as string. The sea shepherds collected us. Collected us for a purpose of irony. Look!"

The boneless fingers hung out, as in a wind, pointing.

Starke turned slowly, and his heart pounded an uneven, shattering drum beat. His jaw clenched and his eyes blurred. That part of him that was Conan cried out. Conan was so much of him and he so much of Conan it was impossible for a cleavage. They'd grown together like pearl material around sand-specule, layer on layer. Starke cried out.

In the hall which this circular room overlooked, stood a thousand men.

In lines of fifty across, shoulder to shoulder, the men of Crom Dhu stared unseeingly up at Starke. Here and there a face became shockingly familiar. Old memory cried their names.

"Bron! Clev! Mannt! Aesur!"

The collected decomposition of their bodily fluids raised them, drifted them above the flaggings. Each of them was chained, like Geil.

Geil whispered. "We have made a union with the men of Falga!"

Starke pulled back.

"Falga!"

"In death, all men are equals." He took his time with it. He was in no hurry. Dead bodies under-sea are never in a hurry. They sort of bump and drift and bide their time. "The dead serve those who give them a semblance of life. Tomorrow we march against Crom Dhu."

"You're crazy! Crom Dhu is *your* home! It's the place of Beudag and Faolan—"

"And—" interrupted the hanging corpse, quietly, "Conan! Eh?" He laughed. A crystal dribble of bubbles ran up from the slack mouth. "Especially Conan. Conan who sank us at Falga . . ."

Starke moved swiftly. Nobody stopped him. He had the corpse's short blade in an instant. Geil's chest made a cold, silent sheathe for it. The blade went like a fork through butter.

Coldly, without noticing this, Geil's voice spoke out:

"Stab me, cut me. You can't kill me any deader. Make sections of me. Play butcher. A flank, a hand, a heart! And while you're at it, I'll tell you the plan."

Snarling, Starke seized the blade out again. With blind violence he gave sharp blow after blow at the body, cursing bitterly, and the body took each blow, rocking in the red tide a little, and said with a matter-of-fact tone:

"We'll march out of the sea to Crom Dhu's gates. Romna and the others, looking down, recognizing us, will have the gates thrown wide to welcome us." The head tilted lazily, the lips peeled wide and folded down languidly over the words. "Think of the elation, Conan! The moment when Bron and Mannt and Aesur and I and yourself, yes, even yourself, Conan, return to Crom Dhu!"

. . .

Starke saw it, vividly. Saw it like a tapestry woven for him. He stood back, gasping for breath, his nostrils flaring, seeing what his blade had done to Geil's body, and seeing the great stone gates of Crom Dhu crashing open. The deliberation. The happiness, the elation to Faolan and Romna to see old friends returned. Old Rovers, long thought dead. Alive again, come to help! It made a picture!

With great deliberation, Starke struck flat across before him.

Geil's head, severed from its lazy body, began, with infinite tiredness, to float toward the ceiling. As it traveled upward, now facing, now bobbling the back of its skull toward Starke, it finished its nightmare speaking:

"And then, once inside the gates, what then, Conan? Can you guess? Can you guess what we'll do, Conan?"

Starke stared at nothingness, the sword trembling in his fist. From far away he heard Geil's voice:

"—we will kill Faolan in his hall. He will die with surprised lips. Romna's harp will lie in his disemboweled stomach. His heart with its last pulsings will sound the strings. And as for Beudag—"

Starke tried to push the thoughts away, raging and helpless. Geil's body was no longer anything to look at. He had done all he could to it. Starke's face was bleached white and scraped down to the insane bone of it, "You'd kill your own people!"

Geil's separated head lingered at the ceiling, light-fish illuminating its ghastly features. "Our people? But we have no people. We're another race now. The dead. We do the biddings of the sea shepherds."

Starke looked out into the hall, then he looked at the circular wall.

"Okay," he said, without tone in his voice. "Come out. Where ever you're hiding and using this voice-throwing act. Come on out and talk straight."

In answer, an entire section of ebon stones fell back on silent hingework. Starke saw a long slender black marble table. Six people sat behind it in carven midnight thrones.

They were all men. Naked except for film-like garments about their loins. They looked at Starke with no particular hatred or curiosity. One of them cradled a harp. It was the shepherd who'd drawn Starke through the gate. Amusedly, his webbed fingers lay on the strings, now and then bringing out a clear sound from one of the two hundred strands.

The shepherd stopped Starke's rush forward with a cry of that harp!

The blade in his hand was red hot. He dropped it.

The shepherd put a head on the story. "And then? And then we will march Rann's dead warriors all the way to Falga. There, Rann's people, seeing the warriors, will be overjoyed, hysterical to find their friends and relatives returned. They, too, will fling wide Falga's defenses. And death will walk in, disguised as resurrection."

Starke nodded, slowly, wiping his hand across his cheek. "Back on Earth we call that psychology. *Good* psychology. But will it fool Rann?"

"Rann will be with her ships at Crom Dhu. While she's gone, the innocent population will let in their lost warriors gladly." The shepherd had amused green eyes. He looked like a youth of some seventeen years. Deceptively young. If Starke guessed right, the youth was nearer to two centuries old. That's how you lived and looked when you were under the Red Sea. Something about the emanations of it kept part of you young.

Starke lidded his yellow hawks' eyes thoughtfully. "You've got all aces. You'll win. But what's Crom Dhu to you? Why not just Rann? She's one of you, you hate her more than you do the Rovers. Her ancestors came up on land, you never got over hating them for that—"

The shepherd shrugged. "Toward Crom Dhu we have little actual hatred. Except that they are by nature land-men, even if they do rove by boat, and pillagers. One day they might try their luck on the sunken devices of this city."

Starke put a hand out. "We're fighting Rann, too. Don't forget, we're on your side!"

"Whereas we are on no one's," retorted the green-haired youth, "Except our own. Welcome to the army which will attack Crom Dhu."

"Me! By the gods, over my dead body!"

"That," said the youth, amusedly, "is what we intend. We've worked many years, you see, to perfect the plan. We're not much good out on land. We needed bodies that could do the work for us. So, every time Faolan lost a ship or Rann lost a ship, we were there, with our golden hounds, waiting. Collecting. Saving. Waiting until we had enough of each side's warriors. They'll do the fighting for us. Oh, not for long, of course. The Source energy will give them a semblance of life, a momentary electrical ability of walk and combat, but once out of water they'll last only half an hour. But that should be time enough once the gates of Crom Dhu and Falga are open."

.  .  .

Starke said, "Rann will find some way around you. Get her first. Attack Crom Dhu the following day."

The youth deliberated. "You're stalling. But there's sense in it. Rann is most important. We'll get Falga first, then. You'll have a bit of time in which to raise false hopes."

Starke began to get sick again. The room swam.

Very quietly, very easily, Rann came into his mind again. He felt her glide in like the merest touch of a sea fern weaving in a tide pool.

He closed his mind down, but not before she snatched at a shred of thought. Her acquamarine eyes reflected desire and inquiry.

"Hugh Starke, you're with the sea people?"

Her voice was soft. He shook his head.

"Tell me, Hugh Starke. How are you plotting against Falga?"

He said nothing. He thought nothing. He shut his eyes.

Her fingernails glittered, raking at his mind. "Tell me!"

His thoughts rolled tightly into a metal sphere which nothing could dent.

Rann laughed unpleasantly and leaned forward until she filled every dark horizon of his skull with her shimmering body. "All right. I *gave* you Conan's body. Now I'll take it away."

She struck him a combined blow of her eyes, her writhing lips, her bone-sharp teeth. "Go back to your old body, go back to your old body, Hugh Starke," she hissed. "Go back! Leave Conan to his idiocy. Go back to your old body!"

Fear had him. He fell down upon his face, quivering and jerking. You could fight a man with a sword. But how could you fight this thing in your brain? He began to suck sobbing breaths through his lips. He was screaming. He could not hear himself. Her voice rushed in from the dim outer red universe, destroying him.

"Hugh Starke! Go back to your old body!"

His old body was—dead!

And she was sending him back into it.

Part of him shot endwise through red fog.

He lay on a mountain plateau overlooking the harbor of Falga.

Red fog coiled and snaked around him. Flame birds dived eerily down at his staring, blind eyes.

His old body held him.

Putrefaction stuffed his nostrils. The flesh sagged and slipped greasily on his loosened structure. He felt small again and ugly. Flame birds nibbled, picking, choosing between his ribs. Pain gorged him. Cold, blackness, nothingness filled him. Back in his old body. Forever.

He didn't want that.

The plateau, the red fog vanished. The flame birds, too.

He lay once more on the floor of the sea shepherds, struggling.

"That was just a start," Rann told him. "Next time, I'll leave you up there on the plateau in that body. *Now,* will you tell the plans of the sea people? And go on living in Conan? He's yours, if you tell." She smirked. "You don't want to be dead."

Starke tried to reason it out. Any way he turned was the wrong way. He grunted out a breath. "If I tell, you'll still kill Beudag."

"Her life in exchange for what you know, Hugh Starke."

Her answer was too swift. It had the sound of treachery. Starke did not believe. He would die. That would solve it. Then, at least, Rann would die when the sea people carried out their strategy. That much revenge, at least, damn it.

Then he got the idea.

He coughed out a laugh, raised his weak head to look at the startled sea shepherd. His little dialogue with Rann had taken about ten seconds, actually, but it had seemed a century. The sea shepherd stepped forward.

Starke tried to get to his feet. "Got—got a proposition for you. You with the harp. Rann's inside me. *Now.* Unless you guarantee Crom Dhu and Beudag's safety, I'll tell her some things she might want to be in on!"

The sea shepherd drew a knife.

Starke shook his head coldly. "Put it away. Even if you get me I'll give the whole damned strategy to Rann."

The shepherd dropped his hand. He was no fool.

Rann tore at Starke's brain. "Tell me! Tell me their plan!"

He felt like a guy in a revolving door. Starke got the sea men in focus. He saw that they were afraid now, doubtful and nervous. "I'll be dead in a minute," said Starke. "Promise me the safety of Crom Dhu and I'll die without telling Rann a thing."

The sea shepherd hesitated, then raised his palm upward. "I promise," he said. "Crom Dhu will go untouched."

Starke sighed. He let his head fall forward until it hit the floor. Then he rolled over, put his hands over his eyes. "It's a deal. Go give Rann hell for me, will you, boys? Give her hell!"

As he drifted into mind darkness, Rann waited for him. Feebly, he told her. "Okay, duchess. You'd kill me even if I'd told you the idea. I'm ready. Try your god-awfullest to shove me back into that stinking body of mine. I'll fight you all the way there!"

Rann screamed. It was a pretty frustrated scream. Then the pains began. She did a lot of work on his mind in the next minute.

That part of him that was Conan held on like a clam holding to its precious contents.

The odor of putrid flesh returned. The blood mist returned. The flame birds fell down at him in spirals of sparks and blistering smoke, to winnow his naked ribs.

Starke spoke one last word before the blackness took him.

"Beudag."

. . .

He never expected to awaken again.

He awoke just the same.

There was red sea all around him. He lay on a kind of stone bed, and the young sea shepherd sat beside him, looking down at him, smiling delicately.

Starke did not dare move for a while. He was afraid his head might fall off and whirl away like a big fish, using its ears as propellers. "Lord," he muttered, barely turning his head.

The sea creature stirred. "You won. You fought Rann, and won."

Starke groaned. "I feel like something passed through a wild-cat's intestines. She's gone. Rann's gone." He laughed. "That makes me sad. Somebody cheer me up. Rann's gone." He felt of his big, flat-muscled body. "She was bluffing. Trying to drive me batty. She knew she couldn't really tuck me back into that carcass, but she didn't want me to know. It was like a baby's nightmare before it's born. Or maybe you haven't got a memory like me." He rolled over, stretching. "She won't ever get in my head again. I've locked the gate and swallowed the key." His eyes dilated. "What's *your* name?"

"Linnl," said the man with the harp. "You didn't tell Rann our strategy?"

"What do *you* think?"

Linnl smiled sincerely. "I think I like you, man of Crom Dhu. I think I like your hatred for Rann. I think I like the way you handled the entire matter, wanted to kill Rann and save Crom Dhu, and being so willing to die to accomplish either."

"That's a lot of thinking. Yeah, and what about that promise you made?"

"It will be kept."

Starke gave him a hand. "Linnl, you're okay. If I ever get back to Earth, so help me, I'll never bait a hook again and drop it in the sea." It was lost to Linnl. Starke forgot it, and went on, laughing. There was an edge of hysteria to it. Relief. You got booted around for days, people milled in and out of your mind like it was a bargain basement counter, pawing over the treads and convolutions, yelling and fighting; the woman you loved was starved on a ship masthead, and as a climax a lady with green eyes tried to make you a filling for an accident-mangled body. And now you had an ally.

And you couldn't believe it.

He laughed in little starts and stops, his eyes shut.

"Will you let me take care of Rann when the time comes?"

His fingers groped hungrily upward, closed on an imaginary figure of her, pressed, tightened, choked.

Linnl said, "She's yours. I'd like the pleasure, but you have as much if not more of a revenge to take. Come along. We start now. You've been asleep for one entire period."

Starke let himself down gingerly. He didn't want to break a leg off. He felt if someone touched him he might disintegrate.

He managed to let the tide handle him, do all the work. He swam carefully after Linnl down three passageways where an occasional silver inhabitant of the city slid by.

Drifting below them in a vast square hall, each gravitating but imprisoned by leg-shackles, the warriors of Falga looked up with pale cold eyes at Starke and Linnl. Occasional discharges of light-fish from interstices in the walls, passed luminous, fleeting glows over the warriors. The light-fish flirted briefly in a long shining rope that tied knots around the dead faces and as quickly untied them. Then the light-fish pulsed away and the red color of the sea took over.

Bathed in wine, thought Starke, without humor. He leaned forward.

"Men of Falga!"

Linnl plucked a series of harp-threads.

"Aye." A deep suggestion of sound issued from a thousand dead lips.

"We go to sack Rann's citadel!"

"Rann!" came the muffled thunder of voices.

At the sound of another tune, the golden hounds appeared. They touched the chains. The men of Falga, released, danced through the red sea substance.

Siphoned into a valve mouth, they were drawn out into a great volcanic court-yard. Starke went close after. He stared down into a black ravine, at the bottom of which was a blazing caldera.

This was the Source Life of the Red Sea. Here it had begun a millennium ago. Here the savage cyclones of sparks and fire energy belched up, shaking titanic black garden walls, causing currents and whirlpools that threatened to suck you forward and shoot you violently up to the surface, in cannulas of force, thrust, in capillaries of ignited mist, in chutes of color that threatened to cremate but only exhilarated you, gave you a seething rebirth!

He braced his legs and fought the suction. An unbelievable sinew of fire sprang up from out the ravine, crackling and roaring.

The men of Falga did not fight the attraction.

They moved forward in their silence and hung over the incandescence.

The vitality of the Source grew upward in them. It seemed to touch their san-daled toes first, and then by a process of shining osmosis, climb up the limbs, into the loins, into the vitals, delineating their strong bone structure as mercury delineates the glass thermometer with a rise of temperature. The bones flickered like carved polished ivory through the momentarily film-like flesh. The ribs of a thousand men expanded like silvered spider legs, clenched, then expanded again. Their spines straightened, their shoulders flattened back. Their eyes, the last to take the fire, now were ignited and glowed like candles in refurbished sepulchers. The chins snapped up, the entire outer skins of their bodies broke into silver brilliance.

Swimming through the storm of energy like nightmare figments, entering cold, they reached the far side of the ravine resembling smelted metal from blast furnaces. When they brushed into one another, purple sparks sizzled, jumped from head to head, from hand to hand.

Linnl touched Starke's arm. "You're next."

"No thank you."

"Afraid?" laughed the harp-shepherd. "You're tired. It will give you new life. You're next."

.  .  .

Starke hesitated only a moment. Then he let the tide drift him rapidly out. He was afraid. Damned afraid. A belch of fire caught him as he arrived in the core of the ravine. He was wrapped in layers of ecstasy. Beudag pressed against him. It was her consuming hair that netted him and branded him. It was her warmth that crept up his body into his chest and into his head. Somebody yelled somewhere in animal delight and unbearable passion. Somebody danced and threw out his hands and crushed that solar warmth deeper into his huge body. Somebody felt all tiredness, oldness flumed away, a whole new feeling of warmth and strength inserted.

That somebody was Starke.

Waiting on the other side of the ravine were a thousand men of Falga. What sounded like a thousand harps began playing now, and as Starke reached the other side, the harps began marching, and the warriors marched with them. They were still dead, but you would never know it. There were no minds inside those bodies. The bodies were being activated from outside. But you would never know it.

They left the city behind. In embering ranks, the soldier-fighters were led by golden hounds and distant harps to a place where a huge intra-coastal tide swept by.

They got on the tide for a free ride. Linnl beside him, using his harp, Starke felt himself sucked down through a deep where strange monsters sprawled. They looked at Starke with hungry eyes. But the harp wall swept them back.

Starke glanced about at the men. They don't know what they're doing, he thought. Going home to kill their parents and their children, to set the flame to Falga, and they don't know it. Their alive-but-dead faces tilted up, always upward, as though visions of Rann's citadel were there.

Rann. Starke let the warmth simmer in him. He let it cool. Then it was cold. Rann hadn't bothered him now for hours. Was there a chance she'd read his thought in the midst of that fighting nightmare? Did she know this plan for Falga? Was that an explanation for her silence now?

He sent his mind ahead, subtly. *Rann. Rann.* The only answer was the move of silver bodies through the fiery deeps.

Just before dawn they broke the surface of the sea.

Falga drowsed in the red-smeared fog silence. Its slave streets were empty and dew-covered. High up, the first light was bathing Rann's gardens and setting her citadel aglow.

Linnl lay in the shallows beside Starke. They both were smiling half-cruel smiles. They had waited long for this.

Linnl nodded. "This is the day of the carnival. Fruit, wine and love will be offered the returned soldiers of Rann. In the streets there'll be dancing."

Far over to the right lay a rise of mountain. At its blunt peak—Starke stared at it intently—rested a body of a little, scrawny Earthman, with flame birds clustered on it. He'd climb that mountain later. When it was over and there was time.

"What are you searching for?" asked Linnl.

Starke's voice was distant. "Someone I used to know."

Filing out on the stone quays, their rustling sandals eroded by time, the men stood clean and bright. Starke paced, a caged animal, at their center, so his dark body would pass unnoticed.

They were seen.

The cliff guard looked down over the dirty slave dwellings, from their arrow galleries, and set up a cry. Hands waved, pointed frosty white in the dawn. More guards loped down the ramps and galleries, meeting, joining others and coming on.

Linnl, in the sea by the quay, suggested a theme on the harp. The other harps took it up. The shuddering music lifted from the water and with a gentle firmness, set the dead feet marching down the quays, upward through the narrow, stifling alleys of the slaves, to meet the guard.

Slave people peered out at them tiredly from their choked quarters. The passing of warriors was old to them, of no significance.

These warriors carried no weapons. Starke didn't like that part of it. A length of chain even, he wanted. But this emptiness of the hands. His teeth ached from too long a time of clenching his jaws tight. The muscles of his arms were feverish and nervous.

At the edge of the slave community, at the cliff base, the guard confronted them. Running down off the galleries, swords naked, they ran to intercept what they took to be an enemy.

The guards stopped in blank confusion.

.  .  .

A little laugh escaped Starke's lips. It was a dream. With fog over, under and in between its parts. It wasn't real to the guard, who couldn't believe it. It wasn't real to these dead men either, who were walking around. He felt alone. He was the only live one. He didn't like walking with dead men.

The captain of the guard came down warily, his green eyes suspicious. The suspicion faded. His face fell apart. He had lain on his fur pelts for months thinking of his son who had died to defend Falga.

Now his son stood before him. Alive.

The captain forgot he was captain. He forgot everything. His sandals scraped over stones. You could hear the air go out of his lungs and come back in a numbed prayer.

"My son! In Rann's name. They said you were slain by Faolan's men one hundred darknesses ago. My son!"

A harp tinkled somewhere.

The son stepped forward, smiling.

They embraced. The son said nothing. He couldn't speak.

This was the signal for the others. The whole guard, shocked and surprised, put away their swords and sought out old friends, brothers, fathers, uncles, sons!

They moved up the galleries, the guard and the returned warriors, Starke in their midst. Threading up the cliff, through passage after passage, all talking at once. Or so it seemed. The guards did the talking. None of the dead warriors replied. They only *seemed* to. Starke heard the music strong and clear everywhere.

They reached the green gardens atop the cliff. By this time the entire city was awake. Women came running, bare-breasted and sobbing, and throwing themselves forward into the ranks of their lovers. Flowers showered over them.

"So this is war," muttered Starke, uneasily.

They stopped in the center of the great gardens. The crowd milled happily, not yet aware of the strange silence from their men. They were too happy to notice.

"Now," cried Starke to himself. "Now's the time. Now!"

As if in answer, a wild skirling of harps out of the sky.

The crowd stopped laughing only when the returned warriors of Falga swept forward, their hands lifted and groping before them . . .

The crying in the streets was like a far siren wailing. Metal made a harsh clangor that was sheathed in silence at the same moment metal found flesh to lie in. A vicious pantomime was concluded in the green moist gardens.

Starke watched from Rann's empty citadel. Fog plumes strolled by the archways and a thick rain fell. It came like a blood squall and washed the garden below until you could not tell rain from blood.

The returned warriors had gotten their swords by now. First they killed those nearest them in the celebration. Then they took the weapons from the victims. It was very simple and very unpleasant.

The slaves had joined battle now. Swarming up from the slave town, plucking up fallen daggers and short swords, they circled the gardens, happening upon the arrogant shining warriors of Rann who had so far escaped the quiet, deadly killing of the alive-but-dead men.

Dead father killed startled, alive son. Dead brother garroted unbelieving brother. Carnival indeed in Falga.

An old man waited alone. Starke saw him. The old man had a weapon, but refused to use it. A young warrior of Falga, harped on by Linnl's harp, walked quietly up to the old man. The old man cried out. His mouths formed words. "Son! What *is* this?" He flung down his blade and made to plead with his boy.

The son stabbed him with silent efficiency, and without a glance at the body, walked onward to find another.

Starke turned away, sick and cold.

A thousand such scenes were being finished.

He set fire to the black spider-silk tapestries. They whispered and talked with flame. The stone echoed his feet as he searched room after room. Rann had gone, probably last night. That meant that Crom Dhu was on the verge of falling. Was Faolan dead? Had the people of Crom Dhu, seeing Beudag's suffering, given in? Falga's harbor was completely devoid of ships, except for small fishing skiffs.

The fog awaited him when he returned to the garden. Rain found his face.

The citadel of Rann was fire-encrusted and smoke shrouded as he looked up at it.

A silence lay in the garden. The fight was over.

The men of Falga, still shining with Source-Life, hung their blades from un-comprehending fingers, the light beginning to leave their green eyes. Their skin looked dirty and dull.

Starke wasted no time getting down the galleries, through the slave quarter, and to the quays again.

Linnl awaited him, gently petting the obedient harp.

"It's over. The slaves will own what's left. They'll be our allies, since we've freed them."

Starke didn't hear. He was squinting off over the Red Sea.

Linnl understood. He plucked two tones from the harp, which pronounced the two words uppermost in Starke's thought.

"Crom Dhu."

"If we're not too late." Starke leaned forward. "If Faolan lives. If Beudag still stands at the masthead."

Like a blind man he walked straight ahead, until he fell into the sea.

. . .

It was not quite a million miles to Crom Dhu. It only seemed that far. A sweep of tide picked them up just off shore from Falga and siphoned them rap-idly, through deeps along coastal latitudes, through crystal forests. He cursed every mile of the way.

He cursed the time it took to pause at the Titan's city to gather fresh men. To gather Clev and Mannt and Aesur and Bron. Impatiently, Starke watched the whole drama of the Source-Fire and the bodies again. This time it was the bodies of Crom Dhu men, hung like beasts on slow-turned spits, their limbs and vitals soaking through and through, their skins taking bronze color, their eyes holding flint-sparks. And then the harps wove a garment around each, and the garment moved the men instead of the men the garment.

In the tidal basilic now, Starke twisted. Coursing behind him were the new bodies of Clev and Aesur! The current elevated them, poked them through obsidian needle-eyes like spider-silk threads.

There was good irony in this. Crom Dhu's men, fallen at Falga under Conan's treachery, returned now under Conan, to exonerate that treachery.

Suddenly they were in Crom Dhu's outer basin. Shadows swept over them. The long dark falling shadows of Falga's longboats lying in that harbor. Shadows like black culling-nets let down. The school of men cleaved the shadow nets. The tide ceased here, eddied and distilled them.

Starke glared up at the immense silver bottom of a Falgian ship. He felt his face stiffen and his throat tighten. Then, flexing knees, he rammed upward, night air broke dark red around his head.

The harbor held flare torches on the rims of longships. On the neck of land that led from Crom Dhu to the mainland the continuing battle sounded. Faint cries and clashing made their way through the fog veils. They sounded like echoes of past dreams.

Linnl let Starke have the leash. Starke felt something pressed into his fist. A coil of slender green woven reeds, a rope with hooked weights on the end of it. He knew how to use it without asking. But he wished for a knife, now, even though he realized carrying a knife in the sea was all but impossible if you wanted to move fast.

He saw the sleek naked figurehead of Rann's best ship a hundred yards away, a floating silhouette, its torches hanging fire like Beudag's hair.

He swam toward it, breathing quietly. When at last the silvered figurehead with the mocking green eyes and the flag of shoal-shallow hair hung over him, he felt the cool white ship metal kiss his fingers.

The smell of torch-smoke lingered. A rise of faint shouts from the land told of another rush upon the Gate. Behind him—a ripple. Then—a thousand ripples.

The resurrected men of Crom Dhu rose in dents and stirrings of sparkling wine. They stared at Crom Dhu and maybe they knew what it was and maybe they didn't. For one moment, Starke felt apprehension. Suppose Linnl was playing a game. Suppose, once these men had won the battle, they went on into Crom Dhu, to rupture Romna's harp and make Faolan the blinder? He shook the thought away. That would have to be handled in time. On either side of him Clev and Mannt appeared. They looked at Crom Dhu, their lips shut. Maybe they saw Faolan's eyrie and heard a harp that was more than these harps that sang them to blade and plunder—Romna's instrument telling bard-tales of the rovers and the coastal wars and the old, living days. Their eyes looked and looked at Crom Dhu, but saw nothing.

The sea shepherds appeared now; the followers of Linnl, each with his harp and the harp music began, high. So high you couldn't hear it. It wove a tension on the air.

Silently, with a grim certainty, the dead-but-not-dead gathered in a bronze circle about Rann's ship. The very silence of their encirclement made your skin crawl and sweat break cold on your cheeks.

A dozen ropes went raveling, looping over the ship side. They caught, held, grapnelled, hooked.

Starke had thrown his, felt it bite and hold. Now he scrambled swiftly, cursing, up its length, kicking and slipping at the silver hull.

He reached the top.

Beudag was there.

Half over the low rail he hesitated, just looking at her.

. . .

Torchlight limned her, shadowed her. She was still erect; her head was tired and her eyes were closed, her face thinned and less brown, but she was still alive. She was coming out of a deep stupor now, at the whistle of the ropes and the grate of metal hooks on the deck.

She saw Starke and her lips parted. She did not look away from him. His breath came out of him, choking.

It almost cost him his life, his standing there, looking at her.

A guard, with flesh like new snow, shafted his bow from the turret and let it loose. A chain lay on deck. Thankfully, Starke took it.

Clev came over the rail beside Starke. His chest took the arrow. The shaft burst half through and stopped, held. Clev kept going after the man who had shot it. He caught up with him.

Beudag cried out. "Behind you, Conan!"

Conan! In her excitement, she gave the old name.

Conan he *was*. Whirling, he confronted a wiry little fellow, chained him brutally across the face, seized the man's falling sword, used it on him. Then he walked in, got the man's jaw, unbalanced him over into the sea.

The ship was awake now. Most of the men had been down below, resting from the battles. Now they came pouring up, in a silver spate. Their yelling was in strange contrast to the calm silence of Crom Dhu's men. Starke found himself busy.

Conan had been a healthy animal, with great recuperative powers. Now his muscles responded to every trick asked of them. Starke leaped cleanly across the deck, watching for Rann, but she was no where to be seen. He engaged two blades, dispatched one of them. More ropes raveled high and snaked him. Every ship in the harbor was exploding with violence. More men swarmed over the rail behind Starke, silently.

Above the shouting, Beudag's voice came, at sight of the fighting men. "Clev! Mannt! Aesur!"

Starke was a god, anything he wanted he could have. A man's head? He could have it. It meant acting the guillotine with knife and wrist and lunged body. Like—*this!* His eyes were smoking amber and there were deep lines of grim pleasure tugging at his lips. An enemy cannot fight without hands. One man, facing Starke, suddenly displayed violent stumps before his face, not believing them.

Are you watching, Faolan, cried Starke inside himself, delivering blows. Look here, Faolan! God, no, you're blind. *Listen* then! Hear the ring of steel on steel. Does the smell of hot blood and hot bodies reach you? Oh, if you could see this tonight, Faolan. Falga would be forgotten. This is Conan, out of idiocy, with a guy named Starke wearing him and telling him where to go!

It was not safe on deck. Starke hadn't particularly noticed before, but the warriors of Crom Dhu didn't care whom they attacked now. They were beginning to do surgery to one another. They excised one another's shoulders, severed limbs in blind instantaneous obedience. This was no place for Beudag and himself.

He cut her free of the masthead, drew her quickly to the rail.

Beudag was laughing. She could do nothing but laugh. Her eyes were shocked. She saw dead men alive again, lashing out with weapons; she had been starved and made to stand night and day, and now she could only laugh.

Starke shook her.

She did not stop laughing.

"Beudag! You're all right. You're free."

She stared at nothing. "I'll—I'll be all right in a minute."

He had to ward off a blow from one of his own men. He parried the thrust, then got in and pushed the man off the deck, over into the sea. That was the only thing to do. You couldn't kill them.

Beudag stared down at the tumbling body.

"Where's Rann?" Starke's yellow eyes narrowed, searching.

"She *was* here." Beudag trembled.

Rann looked out of her eyes. Out of the tired numbness of Beudag, an echo of Rann. Rann was nearby, and this was her doing.

Instinctively, Starke raised his eyes.

Rann appeared at the masthead, like a flurry of snow. Her green-tipped breasts were rising and falling with emotion. Pure hatred lay in her eyes. Starke licked his lips and readied his sword.

Rann snapped a glance at Beudag. Stooping, as in a dream, Beudag picked up a dagger and held it to her own breast.

Starke froze.

Rann nodded, with satisfaction. "Well, Starke? How will it be? Will you come at me and have Beudag die? Or will you let me go free?"

Starke's palms felt sweaty and greasy. "There's no place for you to go. Falga's taken. I can't guarantee your freedom. If you want to go over the side, into the sea, that's your chance. You might make shore and your own men."

"Swimming? With the sea-*beasts* waiting?" She accented the *beasts* heavily. She was one of the sea-*people*. They, Linnl and his men, were sea-*beasts*. "No, Hugh Starke. I'll take a skiff. Put Beudag at the rail where I can watch her all the way. Guarantee my passage to shore and my own men there, and Beudag lives."

Starke waved his sword. "Get going."

He didn't want to let her go. He had other plans, good plans for her. He shouted the deal down at Linnl. Linnl nodded back, with much reluctance.

Rann, in a small silver skiff, headed toward land. She handled the boat and looked back at Beudag all the while. She passed through the sea-beasts and touched the shore. She lifted her hand and brought it smashing down.

Whirling, Starke swung his fist against Beudag's jaw. Her hand was already striking the blade into her breast. Her head flopped back. His fist carried through. She fell. The blade clattered. He kicked it overboard. Then he lifted Beudag. She was warm and good to hold. The blade had only pricked her breast. A small rivulet of blood ran.

On the shore, Rann vanished upward on the rocks, hurrying to find her men.

In the harbor the harp music paused. The ships were taken. Their crews lay filling the decks. Crom Dhu's men stopped fighting as quickly as they'd started. Some of the bright shining had dulled from the bronze of their arms and bare torsos. The ships began to sink.

Linnl swam below, looking up at Starke. Starke looked back at him and nodded at the beach. "Swell. Now, let's go get that she-devil," he said.

•  •  •

Faolan waited on his great stone balcony, overlooking Crom Dhu. Behind him the fires blazed high and their eating sound of flame on wood filled the pillared gloom with sound and furious light.

Faolan leaned against the rim, his chest swathed in bandage and healing ointment, his blind eyes flickering, looking down again and again with a fixed intensity, his head tilted to listen.

Romna stood beside him, filled and refilled the cup that Faolan emptied into his thirsty mouth, and told him what happened. Told of the men pouring out of the sea, and Rann appearing on the rocky shore. Sometimes Faolan leaned to one side, weakly, toward Romna's words. Sometimes he twisted to hear the thing itself, the thing that happened down beyond the Gate of besieged Crom Dhu.

Romna's harp lay untouched. He didn't play it. He didn't need to. From below, a great echoing of harps, more liquid than his, like a waterfall drenched the city, making the fog sob down red tears.

"Are those harps?" cried Faolan.

"Yes, harps!"

"What was that?" Faolan listened, breathing harshly, clutching for support.

"A skirmish," said Romna.

"Who won?"

"*We* won."

"And *that?*" Faolan's blind eyes tried to see until they watered.

"The enemy falling back from the Gate!"

"And that sound, and that sound!" Faolan went on and on, feverishly, turning this way and that, the lines of his face agonized and attentive to each eddy and current and change of tide. The rhythm of swords through fog and body was a complicated music whose themes he must recognize. "Another fell! I heard him cry. And another of Rann's men!"

"Yes," said Romna.

"But why do our warriors fight so quietly? I've heard nothing from their lips. So quiet."

Romna scowled. "Quiet. Yes—quiet."

"And where did they come from? All our men are in the city?"

"Aye." Romna shifted. He hesitated, squinting. He rubbed his bulldog jaw. "Except those that died at—Falga."

Faolan stood there a moment. Then he rapped his empty cup.

"More wine, bard. More wine."

He turned to the battle again.

"Oh, gods, if I could see it, if I could only see it!"

Below, a ringing crash. A silence. A shouting, a pouring of noise.

"The Gate!" Faolan was stricken with fear. "We've lost! My sword!"

"Stay, Faolan!" Romna laughed. Then he sighed. It was a sigh that did not believe. "In the name of ten thousand mighty gods. Would that I were blind now, or could see better."

Faolan's hand caught, held him. "What *is* it? Tell!"

"Clev! And Tlan! And Conan! And Bron! And Mannt! Standing in the gate, like wine visions! Swords in their hands!"

Faolan's hand relaxed, then tightened.

"Speak their names again, and speak them slowly. And tell the truth." His skin shivered like that of a nervous animal. "You said—Clev? Mannt? Bron?"

"And Tlan! And Conan! Back from Falga. They've opened the Gate and the battle's won. It's over, Faolan. Crom Dhu will sleep tonight."

Faolan let him go. A sob broke from his lips. "I will get drunk. Drunker than ever in my life. Gloriously drunk. Gods, but if I could have seen it. Been in it. Tell me again of it, Romna . . ."

. . .

Faolan sat in the great hall, on his carved high seat, waiting.

The pad of sandals on stone, outside, the jangle of chains.

A door flung wide, red fog sluiced in, and in the sluice, people walking. Faolan started up. "Clev? Mannt? Aesur!"

Starke came forward into the fire-light. He pressed his right hand to the open mouth of wound on his thigh. "No, Faolan. Myself and two others."

"Beudag?"

"Yes." And Beudag came wearily to him.

Faolan stared. "Who's the other? It walks light. It's a woman."

Starke nodded. "Rann."

Faolan rose carefully from his seat. He thought the name over. He took a short sword from a place beside the high seat. He stepped down. He walked toward Starke. "You brought Rann alive to me?"

Starke pulled the chain that bound Rann. She ran forward in little steps, her white face down, her eyes slitted with animal fury.

"Faolan's blind," said Starke. "I let you live for one damned good reason, Rann. Okay, go ahead."

Faolan stopped walking, curious. He waited.

Rann did nothing.

Starke took her hand and wrenched it behind her back. "I said 'go ahead.' Maybe you didn't hear me."

"I will," she gasped, in pain.

Starke released her. "Tell me what happens, Faolan."

Rann gazed steadily at Faolan's tall figure there in the light.

Faolan suddenly threw his hands to his eyes and choked.

Beudag cried out, seized his arm.

"I can see!" Faolan staggered, as if jolted. "I can see!" First he shouted it, then he whispered it. "*I can see.*"

Starke's eyes blurred. He whispered to Rann, tightly. "Make him see it, Rann, or you die now. Make him see it!" to Faolan. "What do you see?"

Faolan was bewildered, he swayed. He put out his hands to shape the vision. "I—I see Crom Dhu. It's a good sight. I see the ships of Rann. Sinking!" He laughed a broken laugh. "I—see the fight beyond the gate!"

Silence swam in the room, over their heads.

Faolan's voice went alone, and hypnotized, into that silence. He put out his big fists, shook them, opened them. "I see Mannt, and Aesur and Clev! Fighting as they always fought. I see Conan as he was. I see Beudag wielding steel again, on the shore! I see the enemy killed! I see men pouring out of the sea with brown skins and dark hair. Men I knew a long darkness ago. Men that roved the sea with me. *I see Rann captured!*" He began to sob with it, his lungs filling and releasing it, sucking in on it, blowing it out. Tears ran down from his vacant, blazing eyes. "I see Crom Dhu as it was and is and shall be! *I see, I see, I see!*"

Starke felt the chill on the back of his neck.

"I see Rann captured and held, and her men dead around her on the land before the Gate. I see the Gate thrown open—" Faolan halted. He looked at Starke. "Where are Clev and Mannt? Where is Bron and Aesur?"

Starke let the fires burn on the hearths a long moment. Then he replied. "They went back into the sea, Faolan."

Faolan's fingers fell emptily. "Yes," he said, heavily. "They had to go back, didn't they? They couldn't stay, could they? Not even for one night of food on the table, and wine in the mouth, and women in the deep warm furs before the hearth. Not even for one toast." He turned. "A drink, Romna. A drink for everyone."

Romna gave him a full cup. He dropped it, fell down to his knees, clawed at his breasts. "My heart!"

"Rann, you sea-devil!"

Starke held her instantly by the throat. He put pressure on the small raging pulses on either side of her snow-white neck. "Let him go, Rann!" More pressure. *"Let him go!"* Faolan grunted. Starke held her until her white face was dirty and strange with death.

It seemed like an hour later when he released her. She fell softly and did not move. She wouldn't move again.

Starke turned slowly to look at Faolan.

"You saw, didn't you, Faolan?" he said.

Faolan nodded blindly, weakly. He roused himself from the floor, groping. "I saw. For a moment, I saw everything. And Gods! but it made good seeing! Here, Hugh-Starke-Called-Conan, give this other side of me something to lean on."

.  .  .

Beudag and Starke climbed the mountain above Falga the next day. Starke went ahead a little way, and with his coming the flame birds scattered, glittering away.

He dug the shallow grave and did what had to be done with the body he found there, and then when the grave was covered with thick grey stones he went back for Beudag. They stood together over it. He had never expected to stand over a part of himself, but here he was, and Beudag's hand gripped his.

He looked suddenly a million years old standing there. He thought of Earth and the Belt and Jupiter, of the joy streets in the Jekkara Low Canals of Mars. He thought of space and the ships going through it, and himself inside them. He thought of the million credits he had taken in that last job. He laughed ironically.

"Tomorrow, I'll have the sea creatures hunt for a little metal box full of credits." He nodded solemnly at the grave. "He wanted that. Or at least he thought he did. He killed himself getting it. So if the sea people find it, I'll send it up here to the mountain and bury it down under the rocks in his fingers. I guess that's the best place."

Beudag drew him away. They walked down the mountain toward Falga's harbor where a ship awaited them. Walking, Starke lifted his face. Beudag was with him, and the sails of the ship were rising to take the wind, and the Red Sea waited for them to travel it. What lay on its far side was something for Beudag and Faolan-of-the-Ships and Romna and Hugh-Starke-Called-Conan to discover. He felt damned good about it. He walked on steadily, holding Beudag near.

And on the mountain, as the ship sailed, the flame birds soared down fitfully and frustratedly to beat at the stone mound; ceased, and mourning shrilly, flew away.

# SEVENTEEN

# ONE MINUS ONE (CORPSE-CARNIVAL)

It was unthinkable! Raoul recoiled from it, but was forced to face its reality because convulsions were surging sympathetically through his nervous system. Over him, the tall circus banners in red, blue and yellow fluttered sombre and high in the night wind; the fat woman, the skeleton man, the armless, legless horrors staring down at him with the same fierce hatred and violence they expressed in real life. Raoul heard Roger gasping beside him, tugging at the knife in his chest.

"Roger, don't die! Hold on, Roger!" Raoul screamed.

They lay side by side on the warm grass, a sprinkle of odorous sawdust under them. Through the wide flaps of the main tent, which flipped like the leathery wings of some prehistoric monster, Raoul could see the empty apparatus at the tent top where Deirdre, like a lovely bird, soared each night. Her name flashed in his mind. He didn't want to die. He only wanted Deirdre.

"Roger can you hear me, Roger?"

Roger managed to nod, his face clenched into a shapeless ball by pain. Raoul looked at that face; the thin, sharp lines, the pallor, the arrogant handsomeness, the dark, deep-set eyes, the cynical lip, the high forehead, the long black hair—and seeing Roger was like gazing into a mirror at one's own death.

"Who did it?" Raoul struggled, got his frantically working lips to Roger's ear. "One of the other freaks? The Cyclops? Lal?"

"I—I—" sobbed Roger. "Didn't see. Dark. Dark. Something white, quick. Dark." He sucked in a rattling breath.

"Don't die, Roger!"

"Selfish!" hissed Roger. "Selfish!"

"How can I be any other way; you know how I feel! Selfish! How would any man feel with half his body, soul and life cast off, a leg amputated, an arm yanked away! Selfish, Roger. Oh, God!"

The calliope ceased, the steam of it went on hissing, and Tiny Mathews, who had been practicing came running through the summer grass, around the side of the tent.

"Roger, Raoul, what happened!"

"Get the doctor, quick, get the doctor!" gibbered Raoul. "Roger's hurt badly. He's been stabbed!"

The midget darted off mouse-like, shrilling. It seemed like an hour before he returned, with the doctor, who bent down and ripped Roger's sequined blue shirt from his thin, wet chest.

Raoul shut his eyes tight. "Doctor! Is he dead?"

"Almost," said the doctor. "Nothing I can do."

"There is," whispered Raoul, reaching out, seizing the doctor's coat, clenching it as if to crush away his fear. "Use your scalpel!"

"No," replied the doctor. "There are no antiseptic conditions."

"Yes, yes, I beg of you, cut us apart! Cut us apart before it's too late! I've got to be free! I want to live! Please!"

The calliope steamed and hissed and chugged; the brutal roustabouts looked down. Tears squeezed from under Raoul's lids. "Please, there's no need of both of us dying!"

The doctor reached for his black bag. The roustabouts did not turn away as he ripped cloth and bared the thin spines of Raoul and Roger. A hypodermic load of sedative was injected, efficiently.

Then the doctor set to work at the thin epidermal skin structure that had joined Raoul to Roger, one to the other, ever since the day of their birth, twenty-seven years before.

Lying there, Roger said nothing, but Raoul screamed.

.   .   .

Fever flooded him to the brim for days. Drenching the bed with sweat, crying out, he looked over his shoulder to talk with Roger but—*Roger wasn't there! Roger would never be there again!*

Roger *had* been there for twenty-seven years. They'd walked together, fallen together, liked and disliked together, one the echo of the other, one the mirror, slightly distorted by the other's perverse individuality. Back to back they had fought the surrounding world. Now, Raoul felt himself a turtle unshelled, a snail irretrievably dehoused from its armour. He had no wall to back against for protection. The world circled behind him now, came rushing in to strike his back!

"Deirdre!"

He cried her name in his fever, and at last saw her leaning over his bed, her dark hair drawn tight to a gleaming knot behind her ears. In memory, too, he saw her whirling one hundred times over on her hempen rope at the top of the tent in her tight costume. "I love you, Raoul. Roger's dead. The circus is going on to Seattle. When you're well, you can catch up with us. I love you, Raoul."

"Deirdre, don't you go away, too!"

Weeks passed. Often he lay until dawn with the memory of Roger next to him in the old bondage. "Roger?" Silence. Long silence.

Then he would look behind himself and weep. A vacuum lived there now. He must learn never to look back. How many months he hung on the raw edge of life, he had no accounting of. Pain, fear, horror, pressured him and he was reborn again in silence, alone, one instead of two, and life had to start all over.

He tried to recall the murderer's face or figure, but could not. Twisting, he thought of the days before the murder—Roger's insults to the other freaks, his adamant refusal to get along with anyone, even his own twin. Raoul winced. The freaks hated Roger, even if Raoul gave them no irritation. They'd demanded that the circus get rid of the twins for once and all!

Well, the twins were gone now. One into the earth. The other into a bed. And Raoul lay planning, thinking of the day when he might return to the show, hunting the murderer, to live his life, to see Papa Dan, the circus owner, to kiss Deirdre again, to see the freaks and search their faces to see which one had done this to him. He would let no one know that he had *not* seen the killer's face in the deep shadows that night. He would let the killer simmer in his juices, wondering if Raoul knew more than he had said!

. . .

It was a hot summer twilight. Animal odors sprang up all around him in infinite acrid varieties. Raoul walked across the tanbark uneasily, seeing the first evening star, unused to this freedom, always peering behind himself to make certain Roger wasn't lagging.

For the first time in his life Raoul realized he was being ignored! The sight of him and Roger had gathered crowds anywhere, anytime. And now, the people looked only at the lurid canvasses, and Raoul noticed, with a turn of his heart, that the canvas painting of himself and Roger had been taken down. There was an empty space, as if a tooth had been extracted from the midway. Raoul resented this sudden neglect, but at the same time he glowed with a new sensation of individuality.

He could run! He wouldn't have to tell Roger: "Turn here!" or "Watch it, I'm falling!" And he wouldn't have to put up with Roger's bitter comments: "Clumsy! No, no, not *that* direction. I want to go this way. Come on!"

A red face poked out of a tent. "What the hell?" cried the man. "I'll be damned! Raoul!" He plunged forward. "Raoul, you've come back! Didn't recognize you because—" He glanced behind Raoul. "That is, well, dammit, welcome home!"

"Hello, Father Dan!"

Sitting in Father Dan's tent they clinked glasses. Father Dan was a small, violently red-haired Irishman and he shouted a lot. "God, boy, it's good to see you. Sorry the show had to push on, leave you behind that way. Lord! Deirdre's been a sick cow over you, waiting. Now, now, don't fidget, you'll see her soon enough. Drink up that brandy." Father Dan smacked his lips.

Raoul drank his down, burning. "I never thought I'd come back. Legend says that if one Siamese twin dies, so does the other. I guess Doc Christy did a good job with his surgery. Did the police bother you much, Father Dan?"

"A coupla days. Didn't find a thing. They get after you?"

"I talked a whole day with them before coming West. They let me go. I didn't like talking to them anyway. This business is between Roger and me and the killer." Raoul leaned back. "And now—"

Father Dan swallowed thickly. "And now—" he muttered.

"I know what you're thinking," said Raoul.

"Me? Thinking?" guffawed Father Dan too heartily, smacking Raoul's knee. "You know I never think!"

"The fact is, you know it, I know it, Papa Dan, that I'm no longer a Siamese twin," said Raoul. His hand trembled. "I'm just Raoul Charles DeCaines, unemployed, no abilities other than gin-rummy, playing a poor saxophone, and telling a very few feeble quips. I can raise tents for you, Papa Dan, or sell tickets, or shovel manure, or I might leap from the highest trapeze some night without a net; you could charge five bucks a seat. You'd have to break in a new man for *that* act every night."

"Shut up!" cried Father Dan, his pink face getting pinker. "Damn you, feeling sorry for yourself! Tell you what you'll get from me, Raoul DeCaines—hard work! Damn right you'll heave elephant manure and camel dung, but—maybe later when you're strong, you can work the trapezes with the Condiellas."

"The Condiellas!" Raoul stared, not believing.

"Maybe, I said. Just maybe!" retorted F.D., snorting. "And I hope you break your scrawny neck, damn you! Here, drink up, boy, drink up!"

The canvas flap rattled, opened, a man with staring blind eyes set in a dark Hindu face, felt his way inside. "Father Dan?"

"I'm here," said Papa Dan. "Come in, Lal."

Lal hesitated, his thin nostrils drawing small. "Someone else here?" His body stiffened. "Ah." Blind eyes shone wetly. "They are back. I smell the double sweat of them."

"It's just me," said Raoul, feeling cold, his heart pumping.

"No," insisted Lal, gently. "I smell the two of you." Lal groped forward in his own darkness, his delicate limbs moving in his old silks, the knife he used in his act gleaming at his waist.

"Let's forget the past, Lal."

"After Roger's insults?" cried Lal, softly. "Ah, no. After the two of you stole the show from us, treated us like filth, so we went on strike against you? Forget?"

Lal's blind eyes narrowed to slits. "Raoul, you had better go away. If you remain you will not be happy. I will tell the police about the split canvas, and then you will not be happy."

"The split canvas?"

"The sideshow canvas painting of you and Roger in yellow and red and pink which hung on the runway with the printed words SIAMESE TWINS! on it. One night four weeks ago I heard a ripping sound in the dark. I ran forward and stumbled over the canvas. I showed it to the others. They told me it was the painting of you and Roger, ripped down the middle, separating you. If I tell the police of that, you will not be happy. I have kept the split canvas in my tent—"

"What has that to do with me?" demanded Raoul, angrily.

"Only you can answer that," replied Lal, quietly. "Perhaps I'm blackmailing you. If you go away, I will not tell who it was who ripped the canvas in half that night. If you stay I may be forced to explain to the police why you yourself sometimes wished Roger dead and gone from you."

"Get out!" roared Father Dan. "Get out of here! It's time for the show!"

The tent flaps rustled; Lal was gone.

. . .

The riot began just as they were finishing off the bottle, starting with the lions roaring and jolting their cages until the bars rattled like loose iron teeth. Elephants trumpeted, camels humped skyward in clouds of dust, the electric light system blacked out, attendants ran shouting, horses burst from their roped stalls and rattled around the menagerie, spreading tumult; the lions roared louder, splitting the night down the seams; Father Dan, cursing, smashed his bottle to the ground and flung himself outside, swearing, swinging his arms, catching attendants, roaring directions into their startled ears. Someone screamed, but the scream was lost in the incredible dinning, the confusion, the chaotic hoofing of animals. A swell and tide of terror sounded from the throats of the crowd waiting by the boxes to buy tickets; people scattered, children squealed!

Raoul grabbed a tent pole and hung on as a cluster of horses thundered past him.

A moment later the lights came on again; the attendants gathered the horses together in five minutes. The damage was estimated as minor by a sweating pink-faced, foul-tongued Papa Dan, and everything quieted down. Everybody was okay, except Lal, the Hindu. Lal was dead.

"Come see what the elephants did to him, Father Dan," someone said.

The elephants had walked on Lal as if he were a small dark carpet of woven grasses; his sharp face was crushed far down into the sawdust, very silent and crimson wet.

Raoul got sick to his stomach and had to turn away, gritting his teeth. In the confusion, he suddenly found himself standing outside the geeks' tent, the place where he and Roger had lived ten years of their odd nightmarish life. He hesitated, then poked through the flaps and walked in.

The tent smelled the same, full of memories. The canvas sagged like a melancholy grey belly from the blue poles. Beneath the stomaching canvas, in a rectangle, the flake-painted platforms, bearing their freak burdens of fat, thin, armless, legless, eyeless misery, stood ancient and stark under the naked electric light bulbs. The bulbs buzzed in the air, large fat Mazda beetles, shedding light on all the numbed, sullen faces of the queer humans.

The freaks focussed their vague uneasy eyes on Raoul, then their eyes darted swiftly behind him, seeking Roger, not finding him. Raoul felt the scar, the empty livid stitchings on his back take fire. Out of memory, Roger came. Roger's remembered voice called the freaks by the acrid names Roger had thought up for them: "Hi, Blimp!" for the Fat Lady. "Hello, Popcyc!" This for the Cyclops Man. "And to you, Encyclopedia Britannica!" That could only mean the Tattooed Man. "And you, Venus De Milo!" Raoul nodded at the armless blonde woman. Even six feet of earth could not muffle Roger's insolent voice. "Shorty!" There sat the legless man on his crimson velvet pillow. "Hi, Shorty!" Raoul clapped his hand over his mouth. Had he said it *aloud?* Or was it just Roger's cynical voice in his brain?

Tattoo, with many heads painted on his body, seemed like a vast crowd milling forward. "Raoul!" he shouted happily. He flexed muscles proudly, making the tattoos cavort like a three ring act. He held his shaved head high because the Eiffel Tower, indelible on his spine, must never sag. On each shoulder blade hung puffy blue clouds. Pushing shoulder blades together, laughing, he'd shout, "See! Stormclouds over the Eiffel! Ha!"

But the sly eyes of the other freaks were like so many sharp needles weaving a fabric of hate around him.

Raoul shook his head. "I can't understand you people! You hated both of us once for a reason; we outshone, outbilled, outsalaried you. But now—how can you still hate *me?*"

Tattoo made the eye around his navel almost wink. "I'll tell you," he said. "They hated you when you were more abnormal than they were." He chuckled. "Now they hate you even more because you're released from freakdom." Tattoo shrugged. "Me, I'm not jealous. I'm no freak." He shot a casual glance at them. "They never liked being what they are. They didn't plan their act; their glands did. Me, my mind did all this to me, these pink chest gunboats, my abdominal island ladies, my flower fingers! It's different—mine's ego. Theirs was a lousy accident of nature. Congratulations, Raoul, on escaping."

A sigh rose from the dozen platforms, angry, high, as if for the first time the freaks realized that Raoul would be the only one of their number ever to be free of the taint of geekdom and staring people.

"We'll strike!" complained the Cyclops. "You and Roger always caused trouble. Now Lal's dead. We'll strike and make Father Dan throw you out!"

Raoul heard his own voice burst out. "I came back because one of you killed Roger! Besides that, the circus was and *is* my life, and Deirdre is here. None of you can stop me from staying and finding my brother's murderer in my own time, in my own way."

"We were all in bed that night," whined Fat Lady.

"Yes, yes, we were, we were," they all said in unison.

"It's too late," said Skyscraper. "You'll never find anything!"

The armless lady kicked her legs, mocking. "I didn't kill him. I can't hold a knife except by lying on my back, using my feet!"

"I'm half blind!" said Cyclops.

"I'm too fat to move!" whined Fat Lady.

"Stop it, stop it!" Raoul couldn't stand it. Raging, he bolted from the tent, ran through darkness some ten feet. Then, suddenly, he saw her, standing in the shadows, waiting for him.

"Deirdre!"

She was the white thing of the upper spaces, a creature winging a canvas void each night, whirling propeller-wise one hundred times around to the enumeration of the strident ringmaster: "—eighty-eight!" A whirl. "Eighty-nine!" A curling. "Ninety!" Her strong right arm bedded with hard muscles, the fingers bony, grasping the hemp loop; the wrists, the elbow, the biceps drawing her torso, her tiny bird-wing feet on up, over and down, on up, over and down; with a boom of the brass kettle as she finished each roll.

Now, against the stars, her strong curved right arm raised to a guywire, she poised forward, looking at Raoul in the half light, her fingers clenching, relaxing, clenching again.

"They've been at you, haven't they?" she asked, whispering, looking past him, inward to those tawdry platforms and their warped cargo, her eyes blazing. "Well, I've got power, too. I'm a big act. I've got pull with Papa Dan. I'll have my say, darling."

At the word "darling" she relaxed. Her tight hand fell. She stood, hands down, eyes half-closed, waiting for Raoul to come and put his arms around her. "What a homecoming we've given you," she sighed. "I'm so sorry, Raoul." She was warmly alive against him. "Oh, darling, these eight weeks have been ten years."

Warm, close, good, his arms bound her closer. And for the first time in all his life, Roger was not muttering at Raoul's back: "Oh, for God's sake, get it over with!"

. . .

They stood in the runway at nine o'clock. The fanfare. Deirdre kissed his cheek. "Be back in a few minutes, darling." The ringmaster called her name. "Raoul, you must get up, away from the freaks. Tomorrow, you rehearse with the Condiellas, as Papa Dan suggests."

"Won't the freaks detest me for leaving them on the ground? They killed Roger, now, if I outshine them again, they'll get me!"

"To hell with the freaks, to hell with everything but you and me," she declared, her iron fingers working, testing a practice hemp, floured with resin. She heard her entrance music. Her eyes clouded. "Darling, did you ever see a Tibetan monk's prayer wheel? Each time the wheel revolves its one prayer to heaven—*oom mani padme hum.*" Raoul gazed at the high rope where she'd swing in a moment. "Every night, Raoul, every time I go around one revolution, it'll mean I love you, I love you, I love you, like that—over and over."

The music towered. "One other thing," she added quickly. "Promise you'll forget the past. Lal's dead, he committed suicide. Father Dan's told the police another story that doesn't implicate you, so let's forget the whole sorry mess. As far as the police know Lal was blind and in the confusion of the lights going off, when the animals got free, he was killed."

"Lal didn't commit suicide, Deirdre. And it wasn't an accident." Raoul could hardly say it, look at her. "When I returned, the real killer got panicky and wanted a cover-up. Lal suspected the killer, too, so there was a double motive. Lal was pushed under those elephants to make me think my search was over and done. It's not. It's just beginning. Lal wasn't the kind to commit suicide, he was a Hindu."

"But he hated Roger."

"So did *all* the geeks. And then there's the matter of Roger's picture and mine torn in two pieces."

Dierdre stood there. They called her name. "Raoul, if you're right, then they'll kill you. If the killer was trying to throw you off-trail, and you go on and on—" She had to run, then, off into the music, the applause, the noise. She swang up, up, high, higher into the canvas firmament.

A large-petaled flower floated on the darkness and came to rest on Raoul's shoulder. "Oh, it's you, Tattoo."

The Eiffel Tower was sagging. Twin flowers were twitching at Tattoo's sides as in a high storm. "The geeks," he muttered sullenly. "They've grouped and gone on hands and knees to Father Dan!"

"What!"

"Yeah. The armless lady is gesturin' around with her damn big feet, yellin'. The legless man waves his arms, the midget walks the table top, the tall man thumps the canvas ceiling! Oh, God, they're wild mad. Fat Lady'll bust like a rotten melon, I swear! Thin Man'll fall like a broken xylophone, all shaking!"

"They say you killed Lal and they're going to tell the police. The police just got done talking with Father Dan and he convinced them Lal's death was pure accident. Now, the geeks say either Father Dan kicks you out or they go on strike and tell the cops to boot. So Father Dan says for you to hop on over to his tent, toot sweet. Good luck, kid."

Father Dan sloshed his whiskey into a glass and glared at it, then at Raoul. "It's not what you did or didn't do that counts, it's what the geeks *believe.* They're boiling. They say you killed Lal because he knew the truth about you and your brother—"

"The truth!" cried Raoul, "What *is* the truth?"

Father Dan couldn't face him, he had to look away. "That you were fed up, sick of being tied to Roger like a horse to a tree. That you—that you killed your brother to be free—that's what they say!" Father Dan sprang to his feet and paced the sawdust. "I'm not believing it—yet."

"But," cried Raoul. "*But,* maybe it would've been worth risking, isn't that what you mean?"

Father Dan pulled out his flask viciously and took a long vicious pull at it. "Dammit, I don't know what I mean. All I know is I got half a Siamese twin act on my hands and I'm trying to be decent, and the geeks are walking out unless I fire you."

He sat down, his voice softer, more logical. "Look here, Raoul, it stands to reason, if one of the geeks killed Roger, why in hell are you alive? Why didn't he kill you? Would he chance having you catch up with him? Not on your busted tintype. Hell. None of the geeks killed Roger. That's the way it looks from here."

"Maybe he got scared. Maybe he wanted me to live and suffer. That would be real irony, don't you see?" pleaded Raoul, bewildered.

Father Dan closed his eyes. "I see that I've got my head way out *here.*" He shoved out his hand. "And this business of the torn painting of you and Roger that Lal found. It points to the fact that someone wanted Roger dead and you alive, so maybe you paid one of the other geeks to do the job, maybe you didn't have the nerve yourself—" Father Dan paced swiftly. "And after the job was done, your murderer friend tore the picture triumphantly in two pieces!" Father Dan stopped for breath, looked at Raoul's numbed, beaten face. "Allright," he shouted, "maybe I'm drunk. Maybe I'm crazy. So maybe you *didn't* kill him. You'll still have to pull out. I can't take a chance on you, Raoul, much as I like you. I can't lose my whole sideshow over you."

Raoul rose unsteadily. The tent tilted around him. His ears hammered crazily. He heard his own strange voice saying, "Give me two more days, Father Dan. That's all I ask. When I find the killer, things will quiet down, I promise. If I don't find him, I'll go away, I promise that, too."

Father Dan stared morosely at his boot-tip in the sawdust. Then he roused himself uneasily. "Two days, then. But that's all. Two days, and no more. You're a hard man to down, aren't you, number two twin?"

.   .   .

They rode on horseback down past the slumbering town, tethered up by a creek and talked earnestly and kissed quietly. He told her about Papa Dan, the split canvas, Lal, and the danger to his job. She held his face in her hands, looking up.

"Darling, let's go away. I don't want you hurt."

"Only two more days. If I find the murderer, we can stay."

"But there are other circuses, other places." Her grey eyes were tormented. "I'd give up my job to keep us safe." She seized his shoulders. "Is Roger that important to you?" Before he knew what she intended, she had whirled him in the dark, locked her elbows in his, and pressured her slender back to his scarred spine. Whispering softly, she said, slowly, "I have you now, for the first time, alone, don't go away from me." She released him slowly, and he turned and held her again. She said, so softly, "Don't go away from me Raoul, I don't want anything to interfere again. . . ."

Instantly, time flew backward. In Raoul's mind he heard Deirdre on another day, asking Roger why he and Raoul had never submitted themselves to the surgeon's scalpel. And Roger's cynic's face rose like driftwood from the tide pool of Raoul's memory, laughing curtly at Deirdre and retorting, "No, my dear Deirdre, no. It takes two to agree to an operation. I refuse."

Raoul kissed Deirdre, trying to forget Roger's bitter comment. He recalled his first kiss from Deirdre and Roger's abrupt voice: "Kiss her this way, Raoul! Here let *me* show you! May I cut in? No, no, Raoul, you're unromantic! That's better. Mind if I fan myself?" Another chortle. "It's a bit warm."

"Shut up, shut up, shut up!" screamed Raoul. He shook violently, jolting himself back into the present—into Deirdre's arms—

He woke in the morning with an uncontrollable desire to run get Deirdre, pack, catch a train and get out now, get away from things forever. He paced his hotel room. To go away, he thought, to leave and never know any more about the half of himself that was buried in a cemetery hundreds of miles away—. But he *had* to know.

Noon bugle. The carnies, geeks, finkers and palefaces, the shills and the shanties lined the timber tables as Raoul picked vaguely at his plated meat. There *was* a way to find the murderer. A *sure* way.

"Tonight I'm turning the murderer over to the police," said Raoul murmuring. Tattoo almost dropped his fork. "You mean it?"

"Pass the white top tent," someone interrupted. Cake was handed past Raoul's grim face as he said:

"I've been waiting—biding my time since I got back—watching the killer. I saw his face the night he got Roger. I didn't tell the police that. I didn't tell anybody that. I been waiting—just waiting—for the right time and place to even up the score. I didn't want the police doing my work for me. I wanted to fix him in my own time in my own way."

"It wasn't Lal, then?"

"No."

"You let Lal be killed?"

"I didn't think he would be. He should have kept quiet. I'm sorry about Lal. But the score'll be evened tonight. I'll turn the killer's body over to the police, personally. And it'll be in self-defense. They won't hold me, I'll tell you that, painted man."

"What if he gets you first?"

"I'm half-dead now. I'm ready." Raoul leaned forward, earnestly, holding Tattoo's blue wrist. "You won't tell anyone about this, of course?"

"Who? Me? Ha, ha, not *me*, Raoul."

.  .  .

The choice news passed from Tattoo to Blimp to Skeleton to Armless to Cyclops to Shorty and on around. Raoul could almost see it go. And he knew that now the matter would be settled; either he'd get the killer or the killer'd get him. Simple. Corner a rat and have it out. But what if nothing happened?

He frequented all the dark places when the sun set. He strolled under tall crimson wagons where buckets might drop off and crush his head. None dropped. He idled behind cat cages where a sprung door could release fangs on his scarred spine. No cats leaped. He sprawled under an ornate blue wagon wheel waiting for it to revolve, killing him. The wheel did not revolve; nor did elephants trample him; nor tent poles collapse across him, nor guns shoot him. Only the rhythmed music of the band blared out into the starry sky, and he grew more unhappy and solemn in his death-walking.

He began walking faster, whistling loudly against the thoughts in his mind. Roger had been killed for a purpose. Raoul was *purposely* left alive.

A wave of applause echoed from the big top. A lion snarled. Raoul put up his hands to his head and closed his eyes. The geeks were innocent. He knew that now. If Lal or Tattoo or Fat Lady or Armless or Legless was guilty, they'd have killed both Roger and Raoul. There was only one solution. It was clear as a blast of a new trumpet.

He began walking toward the runway entrance, shuffling his feet. There'd be no fight, no blood spilled, no accusations or angers.

"I will live for a long time," he said to himself, wearily. "But what will there be to live for, after tonight?"

What good to stick with the show now, what good if the freaks did settle down to accepting him? What good to know the killer's name? No good—no damned good at all. In his frantic search for one thing he'd lost another. He was alive. His heart pounded hot and heavy in him, sweat poured from his armpits, down his back, on his brow, in his hands. Alive. And the very fact of his aliveness, his living, his heart pulsing, his feet moving, was proof of the killer's identity. It is not often, he thought grimly, that a killer is found through a live man being alive, usually it is through a dead man's being dead. I wish I were dead. I wish I were dead.

This was the last performance in the circus in his life. He found himself shuffling down the runway, heard the whirling din of music, the applause, the laughter as clowns tumbled and wrestled in the red rings.

Deirdre stood in the runway, looking like a miracle of stars and whiteness, pure and clean and birdlike. She turned as he came up, her face pale, small blue petals under each eye from sleepless nights; but beautiful. She watched the way Raoul walked with his head down.

The music held them. He raised his head and didn't look at her.

"Raoul," she said, "what's wrong?"

He said, "I've found the killer."

A cymbal crashed. Deirdre looked at him for a long time.

"Who is it?"

He didn't answer, but talked to himself, low, like a prayer, staring straight out at the rings and the people: "You get caught. No matter what you do, you're helpless. With Roger I was unhappy; without him I'm worse. When I had Roger I wanted you; now, with Roger gone, I can never have you. If I'd given up the hunt, I'd never have been happy. Now that the hunt is over, I'm even more miserable with what I've found."

"You're—you're going to turn the killer in, then?" she asked, finally, after a long time.

He just stood there, saying nothing, not able to think or see or talk. He felt the music rise, high. He heard, far off, the announcer giving Deirdre's name, he felt her hard fingers hold him for a moment, tightly, and her warm lips kiss him hard.

"Goodbye, darling."

Running lightly, the sequins all flashing and flittering like huge reflecting wings, Deirdre went over the tanbark, into the storm of applause, her face upward, staring at her ropes and her heaven, the music beating down on her like rain. The rope pulled her up, up, and up. The music cut. The trap drum pattered smoothly, monotonously. She began her loops.

A man walked out of the shadows when Raoul motioned to him, smoking a cigar, chewing it thoughtfully. He stopped beside Raoul and they were wordless for a time, staring upward.

There was Deirdre, caught high in the tent by a white beam of steady light. Grasping the slender rope strand, her legs swung up over her curved body in a great circle, over, up and down.

The ringmaster bawled out the revolutions one by one: "One—Two—Three—Four—!"

Over and over went Deirdre, like a white moth spinning a cocoon. *Remember, Raoul, when I go around; the monk's prayer wheel.* Raoul's face fell apart. *Oom mani padme hum. I love, I love you, I love you.*

"She's pretty, ain't she?" said the detective, at Raoul's side.

"Yes, and she's the one you want," said Raoul, slowly, not believing the words he had to speak. "I'm alive tonight. That proves it. She killed Roger and ripped our canvas painting in half. She killed Lal." He passed a trembling hand over his eyes. "She'll be down in about five minutes, you can arrest her then."

They both stared upward together, as if they didn't quite believe she was there.

"Forty-one, forty-two, forty-three, forty-four, forty-five," counted the detective. "Hey, what're you crying about? Forty-six, forty-seven, forty- . . ."

# EIGHTEEN

# THE SEA CURE
# (DEAD MEN RISE UP NEVER)

When Sherry began to scream I gripped the steering wheel and started sweating. I smelled her sweet and warm in the back seat between the stale smell of Willie and the sharp smell of Mark, and my nostrils took Hamphill into account, too. Hamphill smelled soap-clean up in the front seat with me, and he tried to talk to her, calm her. He held her hand:

"Sherry, this is for your own good. Please listen to me, Sherry. We only got you away from your house in time. Finlay's men, the ones who threatened you, would have kidnapped you today. I swear it. In God's name, Sherry, we're only protecting you."

She didn't believe Hamphill. I saw her dark shining eyes caught, held like crazy, wild things, in the rear-view mirror. The car's speed was up to sixty-five. Listen to him, Sherry, I thought, damn you, he loves you, so give him a chance!

"No! I don't believe you," was what she said. "You're gangsters, too! I know you!"

She tried to fling herself out of the car. Maybe she didn't know how fast we were traveling. The ground ran past in a windy blur. She struggled. Mark held onto her. There was a shouting, a sudden scream and silence. . . .

Sherry relaxed too suddenly in the back seat. Willie must have blinked at her, dully, not understanding.

"Stop the car." Hamphill groped at my elbow.

"But, boss . . ." I said.

"You heard me, Hank, stop it."

The car sound died away and all you could hear was the ocean moaning along the skirt of the cliff. We were on top of it. Hamphill stared over into the rear seat and Willie's dull voice said:

"She's gone to sleep, boss. Guess maybe she's tired."

I didn't turn around. I looked at the grey clouds in the sky and the seagulls looping and crying—at Hamphill's long lean face, next to me, bleached to a beaten, shocked white, like a carved wooden mask left to bake and crumble on the sands.

The ocean came in once, twice, three times. Each time, Hamphill breathed through his tiny, constricted nostrils. Then, holding her wrists, searching for a pulse he couldn't find, he shut his eyes—tight.

I stared ahead. "There's the cliff house, boss, just ahead. We better get inside it, in case Finlay and his men are following us. I bet they're damn mad at us for this trick. . . ." I trailed off.

Hamphill didn't know I was alive. He resembled something as old suddenly as that ancient wind-shaped, paint-flaked mansion standing on the rim of the stony cliffs.

Loving Sherry had made him young awhile. Now, the salt sea wind was at him, riming his hair above the ears, peeling away his new youth; the tide pounded his guts and sucked away his thinking.

I started the car and drove the last half mile to the cliff house very slowly. I climbed out of the car and slammed the door to waken the boss from his nightmare.

We walked into the house, the four of us carrying her. The front steps groaned when our feet touched them.

Upstairs, in a west room with a view, we laid Sherry on an old overstuffed sofa. A fine dust puffed from upholstery pores, hovering over her in a powdery, sunlit veil. Death had quieted her features and she was beautiful as polished ivory, her hair like the color of waxed chestnuts.

Very slowly, Hamphill sank beside her and told her what he thought of her, soft, like a kid talking to a fairy goddess. He didn't sound like Hamphill, the beer-baron; or Hamphill, the numbers man; or Hamphill the racing boss. The wind whined behind his voice, because Sherry was dead and the day was over. . . .

■  ·  ·

A car passed on the highway and I shivered. Any minute now, maybe, if we hadn't ditched them, some of Finlay's boys might show up—

The room felt crowded. There were only two people who needed to be in it. I pushed Willie and nodded at Mark. We went out and I closed the door and we stood with our hands deep in our pockets, in the hall, thinking many thoughts.

"You didn't have to scare her," I said.

"Me?" asked Mark, jerking a match on the wall and putting the flame unevenly against his cigarette. "She started yelling like a steam whistle."

"You scared her with your talk," I said. "After all, it wasn't a regular kidnapping. We were shielding her from Finlay. You know how soft the boss was on her—special."

"I knew," said Mark, "that we'd collect money on her, then frame Finlay for the deal, have him jailed, leaving us in the clear."

"You got the general idea," I said gently, "only let me bring out the details. The whole thing depended on Sherry's cooperation, once she learned our intentions were for her own good. There wasn't much time to explain today, when we heard Finlay was coming after her, so we grabbed her and ran. The blueprint was for us to hide here, then trap Finlay, let Sherry get a look at him and tell the police it was Finlay kidnapped her. Then they'd salt Finlay away and the whole business would be over."

Mark flicked ashes on the rug. "Only trouble is, Sherry's dead now. Nobody'll believe we didn't kidnap her ourselves. Ain't that swell!" One of Mark's little pointed, shiny black shoes kicked the wall. "Well, I don't want nothing else to do with her. She's dead. I hate dead people. Let's load her in a canvas tied with weights and put her out in the bay somewhere deep, then get out of here, get our money and—"

The door opened. Hamphill came out of it, pale.

"Willie, go watch over her while I talk to the boys," he said slowly, not thinking of the words. Willie beamed proudly and lumbered in. The three of us went into another room.

Mark has a mouth the shape of his own foot. "When we gonna get the money and scram, boss?" He shut the door and leaned on it.

"Money?" The boss held the word up like something strange found on the beach, turning it over. "Money." He focused dazedly on Mark. "I didn't want any *money*. I wasn't in this for the *money*—"

Mark shifted his delicate weight. "But, you said—"

"I said. *I* said." Hamphill thought back, putting his thin fingers to his brow to force the thinking. "In order to make you play along, Mark, I said about money, didn't I? It was a lie, Mark, all a lie. Yes. All a lie. I only wanted Sherry. No money. Just her. I was going to pay you out of my own pocket. Right Hank?" He stared strangely at me. "Right, Hank?"

"Right," I said.

"Well, of all the—" Angry color rose in Mark's cheeks. "This whole damn setup's nothing but nursemaiding a coupla lovebirds!"

"No money!" shouted Hamphill, straightening up. "No money! I was only kicking down the Christmas tree to get the star on top. And you—you always said it was wrong for me to love her, said it wouldn't work. But I planned everything. A week here. A trip to Mexico City later, after she got to know me, after fixing Finlay so he wouldn't bother her again! And you, Mark, you sniffing your damn nose at me, goddamn you!"

Mark grinned. "You should've said about it, boss, how you never intended getting money from kidnapping her, to make me understand. Why, sure, there was no use lying to me. Why, no, boss; no, of course not."

"Careful," I muttered.

"I'm sure sorry," said Mark, lidding his small green eyes. "Sure am. And, by the way, boss, how long we going to be here? I'm just curious, of course."

"I promised Sherry a week's vacation. We stay here that long."

One week. My brows went up. I said nothing.

"One week here, without trying to get the money, sitting, waiting for the cops to find us? Oh, that's swell, boss, I'm right in there with you, I sure am, I'm with you," said Mark. He turned, twisted the doorknob hard one way, stepped out, slammed it.

I put my right hand against Hamphill's heaving chest to stop his move. "No, boss," I whispered. "No. He ain't living. He never lived. Why bother killing him? He's dead, I tell you. He was born dead."

The boss would have spoken except that we both heard a voice talking across the hall behind the other door. We opened the door, crossed the hall and opened the other door slowly, looking in.

Willie sat on the couch-end like a large, grey, stone idol, his round face half-blank, half-animated, like a rock with lights playing over it. "You just rest there, Miss Bourne," he said to Sherry earnestly. "You look tired. You just rest. Mr. Hamphill thinks a lot of you. He told me so. He planned this whole setup for weeks, ever since he met you that night in Frisco. He didn't sleep, thinking about you—"

. . .

Two days passed. How many sea gulls cried and looped over us, I don't remember. Mark counted them with his green eyes, and for every seagull, he threw away a cigarette butt burnt hungrily down to a nub. And when Mark ran out of smokes, he counted waves, shells.

I sat playing blackjack. I'd put the cards down slow and pick them up and put them down slow again and shuffle them and cut them and lay them down. Maybe now and then I whistled. I've been around long enough so waiting makes no difference. When you been in the game as long as I have you don't find any difference in anything. Dying is as good as living; waiting is as good as rushing.

Hamphill was either up in *her* room, talking like a man in a confessional, soft and low, gentle and odd, or he was walking the beach, climbing the cliff stones. He'd tell Willie to squat on a rock. Willie'd perch there in the foggy sun with salt rime on his pink ears for five hours, waiting until the boss came back and said to jump down.

I played blackjack.

Mark kicked the table with his foot. "Talk, talk, talk, that's all he does upstairs at night, on and on, dammit! How long do we stick here? How long are we waiting?"

I laid some cards. "Let the boss take his vacation any way he pleases," I said.

Mark watched me walk out on the porch. He shut the door after me and though I couldn't be sure, I thought I heard the phone inside being ticked and spun by his fingers. . . .

Late that evening the fog crept in thicker, and I stood upstairs in a north room with Hamphill, waiting.

He looked down out of the window. "Remember the first time we saw her? The way she held herself, the way she took her hair in her hand, the way she laughed? I knew then it would take all the education and smartness and niceness in me to ever get her. Was I a fool, Hank?"

"A fool can't answer that," I said.

He nodded at the sea breaking over rocks, toward a point where fog bands crossed a jut of land that fingered out to sea. "Look beyond that curve, Hank? There's an old California mission out there."

"Under water?"

"About twenty feet under. On a clear day when the sun cuts down, the water's a blue diamond with the mission held inside it."

"Still there, intact?"

"Most of it. They say some of the first padres built it, but the land settled slowly and the little cathedral sank. On clear days you can see it lying there in the water, very quiet. Maybe it's just a ruin, but you imagine you see the whole thing; the stained glass windows, the bronze tower bell, the eucalyptus trees in the wind—"

"Sea weed and the tide, huh?"

"Same thing. Same effect. I wanted Sherry to see it. I wanted to walk along the cliff bottoms, over those big rocks with her, and bake in the sun. Bake all the old poison out of me and all the doubt out of her. The wind does that to you. I thought maybe I could show Sherry the little cathedral and maybe in a day or so she'd breathe easy and sit on a rock with me to see if we could hear the bell in the church tower ringing."

"That's from the bell-buoy at the point," I said.

"No," he said, "that's further over. This bell rings from in the water, but you have to listen close when the wind dies."

"I hear a siren!" I cried, suddenly, whirling. "The police!"

Hamphill took my shoulder. "No, that's only the wind in the holes of the cliff. I've been here before. I know. You get used to it."

I felt my heart pounding. "Boss, what do we do now?"

I shut up. I looked down at the white concrete road shimmering in the night and the fog. I saw the car sweeping down the highway, cutting through the fog with scythes of light.

"Boss," I said. "Take a look out this window."

"You look for me."

"A car. It's Finlay's sedan, I'd know it anywhere!"

Hamphill didn't move. "Finlay. I'm glad he's come. He's the one that caused all this. He's the one I want to see. Finlay." He nodded. "I want to talk to him. Go let him in, quietly."

. . .

The car ground to a stop below; its doors burst open. Men piled out, crossed the drive swiftly, crossed the porch; one ran around back. I saw guns with fog wet on them. I saw white faces with fog on them.

The downstairs bell rang.

I went down the stairs, alone, empty-handed, clenched my teeth together and opened the door. "Come on in," I said.

Finlay thrust his bodyguard in ahead of himself. The guard had his gun ready and was popeyed to see me just standing there. "Where's Hamphill?" Finlay demanded. A second gunsel stayed just outside the door.

"He'll be down in a minute."

"It's a good thing you didn't try any rough stuff."

"Oh, hell," I said.

"Where's Sherry?"

"Upstairs."

"I want her down here."

"Particular, aren't you?"

"Shall I hit him?" Finlay's bodyguard asked him.

Finlay looked up the dark stairs at the light in the opening door above. "Never mind."

Hamphill came down very quietly, one step at a time, pausing on each one with pain, as if his body was old, tired, and it was no longer fun to live and walk around. He got about halfway down when he saw Finlay. "What do you want?" he said.

"It's about Sherry," said Finlay.

I tightened up. The boss said, far away, "What about Sherry?"

"I want her back."

Hamphill said, "No."

"Maybe you didn't hear me right. I said I wanted her back, now!"

"No," said Hamphill.

"I don't want no trouble," said Finlay. His eyes moved from my empty hands to Hamphill's empty hands, puzzled at our strange actions.

"You can't have her," said Hamphill slowly. "Nobody can have her. She's gone."

"How'd you find us?" I asked.

"None of your damn business," said Finlay, glaring. To Hamphill: "You're lying!" To me: "Ain't he lying?"

"Talk quiet," I said. "Talk quiet in a house with someone dead in it."

"Dead?"

"Sherry's dead. Upstairs. Keep your voice down. You're too late. You better go back to town. It's all over."

Finlay lowered his gun. "I'm not going anywhere until I see her with my own eyes."

Hamphill said, "No."

"Like hell." Finlay looked at Hamphill's face and saw how much it looked like bone with the skin peeled away, white and hard. "Okay, so she's dead," he said, finally believing. He swallowed. He looked over his shoulder. "So we can still collect money on her, can't we?"

"No," said the boss.

"Nobody knows she's dead except us. We can still get the money. We'll just borrow a bit of her coat, a buckle, a button, a clip of her hair—"

"You can keep the body, Hampy, old boy, with our compliments," Finlay assured him. "We'll just need a few things like her rings or compact to mail to her father for the dough."

A vein in Hamphill's hardboned brow began to pulse. He leaned forward, stiffening, his eyes shining.

Finlay went on, "You can have the body, we'll leave you here with it, so you guys can take the rap."

"Sounds familiar," I said, remembering our plan to do the same for Finlay. That's life.

"Step aside, Hampy," said Finlay, walking big.

Hamphill fooled everyone the quiet way he stepped aside, turned as if to lead Finlay upstairs, took two steps up, then whirled. Finlay shouted as Hamphill pumped two shots into his big chest.

I shot the gun from one gunsel's hand. The second gunsel, outside, cursed, banged the door open, and sprang inward, his revolver aimed. The second gunsel shot Hamphill in the left arm just as Hamphill clutched Finlay, and they fell downward, collapsing together.

I got the second gunsel easily with one shot. The first one stood holding his awful red hand. Footsteps came in the back door. Willie came lumbering downstairs, bleating. "Boss, you all right?"

"Upstairs!" I said, helping the boss to his feet from Finlay's quiet body. "Willie, take him up!"

The third bodyguard rushed in, maybe expecting to see us all laid out stiff. I made a mess of his hand, too.

Willie helped the boss upstairs and came down with some rope he'd found. There were no more footsteps outside. I pulled the door wide, letting the mist in, cooling my face. It smelled so good I just lay against the wall, smelling and liking it. The car was parked, its lights dark but there was no movement. We'd taken care of everybody.

"Okay, Willie," I said. "Let's tie 'em up."

. . .

Hamphill lay like a long grey stick on the couch in the west room, nursing his wound. I closed the door.

"We got a set-up, if we want to use it," I said.

He swabbed the wound with a white handkerchief.

I looked at him steadily. "This is the way it'll look to the cops: Finlay and his boys fight over money and shoot each other four ways from Christmas. The police find them here, anytime we want to call and tell them."

Hamphill's eyes fluttered weakly, his voice was small. "Later," he gasped. "Later, Hank. Not now."

"We got to talk about it now," I said. "It's important."

"I don't want to leave Sherry."

"Look, boss, you're hit bad. You don't feel well."

"Later, Hank," he sighed.

"Yeah," I said feeling cold, but understanding. "Later. Okay."

Downstairs, Mark looked white as new snow. His hands shook as he sucked deeply on a cigarette he'd found on Finlay's body.

"Where were you when the shooting started?" I asked.

"Down at the boathouse on the beach, walking around. I ran up as quick as I could."

"You must be getting old," I said. "What sort of deal did you make on the phone with Finlay?"

Mark jerked, blew out smoke, drew his shaking hand across his unshaven cheek and looked at his cigarette, then straight at me:

"The fog got me. The waiting got me. My guts got like *that*." He showed a tightened fist to me. "The boss upstairs, talking to her—like water dripping and dripping on my head. So I figured it out neat. You listening?"

"Talk."

"I called Finlay; told him I was double-crossing you guys, that I wanted a cut, that they could have Sherry. I knew Finlay'd come down and we'd get him and his gang and let them take the rap."

"You knew that, did you?"

"You calling me a liar!"

"You were sure quiet about it. We mighta got shot. It mighta worked both ways. We won, you stick with us. If Finlay'd won, you'd be with him huh? Maybe."

"Hell, no! It was a chance, that's all. Either the cops found us here with

Sherry and we got the gas-chamber, or we had it out with Finlay. I couldn't tell you or the boss because if he knew he'd have shot me. I got nervous waiting. I wanted a fall-guy. Finlay was it. I just didn't think he'd get here when he did; that's why I was down on the beach when things popped. I hoped that Finlay would swipe Sherry, even, and then we'd *have* to get out!"

"Okay," I said, nodding. "But there's still one thing gimmixed up. The boss won't move. After all your trouble fixing a frame, he won't move. So what'll you do now, junior?"

Mark swore. "How long'll we stay here? God, next week, next *month?*"

I pushed him away. "It smells in here. Go open the window."

I was dead tired. I checked the ropes on the three men to be sure they were tied tight, then I stretched out on the couch. Mark went upstairs. I could hear the boss up there, too, talking to somebody now, grunting with pain.

I slept deep, dreaming I walked under green water into that little church off the point, where fish swam with me in a congregation, and the underwater bronze bell rang, and a large squid draped itself like a soiled alter cloth across the pulpit . . .

I woke about four in the morning to the ticking of my watch. I had a feeling something was wrong. It was so wrong that I didn't have time to do anything about it. Someone hit me over the head. I fell, face forward, on the floor. That was all for a while . . .

I had a terrific headache when I came to. I blinked around in the dark, found my hands tied. It took five minutes to work out of the rope. I switched on a light.

Two of Finlay's men were gone!

I cursed myself out of the ropes tying my feet, and raced upstairs.

Hamphill lay exhausted, in deep sleep. He didn't stir, even when I called his name. I shut the door softly and went to Sherry's room.

The couch where Sherry Bourne had lain was empty. Sherry was gone. . . .

. . .

The ocean came and dropped itself on the sand and slid out with a foaming sigh as my feet crunched the sand down.

Squinting out, I saw the rowboat—a grey rowboat, barely visible in the moonlight just breaking through the fog.

A large man stood in the boat, with long thick arms and a big head. Willie.

Mark stood on the beach where the waves didn't quite touch his small dark shoes. He turned as I walked up. I looked at Willie in the boat. Mark looked as if he hadn't expected me to show up.

"Where's Willie going?" I said.

Mark looked out at Willie, too. "He's got a load."

"A load of what?"

"Canvas with chains around it and bricks inside."

"What's he doing with that at four in the morning?"

"Dumping it. It's Finlay."

"Finlay!"

"I couldn't sleep downstairs with him there. And if you didn't like my plan, I wanted to get him out of the way. One corpse less, if the cops came." He looked at my head. "Somebody hit you?"

"About half an hour ago, and tied me up. While you were down here fussing around, two of the Finlay boys got free and whacked me." I smiled a little, too, to be friendly. "Then they took Sherry and drove off, just a few minutes ago. What do you think of that story?"

"They stole Sherry!" Mark's eyes widened, his jaw dropped.

"You're a damn good actor," I said.

"What do you mean?"

"I mean, why didn't they shoot me and the boss? We shot Finlay, didn't we? So why'd they hit me over the head when a shot in the guts would be better? It doesn't click. It's too damned convenient, you being down here, twice now, when everything begins to pop. Too damn neat you being down here with Finlay's body, giving them a chance to lam."

"I don't get what you're squawking at," snapped Mark. "If you ask me, you should be glad Sherry's gone. Now we won't have to stay here nursemaiding Hamphill!"

"You're just a little *too* glad," I said.

Willie was way out in the night now, looking back, waving at us.

Mark and I watched as Willie lifted the canvas thing and dropped it over the boat side. It made a big splash with ripples.

"Oh, God," I said. I took Mark quietly by his lapels, holding him close so I breathed in his face. "Know what I think?" I breathed. I gripped him. "I think you wanted to get out of here, bad. So you hit me on the head, tied me up, then you took Finlay's men, toted them out to their car, pushed them inside, drove the car down the road, parked it off behind some shrubs, lights out, left them, and came back. A good setup. You tell the boss they slipped their ropes, swiped Sherry and escaped." I looked at Willie in the boat. "All while you were dropping a body in the ocean—only, not Finlay's body!"

"Yes, it is!" He struggled, but I held him.

"No."

"You can't prove anything. I don't know anything about Sherry!"

"You should've shot me, Mark, it would have been more convincing." I released him. "You got the cards stacked. I can't prove that was Sherry inside the canvas with the chains and weights. Getting rid of Sherry was the most important thing in your life, wasn't it? No evidence. Gone for good. And that meant we could move on. We'd *have* to move on. The boss'd chase after the escaped Finlay gang to get Sherry back, only it'd be a wild goose chase, because Sherry isn't anywhere but out there, about forty feet under, where that little cathedral is!"

Willie turned the boat around and started rowing clumsily back with slow strokes. I started a cigarette and let the wind whip away the smoke.

"Funny, you thought of putting her out there. There's not a better place. If the boss knew, I think he'd like her being there with the bronze bell in the tower and all. It's just your motive for putting her there that spoils it, Mark. You made something dirty out of something that could've been—well—beautiful."

"You aren't going to tell Hamphill!"

"I don't know. In a way I guess it might be best for us to move on. I don't know."

Willie beached his rowboat, grinning.

I said, "Hi, Willie."

"Hello, Hank. That takes care of Mr. Finlay, don't it?"

"It sure does, Willie. It sure does."

"He wasn't very heavy," said Willie, puzzled.

.  .  .

There was a crunching of feet on the sandy cement stairway coming down the cliff. I heard Hamphill coming down, sobbing with pain and moaning something that sounded like "Sherry's gone. Sherry's gone!" He burst toward us from the base of the steps. "Sherry's gone!"

"Gone?" said Mark, playing it. "Gone!" said Willie.

I said nothing.

"Finlay's car's gone, too. Hank, get our car, we've got to go after them. They can't take Sherry—" He saw the rowboat. "What's that for?"

Mark laughed. "I got Willie to give me a hand with Finlay."

"Yeah," said Willie. "Plunk—overboard. He wasn't heavy at all. Light as a feather."

Mark's cheek twitched. "You're just strong, Willie. Oh, Hank, you better go get the car ready."

Maybe I showed something in my eyes. Hamphill glanced first at me, then at Mark, then at Willie, then at the boat.

"Where—where were you, Hank? Did you help load Finlay and drop him?"

"No. I was asleep. Somebody hit me on the head."

Hamphill shambled forward in the sand.

"What's wrong?" cried Mark, stepping back.

"Hold still!" commanded Hamphill. He plunged his hand into one of Mark's coat pockets, then the other. He drew something out into the moonlight.

Sherry's bracelet and ring.

Hamphill's face was like nothing I'd ever seen before in my life. He stared blindly at the boat and his voice was far away as he said, "So Finlay was light as a feather, was he, Willie?"

"Yes, sir," said Willie.

Hamphill said slowly, "What were you going to do, Mark, use the bracelet and ring on your own time, to get the money?" He jerked a hand at Willie. "Willie, grab him!"

Willie grabbed. Mark yelled. Willie coiled him in like a boa-constrictor enfolding a boar.

Hamphill said, "Walk out into the water with him, Willie."

"Yes, boss."

"And come back alone."

"Yes, boss."

"Boss, cut it out. Cut it, boss!" Mark screamed, thrashing wildly.

Willie began walking. The first shell of water poured over his big feet. A second skin of water slid in, foaming soft. Mark shouted and a wave thundered, roared around the shout, folding it as Willie folded Mark. Willie stopped, waiting for the big wave to collapse.

"Keep going," said Hamphill.

Willie went in to his knees, then up, inch by inch, over his big stomach, to his chest. Mark's yelling was further away now because the night wind covered it over, and the waves smashed his voice into so many hysterical fragments. I shivered.

Hamphill stood watching like a frozen god. A wave broke over Willie into custard foam, leveled out, as Willie plunged ahead with Mark and vanished. Six waves came in, broke. A long silence.

Then a huge water wall rushed in, casting Willie, alone, at our feet. He stood up, shaking water off his thick arms. "Yes, boss."

"Go up to the car and wait there, Willie," said Hamphill. Willie lumbered off, happy to be ordered around.

Hamphill looked out at the point, listening. "Now what in hell are you up to?" I said.

"None of your damn business."

He began walking toward the water. I put out my hands. He pulled away from me and there was a gun in one hand. "Get going. Go on up to the car with Willie."

"But—"

"I got a date for a high mass," he said. "And I don't want to be late. Go on. *Now*, Hank."

He walked out into the cold water, straight ahead. I stood watching him as long as I could see his tall striding figure. Then one big wave came and spread everything into a salt solitude. . . .

. . .

I climbed back up to the car, opened the door and slid in beside Willie.

"Where's the boss?" asked Willie.

"I'll tell you all about it in the morning," I said. I sat there and Willie dripped water all over the leather seat.

"Listen," I said and held my breath.

We heard the waves go in and out, in and out, like mighty organ music. "Hear 'em, Willie? That's Sherry taking the soprano and the boss on the baritone. They're in the choir loft, Willie, sending way up high after that *gloria.* That is real singing, Willie—listen to it while you can. You'll never hear anything like it again . . ."

"I don't hear nothing," said Willie.

"You poor guy," I said, started the car and drove away. . . .

# NINETEEN

# SKELETON

It was past time for him to see the doctor again. Mr. Harris turned palely in at the stair-well, and on his way up the flight he saw Dr. Burleigh's name gilded over a pointing arrow. Would Dr. Burleigh sigh when he walked in? After all, this would make the tenth trip so far this year. But Burleigh shouldn't complain; after all he got money for the examinations!

The nurse looked him over and smiled, a bit amusedly, as she tiptoed to the glazed glass door and opened it to put her head in. Harris thought he heard her say, "Guess who's here, Doctor?" And didn't the doctor's acid voice reply, faintly, "Oh my God, *again?*" Harris swallowed uneasily.

When Harris walked in, Dr. Burleigh snorted thinly. "Aches in your bones again! Ah!" He scowled at Harris and adjusted his glasses. "My dear Harris, you've been curried with the finest tooth-combs and bacteria-brushes known to science. You're only nervous. Let's see your fingers. Too many cigarettes. Let me smell your breath. Too much whiskey. Let's see your eyes. Not enough sleep. My response? Go home to bed, stop drinking, stop smoking. Ten dollars, please."

Harris stood there, sulking.

Dr. Burleigh looked up from his papers. "You still here? You're a hypochondriac! That's *eleven* dollars, now."

"But why should my bones ache?" asked Harris.

Dr. Burleigh addressed him like a child. "You ever had a pained muscle, and keep at it, irritating it, fussing with it, rubbing it? It gets worse, the more you bother it. Then you leave it alone and the pain vanishes. You realize you caused most of the soreness. Well, son, that's what's with you. Leave yourself alone. Take a dose of salts. Get out of here now! Take that business trip to Phoenix you've been stewing about for months. Do you good to get away!"

Mr. Harris riffled through a classified phone directory five minutes later, at the corner druggist's. A fine lot of sympathy one got from blind fools like Burleigh! He passed his finger down a list of BONE SPECIALISTS, found one named M. Munigant. Munigant lacked an M.D. or any other academical lettering behind his name, but his office was easily reached. Three blocks down, one block over. . . .

M. Munigant, like his office, was small and dark. Like his office, he smelled of iodoform, iodine and other odd things. He was a good listener, though, and listened with eager, shiny eyes, and when he talked to Harris, he had an accent and seemed to whistle every word, undoubtedly due to imperfect dentures. Harris told all.

M. Munigant nodded. He had seen cases like this before. The bones of the body. Man was not aware of his bones. Ah, yes, the bones. The skeleton. Most difficult. Something concerning an imbalance, an unsympathetic coordination between soul, flesh and bone. Very complicated, softly whistled M. Munigant. Harris listened, fascinated. Now, *here* was a doctor who understood his illness! Psychological, said M. Munigant. He moved swiftly, delicately to a dingy wall and rattled down half a dozen X-rays and paintings of the human skeleton. He pointed at these. Mr. Harris must become aware of his problem, yes. He pointed at this and that bone, and these and those, and some others.

The pictures were quite awful. They had something of the grotesquerie and off-bound horror of a Dali painting. Harris shivered.

M. Munigant talked on. Did Mr. Harris desire treatment of his bones?

"That all depends," said Harris.

M. Munigant could not help Harris unless Harris was in the proper mood. Psychologically, one had to NEED help, or the doctor was of no use. But (shrugging) M. Munigant would "try."

Harris lay on a table with his mouth open. The lights were off, the shades drawn. M. Munigant approached his patient. Something touched Harris' tongue. He felt the jawbones forced out. They cracked and made noises. One of those pictures on the dim wall seemed to leap. A violent shivering went through Harris and, involuntarily, his mouth snapped shut.

M. Munigant cried out. He had almost had his nose bitten off! It was no use. Now was not the time. M. Munigant raised the shades. He looked dreadfully disappointed. When Mr. Harris felt he could cooperate psychologically, when Mr. Harris really *needed* help and trusted M. Munigant to help him, then maybe something could be done. M. Munigant held out his little hand. In the meantime, the fee was only two dollars. Mr. Harris must begin to think. Here was a sketch for Mr. Harris to study. It would acquaint him with his body. He must be aware of himself. He must be careful. Skeletons were strange, unwieldy things. M. Munigant's eyes glittered. Good day to Mr. Harris. Oh, and would he have a bread-stick? He proffered a jar of long hard salty breadsticks to Harris, taking one himself to chew on, and saying that chewing breadsticks kept him in—ah—practice. See you soon, Mr. Harris. Mr. Harris went home.

. . .

The next day was Sunday, and Mr. Harris started the morning by feeling all sorts of new aches and pains in his body. He spent some time glancing at the funny papers and then looking with new interest at the little painting, anatomically perfect, of a skeleton M. Munigant had given him.

His wife, Clarisse, startled him at dinner when she cracked her exquisitely thin knuckles, one by one, until he clapped his hands to his ears and cried, "Don't do that!"

The remainder of the day he quarantined himself in his room. Clarisse was seated at bridge in the living room with three other ladies, laughing and conversing. Harris himself spent his time fingering and weighing the limbs of his body with growing curiosity. After an hour of this he suddenly stood up and called:

"Clarisse!"

She had a way of dancing into any room, her body doing all sorts of soft, agreeable things to keep her feet from ever quite touching the nap of a rug. She excused herself from her friends and came to see him now, brightly. She found him reseated in a far corner and she saw that he was staring at that anatomical sketch. "Are you still brooding, darling?" she asked. "Please don't." She sat upon his knees.

Her beauty could not distract him now in his absorption. He juggled her lightness, he touched her knee-cap, suspiciously. It seemed to move under her pale, glowing skin. "Is it supposed to do that?" he asked, sucking in his breath.

"Is what supposed to do what?" she laughed. "You mean my knee-cap?"

"Is it supposed to run around on top your knee that way?"

She experimented. "So it *does*," she marveled. "Well, now, so it does. Icky." She pondered. "No. On the other hand—it doesn't. It's only an optical illusion. The skin moves over the bone; not vice-versa. See?" She demonstrated.

"I'm glad yours slithers too," he sighed. "I was beginning to worry."

"About what?"

He patted his ribs. "My ribs don't go all the way down, they stop *here*. And I found some confounded ones that dangle in mid-air!"

Beneath the curve of her small breasts, Clarisse clasped her hands. "Of course, silly, everybody's ribs stop at a given point. And those funny little short ones are floating ribs."

"I just hope they don't float around too much," he said, making an uneasy joke. Now, he desired that his wife leave him, he had some important discovering to do with his own body and he didn't want her laughing at him and poking fun.

"I'll feel all right," he said. "Thanks for coming in, dear."

"Any time," she said, kissing him, rubbing her small pink nose warm against his.

"I'll be damned!" He touched his nose with his fingers, then hers. "Did you ever realize that the nose bone only comes down so far and a lot of gristly tissue takes up from there on?"

She wrinkled hers. "So what?" And, dancing, she exited.

He felt the sweat rise from the pools and hollows of his face, forming a salten tide to flow down his cheeks. Next on the agenda was his spinal cord and column. He examined it in the same manner as he operated the numerous push-buttons in his office, pushing them to summon the messenger boys. But, in these pushings of his spinal column, fears and terrors answered, rushed from a million doors in Mr. Harris' mind to confront and shake him. His spine felt awfully—bony. Like a fish, freshly eaten and skeletonized, on a china platter. He fingered the little rounded knobbins. "My God."

His teeth began to chatter. "God All-Mighty," he thought, "why haven't I realized it all these years. All these years I've gone around the world with a—SKELETON—inside me!" He saw his fingers blur before him, like motion films triply speeded in their quaking apprehension. "How is it that we take ourselves so much for granted? How is it we never question our bodies and our being?"

A skeleton. One of those jointed, snowy, hard things, one of those foul, dry, brittle, goudge-eyed, skull-faced, shake-fingered, rattling things that sway from neck-chains in abandoned webbed closets, one of those things found on the desert all long and scattered like dice!

. . .

He stood upright, because he could not bear to remain seated. Inside me now, he grasped his stomach, his head, inside my head is a—skull. One of those curved carapaces which holds my brain like an electrical jelly, one of those cracked shells with the holes in front like two holes shot through it by a double-barreled shot-gun! With its grottoes and caverns of bone, its rivetments and placements for my flesh, my smelling, my seeing, my hearing, my thinking! A skull, encompassing my brain, allowing it exit through its brittle windows to see the outside world!

He wanted to dash into the bridge party, upset it, a fox in a chickenyard, the cards fluttering all around like chicken feathers burst upward in clouds! He stopped himself only with a violent, trembling effort. Now, now, man, control yourself. This is a revelation, take it for what it is worth, understand it, savor it. BUT A SKELETON! screamed his subconscious. I won't stand for it. It's vulgar, it's terrible, it's frightening. Skeletons are horrors, they clink and tinkle and rattle in old castles, hung from oaken beams, making long, indolently rustling pendulums on the wind. . . .

"Darling, will you come in and meet the ladies?" called his wife's sweet, clear voice.

Mr. Harris stood upright. His SKELETON was holding him upright. This thing inside him, this invader, this horror, was supporting his arms, legs and head. It was like feeling someone just behind you who shouldn't be there. With every step he took he realized how dependent he was upon this other Thing.

"Darling, I'll be with you in a moment," he called weakly. To himself he said, "Come on, now, brace up. You've got to go back to work tomorrow. And Friday you've got to make that trip to Phoenix. Quite a drive. Over six hundred miles. Got to be in shape for that trip or you won't get Mr. Creldon to put his money into your ceramics business. Chin up, now."

Five minutes later he stood among the ladies being introduced to Mrs. Withers, Mrs. Abblematt and Miss Kirthy, all of whom had skeletons inside them but took it very calmly, because nature had carefully clothed the bare nudity of clavicle, tibia and femur with breasts, thighs, calves, with coiffure and eyebrow satanic, with bee-stung lips and—LORD! shouted Mr. Harris inwardly—when they talk or eat part of their skeleton shows—their *teeth!* I never thought of that.

"Excuse me," he said, and ran from the room only in time to drop his lunch among the petunias over the garden balistrade.

. . .

That night, seated on the bed as his wife undressed, he pared his toenails and fingernails scrupulously. These parts, too, were where his skeleton was shoving, indignantly growing out. He must have muttered something concerning this theory, because next thing he knew his wife, in negligee, slithered on the bed in animal cuddlesomeness, yawning, "Oh, my darling, fingernails are *not* bone, they're only hardened skin growths."

He threw the scissors away with relief. "Glad to hear that. Feel better." He looked at the ripe curves of her body, marveling. "I hope all people are made the same way."

"If you aren't the darndest hypochondriac I ever saw," she said. She snuggled to him. "Come on, what's wrong, tell mama."

"Something inside me," he said. "Something I ate."

The next morning and all afternoon at the office downtown, Mr. Harris found that the sizes, shapes and construction of various bones in his body displeased him. At ten a.m. he asked to feel Mr. Smith's elbow one moment. Mr. Smith obliged but gave forth a suspicious scowl. And after lunch Mr. Harris asked to touch Miss Laurel's shoulderblade and she immediately pushed herself back against him, shutting her eyes in the mistaken belief that he wished to examine a few other anatomical delicacies. "Miss Laurel!" he snapped. "Stop that!"

Alone, he pondered his neuroses. The war, the pressure of his work, the uncertainty of the future, probably had much to do with his mental outlook. He wanted to leave the office, get into his own business, for himself. He had more than a little talent at artistic things, had dabbled in ceramics and pottery. And soon as possible, he'd go to Phoenix, Arizona and borrow that money from Mr. Creldon. It would build him his kiln and set up his own shop. It was a worry.

What a hypochondriac he was. But it was a good thing he had contacted M. Munigant, who had seemed to understand and be eager to help him. He would fight it out with himself. He wouldn't go back to either Munigant or Dr. Burleigh unless he was forced to. The alien feeling would pass. He sat staring into nothing.

.  .  .

The alien feeling did not pass. It grew. On Tuesday and Wednesday it bothered him terrifically that his outer dermis, epidermis, hair and other appendages were of a high disorder, while the integumented skeleton of himself was a slick, clean structure of efficient organization. Sometimes, in certain lights while his lips were drawn morosely downward, weighted with melancholy, he imagined he saw his skull grinning at him. *It had its nerve, it did!*

"Let go of me!" he cried. "Let go of me! You've caught me, you've captured me! My lungs, you've got them in a vise! Release them!"

He experienced violent gasps as if his ribs were pressing in, choking the breath from him.

"My brain, stop squeezing it!"

And terrible hot headaches caught his brain like a bivalve in the compressed clamp of skull-bones.

"My vitals! All my organs, let them be, for God's sake! Stay away from my heart!" His heart seemed to cringe from the fanning nearness of his ribs, like pale spiders crouched and fiddling with their prey.

Drenched with sweat he lay upon the bed one night while Clarisse was out attending a Red Cross meeting. He tried to gather his wits again, and always the conflict of his disorderly exterior and this cool calciumed thing inside him with all its exact symmetry continued.

His complexion, wasn't it oily and lined with worry?

*Observe the flawless snow-white perfection of the skull.*

His nose, wasn't it too large?

*Then observe the small tiny bones of the skull's nose before that monstrous nasal cartilage begins forming Harris' lopsided proboscis.*

His body, wasn't it a bit plump?

*Well, then, consider the skeleton; so slender, so svelte, so economical of line and contour. Like exquisitely carved oriental ivory it is, perfected and thin as a reed.*

His eyes, weren't they protuberant and ordinary and numb looking?

*Be so kind as to note the eye-sockets of the skeleton's skull; so deep and rounded, sombre, quiet, dark pools, all knowing, eternal. Gaze deeply into skull sockets and you never touch the bottom of their dark understanding with any plumb line. All irony, all sadism, all life, all everything is there in the cupped darkness.*

Compare. Compare. Compare.

He raged for hours, glib and explosive. And the skeleton, ever the frail and solemn philosopher, quietly hung inside of Harris, saying not a word, quietly suspended like a delicate insect within a chrysalis, waiting and waiting.

. . .

Then it came to Harris.

"Wait a minute. Hold on a minute," he exclaimed. "You're helpless, too. I've got you, too! I can make you do anything I want you to, and you can't prevent it! I say put up your carpals, metacarpals and phalanges and—swift!—up they go, as I wave to someone!" He giggled. "I order the fibula and femur to loco-mote and HUMM two three four, Humm, two three four—we walk around the block. There!"

Harris grinned.

"It's a fifty-fifty fight. Even-steven. And we'll fight it out, we two, we shall. After all, I'm the part that thinks!" That was good, it was a triumph, he'd re-member that. "Yes. By God, yes. I'm the part that thinks. If I didn't have you, even then I could still think!"

Instantly, he felt a pain strike his head. His cranium, crowding in slowly, began giving him some of his own treatment right back.

At the end of the week he had postponed the Phoenix trip because of his health. He weighed himself on a penny scale and watched the slow glide of the red arrow as it pointed to: "164."

He groaned. "Why I've weighed 175 for ten years. I can't have lost ten pounds." He examined his cheeks in the fly-dotted mirror. Cold primitive fear rushed over him in odd little shivers. "Hold on! I know what're you're about, *you*."

He shook his finger at his bony face, particularly addressing his remarks to his superior maxillary, his inferior maxillary, to his cranium and to his cervi-cal vertebrae. "You rum thing, you. Think you can starve me off, make me lose weight, eh? A victory for you, is it? Peel the flesh off, leave nothing but skin on bone. Trying to ditch me, so you can be supreme, ah? No, no!"

He fled into a cafeteria immediately.

Ordering turkey, dressing, potatoes, cream, three desserts he soon found he could not eat it, he was sick to his stomach. He forced himself. His teeth began to ache. "Bad teeth, is it?" he wanted to know, angrily. "I'll eat in spite of every tooth clanging and banging and rotting so they fall in my gravy."

His head ached, his breathing came hard from a constricted chest, his teeth pulsed with pain, but he had one small victory. He was about to drink milk when he stopped and poured it into a vase of nasturtiums. "No calcium for you, my boy, no more calcium for you. Never will I eat foods again with calcium or other bone-fortifying minerals in them. I'll eat for one of us, not both, my lad."

"One hundred and fifty pounds," he wailed the following week to his wife. "Do you see how I've changed?"

"For the better," said Clarisse. "You were always a little plump, for your height, darling." She stroked his chin. "I like your face, it's so much nicer, the lines of it are so firm and strong now."

"They're not MY lines, they're his, damn him! You mean to say you like him better than you like me?" he demanded indignantly.

"Him? Who's him?"

.  .  .

In the parlor mirror, beyond Clarisse, his skull smiled back at him behind his fleshy grimace of hatred and despair.

Fuming, he popped malt tablets into his mouth. This was one way of gaining weight when you couldn't eat other foods. Clarisse noticed the malt capsules. "But, darling, really, you don't have to regain the weight for me," she said.

"Oh, shut up!" he felt like saying.

She came over to him and sat down and made him lie so his head was in her lap. "Darling," she said, "I've watched you lately. You're so—badly off. You don't say anything, but you look—hunted. You toss in bed at night. Maybe you should go to a psychiatrist. But I think I can tell you everything he would say. I've put it all together, from hints you've dropped. I can tell you that you and your skeleton are one and the same, one nation, indivisible, with liberty and justice for all. United you stand, divided you fall. If you two fellows can't get along like an old married couple in the future, go back and see Dr. Burleigh. But, *first*, relax. You're in a vicious circle, the more you worry, the more your bones stick out, the more your bones stick out, the more you fret. After all, now, who picked this fight—you or that anonymous entity you claim is lurking around behind your alimentary canal?"

He closed his eyes. "I did. I guess I did. Oh, my darling I love you so."

"You rest now," she said softly. "Rest and forget."

Mr. Harris felt buoyed up for half a day, then he began to sag again. It was all right to say everything was imagination, but this particular skeleton, by God, was fighting back.

Harris set out for M. Munigant's office late in the day. He walked for half an hour until he found the address, and then, at the sight of the name M. Munigant initialled in gold on a glass sign outside, Harris' bones seemed to explode from their moorings, blasted and erupted with pain. He could hardly see in his wet, pain-filled eyes. So violent were the pains that Harris staggered away, and when he opened his eyes again, he had rounded a corner, and M. Munigant's office was out of sight. The pains ceased.

M. Munigant, then, was the man to help him. He must be! If the sight of his gilt-lettered name could cause so titanic a reaction in the deepness of Harris' body, why, of course, M. Munigant *must* be just the man.

But, not today. Each time he tried to return to that office, the terrible pains laid him low. Perspiring, he had to give up, and stagger into a beer saloon for respite.

Moving across the floor of the beer palace, he wondered briefly if a lot of blame couldn't be put on M. Munigant's shoulders; after all, it was Munigant who'd first drawn his attention to his skeleton, and brought home the entire psychological impact of it! Could M. Munigant be using him for some nefarious purpose? But what purpose? Silly to even suspect him. Just a little doctor. Trying to be helpful. Munigant and his jar of bread-sticks. Ridiculous. M. Munigant was okay, okay.

. . .

But there was a sight within the beer parlor to give him hope. A large fat man, round as a butterball stood drinking consecutive beers at the bar. Now here was a successful fellow for you. Harris momentarily repressed a desire to go up, clap him on his shoulder and inquire as to how he'd gone about impounding his bones. Yes, the fat man's skeleton was luxuriously closeted. There were pillows of fat here, resilient bulges of it there, with several round chandeliers of fat under his chin. The poor skeleton was lost, it could never fight clear of that blubber; it may have tried once—but now, overwhelmed, not a bony echo of the fat man's supporter remained.

Not without envy, Harris approached the fat man as one might cut across the bow of an ocean liner.

"Glands?" inquired Harris.

"You talking to me?" asked the fat man.

"Or is there a special diet?" wondered Harris. "I beg your pardon, but, as you see, I'm down to the marrow. Adding weight seems an impossibility. I'd like a belly like that one of yours, it's tops. Did you grow it because you were afraid?"

"You," announced the fat man, "are drunk. But I like drunkards." He ordered more drinks. "Listen close. I'll tell you—"

"Layer by layer," said the fat man, "twenty years, man and boy, I built this." He held his vast stomach like a globe of the world, teaching his audience its gastronomical geography. "It was no overnight circus. The tent was not raised before dawn on the wonders installed within. I have cultivated my inner organs as if they were thoroughbred dogs, cats and other animals. My stomach is a fat pink Persian tom slumbering, rousing at intervals to purr, mew, growl and cry for chocolate titbits. I feed it well, it will 'most sit up for me. And, my dear fellow, my intestines are the rarest pure-bred Indian anacondas you ever viewed in the sleekest, coiled, fine and ruddy health. Keep 'em in prime, I do, all my pets. For fear of something? Perhaps."

This called for another drink for everybody.

"Gain weight?" The fat man savored the words on his tongue. "Here's what you do. Get yourself a quarreling bird of a wife, a baker's dozen of relatives who can flush a covey of troubles out from behind the veriest molehill; add to these a sprinkling of business associates whose prime motivation is snatching your last lonely quid, and you are well on your way to getting fat. How so? In no time you'll begin subconsciously building fat betwixt yourself and them. A buffer epidermal state, a cellular wall. You'll soon find that eating is the only fun on earth. But one needs to be bothered by outside sources. Too many people in this world haven't enough to worry about, then they begin picking on *themselves*, and they lose weight. Meet all of the vile, terrible people you can possibly know, and pretty soon you'll be adding the good old fat."

And with that advice, the fat man launched himself out into the dark tide of night, swaying mightily and wheezing.

"That's exactly what Dr. Burleigh told me, slightly changed," said Harris thoughfully. "Perhaps that trip to Phoenix at this time—"

. . .

The trip from Frisco to Phoenix was a sweltering one, crossing, as it did, the Death Valley on a broiling yellow day. It was only to be hoped that Mr. Crel-don, the man in Phoenix with the money, would be in an inspired mood about lending an amount necessary to setting Mr. Harris up in his ceramics business.

The car moved in the hot sluice of desert wind. The one Mr. H. sat inside the other Mr. H. Perhaps both perspired. Perhaps both were miserable.

On a curve, the inside Mr. H. suddenly constricted the outer flesh, causing him to jerk forward on the hot steering wheel.

The car ran off the road into deepest sand. It turned half over.

Night came on, a wind rose, the road was lonely and silent with no traffic, and Mr. Harris lay unconscious until night roused a sandstorm out of the empty valleys.

Morning found him awake and gritty-eyed, wandering in circles, having somehow gotten away from the road, perhaps because sand had layered it over. At noon he sprawled in the poor shade of a bush, and the sun struck at him with a keen sword edge, seeping into his bones. A buzzard circled.

Harris' parched lips cracked open weakly. "So that's it," he whimpered, red-eyed, bristle-cheeked. "One way or another you'll wreck me, walk me, starve me, thirst me, kill me." He swallowed dry burrs of dust. "Sun cook off my flesh so you can peek forth. Vultures lunch and breakfast from me, and then there you'll lie, grinning. Grinning with victory. Like a bleached xylophone strewn and played by vultures with an ear for odd music. You'd like that, eh? Freedom."

He walked on and on through a landscape that shivered and bubbled in the direct pour of sunlight; stumbling, falling, lying to feed himself little mouths of flame. The air was blue alcohol flame; and vultures roasted and steamed and glittered as they flew in glides and circles. Phoenix. The road. Car. Safety. Water.

"Hey!" somebody called from way off in the blue alcohol flame.

Mr. Harris propped himself up.

"Hey!" somebody called again. A crunching of footsteps, quick.

With a cry of unbelievable relief, Harris rose, only to collapse again into a park ranger's arms.

The car tediously repaired, Phoenix reached, Harris found himself in such an unholy state of mind that any business transaction would have to wait. This business of the Thing within him like a hard white sword in its scabbard tainted his eating, colored his love for Clarisse, made it unsafe to trust an automobile; all in all it must be settled before he could have any love for business or anything! That desert incident had brushed too closely. Too near the bone, one might say with an ironic twist of one's mouth. Harris grimly phoned Mr. Creldon, apologized, turned his car around and motored along a safer route to Los Angeles, thence up the coast to Frisco. He didn't trust that desert. But—careful! Salt waves boomed, hissing on the beach as he drove through Santa Barbara. Sand, fish and crustacia would cleanse his bones as swiftly as vultures. Slow down on the curves over the surf.

If anything happened, he desired casket burial. The two of them'd rot together, that way! Damn Him! And what about this little man—M. Munigant? Bone specialist. Oh God, where was one to turn?

"Darling!" trilled Clarisse, kissing him so he winced at the solidity of her teeth and jaw behind the passionate exchange.

"Darling," he said slowly, wiping his lips with his wrist, trembling.

"You look thinner; oh, darling, the business deal—it didn't go through!"

"I have to go back again. Yes, I have to go back again. That's it."

. . .

She kissed him again. Lord, he couldn't even kiss her any more and enjoy it because of this obsession. They ate a slow, unhappy dinner, with Clarisse trying to cheer him. He studied the phone, several times he picked it up indecisively, then laid it aside. His wife walked in, putting on her coat and hat. "I'm sorry to have to leave now, when you're feeling so low. But I'll be back in three hours from the Red Cross. I simply *have* to go."

When Clarisse was gone, Harris dialed the phone, nervously.

"Mr. Munigant?"

. . .

The explosions and the sickness in his body after he set the phone down were unbelievable. His bones were racked with every kind of pain, cold and hot, he had ever thought of, or experienced in wildest nightmare. He swallowed as many aspirin as he could find in an effort to stave off the assault; but when the door-bell finally rang an hour later, he could not move, he lay weak and exhausted, panting, tears streaming down his cheeks, like a man on a torture rack. Would M. Munigant go away if he didn't answer the door?

"Come in!" he tried to gasp it out. "Come in, for God's sake!"

M. Munigant came in. Thank God the door had been unlocked.

Oh, but Mr. Harris looked terrible. Harris nodded. The pains rushed through him, hitting him with large iron hammers and hooks. M. Munigant's eyes glittered as he saw Harris' protuberant bones. Ah, he saw that Mr. Harris was now psychologically prepared for aid. Was it not so? Harris nodded again, feebly, sobbing. Through his shimmering eyes he seemed to see M. Munigant shrink, get smaller. Imagination of course. Harris sobbed out his story of the trip to Phoenix. M. Munigant sympathized. This skeleton was a—traitor! They would FIX him once and for all! "Mister Munigant," sighed Harris, faintly. "I never noticed before, you have such an odd tongue. Round. Tube-like. I'm ready. What do I do?"

If Mr. Harris would relax in his chair, and open his mouth? M. Munigant whistled softly, appreciatively, coming closer. He switched off the lights peering into Harris' dropped jaw. Wider, please? It had been so hard, the first time, to help Harris, with both body and bone in rebellion. Now, he had cooperation from the flesh of the man anyway, even if the skeleton was acting up somewhat. In the darkness M. Munigant's voice got small, small, tiny, tiny. The whistling became high and shrill. Now. Relax, Mr. Harris. NOW!

Harris felt his jaw pressed violently in all directions, his tongue depressed as with a spoon, his throat clogged. He gasped for breath. Whistle. He could not breathe. He was corked. Something squirmed, corkscrewed his cheeks out, bursting his jaws. Like a hot water douche, something squirted into his sinuses, his ears clanged! "Ahhhh!" shrieked Harris, gagging. His head, its carapaces riven, shattered, hung loose. Agony shot into his lungs, around.

Harris could breathe again. His watery eyes sprang wide. He shouted. His ribs, like sticks picked up and bundled, were loosened in him. Pain! He fell to the floor, rocking, rolling, wheezing out his hot breath.

Lights flickered in his senseless eyeballs, he felt his limbs unloosened swiftly, expertly. Through steaming eyes he saw the parlor. The room was empty.

"Mr. Munigant? Where are you? In God's name, where are you, Mr. Munigant! Come help me!"

M. Munigant was gone!

"Help!"

Then he heard it.

Deep down in the subterranean fissures of his bodily well, he heard the minute, unbelievable noises; little smackings and twistings little dry chippings and grindings and nuzzling sounds—like a tiny hungry mouse down in the red blooded dimness, gnawing ever so earnestly and expertly at what may have been, but was not, a submerged timber . . . !

■ ■ ■

Clarisse, walking along the sidewalk, held her head high and marched straight toward her house on Saint James Place. She was thinking of the Red Cross and a thousand other things as she turned the corner and almost ran into this little man standing there.

Clarisse would have ignored him if it were not for the fact that as she passed he took something long, white and oddly familiar from his coat and proceeded to chew on it, as on a peppermint stick. Its end devoured, his extraordinary tongue darted within the white confection, sucking out the filling, making contented noises. He was still crunching his goodie as she proceeded up the sidewalk to her house, turned the doorknob and walked in.

"Darling?" she called, smiling around. "Darling, where are you?"

She shut the door, walked down the hall into the living room.

"Darling . . ."

She stared at the floor for twenty seconds, trying to understand.

She screamed. That scream came from her like a ghastly white fish torn from her vitals by some ungodly fisherman.

Outside in the sycamore darkness, the little man, pierced a long white stick with intermittent holes, then softly, sighing, lips puckered, played a little sad tune upon the improvised instrument to accompany the shrill and awful singing of Clarisse's voice as she stood in the living room.

Many times as a little girl Clarisse had run on the beach sands, stepped on a jelly-fish and screamed. It was not so bad, finding an intact, gelatin-skinned jelly-fish in one's living room. One could step back from it.

It was when the jelly-fish *called you by name.* . . .

# TWENTY
# RIABOUCHINSKA
# (AND SO DIED RIABOUCHINSKA)

Mr. Ockham had a look about him in death as he had had in life . . . a general appearance which might prompt one to say, "There's a man who'll one day be stabbed, or shot, or booted in the head." And although Mr. Ockham had not met his end in any of the aforementioned ways, he *had* been strangled, and he *was* dead. Dead on the floor of a theatre cellar.

Yes, Mr. Ockham was deceased, and nobody seemed to care, thought John Fabian. Nobody but this Detective Lieutenant Krovitch who had been sent down to have a look around.

John Fabian's hand twitched and struck against a small polished bronze box which lay atop a dusty dressing table. On the box lid were the words: "RIABOUCHINSKA—Property of John Fabian, World's Greatest Ventriloquist."

Fabian sensed Krovitch's eyes moving from the box to him, to Alyce Fabian, his wife, to Bernard Douglas, his press agent.

As Krovitch lit his cigar, it happened.

The voice began to plead inside the bronze box. It was high and soft and hidden away.

"Please let me out, oh please let me out!"

The three others glanced with startled eyes at the box. Fabian felt himself staring, too, his head beginning to ache, his throat becoming sore and raw, and he stepped forward and spoke earnestly:

"No, Ria. This is serious business, darling. Stay where you are."

He laughed, unnaturally.

There was a sharp stab of pain in his head.

From behind the polished lid her calm voice said, "Please don't laugh. You should be kind to me now, after what's happened."

Fabian's face stiffened. He swallowed the panic that rose swiftly in him.

Detective Krovitch spoke, irritably. "If you don't mind, Fabian, we'll have the dummy act some other time. Now let's get this clear. Each of you testify that you don't know who this dead Mr. Ockham is, yet he told the stage-manager tonight that he *knew* Mr. Fabian and wanted to see him about something important—"

The voice in the box pleaded softly. "Please let me out."

Krovitch shouted. "Stop it, Fabian!"

There was hidden laughter, like a silver bell.

"Pay no attention to her, Lieutenant," said Fabian.

"Her?" Krovitch glared. "You mean *you*. What is this? Get together, you two!"

"We'll never be together again," murmured the small voice. "Never again after tonight . . ."

Krovitch held out his hand. "Give me the key to the box, Fabian."

In the silence there was the rattle of the key in the lock, and the squeal of the tiny box hinges.

"Thank you," said Riabouchinska.

Krovitch stood, motionless, just looking down, seeing Riabouchinska lying in her box, and not believing what he saw.

There were nights in life when you dreamed, thought John Fabian, and this is what you dreamed. There were women you saw in life, far down a street, walking, fragile, far away, unattainable, and this tiny figure was one of them. There were voices that you heard singing high in a dark church loft, voices that made the candle-flames shudder and dance to every cadence, and this was one of those voices. On a summer afternoon you watched a spider gracefully spinning its cloudy web, and now that web was Riabouchinska's evening dress, here and now. You had heard of honesty and intelligence and frankness and unafraidness, all your life, and now it looked straight up at you, fearlessly, shiningly, from a puppet's eyes. She was so beautiful that your throat closed and you were sad because you knew that she was only a puppet . . .

John Fabian tenderly picked Riabouchinska up.

"Isn't she beautiful?" he said, with pride. "She's carved from the finest wood, Riabouchinska is. She's appeared in London, Paris, Rome, New York. Everyone in the world knows her and loves her. Many people question Riabouchinska's authenticity. They think she's really alive, that she is a midget. People just cannot believe that she is constructed of wood."

John Fabian's wife, Alyce, stood glaring at him with a look of fine hatred; but he was aware of no one but the life-like figure he held in his arms; and speaking to him, it said:

"Please don't go on about me, John. Alyce doesn't like it."

"Alyce *never has* liked anything about you, Ria."

"Sh! Don't!" cried Riabouchinska, softly. "Not here and not now, John." She changed. She turned to Krovitch in Fabian's delicate hands. "Tell me, Lieutenant, how did it all happen? I mean about poor Mr. Ockham?"

Krovitch stared at them. "What *is* this?"

Fabian said, "You'd best return to your box, Ria."

"But I don't want to," she replied. "I have as much right to listen and talk, I'm as much a part of this murder as Alyce or . . . or Mr. Douglas even————"

The press agent threw down his cigarette. "Don't drag me into this, you little witch!" And the manner in which he replied made it obvious that Riabouchinska was more than an illusion to him, for he reacted to her as to a real person.

"It's just that I want the truth to be told," said Riabouchinska. "And if I'm locked in my bronze casket there will be no truth, for John Fabian is a consummate liar and I must watch him. That's right, isn't it, John?"

"Yes," he said, "I suppose it is."

"John loves me best of all the women in the world. And I love him and try to understand his wrong way of thinking."

Krovitch pounded the table. "We're wasting time! If you think you'll interfere with my investigation, Fabian—"

"Lieutenant, I am helpless."

"But she's in your throat!" snapped Krovitch.

Fabian shook his gaunt head. "No, she is in my heart, which is much deeper. Sometimes, I am powerless. Sometimes she is only herself, nothing of me at all. Sometimes, she tells me what to do and I must do it. She watches over me, reprimands me, is honest where I am dishonest, ethical where I am wicked as old sin. She lives her life, I live mine. She has raised a wall in my head, between herself and me. She lives there, ignoring me if I try to make her say improper things, cooperating if I suggest the correct words and pantomime." Fabian sighed. "So, if you intend going on, I'm afraid Ria must be present. Locking her up will do no good."

Lieutenant Krovitch sat quietly for a moment, then he seemed to make a decision.

"All right. Let her stay. Maybe . . . maybe before the night's over I'll be tired enough to ask even a ventriloquist's dummy questions."

. . .

John Fabian watched Krovitch unwrap a fresh cigar, prepare it, light it. Fabian touched his throat, unobtrusively; the soreness there, and the headache, had subsided for a moment. Krovitch puffed out smoke. "Once more, Mr. Douglas, do you recognize the dead man?"

Douglas looked at the body. "No. He looks familiar. An actor-type, I believe."

Krovitch swore. "One of you three is lying! From the condition of Ockham's shoes, his worn clothing, he needed money. Douglas, are you in love with Mrs. Fabian?"

"Really, Lieutenant!" cried Alyce Fabian.

"I've been watching you—your actions."

"*My* actions?" Her eyes flashed.

Krovitch nodded. "Yes. The way you look at Riabouchinska's box, Mrs. Fabian. The way you hold your breath when she appears. The way your fingers knot when she talks, the way you stare at her."

"If you think for one moment I'm jealous of a piece of wood!"

"Aren't you?" Krovitch softened his voice.

"No!" She was almost hysterical. "I'm not jealous of her!"

"You needn't tell him, Alyce," said John Fabian.

"Let her!" cried Riabouchinska.

Pain struck his head like a hatchet, and John Fabian reeled. They were all staring at the figurine. And now he himself was looking at her, as if her cry had come from an alien throat.

After a long while, Alyce Fabian began to speak.

"I married John seven years ago. He said he loved me. I loved him and I loved Riabouchinska, too. At first, anyway. But then I began to see that he really paid more attention to her than he did to me. He treated her as a real person. I was only an assistant to his act. I began to feel hatred—not for Riabouchinska, because it wasn't her fault—but I felt a terrible hatred for John, because I knew it was all his doing. His cleverness, his sadistic temperament. Each jealousy on my part was a tribute to the perfection of his art! She came out of him like a woman out of a dark god." She paused, and then went on. "But I couldn't hate Ria, she was lovely, almost real, sweet and honest. Everything that John wasn't."

She stopped talking, and the room was silent.

Fabian felt his throat shudder painfully.

"Tell about Mr. Douglas," murmured Riabouchinska, moving her head.

With an effort, Mrs. Fabian finished it out. "When I got no understanding, no love, from John, I turned to Mr. Douglas . . ."

"So. And Mr. Ockham, our dead man, was a blackmailer. It's quite clear now. He came to the theatre tonight to see your husband about you and Mr. Douglas. You killed him to prevent that interview."

"I didn't kill him," said Alyce, tiredly.

"Douglas might have, and not told you!"

"Why kill a man," said Douglas. "John knew all about it!"

"I did indeed," said John Fabian, and laughed.

His head ached with a sudden violence.

He stopped laughing and Riabouchinska went on laughing for him, echoing in the dim concrete room.

.  .  .

The next day, John Fabian sat in his dressing room, with his head held between his tight, cold hands. The pain was larger with every hour. He hadn't slept during the long night. On the table before him were several half emptied aspirin boxes and a fresh glass of water. Fabian roused himself and was about to take another tablet, when footsteps scraped outside and there was a discreet knock at the door.

"Come in," called Fabian, wearily.

Krovitch entered and closed the door. "Fabian, I have something here which might interest you."

With a tight grin on his face, Krovitch held a photograph of a woman before Fabian. Fabian blinked, put out a startled hand, and then fell back in his chair. He shut his eyes and the knife cut into his head, deeper, deeper the pain and the cutting, the hatchet blows and the nausea. Krovitch turned the picture carefully and began reading from the typewritten data on the back:

"Name, Ilya Riamansk; weight, one hundred pounds, blue eyes, black hair, oval face, born 1914, New York City. Of Russo-Slav parentage. Disappeared in 1934. Believed a victim of amnesia."

Fabian shut his eyes tighter. His skull was on fire.

Krovitch laid the photograph down, shaking his head thoughtfully. "Fabian, it was pretty silly of me to search through the files for a picture of a ventriloquist's puppet. They all laughed, at headquarters. And yet, here she is. Riabouchinska. Not papier-mâché, not wood, not a puppet, but a woman who once lived and moved about and—disappeared." He glanced up. "Take it from there, Mr. Fabian."

Fabian half-smiled. "There's nothing to it." Pain, like colors, flashed over his staring eyes. "I saw her picture long ago, liked her looks, and copied my puppet after her."

"Nothing to it, eh?" drawled Krovitch. "Listen, Fabian, this morning I read through a stack of *Billboard* magazines *that* high. In the year 1934 I found an interesting article concerning an act playing on a lesser circuit known as *Fabian and Sweet William*. Sweet William was a little male dummy. As usual in such acts, there was a girl assistant. Ilya Riamansk. There was no picture of her. But I had the name of a real person to go on, and her name being Russian, somewhat like Riabouchinska, I lost no time in digging up this picture. The resemblance, needless to say, between the real woman on the one hand and Riabouchinska on the other, is startling. Would you like to start all over again?"

"She was my assistant, yes. That was all. I simply used her as a model."

Krovitch snorted. "Do you take me for a fool? Do you think I don't know love when I see it? It all starts and ends with Riabouchinska! Why should you love a puppet so intensely? Because you loved the original *woman* intensely! Look here, Fabian, we've fenced enough. You're in a spot, and you know it!"

Fabian lifted up his pale, delicate hands and let them drop. "All right. In 1934 I *was* billed as *Fabian and Sweet William*. Sweet William was a small, bulb-nosed little boy dummy I carved years ago. I was playing in Los Angeles when this girl, Ilya Riamansk, appeared at the stage door one night. She wanted a job. She'd followed my work for years. She was desperate for employment, and she hoped to be my assistant. It was autumn . . ."

He remembered her in the half-light of the stage alley. He remembered how startled he was at her fresh beauty, her eagerness to work with him and for him . . . the way the rain, when it fell softly down through the narrow alley, caught in her dark hair and touched her feverish cheeks. He had given her the job almost without questioning. And in four months he who had always denied and scoffed at love became hopelessly lost to this woman.

Then there were arguments, and things much more than arguments, things done and said that were violent and unfair. He wanted her to marry him; she never quite accepted. He went into hysterical rages at her. Once he destroyed her wardrobe. That much she had taken. But it was somewhat different on that last night when he had fired her, shouted at her, taken hold of her and slapped her, violently, three times, across the face!

Ilya Riamansk vanished that night.

He was desparate when he found she was really gone for good, and there was nowhere to find her. He inserted ads in the papers, put a private detective on the case. People talked. The police came to question him. There was talk of murder. But she was gone with no trace. A record of her was sent to the largest cities. That was the end of it for the police. But not for Fabian. She might be dead, or just run away, but wherever she was, he knew he needed her.

One night he returned home more depressed than usual. He collapsed upon a chair, and before he knew it, he found himself speaking to Sweet William, in the totally dark room:

"William, William, this is all over and done! I can't go on!"

And William cried, "Coward! You can get her back if you want!"

"No, no I can't. No, I can never get her back!"

Sweet William squeaked and clappered at him. "Yes, you can! *Think!*" he insisted. "Think of a way. You can do it. Put me away. Start all over . . ."

"Start all over?"

"Yes," whispered Sweet William. "Buy a length of the finest hard-grained wood you can buy, and begin carving, exactly, and *slowly,* and lovingly. Carving. Make the little arching nostrils, just *so,* and cut her black, thin eyebrows round and high, and make her cheeks in small, duplicate hollows . . ."

"No!" shouted Fabian. "It's foolish! I could never do it!"

"Yes, you could. Yes, you could, could, could . . . could . . ."

The voice faded away like a water ripple in a dark cave. Blackness rushed over Fabian. His head fell forward. He whimpered. Sweet William sighed. And then they both lay silent and solemnly unconscious.

The next morning, John Fabian purchased the hardest, best-grained piece of wood he could buy, but when he reached home, despair seized him. How could he fashion his warm Ilya from this cold wood? How could he shape this dumb block of dead substance into anything faintly approximating her glowing life? It was Sweet William who urged him on, sighing in the night:

"You can do it!"

For twenty weeks he worked. He carved her hands into things as natural and beautiful as shells lying in the sun. And Sweet William lay dust-cloaked in his box, from time to time croaking some sarcasm, some criticism, some hint, some help; but he was dying, soon to be untouched, inanimate wood. As weeks passed and Fabian moulded and scraped and polished the new wood, Sweet William lay longer and longer in stricken silence, and one day as Fabian held the puppet in his hand, Sweet William seemed to look at him a moment with puzzled eyes, and then there was a death rattle in his throat.

And Sweet William was gone!

Now, as Fabian carved, a fluttering, an attempting of speech in his throat began echoing and re-echoing the sounds of Ilya Riamansk. By the year's ending he was thinned and without money. But by then he had searched his stream of consciousness, experimented, and given the doll all the gracious mannerisms and shy gestures of the real woman.

And then, at last, he held Ilya Riamansk in his arms again, they were together, he could talk to her and she could reply. And the first thing he made the little creature say was:

"I love you, John Fabian."

.   .   .

Krovitch sat in his chair, watching John Fabian.

"I see," he said. "And your wife?"

"Alyce? She was another of my assistants. She did her work well and she loved me," said Fabian. "I don't know why I married her."

"I see. What about the dead man—Ockham?"

"I had never seen him before you showed me his body downstairs in the cellar yesterday."

The pain gripped his skull and pressed. He felt something almost scurry, like a tiny animal, in his head, behind his eyes, and his throat was raw, and Riabouchinska stirred in his lap. "That's not true, John Fabian. Don't lie."

Fabian's cheeks were white. The puppet spoke, looking directly at Krovitch:

"John received the first blackmail letter a month ago. It said, simply: RIA-BOUCHINSKA, BORN 1914, DIED 1934—BORN *AGAIN* IN 1935."

Fabian's body froze. He felt the cold senseless motion of his finger hidden up within the puppet body, curled over the wire loop which twitched her beautiful small mouth wide, and he felt his tongue move chill and numb between his dry teeth. His eyes whirled about, seeking an exit from the room, seeking some way where a frustration or a truth did not wait to bar the way. He gave up. He whispered:

"Ockham threatened to expose me to the world!"

"Go on."

Fabian took time to find the right words. "I wanted my love for Ilya kept to myself." His voice rose. "What sort of love would it be in the future if people really guessed the significance of my carving this figurine that talked and moved? People would laugh or be disgusted. Perverted, criminal mind, they'd shout! Ugly, horrible, revolting! And could I play my love scenes with Ria any more, when *they* knew? Not when with every word I uttered someone in the audience would nudge someone else and whisper, "She lived once, you know. Disappeared. They say he loved her. They say he killed her!'"

"How much did Ockham want?"

"A thousand dollars to start with. More later."

"And so you killed him?"

"No, I didn't! I paid him!"

"We found no money on him."

"Nevertheless, I paid him! Alyce and Douglas must've heard our conversation. They've wanted to be rid of me for years now, I'm not blind! Alyce saw a way of eliminating me and getting some money, too. She's nothing but a . . ."

"Just a moment," said Riabouchinska, quietly. "There's something I wish to say. And yet," she wailed helplessly, "I can't say it."

Krovitch backed away. John Fabian's eyes widened in his face, and the pain now was so intense that it threatened to shatter the parts of his head in an explosion of fire and bone. His throat convulsed and shot needles of pain into his chest. The hollows of his face sank in and twisted.

"I—I was in the room when Mr. Ockham came," Riabouchinska began. Her voice was high and blurred now. "I lay in my box and I listened and I heard, and I *know*." The voice shook, then controlled itself. "Mr. Ockham threatened to destroy me, tear me up, burn me into ashes if John didn't pay him a thousand dollars. Then, suddenly, there came a falling sound," she cried. "Mr. Ockham's head must have struck the floor! I heard Mr. Fabian cry out, swearing and sobbing, all in one. I heard a hissing, gasping, choking, horrible sound!"

Fabian shouted. "You heard nothing! You're deaf and dumb and blind and lifeless; you heard nothing! Your ears are carved!"

"But they *hear!*" She spoke with difficulty. "And then the hissing, choking sound stopped. I heard John drag Mr. Ockham to the door, open it, and take Mr. Ockham down the stairs, under the theatre toward the old dressing rooms that haven't been used in years. Down . . . down . . . down he took the body . . ."

Fabian was out of his chair. And there it was, in the mirror, he could see it himself! A scene so incongruous, so impossible, so completely beyond the veil of sanity that Krovitch was recoiling from him. If ever in the time of the world the forces that manipulate man struggled one side against another, this was the time! There, in the mirror! His own face, the shocked pallid face of John Fabian, wrenching, the horrible protrusion of the eyes, the clenching of the teeth as a censor, then relaxing again; the subtle move of the throat, and the high, sad, and accusative voice of Riabouchinska leaping from her tiny, shining lips! And the concussions of pain that sliced his head apart! I know what is happening, thought Fabian, but I do not know!

Now her voice was so high and faint it was barely audible:

"I'm not made to live this way. There is nothing for us now, anyway, because the world will know of us. Even when you killed him and I lay in my bronze box last night, I realized, we *both* realized, that these were our last hours; because while I've accepted your weaknesses and lies, I can't exist in murder. It couldn't have gone on. No one can live side by side with such knowledge . . ."

Fabian took her in his arms and held her high into the warm sunlight. She looked down at him with her clear, honest way of seeing him. There were angry, helpless tears in his eyes. His hand shook and, in shaking, made her tremble, too.

Her mouth closed and opened, silent, gaping and shutting, again and again, with no words.

Fabian began to sob. He closed his fingers unbelievingly about his own throat, his eyes glazed. He looked like a man trying to remember something beautiful— her voice, how it sounded, how to make it sound again, how to make her take back all she had said that was the truth.

"She's gone," he whispered, frantically, clenching his throat. He squeezed his eyes tight. "She's gone. I can't find her. I try—but I can't find her. She's run off behind the dark wall and so deep deep down and far away in the night I'll never be able to find her again. She's gone."

His head no longer ached. It was cool. His throat was relaxed.

Riabouchinska slipped bonelessly from his limp hand, folded over and glided noiselessly down to lie upon the cold floor, her eyes closed, her mouth gently sealed.

Fabian did not even look at her as Krovitch led him away.

# TWENTY-ONE

# SKELETON

Well, I just didn't know *it* was there until this morning," said the man. His name was Arnie and he swabbed bars and shook cocktails.

"That was a helluva time to find out," said his wife, whose name was Lily. Her work around their house consisted of pyramiding cigarette butts in various containers all day and then carrying them to the kitchen to dump them. After that she started on a new pyramid.

Arnie sat in a big green overstuffed chair, and the smoke from his cigarette made a trembling pattern because his hand was doing the same. "All of a sudden I discovered it," he said, amazed. He looked down at himself as if every part of his body was a rare piece of ivory carving. "This morning I got a little twinge in my knee, you understand. Then I touched it, felt it." His eyebrows went up, surprised. "There was a *bone* there!"

"There's always a bone there," said his wife.

"Yeah, but I didn't know it," cried Arnie softly, his cheeks burning. "I didn't know it, and the bone felt funny. It never felt that way before."

"You never *looked* at it before," said his wife.

"Sure, sure. So this morning I looked at it. You were gone out to the store. I was alone. And I began to wonder." He stopped. "Say—honey, can I—" He asked her earnestly, staring at her. "Can I feel your knee-cap?"

"Oh, for God's sake," she said. "A new approach, yet. In the guise of a bone specialist."

"Can't you see I'm not kidding," he said, and his hands trembled again. "I want to know if everybody's made the same; not just *me*."

"I'm the same," she said. "Well—almost. A few changes, maybe. Nothing to throw a wing-ding over."

"Anyway," he put it in a picture for her, framed the epic drama in monotone. "I felt my knees. Then I felt my ankles. Then I grabbed my wrists, my arms, my neck, my head! Then I jumped up, like I'd been shot! Christ All Mighty! I yelled! I got a *skeleton* inside me! Get 'im outa here! A skeleton!"

His wife was looking at him thoughtfully.

"I know what you're thinking," gasped Arnie, lying back in his chair. "You're thinking I'm either drunk or nuts. Maybe I'm both. I had to take a drink. I got a skeleton inside me. Here we go walking around the world, smiling at people, talking at people, shaking their hands, slapping them on the back, and we all got skeletons. Like inside closets. I got to figuring—bodies *are* closets. We keep bones there."

"What you want to go thinking *that* for? You're queer."

"Can I help it? I began to shake. I lay on the couch, not able to move. I thought, I got a skeleton in me. One of those things you read about hanging in castle dungeons, with webs on them; or dangling on stone walls clanking in the wind, bronze chains on their wrists and necks. One of those bony, white, horrible things you see all naked on deserts. God!"

"Yeah," said his wife.

"I was scared. I still am. You go walking around taking yourself for granted, not even knowing yourself. And it's like a snap ending on a story, to find you been hiding a regular Mr. Hyde or a Frankenstein inside you."

"You got something there," said his wife.

"So I finally quit shaking, at least enough so I could examine myself, and began to feel myself, all over."

"I hope you two live happily ever after," laughed his wife. "You and your skeleton."

"Aw, cut it!" he said, glaring at her. "I felt my ribs, and there they were. Like two big spiders standing over my lungs, pressing 'em in, letting 'em out, pressing 'em in again with their long thin white legs. Oh, *baby*. And I felt my neck. Feel your neck, Lily. Get hold of the neck bones. That's it. Now, still holding your neck bones, bend your head way back. *Way* back. Feel? What happens to your neck bones? They go inside somewhere! They're gone! There's nothing to hold your head up but a lot of soft stuff!"

She snapped her fingers away from her neck after the experiment, a shiny light in her grey eyes. "Okay, okay. It's *still* there. It's inside somewhere. Who cares?"

"And I began to feel how the jaw moves and the joints work. Lord, what I learned. There's bone all around your brain. You read that in school, but you don't think about it, it's just something in a book. And now you find bone around your brain. This damned Skeleton *owns* us. It holds everything that's important, practically. Your brain, your lungs, your heart. Gee-zuzz! And I began to get scared again. The only good thing about people is they have skin on. Skin and color and hair."

"And a little weight here or there," said his wife, smudging out a cigarette. "But, Arnie, we'd look awful funny, sweets, if we were just skin and fat. Nothing to hold us up."

"I don't want nothing out of a horror novel holding *me* up!" he cried wildly, hoarsely.

"I can see you're gonna carry on this way a long time," she said, walking over to him. "Honest, Arnie, you're a weird bird. Here." She sat on his lap. "We're all the same. It's okay. Whatever we are it's okay, because that's how we're made. Something's holding me up, too, but it gives me shape, honey. You'll forget about this. You always forget. You get scared of some little thing, the wind at night, the mountains, the snow, and now a skeleton, but you forget, Arnie. It's easy. Here. You want to feel my knee bone? It's the same as yours."

"Can I?" he asked doubtfully, slowly.

"Sure, honey," she said. "Sure."

He touched her knee bone as if it were red hot. It was not red hot. It was only pleasantly glowing and warm.

She leaned against him, kissed him lightly on the forehead, bit his ear tenderly. "You'll forget, Arnie," she murmured, easily. She took the cigarette from his quivering hand, put it in a tray. Then she kissed him on the lips.

Arnie slid his arms around her. Arnie held her tightly, his hands moving. He kissed her for a long time and then kissed her again.

He stopped trembling.

Deep down inside herself, rich and low, she laughed and sighed with relief, her eyes closed. She pretended to try and get up and go away, but he held onto her and kissed her. She laughed again, warmly, drowsily, deeply. She was proving something to him, she didn't know exactly what, but she was proving it.

A few minutes later her hand, with the skelatinous ghostly white bones inside it, the kind that hang in webbed castles, the kind that lie naked on hot deserts or hang rustling in closets, reached over and clicked out the light.

# TWENTY-TWO

# THE BLACK FERRIS

The carnival had come to town like an October wind, like a dark bat flying over the cold lake, bones rattling in the night, mourning, sighing, whispering up the tents in the dark rain. It stayed on for a month by the gray, restless lake of October, in the black weather and increasing storms and leaden skies.

During the third week, at twilight on a Thursday, the two small boys walked along the lake shore in the cold wind.

"Aw, I don't believe you," said Peter.

"Come on, and I'll show you," said Hank.

They left wads of spit behind them all along the moist brown sand of the crashing shore. They ran to the lonely carnival grounds. It had been raining. The carnival lay by the sounding lake with nobody buying tickets from the flaky black booths, nobody hoping to get the salted hams from the whining roulette wheels, and none of the thin-fat freaks on the big platforms. The midway was silent; all the gray tents hissing on the wind like gigantic prehistoric wings. At eight o'clock perhaps, ghastly lights would flash on, voices would shout, music would go out over the lake. Now there was only a blind hunchback sitting on a black booth, feeling of the cracked china cup from which he was drinking some perfumed brew.

"There," said Hank, pointing.

The black Ferris wheel rose like an immense light-bulbed constellation against the cloudy sky, silent.

"I still don't believe what you said about it," said Peter.

"You wait, I saw it happen. I don't know how, but it did. You know how carnivals are; all funny. Okay; this one's even *funnier.*"

Peter let himself be led to the high green hiding place of a tree.

Suddenly, Hank stiffened. "*Hist!* There's Mr. Cooger, the carnival man, now!" Hidden, they watched.

Mr. Cooger, a man of some thirty-five years, dressed in sharp bright clothes, a lapel carnation, hair greased with oil, drifted under the tree, a brown derby hat on his head. He had arrived in town three weeks before, shaking his brown derby hat at people on the street from inside his shiny red Ford, tooting the horn.

Now Mr. Cooger nodded at the little blind hunchback, spoke a word. The hunchback blindly, fumbling, locked Mr. Cooger into a black seat and sent him whirling up into the ominous twilight sky. Machinery hummed.

"See!" whispered Hank. "The Ferris wheel's going the wrong way. Backwards instead of forwards!"

"So what?" said Peter.

"Watch!"

The black Ferris wheel whirled twenty-five times around. Then the blind hunchback put out his pale hands and halted the machinery. The Ferris wheel stopped, gently swaying, at a certain black seat.

A ten-year-old boy stepped out. He walked off across the whispering carnival ground, in the shadows.

Peter almost fell from his limb. He searched the Ferris wheel with his eyes. "Where's Mr. Cooger!"

Hank poked him. "You wouldn't believe! Now *see!*"

"Where's Mr. Cooger at!"

"Come on, quick, run!" Hank dropped and was sprinting before he hit the ground.

.  .  .

Under giant chestnut trees, next to the ravine, the lights were burning in Mrs. Foley's white mansion. Piano music tinkled. Within the warm windows, people moved. Outside, it began to rain, despondently, irrevocably, forever and ever.

"I'm *so* wet," grieved Peter, crouching in the bushes. "Like someone squirted me with a hose. How much longer do we wait?"

"Sh!" said Hank, cloaked in wet mystery.

They had followed the little boy from the Ferris wheel up through town, down dark streets to Mrs. Foley's ravine house. Now, inside the warm dining room of the house the strange little boy sat at dinner, forking and spooning rich lamb chops and mashed potatoes.

"I know his name," whispered Hank, quickly. "My Mom told me about him the other day. She said, 'Hank, you hear about the li'l orphan boy moved in Mrs. Foley's? Well, his name is Joseph Pikes and he just came to Mrs. Foley's one day about two weeks ago and said how he was an orphan run away and could he have something to eat, and him and Mrs. Foley been getting on like hot apple pie ever since.' That's what my Mom said," finished Hank, peering through the steamy Foley window. Water dripped from his nose. He held onto Peter who was twitching with cold. "Pete, I didn't like his looks from the first, I didn't. He looked—mean."

"I'm scared," said Peter, frankly wailing. "I'm cold and hungry and I don't know what this's all about."

"Gosh, you're dumb!" Hank shook his head, eyes shut in disgust. "Don't you see, three weeks ago the carnival came. And about the same time this little ole orphan shows up at Mrs. Foley's. And Mrs. Foley's son died a long time ago one night one winter, and she's never been the same, so here's this little ole orphan boy who butters her all around."

"Oh," said Peter, shaking.

"Come on," said Hank. They marched to the front door and banged the lion knocker.

After awhile the door opened and Mrs. Foley looked out.

"You're all wet, come in," she said. "My land," she herded them into the hall. "What do you want?" she said, bending over them, a tall lady with lace on her full bosom and a pale thin face with white hair over it. "You're Henry Walterson, aren't you?"

Hank nodded, glancing fearfully at the dining room where the strange little boy looked up from his eating. "Can we see you alone, ma'm?" And when the old lady looked palely surprised, Hank crept over and shut the hall door and whispered at her. "We got to warn you about something, it's about that boy come to live with you, that orphan?"

The hall grew suddenly cold. Mrs. Foley drew herself high and stiff. "Well?"

"He's from the carnival, and he ain't a boy, he's a man, and he's planning on living here with you until he finds where your money is and then run off with it some night, and people will look for him but because they'll be looking for a ten-year-old boy they won't recognize him when he walks by a thirty-five-year-old man, named Mr. Cooger!" cried Hank.

"What *are* you talking about?" declared Mrs. Foley.

"The carnival and the Ferris wheel and this strange man Mr. Cooger, the Ferris wheel going backward and making him younger, I don't know how, and him coming here as a boy, and you can't trust him, because when he has your money he'll get on the Ferris wheel and it'll go *forward*, and he'll be thirty-five years old again, and the boy'll be gone forever!"

"Goodnight, Henry Walterson, don't *ever* come back!" shouted Mrs. Foley.

The door slammed. Peter and Hank found themselves in the rain once more. It soaked into and into them, cold and complete.

"Smart guy," snorted Peter. "Now you fixed it. Suppose he heard us, suppose he comes and *kills* us in our beds tonight, to shut us all up for keeps!"

"He wouldn't do that," said Hank.

"Wouldn't he?" Peter seized Hank's arm. "Look."

In the big bay window of the dining room now the mesh curtain pulled aside. Standing there in the pink light, his hand made into a menacing fist, was the little orphan boy. His face was horrible to see, the teeth bared, the eyes hateful, the lips mouthing out terrible words. That was all. The orphan boy was there only a second, then gone. The curtain fell into place. The rain poured down upon the house. Hank and Peter walked slowly home in the storm.

. . .

During supper, Father looked at Hank and said, "If you don't catch pneumonia, I'll be surprised. Soaked, you were, by God! What's this about the carnival?"

Hank fussed at his mashed potatoes, occasionally looking at the rattling windows. "You know Mr. Cooger, the carnival man, Dad?"

"The one with the pink carnation in his lapel?" asked Father.

"Yes!" Hank sat up. "You've seen him around?"

"He stays down the street at Mrs. O'Leary's boarding house, got a room in back. Why?"

"Nothing," said Hank, his face glowing.

After supper Hank put through a call to Peter on the phone. At the other end of the line, Peter sounded miserable with coughing.

"Listen, Pete!" said Hank. "I see it all now. When that li'l ole orphan boy, Joseph Pikes, gets Mrs. Foley's money, he's got a good plan."

"What?"

"He'll stick around town as the carnival man, living in a room at Mrs. O'Leary's. That way nobody'll get suspicious of him. Everybody'll be looking for that nasty little boy and he'll be gone. And he'll be walking around, all disguised as the carnival man. That way, nobody'll suspect the carnival at all. It would look funny if the carnival suddenly pulled up stakes."

"Oh," said Peter, sniffling.

"So we got to act fast," said Hank.

"Nobody'll believe us, I tried to tell my folks but they said hogwash!" moaned Peter.

"We got to act tonight, anyway. Because why? Because he's gonna try to kill us! We're the only ones that know and if we tell the police to keep an eye on him, he's the one who stole Mrs. Foley's money in cahoots with the orphan boy, he won't live peaceful. I bet he just tries something tonight. So, I tell you, meet me at Mrs. Foley's in half-an-hour."

"Aw," said Peter.

"You wanna die?"

"No." Thoughtfully.

"Well, then. Meet me there and I bet we see that orphan boy sneaking out with the money, tonight, and running back down to the carnival grounds with it, when Mrs. Foley's asleep. I'll see you there. So long, Pete!"

"Young man," said Father, standing behind him as he hung up the phone. "You're not going anywhere. You're going straight up to bed. Here." He marched Hank upstairs. "Now, hand me out every thing you got on." Hank undressed.

"There're no other clothes in your room are there?" asked Father. "No, sir, they're all in the hall closet," said Hank, disconsolately.

"Good," said Dad and shut and locked the door.

Hank stood there, naked. "Holy Cow," he said.

"Go to bed," said Father.

. . .

Peter arrived at Mrs. Foley's house at about nine-thirty, sneezing, lost in a vast raincoat and mariner's cap. He stood like a small water hydrant on the street, mourning softly over his fate. The lights in the Foley house were warmly on up-stairs. Peter waited for half-an-hour, looking at the rain-drenched slick streets of night.

Finally there was a darting paleness, a rustle in wet bushes.

"Hank?" Peter questioned the bushes.

"Yeah." Hank stepped out.

"Gosh," said Peter, staring. "You're—you're *naked!*"

"I ran all the way," said Hank. "Dad wouldn't let me out."

"You'll get pneumonia," said Peter.

The lights in the house went out.

"Duck," cried Hank, bounding behind some bushes. They waited. "Pete," said Hank. "You're wearing pants, aren't you?"

"Sure," said Pete.

"Well, you're wearing a raincoat, and nobody'll know, so lend me your pants," asked Hank.

A reluctant transaction was made. Hank pulled the pants on.

The rain let up. The clouds began to break apart.

In about ten minutes a small figure emerged from the house, bearing a large paper sack filled with some enormous loot or other.

"There he is," whispered Hank.

"There he goes!" cried Peter.

The orphan boy ran swiftly.

"Get after him!" cried Hank.

They gave chase through the chestnut trees, but the orphan boy was swift, up the hill, through the night streets of town, down past the rail yards, past the factories, to the midway of the deserted carnival. Hank and Peter were poor seconds, Peter weighted as he was with the heavy raincoat, and Hank frozen with cold. The thumping of Hank's bare feet sounded through the town.

"Hurry, Pete! We can't let him get to that Ferris wheel before we do, if he changes back into a man we'll never prove anything!"

"I'm hurrying!" But Pete was left behind as Hank thudded on alone in the clearing weather.

"Yah!" mocked the orphan boy, darting away, no more than a shadow ahead, now.

Now vanishing into the carnival yard.

Hank stopped at the edge of the carnival lot. The Ferris wheel was going up and up into the sky, a big nebula of stars caught on the dark earth and turning forward and forward, instead of backward, and there sat Joseph Pikes in a black painted bucket-seat, laughing up and around and down and up and around and down at little old Hank standing there, and the little blind hunchback had his hand on the roaring, oily black machine that made the Ferris wheel go ahead and ahead. The midway was deserted because of the rain. The merry-go-round was still, but its music played and crashed in the open spaces. And Joseph Pikes rode up into the cloudy sky and came down and each time he went around he was a year older, his laughing changed, grew deep, his face changed, the bones of it, the mean eyes of it, the wild hair of it, sitting there in the black bucket seat whirling, whirling swiftly, laughing into the bleak heavens where now and again a last split of lightning showed itself.

Hank ran forward at the hunchback by the machine. On the way he picked up a tent spike. "Here now!" yelled the hunchback. The black Ferris wheel whirled around. "You!" stormed the hunchback, fumbling out. Hank hit him in the knee-cap and danced away. "Ouch!" screamed the man, falling forward. He tried to reach the machine brake to stop the Ferris wheel. When he put his hand on the brake, Hank ran in and slammed the tent spike against the fingers, mashing them. He hit them twice. The man held his hand in his other hand, howling. He kicked at Hank. Hank grabbed the foot, pulled, the man slipped in the mud and fell. Hank hit him on the other knee, hard. Hank hit him on the head, shouting.

The Ferris wheel went around and around and around.

"Stop, stop the wheel!" cried Joseph Pikes-Mr. Cooger flung up in a stormy cold sky in the bubbled constellation of whirl and rush and wind.

"I can't move," groaned the hunchback. Hank jumped on his chest and they thrashed, biting, kicking.

"Stop, stop the wheel!" cried Mr. Cooger, a man, a different man and voice this time, coming around in panic, going up into the roaring hissing sky of the Ferris wheel. The wind blew through the high dark wheel spokes. "Stop, stop, oh please stop the wheel!"

.  .  .

Hank leaped up from the sprawled hunchback. He started in on the brake mechanism, hitting it, jamming it, putting hunks of metal in it, tying it with rope, now and again hitting at the crawling weeping dwarf.

"Stop, stop, stop the wheel!" wailed a voice high in the night where the windy moon was coming out of the vaporous white clouds now. "Stop . . ." The voice faded.

Now the carnival was ablaze with sudden light. Men sprang out of tents, came running. Hank felt himself jerked into the air with oaths and beatings rained on him. Terrible faces leered and gaped at him. From a distance there was a sound of Peter's voice and behind Peter, at full tilt, a police officer with pistol drawn.

"Stop, stop the wheel!" In the wind the voice sighed away.

The voice repeated and repeated.

The dark carnival men tried to apply the brake. Nothing happened. The machine hummed and turned the wheel around and around. The mechanism was jammed.

"Stop!" cried the voice one last time.

Silence.

Without a word the Ferris wheel flew in a circle, a high system of electric stars and metal and seats. There was no sound now but the sound of the motor which died and stopped. The Ferris wheel coasted for a minute, all the carnival people looking up at it, the policeman looking up at it, Hank and Peter looking up at it.

The Ferris wheel stopped. A crowd had gathered at the noise. A few fishermen from the wharfhouse, a few switchmen from the rail yards. The Ferris wheel stood whining and stretching in the wind.

"Look," everybody said.

The policeman turned and the carnival people turned and the fishermen turned and they all looked at the occupant in the black painted seat at the bottom of the ride. The wind touched and moved the black wooden seat in a gentle rocking rhythm, crooning over the occupant in the dim carnival light.

A skeleton sat there, a paper bag of money in its hands, a brown derby hat on its head.

# APPENDIX A
# CHRONOLOGICAL CATALOG
# (1944-1945)

The complete chronological catalog, maintained in the archives of the Center for Ray Bradbury Studies, establishes the sequence and dates of composition for all known Bradbury stories up through 1950. There are entries for all published stories, for unpublished stories with verified surviving typescripts, and unpublished stories where no typescript has been located but composition has been verified from secondary sources. Bradbury's thousands of pages of incomplete story openings and fragments, surviving today in the Albright Collection, are rarely datable with precision and are not included in the catalog structure.

Volume 1 of the *Collected Stories* contains the catalog entries from 1935 (the date of Bradbury's earliest surviving high school stories) to April 1943 (the composition date for "The Small Assassin," the first volume's final selection). Volume 1's catalog also extended the record of Bradbury's known story compositions through the end of 1943. Volume 2's catalog provided continuity overlap with volume 1 by covering all known story compositions for 1943 and 1944. For purposes of continuity between volumes in the series, volume 3's catalog includes all known stories written during 1944 and 1945, providing an extended reference for the volume 3 selections, which were all composed between March 1944 and March 1945. Appendix B describes the unpublished stories composed during 1945 (descriptions of the unpublished stories composed through 1944 appear in volume 2).

The chronological catalog is designed to contrast the publishing record of these years with the broader development of his creativity as a short story writer. The left column contains the continuous publication history of Bradbury's short fiction, as established in Eller, "The Stories of Ray Bradbury: An Annotated Finding List 1938–1991" (*Bulletin of Bibliography* 49.1 [March 1992]: 27–51) and as revised and expanded for Eller and Touponce, *Ray Bradbury: The Life of Fiction* (Kent, OH: Kent State University Press, 2004) 439–503. This publication history represents the timeline by which scholars and critics have always studied Bradbury's prolific output of short fiction as it has developed over his seven decades as a published author. The right column presents a chronological catalog, or calendar, of Bradbury's short fiction, which reveals (as far as possible) the dates and true order of composition for both his published and unpublished stories. The catalog also serves as the structural foundation for all volumes in this chronological edition of Bradbury's short stories.

In establishing the chronological catalog, I relied on fourteen years of personal interviews with Bradbury, my continuing study of his personal papers, and a detailed study of his incoming correspondence for these early years as preserved in the collection of Bradbury's principal bibliographer, Professor Donn Albright of the Pratt Institute. I have also studied the record of his outgoing correspondence as it has been preserved in various university collections around the country. Photocopies of the Albright Collection holdings of letters received by Bradbury from the earliest years of his career through the 1960s are deposited here in the Center for Ray Bradbury Studies, along with originals of the post-1960s correspondence gifted to the Bradbury Center by the late author's estate in 2013.

What remains of Bradbury's personal record of composition and submission is preserved in the Albright Collection. His 1942 to 1945 composition and submission log, his 1941 to 1949 sales record, and his two sales-by-publisher indexes are somewhat fragmentary and cryptic in places, but these represent the principal sources of documentation for the chronology. The final primary source of information is a more recent discovery; in October 2010 I located Bradbury's index card file of submissions covering the period from 1941 through 1975. These include a more extensive record of magazine submissions (and rejections) than any of the other primary source documents.

There is one significant third-party source as well. Bradbury's record of sales negotiated by his first New York agent, Julius Schwartz, was prepared and annotated by author and close Bradbury friend William F. Nolan. His access to Schwartz, Bradbury, and other bibliographical sources dates from the early 1950s; in spite of its third-hand status, Nolan's list may represent the most accurate source for actual sales dates and pre-commission payment records. All of the primary and secondary source documents used in establishing the chronological catalog for the period covered by this volume are preserved in the Albright Collection; photocopies of these sources are deposited in the Center for Ray Bradbury Studies, Institute for American Thought, Indiana University School of Liberal Arts (IUPUI).

I have established the chronology for Bradbury's stories by working backward from the publication date to find (a) the date of sale, (b) the date a story was received or first circulated by his agents, and in some cases (c) Bradbury's own annotated date of initial composition. I discovered many of these benchmark dates in letters from Julius Schwartz, who handled nearly all of Bradbury's pulp sales until 1947, and in the letters of Don Congdon, who advised Bradbury beginning in the winter of 1945–46 and became Bradbury's agent in September 1947. Bradbury's own letters to these men and to some of his editors also provide documentation, as do Bradbury's occasional annotations on his typescript carbons. Bradbury's introductions to his more recent story collections, his unpublished notes and contents listings, his published articles and interviews, and my own series of interviews have filled in many gaps in the record.

For *The Collected Stories of Ray Bradbury* volumes, all of the dating documentation for the published stories is provided in the individual story head notes, located in the volume's apparatus section. Entries in both columns of the Chronological Catalog begin with the standard bibliographic reference for the published stories, which indicates year of publication and the sequence within that year; thus, 44-1 identifies "The Sea Shell" as the first story published by Bradbury in 1944. In the left column, seasonal (quarterly) publications precede monthly publications of the same season; monthly publications precede those published by date within the month. The titles of published stories appear in boldface type for ease of analysis. In the right column, these same bibliographical identifiers will serve to illustrate just how radically the public record of publication gives way to the actual chronology of composition. The bibliographical numbers show that eleven of the published stories written during the volume period were first published later—sometimes years and decades later. Unpublished stories in the compositional sequence, which have no identifier prefixes, are marked by an em-dash (—) and are easily spotted. Where a story is better known by a variant title, that variant is given parenthetically (in square brackets []) to aid reader recognition of Bradbury's most significant and popular tales. Subsequent volumes will continue the chronology with similar tables that can be connected to study the larger timeline of Bradbury's early career.

—JE

| Publication Sequence | Compositional Sequence |
|---|---|

-1944-

44-1 **"The Sea Shell."** *Weird Tales,* Jan. 1944.

47-9 **"Jack-in-the-Box."** Jan. 1944. First published *Dark Carnival,* [Apr.] 1947.

09-19 **"Where Everything Ends."** Jan. 1944. With Julius Schwartz cover page. Original lost; photocopy in the Albright Collection. First published *Where Everything Ends* (Bradbury crime fiction omnibus, 2009).

44-12 **"Bang! You're Dead!"** Feb. 1944. First published *Weird Tales,* Sept. 1944.

— "The Douser" (three unpublished and incomplete story fragments). Feb. 1944.

44-14 **"Half-Pint Homicide."** Feb. 1944. First published *Detective Tales,* Nov. 1944. Original title: **"Enter—The Douser."**

46-4 **"Rocket Skin."** Feb. 1944. Rewritten May 1944. First published *Thrilling Wonder Stories,* Spring 1946.

44-2 **"Reunion."** *Weird Tales,* Mar. 1944.

44-16 **"It Burns Me Up!"** Mar. 5, 1944. First published *Dime Mystery,* Nov. 1944. Original title: **"Forgotten Man."**

44-15 **"The Jar."** Mar. 7, 1944. First published *Weird Tales,* Nov. 1944.

---

**Volume 3 Period**

---

44-10 **"Yesterday I Lived!"** Mar. 15, 1944. First published *Flynn's Detective Fiction,* Aug. 1944. Original title: **"No Phones, Private Coffin."**

44-3 **"The Monster Maker."** *Planet Stories,* Spring 1944.

— "These Are the Good Days" (unpublished and unlocated). Mar. 27, 1944.

— "Dress for Janie" (unpublished and unlocated). Apr. 5, 1944. Circulated by Ed Boden, 1944.

| Publication Sequence | Compositional Sequence |
|---|---|
| | 09-5    **"If Paths Must Cross Again."** Apr. 5, 1944. Expanded Dec. 7, 1944. With Julius Schwartz cover page. Original lost; photocopy in the Albright Collection. First published in *We'll Always Have Paris* (NY: Morrow, 2009). |
| | 46-5    **"The Miracles of Jamie."** Apr. 7, 1944. First published *Charm,* Apr. 1946. |
| | —    "The Extra Words" (unpublished and unlocated). Apr. 19, 1944. Returned by *The Saint,* Mar. 1945; to Saint's Choice, Feb. 5, 1946; to Fiction House syndicate (Paul Payne), Mar. 27, 1947. |
| | —    "Room of the World." Apr. 26, 1944. Rejected by *Yale Review.* Two-page fragment is in the Albright Collection. |
| | 45-12    **"The Long Way Home."** May 2, 1944. First published *Dime Mystery,* Nov. 1945. Original title: **"The Long Way Around."** |
| 44-4    **"I, Rocket."** *Amazing Stories,* May 1944. | |
| 44-5    **"The Lake."** *Weird Tales,* May 1944. | 44-18    **"Four-Way Funeral."** May 8, 1944. First published *Detective Tales,* Dec. 1944. Original title: **"The Very Bewildered Corpses."** |
| | —    "To Remember Is to Forget" (unpublished and unlocated). May 10, 1944. Single-page fragment, dated May 5, 1944, is in the Albright Collection. |
| | 05-7    **"The Reincarnate."** June 3, 1944. With Julius Schwartz cover page. Original lost; photocopy in the Albright Collection. First published in *Dark Delicacies* (NY: Carroll & Graff, 2005). |
| | —    "A Noise Like Love" (unpublished). June 14, 1944. |
| | —    "Long Live the Douser!" (unpublished). June 23, 1944. With Julius |

| Publication Sequence | Compositional Sequence |
|---|---|

<table>
<tr><td></td><td>Schwartz cover page. Original lost; photocopy in the Albright Collection.</td></tr>
<tr><td>44-6 "Morgue Ship." Planet Stories, Summer 1944.</td><td>04-7 "Chrysalis" (distinct from 46-11). June 1944. TS, 15 pp. First published in The Cat's Pajamas (NY: Morrow, 2004).</td></tr>
<tr><td>44-7 "There Was an Old Woman." Weird Tales, July 1944.</td><td>— "The Boss" (unpublished). ca. Jul. 1944 (vt: "Top Man").</td></tr>
<tr><td>44-8 "Killer, Come Back to Me!" Detective Tales, July 1944. Original title: "Autopsy."</td><td>45-1 "The Poems." July 10, 1944. First published Weird Tales, Jan. 1945.</td></tr>
<tr><td>44-9 "The Long Night." New Detective, July 1944.</td><td>46-3 "Defense Mech." July 19, 1944. First published Planet Stories, Spring 1946.</td></tr>
<tr><td>44-10 "Yesterday I Lived!" Flynn's Detective Fiction, Aug. 1944. Original title: "No Phones—Private Coffin."</td><td>45-3 "Hell's Half-Hour." Aug. 5, 1944. First published New Detective, Mar. 1945. Original title: "Mr. Priory Meets Mr. Caldwell."</td></tr>
<tr><td></td><td>45-2 "I'm Not So Dumb." Aug. 8, 1944. First published Detective Tales, Feb. 1945, with exclamation point closing the title.</td></tr>
<tr><td></td><td>45-13 "Invisible Boy." Aug. 11–Sept. 14, 1944. First published Mademoiselle, Nov. 1945.</td></tr>
<tr><td>44-11 "The Trunk Lady." Detective Tales, Sept. 1944.</td><td>— "Solution From a Bottle" (unpublished). Aug. 19, 1944. With Julius Schwartz cover page. Original lost; photocopy in the Albright Collection.</td></tr>
<tr><td>44-12 "Bang! You're Dead!" Weird Tales, Sept. 1944.</td><td>50-1 "Ylla." Fall 1944. First published Maclean's (Canada), Jan. 1, 1950, as "I'll Not Ask for Wine."</td></tr>
<tr><td></td><td>45-4 "The Tombstone." Oct. 13, 1944. First published Weird Tales, Mar. 1945.</td></tr>
<tr><td>44-13 "And Then—The Silence." Super Science Stories (Canada), Oct. 1944.</td><td>45-6 "The Watchers." Oct. 13, 1944. First published Weird Tales, May 1945.</td></tr>
<tr><td></td><td>45-8 "Corpse-Carnival" (as by D. R. Banat). Oct. 27, 1944. First published Dime Mystery, July 1945. Original title: "One Minus One."</td></tr>
</table>

| Publication Sequence | Compositional Sequence |
|---|---|
| | — "The Lady Up Ahead" (unpublished). Oct. 27, 1944. With Julius Schwartz cover page. Original lost; photocopy in the Albright Collection. |
| | 46-9 **"Lorelei of the Red Mist"** (with Leigh Brackett). Sept.–Oct. 1944. First published *Planet Stories,* Summer 1946. |
| 44-14 **"Half-Pint Homicide."** *Detective Tales,* Nov. 1944. Original title: **"Enter—The Douser."** | 45-7 **"Dead Men Rise Up Never."** Nov. 6, 1944. First published *Dime Mystery,* July 1945. Original title: **"The Sea Cure."** |
| 44-15 **"The Jar."** *Weird Tales,* Nov. 1944. | |
| 44-16 **"It Burns Me Up!"** *Dime Mystery,* Nov. 1944. | 45-11 **"Skeleton"** (distinct from 45-5). Nov. 30, 1944. First published *Weird Tales,* Sept. 1945. |
| | — "The Gull" (unpublished). ca. Dec. 1944; sent to Don Congdon, Nov. 9, 1947. |
| 44-17 **"Undersea Guardians."** *Amazing Stories,* Dec. 1944. | — "One in the Dark" (unpublished). 1944. |
| 44-18 **"Four-Way Funeral."** *Detective Tales,* Dec. 1944. Original title: **"The Very Bewildered Corpses."** | — "Appointment for Dinner" (as by D. R. Banat; unpublished). ca. 1944. With Julius Schwartz cover page. Original lost; photocopy in the Albright Collection. |
| 44-19 **"Lazarus Come Forth."** *Planet Stories,* Winter 1944. | |

-1945-

| | — "From Now On" (unpublished). Jan. 10, 1945. |
|---|---|
| 45-1 **"The Poems."** *Weird Tales,* Jan. 1945. | 53-12 **"And So Died Riabouchinska."** Jan. 19, 1945. Submitted to Julius Schwartz, Feb. 1945. Accepted by *The Saint's Choice,* Mar. 20, 1946, but not published. Circulated widely until finally published in *The Saint Detective Magazine,* June–July 1953. Original title: **"Riabouchinska."** |
| 45-2 **"I'm Not So Dumb!"** *Detective Tales,* Feb. 1945. | |
| | — "The Cricket Cage" (unpublished). Feb. 8, 1945. Begun in late |

| Publication Sequence | Compositional Sequence |
|---|---|

**Compositional Sequence**

1944. With Julius Schwartz cover page. Original lost; photocopy in the Albright Collection.

45-5    **"Skeleton"** (distinct from 45-11). Feb. 20, 1945.

48-6    **"The Black Ferris."** Mar. 1945 (Bradbury to Derleth); preliminary fragments summer 1945–46 (bound notebook); full draft sent to Congdon Sept. 19, 1947.

---

### Volume 4 Period

45-9    **"The Dead Man."** Mar. 3, 1945.

—    "You Wouldn't Think It to Look at Him!" (unpublished). Mar. 20, 1945.

46-8    **"Her Eyes, Her Lips, Her Limbs."** Apr. 5, 1945.

46-14    **"The Creatures That Time Forgot"** (**"Frost and Fire"**). May 19, 1945.

47-17    **"I See You Never."** Apr. 28, 1945.

46-15    **"Homecoming."** Apr. 30, 1945.

46-13    **"The Electrocution"** (as William Elliott). Apr. 28, 1945.

45-10    **"The Big Black and White Game."** June 1, 1945.

46-2    **"The Traveler."** July 20, 1945.

46-6    **"One Timeless Spring."** July 1945.

97-5    **"House Divided."** Aug. 17, 1945.

46-18    **"A Careful Man Dies."** Aug. 1945.

**Publication Sequence**

45-3    **"Hell's Half Hour."** *New Detective,* Mar. 1945. Original title: **"Mr. Priory Meets Mr. Caldwell."**

45-4    **"The Tombstone."** *Weird Tales,* Mar. 1945.

45-5    **"Skeleton."** *Script,* Apr. 28, 1945 (distinct from 45–11).

45-6    **"The Watchers."** *Weird Tales,* May 1945.

45-7    **"Dead Men Rise Up Never."** *Dime Mystery,* July 1945. Original title: **"The Sea Cure."**

45-8    **"Corpse Carnival"** (as D. A. Banat). *Dime Mystery,* July 1945. Original title: **"One Minus One."**

45-9    **"The Dead Man."** *Weird Tales,* July 1945.

45-10    **"The Big Black and White Game."** *American Mercury,* Aug. 1945.

45-11    **"Skeleton."** *Weird Tales,* Sept. 1945 (distinct from 45–5).

| Publication Sequence | Compositional Sequence |
|---|---|

| | |
|---|---|
| 45-12 **"The Long Way Home."** *Dime Mystery,* Nov. 1945. Original title: **"The Long Way Around."** | 46-7 **"The Smiling People."** Dec. 1945. |
| | 88-8 **"West of October."** ca. 1945. |
| 45-13 **"Invisible Boy."** *Mademoiselle,* Nov. 1945. | 97-6 **"I Wonder What's Become of Sally?"** ca. 1945. |
| | 97-7 **"Thunder in the Morning."** ca. 1945. |
| | — "Clay in the Rain" (unpublished). ca. 1945. |
| | — "The Dancer" (unpublished). ca. 1945. |

# APPENDIX B
# SUMMARY OF BRADBURY'S UNPUBLISHED FICTION

## 1945

"From Now On." Jan. 10, 1945. 11,500 words. Science fiction story.

In 2015 Los Angeles, John Remington wakes to discover that he is unable to see his wife although she is beside him. He can feel and hear her, however. He is invisible to her as well. The couple learns through the media that throughout the world, humans have become invisible. They are briefly comforted, but they panic when they cannot find their baby daughter. After locating the child, they realize that they cannot track her movements by clothing her because the clothing disappears when it touches her skin. The couple then wakes their teenage daughter, who has become invisible as well.

Remington drives to work—all of the cars appear driverless. A pedestrian is struck and killed, but no one can find him because he is invisible. Remington arrives at his antique shop only to witness his merchandise floating out the door, carried away by invisible looters. When the criminals hear his voice, they unsuccessfully attempt to shoot him, but they are successful in driving off in their large van filled with the stolen antiques. Because of the chaos caused by ubiquitous human invisibility, however, the police are unable to respond to this relatively minor crime. Remington and his coworker discover that one thief was left behind, and they tie him up while brainstorming ways they might burglarproof and restock their store.

When Remington appeals to his insurance company, he learns that his policy has lapsed, and his insurance agent treats him rudely and insults his voice. Angry, he returns to his shop and calls his wife, who cheers him by focusing on the absurdities of the situation. When he finally laughs, he is greatly relieved. The family learns to appreciate the magic of invisibility.

In the outside world, wars that have been raging continue for a time but, because of the confusion, conflict had to be suspended until new rules accounting for human invisibility could be decided. Police install new devices to help detect crime, but mostly people cope with the dire situation with common sense and humor.

Remington still has many problems, one of which is that his wife, now unable to see his physical attractiveness, begins to consider his voice annoying. He realizes that his insurance agent had treated him badly because of his voice and discovers that attractiveness must now be linked to voice rather than appearance. He had always used his looks to help him succeed, but this aspect was now utterly useless to him. Meanwhile, Remington's older daughter discovers the opposite. Her plain appearance has disappeared, but her voice is beautiful and attractive to boys. When her father catches her kissing a boy, she threatens to run away. Later, Remington suspects that his wife has been spending time with another man.

He realizes that visibility was what made people insecure and vulnerable to social pressure to follow rules and laws. Nothing could prevent cheating at games or committing crimes. Nothing could prevent his wife and daughter from leaving him. In order to prevent himself from losing his family, Remington concocts a strategy to make them feel insecure again. He works first on his daughter, leading her to believe he has committed murder. He asks his daughter to spy on her mother, indicating that if she refuses, he might have to commit further crimes. When the teenager becomes worried, Remington knows he has succeeded in making her feel that the secret to being secure was being obedient, i.e., good.

One evening Phyllis, his wife, invites another couple over for cocktails. At the end of the pleasant night, the couple informs the Remingtons, to their great surprise, that they are African American. At the time this story was written, de jure racism in the United States would have made such interracial socializing scandalous. The event causes Remington to muse about the end of racism, a positive outcome of human invisibility, which he believes would happen if only everyone spoke the same language in the same accent.

Remington embarks on a voice instruction program to make himself more attractive to his wife and more successful in his business. Improving his voice works to improve his marriage and his livelihood. The story ends with the Remingtons embracing.

"From Now On" is the first entry under 1945 in Bradbury's composition and submission log. Shortly after completing the story on January 10, he sent it on to Julius Schwartz in New York for circulation under the name "William Elliott," a pseudonym he had fashioned after the names of the modernist poets William Carlos Williams and T. S. Eliot. Later that year Bradbury would use this name for some of his direct major market submissions, but "From Now On" went out to the pulp market. Schwartz sent it to *Astounding*'s John W. Campbell, who found it interesting but weak in terms of plot. This was a long typescript, more than 11,000 words, and good structure would be crucial in selling the story.

Schwartz had seen the same impasse develop over "Chrysalis" (volume 1, selection 11), another science fiction tale that verged on novella length. That time he had brought in Henry Kuttner to advise Bradbury, and in the spring of 1945 he sent "From Now On" to Kuttner for the same kind of critique. Kuttner had known Bradbury since 1937, and he had seen his friend take major strides forward in the genre fields. But in Kuttner's estimation "From Now On" was a step backward, depending on a self-indulgent style to cover the lack of plot and action. Kuttner pinned Bradbury's ears back in his three-page written critique, and was sure that no pulp editor would take it as written. Bradbury had a number of new stories circulating and was beginning to engage more actively with the mainstream magazines as well; in the end he never made time to attempt the drastic rewriting that he knew the story required. "From Now On" was returned to Bradbury with other unsold tales and never circulated again.

## "The Cricket Cage." Feb. 8, 1945. 5,200 words. Romantic crime story.

Conrad, a music producer, travels to the West Indies to look for music and performers for his new company label. He finds Bethalady, a young, beautiful, talented singer. While watching her perform, Conrad makes eye contact and they form a bond. But Conrad is warned by his lawyer companion, Jolle, that Bethalady belongs to a gangster, Brezzo, who "owns the town, the ships . . . the police, and her." After the song Conrad meets Bethalady backstage, but they are interrupted by Brezzo. He forces Bethalady to state that she has no desire to leave the island—or him. Brezzo's thug tries to stab Conrad, but Brezzo stops him. Conrad and his lawyer return to Conrad's house, which overlooks the harbor. Jolle informs Conrad that Brezzo's cutter is used for smuggling drugs via the harbor and that local police are paid not to inform island authorities about the crime. The next day, Conrad meets Bethalady, but she warns him that Brezzo will never let her go. Later, however, she goes to Conrad's house, and they try to escape together, but Brezzo and his men find them and take Bethalady away.

Conrad looks for Bethalady the next morning but cannot find her at the bar where she sings. He bribes the bar's janitor who tells him where to find Bethalady. He discovers her drugged in a secluded hut in the jungle. Conrad tries to convince her to leave with him, but she is addicted to the drugs Brezzo has been feeding her, and she attacks Conrad for trying to take her away. Conrad decides that he needs to obtain enough of the drug cocktail to allow Bethalady to get away from the island without pain of withdrawal and enough for her to taper off when she is safe. He attempts to steal drugs from Brezzo's cutter and arms himself to shoot Brezzo if he is caught. When Brezzo, his men, and Bethalady appear on the cutter, Conrad shoots at Brezzo and his gang. After only hitting Brezzo and one of his henchmen, Conrad dives into the harbor. In the water, a fight between Conrad and Brezzo, wounded in the leg, ensues. Conrad is victorious, and he forces Brezzo to take him and Bethalady to a place from which they can escape. Brezzo complies, and the story ends with the two lovers, Conrad and Bethalady, on a plane, embarking on a new life together. She had been a singing cricket trapped in Brezzo's cage; now her cage would be Conrad's love and protection.

Bradbury's composition and submission log lists "The Cricket Cage" as completed on February 8, 1945, but an incomplete and deleted entry suggests that he was working on the story at the beginning of January. Schwartz thought the story had some interesting writing, but the recurring calypso music seemed to carry the story better than the narrative itself. On February 24, he wrote to say that he would try the story with *Adventure*. Bradbury had been hoping to crack the pages of *Short Story*, but Schwartz felt the tale just wasn't strong enough. In the end it never sold at all and was returned to Bradbury with other unsold tales in 1947.

## "You Wouldn't Think It to Look at Him." Mar. 20, 1945. 1,300 words. A light psychological study of human nature.

The narrator of this story sits in a bar having a drink, and Dave, the bartender, points out another man in the room, saying, "You wouldn't think it to look at him, . . . Would you?"

The narrator sees a tall, fit-looking, handsome man and tries to figure out what his secret is. But when the narrator asks counter-questions of Dave, Dave won't talk. At last, put out by Dave's lack of cooperation, the narrator takes his drink to the man's table to see if he can get answers there. The stranger is as evasive as Dave had been, but it seems that most people look at him, a complete stranger, and assume right away they can identify his profession, his lifestyle, his religion, or whatever other characteristics they might want to attribute to someone they'd never seen before.

As the tall man and the narrator converse, it becomes obvious that the man and Dave, the bartender, have been playing a game with the bar's patrons. The narrator realizes that the bar patrons' perceptions of the tall man are based on their own concerns, prejudices, and fears. From his own point of view, the narrator finally describes the tall stranger as "Intelligent. Right. Good." As he leaves the bar, he bids goodbye to the stranger, saying, "I'll look for all of you." The stranger replies, "Don't be surprised if you only find yourself," indicating that what the bar's customers see in this blandly handsome man reveals more about themselves than it does about him.

"You Wouldn't Think It to Look at Him" shares elements with another un-published tale of the period, "From Now On"—an unexpected encounter trig-gers an examination of how we value others, and how we often fail to reflect on our own inability to look beneath surface appearance. The stranger at the bar presents a reflection of the beholder, and in this way anticipates Masks, Brad-bury's fragmentary 1946–47 novel project about the way masks can be used to hide identity and project power over others. Bradbury felt that "You Wouldn't Think It to Look at Him" had a chance with the major market magazines; be-cause Schwartz only represented him in the pulp fields, and shortly after fin-ishing it on March 20, 1945, Bradbury circulated it on his own. It was a very short piece, and shortly after completing it he tried it with *Script*, a Hollywood slick with a long history as a New Yorker-style magazine. He had placed simi-larly short and light pieces with *Script* before, but the story was soon rejected. His special submissions log shows that on April 4 he sent it out to the *New Yorker*, where it was rejected again. There is no record of further submissions, and the story went into Bradbury's inactive files.

## "Clay in the Rain." ca. 1945. 1,819 words. Sentimental crime story.

Two policemen, Charlie and Roger, talk as Charlie bores a hole in a wall using a hand drill. They are trying to arrest a prostitute in the act of solicitation. Charlie remembers that Roger used to know the woman and liked her. Roger admits as much, and he launches into a speech about how pretty Mexican girls are when they are young, but they lose their beauty at a fairly young age because they "live quick." When the surveillance hole is ready, Charlie takes the first watch and reports to Roger that two people have entered the room. As Charlie describes the details of the room—the young man seated on a chair and the older woman undressing—Roger indulges in reverie about his past with the same woman when she was young and beautiful.

After twenty minutes, Roger instructs Charlie to rap on the door and ar-rest the woman. Roger warns the young man not to "do any time traveling," as he himself has obviously done on this night. As they drive the woman to jail, Roger glances at her in the rearview mirror. She has aged; she has grown fat and wrinkled. As he looks at her from that vantage point, she seems like someone he had never known. Although this distance from their former selves enables Roger to arrest a woman he once loved, his memories of her beauty and of that time in his youth with her are damaged forever.

The typescript's seven pages are undated. The manila folder containing the story is dated "1945" and annotated in Bradbury's hand "The detective who once loved the girl he must now spy on & arrest." The paper is of a type he used in 1945, and the content is consistent with his emphasis on writing crime stories during much of 1944 and 1945.

## "The Dancer." ca. 1945. 554 words. Short lyrical vignette.

The story begins with an intense, poetic evocation of music—"a hundred violins and cellos and violas, and the drumming murmur of kettle-drums rolling into a pomm-pomming rhythm." Bradbury describes a beautiful dancer—exquisite, electric, artistic, perfect—with layers of skirting, including the cascading skirt of her long hair, whirling out in centrifugal force. The dancer finishes and the applause begins; the audience demands an encore. Abruptly, a voice belonging to a Mrs. Logan intrudes into the descriptive prose, asking what Annette is doing. Annette is sitting beside a phonograph listening to music.

Another voice, that of Mrs. Watriss, answers that Annette is dancing—dancing in her mind. It is revealed that Annette with twisted and paralyzed limbs, and her "wretched mask of a face," can only dance in her mind. At the end of the story, Annette's physical limitation is emphasized when she must call out to Mrs. Watriss to turn over the record so that she can hear the other side. It is clear that the perfect dance described has taken place only in Annette's imagination. In order to perform her imaginary encore, she needs the help of an able-bodied person to flip the record.

The dating rationale for "The Dancer" is based on converging elements of circumstantial evidence. The paper is of a stock that Bradbury used during this period, and the address typed in the upper left corner of the opening page is the Venice Beach home where he still lived with his parents from the spring of 1942 to the fall of 1947. Bradbury's strong interest in ballet continued as he attended major touring performances late in the war, but the strongest evidence for dating emerges from his Christmas 1944 letter to Henry Kuttner, in which he reveals the influence of "No Woman Born," a story recently published by Kuttner's wife, C. L. Moore. "No Woman Born" tells of an internationally renowned singer and dancer who has been horribly crippled in a theater fire. She wills her body, replaced in parts by amazing machineries, to return to the stage and perform yet again. "I still get chills up my spine when I think of it." He went on at length about this tale, noting his own recent reading of a variety of works on ballet: "Her descriptions of the dance were far better than stuff I've read on the dance by accomplished balletomaniacs." Bradbury's letter indicates a peak in his fascination with ballet and imaginary performance, and provides the key for attributing composition of "The Dancer" to 1945.

"One Woman Show," a distinct and much longer variation on "The Dancer," survives in a sixteen-page 1952 typescript preserved in the Albright Collection. Albright was able to persuade Bradbury to publish "One Woman Show" in his

2002 collection, *One More for the Road*. The story centers on a marvelous dancing legend who can mesmerize vast audiences, but when a critic gets past the protective shield of the dancer's husband, he realizes that, off the stage, she is drained of all personality and energy, unaware of the world around her, a cripple who can only come to life in her one-woman show.

# ANNOTATIONS

## 1. No Phones, Private Coffin (Yesterday I Lived!)

1.0 [*title*] Bradbury's original title, "No Phones, Private Coffin," alludes to the cemetery adjacent to the studio where actress Diana Coyle is buried, and the irony that many studio stars had crossed over the wall: "all of them looked forward to an office in Hollywood Cemetery—with no phones."

1.2 Hollywood Cemetery] Hollywood Forever Cemetery, originally Hollywood Memorial Park Cemetery, is closely associated with Paramount Studios. The adjacent studio purchased forty acres of the original hundred-acre cemetery in 1920. Paramount shared its back-lot north wall with the cemetery for decades, including the years (roughly 1934–1939) when Bradbury would seek autographs at the front gate and sneak over the north wall from the cemetery to roam the studio grounds.

1.3 the studio projection room] the story begins and ends here, and given Bradbury's close teen-age association with the studio grounds, the setting is almost certainly modeled on Paramount. Note, however, that the A-List stars that Jamie Winters parades through his collection of flubbed outtakes are all MGM stars, and unlikely to have cutting room sweepings on file over at Paramount. This conflation of studios is not distracting, however, and the story is one of the more believable of his detective tales from this period.

2.21 flatfoot] slang for uniformed or plain-clothes police officer; first documented use in 1913.

3.4 San Fernando . . . year,] California city located in the San Fernando Valley. It was named for the Mission San Fernando Rey de España. Unlike many of the towns in the San Fernando Valley annexed by Los Angeles in the 1910s in order to benefit from the Los Angeles Aqueduct, San Fernando's plentiful groundwater allowed it to remain an independent city, retaining its independence even after the San Fernando Valley transformed from an agricultural to a suburban area in the years following World War II. In the context of the story, the abundant waters and the resulting independence make San

Fernando the ideal escape dream for Cleve, who bridles at outside authority all through the story.

3.37–38 smelling salts] Chemical compounds, commonly employing ammonium carbonate, used to arouse consciousness in people who have fainted or to prevent fainting. One of the many elements of formula mystery writing that Bradbury brought into the story line. In this case, the intent is to show that nothing can bring Diana Coyle back to life.

4.36 detective named Foley] This may be a name familiar to Bradbury; its subsequent use in "The Black Ferris" (selection 22) and as expanded in *Something Wicked This Way Comes* (1962) suggests Bradbury's Waukegan childhood memory of the old Foley house, which stood about two blocks east and north of his grandfather's Washington Street home. In the context of Hollywood, "Foley" may be a play on Foley mixing, the sound effects added to film soundtracks. Jack Foley pioneered his eponymous technique in the earliest sound pictures of 1927, and continued to lead the field for forty years. During the mid-1930s, Bradbury's many clandestine trips over Paramount's north wall may have introduced him to this art.

5.5 film laboratory] Bradbury's eerie description blends the daytime world of the studio with the nighttime world of the adjacent cemetery: "It was a huge dark mortuary building with dead-end passages and labyrinths of black walls to cut the light." The narrative goes on to describe the shadowy terrors involved in negotiating these passages, and the entire paragraph closely resembles the path through the mysterious labyrinths connecting the two worlds of studio and cemetery in his 1989 mystery novel, *A Graveyard for Lunatics*.

5.18 "Here you are, Mr. Foley.] The words of Juke Davis as he starts the film preview for Detective Foley reinforce the possibility that Bradbury is playing with Foley mixing, an allusion to the addition of special effects in film soundtracks: "'There's no sound-track. I'll develop and splice it in later,' said Davis. 'Here you are, Mr. Foley. Here's your film.'" Two possible biographical origins of Foley's name are identified at 4.36 above.

5.41 nicotine] A toxic alkaloid that acts as a stimulant in small doses; the active ingredient in tobacco.

6.1–2 Black Leaf Forty nicotine sulfate] A commercially available alkaloid parasiticide. Bradbury is trying to blend a touch of science into the forensics of this murder tale for effect.

7.18–19 Sometimes it seemed everyone in movietown tried to scale that wall.] This entire paragraph may have inspired the opening scene of his 1989 detective novel, *A Graveyard for Lunatics*. The novel opens with a manikin on a ladder, leaning into the studio from a ladder propped against the cemetery wall: a prank foreshadowing murders to come.

8.19 Gable's last picture] The Gable reference may allude to the three-year break in Clark Gable's studio work; at the time that Bradbury wrote this story (1944), the last Gable film was *Somewhere I'll Find You* (released September 1942). Here Bradbury is conflating his Hollywood Paramount setting with an A-list star from Metro-Goldwyn-Mayer, a Culver City studio. Loaning clips between studios is possible, but there is little evidence for this.

8.22–23 Garbo . . . Tracy . . . Powell] These A-list stars, like Gable, appeared in MGM productions. Gable was out of pictures throughout the war years, Garbo had retired from films in 1941, and William Powell appeared in far fewer films during and after the war. These choices may be designed to reinforce the sense of loss and memory surrounding the death of Diana Coyle.

10.17–18 I'm going downtown . . . murder of Diana Coyle] Previously Cleve called the footage Winters shows him "all good evidence," (10.10) but the tapes show circumstantial "evidence" at best.

10.22 *gas-chamber*] Used widely by the Third Reich in the 1930s and 40s for mass euthanasia, the gas chamber was usually a closed room or van where carbon monoxide or hydrogen cyanide was used for execution. The United States employed gas chambers for capital punishment beginning in 1924, but Bradbury's allusion may draw on the increasing public awareness late in World War II of the euthanasia programs of Nazi Germany. Cleve's drowsy stream of consciousness begins with "Toddle off to your gas chamber"; "toddle" is an unusual verb for Bradbury, but it may also be a play on "tod," the German word for death.

11.21 The screen flickered] Scene shifts back to present unexpectedly (see 1.4, 1.10)

12.5 black-balled] Rejected by secret ballot, using black or white marbles or balls to signify acceptance (white) or rejection (black). The term is used for any rejection by secret ballot, regardless of whether black and white balls are used. Hollywood has always been an unforgiving world, and Jamie's fear of becoming unemployable was his prime motivation for the murder.

12.35 And Cleve . . . and again!] Cleve beats Winters rather than report the killer to the police despite his constant attempts to work with (and as) the police. And, like the other "evidence" on the tapes, Diana's death confession (looking into the camera) is only Cleve's interpretation of circumstantial evidence. Cleve follows the same pattern as other detectives and detective-like characters in Bradbury's crime stories of this period: reliance on the patterns of the conventions of the detective story rather than due process of the law. Cleve decides guilt and enforces his own justice based on his interpretation of circumstantial evidence.

## 2. If Paths Must Cross Again

13.29 Brentwood, Illinois, population 34,901!] A town about twenty miles southwest of Bradbury's hometown of Waukegan, Illinois. Brentwood is much smaller than the population figure given in the story, but that figure is close to the actual population of Waukegan around the time that Bradbury's family moved away in 1934.

13.31 YMCA] Young Men's Christian Association. Traditionally, the YMCA provided very affordable lodging and gymnasium facilities across the country. In Bradbury's day many traveling professionals and temporary workers took advantage of such savings. Bradbury had stayed in a Manhattan YMCA when he attended the 1939 World Science Fiction Convention in New York, and would stay there again in 1946. During Bradbury's childhood, the Waukegan facility, Northern Lake YMCA, was located a couple of miles north of Central School on Western Avenue. He has adjusted memories and locales to provide the elusive memory links between the two lovers.

13.31 Central School] Located in the downtown grid of Waukegan until 1965, when the building was razed and replaced with a new public library building. Originally a high school, Central School was an elementary school in Bradbury's day; he attended grades 1 through 6, part of 7th grade, and nearly all of 8th grade before his father moved the family to Los Angeles in 1934.

15.27 Harold Lloyd's . . . DANGER] *Welcome Danger* is a 1929 pre-code American comedy film directed by Clyde Bruckman and starring Harold Lloyd. Both a sound version and a silent version of *Welcome Danger* were released at a time when Ray Bradbury saw every film that came to Waukegan theaters. He would allude to *Welcome Danger* most famously in one of his best-known terror tales, "The Whole Town's Sleeping" (*McCall's*, Sept. 1950: 34); he later changed the reference to the better-known Charlie Chaplin when he revised the *McCall's* story for *Dandelion Wine* (1957).

15.30 Ruth Etting . . . Moon] Ruth Etting (1897–1978) was an American singer and actress popular in the 1920s and 1930s. "Shine On, Harvest Moon" was one of her best-known songs, along with "Ten Cents a Dance," and "Button Up Your

Overcoat," among others. Bradbury heard most of the hits of the 1920s and 1930s on his family's radio in Waukegan or through phonograph recordings.

15.31 Follow the bouncing ball!] Bradbury refers to the ball on film screens that bounces above the lyrics of songs so that the audience can sing along.

## 3. The Miracles of Jamie

18.8 life . . . hoop] Jamie tries to reverse the reality that life forces people to jump through hoops, i.e., overcome obstacles. Jamie wishes life to "jump through hoops" for him.

18.21 Arizona State Day parade] Bradbury lived in Tucson, Arizona, from October 1932 until May 1933, during most of his seventh-grade year. He would have experienced the city's Statehood Day parade in February 1933. The parade memory and Bradbury's recollection of his best friend in Tucson, John Huff, are both worked into Jamie's desert world.

18.26 Jamie Winters] Just weeks before composing this story, Bradbury used the same full name for the murderous camera man in "Yesterday I Lived" (selection 1)

18.30–31 Jesus . . . himself] Jamie's boyhood logic leads him to hide his belief in his divinity not because he fears sharing Jesus' fate, but because he fears the unspoken ridicule and alienation that would result from such a proclamation. Bradbury had a keen appreciation for the fear of "otherness" in people, and would work that fear into a number of his darker stories.

19.8 Sam Browne belts] The "Sam Browne" belt is a wide leather belt with a narrower right shoulder strap. General Sir Samuel Browne (1824–1901) served in the British Army Cavalry in India, receiving the Victoria Cross for his action in Seerporah on 31 August 1858, the most prestigious combat award for the British and Commonwealth military. The sword wound he received in combat rendered him unable to wear a standard belt. The belt became a common accouterment of the British Army, and was also worn in certain uniform combinations by American army and police units extensively during Bradbury's youth. The imitation of uniforms by the students feeds Jamie's tendency to overplay his speculations about life and death.

19.32 "The Stars and Stripes Forever."] A melody in the standard military march form, composed by John Philip Sousa on Christmas Day, 1896; since then it has often been the opening or closing selection for many parade celebrations, and was declared the official National March of the United States by a 1987 act of the U.S. Congress. Even in the 1930s or 1940s, it would be anyone's best guess for the band to play in Jamie's parade.

19.35 "Columbia, Gem of the Ocean,"] An American patriotic song popular from the mid-nineteenth century; prior to the twentieth-century adaptation of the "Star Spangled Banner," this song was often used in ceremonies as an unofficial national anthem. Jamie rationalizes his missed prediction of marching band selections to protect his confidence in his miracles. Bradbury would later have his Martians play "Columbia, the Gem of the Ocean" at the conclusion of his most famous *Martian Chronicles* tale, "Mars Is Heaven!" ("The Third Expedition").

19.41–20.1 J.C. Penney . . . Morble Company] In 1907, James Cash Penney (1875–1971), established what would become one of the largest department stores, specializing in inexpensive general merchandise, in the U.S. Information on the Morble Company could not be located.

20.1 Each cadence was like a whip thud] Jamie's obsession with the largely unknown childhood years of Jesus may include the one incident recorded in all four Gospels—driving the money changers from the Temple. John 2:13–16 notes that this ousting was done with "a whip of cords." Jamie is driving his marching classmates with intensity, and Bradbury may have intended a gentle irony here.

21.1 blond] In French, blond is the masculine term for fair-haired; blonde is the feminine. British English generally adheres to the French distinction, but in American English, blond is preferred in both masculine and feminine cases.

21.22 Santa Catalina foothills] Located north and northeast of Tucson, Arizona, the Catalina Mountains have the highest elevation in the Tucson area.

23.27 Schabold] The name "Schabold" also appears in Bradbury's "Enter—The Douser" ("Half-Pint Homicide") completed in February 1944 (volume 2, selection 22). The Schabold twins were childhood friends of Bradbury in Waukegan, sharing his passion for magic tricks. As children, the three occasionally staged magic performances.

24.33 walls of Jericho] According to Joshua 6:1–27, Jericho was the first city of Canaan to be taken by the descendants of Abraham, who marched around the city walls once every day for six days. On the seventh day, they marched seven times around the walls, the priests blew their shofars (ram's horns) and Jericho's walls fell.

24.35–36 Bring her . . . Lazarus come forth.] Jamie attempts to bring his mother back to life, as Jesus did for Lazarus in John 11:43. This passage also alludes to his earlier science fiction story "Lazarus Come Forth" (volume 2, selection 16), concerning the substitutional death of a crewman from a "morgue ship" collecting bodies from an interplanetary war.

## 4. The Long Way Around (The Long Way Home)

26.3 comptometers] Thanks to patents, the Felt and Tarrant Comptometer (1885) remained the dominant adding machine throughout Bradbury's childhood and early writing career. The proprietary name "Comptometer" was prominently displayed on the casing of every machine. Bradbury would also have known Elmer Rice's Pulitzer Prize-winning stage play *The Adding Machine* (1923), which explored the dehumanizing aspects of modern technology. Guidney appears to be a CPA with the Sternwell firm; as his employer's name suggests, machine and management have drained away most of Guidney's life force well before the beginning of the story.

27.26 Sternwell. . . . Murder.] Bradbury's eccentric protagonist acts out the author's own method of word association—not to produce story ideas, but to come up with a dangerous adventure that might revitalize his marriage.

27.26] Sternwell] Guidney's spontaneous wish-fulfillment centers on killing the owner of his company. Sternwell's name and the comptometers that Guidney operates provide strong clues to the quiet desperation that, along with his wife's manipulating personality, drive him to make up the story that he has killed his boss. The opening premise parallels that of Elmer Rice's 1923 prize-winning play *The Adding Machine,* where Mr. Zero is tried and executed for killing his employer.

29.10 gun-moll] An American slang expression meaning a female thief or armed woman. Its first recorded usage was in 1908. Guidney sees his wife's sudden change to a quiet, focused demeanor as playing into his imaginary world; in reality, her new "gun moll" mannerisms hide her intent to frame him for murder.

30.36 rough-dried] Dried imperfectly.

31.31 Temple Street] From 1942 until early 1946, Bradbury maintained a day writing office in a tenement at the corner of Temple and Figueroa in Los Angeles. Many of the characters he observed in this crowded and richly diverse neighborhood were worked into various crime stories and his late-life detective novels, beginning with *Death Is a Lonely Business* (1985).

32.7 Jack the Ripper . . . the chill hand of Fate] Guidney's deadly serious comparison of his own clumsy and exaggerated crimes to those of Jack the Ripper, perhaps the most infamous of all serial killers, is laughable, but his further allusion to the chill hand of Fate also suggests the masterful terrors of Cornell Woolrich, whose unremarkable everyday characters often fall prey to random and unexpected acts of violence. Woolrich (often writing as William Irish) was a Bradbury reading favorite throughout the 1940s; *Phantom Lady* (1942) illustrates the kind of nightmare complications that Bradbury was striving for on the more limited level of dark humor short fiction.

32.8–11 shopping district . . . the alleys.] A microcosm of Bradbury's day office neighborhood, extended into the fantastic.

32.13 prowl cars] police car

34.8–9 "A murderer . . . couldn't he?"] A recently fired pistol may still smell of powder or cordite. And the proprietor of the gun shop has just described a woman (presumably Lydia), but Charlie uses the gender specific personal pronoun "he."

34.35 Kelly could.] It seems unlikely that the arresting officer would wait outside the murder suspect's tenement flat while the suspect enters to say goodbye to his wife. But Kelly is a local beat cop, comfortable with his control of characters and environment; this attitude also underlines Kelly's accurate sense of Guidney's lack of true criminal intent.

35.12 stumble-bums] American slang for drunks, or awkward persons. The first documented usage occurs in Ernest Hemingway's 1932 novel, *Death in the Afternoon.*

36.4–5 I heard . . . her now] There are loose ends, especially Guidney's earlier assault on officer Kelly. But Bradbury was immersed in all of the Hollywood film genres, including the mystery comedies where the true confession leads right into the rising soundtrack and credits. Bradbury saw the entire run of Dashiell Hammett's *The Thin Man* film adaptations by MGM (five films through 1944), and had read the novel as early as 1940; he was also well versed in the nearly thirty *Charlie Chan* detective film adaptations of Earl Derr Biggers's novels by Fox (and later by Monogram) that had been released by 1944. These would have been the most likely influences on his decision to leave loose ends at the conclusion of "The Long Way Around."

36.8 The white rat with the shiny pink eyes] Lydia's unbridled terror, leading her to confess outright to the murder, depends on the "weapon" being a pink-eyed, white laboratory rat, much larger than the small tenement mice that have terrified her in the past. The irony is heightened by the docile nature of the typical lab rat, here handled very easily by Charlie.

## 5. The Very Bewildered Corpses (Four-Way Funeral)

37.18 Square] the park and square complex where Douser meets Lajos is probably Pershing Square, a public park in downtown Los Angeles and a favorite walking area for Bradbury as early as 1940.

38.6–7 Earl Lajos] Possibly from Lajos Egri, whose book on dramatic characterizations (1942; revised 1946) was an important guide as Bradbury began his professional career. From an early age, Bradbury was also fascinated by the French illustrator Henri Lajos; the Lajos serial art for the H.G. Wells *Harper's Magazine* serialization of *When the Sleeper Wakes* (1898–99) was handed down to him by grandfather Bradbury. No deep allusive thread dictated the naming; Bradbury often used familiar or family names in his stories regardless of character attributes. Lajos is a Hungarian surname.

38.8 "Vice . . . vice,"] This double meaning spans the figure of speech and a reference to the various crimes in the criminal code classified as vice crimes investigated by a "vice squad" in many metropolitan police departments.

38.24 Having no . . . bother criminals] Lajos's comment suggests that Douser was once, like his late brother, a policeman. It's not clear at all if Douser even has a private detective's license, although that is the assumption throughout the several Douser Mulligan stories that Bradbury published or drafted.

38.31 "Speak on, MacDuff!"] Douser's verbal duel prompts his wisecrack paraphrase of Macbeth's answer to Macduff's deadly challenge in Shakespeare's *Macbeth,* act 5, scene viii, lines 32–33: "Before my body I throw my warlike shield. Lay on, Macduff."

38.33 scot-free] The third-person narrator here mimics Douser's lousy puns, playing on the reference to *Macbeth* in the preceding lines of dialog.

38.39 snow-hounds] Possibly police or crime world shorthand for heroin users.

38.41 first water] The best or highest quality, possibly taken from Shakespeare's *Pericles.* The expression is often used to express the clarity of a diamond.

39.25 commoner] A pun on the reduction of the king-sized cigarette to the size of a "commoner."

39.33 black button eyes] Inanimate eyes with a comic strip or marionette look. Bradbury's fascination with automata would grow into such major stories as "Riabouchinska" (1945; "And So Died Riabouchinska," 1953), "I Sing the Body Electric" ("The Beautiful One Is Here," 1968), and three so-called "mari-

onette" stories: "Marionettes, Inc." (1949), "Changling" (1949), and "Punishment Without Crime" (1950).

40.31–32 a thing . . . roller skates] Bradbury went all over on skates, in
Waukegan (where his dog pulled him downtown to buy the Saturday paper
with weekend comics) and Los Angeles (sometimes as far as the Hollywood
motion picture studios and radio stations). His meaning here is "no way."

40.33–34 Hart, Schaffner, and Marx trachea] Hart Schaffner and Marx, cur-
rently Hartmarx, began as a small clothing store in Chicago in the 1870s. Its
popularity rose around the turn of the century because the store's off-the-rack
suits provided an affordable alternative to the custom tailored suit.

40.34 the royal jools off a king-size] Refers to Drum having smoked his
king-sized cigarette down to the butt.

41.5 Sam Spade] Fictional private detective created by Dashiell Hammett
(1894–1961) for his 1930 novel, *The Maltese Falcon*. He is an archetypal private
detective who often rolled cigarettes to extend a dramatic pause. Spade was to
appear in three short stories by Hammett and adaptations for television, film,
and radio. The best-known portrayal of the character is found in the 1941 *Maltese Falcon* film adaptation directed by John Huston and starring Humphrey
Bogart as Spade. Henry Kuttner led Bradbury to Hammett's novels around
1940. Bradbury's dream of writing in Hollywood dates to his desire to work
for director John Huston after seeing the 1941 film version. This dream became
reality when he scripted Huston's production of *Moby Dick* in the 1950s.

41.14 bolixing] Usually spelled "bollixing," the word means bungling or
messing up a plan.

41.16 kid] Possible reference to Humphrey Bogart's line from the film *Casa-
blanca* (1942), "Here's looking at you, kid." Bradbury, the inveterate moviegoer,
would have known all of Bogart's turns of phrase.

41.22–23 Drum-tiddie-Um-Tum] The rhythm suggests the comedy punch
line cue spoken or played in Vaudeville acts, films, and cartoons: "Shave and a
hair cut, two bits."

41.24–25 Chanel Number Five] The first and most profitable of the per-
fumes created by French designer Coco Chanel (1883–1971).

41.27 fain] A possible example of "Runyonese" dialogue, a style coined by author Damon Runyon (1880–1946) and characterized by a reliance on slang terms
and the use of the present tense.

42.5 palaver] Talk that is lengthy and often of little substance.

42.22 *Love, It's Nice*] A film title that appears to be of Bradbury's invention.

43.21 palamino horse] Gold or tan colored horse with a white mane and tail; popular in horse shows and parades due to its distinct appearance.

43.23 sobbing . . . woman] The sexism in the story reflects the era in which it was written. Lajos is portrayed as a vain, effeminate criminal.

45.29 rods] The act of shooting the "rod" or handgun.

46.5 so many bewildered corpses] Lifted as the title line by Bradbury's editors; the last moments of life were horrifying and unpredictable, noir in the style of Cornell Woolrich, a Bradbury favorite.

46.6 Whistling . . . story] The story refers to the genre and conventions of detective fiction throughout. Bradbury may refer to *The Whistler* radio show, a mystery drama that ran from 1942 to 1955 on the west-coast CBS network. The show opened with the sound of whistling.

46.22 A man . . . bank robber] Douser's observations about a person's criminality are seemingly arbitrary, but they always ring true. He's a douser, a diviner in the sense of a dousing rod, thus explaining his nickname.

## 6. The Reincarnate

47.1 After a while you will] Bradbury occasionally experimented with second-person narratives, most successfully with "The Night" (volume 2, selection 5). His influences included second-person narrative experiments in some of the short stories of Somerset Maugham, but Bradbury soon moved away from these experiments; "The Night" was eventually re-written in the third person for *Dandelion Wine* (1957), but "The Reincarnate" remained a second-person narrative in his inactive files. Bradbury's late-life revisions for the long-delayed publication (*Dark Delicacies*, 2004) were extensive, but he nonetheless retained the second-person point of view.

47.4–7 The first . . . tenth month.] Bradbury here inverts the death process through ten months of decay; time runs backwards, and the first moments after death are equated to the miracle of birth: "It is new to you. You are born again." (47.12).

47.17 an emotional hand to slap you] The birth-death analogy continues through this parallel to the breath-giving slap of an obstetrician. The figurative "emotional hand" is the dead narrator's desire to see his wife again. This figurative slap foreshadows the real birth-slap he experiences through the birth of his own child (59.23).

48.8 a sort of dream town on the rim of a lake] The town will soon coalesce in the narrator's mind as Bradbury's unnamed hometown, Waukegan, Illinois, on the western shore of Lake Michigan north of Chicago.

48.12 tethered . . . at these iron tying posts] The tying posts in the green springs (changed to water fonts in *Dark Delicacies*) suggests riding through the many Waukegan Parks; Bradbury was most familiar, as a child, with nearby lower Powell park and its geographically defining ravine (since re-named Ray Bradbury Park).

48.23 Remember . . . burning?] An early forerunner of the burning book images that Bradbury was beginning to see as the death struggle of a living thing. By 1946–47, extended images of such "dying" pages surface in his unfinished novel, *Where Ignorant Armies Clash by Night*.

49.25–26 We newly dead . . . a persecuted minority.] Bradbury's unnamed speaker for the dead will eventually grow into the "Pillar of Fire" protagonist William Lantry (1948), who is disinterred into a future where supernatural literature has been obliterated from human memory.

49.31–32 persecuted . . . Germany!] In 1939 Germany invaded Poland and an additional three million Jews came under Nazi control—Nazi policy moved from expatriation to containment. The Holocaust would not end until the year following the writing of this story with the deaths of roughly six million Jews. In the *Dark Delicacies* revisions (2004) the reference is to Jews and the history of Jewish oppression in general and not to any specific historical event (*DD* 3.24). The other dead man's political rhetoric is less direct and revolutionary in *Dark Delicacies;* however, *Dark Delicacies* changes the words from "pour out to overflow the villages!" (50.19) to "Pour out to drown the unbelievers." (*DD* 4.1–2).

50.5–6 hatred for the living] The rise of the dead to celebrate and restore the supernatural world will become the goal of the resurrected William Lantry in "Pillar of Fire" (1947; published 1948). In this more mature and long tale, Bradbury is critical of censorship and the inevitable death of the imagination that such authoritarian initiatives may cause.

50.11 Elysian Park] Actual park in Los Angeles and the second largest park in the city and its oldest, having been founded in 1886 by the Elysian Park Enabling Ordinance. By 1944 Bradbury had lived in Los Angeles for a decade, but "The Reincarnate" is a Waukegan story; his use of Elysian Park is a mythological reference to Elysium, or the Elysian Fields, the Greek afterlife for mortals who are related to the gods. This allusion also connects with the Reincarnate's rebirth at the end of the story (see also 58.7).

50.29 rococo magnificence] In his fiction, Bradbury often transformed the small Washington Street house where his grandparents kept boarders into the Sheridan Road (formerly State Street) mansion of his Great-Grandfather Bradbury, a Victorian home that may have contained rococo elements in its décor. In later years Bradbury would often use "rococo" to describe the ornate style of certain modern writers, including Frederic Prokosch and Karen Blixen (Isak Dinesen).

50.29–30 the house where Grandma sheltered her boarders.] Grandmother Bradbury's home at 619 Washington Street in Waukegan was next door to 11 South St. James Street, where Bradbury lived, for the most part, from 1920 to 1934—from birth until the summer of his fourteenth year. He spent many hours with these boarders, and wrote certain aspects of them into his stories and novels.

50.30–31 Fourth of July,] These memories extend back to Grandfather Bradbury (d. 1926), who first showed him the rockets and fire balloons of Independence Day from the porch.

50.33 uncle Bion] Bion Bradbury, younger brother to Ray's father Leo, lived just around the corner from the other two Bradbury households at 616 (or 618) Glen Rock Avenue. Bion was a machinist by trade, and he fashioned a miniature canon for Fourth of July celebrations.

51.2 Boston-baked beans . . . bacon.] The great boarding-house meals of Bradbury's youth are celebrated in "Dinner at Dawn" (1954), subsequently an untitled story-chapter of *Dandelion Wine* (1957).

51.5 Kim's house] Bradbury left Waukegan near the end of his eighth-grade year, and there is no indication that any of his early adolescent attachments carry over into Kim's character. He would save memories of his good childhood friend Isobel Skelton for *Farewell Summer* (2005), the long-delayed Green Town Illinois novel from which *Dandelion Wine* (1957) had been extracted.

51.15 Your breath] The lifeless "Reincarnate" Paul is breathing, an impossibility in his state; his cold dead body should not produce warm breath to fog Kim's window, or to expend as he struggles with her at 56.4, or to struggle back to his grave at 59.8. Elsewhere in the story (i.e., 58.26, "Your breath, or the illusion of breath, slows."), Bradbury begins to show that breathing, like eating and swallowing, begin to erode Paul's will to remain a functional shade among the living.

51.25–26 from deep under a sea you hear a song] His extensive reading of Edgar Allan Poe's poems may be suggested here, including "The City in the Sea" (1845; earlier version published as "The Doomed City" in 1831), "Ulalume" (1847), and "Annabel Lee" (1849). The water-born elements of these poems center on a beloved lady lost to death; in "The Reincarnate," the pattern is reversed, and the male narrator must reach back to the living.

52.24 Six months] Paul is in the "prime" (47.5) of his decomposition, but quickly falls apart by the end of the evening, which should not be happening until between the eighth and tenth month (47.6–7).

52.32 horrible . . . chrysalis] Bradbury's fascination with the fear of otherness resulted in two stories titled "Chrysalis": a science fiction tale (volume 1, selection 11) and a condemnation of racial intolerance (volume 3, selection 7). "The Reincarnate" explores similar themes of transformation and "metamorphosis" (52.31–32).

53.4–5 I'm the quick . . . dead.] A biblical allusion to Acts 10:42; 2 Timothy 4:1; 1 Peter 4:3–5, and possibly the Apostle's Creed, from the *Book of Common Prayer*.

53.5 We're opposed by our very natures.] The debate revolves around the love of life claimed, through typical Bradbury ambivalence, by both the living and the dead. Bradbury knew the Bible well, and it is likely an intended irony that the "Reincarnate" is Paul, the name of the most influential apostle, a great proclaimer of love.

53.29 White City] May refer to the White City resort of Altadena, California, which was a popular Victorian tourist destination, with a 70-room hotel, dance hall, observatory, petting zoo, casino, and tavern. Located three miles up Echo Mountain, the resort and its incline railway were abandoned in 1938 after a series of natural disasters.

53.41 "I have been taught to be afraid,] Kim reflects the general educational and social biases against supernatural literature in mid-century America. During the late 1940s Bradbury would publish stories that directly attacked the growing fear of non-conformist literature and the supernatural, including "Pillar of Fire," "Usher II" (originally "Carnival of Madness"), and "The Exiles" (originally "The Mad Wizards of Mars").

55.26 You can smell nothing] Bradbury's extensive studies of sensation, later evident in "Skeleton" (selection 19), are evident here. He uses loss of smell, touch, hearing, and finally sight to mark the transition away from contact with the world of the living. The Bradbury twist is seen in the unexpected transition back into life through his soon-to-be-born son.

57.7–8 I'll be . . . another month] Kim is roughly eight months pregnant and should be showing, but Paul does not notice.

58.7 a ravine path in Elysian park] The southern extension of Powell Park includes the north-south branch of the ravine that Bradbury knew best as a child in Waukegan; this section of the ravine runs to the south under Washington Street just east of the Bradbury homes. This lower portion of Powell Park was renamed Ray Bradbury Park during the 1980s. Elysian Park is also a well-known Los Angeles attraction in the Chavez Ravine area where Dodger Stadium now stands. Even though the story uses many Waukegan landmarks, Bradbury may be deliberately conflating both locales (see also 50.11).

59.8 The coffin is now a round dim shell, no longer square] "Interim," a subsequent Bradbury variation on the coffin-to-womb terror, appears as a single-page narrative sketch in *Dark Carnival* (1947) and the July 1947 issue of *Weird Tales.*

59.28 cuddled and nursed] Bradbury always claimed that he retained neonatal memories of birth, nursing, and circumcision. His late-life discovery that he was a delayed "tenth month" baby reinforced this conviction (Eller, *Becoming Ray Bradbury,* 9; Weller, *Bradbury Chronicles,* 11).

## 7. Chrysalis

60.1 Walter] This name has no traceable biographical origins, but the earliest TSπ reading is Henry. During the war years, Bradbury kept a day office in a tenement at Temple and Figueroa owned by the mother of his friend, Grant Beach. One of Bradbury's friends in the tenement was a blind black man named Henry. Although the name drops out of "Chrysalis," Bradbury would revive Henry for all three of his late-life detective novels.

61.10 This is the white place.] Bradbury visited Santa Monica Beach with his family during the mid-1930s; during the early 1940s, he regularly met with his friend and mentor Leigh Brackett there on Sunday afternoons, where she played volleyball and critiqued his stories. The beach was racially segregated during these years, and Bradbury observed how these restrictions were more or less enforced. Bradbury had always objected to any form of intolerance and injustice, and "Chrysalis" is one of a dozen stories drafted or sketched out during the mid-1940s to explore the complexities of racism in America.

61.15 the Palisades] Pacific Palisades, north of Santa Monica, is defined by the rising landscape where the California coast turns to the west toward Malibu. Walter's mother apparently works in a Palisades resort hotel within an expensive area where Hollywood stars often built homes to get away from the downtown traffic.

61.39–62.2 About ten . . . massages.] This short episode of Bill eagerly check-ing the early development of his summer suntan is important because it stands in contrast to Walter's anxiety over his dark skin color. Walter's wish for white skin opens the story, but the TS1 opening presented here is less explicit than the first paragraph of TS2 (published in Bradbury's 2004 collection, *The Cat's Pajamas*), where Walter tries a series of bleaching creams and lotions.

62.26–27 "Flop down!" . . . immediately obeying] Bradbury's use of the word "obey" makes Bill's comment interesting. Bill's words could be an invita-tion or an imperative; the use of a word like *obey* implies a level of submission to another. A major component of the interaction between the boys is Bill's discovery of racial insensitivities that are a part of his everyday speech and knowledge (see 63.24: "I never thought of that").

64.4 Mammoth Cave] The longest cave system known to exist in the world, Mammoth Cave is mostly located in Edmondson County, Kentucky, but it ex-tends to Hart and Barren Counties to the east. Its official name is Mammoth-Flint Ridge Cave System, and it was established as a U.S. National Park in 1941. The park is nearly 53,000 acres.

64.30 A great thing . . . a progression] Bradbury refers to the progression of Bill's summer tan, which eventually turns his skin a darker shade than Walter's. But as other white boys also choose to become dark-skinned, Walter feels equal to them, a part of their group, for the first time. Bradbury uses this episode to emphasize the cruel absurdity of prejudice based on skin color.

64.42 playing volleyball] During the war years, Bradbury observed that the Santa Monica Beach volleyball games sometimes included black athletes from the segregated beach. One of them explained the severity of sunburn to black sunbathers for Bradbury, a revelation that became the germinal seed for this story.

## 8. The Poems

68.20 skeined] wound yarn or thread, a metaphor that may relate to the way Bradbury came to see the process of compressing words into poetic or story form.

70.11 Can I etch life, burn it onto paper,] Bradbury's lifelong fascination with the act of transmitting the creativity of the mind through his fingers to paper is first apparent in his unpublished 1942 poem, "My Typewriter Wife," where his creativity pushes life out of the "womb" of nested keys, "Line after night-black line, page after page."

70.17 cage the wind.] Bradbury's 1943 story "The Wind" (volume 1, selection 7) is a more fully developed fantasy involving an explorer who discovers the secret and malign intelligence of the winds. His interest in controlling the wind began with his childhood reading of two stories by his mentor Edmond Hamilton, "Child of the Winds" (1936) and "Bride of the Lightning" (1939). The poet's awareness of the wind surfaces again at 71.19.

71.1 Holy Grail] The impossible made possible; the Grail is only made immanent through spiritual revelation. Over time, the concept of writing as a God-given talent became an abiding Bradbury belief. But the metaphor of the Holy Grail for the poet's gift is here an ambiguous one; David's poetry reveals in words only what it erases in reality, and the fact that he appears to desire fame at the cost of the natural world indicates that his talent may be a gift from a malevolent source.

71.7 destroy the universe and immortalize it] Romantic poetry attempted to capture the sublimity of nature through the poet's individual and personal emotional responses to it, expressed in established poetic forms. Bradbury had not read much Romantic poetry at the time this story was written. He would begin concentrated study of the Romantics in 1946–47, under the influence and guidance of his wife Maggie and of author Edmond Hamilton.

71.10 cosmic music] Bradbury's 1940–41 unpublished story "Black Symphony" explored the controlling quality of music: a lone teacher is unaffected by the music that the totalitarian government uses to control humanity, but his attempts to liberate his students fail. Paul's attempt to control the cosmos plays out in a similar symphony of words.

71.15 Keats and Shelley and Browning] John Keats (1795–1821) numbered among the second generation of English Romantic poets. He was best known for his odes, and although his work was not well received during his short lifetime, he became one of the most influential poets of the Romantic Movement after his death. Percy Bysshe Shelley (1792–1822) was a major English Romantic poet and member of a circle of poets that included Lord Byron, Leigh Hunt, Thomas Love Peacock, and Mary Shelley, his second wife. Among his most famous works are *Queen Mab: A Philosophical Poem* (1813), *Ozymandias* (1818), and *Ode to the West Wind* (1819). Shelley was an important influence on Robert Browning (1812–89), whose dramatic monologues and epic poems brought him fame. His works include *My Last Duchess* (1842), *Childe Roland to the Dark Tower Came* (1855), and his epic poem *The Ring and the Book* (1868–69). He married successful poet Elizabeth Barrett (1806–61) in 1846. It is unclear whether Bradbury refers to Robert or Elizabeth Barrett Browning in this story.

The intensity, passion, and focus on imagination that characterize Romanticism are also traits that Bradbury's poet-protagonist Paul has or is trying to emulate.

73.5 microbe-infested] Most living creatures are infested with microbes, but the poet uses this reason to minimize the living creature's value. During this period Bradbury would also write "The Watchers" (selection 15), where the principal characters suspect that microbes form a malign "overmind" that is inimical to humanity.

76.26 she began to dictate] The poet's wife, at the end of the story, takes on great agency as his Muse in order to stop his destroying the subjects of his poems; characters are the active agents in Bradbury's concept of creativity; he would often speak of letting his characters write their stories. The turning point that the poet's wife acts out here may originate in Bradbury's 1943 reading of Maren Elwood's *Characters Make Your Story*, which encouraged him to lessen his reliance on narrative description. He found that the most important lesson he took away from Elwood's book was "to let your characters act, and explain themselves with action" (Bradbury-Eller interviews, Oct. 10, 2005).

## 9. Defense Mech

78.1 how far from Earth we are?] Bradbury's abiding conviction that the limitless distances create a paralyzing sense of loneliness and alienation would peak in such stories as "No Particular Night or Morning" (*The Illustrated Man*, 1951). Specific Martian stories of isolation and homesickness include "The Long Years" (1948), "The Visitor" (1948), and "The Strawberry Window" (1954).

78.23 Halloway] A name that becomes central to *Something Wicked This Way Comes:* the father-and-son protagonists, Charles and Will Halloway.

78.26 weight in uranium] The central importance of uranium in the development of the atomic bomb was hardly known to the public at the time this story was written, but its scarcity and importance in radiation experiments and x-ray technology had been generally known since the days of Roentgen and the Curies.

79.4 reversion to childhood] Severe mental trauma has been known to cause behavioral regression in children and adults. Bradbury's early 1940s readings in psychology would have included relevant case studies.

79.9 old cool . . . *chikk*] During the nineteenth and early twentieth centuries, before domestic refrigerators were common, perishables were kept cold in an icebox. Ice, harvested from natural bodies of water, was loaded into a wagon or truck and delivered to homes and other establishments by icemen who trans-ferred the ice from the truck to the icebox.

80.2 bulgers] An imagined design for segmented and rigid spacesuits com-mon in the science fiction of the 1930s through the 1950s, when a more flexible space suit design was developed for actual manned spaceflight.

80.22–23 ethics of my profession] Bradbury refers to the ethics of the medi-cal profession, which include respect for the patient's autonomy, beneficence, nonmaleficence, justice, truthfulness, and honesty.

80.25 a protective defense mechanism] A psychological defense an indi-vidual uses to cope with severe problems in order to function.

80.32 tetched] Psychologically unstable; the American dialect expression dates from the 1930s.

81.36–37 copperheads . . . crawfish] The alien dangers of Mars are translated in his mind into more familiar creatures such as the copperhead (a common North American pit viper) and crawfish (common freshwater crustaceans re-sembling small lobsters).

82.20 yellow street car] Bradbury was very fond of the Los Angeles Street-cars, which were discontinued by the early 1960s. All of the downtown lines used yellow street cars, and this term became the generic descriptor for all lo-cal street cars during this era in Los Angeles rapid transit history.

82.35 nine-day miracle] Bradbury may refer to the concept, first documented in Chaucer, of the "nyne days' wonder." A "nyne days' wonder" is an unusual occurrence that garners widespread attention for a short period of time and is quickly forgotten thereafter. Otherwise, Bradbury may refer to an extension of the seven days of creation and the eight days of Chanukah; by the mid-1960s, as Bradbury found himself a prominent spokesman for the Space Age, he would extend his developing concept of the eighth day of man and the ninth day of the developing Apollo lunar program into his poem-cantata, "Christus Apollo."

85.41 iced] Synonym for "killed."

87.13–14 Irishmen . . . Italians] The hypnotized Halloway highlights these ethnicities as threatening because he remembers them as recent immigrants with unknown values and intentions. Bradbury often probed the deep-seated human fears of difference that he felt would cripple Humanity's chances of making successful first contact with intelligent life from other worlds.

88.16–19 the Martians . . . came?"] The ethics of Earth's imperialism on Mars is never questioned in the story. Martians have some level of technology, social organization, and culture but the crew from Earth does not seem to recognize anything Martian as having authority in the area. Halloway's performance during the Martian trial also reinforces human superiority (and possibly implicitly justifies the human claim to the planet), which allows the reader to feel sympathy for Berman and Halloway while feeling nothing for the Martians killed. This begs the question: could the Martians be justified in their treatment of the crew (the "blood-letting jamboree" noted at 86.1)? How would humans treat a group of Martians who had come and done the same on Earth?

## 10. Mr. Priory Meets Mr. Caldwell (Hell's Half-Hour)

89.5 Chris Priory] The name originates in "King of the Gray Spaces" (vt "R Is for Rocket"), his earliest quality science fiction tale (volume 1, selection 19). Both of these "Priory" characters epitomize great potential for achievement and a dedication to tasks that one might find in a priory or its governing monastery.

92.1 like waltzing mice] A lay term for mice with a neurological disorder that prevents them from moving in a straight line. These mice have a tendency to run in circles.

92.9 a gigantic pendulum] Bradbury's fascination with the movement of a pendulum dates to his childhood memories of the large clock in his grandfather's home and the clock store on Main Street in Waukegan. By the time he wrote "The Pendulum" for his fanzine *Futuria Fantasia* (Fall 1939) and revised it, with Henry Hasse, for his first professional pulp sale (1941), he had come to see the pendulum as a root metaphor for time machines. Above all, he was fascinated by the concept of duration; the unusually long time it takes to kill the victim stands as the crucial clue that Chris Priory follows in identifying the blind Mr. Melton as the murderer.

92.38 Douglas] The narrator, playing Watson to Priory's Holmes, is given a favorite Bradbury name. Douglas was Bradbury's middle name, and he developed Douglas Spaulding as the older boy in *Dandelion Wine* and related stories based on his hometown Waukegan. Here the use of the name suggests a playful authorial connection with the narrator, who echoes the "Dr. Watson" narrations of one of Bradbury's favorite writers, Sir Arthur Conan Doyle.

93.33–35 but the very . . . our murderer?"] Chris Priory speaks in terms of evidence, but he is relying on circumstantial coincidence (which happens to work out). Priory seems to be playing fast and loose with police procedure, and this strategy is what Bradbury consistently does to make his detective stories work.

94.35–36 his old eye ailment recurred . . . progressively blind] Bradbury's childhood development of nearsightedness was initially misdiagnosed as progressive blindness; he soon realized he was myopic, but the fear of continuing loss of sight plagued him until 1944, when he began a regimen of eye exercises based on the controversial Bates method of therapy. Further background to Bradbury's abiding fear of blindness is provided in the volume introduction and in this selection's apparatus headnote essay.

## 11. "I'm Not So Dumb!"

97.1 Spaulding's Corner] The Spauldings were Bradbury's paternal grandmother's family, a surname used many times in his fiction and even as a pseudonym. There are places in Waukegan named for his Spaulding ancestors.

97.18 Italian labor crew] During World War II, Italian prisoners captured in North Africa and Southern Italy were placed in Stateside prisoner-of-war camps.

97.24 skyhook and shore line] Fool's errands for new Navy recruits (skyhook) and Boy Scouts (shore line).

97.26 pentagonal monkey-wrench] A fool's errand.

100.29 phitted] More as "fought," not, as styled in *MeM* (1984), as "fightin'," which breaks the narrative out of dialect.

102.31–32 left-handed screw driver] A fool's errand.

## 12. Invisible Boy

103.11 miracle bag] Old Lady's magic is a form of folk or Appalachian-based enchantment, but Bradbury deliberately leaves the deeper aspects vague to focus on the story's central conceit: a practicing witch who has no powers at all.

103.22 Ozark] Mountain range in Missouri and Arkansas, a geographic region, and an American cultural group.

104.11 miracles] "Invisible Boy" shifts between magic and miracles despite differences in the meanings of the words, which may indicate Bradbury's use of the words as synonyms in this story, whereas in "The Miracles of Jamie," the young boy clearly interprets his perceived feats as miracles in a religious sense.

104.15 spunks] Sparks.

104.25 mouse-ear root] Mouse-ear chickweed is a perennial root herb that reproduces by seeds and grows in vines.

104.32 salvation tambourine] The tambourine was a mainstay of music performed by local Salvation Army bands. These bands depended in part on easy mobility and quick setup, and the hand-carried tambourine was an ideal percussion accompaniment that required little training. As a teenager and young man, Bradbury attended and studied a wide range of religious services and related salvation shows.

105.24 gingham] Patterned textile, mostly used for women's domestic day garments.

106.16 shiny tips of her eyes] A reference to the pointed corners of her eyes; Old Lady preserves the illusion of the boy's invisibility by not looking directly at him.

107.13 hairy . . . Chautauqua] A Chautauqua was a community event in rural America popular in the early twentieth century. They fell out of vogue after the automobile and radio became more popular and rural Americans had greater access to urban-centered cultural events.


## 13. Ylla (I'll Not Ask For Wine)

111.2–3 red cake . . . spider web] Bradbury eventually shifts such "red cake" food away from the homey Waukegan fare of his youth to "golden fruits" in later versions, more in line with his exotic golden-eyed Martians. But the major changes involve transforming spider webs to magnetic dust, cooking fires to lava boils, and guns to the deadly bee stinger weapons. These changes were suggested by *Mademoiselle*'s fiction editor Marguerita (Rita) Smith, who read early versions twice without ever being able to convince her publishers to buy the story, and by *Cosmopolitan* editor Arthur Gordon. Although spider webs (common to Bradbury's Elliot family of "Homecoming" and other weird tales) reinforce the insect motif of Martian life, the magnetic dust, lava, and exotic weapons provide more of an alien feel to the Martian culture he was beginning to define in his science fiction—a culture that resembled, in some ways, the equally-doomed native American cultural landscape.

111.9 told tales of when the sea was alive] This paragraph closely resembles the setting of his nearly simultaneous co-authored work on "Lorelei of the Red Mist," which continued Leigh Brackett's vision of semi-barbaric Venus and its mystical seas (selection 16). Bradbury here suggests a similar but long-dead past for his Martians. In his revisions from the TS1 copy-text toward S1, Bradbury altered his vision of ancient Mars to show some continuity in weaponry with the insect-like technology of the present Mars, with memories of "tales of when the sea was red steam on the shore and ancient men had carried clouds of metal insects and electric spiders into battle."

111.12 ten centuries] Bradbury hints at the slow decline of his etiolated Martians. Ylla and Yll seem to represent the entire thousand-year line of the household, occupying the house like Poe's isolated and dwindling line of Ushers.

111.13 the true Martian] In crafting his Martians, Bradbury was inspired in part by his childhood encounters with images of ancient Egyptian representations of the human form, especially King Tutankhamen's death mask. To these elements he would envision the yellow or golden (111.30) eyes of an incredibly old and jaded race of aliens who are also, in many respects, chillingly human.

111.16 wine room] Martian awareness of wine ensures that Ylla will understand the late Renaissance Ben Jonson (1572–1637) poem and song "To Celia" (1616) that reaches her mind from Captain York's approaching spacecraft; the first line of this fragment becomes the S1 first publication title, "I'll Not Ask for Wine."

111.18 Something was going to happen.] The indescribable feeling of impending revelation is similar to the sudden realization of being alive that Bradbury's young protagonist Douglas Spaulding will feel, a decade later, in the short story "Illumination," one of the opening untitled chapters of *Dandelion Wine*.

113.3–10 'I've come . . . our planet.'] York is not consciously communicating with Ylla; she is picking up the unspoken imaginings or rehearsals of his first contact speech as the Earth ship comes within range of her receptive mental powers.

113.37–39 "Drink . . . for wine."] Captain York's idle thoughts project early modern English dramatist and poet Ben Jonson's poem "To Celia" (see annotation 111.16). TS1 and S1 both present Bradbury's transcription of these lines. The British *Argosy* S2 (1950) contains the variant "but in" (for "within"); both S2 and editions of *The Silver Locusts* (the title for some British editions of *The Martian Chronicles*) contain the variant "look for wine." These variants may be based on variants in early editions of Jonson's works.

114.27 twin moons] The two moons of Mars, discovered in 1877, are named Phobos (panic) and Deimos (fear), after the children of the Greek god Ares, who was called Mars in Roman mythology. The names, and the rapid progression of these moons through the Martian sky, play into the emotional mix of expectancy and dread that underlies Ylla's consciousness.

118.25 a thunder storm coming] Ylla's remembered sensation of a thunderstorm is heightened by the implication that such a storm on arid Mars is a rare event. Bradbury would reverse the phenomena for "All Summer in a Day" (1954), where Earth's colonists on Venus eagerly await the one-half hour of the year when the sun breaks through the constant rain. Bradbury wrote both of these tales in the last decades before space probes and landers would relegate such planetary climates (as seen in the Burroughs-Klein-Moore/Kuttner-Brackett-Heinlein-Bradbury creative arc) to realms of pure fantasy and (as most recently seen in S. M. Sterling) to alternate realities.

120.19–34 "Remember what?" . . . "I'll be all right, tomorrow."] During 1944 and 1945 Bradbury sometimes experimented with a kind of understated, tense, Hemingway-esque style, especially when dealing with the subject of death. The closing passage between Ylla and Yll reads like Hemingway prose in such stories as "Hills Like White Elephants," where there is a subtext between the male and female characters. This was also a time when Bradbury, still single, was experimenting with various ways to present married relationships, the reality of which he could only imagine.

120.21 forgotten it] Her lost awareness implies that Ylla's mind and York's mind had been connected while he lived, a connection now sundered by the murder she cannot consciously acknowledge.

120.34 tomorrow] In this tale, Mars has scientists and some level of technology, and early in the story Mr. K mentions that these scientists have done an atmospheric study of Earth and found it incapable of supporting life because of its oxygen-rich atmosphere. It is likely that Martian scientists would detect the Earth ship approaching the planet, or that someone would have at least seen or heard it besides Mr. and Mrs. K. The isolated tale of Ylla works as a stand-alone story, but broader Martian contact radiated out from this first encounter by late September 1949, when Bradbury revised three other contact stories to appear as second, third, and fourth expeditions in *The Martian Chronicles*: "The Earthmen," "Mars Is Heaven!" ("The Third Expedition"), and the thematic center of the book, "And the Moon Be Still as Bright," all published as separates in 1948.

## 14. The Tombstone

121.17 Oklahoma man] Bradbury likely refers to the migrant farm workers from Oklahoma, commonly known as Okies, who were forced to leave their state in search of work during the Great Depression of the 1930s. As a boy, he experienced their challenges (and their company) during his own family's 1932 and 1934 migrations west from Waukegan.

122.3–4 defense plant] A World War II era "home front" allusion; in his postwar revisions for *Dark Carnival* (1947), his first story collection, Bradbury changed the reference to "an envelope factory," a touch that enhances the ephemeral background of Leota and her husband.

122.8–9 inferiority complex . . . scuttled off] An allusion to T. S. Eliot's *The Love Song of J. Alfred Prufrock* (1920), an archetypal modernist quietic; "I should have been a pair of ragged claws | Scuttling across the floors of silent seas." Bradbury was in the midst of an extensive reading program in nineteenth century and modernist prose and poetry when he wrote the stories of this period.

122.21 up-crik] A dialect variation of the common cliché "up the creek."

123.23 rubbing his bones together] an allusion to the folk-tale noises of a walking skeleton, where cartilage no longer prevents the bones from generating noise between bone joints. The sound is often detectable in the living who have lost cartilage due to aging or arthritis.

124.11–13 making queer . . . her craw] Leota may refer to glossolalia, or speaking in tongues, a religious expression practiced by Pentacostal and Charismatic Christians.

## 15. The Watchers

126.12 the cricket upon your hearth!] *The Cricket on the Hearth* (1845) is a novella by Charles Dickens in which a cricket is seen as an angel in the home. More sentimental and with less social commentary than many of his other novels, *The Cricket on the Hearth* idealizes Victorian family/home stability. Bradbury may be using this as an ironic nod to the author and his work, or may simply be relying on the association or possible contrast with the other insects that Tinsley suspects of spying on him. The title metaphor of Bradbury's "The Cricket on the Hearth" (c.1950; published 2002) would refer to a hidden microphone in a fireplace during the McCarthy era.

126.31 Clyde Beatty] Beatty (1903–65) began his circus career as a cage cleaner before becoming a famous lion tamer who owned his own show. He also worked with tigers, hyenas, and cougars.

127.4 corpses] A term not generally employed when talking about insects or bugs. "Corpse" can be used to mean any dead body, but the referent is generally people or animals. Bradbury's use here plays into the magnified fear of the insect world, and eventually of their microbial "masters," in the minds of the central characters.

127.12 as soon as war conditions permit] Rationing, especially of paper, had a signficant impact on Bradbury's early breakthrough into the pulp magazines, as several of his editors had to sacrifice certain titles, most notably *Flynn's Detective* (Popular Publications) and *Unknown* (Street and Smith), where Bradbury had made sales.

128.14–15 tinker's chance in hell] A conflation of "no chance in hell" and "a tinker's damn."

128.19 delusions of persecution] Mental illness known as paranoia. Such delusions also characterize schizophrenia, a more complex condition.

129.3–4 "Ninety-nine . . . insect life—"] The statement that 99% of life on earth is insect life is verified by several scientific studies.

129.19–20 darning needles . . . brown ants] Bradbury often referred to the "darning-needle dragonfly," especially in *Something Wicked This Way Comes* (1962).

129.37 spread the memory . . . and pinned it down] Similar to the opening and closing narrative frame of Bradbury's 1943 story "Autopsy" ("Killer Come Back to Me!," volume 2, selection 14). In that tale, the pathologist conducting the autopsy of the crime boss "reads" his history by laying out the internal organs like tea leaves in a fortune teller's teacup.

129.39 Lake Arrowhead] Located in the mountains above San Bernardino; Bradbury refers to the smaller lakes of the area as well. His family would sometimes vacation in this region beginning in his high school years.

131.13–14 They who control the animals and insects, killed him] The sentient quality attributed to the microbial world is similar to that of the global air currents at the center of Bradbury's 1943 tale "The Wind" (volume 1, selection 7).

132.40 'Scarlet Letter'] Bradbury refers to Nathaniel Hawthorne's novel, *The Scarlet Letter* (1850) set in seventeenth-century Salem, Massachusetts. The protagonist, a young woman named Hester Prynne is shamed by her Puritan community for having committed adultery while her husband is at sea. She is forced to wear a scarlet "A" (standing for "adulteress") on her dress and stand on the scaffold each day until she admits the identity of her daughter's father, which she never does.

134.37 women are superstitious] The "mind culture" that Bradbury's character here attributes to women is probably influenced by his reading of A. Merritt (*Burn Witch Burn*, 1932) and Fritz Leiber, Jr. (*Conjure Wife*, in *Unknown Worlds*, April 1943).

134.37 still a woman . . . superstitious] The implication is that women have a lower terror threshold than men, a premise common in early science fiction, horror, and dark fantasy.

136.38 you still have—microbes] The unexpected supremacy of microbes is no doubt inspired by Bradbury's love of H.G. Wells's early scientific romances; the fate of Bradbury's humans is a reversal of the fate that awaits Wells's technologically superior Martians in *The War of the Worlds* (1899).

136.39–137.10 Bacteria . . . instantly!] This dark depiction of the microbial world is carefully constructed, and at least invites Coleridge's "willing suspension of disbelief." In spite of his lack of college or scientific studies, Bradbury had some familiarity with biology. It was his best science subject at Los Angeles High School; during the second semester of his senior year (spring 1938), he opted to drop a second semester of astronomy and instead took an additional course in physiology.

137.13–17 Bill, is that you . . . disease you are!] The rapid death and decay of Tinsley convinces the narrator that microbes, not insects, form the collective sentient entity that silently controls the world. But the narrator is no more reliable than Tinsley. Is Tinsley's disfigurement the result of a microbial horror, or simply scars from the scalding shower he has endured to sterilize his skin? The power of suggestion is strong in both Tinsley and his narrator-friend, just as it was a self-acknowledged factor in Bradbury's own receptivity to hypnosis.

137.25 to drive Bill's car into the ditch and set fire to him and it.] The reader may infer that, by not reporting Tinsley's death to the police, the narrator believes he is protecting the rest of humanity from the death that comes with knowledge of the secret microbial world.

138.21 etaoin shrdlucmfwyp cmfwym] The letter sequence "etaoin shrdlu" includes the twelve most common letters in the English language. The linotype keyboard, long a mainstay of newspaper typesetting, was based on this unique lettering pattern. It occasionally appeared in newspapers by accident or design. Bradbury was an excellent touch-typist from high school on, and enjoyed typesetting humor that built on such unpronounceable nonce words. There are at least two other possible influences. Bradbury had already alluded to Elmer Rice's 1921 Pulitzer Prize-winning play, *The Adding Machine,* in his story "The Long Way Around"; Rice's play includes a character named Shrdlu. He would later know Fredric Brown, and may have read Brown's 1942 linotype-come-alive story "Etaoin Shrdlu."

## 16. Lorelei of the Red Mist

139.1 The Company dicks were good.] Brackett's mastery of detective fiction narrative occasionally led her to build her interplanetary science fiction around crime plots, as seen here in Starke's opening reference to the company detectives pursuing him, literally, into the beginning of the novella.

139.1 Hugh Starke] The original persona of the reluctant hero in "Lorelei of the Red Mist" is distinct from Eric John Stark (no "e"), who was later a prominent Leigh Brackett hero through three interplanetary novellas (1949–1951) and a trilogy of interstellar novels of the mid-1970s.

139.5–6 Venus was a frontier planet] Brackett was still working in the Burroughs tradition of a wet and warm Venus, decades before the Soviet and American probes would verify the extreme atmospheric pressures and temperatures of the planet. For "Lorelei," she envisioned a world partially settled (at least for mineral exploitation), and partly still a semi-barbaric world of native humans, sea creatures, and hybrids in regions protected by severe magnetic and electrical disturbances that form a barrier to exploration. The planet is not exactly uncharted, but the Venusians "weren't sending out any maps" (139.6–7). Brackett's peers would build similar habitable visions of Venus for some years to come, including Heinlein (as in *Between Planets,* 1951) and Henry Kuttner and C. L. Moore (for example, their *Clash by Night* (1943) and its sequel). Bradbury's few stand-alone Venusian tales include "Death by Rain" (collected in *The Illustrated Man* as "The Long Rain," 1950), and his often-anthologized "All Summer in a Day" (1954).

139.15 lone-wolf] The typical down-and-out Brackett protagonist is often a lone-wolf personality; Bradbury had created acknowledged variations on Brackett's "isolato" protagonists in his earlier *Planet Stories* tales, including "Morgue Ship" (volume 1, selection 16) and "Lazarus Come Forth" (volume 2, selection 16).

140.8–9 red mist] A possible trigger source for the novella's third and final title, and, given the metaphorical elements, very likely Bradbury's.

140.25 tabard] A loose-cut, sleeveless garment, worn by a knight over his armor, and emblazoned with his coat-of-arms.

144.13 Conan] Not the famous genre literature character created in the pulps by Robert E. Howard, but the same name.

146.6 Crom Dhu]May actually refer to Crom Dubh. Crom Dubh, meaning "dark crooked one" in Celtic, is a mythical figure in Irish folklore.

147.3 "Her people have that power.] Brackett's premise that Rann can move minds into other bodies may have influenced Bradbury's subsequent development of Cecy Elliott in "Homecoming" (1946–47) and "The April Witch" (1952).

148.10–11 looked fey] Formerly meaning on the point of death or descending into the stupefaction of death, but in the context of the narrative, "fey" more likely means able to foresee events or bearing other attributes of what is often called a sixth sense. Given Romna's small size as a "swamp edger" (an established Brackett variation on interplanetary humanoids), this allusion may also refer to the physical and mental characteristics of fairies or elves.

148.15–17 Starke said . . . called Falga."] Starke's ignorance of Venusian geography and politics is not surprising. As the narrative opens, it's clear that "Venus was a frontier planet, and still mostly a big X, except to the Venusians" (139.5–6). This earlier passage indicates that while industrial giants like the T-V Mining Corporation are colonizing parts of the planet with workers, there is little substantive interaction with the indigenous cultures of Venus.

148.31 After a . . . third people] Romna gives a local account of how the rover peoples came from the North, providing a native perspective that is not present in the novella's opening account—an opening based on colonial Earth's limited knowledge of Venus.

150.31–33 a heavy gas, . . . mixture.] Since Starke's mind holds the technologically advanced perspective of an interplanetary criminal, he provides the perfect opportunity for Brackett to present the one flash of scientific verisimilitude that the reader needs to "suspend disbelief" and accept the physics of the red mist sea. This superficial nod to science was not necessary for *Planet*'s editors, but she had learned to provide that touch of science for John W. Campbell at the higher-tier *Astounding,* where such a touch was more or less required.

153.35 have scurvy . . . fruit] A lack of grain foods is not a factor in developing scurvy, which is actually caused by a lack of vitamin C.

154.12 dun] From time to time Brackett invokes Celtic words to describe clothing (kilt and tabard) and structures; Faolan's stronghold is a more substantial stone variation of the Scottish and Irish "dun," a double-ringed palisaded fortress dating back to Neolithic origins. Bradbury continues Brackett's use of "dun" at 166.5.

159.12–13 the color of shoal-water] Shallow transparent water or surface turbulence caused by the appearance of fish near the surface.

166.26 He saw the flock, herded by more of the golden hounds.] According to Leigh Brackett (Introduction to *The Best of Planet Stories #1*) this passage marks the point in the middle of the novella where Bradbury took over the writing.

166.26–27 the shepherd, with the harp] The Brackett hand-off note (undated, but September 1944) refers to the "sea-beasts," but the shepherd and his harp (a more powerful variation on Brackett's character Romna) appear to be Bradbury's transition into alliance with the original undersea civilization. The shepherd "king" (older than the youth he first appears to be) and his harp may also allude to the biblical King David, often depicted with the harp of his early shepherd's life.

166.29 One hundred, two hundred] The "flock" of most recently slain Falgan warriors are, presumably, the ones slain at the gates of Crom Dhu the day before, just as Starke awakens in Conan's body. This plot twist is the first thread that Bradbury connects to Brackett's first-half narrative.

168.1–13 Long ago . . . archway] Bradbury's first fully descriptive passage in his portion of the novella presents his undersea city in color-rich detail resembling the fantasy cities of A. Merritt. Bradbury, who met Abe Merritt in 1939, had been an enthusiastic reader of Merritt's pioneering fantasies and his finely detailed (if sometimes overwritten) use of similar precious stone metaphors.

168.9 radium-skinned] Bradbury would have been familiar with radium-painted clock faces, a radium-copper-zinc mixture that produced the green glow he uses to describe the light-producing creatures beneath the red sea of Venus.

168.36 The part . . . the name] As he took up the narrative, Bradbury chose to give Starke some of Conan's memories. Brackett seems to have left Conan's consciousness suppressed under Starke's persona, but still inaccessible. Bradbury's Starke benefits from Conan's memories without having to deal with any of his personality.

169.3 Aesur] May refer to Aesir, the Old Norse plural noun denoting the pantheon of Norse gods.

169.23 "In death, all men are equals."] This is a paraphrase of a maxim that may be falsely attributed to Publilius Syrus, an Assyrian slave and writer of Latin maxims in Italy during the first century B. C. It is said that the wisdom of his maxims moved his master to free him from slavery.

174.13 baby's nightmare before it's born.] Bradbury was fascinated by theories of prenatal memory and post-natal nightmares of birth trauma, as evidenced in such earlier stories as "The Small Assassin" (volume 1, selection 23) and "The Reincarnate" (selection 6). This motif in his work leads on into the volcanic Source energy's "seething rebirth" for the dead warriors of both Falga and Crom Dhu (175.21 [the source life of the Red Sea.]). The undersea world and its resources represent Bradbury's earliest (and perhaps his most substantial) contribution to the novella narrative.

175.24 cannulas] Bradbury had used a copy of *Hartrampf's Vocabularies* (1929) since the late 1930s as a synonym and antonym finder. As late as the mid-1940s, words beyond Bradbury's usual vocabulary range can sometimes be sourced to Hartrampf; "canula" is one of many words cross-referenced to "artificial conducting mediums" in that reference book.

175.26 gave you a seething rebirth!] Another description using the motif of rebirth that pervades this story in many forms, beginning with Starke's new body and continuing through to Starke's eventual adoption of the Starke/Conan persona.

175.36 The ribs . . . like silvered spider legs.] A simile Bradbury used again in both his *Weird Tales* "Skeleton" (selection 19) and his *Script* "Skeleton" (selection 21).

177.6 "This is the day of the carnival.] The carnival tradition, often an inversion or a dark reflection of the real world order, was never very far beneath the surface in Bradbury's work. Here he has chosen Falga's carnival day for the destruction of the city and its citadel.

180.5 the tidal basilic] Bradbury's similar search for "artificial conduits" in his copy of *Hartrampf's Vocabularies* (175.24, "cannulas") also led him to "basilic" in the adjacent section on synonyms for "organic passages." His choice also has a rich mythological connotation that allows him to describe Conan's struggle with the red sea's tidal flow metaphorically, as a struggle with a basilisk, a mythical reptile whose breath and gaze were fatal to its prey.

## 17. One Minus One (Corpse-Carnival)

189.18 bared the thin spines] This is the first hint that Raoul and his brother are conjoined along a line of soft tissue close to (and paralleling) their separate spinal columns. The physical orientation of attachment explains not only how they are lying as the story opens (on their sides, facing away from each other), but also how the murderer could have attacked without being seen by Raoul.

189.29 Roger *had* been there for twenty-seven years.] Bradbury's older brother, Leonard Jr. ("Skip," born 1916), had a twin, Samuel, who died in the Great Influenza epidemic of 1918. Marvin Mengeling (in *Red Planet, Flaming Phoenix, Green Town,* 2002) maintains that Ray Bradbury, born four years after the twins, grew into the eerie feeling that he was seen as the "replacement" twin by the rest of the family. The two surviving boys would share the same bed in the Bradbury household until Ray Bradbury was twenty-seven years old (two years after the composition of "One Minus One"). This passage seems to capture the world of the Bradbury boys, one an athlete and fighter, the other a reader and dreamer, and projects that world into the story.

190.2–3 Often he lay . . . Long silence.] Almost like a phantom pain, Raoul still experiences his brother's physical presence; this feeling serves as threshold to his sense that Roger's lingering presence was also inseparable from his own mind and personality.

190.7 one instead of two] This phrase, along with Raoul's growing realization that Roger seemed to be his own darker self, may have inspired Bradbury's original submitted title, "One Minus One."

190.23 tanbark] Tree bark that contains tannins, used primarily for tanning leather. Several types of trees produce tanbark, which may be refined into mulch or peat moss. This absorbent mulch was often spread underfoot in circus grounds; Bradbury brings this texture into the story from his many experiences with circuses as a boy in Waukegan.

191.6–7 Legend says that if one Siamese twin dies, so does the other.] Depending on how the twins are joined, there is truth to this. Many Siamese twins share organ systems or will have dependent systems where the organs of one twin dominate the organs of the other. From his youth Bradbury was steeped in circus lore, and would have known of P. T. Barnum's celebrated Siamese twins Chang and Eng, who died hours apart in 1874 at the age of 63 (at death it was learned each man's liver was involved, ensuring that they could not have been separated in life). Bradbury's fictional twins can be separated, but their work as carnival oddities (and what Raoul expresses as their inextricably intertwined minds and personalities) has kept them conjoined. The late-life alcoholism of Chang (a condition that precipitated the death of both twins), as well as Chang's deteriorating psychological health, also may have been known to Bradbury as he wrote.

191.18 DeCaines] Caines is a town in northern Italy, located in the provine of Bolzano. It has a tiny population. The name DeCaines can be Spanish, French, or Italian, meaning in all those languages, "from the town of Caines."

193.12 Mazda beetles] Mazda Motor Corporation is a Japanese automaker founded in 1920 in Hiroshima, Japan. Its name was originally Toyo Cork Kogyo Co., Ltd., and it manufactured machine tools and weapons before introducing its first car in 1931. The company supplied the Japanese military with weapons throughout the duration of World War II. "Beetle" is a word Bradbury often uses as a synonym for automobiles, but it's unclear if his usage here relates to the Japanese vehicle maker.

193.20 Venus De Milo] Raoul remembers how his late brother Roger had given insulting names to all of the circus sideshow exotics, cruelly alluding to the armless lady as the Venus De Milo, a centerpiece of the Louvre and perhaps the best-known classical Greek carving in the Western world. The statue's arms were recovered during excavation but subsequently lost, adding a tantalizing parallel to the circus lady's condition.

193.25–30 Tattoo, . . . Ha!"] Except for the ability to muscle-flex the image of the Eiffel Tower on his back, Tattoo's body art is, for the most part, a static display. By the summer of 1950, Bradbury would develop the enchanted story-telling tattoos, revealing both past secrets and future terrors, in the Prologue / Epilogue framework of his 1951 story collection, *The Illustrated Man*.

193.39–194.1 I'm no freak." . . . my mind did all this to me] Tattoo, the illustrated man of "One Minus One," freely chose to adapt the tattoos that define his professional role, and is thus able to avoid any kind of psychological enslavement to them. Bradbury would explore the psychological and supernatural terrors of the tattooed image in "The Illustrated Man" (1950, distinct from the *Illustrated Man* story collection structure) and in *Something Wicked This Way Comes* (1962), in which Mr. Dark's tattoos are the enslaved souls of the people drawn into his nightmare carnival world. Both works have their origins in the period just after Bradbury composed "One Minus One."

194.24 She was the white thing of the upper spaces,] Bradbury's first planted clue for the reader loses its subtlety in the same paragraph, when Bradbury goes on to describe Deirdre's dominant arm strength as a high-trapeze spinner: "Her strong right arm bedded with hard muscles, . . ." There remains little doubt as to the identity of Roger's murderer; the reader awaits only the revelation of motive.

195.15 Tibetan monk's prayer wheel] Prayer wheels, large and small, are used by Buddhists of Tibet and the Himalayas to add to their prayers. Individual prayers or mantras are printed and attached to the wheel and the wheel is spun in prayer. Each revolution of the wheel holds the equivalent of saying the prayer one time. Bradbury explored many religious traditions, but his knowledge of Eastern religions (gained through the British expatriate writer and lecturer Gerald Heard) was still more than five years in the future.

195.16 *oom mani padme hum*] Words of a mantra used in prayer and meditation, especially in Tibetan Buddhism. "Oom" functions as an invocation; "mani" means jewel; "padme," a lotus flower; a discrete meaning for "hum" remains unclear.

196.10 toot sweet] From French: tout de suite, part of a command meaning "right away" or "immediately."

197.34–35 uncontrollable desire . . . get away from things forever.] Bradbury's belief in the power of the subconscious goes back to his reading of Dorothea

Brande's *Becoming a Writer* in 1939. He soon came to believe that the author must let the creative upwellings of his subconscious shape the first draft of his character's actions before bringing the self-conscious act of revision into play. Here Bradbury has Raoul react to the recurring truths of his subconscious, where the identity of Roger's killer is already known.

199.11–12 a live man being alive] An early and somewhat obvious example of the so-called "Bradbury twist"; Raoul is able to track the murder back to his lover Deirdre because she has killed half of him by killing his Siamese twin. The twist is an inversion of the usual trail to the killer, which runs through "the dead man's being dead."

200.15–18 "Yes, and she's . . . arrest her then."] As with most Bradbury detective stories in the volume, the strongest evidence is only circumstantial. With no witnesses or murder weapon, and still no confession, it is still only likely that Dierdre murdered Roger.

## 18. The Sea Cure (Dead Men Rise Up Never)

203.32–37 "No money! . . . goddamn you!"] The phrase "kicking down the Christmas tree to get the star on top" is Bradbury's way of presenting a gangster's version of the cliché "cutting off your nose to spite your face."

205.13 old California mission] During 1944, Bradbury had accompanied his friend Grant Beach on a driving tour through a number of the Spanish mission stations along the Mexican and Southern California coast.

205.18 some of the first padres built it] An indirect reference to Junípero Serra and his successors, who established the California missions under Spanish colonial rule (there are twenty-one in all).

205.21 eucalyptus trees] This image plays into an effective comparison of the original mission flora to the seaweed in tidal motion around the now-submerged church, but it also creates an unintended anachronism. The California range of cultivated and natural eucalyptus groves that Bradbury knew originated with specimens brought by Australian prospectors during the California gold rush in 1850; they were not present during the Spanish period when this fictitious early mission apparently subsided into the sea.

205.31 This bell rings from the water] Rapture of the deep (nitrogen narcosis) can create the sound of bells. The image more likely comes to Bradbury through his early reading of Poe; by the war years, his reading of Poe's fiction was beginning to extend to the poems, peaking under the influence of his friend and occasional mentor, Edmond Hamilton. Poems expressing fantasies similar to those of Hamphill include "The Sleeper," "Ulalume," "The City in the Sea," and the late-life poem "Annabel Lee."

205.33 siren] A play on the legend of the siren song, intended to pull Hamphill back to reality (a possible police call) from his obsession with the underwater bells he thinks he hears from the submerged mission ruins.

206.15 gunsel] A criminal armed with a gun.

209.5 swipe Sherry] This second possibility in Mark's alleged counterscheme—letting Finlay's gang leave with Sherry's body and continue the ransom scam—is as vague and unclear as the first possibility—killing and framing Finlay's entire gang for Sherry's death. The vagueness may be intended to suggest that Mark's explanation is simply a nervous cover story for his true intent: to betray his own gang.

## 19. Skeleton (*Weird Tales*)

214.24 a dose of salts] Epsom salts, or magnesium sulfate, has long been used to treat a number of ailments from constipation, to asthma, to preeclampsia. This is an early indicator of Harris's extreme hypochondria.

215.1–2 smelled of iodoform, iodine] Iodoform is an organoiodide compound with a distinctive odor, most often used as a disinfectant. Iodine is a chemical element ("I," Periodic Table number 53). Iodine is primarily used in compounds promoting nutrition in health care and in creating polymers in manufacturing.

215.16 of a Dali painting] M. Mugnaint shows the protagonist Dali-esque pictures and paintings of diseased bones. Salvador Dalí (1904–89) was the best-known of the Surrealist school of artists. In this story, Bradbury may be referencing Dali paintings such as *The Metamorphosis of Narcissus* (1937), which featured hand and body bone structures.

215.37 chewing breadsticks] The foreshadowing here is subtle. Only in retrospect will the reader realize that the breadsticks keep Munigant "in—a—practice" for chewing human arm and leg bones.

216.5 Clarisse] This becomes a recurring character name, best known through Clarisse McClellan, who awakens the conscience of Fireman Montag in *Fahrenheit 451*.

216.33 floating ribs] The two lowest ribs are called "floating ribs." To the protagonist, however, this nomenclature confirms that his bones are moving out of control.

216.35 he desired that his wife leave him,] A psychological inversion of the norm. He doesn't desire his beautiful wife—he desires her absence so that he can explore and manipulate his own body.

217.18 dice!] Often referred to as "bones," dice were traditionally carved from ivory (tusk dentin) or bone.

217.22 inside my head is a—skull] The description that follows (217.22–27) shows the abiding influence of Poe and his obsession with the terror of the intellect trapped within a mortal body that will eventually die and decay. Bradbury knew such descriptions from Poe's stories "Ligeia" and "The Fall of the House of Usher," and from various poems.

217.26 my smelling, my seeing, my hearing] Early in his career, Bradbury collected many books on the senses; these included scientific texts on olfactory processes, the anatomy of the eye, the process of sight, and books on hearing and touch. Many of these readings clearly play into "Skeleton."

217.33–35 Skeletons . . . rustling pendulums on the wind] Bradbury playfully brings together three of his favorite story elements. "The Pendulum" was his first professional sale, invoked here to bring time to bear on the skeleton and its time-controlled deterioration from a living armature into death. "The Wind" (1943), in which Bradbury characterized global air currents as dangerous sentient entities, was one of his earliest sales to Weird Tales.

218.5 ceramics business] Bradbury's high-school ceramics experience expanded into work with his friend Grant Beach. During the war years, he encouraged Beach and his mother to overcome depression (caused by the death of Beach's father) through learning the art of molding and firing ceramic art. As he wrote this story, he was still assisting Beach in his home ceramics shop near Temple and Figueroa, where Bradbury also kept his daytime writing office between 1942 and early 1946. Bradbury periodically helped Beach sell his ceramics at a gallery across from the Farmer's Market in Los Angeles.

218.26 tell mama."] His neurotic obsession has turned so far inward that his beautiful wife has become a mother figure, a role that she embraces even as she continues to approach her husband with an air of languid sexuality.

218.35 neuroses] His reading of the works of psychiatrist Dr. Karen Horney (1885–1952), in particular, The Neurotic Personality in Our Time (1937), informs his creative interpretations of progressive neurotic behavior here and in other stories of the period. Through her work in particular Bradbury gained insight into the neurotic cycles of anxiety and hostility seen in Mr. Harris and other Bradbury characters of this period (see also "The Watchers," selection 15). He also gained a general understanding of Freud's views on neuroses (and the basic nervous tendencies of most people) from his Modern Library edition of selected works by Freud.

219.18–19 bivalve in the compressed clamp of skull-bones.] The simile is based on the soft body of a bivalve, such as a clam or an oyster, nested between its two hardened shells. Bradbury deleted this passage in his 1955 *October Country* revisions.

219.24 Red Cross meeting] Bradbury was classified 4F (for poor eyesight) when the selective service draft was initiated in 1940. His wartime alternative service involved writing blood drive advertising copy for newspapers and radio spots; his mother was also a Red Cross volunteer.

219.37–38 *skull sockets . . . plumb line.*] This description may allude to Poe's short story "The Gold Bug." Bradbury had a good reading knowledge of Poe's major tales, and would have known that the location of the buried treasure in Poe's story depended on dropping the gold bug, like a plumb line weight, through the right eye socket of a skull mounted in a tall tree. In his 1955 *October Country* revisions, Bradbury removed this passage from "Skeleton."

220.3 like a delicate insect within a chrysalis] The natural wonder of the hard chrysalis shell protecting the developing insect was a favorite Bradbury metaphor, prompting him to write two stories titled "Chrysalis" (volume 2, selection 11 and volume 3, selection 7) before his composition of "Skeleton." The image here brings yet another inversion into the story: a hard skeleton creature hidden within the soft and "disorderly" exterior of skin and fat. This inversion is itself embedded within a more general metaphorical pattern in Bradbury's most suspenseful works—something hidden beneath the surface, waiting to come out.

220.9 carpals, metacarpals, and phalanges] Bradbury received high marks in his biology and physiology high school classes; this experience provided him with the anatomical nomenclature that pervades the story, adding a rare scientific element to his fiction.

223.9 quid] A British colloquialism for the pound sterling that came to mean money in general, both in Britain and in the United States.

223.22 from Frisco to Phoenix] Harris' enroute disaster in Death Valley is close to the straight-line route between San Francisco and Phoenix, and his earlier mileage estimate (over six hundred miles) at 218.3 approximates the actual straight-line distance of 654 miles. Highway connections through Death Valley did not develop in straight lines, however, and the driving distance (then and now) would be considerably greater than Bradbury's estimate. In his 1955 *October Country* revisions, Bradbury changed Harris' home city to Los Angeles and shifted the auto accident to the Mojave desert, more than one hundred miles to the southeast. This route drifts far to the north from Los Angeles, but it is drivable. Bradbury modifies the return trip to avoid the northern route entirely.

224.1 xylophone] In both "Skeleton" and "One Minus One" (selection 17), Bradbury uses the image of the xylophone as an anatomical metaphor. He was already an enthusiast of Lionel Hampton's genius with this instrument, having seen him play in San Francisco on Bradbury's round-about way home to Los Angeles from the inaugural 1939 New York Science Fiction convention. In decades to come, Hampton (1908–2002) would become an enthusiastic reader of Bradbury's fiction.

224.19–21 safer route . . . Santa Barbara.] Santa Barbara is a city in California located approximately 90 miles west-northwest of Los Angeles, somewhat out of the way for Harris's return trip from Phoenix.

226.12 Saint James Place] In 1934, Bradbury's father moved the family to 1619 South St. Andrews Place, a subdivided house that the family rented throughout Bradbury's high school years. As a child in Waukegan, he had lived at 11 South St. James Place from birth until his fourteenth year. Although the story is set in Los Angeles, Bradbury is probably combining the two addresses from earlier times.

## 20. Riabouchinska (And So Died Riabouchinska)

227.1 Ockham] The nature of the story's plot and Bradbury's range of reading during this period suggest that the deceased Mr. Ockham's name may be an allusion to the medieval cleric and philosopher William of Ockham (c. 1287–1347), or more specifically, to the attribution "Ockham's Razor." Among its many interpretations and formulations since the nineteenth-century first expression as "Ockham's Razor" is the broad public interpretation that the simplest explanation of a phenomenon is most likely to be the true one. Despite the complexities of Fabian's psychological dependence on his creation Riabouchinska's ability to "express" his repressed truths, the simplest answer lies in the dead man's name: the simplest explanation, and the true one, is that Fabian murdered his blackmailer Ockham. Bradbury's reading in philosophy was sporadic, but in 1944 he read extensively in his copy of Bertrand Russell's *The History of Western Philosophy* (1945). This reading of Russell (1872–1970) led him to Henri Bergson (1859–1941) and the idea for his story "The Creatures That Time Forgot" (better known as "Frost and Fire"); Russell also extended

Ockham's razor in his own writing, and Bradbury may have encountered the modern concept through this source.

227.5 floor of a theatre cellar.] The perfect place to hide a corpse—a theatre cellar is often labyrinthine, and is always out of sight of the audience (in this case, readers, who are brought in with very limited omniscience). Bradbury would be very familiar with such settings; as a Hollywood Bowl usher on symphony nights (1940–41), Bradbury knew the dressing areas beneath the stage (in fact, his own staff photo was displayed with those of the other ushers in this area). Subterranean worlds appear in many of his fictions, including the immense Los Angeles storm drains with its conduits to the ocean in "The Cistern" (1947) and *Let's All Kill Constance!* (2002). The basement complex of the Hollywood landmark Grauman's Chinese Theatre is also prominent in the latter novel.

227.10–11 RIABOUCHINSKA] Bradbury attended the major ballet tours as they came through Los Angeles, and actively followed the careers of George Ballanchine's principal dancers with the Ballet Russe from the late 1930s through the 1940s. He would have been familiar with the career of Russian-American prima ballerina Tatiana Riabouchinska (1917–2000), who danced on tour with the Ballet Russe (the successor to the Ballet Russe de Monte Carlo) until 1942. She had joined the company in her mid-teens, and was known as one of Ballanchine's trio of "Baby Ballerinas." The doll-like perfections of Fabian's Riabouchinska suggest the inspiration, as does Bradbury's devotion to ballet during these years (he would eventually name his youngest daughter after another prima).

227.28 Each of you testify] Testimony is given in court and under oath. At this point *claim* may be a more appropriate term, but Bradbury is intentionally heightening the story's central irony—no one tells the truth freely except Riabouchinska, who represents the principal manifestation of Fabian's schizophrenia.

229.14–21 Fabian shook his . . . will do no good."] Fabian is describing, through metaphors, the compartmentalized boundaries of his schizophrenia.

229.24–25 maybe before . . . dummy questions."] Any statement made by someone playing a character, like a ventriloquist, may not be admissible as evidence later in court. Detective Krovitch knows this, as is evident from his background and his method of interrogation, but he accepts Fabian's schizoid point of view in the interest of reaching the truth.

231.23 *Billboard* Magazines] Krovitch has researched Fabian's past through the entertainment industry's premier news magazine at the time the story was written. *Billboard* had originated in the late nineteenth century as a clearing house for entertainment poster information; a generation later, the young Ray Bradbury grew up mesmerized by the circus, theatre, and motion picture posters of the interwar years and occasionally worked them into his fiction (the time-machine kite of Bradbury's 1972 novel *The Halloween Tree* would be made of animal images torn from old circus billboards). By the 1940s, *Billboard* was turning more and more to the music industry, but the older issues Krovitch read would still have the stage act billing news of earlier times.

## 21. Skeleton (*Script*)

236.10 ivory carving] A similar bone and ivory simile appears in his *Weird Tales* "Skeleton" (selection 19). Various elements common to both stories suggest that his *Script* "Skeleton" evolved as a brief and playfully sexual contrast to the dark terrors of the longer tale.

237.9–12 One of those things . . . deserts.] The same reverie or dream-like progression of image associations seen here in the husband also appears in Mr. Harris's mind in his earlier "Skeleton" story.

237.16 Mr. Hyde or a Frankenstein] A dual reference to Mary Shelley's *Frankenstein* (1818; revised 1831) and Robert Louis Stevenson's *Strange Case of Dr. Jekyll and Mr. Hyde* (1886). Mr. Hyde was another face that allowed Dr. Jekyll to sin in ways he had only dreamed about before. Frankenstein was a doctor who created life in the form of a monster. Sometimes the doctor and the monster are confused in reference. Hyde and Frankenstein could each be said to have taken something monstrous hidden beneath the surface and brought it into a full and terrifying manifestation.

237.23 two big spiders standing over my lungs,] The same image springs to the mind of Harris in the earlier "Skeleton" story.

238.4 She sat on his lap.] Here, as in the earlier "Skeleton" tale (selection 19), the wife brings her husband to the same threshold for recovery; both wives use touch, even settling on the husband's lap. Harris's wife Clarisse is ultimately unsuccessful in the earlier story, but here the wife is able to convey the larger truth to her husband effectively and successfully—not rationally as Clarisse attempted in the first story, but seductively, through words *and* actions.

## 22. The Black Ferris

239.1 carnival . . . October wind.] The sinister aspect of this carnival is foreshadowed by its arrival out of season, in October; the regular season would be

Memorial Day weekend through Labor Day weekend, (late May to early September). The dark implications move even closer to Halloween as Bradbury expanded the story, over many years, into *Something Wicked This Way Comes* (1962).

239.6 lake shore] Bradbury's Lake Michigan home town, Waukegan, opens out onto beachfront recreational areas near open ground where the circuses and carnivals pitched their attractions. They would arrive in and depart from the lakeshore rail yards; as a boy, Bradbury often met the trains when they arrived and "assisted" the roustabouts in return for free admission on opening night.

239.13 and none of the thin-fat . . . platforms.] The story opens with a quick reference to the carnival and sideshow freaks. Bradbury seems to be most at home when writing about the carnival and keeps that idea of suspense, mystery, and weirdness as a tone for this story.

239.31 shiny red Ford] Between 1908 and 1914, Model T Fords were available in four or five dark colors, not including black. From 1914 to 1926, all Model T Fords were painted black, the least expensive color. When Ford's sales suffered in the 1920s the company began offering a wider range of colors in order to compete with other American automakers that had been offering color choice for years.

240.21 the ravine] One of the most enduring of Bradbury's locales for unseen terror and for the great divide between youth and old age, the ravine topography of downtown Waukegan was both a daytime playground and a night-time dread. One branch ran east-west just south of his Uncle Bion's house on Glen Rock, around the corner to the south of the Bradbury home. But the main branch that Bradbury frequented was the north-south run just east of his block that meandered down through Powell Park and the smaller lower Powell Park (renamed Ray Bradbury Park) before passing under the main east-west corridor of Washington Street. The ravine is geologically significant, and is known as one of the best ravine formations for study in the Great Lakes region. Bradbury's best-known ravine tales were bridged into *Dandelion Wine* (1957) and its original novel source, *Farewell Summer* (2005), forming, along with *Something Wicked This Way Comes,* his enduring Greentown trilogy.

240.28 Mrs. Foley's ravine house] The house in "The Black Ferris" is modeled on the old Foley house in Waukegan, a large home just north of Washington Street above the ravine where Bradbury often played. The house was two blocks from Bradbury's childhood home, and he walked past it on his way to school for years. It was eventually burned down by the fire department.

240.33 Joseph Pikes] Bradbury resurrected the name "Pikes" in interesting ways for "Carnival of Madness" (*Thrilling Wonder Stories,* April 1950), better known as "April 2005: Usher II" (*The Martian Chronicles,* 1950). In this story-chapter of the *Chronicles,* Pikes is the murderous assistant to the millionaire William Stendahl, who has just built his Usher II mansion on Mars; together they fashion fantastic creatures out of Edgar Allan Poe stories to attack the arbiters of censorship.

241.12–13 Henry Walterson] In the final novelization *Something Wicked This Way Comes,* Henry is transformed into the far more complicated character of Jim Nightshade, a fatherless boy who yearns for a quick transformation to adulthood—as only the dark carnival can provide.

242.19–23 "He'll stick around . . . pulled up stakes."] Hank, like Bradbury's other detectives in this volume, strings together a wild interpretation that happens to be correct: the carnival always leaves a town before its predatory secrets are discovered by the authorities. In the *Something Wicked* expansions, the carnival returns at great intervals, after living memory has faded away, to prey on new generations of victims.

242.41–243.2 "Now, hand . . . Hank, disconsolately.] It's reasonable (and slightly humorous) that Hank's father would enforce his son's restriction by confiscating all his clothes. The fact that Hank's wardrobe is kept in the hall closet seems a bit odd, but Bradbury stretches credibility beyond bounds as Hank shows up at his rain-soaked rendezvous naked, lacking even underwear or pajamas; we are to assume that his room locks only from the outside, forcing a window escape without a stitch of clothing. The comic effect is greatly diminished by this incongruity. During his long years of revision and expansion into his unproduced "Dark Carnival" screenplay and his novel *Something Wicked This Way Comes,* Bradbury would develop better-crafted predicaments for his two young protagonists.

244.18 "Here now!" yelled the hunchback.] Early in the tale Bradbury established that the grotesque Ferris operator is blind, but he is now able to see Hank's approach. The narrative logic is further distorted by Hank's savage and extended attack on the blind man, for both Hank and Pete are established early on in the story (through dialog and behavior) as being very young. Bradbury would eventually eliminate the Hunchback complications in the novelized chapter version of this tale.

244.37–39 Hank leaped up . . . weeping dwarf.] Hank's brutality is surprising. He has been beating and smashing a *blind* hunchback with a tent spike, and now he is smashing the equipment that allows the Ferris wheel to run. In a very real sense his actions against the hunchback are savage and contribute to the carnival

master's manslaughter death—quite an evening for a young boy. Bradbury eliminated such incongruities as he absorbed the story into the novel structure of
*Something Wicked This Way Comes,* making the boys older and shifting the carnival master's destruction to a more elemental struggle between good and evil.

245.22–23 The wind touched . . . crooning] Bradbury often gave the wind
animate characteristics, beginning with his eponymous 1943 story "The Wind"
(volume 1, selection 7) and, occasionally, to provide a suggestion of eeriness or
closure in such tales as "The Mad Wizards of Mars" (*Macleans,* Sept. 15, 1949),
better known as "The Exiles" (*The Illustrated Man,* 1951).

TEXTUAL RECORD

# Textual Commentary

The deeply interwoven roles of storyteller and truthseeker formed the great creative core of Ray Bradbury's seven-decade writing career. His many successful forays into other forms of writing and media adaptation almost invariably radiated out from the enduring armature provided by the nearly 450 distinct short stories that he published during his long and productive life. Ironically, the individual story texts themselves proved far less stable over time; many of his pulp and major market magazine stories were revised or completely rewritten and republished, sometimes under different titles, in more than two dozen carefully crafted story collections, including *The Illustrated Man, The Golden Apples of the Sun,* and *The October Country.*

Others were revised and bridged into novels and novelized story cycles such as *The Martian Chronicles* (1950), *Dandelion Wine* (1957), and *Something Wicked This Way Comes* (1962). Even his classic 1953 novel, *Fahrenheit 451,* one of the most widely read books of our time, evolved from story fragments and a short novella. In three retrospective story compilations—*The Vintage Bradbury* (1965), *The Stories of Ray Bradbury* (1980), and *Bradbury Stories* (2003), all still in print—he cast successively wider nets in order to gather more than 200 stories that he considered broadly representative of his best work.

His novels, along with his many stage, cinema, radio, and television story adaptations, sometimes obscure the underlying reality: his achievements as a creative writer derived in large measure from his early mastery of the short story form. Throughout his career, he took great care to showcase his subsequent intentions for the early stories as he gathered many—and excluded others—to fashion his periodic story collections and definitive compilations. His tendency to revise and even rewrite for these collections further obscures the key to understanding his maturing creativity: *the date of composition—and the sequenced order of composition—for the individual stories.* Each original story represents an upwelling of ideas and associations from his unconscious, triggering a creative burst that sometimes led to variations on the same themes and topics in other stories composed during a single concentrated period of days or weeks or months. Even the dates of first publication (usually in periodicals) mask the order and chronology of composition, for many of his stories had long circulation histories before reaching print; others never made it into magazines and first appeared—often years or even decades later—in Bradbury's story collections.

When brought to light, the true compositional order of Bradbury's stories yields significant new information about his development as a unique stylist and master of short fiction. The best of his genre stories were actually written far earlier than previously known, a discovery that provides more accurate documentation for the incredibly brief span of years during which Bradbury developed from a promising but inconsistent and self-conscious young writer into a masterful teller of fantasy, science fiction, and horror tales. The years of research behind *The Collected Stories of Ray Bradbury* series reveals that such quality stories as "The Lake" (volume 1), "King of the Gray Spaces" (volume 1), and "The Man Upstairs" (volume 2) were written years ahead of publication. Other stories destined to anchor enduring Bradbury classics were also written far earlier than first magazine publication might suggest; these include "The Million Year Picnic" (volume 2) and "Ylla" (volume 3), which would become the closing and opening stories, respectively, of *The Martian Chronicles,* and "The Black Ferris" (volume 3), which would unmask the central terrors of *Something Wicked This Way Comes.*

But the most important task of *The Collected Stories of Ray Bradbury* volumes is to present the chronological sequence of stories through reliable texts that reflect Bradbury's earliest settled intention for each tale—an intention that, for the most part, is not otherwise available today. The following section of the "Textual Commentary" describes the theory and method of critical editing used (1) to identify and recover the earliest form of each story and (2) to provide a record of the subsequent history of each text as Bradbury's authorial intentions changed over time. The commentary concludes with an overview of the challenges found in recovering the texts for this volume, and this discussion will lead into the short textual histories and apparatus documentation for each story.

## Textual Principles and Procedures

The volumes of *The Collected Stories of Ray Bradbury* present a critical edition of Bradbury's published short fiction, presented for the first time in the chronological order of composition. The edition is "critical" because it is based on the identification and examination of the versions of each story over which Bradbury may have exercised at least some degree of authorial control. The *Collected Stories* editors collate (compare) Bradbury's known typescripts (he composed almost exclusively at the typewriter), his serial printings, and all Bradbury story collections, retrospective compilations, as well as novels or novelized story cycles containing the published stories of the volume period. During the process, the editors also identify and record all variant readings. For the stories that Bradbury brought into book-length collections, all true editions (distinct type-settings) are also collated, along with any known galleys or page proofs. Since successive printings (also known as impressions) within an edition may have been revised or corrected by Bradbury, the final impression is collated against the first; if variants surface, the intermediate impressions are examined to pin-point the date of introduction and to determine whether the variation is edito-rial or authorial. This systematic recording of the variant textual history leads to the essence of critical editing: the exercise of editorial judgment in classifying the variants and establishing the text that best reflects the author's intention at a specific period in each story's publishing life.

Bradbury established his final intentions for his stories through a lifetime of reconfigurations. This summative process is a form of textual autobiogra-phy, reflecting the author's highly subjective backward glance from one or more vantage points further along the corridors of time.[1] But the author's first sub-mitted typescript—the form first circulated by Bradbury or his agent during the volume period—represents the desired form of the text for the critical edition series. In the case of volume 3 stories such as "Ylla" ("I'll Not Ask for Wine") and "Riabouchinska" ("And So Died Riabouchinska"), serial sales came years after initial circulation, and only after significant revision. In such cases, the earliest circulating form is still the ideal starting point (if it survives), for it represents Bradbury's first settled intention, closest in time to his composing hand.

To be sure, the further evolution of the author's text is crucial to under-standing a writer like Bradbury, and the volume apparatus contains a full record of his later substantive revisions. Bradbury's rich and often masterful process of refashioning his *oeuvre* made him one of the most recognizable names in modern American culture, and in many ways his legacy rests with his perennially popular collections, his novels, and the multimedia adapta-tions they have inspired. But his literary legacy also depends on recovering his creative origins and early development as an author, and *The Collected Stories of Ray Bradbury* series is designed to recover, document, and preserve the early versions as historical artifact, worthy of study by all who wish to discover the making of a master storyteller.

## Selecting and Emending the Copy-Text

The critical edition is based on a clear-text presentation of Bradbury's published stories in chronological order of composition. The selection of the copy-text for each story—the form of the text serving as the basis for the critical edition—fol-lows Sir Walter W. Greg's copy-text rationale, as modified for nineteenth- and twentieth-century literary authors by Fredson Bowers and G. Thomas Tanselle.[2]

As Greg and others have pointed out, the concept of the copy-text is a pragmatic rationale that can be applied to multiple-text situations, such as we find with the vast majority of Bradbury's stories. Greg offers two classifications of textual variants: substantives (variants in words, phrases, or larger continuous blocks of text), and accidentals (isolated variants in spelling, punctuation, case, word division, and marks of emphasis). Paragraphing, depending on the impact it has on the text, may be considered either an accidental or a substantive variant; given the large amount of editorial imposition and authorial revision found in Bradbury's texts, variations in paragraphing are regarded as substantives. Variants in number (singular or plural forms), verb tense, and the use of the possessive apostrophe all change meaning and are also regarded as substantives.

The copy-text is the most authoritative source for accidentals. In reading stages of presswork, authors pay varying degrees of attention to proofing spelling, punctuation, and capitalization, or such meaningful font characteristics as italics. Bradbury almost always read galleys and page proofs for his books but rarely (if ever) had the chance to read copy for his magazine appearances. In the absence of marked-up presswork, the cryptic nature of accidentals makes it even more difficult to distinguish changes made by intermediaries (primarily compositors or editors). For periodicals, and especially for the genre periodicals that published most of Bradbury's early stories, the short turnaround time from typesetting to market release kept even editorial proofing to a minimum. Unless there is external (or strong internal) evidence to the contrary, the copy-text should be the version closest to the author's unmediated hand—ideally, the author's submitted manuscript or typescript that was used as setting copy. When none of the authorial or presswork stages have been located (and this is usually the case with Bradbury's initial magazine appearances), the first magazine (serial) printing stands as the copy-text, for it is closer to Bradbury's initial intention than any subsequent form.

The copy-text, therefore, provides the basis for the punctuation, spelling, and words of the literary work. All accidental variants found in later forms of the text must be assumed to be editorial corruptions or stylings unless there is supportable evidence that they represent the work of Bradbury's revising hand. Accidentals found in magazine reprints or in Bradbury's subsequent story collections will be rejected, except on the occasions where the variant corrects an obvious error in spelling, punctuation, or capitalization. Where such errors were never corrected in subsequent publications, or where no subsequent publications exist, the present editors emend the readings and record the emendations in the backmatter emendation lists, using the siglum (symbol) of the critical edition, CE. Such emendations correct only unacceptable errors; Bradbury's discernible preferences in spelling, as well as his habit of creating strings of hyphenated word compounds, are not emended. Unfortunately, most copy-texts will be first magazine printings, which may already have undergone some degree of house styling. On occasion, Bradbury's preferences can be documented in pre- or post-copy-text typescript fragments or from his large body of surviving unpublished story manuscripts of the volume period. In the rare situations where a strong Bradbury spelling or punctuation preference appears to be styled away in the copy-text, Bradbury's preference is restored by emendation. All emendations are recorded in the emendations list included in the apparatus for each story. Discussions of difficult passages, whether emended or retained, appear in the textual notes found within each apparatus section.

In many critical editions, presenting the author's final intention is the goal, and so revisions and corrections in later (magazine and book) stages of publication that can be reliably determined to be authorial would be emended into the copy-text. However, the goal of the present critical edition is to establish a text that best reflects the author's intention for *initial* publication; in this way, each story in the chronological presentation of *The Collected Stories of Ray Bradbury* stands as an exemplar of Bradbury's development as a published author at that particular moment in time. Bradbury's typescript errors transmitted into the first published form, as well as the almost inevitable compositorial typesetting corruptions, are not generally distinguishable in the absence of the submitted typescript, but all discernible errors of this kind are corrected by emendation, since such emendations reflect Bradbury's obvious intention. But his subsequent stages of revision found in his story collections and novelizations represent entirely different intentions that will not be emended into the copy-texts of the critical edition.

Although the final stages of revision are manifest in the Bradbury collections, retrospectives, and novels that remain in print today, many of the intermediate stages (such as those in *Dark Carnival,* his first story collection) are not readily available, and the earliest magazine reprintings of the texts are rarely available outside of academic libraries and specialized research archives. Most of these progressive stages of publication, which often include revisions and corrections, had never been fully studied until the *Collected Stories* editors began to prepare the historical collations for the critical edition. Although the texts of the present edition consistently reflect the first-publication versions, the textual apparatus for each story includes a historical record of the substantive variants as they were introduced down through successive forms of the text. In this way, students of Bradbury's evolving creativity can read the original forms and use the apparatus to see the substantive post-copy-text revisions.

The long textual histories of "Ylla" and "Riabouchinska" test the limits of word-for-word comparison, but the record is nevertheless recoverable in useful ways through the volume's Historical Collation lists. "The Black Ferris," however, completely rewritten and extended to form part of three chapters in his 1962 novel *Something Wicked This Way Comes,* is a distinctly separate work from the original story presented here. The novel text, which represents completely different intentions, is so divergent that it cannot be represented in the historical collation of "The Black Ferris." That novel is, however, widely available in print today, and the embedded episode (centering on a mysterious carousel rather than a Ferris wheel) can be compared in more general ways to the seldom-seen original magazine version and its subsequent stand-alone reprint history as recorded in *The Collected Stories of Ray Bradbury.*

## Establishing the Date Chronology of the Stories

The publication history of Bradbury's stories (through 2003) can be found in the year-by-year listing in Appendix A of Eller and Touponce, *Ray Bradbury: The Life of Fiction* (2004) 439–503; anthology publications are included, although only the first textbook appearance of each story is noted. A broader history of Bradbury's stories is documented in "Ray Bradbury: Adaptations in Other Media," an indexed listing in *The New Ray Bradbury Review* 1 (2008): 178–220. These are the most accessible comprehensive sources; they radiate out from the unpublished *October's Friend,* a bibliographical finding list for the Albright Collection prepared by Jim Welsh and Professor Donn Albright of the Pratt Institute. For more than four decades, Albright has been Bradbury's principal bibliographer and the foremost collector of all publications and materials associated with Bradbury's life and career.

Accurate records of this sort provide a useful starting point through the bewildering maze of Bradbury's publishing world, but even with these tools the completion dates and compositional sequence of Bradbury's short stories remain in almost total darkness. Surviving typescripts of some of the published stories, preserved in a few institutional and private collections, offer a fragmentary glimpse of the stages leading up to first publication and, very rarely, of the stages leading up to serial reprintings or to appearances in Bradbury collections. Some, but not many, include notational dates of composition and revision. But the broad underlayment of Bradbury's compositional history survives in the large body of unpublished short fiction preserved in the Albright Collection along with thousands of pages of unpublished fragments. More than 230 of the unpublished stories are identified in appendix B of *Ray Bradbury: The Life of Fiction,* but further discoveries and the subsequent publication of more than two dozen of these stories in recent Bradbury trade and limited collections has outdated this reference to some degree. The unpublished stories themselves (or their folders) occasionally contain dates of composition, but not consistently enough to recover the missing sequence of composition. Bradbury's focused ability to write a story a week or more during the first decade of his professional career resulted in an incredible record of productivity, but the creative continuity of his early career cannot be recovered from the stories alone.

However, a half-dozen closely related composition and publishing records do survive in the Albright Collection, and together with known correspondence related to Bradbury's stories—from his agents, editors, publishers, and the few fellow writers who from time to time served as mentors or confidants—they can be used to recover the true progression of his creativity. The earliest of these is a typed single-leaf list of stories drafted or in progress during the summer after Bradbury graduated from high school. The thirty-two story titles are undated, but most are identifiable; the few that were already published in amateur fanzine publications are so indicated; others subsequently published in fanzines are not annotated as published, suggesting he typed the list in July or August 1938. This list, fully described in volume 1's "Textual Commentary," provides dating information for many of the amateur pieces included in that volume.

In early 1942 Bradbury began keeping a composition and submission log of sorts. It does not include his first three professional sales, which were made between July and December 1941. The seven extant pages are complete but are heavily damaged and yellowed; nevertheless, they contain a fairly readable series of typed entries for stories composed from January 1942 through July 1945. The final two pages contain an overlapping log of "Special Submissions" running from March through August 1945, documenting the stories he was beginning to submit—on his own and in rapid-fire fashion—to the major market magazines. From 1944 on, his typed running header indicates that the log included submission dates rather than completion dates, but this distinction has little effect on the recovery of the chronology. During his early professional years, he would usually rush through an initial draft in the first blaze of creative insight, never stopping to let his rational mind take control until he was finished. He would revise over the next few days, and unless a story became problematic he would mail it cross-country to Julius Schwartz, his first agent, in New York within five to seven days of the first draft. In other words, the completion date and the submission date were often one and the same, a characteristic that gives the composition and submission log a high degree of consistency as a chronological source. Generally speaking, submission-to-market time was also only a matter of a few days; the coast-to-coast deliveries of Bradbury's stories usually took no more than two days, and Schwartz was only blocks away from the editors he had worked with for years.

Bradbury kept a parallel record of sales that is slightly older. This document begins with the three stories he sold in 1941 and continues on through ten leaves (rectos only) to document his sales through 1949. Once again, the highly acidic leaves are yellowed and moderately damaged, but the typed record is more or less continuous and inclusive. Dating becomes intermittent on the 1948 and 1949

pages, but by this time his incoming editorial correspondence and surviving letters from Don Congdon, who became his representative in all markets during
September 1947, provide most of the missing dates. These two key documents—
Bradbury's composition and submission log and his sales record—are closely
related, and together they stand as the primary documents used in establishing
the composition sequence for all the published stories as well as many of the
unpublished stories that Bradbury wrote during World War II.

In January 1943 Bradbury began to keep a sales-by-publisher index. His first
index is only a single typed page, with additional sales carried only through
March 1943. His first eleven sales entries are undated, but the document itself
can be dated by cross-referencing its contents with the dates of sales within the
cumulative sales log. At some point—the final entries, the paper, and the typeface all suggest circa 1950—Bradbury prepared an expanded sales-by-publisher
index with separate sequences for each of the publishing syndicates where he
had sold stories: Popular; Fiction House; Story Inc. (publishers of *Weird Tales*);
Fictioneers Inc. (Popular's subsidiary syndicate); Ziff-Davis; and Street & Smith.
His first nine sales to major market and academic periodicals, completed on his
own before engaging Congdon to represent him, conclude the last page of pulp
syndicate entries. It is followed by a single-page index of his first eleven major
market and academic sales through March 1948. Each entry includes publication
dates and what appears to be a rough recall of the sale payment. There is also a
column for rights on every page; the first page notes that all rights were sold
with the stories appearing in Standard Magazine's titles (*Thrilling Wonder Stories*
and *Startling Stories*) but question mark placeholders in all the other syndicates'
rights columns indicate that Bradbury had questions about these matters. Bradbury would not like the answers, however; by 1950, he and Don Congdon began
to realize that Schwartz had initially sold all rights to the pulp magazine stories,
which made it difficult to reprint some of the stories in major market magazines
(or even to adapt them for other media). In many cases, the subsequent rights
buyout ended up being far greater than the penny-a-word rates (or less) that the
syndicates had originally paid for the stories.

The payment listings in the extended sales-by-publisher index appear to
come from Bradbury's typed and holograph annotations in the 1941–49 sales
log. In both documents, the payment amounts may have been recorded from
memory. The best source of sales payments appears to be his listing of sales
negotiated by Schwartz. It contains all seventy stories that Schwartz sold for
Bradbury, concluding with the January 1948 *Weird Tales* payment for "The
Black Ferris." The Schwartz listing was prepared around 1950 by William F.
Nolan, who became Bradbury's first bibliographer around that time, roughly
two years before setting out on his own professional writing career. The three-
page typescript bears an opening page title and data headings in Nolan's hand.

It contains a few typographical errors, but the payments listed agree with the amounts quoted in Schwartz's postcards and letters to Bradbury at the time of sale. The pre-commission payments given in the critical edition are based on this source; payment variations in Bradbury's other record documents are always minor and are given in each story's apparatus head note essay.

The last (but only recently unearthed) chronology survives within a metal notecard file box discovered in 2010, shortly after volume 1 went to press. The box contains individual notecards dating back to Bradbury's first story sales in 1941; cards for 1941 and early 1942 are place holders, suggesting that the file was actually started later in 1942. Most cards provide a date of submission for circulation, and subsequent dates for rejections and re-submissions. This file is the most comprehensive record of Bradbury's short fiction, and continues through the mid-1970s.

## Producing the Critical Edition

Establishing the genealogy for Bradbury's early stories begins with careful study of the seven composition and sales documents already described, and continues on through the study of the published and unpublished bibliographical sources to verify the initial publication dates and venues for each story. The known correspondence between Bradbury and his agents, editors, publishers, and other writers of the period further confirms and extends the data in Bradbury's surviving composition and sales records. At this point, the chronology of story composition can be established, and the volume contents can be identified and sequenced. Attention now turns to finding all relevant forms of the text that may survive. Existing typescript stages and prepublication presswork are located and photocopies are secured. All published forms of each story are identified and copies of relevant forms—those over which Bradbury may have exercised authorial control—are acquired in original or photocopy form. Although Bradbury generally allowed his agents to handle all aspects involving serial reprints, these forms are also gathered for collation along with all editions of the relevant Bradbury story collections.

Bradbury had no control over anthology and textbook appearances beyond the point of sale and generally took little interest in them as textual artifacts. He expected all editors to publish his stories accurately and in their entirety; in a few cases he disputed unauthorized editorial variations or abridgments. Such cases are rare and none affect texts in this volume. But the significant variant histories found in magazine reprints and in Bradbury's revisions for his story collections sometimes resurface in anthologies and textbooks; the anthologized forms are not included in the word-for-word collation schedule, but they are listed in the story's head note.

Once the copy-text representing Bradbury's earliest surviving intention is identified for each story, the process of producing a copy-text transcription begins. For magazine copy-texts, editorial teasers—one or two-sentence paraphrases from the story text inserted below or above the title line to catch the attention of bookstore or newsstand browsers—are not transcribed, but they are described in the selection's textual notes. For all stories, the transcriber initially works from a photocopy of the copy-text, keyboarding a full literal transcription file; the transcriber then conducts an initial proofreading and correction in isolation prior to producing a printout and entering the transcription into the perfection process. A team of two editors takes the initial transcription printout through a vocal proofreading, marking any errors in the literal transcription for correction. The file is corrected electronically and reprinted before being team-checked to ensure that the corrections were entered properly without corrupting other points of the transcription. If any errors remain, the printout is corrected, reprinted, and checked until it is ready to stand as the corrected transcription.

The editors then read the corrected transcription against the actual copy-text, using the original publications or typescripts located in the Center for Ray Bradbury Studies or the Albright Collection. Any errors caused by photocopy limitations are noted and marked on the corrected transcription. At this point the copy-text transcription is considered "perfected"; this term does not indicate conventional correctness but rather that a transcription has been rendered—as far as humanly possible—to reflect the exact reading of the copy-text source, including any errors that the original itself contains. The perfected transcription is now ready for the editing phase, and at this point, collations of the later forms of the text come into play.

In fact, variations in the post-copy-text forms can play a role in determining whether a reading should be emended in the process of fully restoring the author's initial intention for the text. This is crucial in the case of Bradbury's early published stories, where very few of his submitted typescripts are known to survive and where pulp magazine compositors and editors—working with small budgets and tight deadlines—sometimes introduced a significant number of errors. Serial reprintings (especially in the reset Canadian issues of *Weird Tales* and *Super Science Stories*) inevitably add a new layer of compositorial corruption, but they also often correct typographical errors found in the originals and become a source (but not an authority) for emendation decisions. In some instances, collation will reveal that the second serial forms were set from Bradbury's submitted typescript or perhaps the unedited first serial galleys, neither of which survive today; this usually happened in the Canadian reprints, which sometimes contain text silently omitted from initial American serialization due to space limitations. Bradbury's own revisions for his subsequent collections also include corrections to readings where the error might not be apparent to editors working solely with the first published form of the text. In this respect, post-copy-text variants are extremely useful in turning the preliminary list of emendations into the final volume apparatus form.

The collation process is equally important in building the historical record of post-copy-text substantive variations included in the apparatus for many of the volume's story selections. In each case, sight collations are performed and recorded for forms of the text in the vertical line of descent (that is, for each distinct typesetting down through time). The collation process for each story involves reading the standard of collation (the earliest surviving form) against the successive serial or book typesettings.[3] Since Bradbury developed working relationships with his British publishers and was sometimes involved with transatlantic proofreading, the sight-collation process includes the reset British editions (or distinct British collections) that contain versions of the stories in this volume. A different member of the editorial staff checks each sight collation to ensure accuracy.

One characteristic of the author's creativity led to a modification of the sight-collation methodology: the deep revisions that Bradbury made in collecting stories for *Dark Carnival* made it necessary to perform two sequences of collation for these selections. The first serial publication served as the standard of collation against *Dark Carnival* and any serial reprintings that descend directly from the first serialization. The *Dark Carnival* text then became the standard of collation against editions of *The October Country,* subsequent Bradbury collections, and serial reprintings that descend from the heavy layer of revisions found in *Dark Carnival.* Further substantial Bradbury revisions in *The October Country* require yet a third sequence of collation for its many editions as well as subsequent Bradbury collections that descend directly from *The October Country*'s texts. Similar but less complicated situations also exist for stories, such as "Invisible Boy," that Bradbury heavily revised for inclusion in *The Golden Apples of the Sun.* The first edition of that collection serves as the standard for collation against its many reprintings, reissues, and subsequent reset editions.

Machine collation allows a comparison of successive printings within a single typesetting of Bradbury's story collections. In this way the "horizontal" progression across the various reimpressions and reissues of a single typesetting can be expeditiously examined to determine if there are any hidden states of variation, for each successive impression may contain authorial or editorial corrections as well as line shifts across pages or even unintentional line drops and transpositions. For these reasons, the first and last impressions of each successive Ballantine edition of *The October Country* have been machine collated on a Lindstrand Comparator to determine if any impressions introduce variant states of the texts in question. The same process was repeated for other Bradbury collections with multiple impressions; since "Ylla" became the first story-chapter of *The Martian Chronicles*, successive impressions within the various *Chronicles* editions were also machine collated. Any accidental or substantive variants discovered as a result of the machine collation were then combined with the sight collation record to form the full historical collation of variants for every story included in the present volume. This collation is created and maintained by the Center for Ray Bradbury Studies in Indiana University's School of Liberal Arts (IUPUI). The substantive variants are extracted from the full historical collation to create the listing of post-copy-text substantives found in the apparatus for each story in the present volume.

With a full post-copy-text history of variants now in hand, the textual editor marks up the perfected copy-text transcription of each story for emendation according to the conservative guidelines summarized in earlier sections of the "Textual Commentary." The emendations are then entered into the electronic file along with the correction of any final "perfection" errors discovered and marked while proofing the corrected transcription against the copy-text originals at archive. An "edited" copy of the transcription is printed out and members of the editorial team check this printout against the markup. Further corrections and printouts are checked as necessary for each story until all the volume selections are fully corrected as edited. At this point, the transcription files are consolidated with the front- and backmatter files and the preliminary formatting tags are checked for consistency by the production and transcription team before submission of the book file to The Kent State University Press for layout. Since the volume represents a critically-established text with apparatus, the staff editors receive proofs back from the press in order to check for textual stability and to key actual page-and-line numbers into the apparatus lists, the textual notes, and the content annotations. During this phase the editorial team performs a final word-for-word proofreading of the Bradbury texts against the marked-up editing copy to ensure that the words and punctuation remain as established for the critical edition. The Press then lays out the keyed backmatter, and the editorial staff checks backmatter proofs. After a final check of post-layout corrections against blues, the volume is ready for publication.

## The Contents and Structure of the Critical Edition

Volume 3 of *The Collected Stories of Ray Bradbury* includes twenty-two selections (twenty-one stories and a co-authored novella) that eventually sold and reached publication. All were written between March 1944 and March 1945. In some cases, publication came years or even decades later, but the volume sequence is based on the order of composition.

The Bradbury stories lead into Appendix A—the "Chronological Catalog" of the period covered by this volume. The left-hand column offers a listing of

Bradbury's published fiction in the order of publication, presenting his stories in the sequence by which they were encountered by the reading public. The right-hand column reveals the hidden chronology of this period—all known Bradbury stories, published and unpublished, arranged in chronological order of composition. This listing reflects the chronological underpinnings of the entire critical edition series and documents all that is known about the circulation history of the unpublished stories. For ease of reference to adjacent volumes in the series, the chronology extends before and after the volume period to provide full coverage for the years 1944 and 1945. Subsequent volumes in the series will continue this overlapping time line of creativity through the 1940s.

Appendix B reveals another historical dimension of Bradbury's development—a detailed sequence of content summaries for the unpublished pieces that have been recovered and survive today in the Albright Collection. Volume 1 provided summaries of unpublished stories written through 1943; volume 2 covered the unpublished stories of 1944; and volume 3 includes summaries for the unpublished stories of 1945.

"Annotations," a detailed series of content references for all the published story texts, follows the appendices. These annotations gloss possible biographical allusions to persons, places, and possible references to books and films that he had read or seen by that time in his life. The annotations also recover cultural allusions that have slipped from common knowledge, and show how specific descriptions or situations may echo earlier tales or serve as possible forerunners to later works in the Bradbury canon.

"Editorial Symbols and Abbreviations" prefaces the textual apparatus of the volume. Editorial decisions concerning the texts, discussions of editorial cruxes, and relevant historical information appear in twenty-two self-contained apparatus sections, one for each of the volume's story selections. Each apparatus section begins with a narrative headnote that pinpoints (as closely as possible) the story's date of composition, its circulation and sales history, the record of subsequent revision and publication, and the editorial rationale for the copy-text selection. Abbreviations (or sigla) for each form of the text will be identified here. The headnote commentary also tells "the story of the story," presenting the people and circumstances that influenced composition and circulation. This comprehensive head-note essay concludes with a list of all sources used to uncover the history of the text and other references that may help the reader situate the historical or literary context of the story. Textual notes, describing specific problematic points within the copy-text and any editorial decisions made to retain or emend a problem reading, follow the essay.

A list of "Emendations" follows the textual notes; it records all editorial changes, both accidentals and substantives, made by the present editors in establishing the text of the critical edition. Emendations made for the first time in the critical edition are identified by the siglum CE. Each entry in the list begins with the emended reading to the left of a terminal bracket; a siglum indicating the source of the emended reading appears to the right of the bracket, followed by a semicolon and the original copy-text reading, followed by its siglum. Additional variant readings found in intervening texts published after the copy-text but before the source of the accepted reading appear (followed by their respective sigla) to the right of the original copy-text reading. Any intervening forms not listed may be assumed to agree with the copy-text reading. Character spacing, font size, and drop-capital letters or all-capital words representing story or section openings, are purely visual aspects of the text and are silently regularized without emendation.

For selections where collation reveals substantive variations in subsequent forms of the text, a listing of post-copy-text substantives follows the emendations list. This is the most significant portion of the full historical collation, and it provides valuable insights into the way Bradbury revised certain stories to fulfill subsequent authorial intentions for his work. It also allows us to detect where later typesetters and editors contributed to the transmission of error through subsequent published versions of Bradbury's stories. Each entry in this historical record begins with the copy-text reading to the left of a terminal bracket followed by its siglum and a semicolon. To the right of the semicolon the successive record of substantive variation appears in chronological order, separated by the respective sigla followed by semicolons. Sometimes Bradbury, over time, embedded successive layers of substantive revision within a single passage; in such cases, the embedded revisions begin with a black diamond symbol and terminate with the bracketed siglum of the embedded revision's source.

Occasionally, words that may be true hyphenated compounds are broken across lines in the copy-text. Such words are listed at the end of a story's apparatus, to the left of a terminal bracket, followed by the resolution of the reading (either as a true hyphenated compound or as a single word). Some compound words will inevitably end up being hyphenated across lines in the present critical edition; a single list at the end of the volume records all such compounds that, if quoted or transcribed from the present text, should retain their hyphens. Any other possible compounds laid out as end-line hyphenations in the present edition should be transcribed as single words.

Bradbury's texts, consistently edited to present his earliest intentions for his fiction as standalone stories, are thus supported by a full apparatus describing the historical transmission of each published story text, identifying the source and extent of every editorial emendation to the copy-text, and presenting (in list form) the subsequent history of substantive variation. The new text, as annotated, documented, and represented in this way, constitutes a critical edition of Bradbury's earliest published fiction.

## Overview of the Volume Period: 1944 and 1945

Between March 1944 and March 1945, Bradbury's creative arc ran roughly parallel to the very public way that he continued to publish regularly in the horror
and detective pulps and slightly less so in the science fiction and fantasy magazines. Nineteen of his stories reached the pages of the genre pulps in 1944, and
thirteen more were published the following year. The wartime constriction of
the pulp market more or less explains his 1945 drop-off, but this was compen-
sated for later in the year when he began to reach the mainstream magazines.
His major market breakthrough was still only a dream at the moment; by the
spring of 1945 the previous twelve months had secured twenty-four sales, all
through his pulp agent Julius Schwartz in New York.

Hidden away behind this record of sales and publication, Bradbury actually completed thirty-seven stories from one spring to the next, and sent most
of them east to Schwartz. Only fourteen of these would sell to the pulps on
Schwartz's watch, but before the end of 1945 Bradbury, acting on his own, would
sell two others—"The Miracles of Jamie" and "Invisible Boy"—to major market
magazines. "Ylla" would eventually follow into the mainstream and on into *The
Martian Chronicles*. He had the satisfaction of giving "Skeleton," a humorous
echo of his *Weird Tales* story of the same name—to *Script*, a Hollywood magazine where he had placed his first professional short-short tale. But four of the
thirty-seven would be deferred for many years, and fifteen would never sell at all.

To be sure, these figures are part of a broader continuum of constant ex-
perimentation with style and subject, punctuated by a fair share of success as
Schwartz continued to sell his off-trail stories to *Weird Tales* and to four of the
detective magazines managed by Popular Publications. The little science fiction he produced during this year was highlighted by writing the second half
of the novella "Lorelei of the Red Mist" for friend and mentor Leigh Brackett,
an indicator that he was at last ready to come out from under her influence in
this field. He was still self-indulgent at times, and thin on plot development.
He also refused to bend to genre norms in his range of subjects, preferring to
probe the remembered hopes, fears, loves, and hates of his own childhood for
his tales. He focused his frustrations on editorial pressure to slant his work for
a particular market, but his eventual success and transcendance of this market
was more a result of his revising hand and his growing maturity as a storyteller
than a victory over editors and publishers.

Most of the evidence for this development is veiled by the mists of time, but
much of that year of creativity can be glimpsed today by recovering the earliest versions of these stories that still survive and reading them in the order of
composition. Seventeen of the twenty-two stories that eventually reached print
from this period can be recovered from the pages of the magazines where they

first appeared. Only one of these magazines—*Mademoiselle,* publisher of "Invisible Boy"—still surives today, or indeed survived the great die-off of magazines in the middle of the twentieth century. These elusive magazine versions, free of the revisions, stylings, and typesetting errors introduced as Bradbury collected many of them for his story collections and novels, form the basis for seventeen of the story texts in volume 3.

For one of these seventeen, we can take a tantalizing step further back in time toward Bradbury's unmediated hand. A dated typescript page survives for the opening of "I'm Not So Dumb!" It is a carbon or a very late discard from the finished version that he submitted to Schwartz for circulation, apparently retained as evidence of authorship (in fact, Bradbury retained a number of such dated pages for stories outside of this period). This page was typed by the author, and serves as copy-text for the first few hundred words of the tale.

Five stories have been recovered from far deeper origins. These all took years to reach print, and that may be why complete typescript versions have survived. Two early forms of his nostalgic wartime story "If Paths Must Cross Again" show composition dates of April and December 1944. More than half a century later, Bradbury placed his expanded December 1944 rewrite in his 2009 story collection, *We'll Always Have Paris.* But the initial shorter version of April 1944 is also complete, and contains an interesting experiment with indirect dialog and an unexpected concluding revelation that he eliminated from the later version. The April 1944 text, recovering Bradbury's intention at the time he first submitted the story for circulation, stands as copy-text in the present edition, allowing us to establish the critical text directly from Bradbury's unstyled spellings and punctuation.

"The Reincarnate" typescript is unrevised, but five decades later Bradbury revised a photocopy for publication in the genre anthology *Dark Delicacies* (2004). The unrevised original, reflecting Bradbury's intentions during initial circulation in the mid-1940s, serves as copy-text for the present edition. Both "If Paths Must Cross Again" and "The Reincarnate" have Julius Schwartz's circulating cover sheets, and were returned to Bradbury with a number of other unsold typescripts in 1947; all of these originals were lost sometime in the late 1970s, but not before a photocopy record was preserved in the Albright Collection.

"Chrysalis" was one of a number of stories and narrative sketches critical of the racism that Bradbury observed in 1940s America. He cirulated it in the mainstream markets until it became apparent that no one was willing to publish such a story. The publication of this story in Bradbury's 2004 collection *The Cat's Pajamas* was based on a revised version from the 1940s. But a carbon survives that contains opening pages from an even earlier version that stands as close as we can come to the orginal complete draft of 1944. This bridged typescript stands as copy-text for the present edition.

Bradbury's early version of "Ylla," destined to lead millions of readers into *The Martian Chronicles* since 1950, has a surviving typescript history that greatly predates the story's first publication (as "I'll Not Ask for Wine") in the popular Canadian weekly *Macleans*. In May 2015 a fragment dating back to 1947 or earlier was reunited with pages in the Albright Collection to form the earliest known complete typescript of a *Martian Chronicles* tale. This discovery, made in the preparation of the present edition, reveals the very early glimmerings of the Martian culture that Bradbury would refine significantly for the *Macleans* and *The Martian Chronicles* versions, both of which descended in parallel lines from this long-lost source. The present edition text is based on this recovered typescript.

"Riabouchinska" is almost as well-known as "Ylla," but it descends through an even more complicated line of typescripts. Bradbury's story of a ventriloquist's beautiful mannikin that seems to be the only witness to a murder circulated for eight years before Bradbury finally placed it in the digest-size *Saint Detective Magazine* in 1953. The trail includes four drafts of an original version that never reached print at all. The first complete draft, which may stand very close to the January 1945 initial composition, provides the copy-text for this long-deferred version of the tale.

But most of the stories in volume 3 have no surviving pre-publication materials, and we must rely on the initial periodical publications for the respective copy-texts. Five selections were first published in *Weird Tales*, the oldest of the traditional horror magazines. In order of composition, these include "The Poems," "The Tombstone," "The Watchers," "Skeleton," and "The Black Ferris." Tantalizing fragment sketches for "The Black Ferris" survive in the 1945–46 notebook that forms the earliest step toward the now-classic 1962 Bradbury novel, *Something Wicked This Way Comes*. Those fascinating but very fragmentary intimations, along with evidence of composition indicated in a March 1945 letter to Arkham House publisher August Derleth, provide the dating rationale, but we must rely on the May 1948 publication in *Weird Tales*. Fortunately, very little styling was imposed on the *Weird Tales* texts, and Bradbury's own spelling preferences (as well as his inconsistencies) are often discernible, making the few points (beyond typesetting errors) where emendation is necessary easy to negotiate.

The chilling horrors of "Skeleton" were revised and showcased in *Dark Carnival*, Bradbury's first story collection, along with "The Tombstone." The post-copy-text revisions that Bradbury made in all of his *Dark Carnival* stories represent a later intention, and are relegated to the lists of variants included in the apparatus. Bradbury eventually revised "The Skeleton" yet again for *The October Country* (1955), his final refashioning of his best early weird stories. This further layer of heavy revision offers a fascinating journey through Bradbury's maturing process of creativity, and is recorded in the Historical Collation for "Skeleton."

The seven crime stories included in the present volume were successfully circulated among the editors of the various detective magazines sold by Popular Publications. They were not typical of the crime genre; Popular's editors, especially general editor Alden Norton, rejected a few Bradbury submissions for weak plots and downright disregard of the mystery story formula, but they all admired his originality and off-trail surprises. The seven Bradbury purchases appeared in *Detective Tales, New Detective,* and *Dime Mystery.* Only "I'm Not So Dumb" retained its submitted title in print (with an editorially imposed exclamation mark); the editorially imposed titles of the others have been relegated (by emendation) to subtitles in the present edition, and Bradbury's intended titles restored.

Eight stories circulated among various detective magazines (including *Ellery Queen*), but were never sold; they are described in Appendix B of this volume. In order of composition, the seven crime tales published from this period are "The Long Way Around" ("The Long Way Home"), "The Very Bewildered Corpses" ("Four-Way Funeral"), "Mr. Priory Meets Mr. Caldwell" ("Hell's Half-Hour"), "I'm Not So Dumb(!)," "One Minus One" ("Corpse Carnival"), and "The Sea Cure" ("Dead Men Rise Up Never"). Three had just enough of a horror angle that they appeared in Popular's more gruesome *Dime Mystery,* and these were reprinted directly (from uncut galleys or Bradbury's typescript) in the Canadian magazine *Strange Detective Tales:* "The Long Way Around," "One Minus One," and "The Sea Cure." In all three cases, the *Strange Detective Tales* reprints restored cuts made by Popular's editors in the originals. The Canadian issues eliminated the illustrations and had fewer advertisements, allowing more space for Bradbury's stories. The missing lines and short paragraphs recovered from the Canadian versions are restored by emendation, thereby presenting the complete stories for the first time in an American publication.

Pressure from Schwartz and from Popular's detective magazine editors reduced Bradbury's production of science fiction for a time. Both of Bradbury's successful science fiction compositions from this period eventually fell to the reliable but second-tier genre magazine *Planet Stories.* Under the editorship of Malcolm Reiss and subeditor Wilbur Peacock, the magazine had previously published several Bradbury stories that showed the influence of his friend and mentor, *Planet Stories* mainstay Leigh Brackett. His July 1944 submission, "Defense Mech," was more of a whimsical experiment in illusion and reality that playfully parodies Brackett's against-the-odds heroes; after *Planet's* wartime backlog cleared, "Defense Mech" reached print in the spring 1946 issue. Bradbury's best *Planet Stories* effort to date appeared in the next quarterly issue—his collaboration with Leigh Brackett included the entire second half of a 10,000-word novella, "Lorelei of the Red Mist." This milestone, along with

Bradbury's long-delayed Martian tale "The Million Year Picnic" (volume 2, selection 11) dominated the cover and contents of the summer 1946 issue.

Most of the volume 3 stories were reprinted, with varying degrees of accuracy, in a wide range of other magazines; substantive variants, resulting from editorial impositions, abridgement, or typesetting error, are relegated to the Historical Collation lists for each story. These lists provide more than a record of editorial misadventure, however; they also reveal the fascinating way that Bradbury revised many of these stories over time to fashion more mature presentations of his early work in a wide range of story collections, novelized story cycles, and even novels. The stories themselves, restored to seldom-seen original versions, offer a new way of seeing a remarkably creative young writer negotiate his way through the complex worlds of pulp fiction on the eve of his first ventures into the literary mainstream.

Jonathan R. Eller

Center for Ray Bradbury Studies

Indiana University School of Liberal Arts

## Notes

1. In establishing the texts for *The Collected Poems of Robert Penn Warren* (1998), Professor John Burt of Brandeis University was faced with a similar challenge. Although he concentrated on recovering the forms of the poems as first gathered into a Warren collection, his copy-text decisions invariably represented an early settled intention for each poem. Burt suggested that such a process of recovering the author's intentions at earlier career stages is analogous to recovering "an author's diary, representing the author's intellectual life as it unfolded, with no certainty, but with many provisional intuitions, about how each event will fit into the big picture."

2. Sir Walter Greg, "The Rationale of Copy-Text," *Studies in Bibliography* 3 (1950–51): 19–36, reprinted in *The Collected Papers of Sir Walter W. Greg*, ed. J. C. Maxwell (Oxford: Clarendon Press, 1966), 374–91.

3. The term "standard of collation" has no authoritative significance; it is merely a methodological distinction designed to establish a stable chronological focus for the collation process.

# Editorial Symbols and Abbreviations

## Editorial Symbols

Bradbury's stories are presented in a clear-text format. The following symbols and abbreviations appear within the apparatus sections:

### Page and line references

The page and line numbers, separated by a period, refer to the present edition. For each story, the title block is not included in the line count; however, extra lines and section break spacings are counted. Lines may occasionally contain more than one occurrence of a word; if such a word anchors an apparatus list entry, a parenthetical number follows the line number to indicate which occurrence serves as the lemma anchor. For example, "1.16 (2) amber" refers to page 1, line 16, and the second occurrence of "amber" in the line.

### *Also*

The term *Also* appears in rejected readings to identify subsequent points in the text that contain the identical variant word or phrase. Plural forms and other suffix endings of a variant word may be identified by the term *similarly.* Such editorial comments will always be presented in italic type.

### The Asterisk [*]

An asterisk preceding the page-line number of an emendation or historical collation entry indicates that the reading is discussed in a textual note.

### The Lemma Bracket []]

The lemma or anchoring text of an apparatus list entry is followed by the closing half of a roman bracket pair.

### The Pilcrow [¶]

A pilcrow, or paragraph symbol, used in the lemma or in any other part of an emendation or historical collation entry, indicates a paragraph indention.

## The Caret (^)

A caret, lowered to the base line, indicates an absence of punctuation in a rejected reading. The accepted reading anchoring an entry in the emendations list is presented in clear text.

## The Tilde (~)

A wavy dash or tilde in the rejected reading (to the right of the anchoring bracket) represents the same word in the accepted reading (emendations list) or the original copy-text reading (historical collation) to the left of the bracket. The tilde is only used for words where the rejected reading is limited to punctuation or paragraphing.

## The Solidus (|)

The vertical line or solidus is used in the rare situations where line breaks in a story title or closing (e.g., "The End") need to be represented in the apparatus lists.

## The Black Diamond (◆)

A small black diamond within a large rejected reading indicates that the words following the diamond are part of a further variation from an earlier or later version of the text. Such embedded variants are bounded on the right by a pair of square brackets enclosing the siglum or abbreviation of the embedded variant's source.

## The Clear Diamond (◊)

A small clear diamond appears at the beginning of a post-copy-text substantive (in the Historical Collation apparatus lists) when the text of the substantive reading's anchor text does not correspond to the current edition due to an editorial emendation. The diamond alerts the reader that the substantive contains the original reading, while the corresponding emendation entry contains the new, critically edited text.

## Bibliographical Abbreviations

Unless otherwise indicated in source citations, letters to and from Bradbury are in the Albright Collection, with photocopies deposited with the Center for Ray Bradbury Studies. The following abbreviations for reference texts are used in the narrative headnotes to identify sources of information used in preparing the headnotes for each story:

### Ashley, *History*

Ashley, Mike. *The History of the Science Fiction Magazine: Part 2 1936–1945.* London: New English Library, 1975.

### Ashley, *Time Machines*

Ashley, Mike. *The Time Machines.* Liverpool: Liverpool University Press, 2000.

### Carter

Carter, Paul A. *The Creation of Tomorrow: Fifty Years of Magazine Science Fiction.* New York: Columbia University Press, 1977.

### Clute and Nicholls

Clute, John, and Peter Nicholls, comp. *The Encyclopedia of Science Fiction.* New York: St. Martin's, 1993; update, 1995.

### Eller, *Becoming Ray Bradbury*

Eller, Jonathan R. *Becoming Ray Bradbury.* Champaign, IL: University of Illinois Press, 2011.

### Eller, *Ray Bradbury Unbound*

Eller, Jonathan R. *Ray Bradbury Unbound.* Champaign, IL: University of Illinois Press, 2014.

### Eller and Touponce, *Life of Fiction*

Eller, Jonathan R. and William F. Touponce. *Ray Bradbury: The Life of Fiction.* Kent, OH: The Kent State University Press, 2004.

### Greenberg and Olander

Greenberg, Martin Harry and Joseph D. Olander. *Ray Bradbury.* New York: Taplinger, 1980. Multi-author essays on Bradbury's works (individual authors cited by name).

### Johnson

Johnson, Wayne L. *Ray Bradbury.* New York: Frederick Unger, 1980.

### Mengeling

Mengeling, Marvin E. *Red Planet, Flaming Phoenix, Green Town: Some Early Bradbury Revisited.* Bloomington: 1st Books, 2002.

## Mogen

Mogen, David. *Ray Bradbury*. Boston: Twayne, 1986 (Twayne U. S. Authors series).

## Moskowitz

Moskowitz, Sam. *Seekers of Tomorrow: Masters of Science Fiction*. New York: Ballantine, 1967.

## Nolan

Nolan, William F. *The Human Equation*. Nashville: Charter House, 1971.

## Touponce, *Ray Bradbury*

Touponce, William F. *Ray Bradbury*. Mercer Island: Starmont, 1989. Starmont Reader's Guide 31.

## Tymn and Ashley

Tymn, Marshall B. and Mike Ashley, comp. *Science Fiction, Fantasy, and Weird Fiction Magazines*. Westport, CT: Greenwood Press, 1985.

## Weinberg

Weinberg, Robert. *The* Weird Tales *Story*. West Linn, OR: FAX Collector's Editions, Inc., 1977.

## Weller, *Chronicles*

Weller, Sam. *The Bradbury Chronicles*. New York: Morrow, 2005.

## Weller, *Echoes*

Weller, Sam. *Listen to the Echoes*. Brooklyn, NY: Melville House, 2010.

## Unpublished Interview Abbreviations

### Albright-Bradbury interviews (date)

Conducted March 2001 (The *Dark Carnival* interview), March 2003, March 2004, March 2006, April 2008 (*Masks* interview).

### Eller-Bradbury interviews (date)

Conducted October 1998, March 2002, October 2002, October 2004, October 2005, October 2006, October 2007, October 2008, April 2009, October 2009, March 2010, October 2010, March 2011, October 2011, March 2012.

## Sigla

The following abbreviations or sigla are used to designate the sources of readings in the head-note essays and apparatus lists of the individual story entries:

S A serial (magazine or newspaper) version of a story text; S1 indicates first serial publication, S2 indicates second serial appearance, etc.

TS A typewritten version of a story text; multiple typescript situations are indicated in genealogical order as TS1, TS2, etc.

TSπ A page or pages from preliminary drafts of a story that fall into the category of pre-copy-text materials. The designation pi (π) stands for "preliminary," much as the same symbol identifies the preliminary leaves of a book in bibliographical descriptions.

G A galley stage of presswork with no authorial revisions or corrections.

RG A galley stage of presswork overwritten with a subsequent layer of revisions by the author in holograph or typescript form.

BB *Bloch and Bradbury* (New York: Tower Publications, 1969). First edition, trade paperback. Dual-author story collection. See *FD&OF*.

BB$^{1972}$ Bloch and Bradbury (Chicago: Peacock, 1972). Mass market edition, expanded (no new Bradbury stories). See *FD&OF*.

BS *Bradbury Stories* (New York: William Morrow, 2003). Retrospective story compilation. Reissued as book club (hardbound) and as trade paperback. See *RBS*.

CP *The Cat's Pajamas* (New York: William Morrow, 2004). First edition, hardbound and trade paperback. Story collection. See *CP+4*.

CP+4 *The Cat's Pajamas Plus Four.* Expanded limited edition of *CP*.

CS1 *Classic Stories 1* (New York: Bantam, 1990). Mass-market paperback. Remixed story collection; combines *GA* and *RR* stories in original volume order but deletes seven stories to avoid overlap with each other and with *CS2*. See *GA&OS*.

CS2 *Classic Stories 2* (New York: Bantam, 1990). Mass-market paperback. Remixed story collection; combines *A Medicine for Melancholy* (New York: Doubleday, 1959) and *SS* stories in original volume order but deletes seven stories to avoid overlap with each other and with *CS1*. See *MM&OS*.

DC *Dark Carnival* (Sauk City, WI: Arkham House, 1947). First edition, hardbound. Story collection. Some stories subsequently revised or rewritten for *OC*.

$DC^{1948}$    *Dark Carnival* (London: Hamish Hamilton, 1948). Second edition, hardbound. Abridged contents.

$DC^{2001}$    *Dark Carnival* (Colorado Springs, CO: Gauntlet, 2001). Third edition, hardbound. Expanded contents.

*FD&OF*    *Fever Dream and Other Fantasies* (London: Sphere, 1970). British mass market paperback edition of *BB*.

$GA^{1953a}$    *The Golden Apples of the Sun* (Garden City, New York: Doubleday, 1953). First edition, hardbound. Story Collection. See *CS1* and *T22*.

$GA^{1953b}$    *The Golden Apples of the Sun* (London: Rupert Hart-Davis, 1953). British edition, hardbound. Reissued (London: Grafton, 1986).

$GA^{1954}$    *The Golden Apples of the Sun* (New York: Bantam, 1954). Mass-market paperback edition.

$GA^{1956}$    *The Golden Apples of the Sun* (London: Corgi, 1956). British mass-market paperback edition.

$GA^{1961}$    *The Golden Apples of the Sun* (New York: Bantam, 1961). Reset mass-market paperback. Reissued in Britain (London: Earthlight, 1999).

$GA^{1964}$    *The Golden Apples of the Sun* (London: Corgi, 1964). Reset British mass-market paperback. Reissued (London: Panther, 1977).

$GA^{1979}$    *The Golden Apples of the Sun* (New York: Bantam, 1979). Reset mass-market paperback.

*GA&OS*    *The Golden Apples of the Sun & Other Stories* (New York: Avon, 1997). A trade-paperback edition of *CS1*. Reissued by William Morrow as *GA&OS* and as *A Sound of Thunder*.

$LAM^{1976}$    *Long After Midnight* (New York: Knopf, 1976). First edition, hardbound. Story collection.

$LAM^{1976BC}$    *Long After Midnight* (New York: Knopf, 1976). Reset book club edition, hardbound.

$LAM^{1977}$    *Long After Midnight* (London: Hart-Davis, MacGibbon, 1977). British edition, hardbound. Reissued in Britain (Panther, Granada, 1978) as a mass-market paperback.

$LAM^{1978}$    *Long After Midnight* (New York: Bantam, 1978). Mass-market paperback edition. Reissued in Britain (London: Earthlight, 2000).

*MF*    *Match to Flame: The Fictional Paths to Fahrenheit 451* (Colorado Springs: Gauntlet, 2006). Hardbound limited press edition. Themed story collection.

$MC^{1950}$    *The Martian Chronicles* (Garden City, New York: Doubleday, 1950). First edition, hardbound. Novelized story cycle. Fifteen story-chapters with eleven short bridging chapters.

$MC^{1951}$    *The Martian Chronicles* (New York: Bantam, 1951). Mass-market paperback edition (two printings). Contents identical to $MC^{1950}$.

$MC^{1953}$    *The Martian Chronicles* (London: Science Fiction Book Club, 1953). Book club hardbound edition. Sixteen story-chapters with eleven short bridging chapters. Contents of $SL^{1951}$, but adds "May 2003: The Wilderness."

$MC^{1954}$    *The Martian Chronicles* (New York: Bantam: 1954). Mass-market paperback edition (94 printings). Contents identical to $MC^{1950}$.

$MC^{1963}$    *The Martian Chronicles* (New York: Time, Inc., 1963). Trade (large format) paperback (Time Reading Program special edition). Seventeen story-chapters and eleven short bridging chapters. Contents of $MC^{1950}$, but adds "November 2002: The Fire Balloons" and "May 2003: The Wilderness." The first "complete" edition.

$MC^{1974}$    *The Martian Chronicles* (Avon, CT: Heritage Press, 1974). Limited hardbound illustrated book club edition. Second issue by Easton Press (1989). Contents identical to $MC^{1950}$.

$MC^{1979}$    *The Martian Chronicles* (Bantam, 1979). Trade (large format) illustrated edition. Contents identical to $MC^{1950}$.

$MC^{1990}$a    *The Martian Chronicles* (Garden City, NY: Doubleday, 1990). Fortieth anniversary hardbound edition. Contents identical to $MC^{1950}$, but adds "November 2002: The Fire Balloons."

$MC^{1990}$b    *The Martian Chronicles* (London: Grafton [HarperCollins] 1990). Mass-market paperback edition; the so-called 8th printing of $SL^{1977}$ (as identified by "8" on the copyright page). Second issue (London: Flamingo [HarperCollins], 1995) is a trade (large format) paperback (12 printings). Contents identical to $SL^{1951}$.

$MC^{1997}$    *The Martian Chronicles* (New York: Avon, 1997). Small format hardbound (printings 1–6). Reissued by Morrow (printings 7–12). Reissued by Morrow for Book-of-the-Month Club (1 unsequenced printing). Reissued by Morrow (printings 13 and subsequent). Contents of $MC^{1950}$, but deletes "June 2003: Way in the Middle of the Air" and shifts the dates in the chapter title prefixes a quarter century further into the future.

$MC^{2006}$    *The Martian Chronicles* (New York: Bantam, 2006). Mass-market paperback, printings 95 and subsequent, cumulative from the $MC^{1954}$ print count. Contents identical to $MC^{1950}$.

$MC^{2008}$    *The Martian Chronicles* (London: Harper Voyager [HarperCollins], 2008). Trade (large format) paperback. Contents identical to $SL^{1951}$.

$MC^{2009}$    *The Martian Chronicles* (Burton, MI: Subterranean Press / Hornsea, U.K.: PS Publishing, 2009). Limited hardbound edition; subtitled "The Complete Edition." Includes additional Martian tales tangential to the actual *Chronicles*, and two of Bradbury's screenplay adaptations.

$MC^{2011}$  *The Martian Chronicles* (New York: HarperPerennial, 2011). Trade (large format) paperback reissue of $MC^{1997}$.

$MC^{2012}$  *The Martian Chronicles* (New York: Simon & Schuster, [March] 2012). Mass-market paperback. Contents identical to $MC^{1950}$.

MeM  *A Memory of Murder* (New York: Dell, 1984). Mass-market paperback. Story collection.

$MJ^{1964a}$  *The Machineries of Joy* (New York: Simon & Schuster, 1964). First edition, hardbound. Short story collection.

$MJ^{1964b}$  *The Machineries of Joy* (London: Hart-Davis, 1964).

$MJ^{1965}$  *The Machineries of Joy* (New York: Bantam, 1965). Mass-market paperback edition. Reissued in Britain (London: Earthlight, 2000).

$MJ^{1966}$  *The Machineries of Joy* (London: Corgi, 1966). British mass-market paperback edition.

MM&OS  *A Medicine for Melancholy & Other Stories* (New York: Avon, 1998). A trade-paperback edition of CS2. Reissued by William Morrow.

$OC^{1955}$  *The October Country* (New York: Ballantine, 1955). First edition, hardbound, 36 lines per page. Story collection. Reissued hardbound (London: Rupert Hart-Davis, 1956); reissued as a mass-market paperback with 40 lines per page (New York: Ballantine, 1956); original 36-line page break reissued as a trade paperback (New York: Ballantine, 1996, first three printings), and twice as a mass-market paperback (New York: Ballantine, 1996 and London: Earthlight, 1998).

$OC^{1961}$  *The October Country* (London: Ace, 1961). Second edition, mass-market paperback. Abridged contents. See *SA*.

$OC^{1963}$  *The October Country* (London: Four Square, 1963). Third edition, mass-market paperback. Reissued by New English Library. Abridged contents. See *SA*.

$OC^{1970}$  *The October Country* (New York: Knopf, 1970). Fourth edition, hardbound.

$OC^{1976}$  *The October Country* (London: Panther, 1976). Fifth edition, mass-market paperback. Reissued by Panther/Granada, 1984. Abridged contents. See *SA*.

$OC^{1984}$  *The October Country* (London: Grafton, post-1984). Sixth edition, mass-market paperback. So-called Panther "4th printing." Contains all OC selections.

$OC^{1996}$  *The October Country* (New York: Ballantine, 1996). Seventh edition, trade paperback. So-called fourth ("4") and subsequent printings of the 1996 Ballantine first edition trade paperback (see *OC*).

$OC^{1997}$    *The October Country* (Springfield, PA: Gauntlet, 1997). Eighth edition, hardbound.

$OC^{1999}$    *The October Country* (New York: Avon, 1999. Ninth edition, hardbound (small format). Reissued by William Morrow.

$RB$    *Ray Bradbury* (London: Harrap, 1975). Trade paperback (single-author textbook anthology).

$RBS1$    *Ray Bradbury Stories* v. 1 (London: HarperCollins, 2008). Trade paperback retrospective story compilation. A resetting of *SRB*.

$RBS2$    *Ray Bradbury Stories* v. 2 (London: HarperCollins, 2008). Trade paperback retrospective story compilation. A resetting of *BS*.

$RR$    *R Is for Rocket* (Garden City, New York: Doubleday, 1962). First edition, hardbound. Remixed story collection. Reissued (U.K.) by Rupert Hart-Davis, 1968.

$RR^{1965}$    *R Is for Rocket* (New York: Bantam, 1965). Second edition, mass-market paperback. Multiple issues and reprintings.

$RR^{1972}$    *R Is for Rocket* (London: Pan, 1972). Third edition, mass-market paperback.

$S$    *Skeletons* (Burton, MI: Subterranean, 2008). Two-story limited edition chapbook.

$SA^{1962}$    *The Small Assassin* (London: Ace, 1962). First edition, mass-market paperback. Contains seven *OC* stories deleted from the abridged British Ace paperback ($OC^{1961}$).

$SA^{1976}$    *The Small Assassin* (London: Grafton, 1976). Second edition, mass-market paperback.

$SL^{1951}$    *The Silver Locusts* (London: Hart-Davis, 1951). British hardbound edition of $MC^{1950}$. Fifteen story-chapters with eleven short bridging chapters. Deletes "Usher II" and adds "The Fire Balloons" to the $MC^{1951}$ contents.

$SL^{1956}$    *The Silver Locusts* (London: Corgi, 1956). British mass-market edition of $SL^{1951}$.

$SL^{1963}$    *The Silver Locusts* (London: Corgi, 1963). British mass-market paperback reissue of $MC^{1951}$ under the *SL* title.

$SL^{1969}$    *The Silver Locusts* (London: Corgi, 1969). British mass-market paperback reissue of $MC^{1951}$ under the *SL* title.

$SL^{1974}$    *The Silver Locusts* (London: Hart-Davis, MacGibbon, 1974). Hardbound reissue of $SL^{1951}$. Subsequent reissue by Collins (London: Granada, 1980) is titled *The Martian Chronicles*.

$SL^{1977}$    *The Silver Locusts* (London: Panther (Granada), 1977). Mass-market paperback edition of $SL^{1951}$. Second issue by Collins (London: Grafton, 1979) is titled *The Martian Chronicles* (*SL* subtitle appears parenthetically on title page only).

*SRB*   *The Stories of Ray Bradbury* (New York: Alfred A. Knopf, 1980). First edition, hardbound retrospective story compilation. Reissued as hardbound (U.K.) Granada, 1981.

*SRB*[1983]   *Stories of Ray Bradbury* (London: Granada, 1983). Second edition, trade paperback, in two volumes.

*SS*[1966]   *S Is for Space* (Garden City, New York: Doubleday, 1966). First edition, hardbound. Remixed story collection. Reissued (U.K.) by Rupert Hart-Davis, 1968. See *RBS1*.

*SS*[1970]   *S Is for Space* (Garden City, New York: Bantam, 1970). Second edition, mass-market paperback. Multiple issues and reprintings. See *RBS1*.

*SS*[1972]   *S Is for Space* (London: Pan, 1972). Third edition, mass-market paperback.

*T22*   *Twice 22* (Garden City, New York: Doubleday, 1966). First edition hardbound, trade and book club. Combines *GA* and *MM* in original volume order.

*VB*   *The Vintage Bradbury* (New York: Random House, 1965). Hardbound retrospective story compilation. Various issues include Vintage Library (hardbound), Vintage mass-market paperback, Vintage trade paperback.

# TEXTUAL APPARATUS
## Story Commentaries, Notes, and Variants

### 1. No Phones, Private Coffin (Yesterday I Lived!)
### (Mar. 15, 1944)

Six of the seven stories Bradbury composed during the winter of 1944–45 were detective tales. The last of these, "No Phones, Private Coffin," first surfaces as a single-line entry for a 5,200-word story in Bradbury's composition and submission log for March 15, 1944, with a subsequent parenthetical typed notation (SOLD!) entered without a date. His sales record sheets indicate that *Flynn's Detective Fiction* magazine purchased the story on April 17, 1944 for a net payment of $70.00 (the actual payment less agent's fee was $70.20); Nolan's list of sales by Julius Schwartz documents an actual sale date of April 14 and a pre-commission payment of $78.00 from *Flynn's* editors, along with the published title "Yesterday I Lived" (lacking the closing exclamation point). No entries for his detective sales to the Popular Publications crime pulps appear in Bradbury's expanded sales-by-publisher index, but his notecard file box contains an entry confirming first publication in the August 1944 issue of *Flynn's Detective Fiction* (designated S1) under the editorially imposed title "Yesterday I Lived!"

Bradbury's notecard file entry shows that he submitted the story under its published title for consideration by the producers of NBC's popular Mollé Mystery Radio Theatre on July 22, 1946; Mollé had scripted and broadcast an earlier Bradbury detective yarn, "'Killer, Come Back to Me!'" (originally "Autopsy," volume 2, selection 14), in May 1946, but "Yesterday I Lived!" was declined. Bradbury preferred to leave most of his detective tales as a legacy of his pulp fiction years, and with few exceptions he never intended to bring them into his subsequent story collections; however, Julius Schwartz had not limited Popular Publications to first serial rights, and most of his detective tales were gathered into Dell's 1984 mass-market paperback collection, *A Memory of Murder* (designated *MeM*). Bradbury was able to salvage some degree of control by lightly revising these stories and preparing a volume introduction that placed them in the proper historical context. The publication of *MeM* also allowed him to regain copyright control, and no subsequent impressions or editions of the collection ever reached print.

Given Bradbury's reluctance to include any of his detective tales in his story collections, it's not surprising that most of them never appeared in multiple-author genre anthologies. "No Phones, Private Coffin" is an exception, however; it was anthologized once (under its published title, "Yesterday I Lived!") in *Great Detectives*, edited by David Willis McCullough (New York: Pantheon, 1984). The traditionally selective Pantheon Books publishing imprint was under pressure from parent Random House to turn a profit, and this collection of English and American "mysteries" coincided with the publication of *MeM* by Dell, another Random House company. Collation of variants in the *Great Detectives* anthology text reveals that it was in fact typeset directly from *MeM*; there's no textual or secondary source evidence that Bradbury was involved at all with the anthology publication.

The March 1944 composition of "No Phones, Private Coffin" was followed by a month of mainstream shorts and sketches aimed at the slicks and handled, on a trial basis, by New York agent Ed Bodin. None of these new pieces sold and his experiment with Bodin's agency soon ended, but while these experiments played out "No Phones" quickly won Bradbury a new level of success in the detective pulps through his long-term author-agent relationship with Julius Schwartz. This came even as Bradbury was working through a minor affectation he had tried in opening some of his recent stories; in a March 11 letter, Schwartz had cautioned him against being so clever with his story openings: "it becomes much too vague and I hardly know what the hell you're talking about. Take it easy, kid. Don't be ashamed to be more simple and direct in telling your yarns."

This kind of cleverness persisted in the opening of "No Phones, Private Coffin," but on March 25, 1944, Schwartz wrote back to say he was nevertheless captivated by it: "For some reason, it affected me a good deal when I read it. The beginning was a bit mysterious and vague . . . but once I got into it, I loved it." Now that Bradbury was becoming a featured author in the Popular Publications stable of detective magazines, Schwartz took care to balance submissions between Mike Tilden, who edited *Detective Tales* and *Dime Mystery*, and Alden H. Norton, supervisory editor for all of Popular's magazines and editor-in-chief of *Flynn's Detective Fiction*. Since Tilden had one of Bradbury's "Douser" stories in hand, Norton received "No Phones." To this point, Norton had reluctantly rejected Bradbury tales for *Flynn's* because of that persistent element of vagueness that Schwartz had also noted; the March 25 letter from Schwartz praising "No Phones" also relayed Norton's rejection of "Where Everything Ends" (volume 2, selection 20) along with Norton's comments on Bradbury's potential: "As I've told you many times, if this Bradbury guy can combine undeniable talent for good writing with a few plots that can really hang together he will be outstandingly good."

On April 8, 1944, Schwartz wrote to say that Norton had actually called him with praise for "No Phones, Private Coffin," and would take it for the August 1944 issue of *Flynn's*. Norton's acceptance meant that Bradbury had now found success at all levels of Popular's thriving detective pulp family of magazines; *Flynn's* had become an excellent seller for the Popular syndicate, but "No Phones," editorially retitled "Yesterday I Lived!," would be Bradbury's only story in the magazine; much to Norton's annoyance, the wartime paper shortage led Popular's executives to suspend *Flynn's* to maintain the syndicate's love pulps.

Despite the future loss of this venue, Bradbury's break into *Flynn's* was an indication that he could attain a level of quality in his often off-trail murder mysteries. Significant post-publication praise came from his friend and mentor Henry Kuttner, now living in New York after his summer 1944 discharge from the army. C. L. Moore, the other half of the prolific Kuttner-Moore writing team, shared her husband's view that Bradbury's Hollywood murder mystery, along with "The Trunk Lady" (volume 2, selection 18) exhibited the best narrative control and plot development among his off-trail detective genre stories.

In the absence of Bradbury's submitted typescript, the first publication in *Flynn's Detective Fiction* (S1) represents the closest form to the author's composing hand. Bradbury's submitted title, an allusion to the sometimes savage irony that Bradbury's heartbroken detective brings to the murder investigation of the actress he loved, is retained; the editorially-imposed "Yesterday I Lived!," which turns the focus to the victim's point of view, appears parenthetically after the title in the present edition as a bibliographical bridge to the story's publishing history. The many variants in *MeM* (including a few substantives) all appear to result from editorial styling imposed by Dell editors; the lack of even light authorial revision in *MeM* suggests that, in Bradbury's mind, the story remained, after forty years, one of the better tales he had published in this genre.

The detective fiction that Bradbury had turned to writing late in the summer and fall of 1944 almost invariably reached print; after two early misses, the next eight all sold during his four-year run in the detective pulps. "No Phones, Private Coffin" was the last and perhaps the best of these first eight. From here on out, the detective stories he continued to write at intervals would be interspersed among new fantasy and science fiction tales and a growing mastery of realism.

Sources: Author's composition and submission log (1942–45); author's sales record (1941–49); author's agency listing (Nolan, c. 1950); author's notecard story file (ca. 1943–1975); Eller-Bradbury interviews, Oct. 2007; Schwartz to Bradbury, Mar. 25, Apr. 8 and 15, Aug. 20, and Sept. 9, 1944; Mogen, 151.

—JE

## Textual Notes

1.0 The teaser inserted below the S1 title was constructed by Bradbury's editors, and is not part of his text: "Over and over again she died for him—the only woman he'd ever loved—while silent, unnoticed and hating, he waited for her dead hand to reach through the years and spell out the name of her murderer." The police investigators run the studio footage of Diana Coyle's collapse and death over and over again, but studio desk sergeant Cleve Morris can only bear to watch it once; it will play in his mind for the next three years, while her murder remains unsolved.

1.22 Diana," when] Both S1 and *MeM* present a full stop between the remembered greetings and the descriptive phrase that follows, creating a confusing and incorrect reading. Retaining the stop and capitalizing "when" would further confuse the reading. The comma supplied by the *Great Detectives* anthology editors reflects Bradbury's probable intention, but he was not involved in the preparation of this text; the emendation is therefore supplied on the authority of the present editors.

1.23 winking,] Here and at 6.4 (evening,), Bradbury sets off the next sentence of dialog with a comma rather than a full stop. *MeM* editors imposed the more correct full stop, but Bradbury's consistent usage of the comma is retained at both points.

2.1 sank,] At several points in the story's third-person narrative, Cleve's thoughts drift into an anecdotal second person present tense. *MeM*'s editors extended the second-person point-of-view by changing "sank" to "sinks." Context indicates that Bradbury intended to break back into the third-person narrative at this point, and his use of "sank" is retained.

2.36 Kroll,] The comma emended in from *MeM* corrects the pronoun antecedent error for "hanging onto him"; without this emendation, it appears that both Kroll and Tally Durham are "hanging onto" Jamie Winters; in actuality, Tally is hanging onto Georgie Kroll. The emendation is required to avoid reader confusion.

4.39 film,] The comma emended into the copy-text at this point establishes "the director and producer of the film" as an appositive for R. J. Guilding, and clarifies an otherwise confusing reading.

6.2 store,] The S1 reading reflects Bradbury's occasional placement of a comma between a subject and predicate; such usage here and at other points in the story is not confusing, and is retained to preserve the stylistic flavor of the original text.

7.36 wreathes, were telling] The S1 comma appears awkward, but it correctly sets off the second part of a compound predicate ("the newspapers had tapered off the black wreathes, were telling her life story on page two the following Wednesday;"). No emendation is required.

10.23 rings.] Once again, Cleve's thoughts shift into an anecdotal second person present tense from the dominant third-person narrative. *MeM*'s editors
intrude into this narrative shift by changing "rings" to "rang." The present edition retains the S1 reading to preserve Bradbury's intended narrative
strategy at this point in the story.

10.39 up up through] Bradbury's doubling of "up up" is more likely an intended
emphasis rather than a typing error. The *MeM* reading ("up through") is
therefore not a necessary correction, and is rejected.

## Emendations

*[title]* No Phones, Private Coffin (Yesterday I Lived!)] CE; YESTERDAY I LIVED!
  | By RAY BRADBURY S1

1.16 her.] *MeM*; ~^ S1

*1.22 Diana,"] CE; ~." S1

*2.36 Kroll,] *MeM*; ~^ S1

*4.39 film,] *MeM*; ~^ S1

6.21 Winters's] *MeM*; Winters S1

8.21 Winters's] *MeM*; Winter's *Also* 9.12 S1

9.18 Denim."] *MeM*; ~.^ S1

10.11 Tally's or Georgie's] *MeM*; Tally or Georgie S1

## Historical Collation: Post-Copy-Text Substantives

*[title]* YESTERDAY I LIVED!] S1, *GD*; Yesterday I Lived! *MeM*

*2.1 sank] S1; sinks *MeM*

2.17 like to kiss] S1; like to have kissed *MeM*

3.17 up all around] S1; up around *MeM*

5.6 Always was.] S1; Always had been. *MeM*

5.20 Cleve, the] S1; Cleve and the *MeM*

7.5–6 snapped: ¶ "Diana] S1; snapped, ^ "Diana *MeM*

7.23 onto] S1; on to *MeM Also* 8.7, 8.38

8.8 one another] S1; each other *MeM*

8.11 miscue] S1; missed cue *MeM*

10.2–3 saying: ¶ "Honest] S1; saying, ^ "Honest *MeM*

*10.23 rings] S1; rang *MeM*

*10.39 up up] S1; up *MeM*

11.35–36 lecture: ¶ "It's] S1; lecture: ^ "It's *MeM*

## Line-End Hyphenation

3.36 salt-/shaker] salt-shaker

4.25 on-/stage] onstage

12.5 black-/balled] black-balled

## 2. If Paths Must Cross Again (Apr. 5, 1944)

Bradbury's composition and submission log indicates that he completed a short 1,100-word version of this story by April 5, 1944. This entry appears third within a group of four consecutive stories listed as submitted to New York agent Ed Bodin for circulation among major market magazines between March 27 and April 7, 1944. A subsequent entry, dated December 7, 1944, documents completion of a longer 2,000-word version; his typed notation "(quality?)" suggests that he was still hoping for a sale to one of the major market slicks. There is no entry for "If Paths Must Cross Again" in Bradbury's 1941–49 sales listing, nor does it appear in Nolan's list of sales by Julius Schwartz. In fact, no record for this story appears in any of Bradbury's subsequent sales records; it remained unpublished until 2009, when his friend and principal bibliographer, Donn Albright, convinced him to include it in his final story collection, *We'll Always Have Paris*.

Bradbury's dream of reaching the mainstream magazine market had prompted him to submit stories as early as his sixteenth year, but his trial relationship with Ed Bodin represents his first sustained major market gambit. But Bodin was unable to place any of the four stories that Bradbury submitted in the spring of 1944; he may not have even circulated the initial submission for "If Paths Must Cross Again" (TS1), which was by far the shortest of the four at 1,100 words. Bradbury's more settled early intention for this tale survives as an 1,800-word typescript (TS2), which he sent on to Julius Schwartz in early December 1944.

Schwartz felt that it was "a neat yarn," and must have known that his young friend had mainstream aspirations for the tale. It first went out to *This Week*, which, since the mid-1930s, had become a leading Sunday magazine supplemental insert for a number of major newspapers. *This Week* paid major market rates for fiction from a wide range of established writers; Schwartz's long-time friend and colleague Mort Weisinger had recently secured $450 for a very short tale, an amazing payday for genre writers who normally sold fiction for a penny or two a word. Nevertheless, it was risky to submit work by a young writer who was just making his mark in the genre pulps, and he did not hide that fact from Bradbury: "I'm not too hopeful of a sale here, but when I gets a hunch I follows it thru . . ."

Schwartz also considered *Argosy*, a major market pulp dating back to the early 1880s that had recently converted to a slick-paper format. But *This Week* had already cut back on its fiction content, and *Argosy* would soon do the same. "If Paths Must Cross Again" represented a distinct departure from the science fiction, fantasy, weirds, and detective tales that Bradbury was producing for the genre pulps; Schwartz was almost exclusively a pulp agent, and had gone as far as he could into the mainstream with this story. It ended up back in Bradbury's inactive files for the next six decades.

The whirlwind wartime romance that frames this story is encapsulated in a single scene of revelation: on their last date before the young officer heads out to join his military unit, the couple discovers that they almost certainly had crossed paths years earlier, when she was a high school student in a small Illinois town and he was staying at the nearby YMCA on business. The memories clearly derive from Bradbury's boyhood Waukegan, but the evening's conversation forms a mixture of romance, remembrance, uncertainty, and a fear that the war will separate them forever. Will they only meet again, reincarnated, in other lifetimes?

The 1,100-word version of April 1944 opens out through a conventional lover's conversation over a nightclub dinner, and the ending is easily predictable: "All the rest of the evening he was a boy in horn-rims with books under his arm, and she was a golden-haired girl with a very blue ribbon tied in her long bright hair . . ." (ellipses Bradbury's). There is no indication that Ed Bodin's agency even circulated the story in this form; in fact, Schwartz's December letter cautioned Bradbury about Bodin's diminishing reputation in New York editorial circles.

But Bradbury had already completely rewritten the tale, and this was the version that, by late December 1944, Schwartz was actively circulating. The dinner and its revelations remain largely unchanged, but the dialog itself is replaced throughout by paraphrase. "If Paths Must Cross Again" had become an experiment, as Bradbury quickly settled on a conversation related through a paragraph-by-paragraph alternation between the conscious thoughts of each character. In this version, there is a far more sophisticated "Bradbury twist" ending: "They arose and she kissed him insistently, and his sunburnt hands went through her tumbling dark hair, holding her, and she was happy that he'd never know that as a girl in 1934 she had never owned a blue ribbon for her hair, and had *never* worn one in all her life."

With her dark, ribbonless hair, she is not the golden-haired girl he remembers; but she has taken control of the situation, and wants him to have this doubled remembrance of her as he goes off to the war. This longer version is more ambitious, more carefully crafted, and represents his settled intention for circulation as 1944 came to a close. Both versions remained inactive until 2009, when Bradbury, on Donn Albright's recommendation, published the short preliminary TS1 version in *We'll Always Have Paris*. Copy-text for the present edition is TS2, the more developed form that Bradbury opted to market actively toward the end of 1944. The suggestion of reincarnated love found in "If Paths Must Cross Again" would surface again in "Lime Vanilla Ice," a Green Town story pulled into *Dandelion Wine* (1957), a novelized story cycle that extended the nostalgic feel of time and memory previewed in this early story.

Sources: Author's composition and submission log; Schwartz to Bradbury, Dec. 25, 1944.

—JE

Emendations
14.10 Right] CE; right TS2
16.24 Oh,] CE; oh, TS2
17.3 *not present*] CE; the end TS2

Historical Collation: Post-Copy-Text Substantives
*[title]* "If Paths Must Cross Again" | by | Ray Bradbury] TS2; If Paths Must
    Cross Again *WAHP*

## 3. The Miracles of Jamie (Apr. 7, 1944)

This story would become the fourth major market magazine sale for Bradbury,
reaching print in the April 1946 issue of *Charm,* but it was the first of this very
significant group of stories to be written. On April 7, 1944, Bradbury listed a
2,300-word version of "The Miracles of Jamie" in his composition and submission log. It is the final entry within a group of four consecutive stories logged
as submitted to New York agent Ed Bodin for circulation among major market
magazines between March 27 and April 7, 1944. Nothing came of the Bodin
consignments, but Bradbury continued to regard this story as a potential major
market sale over the next year; his supplemental list for "Special submissions
during the year 1945," a record of his own direct submissions to radio networks
and to major market magazines, shows that he sent "The Miracles of Jamie" to
*Tomorrow* on August 2, 1945. Bradbury's notecard file for this story shows that
it next went to *Charm* on August 16, and his 1941–49 sales listing includes a $175
sale on September 24, 1945. His income tax worksheet, listing fourteen stories
sold during 1945, confirms the $175 sale to *Charm.* Bradbury negotiated his own
major market sales at this time, thus the story does not appear in Nolan's list
of genre market sales by Julius Schwartz. Bradbury's sales-by-publisher listing
concludes with a summary of "slick sales" that includes "Miracles of Jamie" [*sic*]
as "sold on the basis of first North American rights only." Finally, a single-page
summary of "Stories Published in Quality Magazines" (c. 1948) lists "The Miracles of Jamie" as published in the April 1946 issue of *Charm* (S1).

Curiously, this quality story remained uncollected for three decades. Bradbury pulled most of his often award-winning early experiments in realism into
*The Golden Apples of the Sun* (1953), but he held out "The Miracles of Jamie"
and the more sentimental "One Timeless Spring" until his 1976 collection, *Long
After Midnight* (*LAM*). An undated typescript originated with Bradbury and
survives in the Albright Collection (TS); the paper, typeface and running head
indicate that it was prepared in the 1950s or early 1960s by Bradbury or under his supervision (the typescript's manila folder is titled in Bradbury's hand).
This clean fair copy incorporates several dozen isolated substantive revisions by
Bradbury, all of which are recorded in the present volume's Historical Collation.

Page numbers (typed in the upper right margins of each page) run from 188 to 199, indicating that the typescript and its revisions were at one time intended for a Bradbury story collection. "The Miracles of Jamie" does not appear as a title in any of the working content sheets for the collections within the date range of the typescript, but it is possible that it was briefly considered for *The Golden Apples of the Sun* (1953), *A Medicine for Melancholy* (1959), or *The Machineries of Joy* (1964), all of which contained a few earlier stories.

By the 1970s, his growing occupation with stage and screen adaptations of his works and the relative scarcity of newer stories led Bradbury (with the recommendations of friend and writer Bill Nolan) to include a number of older uncollected tales. "The Miracles of Jamie" was finally collected in *Long After Midnight,* but the earlier typescript revisions were not incorporated in this version. Bradbury appears to have worked directly from the S1 *Charm* text in making relatively few substantive revisions for his new collection, and all further publication of "The Miracles of Jamie" radiates from this source. Knopf's *Long After Midnight* first edition served as setting copy for the Bantam mass market American paperback (1978), the British hardbound edition from Hart-Davis, MacGibbon (1977), and Morrow's hundred-story compilation, *Bradbury Stories (BS,* 2003). The Hart-Davis, MacGibbon typesetting of *LAM* was reissued by Granada (1978) as Bradbury's long-time Hart-Davis publishing legacy in Britain was fully absorbed by the larger consortium. The Bantam paperback typesetting of *LAM* was reissued for the mass market British paperback from Earthlight (1999). "The Miracles of Jamie" remains available in successive reprintings of *Bradbury Stories.*

Most of the stories that Bradbury composed during the spring of 1944 played into his long-standing success with *Weird Tales,* or his more recent streak of sales to Popular Publication's stable of detective pulps. But his early April draft of "If Paths Must Cross Again" (selection 2) seemed to lead him into more realistic themes, and the "what if" for this story leads back to his Waukegan childhood and the vaguely Baptist roots of his family life. In a private 2002 interview, he defined the basic childhood assumption that emerged from his memories to spark the story: "I think every young boy has often thought, if he's a Christian, 'Well, Christ is coming back, isn't he? What if it's me? What if it's me and I don't know it?' So it came from me thinking [about] that when I was a certain age, and then being disillusioned. So in a way, it's a true story."

Bradbury set the tale within his eight-month 1932–33 sojourn in Tucson, Arizona, where his father had tried unsuccessfully to find work during the Great Depression. Bradbury always remembered how, as a seventh-grader, everything seemed so new and frontier-beautiful in Tucson, a rebirth of sorts that seemed the natural setting for the new story. Jamie's rising hopes as he orchestrates seeming miracles at school soon focus on a chance to save his mother from the cancer that is consuming her. A schoolyard bully brutally ends his dreams, and Jamie's haunting new knowledge that he cannot heal his mother concludes a kind of realistic narrative that Bradbury had rarely been able to negotiate with such mastery.

It was a turning-point story that nonetheless took two years to reach print. During 1944 his mentor Henry Kuttner periodically recommended that he submit some of his newer stories to the major market periodicals on his own. Both Kuttner and Julius Schwartz, Bradbury's pulp agent, urged him to find an agent to handle this market for him, but he was producing a story a week in Los Angeles, and had little time for cross-country networking with prospective agents by mail. He knew he had stories that could succeed in the larger market, but he was unsure of a strategy; so far, a sale to *American Mercury* ("The Big Black and White Game") represented his only breakthrough. By the early summer of 1945, Grant Beach, who had read most of his friend's stories while Bradbury kept a writing room in Mrs. Beach's tenement, suggested that Bradbury simply send the better stories scattershot to the major magazines, without trying to match content with perceived readership. He tried this during August 1945, and three stories soon sold. *Charm*'s editors couldn't fit him in until the April 1946 issue, obscuring the significant fact that "The Miracles of Jamie" had been written well before the other three stories that define his initial major market success.

As no prepublication forms of the text have been located, S1 stands as copytext. The variants of TS (prepared from S1 some years later) represent a subsequent intention that never reached print; these fall beyond the range of his first settled intention in S1, but the accidentals are relevant to tracking Bradbury's spelling preferences at key points in the original publication. The substantive variants of TS, along with the separate set of revisions that Bradbury made for *Long After Midnight* and subsequent collections and reissues, are all recorded in the Historical Collation below.

Sources: Author's sales record (1941–49); author's composition and submission log (1942–45) and supplement (1945); author's sales-by-publisher indexes (c. 1950); author's note card files (c. 1943–1975); author's income tax notes (1945); Eller-Bradbury interviews, Mar. 2002; Dimeo, in Greenberg and Olander, 159–60; Johnson, 19; Moskowitz, 362.

—JE

## Textual Notes

18.15 glory water] Bradbury's post-copy-text TS revision to "holy water" eliminates the partial doubling created by the vowel form ("gloried") earlier in the sentence. In his unrelated revisions for *LAM*, he solved the problem by retaining "glory" and changing "gloried" to "basked." Both of these separate lines of revision represent subsequent intentions, and appear only in the Historical Collation.

19.27 feet] The S1 reading presents the image as Bradbury first intended it, with "feet bent up and straightened down" in the form of synecdoche (representing the complete formation of Jamie's marching students), and is retained here to preserve his first intention. Later, in preparing the unpublished TS from its S1 source, Bradbury shifted the image from "feet" to the more easily visualized "legs bent up and straightened down"; this revision is the result of a subsequent intention, however, and is relegated to the Historical Collation.

19.38–39 The street . . . People sweated] For his unpublished TS version, Bradbury apparently decided to delete his S1 reference to the Tucson rodeo. The *LAM* version, which appears to have been revised directly from S1, retains the passage. The deletion is not part of Bradbury's earliest settled intention, and is relegated, along with his many TS revisions, to the Historical Collation.

21.1 grey] It is likely that the S1 editors styled Bradbury's preferred spelling to "gray" at this point in the text. His known preference for the British spelling "grey" for "gray" is well documented for the 1940s, and was actually restored when he prepared the subsequent TS directly from the styled S1 text. The TS variants, part of a failed effort to pull the story into one of his subsequent story collections, fall beyond the range of his first settled intention as represented by S1, but the persistent evidence for this particular spelling preference forms the basis for emendation on the authority of the present edition.

21.12 picking up] The sense of "seizing" (TS) the weighty bully Billiard "by the left foot" is more believable that the original S1 "picking up" by the left foot, but the point of the tale is the concept of "miracles," and neither reading is better than the other in the story context. TS, which also represents a later intention, is relegated to the Historical Collation.

## Emendations

[title] The Miracles of Jamie] CE; The Miracles of Jamie | A SHORT STORY BY RAY BRADBURY S1

20.6 denimed] *LAM*[1976]; denimmed S1

*21.1 grey] TS; gray S1

## Historical Collation: Post-Copy-Text Substantives

[title] The Miracles of Jamie] S1, *LAM*[1976, 1976BC, 1978]; THE MIRACLES OF JAMIE TS, *LAM*[1978UK], BS

18.11 Ma and Pa] S1; Mom or Dad TS

18.11 Seventh Grade] S1; seventh grade TS, *LAM*[1976], *LAM*[1976BC], *LAM*[1978US], BS; class *LAM*[1978UK]

*18.14 gloried] S1; basked *LAM*[1976], *LAM*[1976BC], *LAM*[1978US], *LAM*[1978UK], BS

*18.15 glory] S1; holy TS

18.19 Ma] S1; Mother TS

18.22 principal] S1; headmaster *LAM*[1978UK] *Also* 19.20, 19.25

18.23 to him] S1; at him TS

*19.27 feet] S1; legs TS

19.30 onto] S1; on to *LAM*[1978UK] *Also* 24.9

19.35 Later, when] S1; When TS

19.35 Gem] S1; The Gem TS

19.35–36 thought quickly] S1; quickly thought TS

19.37 that his] S1; his TS

*19.38 The street was lined] S1; People lined the TS

21.3 well-rooted, established.] S1; well-rooted and established. TS

21.8 shins, knocking them] S1; shins and sitting TS

*21.12 picking up] S1; seizing TS

21.24 prickly pears] S1; cacti *LAM*[1978UK] *Also* 24.11

21.30 don't," he said.] S1; don't." TS

21.31 do," retorted Billiard.] S1; do." TS

22.4 two.] S1; two! TS

22.16 Ma] S1; Mom TS *Also* 23.11, 23.13, 24.25

22.19 "How you] S1; "You TS

22.31 Jamie staggered] S1; Jamie had staggered TS

22.35–36 calm down.] S1; calm. TS

22.37 yes, yes, he] S1; he TS

22.40 Sure. That] S1; Surely, that TS

23.10 indirectly by] S1; by indirect TS

23.15 by him] S1; by over him TS

23.16 Mama] S1; Mom TS

23.22 Mama] S1; Mother TS *Also* 23.28, 24.6, 24.13, 24.16

23.26 be] S1; alone TS

23.27 get down] S1; run down TS

23.28 walking easy] S1; easy TS

23.39 got up] S1; leaped up TS

24.1 back," cried Jamie.] S1; back!" he cried. TS

24.2 it."] S1; it!" TS

24.7 little black] S1; small grey TS

24.9 onto] S1; on TS

24.13 Mama's] S1; Mother's TS *Also* 24.28

24.17 in his mind to her.] S1; to her in his mind. TS

24.19 get up] S1; get right up TS

24.20 it wouldn't] S1; wouldn't *LAM*[1976], *LAM*[1976BC], *LAM*[1978US], *LAM*[1978UK], *BS*

24.21 Ma. Get] S1; Ma, get TS

24.27 a jerking] S1; jerking *LAM*[1978]UK
24.30 up.] S1; up! TS *Also* 24.38
24.36 forth.] S1; forth! TS

## Line-End Hyphenation
20.39 by-/product] byproduct

## 4. The Long Way Around (The Long Way Home)
## (May 2, 1944)

From April through June, 1944, Bradbury composed, on average, a story a week, but with the exception of "The Miracles of Jamie" (selection 3), most of these were unremarkable. Only one sold that summer (his "Douser" detective sequel, "The Very Bewildered Corpses," selection 5), and most of them never sold at all. "The Long Way Around" took a year (and two rewrites) to sell; it appears in Bradbury's composition and submission log with a completion date of May 2, 1944, and Bradbury's typed annotation "4,000 words (pulp)." His author's sales record has a handwritten entry for "Long Way Around" [*sic*] with a payment received date of July 16, 1945, noting the name of his editor for many of his detective pulp sales at Popular Publications, Mike Tilden. Bradbury's income tax notes for 1945 list confirm the July 16 payment date from *Dime Mystery;* for both of these payment entries, the post-commission amount is grouped with payment for "The Creatures That Time Forgot," which was bundled into the same check by his agent; the amount for "The Long Way Home" can be inferred, less the ten percent commission, as $51.30. Nolan's list of sales by Julius Schwartz, Bradbury's pulp agent, shows the actual sales date as July 10, 1945, and the pre-commission payment from *Dime Mystery* of $57.00.

"The Long Way Home" is perhaps the weakest of his detective tales to reach print, but circumstances combined to make the sale more than a year after composition. Schwartz had Bradbury's typescript in hand by May 9, 1944, noting that the solution "isn't too difficult to guess but writing and suspense very good." Popular Publications editors were still considering other Bradbury tales for their detective magazines, so Schwartz was considering submitting the new story to *Black Mask*. Although the Schwartz correspondence record is fairly complete, there appears to be at least one missing letter; nothing came of the *Black Mask* option (Schwartz was never able to crack that market for Bradbury), but an unrecorded submission to Mike Tilden at Popular apparently resulted in a rewrite sometime over the next year. On May 12, 1945, Schwartz sent Bradbury a cover note forwarding Mike Tilden's letter turning down the rewrite, but encouraging resubmission. On July 11, 1945, Schwartz relayed Tilden's acceptance of "the last version," implying that the road to publication had been a long one; neither the interpolated drafts, nor Tilden's letter, appear to have survived.

Tilden's willingness to finally accept a lesser Bradbury tale may have been encouraged by the pulp market itself; for months, Bradbury had received repeated messages from Tilden (relayed through Schwartz) urging him to submit more stories. The Popular Publications senior editor, Alden Norton, acknowledged Bradbury's talent, but was wary of the off-trail stories he was submitting. But Tilden, who had to fill the pages of the remaining detective pulps after paper shortages led Norton to discontinue *Flynn's Detective Fiction*, had few reservations about Bradbury's off-trail originality. In fact, Bradbury's highly emotional and carnivalesque stories often fell in line with the "shudder pulp" reputation of *Dime Mystery*, one of the surviving Popular titles. This pulp had been toned down during the war years, but Bradbury's odd little story, after revisions, fit well enough to appear in the November 1945 issue of *Dime Mystery* (S1), with the editorially modified title "The Long Way Home." In Canada, "The Long Way Home" was reset and published in the December 1945 issue of *Strange Detective Mysteries* (S2). Both S1 and S2 appear to have been set directly from Bradbury's final revised submitted copy; the Canadian S2 contains a number of substantive additions (especially in the final third of the story) that appear to be restorations of brief lines and words cut from the S1 text.

The story's final shocker, involving the surprising revelation of the murderer and her pathological fear of rodents, offers a lesser example of the odd and quirky twist that Bradbury often brought to his weird and detective tales. The emotional suspense is fairly well maintained by the way that the protagonist's very dull life is suddenly thrown into the terrifying world of a murder he imagined, but would never dream of committing. It touches on the Cornell Woolrich noir formula that fascinated Bradbury: what if absolutely unbelievable and horrifying events suddenly enter the lives of ordinary people?

It's telling that Bradbury did not include this story in the list of his published detective tales that he sent to *Ellery Queen* editor (and author) Fred Danay in June 1949. Eleven others made the cut, yet Bradbury eventually held back even these stories from further publication. But Julius Schwartz had not limited the Popular Publications rights to first serial only, and nearly four decades later editors holding those rights developed a collection through Dell that Bradbury was unable to prevent. He found a compromise by limiting the 1984 publication of *A Memory of Murder* (*MeM*) to a single mass market paperback printing, and writing an introduction that placed these stories in the context of his early experiments with the detective genre. He lightly revised some of the stories for *MeM*, but "The Long Way Home," appearing with its S1 title, shows no evidence of authorial revisions beneath Dell's layer of editorial stylings.

S1, representing Bradbury's earliest known version of the story, serves as copy-text. Analysis of the S1 and S2 variants, combined with a study of the layout in both magazines, reveals that the S1 compositors appear to have cut nearly twenty sentences and single-sentence paragraphs of dialog to allow for layout of the uncredited headpiece art and three blocks of advertisements without overrunning the story's allotted page count. In general, variants in many of the Canadian versions of Bradbury's stories reveal that the American syndicates sent on Bradbury's original submitted copy (or perhaps their own uncut galleys) for second serial typesetting; in this case, lack of title art and any advertisements in the Canadian issue allowed the S2 typesetters to compose the entire story. The major S2 variants, which in context are clearly part of Bradbury's submitted narrative and often bridge clearly identifiable lacunae in S1, are thus restored by emendation. Discussion of particular points involving these passages and others appear in the textual notes below.

Sources: Author's sales record (1941–49); author's composition and submission log (1942–45); author's note card files (c. 1943–1975); author's income tax notes (1945); Nolan's list of sales by Julius Schwartz (c. 1950); Schwartz to Bradbury, undated [May 9, 1944], May 12 and July 11, 1945; Eller and Touponce, 311–313; Mogen, 150.

—JE

## Textual Notes

[title] The S1 teaser following the title art is entirely editorial: "Every day, meek, rabbitty little Charley Guidney was shoved around by his boss at the office; and every night by his marital boss at home. So he dreamed up a murder that had never happened, but which, nonetheless, came strangely true!" S2's teaser is substantively the same, but a different teaser appears in the Canadian issue's table of contents: "Hen-pecked at home, trampled on at the office, meek little Charlie Guidney reaped the strange fruit of his wildly imaginative imagination!"

26.30 grey] Although Bradbury's submitted typescript has not been located, both S1 and S2 retained his preference for the British spelling.

31.15 Now . . . town] Guidney's thoughts, expressed without quotation marks, first appear in S2; the passage explains Guidney's next action, and may have been cut in space-starved S1 as a non-essential passage. The S2 restoration is emended into the copy-text.

33.24–25 "I don't sell guns,"] This fourth shopkeeper's comment may have seemed expendable to the S1 compositor, but the S2 restoration may offer a clue to where Guidney purchases the white rat he uses to terrify his wife into a confession: the fourth store may be a pet store, but the reader can only speculate.

34.36 "Charlie!"] The great majority of lines missing from S1 were cut from the closing confrontation between Guidney and Lydia. Dialog amounting to more than ten lines of double-columned text were restored in S2 in this final section, contributing to the contextual evidence that these passages were cut from S1 to conserve space. All of these passages are restored by emendation.

## Emendations

[*title*] The Long Way Around (The Long Way Home)] CE; The Long Way Home | By RAY BRADBURY S1

29.20 *me!*"] S2; ~!^ S1

*31.15 street. Now I'll have . . . leave town.] S2; street. S1

31.25 and talked] S2; talked S1

32.26–27 arms. He seemed . . . any crisis.] S2; arms. S1

*33.24–25 third. "I don't sell . . . a fourth.] S2; third. S1

33.41 it! Just wait! . . . the cops!"] S2; it!" S1

34.5–6 focus. "Do you read the papers?" ⌥ "What's . . . do with it?"] S2; focus. S1

34.14 any .22's] S2; an 22's S1

34.15–16 chair. "The murderer . . . for that matter. . . ."] S2; chair. S1

*34.35–37 him. ⌥ "Charlie!" ⌥ "Hello, Lydia."] S2; him. S1

35.3  5 Lydia? Didn't you . . . Didn't you?"] S2; Lydia?" S1

35.13–14 home." ⌥ "Charlie, . . . you saying?"] S2; home.^ S1

35.31–32 over? I was . . . and you—"] S2; over?" S1

35.33–36 cried. ⌥ He felt . . . horrible little man!"] S2; cried. S1

## Historical Collation: Post-Copy-Text Substantives

[*title*] THE LONG WAY HOME | By | RAY BRADBURY] S1, S2; The Long Way Home *MeM*

26.12(2) Sternwell.] S1; ~! S2

26.22 foods!] S1; ~. S2

26.24 at all the] S1; at the S2

27.4–5 as shiny as] S1; shiny as S2

27.5 began. ^ "Your] S1; ~. ⌥ "~ *MeM*

27.9 ^ She] S1; ⌥ ~ S2

27.31–32 frantically searching for something to say,] S1; *om.* S2

28.22 All of a sudden I—"] S1; *om.* S2

28.27 this moment] S1; a moment S2

28.39 agree on] S1; agree to *MeM*

29.20 *me.*] S1; ~! S2

◊29.20 *me!*] S1; me!" S2

30.18 backward] S1; back *MeM*

30.20 him,] S1; ~! S2

*◊31.15 *not present*] S1; Now I'll have to tell Lydia I fooled Kelly, or she won't leave town. S2

31.21 Kelly?" ^ Kelly] S1; ~?" ⁋ ~ *MeM*

31.22 he?" ^ Charlie] S1; ~?" ⁋ ~ *MeM*

31.23 there?" ^ Kelly] S1; ~?" ⁋ ~ *MeM*

31.23 *it*] S1; it S2

◊31.25 him talked] S1; him and talked S2

32.23 lit] S1; lighted *MeM*

◊32.26–27 *not present*] S1; He seemed unaware of any crisis. S2

32.28 it?] S1; ~" S2

32.34–37 On a . . . look!] S1; *om.* S2

32.40 The little . . . talked.] S1; *om.* S2

32.41 Johnny?] S1; Jimmy? S2

33.13 propels] S1; propelled *MeM*

33.14 of a workaday] S1; of workaday S2

33.21–22 could: ⁋ "Mister] S1; ~: ^ "~ S2, *MeM*

*◊33.24–25 *not present*] S1; "I don't sell guns," said a fourth. S2

◊33.41 *not present*] S1; Just wait! I'll tell the cops!" S2

◊34.5–7 *not present*] S1; "Do you read the papers?" ⁋ "What's that got to do with it?" S2

◊34.14 an 22's] S1; any .22's S2; any twenty-twos *MeM*

◊34.15–16 *not present*] S1; "The murderer didn't plan on my checking with you, or anyone checking with you, for that matter. . . ." S2

34.31 first?"] S1; first, please?" S2

◊34.35 turned to him.] S1; turning. S2

*◊34.36–37 *not present*] S1; "Charlie!" ⁋ "Hello, Lydia." S2

◊35.3–5 *not present*] S1; Didn't you guess I was in a mental rut, going berserk, wanting to leave town forever? Didn't you? S2

◊35.14 *not present*] S1; "Charlie, what *are* you saying?" S2

35.26 him?] S1; them, eh? S2

35.27 boredom, Lydia?] S1; boredom, eh, Lydia? S2

◊35.32 *not present*] S1; I was only trying to get us out, and you—" S2

◊35.34–36 *not present*] S1; He felt of the weapon in his pocket. "Tell the truth!" ⁋ "You're a murderer!" she screamed. "And you're trying to blame me! Get out, you hateful, horrible man!" S2

35.39–40 She stared, unbelieving, . . . escape him.] S1; *om.* S2

## Line-End Hyphenation

27.17 pay-/check] paycheck

31.3 head-/quarters] headquarters

31.16 mouth-/piece] mouthpiece

34.17 shop-/keeper] shopkeeper

## 5. The Very Bewildered Corpses (Four-Way Funeral)
## (May 8, 1944)

Six days after Bradbury completed the well-traveled "The Long Way Around," he finished his next detective story; it was marginally better than the former story, but it had the added cachet of being a sequel to Bradbury's initial "Douser" Mulligan detective story (volume 2, selection 22), which Mike Tilden had already purchased for a fall issue of *Detective Tales*. Bradbury's composition and submission log includes an entry for "The Very Bewildered Corpses" dated May 8, 1944. This entry is annotated "(sequel)" beneath the title, and further described as "4,000 words (DOUSER)." Bradbury subsequently rolled the log sheet back through his typewriter to proclaim "SOLD!" between the entry lines. His author's sales record shows a post-commission payment of $45.00 received on June 22 from Schwartz for the sale to *Detective Tales*. Nolan's listing of sales pulp by Julius Schwartz confirms the actual sale date as June 19, 1944 for a pre-commission amount of $50.00. There are no known sale-by-publisher sheets for the Popular Publications syndicate.

Mike Tilden's quick purchase of "The Very Bewildered Corpses" was probably a matter of timing; he already had the prequel, "Enter—the Douser," scheduled to run in the November 1944 issue of *Detective Tales* under the editorially-imposed title of "Half-Pint Homicide." Tilden placed the sequel in the December 1944 issue of *Detective Tales* (S1), imposing still another "wise-guy" genre title to fit detective "Douser" Mulligan's verbal (and literal) take-down of four rival crime bosses: "Four-Way Funeral." The "Douser" is certainly an unconventional private eye, sharing some of the hard-boiled sarcasm and quick wit of a Dashiell Hammett or Raymond Chandler protagonist. He's a "divvy," a sleuth with a sixth sense who knows more about his chosen criminal kingpins than they expect; in the end, his strategy of offering well-timed insults infuriates his criminals to the point that they unwittingly self-destruct, allowing Douser to escape in the nick of time. It was a carnivalesque extension of the hard-boiled detective noir into often low-brow (and middle-brow) underworld humor and criminal absurdity, yet the story had enough plot and drama to extend the Douser run of tales.

But Tilden would turn down the next installment ("Long Live the Douser!"), and "The Very Bewildered Corpses" ("Four-Way Funeral") was not picked up by the syndicate's Canadian affiliates. In June 1949, when Bradbury offered a broad selection of his detective tales to *Ellery Queen*'s Fred Danay for reprint or anthology consideration, he included this story, even though it lacked the suspenseful and dark twists of his best murder mysteries. But he soon relegated most of these tales to an earlier phase of creativity, and most (including "The

Very Bewildered Corpses") never appeared in his own story anthologies. But Julius Schwartz had not reserved rights to the Popular Publications tales, and Bradbury was not able to prevent a later generation of editors from publishing this story and all but one of the other Popular syndicate stories in a 1984 Dell mass-market paperback titled *A Memory of Murder* (*MeM*). Bradbury regained a degree of control by writing a contextual introduction and lightly revising some of the stories; "The Very Bewildered Corpses" appeared, again under the editorially imposed title "Four-Way Funeral," but the few substantives all appear to be editorial styling rather than authorial revisions.

Establishing the original text for the present edition is fairly straightforward. S1 serves as copy-text; with no further serial publication history, and a lack of discernible authorial revisions in *MeM*, the minimal emendations required to correct obvious error in punctuation derive solely from three punctuation corrections in *MeM* that Bradbury may have overseen. The present text retains Bradbury's original title, emending in the imposed editorial title as a parenthetical subtitle to avoid bibliographical confusion.

Sources: Author's composition and submission log (1942–45); Author's sales record (1941–49); Nolan's Schwartz agency sales listing (c. 1950); author's notecard story files (c. 1943–1975); Schwartz to Bradbury, June 20, July 4, and Sept. 2, 1944; Eller and Touponce, 310–18, 331–40; Mogen, 150.

—JE

## Textual Notes

[*title*] The editorial teaser, set within the title and the uncredited title art, derives in part from 40.18–19 and reads: "'We know how you bother people,' they told him, 'but you can't pit us among ourselves, because we're good pals together.' Which was just enough of a challenge to that half-pint of homicide, Douser, to start him on a new—and very lethal—little game . . .'"

37.7 grey] *Detective Tales*' copy editor has retained Bradbury's preferred British spelling; it is retained as well in the present edition.

37.18 Square] This is almost certainly a reference to Pershing Square, and Bradbury's inconsistent intention in the narrative appears to favor capitalizing this implied reference.

39.21 all ready] It's not at all clear if Bradbury means "already" (in the context of "presently" or "now"), or if he means that the Douser was like a dead pigeon all ready to devour. Given the uncertainty, the somewhat unconventional copy-text reading is retained.

46.5 so many bewildered corpses] Bradbury's intended title originates here.

## Emendations

*[title]* The Very Bewildered Corpses (Four-Way Funeral)] CE; Four-Way Funeral
  | A "Douser" Story | By RAY BRADBURY S1

37.31 park] *MeM*; Park S1 *Also* 40.14

42.15 tall,] *MeM*; ~. S1

45.20 around,"] *MeM*; ~,^ S1

## Historical Collation: Post-Copy-Text Substantives

*[title]* Four-Way Funeral | A "Douser" Story | By RAY BRADBURY] S1; Four-
  Way Funeral *MeM*

39.24 Drum, the actor, crushed] S1; Drum crushed *MeM*

40.4 jools] S1; jewels *MeM*

42.22 like that] S1; like he did in that *MeM*

43.23 like] S1; as *MeM*

43.29 like] S1; as if *MeM*

46.2–3 as Marsons tried to grope back to reality. Marsons rolled] S1; as Marsons rolled *MeM*

## Line-End Hyphenation

38.33 un-/hampered] unhampered

42.21 un-/pronging] unpronging

46.19 drug-/store] drug-store

## 6. The Reincarnate (June 3, 1944)

The history of this story stretches across sixty years, but it dropped out of Bradbury's active files very early in its creative life. As early as 1942, Bradbury read
a draft of "The Reincarnate" to a writing group he briefly attended. Bradbury's
composition and submission log reveals that he finally finished a marketable
draft of the story on June 3, 1944, and sent it off to Julius Schwartz in New
York for circulation. Bradbury appended the status note "bounced" to the entry before finally crossing it out completely. Indeed, "The Reincarnate" only
circulated briefly during the summer of 1944, and it drops out of the surviving
records at that point in time.

    In 1942, as his first sales made it possible to leave the afternoon newspaper
stand where he had sold the Los Angeles *Herald Examiner* on weekdays since
1938, he spent a brief period attending a small and informal writing group led by
Virginia Perdue, whose career as a Doubleday Doran Crime Club author was at
its peak. Perdue had been crippled in an automobile accident some years earlier,
and recurrent pain played into her very negative reaction to Bradbury's reading

of an early draft of "The Reincarnate." This was a story about reincarnation set in his home town of Waukegan, Illinois, offering an early exploration of the boundary between life and death that Bradbury found so fascinating as a Waukegan child and, indeed, throughout his long writing career. Even though she was a crime mystery writer, Perdue was chilled by the prospect of coming back into the world after the great physical pain she had already known in this life. The encounter dampened Bradbury's enthusiasm for his story, and nearly two years would pass before he had a more mature draft in hand.

"The Reincarnate" was finally ready to circulate during a period of months when Bradbury failed to produce any strong stories at all. Between mid-April and late June 1944 he had completed two of the weakest off-trail murder mysteries he would ever sell, "The Long Way Around" (selection 4) and "The Very Bewildered Corpses" (selection 5), and six stories that never sold at all (see Chronological Catalog). Bradbury sent "The Reincarnate" on to Schwartz shortly after completing it on June 3, who in turn sent it on to Monty Buchanan, the Standard Publications editor who served as assistant editor for Dorothy MacIlwraith at *Weird Tales*. On July 4, Schwartz relayed to Bradbury that Buchanan was "doubtful" about the story, and had deferred to MacIlwraith for a decision. Within the month, *Weird Tales* rejected the story, and there is no evidence that Schwartz ever circulated it again. In 1947, Schwartz returned the submitted 23-page ribbon copy typescript (under the standard agency cover page), along with more than twenty other Bradbury stories that had circulated but never sold.

"The Reincarnate" ribbon copy typescript (TS1) disappeared from Bradbury's basement along with the rest of the returned story typescripts in the late 1970s, but not before Donn Albright, Bradbury's long-time friend and principal bibliographer, made photocopies of all of the stories in that folder. Albright considered "The Reincarnate" important not only as a variation on the birth-death-rebirth cycle that Bradbury had often explored, but also because aspects of the story also reflected Bradbury's emerging mid-1940s concern that the tradition of supernatural literature, always an isolated target for censorship and intolerance, would be at risk in the coming postwar world. At his urging, Bradbury partially revised the story in 2004 on a carbon copy of the original typescript (TS2). Although he revised many words and phrases in the first third and the final third of the story, Bradbury retained the second-person narrative voice that gives the story a disembodied feel consistent with Paul's self-willed rise from the dead.

This revised version was first published in the multiple-author *Dark Delicacies* anthology (*DD*) edited by Del Howison and Jeff Gelb (New York: Carroll & Graff, 2005). The following year, Donn Albright, assisted by Jon Eller as textual editor, gathered many of Bradbury's so-called anti-censorship and "death of the imagination tales" into the limited press collection *Match to Flame* (Colorado Springs: Gauntlet, 2006). For *Match to Flame* (designated *MF*), Albright

published the TS1 photocopy of the unrevised ribbon copy that he had preserved. Most of the stories collected in *MF*, including the unrevised version of
"The Reincarnate," were repackaged without the editorial matter for *A Pleasure to Burn* (*PB*), another limited press collection (MI: Subterranean Press,
2010). A trade edition of *PB* (New York: Harper Perennial, 2011) succeeded the
limited press edition; *MF* and both editions of *PB* are based on the unrevised
version of "The Reincarnate."

Copy-text for the present edition is the Albright Collection's TS1 photocopy
of the lost ribbon copy. The revisions made to the first seven pages and the final
four pages of the author's surviving carbon copy by Bradbury represent a far
later intention, separated from the original circulating text of 1944 by sixty years.
These 2004 holograph revisions, preserved in Bradbury's carbon copy (S2) and
also in a subsequent faxed amanuensis typescript prepared by Bradbury's daughter Alexandra in 2004 (TS3 and an accompanying faxed fragment), are recorded
in the Bradbury Center's collation files; the substantive variants appear in the
present volume's Historical Collation. Any editorial substantives introduced by
successive editors of *DD*, *MF*, and *PB* also appear in the Historical Collation.

As early as 1947, Bradbury was aware that editor, author, critic, and friend An-
thony Boucher had commented, perhaps in jest, on his apparent "back-to-the-
womb" complex in such stories as his single-page graveyard horror "Interim,"
(in *DC*), and his far more accomplished tale "The Small Assassin." But the Reincarnate's climb out of the grave, his slow recovery of awareness and motor skills,
and his almost crafty ability to mimic breathing and swallowing, all prefigure
William Lantry, dark protagonist of "Pillar of Fire" (1947; published 1948), one of
Bradbury's best cultural and literary cautions against the death of the imagination. Although unpolished and, in places, lacking consistency of narrative, the
early version of "The Reincarnate" presented here provides a long-neglected link
in Bradbury's maturing ability to explore the unstable boundaries between life
and death, and the thin thread by which supernatural literature survives in an
increasingly technological age of wonders.

Sources: Author's composition and submission log (1942–45); Schwartz to
Bradbury, June 20, July 4, and Aug. 5, 1944; Eller, *Becoming Ray Bradbury*, 56.
Eller and Touponce, 91.

—JE

## Textual Notes

47.14 Bradbury's use of "earth" references burial ground, not the planet Earth
    itself; his preference for lower-case is therefore retained throughout.

58.26 or the illusion of breath] Even in this unrevised version, there is evidence
    late in the story that Bradbury realized the need to show that Paul's apparent
    breathing was just an illusion in his mind. Speech requires breath, however,

and Bradbury did not remove the other references to breathing elsewhere in this early draft of the story.

## Emendations

[title] The Reincarnate] CE; The Reincarnate | by | Ray Bradbury TS1

*47.14 earth's] DD; earths TS1

48.12 tying posts] CE; typing posts TS1

48.15 its] TS4; its' TS1

48.30 eyes] TS2; eye TS1

49.7 friend's] DD; friends TS1

49.14 volumes] TS4; volumnes TS1

50.5 them] MF; the TS1

50.30 sheltered] MF; shelthered TS1

50.30 Fourth] MF; Forth TS1

51.2 Boston-baked] MF; Bosten-baked TS1

51.5 This] TS4; this TS1

51.54 heart's] MF; hearts' TS1

51.38 focused] MF; focussed TS1 *Also* 54.16

51.39 does] MF; do TS1

52.2 triumphant] MF; triumpahtn TS1

52.10 at] MF; as TS1

53.26 gaiety] MF; gayety TS1 *Also* 53.32

55.9 food?] CE; ~. TS1

55.12 it?] CE; it. TS1

55.14 How to describe] CE; How describe TS1

56.3 stretches] MF; stetches TS1

57.40 knives] MF; knifes TS1

58.1 Your ears] MF; You ears TS1

58.1 blocked] MF; blocced TS1

58.5 things] MF; thing TS1

58.11 decimate] MF; dessimate TS1

59.8 breathe] MF; breath TS1

59.11 Your huge] MF; You huge TS1

59.40 *not present*] DD; THE END TS1

## Historical Collation: Post-Copy-Text Substantives

[title] "The Reincarnate" | by | Ray Bradbury] TS1, TS2; THE REINCARNATE | Bradbury TS3; "The Reincarnate" TS4; THE REINCARNATE | RAY BRADBURY DD; the reincarnate MF; The Reincarnate PB[2010]; THE REINCARNATE PB[2011]

47.1 awhile] TS1; a while DD

47.1 the inferiority complex. Maybe.] TS1; being afraid TS2, TS4, DD

47.2 can do . . . at night.] TS1; can, just be careful to walk at night. TS2, TS4, *DD*

47.2–3 hot sun . . . particularly helpful.] TS1; sun is terrible. summer nights are no help. TS2, TS4, *DD*

47.3–4 So the best . . . chilly weather.] TS1; You must wait for cold weather. TS2, TS4, *DD*

47.5 The seventh] TS1; In the seventh *DD*

47.5–6 and the maggots will begin. By the end of] TS1; with dissolution. In TS2, TS4, *DD*

47.6 dwindle] TS1; fade TS2, TS4, *DD*

47.7 lie exhausted and weeping] TS1; lie weeping TS2, TS4, *DD*

47.9–11 thought about, . . . skull fall away.] TS1; finished. Many likes and dislikes must be turned in your mind before your mind melts. TS2, TS4, *DD*

47.12 born again.] TS1; re-born TS2, TS4 reborn *DD*

47.12–13 womb is silk-lined and fine smelling] TS1; birthplace is silk-lined and smelling TS2, TS4, *DD*

*◊47.14 earths] TS1; earth's *DD* Earth's *MF*

47.14 Your womb] TS1; This place TS2, TS4, *DD*

47.16 mother soil] TS1; carth TS2, TS4, *DD*

47.16 And there] TS1; There TS2, TS4, *DD*

47.17 an emotional hand to slap you on the back] TS1; an anger to slap you awake TS2, TS4, *DD*

47.18–24 an emotion. Then the . . . forth to] TS1; a need. Then you quiver and rise to strike your head against ◆silken [satin-lined TS4, *DD*] wood. Life calls you. You grow with it, You claw upward, slowly, and find ways to displace earth an ◆inch, [inch at a time TS4, *DD*] and one night you crumble the darkness, the exit is complete, and you burst forth to TS2, TS4, *DD*

47.25–29 lead you as a slender antenna . . . told:] TS1; burn you. You take a step, like a child, stagger, clutch for support—and find a marble slab. Beneath your fingers the carved story of your life is briefly told: TS2, TS4, *DD*

47.30–48.1 wood. Learning . . . on, outward] TS1; wood, trying to walk. You go outward TS2, TS4, *DD*

48.2 sidewalks, past brick walls, down stony paths.] TS1; sidewalks. TS2, TS4, *DD*

48.3–6 You feel . . . there is undone.] TS1; You feel something is left undone. Some flower yet unseen somewhere you must see, some lake waiting for you to swim, some wine untouched. You are going, somewhere, to finish whatever stays undone. TS2, TS4, *DD*

48.7 All the] TS1; The TS2, TS4, *DD*

48.8 a sort of dream town] TS1; a dream TS2, TS4, *DD*

48.8 become] TS1; grow TS2, TS4, *DD*

48.9 walking now, and can go] TS1; ◆walking. You [walking, you TS4, *DD*] go TS2, TS4, *DD*

48.10–17 You know every . . . machine-gun] TS1; You know every lawn of this street, every place where asphalt bubbled from cement cracks in the oven weather. You know where the horses were tethered sweating in the green spring at these iron water fonts so long ago it is a fading mist in your brain. This cross street, where a light hangs like a bright spider spinning light across darkness. You excape ◆◆its' [its TS4, *DD*] [it's *MF*] web into syca-more shadows. A picket fence sounds under your fingers. Here, as a child, you rushed by with a stick raising a machine-gun TS2, TS4, *DD*

48.18 memories of people] TS1, TS2; memories TS2, TS4, *DD*

48.19–25 there, remember? . . . mute agony.] TS1; here, a lady with withered hands who gave you a withered lecture on trampling her petunias. Now she is completely withered like an ancient paper burned. TS2, TS4, *DD*

48.26–27 for the walking . . . one another.] TS1; for ◆sound [the sound TS4, *DD*] of someone walking. You turn a corner and unexpectedly collide with a stranger. TS2, TS4, *DD*

◊48.30–33 The stranger's eye . . . you before."] TS1; The stranger's eyes are deep-seated fires. He is tall, thin and wears a dark suit. There is fiery whiteness in his cheekbones. ◆he [He TS4, *DD*] smiles. "You're a new one," he says. TS2, TS4, *DD*

48.34–35 And you . . . his differentness.] TS1; ◆you [You TS4, *DD*] know then *what* he is. He is walking, 'different' like yourself. TS2, TS4, *DD*

48.36 asks, politely.] TS1; asks. TS2, TS4, *DD*

48.37–38 time to talk," . . . step aside."] TS1; time," you say. "I am going *some-where.* ◆step [Step TS4, *DD*] aside." TS2, TS4, *DD*

48.39 holds onto] TS1; holds TS2, TS4, *DD*

48.39 *what*] TS1; what *MF*

48.40 closer] TS1; close TS2, TS4, *DD*

48.40 are of the same legion? The dead who walk. We] TS1; are the same? We TS2, TS4, *DD*

48.41–49.1 brothers." ⁋ You fidget impatiently. "I] TS1; brothers." ⁋ "I TS2, TS4, *DD*

49.2 and neither] TS1; nor TS2, TS4, *DD*

49.3 but cannot lose him, for he] TS1; but he TS2, TS4, *DD*

49.5 "Do you?"] TS1; "Yes?" TS2, TS4, *DD*

49.6–9 says, casually. . . . light and dark.] TS1; says. "To some ◆child-hood [childhood TS4, *DD*] place. Some river. ◆some [Some TS4, *DD*] house. ◆some [Some TS4, *DD*] memory. ◆some [Some TS4, *DD*] woman, perhaps. To some old ◆friends [friend's *DD*, *MF*] bed. Oh, I know, I know everything about our kind. I ◆know," he [know." He TS4, *DD*] nods at the passing light and dark. TS2, TS4, *DD*

49.10 "You know, do you?"] TS1; "◆do [Do TS4, *DD*] you?" TS2, TS4, *DD*

49.11–15 the dead . . . a house] TS1; we lost ◆ones [one's *DD*] walk. Strange, when you consider all the books written about ♦ghost [ghosts TS4, *DD*] and lost walkers, and never once did the authors of those worthy ♦volumnes [volumes TS4, *DD, MF*] touch the true secret of ♦why the we [why we TS4, *DD*] walk. ♦But Always [But its always TS4, *DD*] for—a memory, a friend, a woman, a house TS2, TS4, *DD*

49.18 paces you:] TS1; follows: TS2, TS4, *DD*

49.19–20 later this . . . our victory."] TS1; later, friend. We will meet with the others, tonight, tomorrow and all the nights until at last, we ♦win! [win!" TS4, *DD*] TS2, TS4, *DD*

49.21 Hastily. "Who] TS1; "Who TS2, TS4, *DD*

49.22–23 "The other . . . intolerance."] TS1; "The dead. ♦ "We [^We TS4, *DD*] join against" a pause, ♦ "intolerance: ["intolerance." TS4] TS2, TS4, *DD*

49.25–27 "We are . . . declares heatedly.] TS1; "We newly dead and newly interred, are a minority, a persecuted minority. They make laws against us! TS2, TS4, *DD*

49.28 The concrete slows under your heels.] TS1; You stop walking. TS2, TS4, *DD*

49.29–41 takes your . . . others?"] TS1; grasps your arm. "Are we wanted? No! Feared! ♦driven [Driven TS4, *DD*] like sheep into a quarry, screamed at, stoned like the Jews. ♦wrong [Wrong TS4, *DD*], I tell you, unfair!" He lifts his hands in a fury and strikes down. "Fair, fair, is it fair? Fair that we, in our graves while the rest of the world sings, laughs, dances, Fair, is it fair, they love while we lie cold, that they touch while our hands become stone, No! I say down with them, down! ♦ "Why [^Why TS4, *DD*] should we ♦die, why [die? Why TS4, *DD*] not the others?" TS2, TS4, *DD*

50.1 "Perhaps you are right."] TS1; "Maybe . . ." TS2, TS4, *DD*

50.2–7 "They throw . . . that right?"] TS1; "They slam the earth in our faces and carve a stone to weigh us, and shove flowers in an old tin and bury it once a a ♦year. [year! TS4, *DD*] Sometimes not that! Oh, how I hate the living. The fools. The damn fools! Dancing all night and loving, while we are ♦abandoned! [abandoned. TS4, *DD*] Is that right?" TS2, TS4, *DD*

◊50.5 hate the,] TS1; hate them *MF*

50.8 thought about it," you say, vaguely.] TS1; thought." TS2, TS4, *DD*

50.9 snorts, "well, we'll] TS1; cries, "we'll TS2, TS4, *DD*

50.10 "What will you do?"] TS1; "How?" TS2, TS4, *DD*

50.11–19 us gathering . . . will come?"] TS1; us tonight in the Elysian grove. I lead! We will kill! ♦"They [^They TS4, *DD*] have neglected us too long, If we can't live, then ♦won't! [they won't! TS4, *DD*] And you will come, friend?" I have spoken with many. ♦Come help. Join [Join TS4, *DD*] us. The graveyards will open tonight and the ♦lost ones [Lost Ones TS4, *DD*] pour out to drown the ♦♦world. [[*underlined blank space*] TS4] [unbelievers *DD*] You will come?" TS2, TS4, *DD*

50.20–21 "I don't . . . I will come."] TS1; ♦Yes ["Yes TS4, *DD*]. Perhaps. "But I must go. I must find some place ahead. I will join you." TS2, TS4, *DD*

50.22 says, as you] TS1; says. You TS2, TS4, *DD*

50.23 good.] TS1; ~! TS2, TS4, *DD*

50.26–28 now, as quick . . . in your condition.] TS1; now, quickly. Thank God the night is cold. TS2, TS4, *DD*

50.29–34 gasp happily. . . . hand-rolled cigarette.] TS1; gasp. There, ♦♦how magnificent, [[*underlined blank space*] magnificence, TS4] [glowing in the night, but with simple magnificence, *DD*] the house where Grandma fed her boarders. Where you as a child sat on the porch watching sky rockets climb in fire, the pinwheels sputtering, the ♦♦gun powder [gun-powder TS4] [gunpowder *DD*] drumming at your ears from the brass cannon ♦♦your uncle lit [[*underlined blank space*] TS4] [your uncle Bion fired *DD*] with his hand-rolled cigarette. TS2, TS4, *DD*

50.35–51.4 Now, standing, . . . upon its teeth. . . .] TS1; Now, trembling with memory, you know why the dead walk. To see nights like ♦this when [this. Here, when TS4, *DD*] dew littered the grass, and you crushed the damp lawn wrestling, and you knew the sweetness of now, now, tomorrow is gone, yesterday is done, tonight ♦live! [lives! *DD*] ¶ Inside that grand tall house Saturday feasts ♦happened, [happen! TS4, *DD*] TS2, TS4, *DD*

◊51.2 Bosten-baked] TS1; Boston-baked *MF*

◊51.5 here, here, man, remember? this] TS1; here, here, remember? ♦this [This TS4, *DD*] TS2, TS4, *DD*

51.6–9 room. Do you . . . her again!] TS1; room. TS4, *DD*

51.10–14 walk. You think . . . see again?] TS1; walk. TS4, *DD*

51.15–17 Your breath . . . ¶ As] TS1; You approach her window and feel your breath falling upon the cold glass. As TS4, *DD*

51.17 form] TS1; shape TS4, *DD*

51.17–20 emerges. The pink . . . You wait.] TS1; emerges: Things spread on the little soft bed, the cherry wood floor brightly waxed, and throw-rugs like heavily furred dogs sleeping there. TS4, *DD*

51.21 comes into] TS1; enters TS4, *DD*

51.22–24 Her hair . . . her figure.] TS1; She looks tired, but she sits and begins to comb her hair. TS4, *DD*

51.25–26 shell of glass, and as from deep under a sea you hear a song. She sings] TS1; ♦pain [pane *DD*], and as from a deep-sea you hear her sing TS4, *DD*

51.26–30 leaves her mouth. . . . cold thunder!] TS1; is sung. TS4, *DD*

◊51.29 hearts'] TS1; heart's *MF*

51.31 Thoughtless, you tap upon the window.] TS1; You tap on the windowpane. TS4, *DD*

51.32 on stroking] TS1; on, combing TS4, *DD*

51.32–33 gently, thinking that you are only the autumn wind outside the glass.] TS1; gently. TS4, *DD*

51.34 anxiously, a bit afraid.] TS1; anxiously. TS4, *DD*

51.35 sets] TS1; puts TS4, *DD*

51.35–36 investigate, calm and certain.] TS1; come to the window. TS4, *DD*

51.37–38 nothing. You are . . . she looks *through*.] TS1; nothing; you are in shadow. Then she looks more closely. TS4, *DD*

◊51.38 focussed] TS1; focused *Also* 54.16 *MF*

◊51.39 light. She still do not recognize.] TS1; light. TS4, *DD*

◊51.39 do not] TS1; does not *MF*

51.40 You] TS1; ◆you [You *DD*] TS4, *DD*

51.40 "It is I! I am here!"] TS1; It's me! Kim!" TS4, *DD*

52.1–7 Your eager face . . . bolt of power!] TS1; You push your face forward into the light. Her face pales. She does not cry out; only her eyes are wide and her mouth opens as if somewhere a terrific lightning bolt in a sudden storm had hit the earth. She pulls back slightly. TS4, *DD*

◊52.2 triumpahtn] TS1; triumphant *MF*

52.8 "It is I!"] TS1; "Kim." TS4, *DD*

52.9 name. She forms it with a numb mouth. Neither of you can] TS1; name, but you can't TS4, *DD*

◊52.10 run, but instead, as your insistence, she pulls up the window] TS1; run but instead she moves the window up TS4, *DD*

◊52.10 as your] TS1; at your *MF*

52.11 you climb upward] TS1; stands back as you climb in and TS4, *DD*

52.11 slam] TS1; close TS4, *DD*

52.12 crucified by fear against the wall.] TS1; her face half-turned away. TS4, *DD*

52.13–23 You sob . . . forest, Kim. . . ."] TS1; You try to think of something to say, but cannot, and then you hear her crying. ¶ At last she is able to speak. TS4, *DD*

52.24 breathes, not believing it.] TS1; says. TS4, *DD*

52.25–27 I saw the lid . . . here now—"] TS1; When you went away I cried. I never cried so much in my life. But now you can't be here." TS4, *DD*

52.28–32 I *am* here!" . . . metamorphosis—"] TS1; "I am!" TS4, *DD*

52.33 "Why, why, why] TS1; "But why? I don't understand," she said. "Why TS4, *DD*

52.34–35 "I was lost . . . in my dream.] TS1; "I was lost. I was very dark and I started to dream; I don't know how. And there in the dream you were and I don't know how, but TS4, *DD*

52.35–36 back, somehow."] TS1; back." TS4, *DD*

52.37 "But you] TS1; "You TS4, *DD*

52.38 "Until daybreak."] TS1; "Until sunrise. I still love you." TS4, *DD*

52.39–53.15 "Paul, don't take . . . But, but—"] TS1; "Don't say that. You mustn't, anymore. I belong here and you belong there, and right now I'm terribly afraid. A long time ago we had a lot of things to love, a lot of things we did together. The things we did, the things we joked and laughed about, those things I still love, but—" TS4, *DD*

53.16 thoughts and] TS1; thoughts. I TS4, *DD*

53.16 Kim!"] TS1; Kim. Please try to understand." TS4, *DD*

◊53.17–32 "But we are . . . rapid, pitiable gayety:] TS1; "You don't want pity, do you?" ⸮ "Pity?" You half turn away. "No, I don't want that. Kim, listen to me. I could come visit every night, we could talk just like we used to. It would be like a year ago. Maybe if we kept talking you would understand and you'd let me take you on long walks or at least be a little bit closer." TS4, *DD*

◊53.26 gayety] TS1; gaiety *Also* 53.32 *MF*

53.33 use."] TS1; use," she said. "We can't be closer." TS4, *DD*

53.34–35 "Kim! One . . . That's all."] TS1; "Kim, one hour every evening, or half an hour, any time you say. Five minutes. Just to see you. That's all, that's all." TS4, *DD*

53.36–38 You bury your . . . tightly closed,] TS1; You try to take her hands. She pulls away. ⸮ She closes her eyes tightly TS4, *DD*

53.38–39 simply: ⸮ "I am afraid."] TS1; simply, "I'm afraid." TS4, *DD*

53.41 afraid, that's all."] TS1; afraid." TS4, *DD*

54.1–5 "Damn the people a . . . stop it, Kim!"] TS1; "Is that it?" ⸮ "Yes, I guess that's it." ⸮ "But I want to talk." ⸮ "Talking won't help." TS4, *DD*

54.6–7 like movements on a disturbed water pool calming and relaxing.] TS1; and she becomes more calm and relaxed. TS4, *DD*

54.7 upon] TS1; on the edge of TS4, *DD*

54.7 old] TS1; very old TS4, *DD*

54.8–13 "All right, darling." . . . won't be afraid."] TS1; "Perhaps," a pause, "maybe. I suppose a few minutes each night and maybe I'd get used to you and maybe I wouldn't be afraid." ⸮ "Anything you say. Tomorrow night, then? You won't be afraid?" TS4, *DD*

54.14–16 "Oh, no." . . . must feel.] TS1; "I'll try not." She has trouble breathing. "I won't be afraid. TS4, *DD*

54.17–18 I'll have to make an excuse to mother and dad to get out past them."] TS1; Let me get myself together and we can say goodnight. Go to the window, step out, and look back." TS4, *DD*

54.19–23 You raise the . . . out the time.] TS1; "Kim, there's only one thing to remember: I love you." ⸮ And now you're outside and she shuts the window. ⸮ Standing there in the dark you weep with something deeper than sorrow. ⸮ You walk away from the house. TS4, *DD*

54.24–27 street, past a . . . He goes] TS1; street a man walks alone and you recall he's the one that talked to you earlier that night. He is lost and walking like you, alone, in a world that he hardly knows. He moves TS4, *DD*

54.28 Kim is beside you now.] TS1; And suddenly Kim is beside you. TS4, *DD*

54.31–33 An ice-cream . . . spoon poised.] TS1; She turns you in at an ice cream parlor and you sit at the counter and order ice cream. ⁋ You sit and look down at the sundae and think how wonderful, it's been so long. TS4, *DD*

54.34(1) You] TS1; You pick up your spoon, then you TS4, *DD*

54.34–35 mouth, sucking . . . embers down.] TS1; mouth and then pause and feel the light in your face go out. TS4, *DD*

54.35 back, removed.] TS1; back. TS4, *DD*

54.36–37 "What's wrong?" . . . you, concerned.] TS1; "Something wrong?" the soda clerk behind the fountain says. TS4, *DD*

54.40 "No. It's] TS1; "No, it's TS4, *DD*

54.41–55.2 "Fly in it?" . . . eating it?"] TS1; "You ain't eating," he says. TS4, *DD*

55.2 tain't] TS1; ain't *MF*

55.3 "I don't want to."] TS1; "No." TS4, *DD*

55.3 it] TS1; the ice cream TS4, *DD*

55.3–4 and your lump . . . "I am sick] TS1; and feel a terrible loneliness move in your body. TS4, *DD*

55.4(2) I] TS1; ⁋ "I TS4, *DD*

55.5 hungry. I can't eat."] TS1; hungry." TS4, *DD*

55.8 ahead into] TS1; at TS4, *DD*

55.8–16 them that your . . . a cold pit?] TS1; her that you can't swallow, can't eat? How can you explain that your whole body seems to become solid and that nothing moves, nothing can be tasted. TS4, *DD*

55.17 Rising, you have no coin in your hand, and Kim pays, and together] TS1; Pushing back, you rise and wait for Kim to pay for the sundaes and then TS4, *DD*

55.17 swing] TS1; wing *MF*

55.18 stars.] TS1; night. TS4, *DD*

55.20 right. I understand,"] TS1; right," TS4, *DD*

55.20–22 Taking your arm, . . . it is lost.] TS1; You walk down toward the park. You feel her hand on your arm, a long way off, but the feeling is so soft that it is hardly there. TS4, *DD*

55.23 It now moves] TS1; You move TS4, *DD*

55.23 below you,] TS1; in something like TS4, *DD*

55.24–25 Just to be . . . Lilacs in bloom."] TS1; Kim says, "Isn't that great? Smell. Lilac." TS4, *DD*

55.26–27 You test the . . . is no use.] TS1; You touch the air but there is nothing. Panicked, you try again, but no lilac. TS4, *DD*

55.28 pass you] TS1; pass TS4, *DD*

55.28 dark, and as they] TS1; dark. They TS4, *DD*

55.28–29 nodding to Kim and you, as they gain distance behind,] TS1; smiling to Kim. As they move away TS4, *DD*

55.29 comments,] TS1; says, TS4, *DD*

55.30–38 "—Don't you . . . screaming from you.] TS1; "Smell that? Something rotten in Denmark." ¶ "What?" ¶ "I don't see—" ¶ "No!" Kim cries. And suddenly, at the sound of those voices, she bursts away and runs. TS4, *DD*

55.39 Wordless, you struggle against her.] TS1; Silently you struggle TS4, *DD*

55.39–41 She twists, . . . run away.] TS1; You can hardly feel her fists. ¶ "Kim!" you cry. "Don't. TS4, *DD*

55.41–56.8 afraid." ¶ Her . . . out in whispers:] TS1; afraid." TS4, *DD*

◊56.3 stetches] TS1; stretches *MF*

56.9–10 "Let go . . . do that."] TS1; "Let go!" she cries. "Let go." ¶ "I can't." TS4, *DD*

56.11 Again the wordless, dark movement of bodies and arms.] TS1; Again the word was ◆ *[underlined blank space]*. ["Can't." *DD*] TS4, *DD*

56.12 hangs limply] TS1; hangs, lightly TS4, *DD*

56.12 trembles very deeply] TS1; trembles. ¶ TS4, *DD*

56.13 teeth chattering.] TS1; shivering. TS4, *DD*

56.13 "I want you, Kim. Don't] TS1; "Kim, don't TS4, *DD*

56.13 had] TS1; have TS4, *DD*

56.14–20 To go to . . . or—or—"] TS1; Travel, anywhere, just travel. Listen to me. Think. To have the best food, to see the best places, to drink the best wine." TS4, *DD*

56.21 Kim speaks.] TS1; Kim interrupts. You see her mouth move. TS4, *DD*

56.22 "What did you say?"] TS1; "What?" TS4, *DD*

56.24 "Speak louder," . . . hear you."] TS1; ◆ "Louder," ["Louder?" *DD*] you ask. "I can't hear." TS4, *DD*

56.24–25 speaks and you cry out, bending near. And] TS1; speaks, her mouth moves, but] TS4, *DD*

56.25 nothing at first, and] TS1; nothing. ¶ And TS4, *DD*

56.26 behind a thick cotton wall, her voice] TS1; as from behind a wall, a voice TS4, *DD*

56.27 "Paul, it's] TS1; "It's TS4, *DD*

56.27 see? You understand now?"] TS1; see?" TS4, *DD*

56.28–32 You release her. . . . not feel it.] TS1; You let her go. ¶ "I wanted to see the light, flowers, trees, anything. I wanted to be able to touch you but, Oh God, first, there, with the ice cream I tasted, it was all gone. And now I feel like I can't move I can hardly hear your voice, Kim. A wind passed by in the night, but you hardly feel it." TS4, *DD*

56.33–57.5 "Paul, this is . . . I want life!"] TS1; "Listen," she said. "This isn't the way. It takes more than wanting things to have them. If we can't talk or hear or feel or even taste, what is there left for you or for me?" ¶ "I can still see you and I remember the way you were." ¶ "That's not enough, there's got to be more than that." ¶ "It's unfair. God, I want to live!" TS4, *DD*

57.6 "You will live, Paul,] TS1; "You will, TS4, *DD*

57.6–7 that. But not . . . half a year,] TS1; that, but not like this. You've been gone six months TS4, *DD*

57.7–8 in another month—"] TS1; soon." TS4, *DD*

57.9 are] TS1; turn TS4, *DD*

57.9 shoulders,] TS1; wrist TS4, *DD*

57.10 soft, moving] TS1; moving TS4, *DD*

57.11 Our child. *Our* child.] TS1; *Our* child. TS4, *DD*

57.12 back. You are] TS1; back, you're TS4, *DD*

57.12–14 Paul. You are . . . best, eventually.] TS1; you'll always be alive. Now turn around and go back. Believe, everything will work out. Let me have a better memory than this terrible night with you. TS4, *DD*

57.16–18 You cannot even . . . at Kim, and] TS1; In this moment you cannot even weep; your eyes are dry. You hold her wrists tightly and then suddenly, TS4, *DD*

57.19–20 Bending over her, . . . Quick. The shock."] TS1; You hear her whisper, "The hospital. Yes, I think the hospital. Quick." TS4, *DD*

57.21–24 You walk down . . . hear the word.] TS1; You carry her down the street. A fog fills your left eye and you realize that soon you will be blind. It's all so unfair. ¶ "Hurry," she whispers. "Hurry." TS4, *DD*

57.25 stumbling. A car passes. You shout at it.] TS1; stumbling. ¶ A car passes and you shout. TS4, *DD*

57.26–27 and the man . . . toward the hospital.] TS1; are in the car with a stranger, roaring silently through the night. TS4, *DD*

57.28–30 In the middle . . . for you somewhere."] TS1; And in the wild traveling you hear her repeat that she believes in the future and that you must leave soon. TS4, *DD*

57.31–34 Your left eye . . . she to you!] TS1; At last you arrive, but by then you're almost completely blind and Kim has gone; the hospital attendant rushed her away without a goodbye. TS4, *DD*

57.34 outside,] TS1; outside the hospital, TS4, *DD*

57.34–58.5 and then turn . . . try to capture.] TS1; then turn and try to walk away. The world blurs. ¶ Then you walk, finally, in half-darkness, trying to see people, trying to smell any lilacs that still might be out there. TS4, *DD*

◊57.40 knifes] TS1; knives *MF*

◊58.1 You ears] TS1; Your ears *MF*

◊58.1 blocced] TS1; blocked *MF*

◊58.5 thing] TS1; things *MF*

58.6–25 Sour-sick, an . . . the persecuted swine."] TS1; *om.* TS2; You find your-self moving down a ravine past the park. The walkers are there, the night walkers that gather. Remember what that man said? All those lost ones, all those lonely ones are forming tonight to move over the earth and destroy those who do not understand them. ⁋ The ravine path rushes under you. You fall, pick yourself up, and fall again. ⁋ The stranger, the walker, stands before you as you walk toward the silent creek. You look and there is no one else anywhere in the dark. ⁋ The strange leader cries out angrily, "They did not come! Not one of those walkers, not one! Just you. Oh, the cowards, damn them, the damn cowards!" TS4, *DD*

◊58.11 dessimate] TS1; decimate *MF*

58.26–30 His words . . . understand, yet."] TS1; "I'm glad they didn't listen. There must be some reason. Perhaps—" it. . perhaps something happened to them that we can't understand." TS2, TS4, *DD*

58.31–35 The Leader . . . tired—"] TS1; The ◆Leader [leader *DD*] shakes his head. I had plans. But I am alone. Even if all the lonely ones should rise, they are not strong. One blow and they fall. We grow tired. *I* am tired—" TS2, TS4, *DD*

58.36–38 behind you. His . . . mute purpose.] TS1; behind. His whispers die. The pulse beats in your head. You walk from the ravine, and into the grave-yard. TS2, TS4, *DD*

58.39–59.3 grave-stone . . . darkness.] TS1; ◆grave-stone [gravestone TS4]. The raw earth awaits you. You slide down the small tunnel into satin and wood, no lon-ger afraid, or excited. You lie suspended in warm darkness. TS2, TS4, *DD*

59.3 can actually] TS1; ◆cann [can *DD*] actually TS4, *DD*

59.4–7 sustenance, of . . . of moves.] TS1; sustenance, like a great yeast, being washed away by a whispering tide. TS2, TS4, *DD*

59.8–10 The coffin is . . . moves.] TS1; You breathe quietly, not hungry, not wor-ried. You are deeply loved. You are secure. This place where you are dream-ing shifts, moves. TS2, TS4, *DD*

◊59.11–12 You huge . . . singing tide.] TS1; ◆You [Your *DD*] body is melting, it is small, compact, weightless. Drowsy. TS2, TS4, *DD*

◊59.11 You huge] TS1; Your huge *MF*

59.14–17 plays at . . . Quiet contraction.] TS1; moves out to sea. You run to fetch, the waves take it away. Someone beautiful. Someone. A time, a place. Sleepy. ◆darkness [Darkness TS4, *DD*], warmth. Soundless earth. Dim tide. Quiet. TS2, TS4, *DD*

59.18–19 A river of . . . faster, faster] TS1; A dark river bears you ◆of faster [faster TS4, *DD*] TS2, TS4, *DD*

59.20–21 an open-ness and are suspended upside down in brilliant yellow light!] TS1; the open. You are suspended in hot yellow ◆light! [light. TS4, *DD*] TS2, TS4, *DD*

59.22–24 new white . . . out of you.] TS1; snow mountain. The sun blazes and a
huge red hand seizes your feet as another hand strikes your back to force a
cry from you. TS2, TS4, *DD*

59.25–28 below, tired; . . . breast.] TS1; ◆near; wetness [near. Wetness TS4, *DD*]
beads her face, and there is a wild singing and a sharp wonder to this room
and this world. You cry out upside-down, and are swung right side up, cuddled and nursed. TS2, TS4, *DD*

59.29–30 Amid your . . . over and over:] TS1; In your small hunger, you forget
talking, you forget all things. Her voice, above, ◆whispers. [whispers: TS4,
*DD*] TS2, TS4, *DD*

59.31 "My little new born baby. I will name you Paul, for] TS1; "Dear baby. I will
name you for TS2, TS4, *DD*

59.32–39 you do not . . . *Kim!*"] TS1; are nothing. Once you feared something
terrifying and black, but ◆now. It [now it TS4, *DD*] is forgotten in this
warmth and feeding content. A name forms in your mouth, you try to say
it, not knowing what it means, it, only able to cry it happily. The word vanishes fades an erased ghost of laughter ◆in the your [in your TS4, *DD*] head:
§ "*Kim! Kim! Oh, Kim!*" TS2, TS4, *DD*

◊59.40 THE END] TS1; *om. DD, MF*


## 7. Chrysalis (June 1944)

This story is distinct from Bradbury's older story "Chrysalis" (volume 1, selection 11), a very fine science fiction tale that followed the usual path through
Bradbury's surviving files of genre submissions and sales. But Bradbury's second "Chrysalis," a very personal story of interracial friendship in a world of
intolerance, was meant from the start to reach the broader literary market. His
author's notecard story files include a double-sided card of submissions made
directly by Bradbury to a wide range of periodicals; beneath the first entry is
the overstruck date of composition, June 1944. His composition and submission log sheets show that it first went out to the *Prairie Schooner* literary magazine on July 28; this entry is cancelled in pencil, replaced later in the log by this
October 1944 update: "CHRYSALIS (quality) OCTOBER 19th (TOMORROW)
rejected on October 30th."

The notecard record, however, dramatically conveys just how difficult it was
to place a story about race in the mid-1940s. Bradbury's self-submissions without benefit of a slick-market agent, and even the fact that he had not yet broken
out of the genre magazines, only made the challenge more difficult. His notecard
file records the following three-year history of disappointment, differing slightly
from the log entries: *Tomorrow* (July 1944); *Prairie Schooner* (August 1944);
*The Atlantic Monthly* (Aug. 31, 1945); *American Mercury* (Dec. 1945); *Harper's*

*Monthly* (Jan. 1, 1946); *Atlantic Monthly* rewrite (February 5, 1946); *Project X*, a cancelled magazine venture by Marshall Fields (April 27, 1946); *The Kenyon Review* (June 10, 1946; rejected July 1); *Harper's Bazaar* (July 9, 1946; rejected July 29); *Esquire* (Aug. 12, 1946); *Town and Country* (October 13, 1946); *Charm* (October 28, 1946); *Story* (Dec. 3, 1946); *Partisan Review* (Jan. 9, 1947); *'47* (Feb. 11, 1947); *Ladies Home Journal* (Mar. 11, 1947); and *McCall's* (Apr. 24, 1947).

This odyssey of submissions played out as Bradbury came to know and trust Don Congdon, an editor at *Collier's* and later Simon & Schuster before joining the Harold Matson Agency in New York. On August 20, 1947, just a month before formally signing Congdon as his new literary agent, Bradbury sent him the well-travelled (and at least once-revised) typescript of "Chrysalis." Congdon managed a very successful record of sales for Bradbury from the beginning, but there is no indication that "Chrysalis" drew any further interest. Meanwhile, Bradbury would write a half-dozen unfinished stories about racial intolerance, usually from the minority perspective, but the lack of interest in "Chrysalis" discouraged Bradbury from really finishing or marketing these other tales. Even the stories of race that he himself placed in *The Martian Chronicles* ("Way in the Middle of the Air") and *The Illustrated Man* ("The Other Foot") failed to find magazine markets in America prior to book publication.

The story languished in Bradbury's inactive files until early in the twenty-first century, when Bradbury's friend and principal bibliographer Donn Albright convinced him to submit "Chrysalis" for his 2004 story collection *The Cat's Pajamas* (*CP*). There were many older stories in the collection, some never before published, and his editor, Morrow's editor-in-chief Jennifer Brehl, agreed to include "Chrysalis" as well. The story was subsequently included in a limited Press expanded edition of *Cat's Pajamas* (*CP+4*), edited by Brehl's husband, veteran editor Peter Schneider.

"Chrysalis" is based on Bradbury's extensive time on Santa Monica Beach and Ocean Pier, which he frequented often between 1934 and 1950, from the age of thirteen until he was nearly thirty. The beach areas were segregated, but Bradbury occasionally met black athletes playing volleyball with white players, and he learned that sunburn is a greater danger to the less reflective pigmentation of black sunbathers. As he noted in a 2004 private interview, ". . . that was a revelation to me. And at the end of summer I was peeling my own skin off. I was taking off my 'darkness,' and bringing out the 'white.' And of course the black person couldn't peel off his sunburn." The metaphor of the chrysalis-like skin transformations became the central metaphor of this rich and understated story.

TS1 and TS2 are, for the most part, carbon copies of the same typescript. The *Cat's Pajamas* version is based on TS2, which appears to date from the post-revision period of circulation in 1946–47. TS1 opens with a page from an earlier unlocated typescript, where the black sunbather Walter was originally

Henry, a name associated with a blind black man who was a friend of Bradbury's during the period (1942–45) that he kept a writing room in a downtown
Los Angeles tenement. Bradbury grafted this page (designated TSπ) onto page
two of the other surviving carbon (TS1), and bridged the narrative by cancel-
ling overlapping passages to form the earliest surviving form of "Chrysalis."
The TSπ / TS1 structure contains Bradbury's earliest known intentions for the
story, and serves as copy-text for the present edition. The minimal and isolated
emendations required to complete Bradbury's intended bridging of the two
stages are fully described in the textual notes below.

The racially-charged language in this story serves to present Bradbury's
strong criticism of racism and intolerance at a time when political and social
movements were still reluctant to explore these issues publically in America; his
usage here, as in his better-known *Martian Chronicles* story-chapter "Way in
the Middle of the Air," conveys a story that is meant to hit hard at de jure racism
at a particular time in American history, and is retained in the present edition.

Sources: Author's composition and submission log (1942–45); author's notecard story file (c. 1943–1975); Eller, *Becoming Ray Bradbury,* 233–35; Bradbury–
Eller interviews, 2004.

—JE

## Textual Notes

60.1–9 Walter looked . . . bare feet.] The TSπ Henry/Walter opening probably
   pre-dates the long TS2 opening and its recounting of Walter's obsession with
   chemical bleaching of his skin (see Historical Collation). As TSπ opens,
   Henry / Walter has internalized his desire to blend into the white man's world,
   suggested only by the countless white grains of sand falling over his bare feet.

60.16–22 Walter looked . . . whiten and dry.] The early TSπ opening page (originally Henry instead of Walter) was bridged into the continuous intermediate draft of TS1 after the drowning reverie. This TSπ reverie superseded a
   similar passage at the top of TS1 (unnumbered page 2), where the two fragments were bridged; the superseded passage in TS2 was marked through by
   the kind of vertical broad-stroke (crayon) arrows used by Bradbury during
   these years. The superseded description of Walter's drowning reverie appears in the Historical Collation below.

60.30 copper wire hair.] Following this sentence, TS2 continued with a slightly revised variant of a sentence in the TSπ opening paragraph ("As he
   looked . . . lightly together."). In bridging TSπ onto page 2 of TS1, he removed
   (by arrowed deletions on TS1) most of the doubled passages, thus giving priority to the TSπ fragment that opens this earliest surviving version of "Chrysalis." The doubled sentence in TS1 is deleted by emendation to complete
   Bradbury's intention for the TSπ / TS1 bridge.

61.28 Walter] At this point, the variant openings of TSπ / TS1 and TS2 merge into the word-for-word collatable carbons of a single typescript.

66.25–37 Where the summer . . . said Bill.] Much of TS2 is a top carbon of TS1, but at this point Bradbury revised the transition from this magical summer to the realities of fall. The TS2 transition (recorded in the Historical Collation) is more somber, and changes Bill's autumn destination from the San Diego shipyard to Chicago.

## Emendations

*60.1 Walter] CE; Henry TSπ *Also* 60.7, 60.16

60.10 boardwalk] *CP*; board walk TSπ

*60.30 copper-wire hair.] CE; Copper-wire hair. As he looked at the sea, his eyes moved in soft starts and stops and wonderings, his thumbs and forefingers rubbed lightly together. TS1

61.16 goddamn] CE; godamn TS1

61.30 boardwalk] *CP*; board-walk TS1

62.12 boardwalk] *CP*; board walk TS1

62.13 pedaled] *CP*; peddled TS1

65.31 hot dogs] *CP*; hot-dogs TS1 *Also* 65.40, 66.10

66.7 hot dog] *CP*; hot-dog TS1 *Also* 66.11

67.23 *not present*] CE; THE END TS1

## Historical Collation: Post-Copy-Text Substantives

*[title]* CHRYSALIS] TSπ; CHRY*a*LIS *CP*

*◊60.1–61.27 Henry looked . . . out at Walter.] TS1; Long after midnight he arose and looked at the bottles fresh from their cartons, and put his hands up to touch them and strike a match gently to read the white labels, while his folks slept unaware in the next room. Below the hill on which their house stood the sea rolled in and while whispering the magic names of the lotions to himself he could hear the tides washing the rocks and the sand. The names lay easy on his tongue: ◆MEMPHIS WHITE OIL, Guaranteed, Tennessee Lotion Salve. Higgen's BLEACH? BONE WHITE SOAP, [*MEMPHIS WHITE OIL, GUARANTEED, TENNESSEE LOTION SALVE . . . HIGGEN's BLEACH BONE WHITE SOAP—CP*] the names that were like sunlight burning away dark, like water bleaching linens. He would uncork them and sniff them and pour a little on his hands and rub them together and hold his hand in matchlight to see how soon he would have hands like white cotton gloves. When nothing happened, he consoled himself that perhaps tomorrow night, or the next, and back in bed he would lie with his eyes upon the bottles, racked like giant green glass beetles above him, glinting in the faint ◆streetlight. [streetlight. ¶ Why am I doing this? he thought. Why? *CP*] ¶

"Walter?" That was his mother calling softly, far away. ❡ "Yes'm?" ❡ "You awake, Walter?" ❡ "Yes'm." ❡ "You better go to sleep," she said. ❡ In the morning he went down for his first view, close up, of the constant sea. It was a wonder to him, for he had never seen one. They came from a little town deep in Alabama, all dust and heat, with dry creeks and mudholes, but no river no lake nearby, nothing much at all unless you traveled, and this was the first traveling they had done, coming to California in a dented Ford, singing quietly along the way. Just before starting the trip Walter had finished out a year's time saving his money and sent off for the twelve bottles of magical lotion ◆which [that *CP*] had arrived only the day before they left. So he had had to pack them into cartons and carry them across the meadows and deserts of the states, secretly trying one or the other of them in shanties and rest rooms along the way. He had sat up front in the car, his head back, his eyes closed, taking the sun, lotion on his face, waiting to be bleached as white as milkstone. "I can see it," he said, each night, to himself. "Just a little bit." ❡ "Walter," said his mother. "What's that smell? What you wearing?" ❡ "Nothing, mom, nothing." ❡ Nothing? He walked in the sand and stopped by the green waters and pulled one of the flasks from his pocket and let a thin twine of whitish fluid coil upon his palm before he smoothed it over his face and arms. He would lie like a raven by the sea all day today and let the sun burn away his darkness. Maybe he would plow into the waves and let them churn him, as a washing machine churns a dark rag, and let it spit him out on the sand, gasping to dry and bake in the sun until he lay there like the ◆long gaunt skeleton of some prehistoric mammal, chalk-white and gleaming [thin skeleton of some old beast, chalk-white *CP*] and fresh and clean. ❡ ◆GUARANTEED [*GUARANTEED CP*] said the red letters on the bottle. The word flamed in his mind. ◆GUARANTEED! [*GUARANTEED! CP*] ❡ "Walter," his mother would say, shocked. "What happened to you? Is that *you*, son? Why you're like milk, son, you're like snow!" ◆❡ His mother and father would dance happily for him, swinging him around, touching him and not believing the miracle. [*om. CP*] ❡ It was hot. Walter eased himself down against the board walk and took off his shoes. Behind him, a hot dog stand sent up shimmers of fried air, the smell of onions and hot rolls and frankfurters. A man with a grained, ropy face looked out at Walter and Walter nodded shyly, looking away. A moment later a wicket gate slammed and Walter heard the blunt footsteps approaching The man stood looking down at Walter, a silver spatula in one hand, a cook's cap on his head, greasy and grey. ❡ "You better get along," he said. ❡ "I beg your pardon, sir?" ❡ "I said the ◆nigger's [niggers' *CP*] beach is down there." The man tilted his head in that direction without looking that way. looking only at Walter. "I don't want you standing around in front of my place." ❡ Walter blinked up at the man, surprised. "But this is California," he said. ¶ "You tryin to get tough with me, nigger?" asked the man. ¶ "No, sir, I just said this ain't the South, sir." ¶ "Nigger, anywhere where I am is South," said the man, and walked back into his hot dog stand to slap some burgers on the griddle and stamp them flat with his spatula, glaring out at Walter. TS2, *CP*

61.32 white boys] TS1; whites *CP*

61.34 dark] TS1; brown TS2, *CP*

61.39–62.11 About ten . . . head, slow.] TS1; *om.* TS2, *CP*

62.12 On the third day,] TS1; *om. CP*

◊62.13 peddled] TS1; pedaled *CP*

62.18 Walter smiled] TS1; Walter walked closer, smiled *CP*

62.20 The white boy] TS1; The boy *CP*

62.22 day," said the boy.] TS1; day." *CP*

62.28 white boy] TS1; boy *CP*

62.28–31 this week. Wait'll . . . is that why,"] TS1; today. ¶ "End of the season," said Walter carefully. ¶ "Yeah. School started a week ago." ¶ A pause. Walter said, "You graduate?" ¶ "Last June. Been working all summer; didn't have time to get down to the beach." ¶ "Making up for lost time?" ¶ "Yeah. Don't know if I can pick up much tan in two weeks, though. Got to go to Chicago October first." ¶ "Oh, TS2, *CP*

62.37–40 soft and shining . . . asked Walter.] TS1; softly, shining. ¶ "You like the beach?" asked Walter. TS2, *CP*

62.41 last summer] TS1; summer before last TS2, *CP*

63.2 a—"] TS1; a nig——" TS2, *CP*

63.9 white-washed stomach] TS1; stomach TS2, *CP*

63.21–22 rain-rubbers] TS1; tan rain-rubbers TS2, *CP*

63.22 Rain-rubbers] TS1; Tan rain-rubbers TS2, *CP*

63.24–25 know colored people got sunburned."] TS1; know." *CP*

63.28 comprehend it.] TS1; comprehend TS2, *CP*

63.28 I'm a nut.] TS1; *om. CP*

63.31 He got up, then.] TS1; He rose. *CP*

64.1 dark boy] TS1; boy *CP*

64.5–6 and hid] TS1; and eagerly hid TS2, *CP*

64.7 Georgia] TS1; Alabama *CP*

64.10 sure] TS1; *sure* TS2, *CP*

64.13 shaking down] TS1; down TS2, *CP*

64.16 black] TS1; brown TS2, *CP*

64.25 great cry, and turned upon his pillow, burying his face. . . .] TS1; great sigh, and buried his face in his pillow. *CP*

64.31 the passing] TS1; this dying TS2, *CP*

64.33 Summer] TS1; Autumn TS2, *CP*

64.40 More white . . . for them.] TS1; On Saturday and Sunday, more white
  boys appeared. TS2, *CP*

65.1 plunged them] TS1; had plunged them all TS2, *CP*

65.16 snatzy.] TS1; snazzy. *CP*

65.26 "Here, take] TS1; "Take *CP*

65.27 reluctantly] TS1; with reluctance TS2, *CP*

65.40 twisted] TS1; turned TS2, *CP*

65.40 some] TS1; those TS2, *CP*

65.42 "No. I] TS1; "I TS2, *CP*

66.1 Bill argued awhile, then quieted, with white lines around his hard mouth.]
  TS1; *om. CP*

66.2 "Okay, anything you say. Damn it. I'll get the dogs myself.] TS1; "Okay.
  Damn it. I'll get the dogs *CP*

66.2 stay] TS1; wait TS2, *CP*

66.3 the counter] TS1; the shadowy counter TS2, *CP*

66.4 and vividly] TS1; *om. CP*

66.5–6 It stood in . . . years after.] TS1; *om. CP*

66.7–8 shouted, bitterly: ⁋ "God-damn you, nigger! You back here again!"]
  TS1; shouted, "Damn you, blackie! You here again!" *CP*

◊66.10 counter into the steam of the hot-dogs.] TS1; counter, waiting. *CP*

66.11 "Oh, well,] TS1; "well, *CP*

66.11–13 Just sort of . . . that goddamn nigger.] TS1; There's a glare from the
  water—you looked just like— *CP*

66.14 Bill leaned across the counter, siezed the man's arm.] TS1; Bill seized the
  man's elbow. *CP*

66.14 it.] TS1; ~? TS2, *CP*

66.14 blacker] TS1; darker *CP*

66.15 Why you kissing *my* big toe?] TS1; Why are you kissing *my* butt? *CP*

66.16 "I tell you, Bill,] TS1; "Hey, Bill, *CP*

66.18 hell!" said Bill.] TS1; hell!" *CP*

66.19 He came] TS1; Bill came *CP*

*66.25–37 Where the summer . . . said Bill.] TS1; The two weeks ended. Au-
  tumn came. There was a cold salt fog for two days and Walter thought he'd
  never see Bill again. He walked down along the boardwalk, alone. It was
  very quiet. No horns honking. The wooden frontings of the final and last
  hot dog stand had been slammed down and nailed fast, and a great lonely
  wind ran along the chilling grey beach. ⁋ On Tuesday there was a brief bit
  of sunlight and, sure enough, there was Bill, stretched out, all alone on the
  empty beach. ⁋ "Thought I'd come down just one last time," he said, as Walt
  sat down beside him. "Well, I won't see you ◆no more." [again." *CP*] ⁋ Going
  to Chicago?" ⁋ "Yeah. No more sun here, anyway; least not the kind of sun

I like. Better get along East." ¶ "I suppose you better," said Walter. ¶ "It was a good two weeks," said Bill. TS2, *CP*

66.38 year] TS1; two weeks TS2, *CP*

67.1 beginning] TS1; starting TS2, *CP*

67.1 *not present*] TS1; "Wish I'd had time to make it a good permanent one." TS2, *CP*

67.1–2 Peering over . . . damn stuff's] TS1; ◆Peering over He peered over [He peered over *CP*] his shoulder at his back and made some gestures at it with elbows bent, fingers clutching. "Look, Walt, this damn stuff is TS2, *CP*

67.3 off a couple patches of it for me?"] TS1; ◆off a couple of patches of the stuff for me?" [off some of the stuff?" *CP*] TS2

67.7 *not present*] TS1; strip by strip, TS2, *CP*

67.7 off Bill's shoulders,] TS1; off of Bill's muscled back, shoulder-blades TS2, *CP*

67.8 the pearly pink] TS1; the pink *CP*

67.9 realized he] TS1; realized that he TS2, *CP*

67.10 took it] TS1; was accepting it TS2, *CP*

67.10–11 didn't worry about . . . in Walter,] TS1; not worried about it, and a great light shone in Walter instantly. TS2, *CP*

67.14–15 really wasn't] TS1; wasn't really TS2, *CP*

67.15–16 They had both . . . each of them.] TS1; He just thought it was there. TS2, *CP*

67.18 here all June and July and August for this,"] TS1; lying here all July and August for that," TS2, *CP*

67.19 And I] TS1; I TS2, *CP*

67.19 *all my life* and I guess] TS1; all my life and TS2, *CP*

67.21 with himself] TS1; *om.* TS2, *CP*

67.22 "Come on now,] TS1; "Now, TS2, *CP*

◊67.23 THE END] TS1; *om. CP*


## 8. The Poems (July 10, 1944)

In spite of his new-found success in the detective pulps and his established popularity in the pages of *Weird Tales,* Bradbury's relatively uninspired output of stories during the spring of 1944 is evident from the fact that ten of the thirteen stories written between late March and early July failed to sell (see the Chronological Catalog). But his luck turned in July and August 1944, as the next five stories that emerged from his typewriter sold within a year of submission. "The Poems" was the first of these; Bradbury's composition and submission log confirms that he completed a 4,000-word draft on July 10, 1944, with a holograph note "SOLD!" written in his hand. His author sales record confirms the sale to *Weird Tales* and a post-commission payment of $36.75 received from his agent on November 7. Nolan's list of sales by Julius Schwartz confirms a pre-commission payment from *Weird Tales* of $40.00 on November 1, 1944. Bradbury's sales-by-publisher listing confirms the $40.00 payment and first publication in the January 1945 issue of *Weird Tales* (S1). The title art, showing the gifted young poet-protagonist bringing his poems to life, was by A. R. Tilburne; the tailpiece was a John Anderson sketch of a skull, paper, quill pen, and inkwell.

"The Poems" was reset (without title or tailpiece art) and sequenced within a different mix of stories in the March 1945 Canadian issue of *Weird Tales* (S2). But Bradbury withheld this story from his 1947 *Dark Carnival* collection, leaving it among the five *Weird Tales* stories omitted from the collection that showcased what he considered the best of these early genre tales. The story remained relatively inaccessible until 2001, when Bradbury's friend and bibliographer Donn Albright convinced him to include most of the omitted stories in an expanded limited press edition of *Dark Carnival* ($DC^{2001}$). The story reached a wider audience when Bradbury included it in his 2003 hundred-story retrospective, *Bradbury Stories* (*BS*).

*Weird Tales* editor Dorothy MacIlwraith and assistant editor Monty Buchanan, a Bradbury enthusiast who had a good working relationship with Julius Schwartz, had already lined up Bradbury stories for all six 1944 issues of *Weird Tales*, and wanted to see more submissions from their unpredictable and often off-trail young genre star. They had even secured a writer's profile from him for the November issue. But they also wanted Bradbury to give them more traditional horror tales. On September 9, 1944, Schwartz wrote to confirm sale of "The Poems," but also to catechize him: "Buchanan is taking 'The Poems' but warned me (and you) this is the last of the 'arty' type of story. Even the readers are beginning to kick a bit on the type of material you have been turning out, he tells me. He begs—nay, demands—you go back to the formula of your first successes. No children psychology—but good old weird-horror yarns."

On the surface, "The Poems" did, indeed, seem "arty": a young poet whose poems are so powerful that they literally pull his subjects—people, fauna, even panoramic landscapes—into the composition itself, leaving only a shadowland behind. His young wife, a powerful intellect in her own right, sees the danger of such a Romantic-Age ego, and pulls him back from the brink. But in reality, "The Poems" presents a parody of the self-conscious poet; Bradbury had gradually been learning to release his imagination from self-conscious limitations or logical restraints. He had also been writing verse of his own, and he turned to poetry to illustrate the need to allow the Muse to move unhindered by ego. The reader eventually realizes that the poet's wife is the Muse of the story. Bradbury's exploration of the pressures of authorship also anticipates his later celebrations of the author's triumph over literary critics in such early 1950s stories as "The Dwarf" and "The Wonderful Death of Dudley Stone."

Bradbury may have held this story out of *Dark Carnival* because he knew that the poet's descriptions and word choice might be taken as a serious attempt to portray his own powers rather than the intended parody of such writing. The story overflows at times with sentiment, but it's important to remember that Bradbury's own reading of the Romantic Age poets was still expanding; it would not reach full bloom until 1946 and 1947, under the guidance of his future wife Marguerite McClure and his old friend and mentor Edmond Hamilton. His interest in symphonic music was more advanced, and elements of this influence (as well as the influence of C. L. Moore) are detectable in the lyric tone of this tale.

S1 stands as copy-text for the present edition. Eventually he prepared (or had prepared) a typescript (TS) that was included in a grouping of his uncollected stories; given the other titles in this grouping, TS may have been prepared (probably from S1) in the late 1940s or early 1950s. It is close enough to the author's hand to be a source of correction for typing or composing errors in S1, but S2 has priority chronologically and may even have been prepared from S1's setting copy in the Canadian offices.

Sources: Author's sales record (1941–49); author's composition and submission log (1942–45); author's sales-by-publisher indexes (c. Feb. 1943 and c. 1950); Schwartz to Bradbury, Sep. 2 and 9, 1944; Eller-Bradbury interviews, ca. 2002; Moskowitz, 360.

—JE

## Textual Notes

*[title]* The editorial teaser in S1, placed at the foot of the opening page, is a condensation of the description at 68.13–14. The teaser text reads: "The square of paper was a brilliantly sunlit casement through which one might gaze into another and brighter land."

70.29 smelling far oceans tainted on it] Although "tainted" may be an S1 compositor's misreading of "painted," it is more likely that Bradbury intended "tainted" in the obsolete sense of colored, dyed, or stained. The effect is synesthetic, a crossing of senses that Bradbury was never afraid to try in his prose.

74.29 tied to] The S1 reading, "tried to," is almost certainly a compositor's error for "tied to," as corrected in S2 and carried forward into *BS*[2003]. The TS reading "tired of" misses the point of the poet; his creativity has been tied to discrete and localized objects when he desires to paint broad and all-inclusive panoramas, extending eventually to the cosmos itself.

## Emendations

*[title]* The Poems] CE; The Poems | By | RAY BRADBURY S1
68.10 "Damn] S2; ^~ S1
70.10 focused] S2; focussed S1

70.39 It's] S2; Its S1
71.15 shaming] S2; shamming S1
71.34 critics'] TS; ~^ S1
*74.29 tied to] S2; tried to S1
75.40 pen.] S2; ~^ S1
77.15 immortal] TS; importal S1

## Historical Collation: Post-Copy-Text Substantives

*[title]* The Poems | By RAY BRADBURY] S1, S2; THE POEMS | by | Ray Brad-
bury TS; THE POEMS $DC^{2001}$, $BS^{2003}$
◊70.10 focussed] S1; focused S2, $BS^{2003}$
◊71.15 shamming] S1; shaming TS
72.20 was accident] S1; was an accident $DC^{2001}$
72.36 them mention] S1; them a mention $DC^{2001}$
73.8 like it!] S1; like! S2
*◊74.29 tried to] S1; tired of TS; tied to S2, $BS^{2003}$
75.33 heart] S1; heat $DC^{2001}$
76.4 next!" she said.] S1; next!" $DC^{2001}$
◊77.15 importal] S1; immortal TS, $BS^{2003}$

## Line-End Hyphenation

71.21 over-/stepped] over-stepped
71.26 rain-/drop] raindrop
75.21 cart-/wheel] cartwheel

## 9. Defense Mech (July 19, 1944)

This experimental narrative requires the reader to accept a most improbable but entertaining hypnosis-induced defense mechanism as the basis for one of Bradbury's earliest Martian "first contact" stories. Bradbury spent much of the summer and early fall of 1944 writing (and very often selling) a range of detective stories and weird tales, but "Defense Mech" continued his intermittent string of early-career science fiction sales to the reliable second-tier Fiction House pulp magazine *Planet Stories*. Bradbury's composition and submission log includes an entry dating the story to July 19, 1944, indicating as well a length of 4,000 words, a note indicating first submission (by Schwartz) to *Astounding*, and a holograph "SOLD!" between the columns. But that sale did not go to John W. Campbell's first-tier *Astounding*; his author's sales record shows receipt of a post-commission payment of $39.75 from *Planet Stories* on November 1. Nolan's list of sales by Julius Schwartz confirms a sale date October 30, 1944, and a pre-commission payment of $45.00. Bradbury's sales-by-publisher record lists the post-commission payment of $39.75 and publication in the Spring 1946 issue of *Planet Stories*

(S1). His earliest science fiction tales were uneven in quality, and Bradbury never placed any of his early *Planet Stories* appearances (including "Defense Mech") in his story collections. "Defense Mech" never appeared in another magazine or in anthology; S1 is the only surviving form of the text.

For all its oddness, Julius Schwartz was immediately drawn to the tale; neither version has been located, but on August 5, 1944, Schwartz sent an intriguing response: "Your idea is terrific—brand new; one of the best I've come across in years. Which version do I like best? THE FIRST? Why? To me it's more punchy, more alive, more hell-for-leather, more *dreadful* (in feeling). Your second is tamer, more logical, more apologetic . . . maybe even more commercial" (ellipses Schwartz's). Swartz, who had recently been trying to school Bradbury on the best variations in jazz, felt that the first draft was more like Chicago-style jazz: "tougher, more devil-may-care—more 'to hell with the audience, we play the way *we* like!'"

Schwartz knew he was taking a risk sending this story to *Astounding*'s John Campbell, who was a notorious champion of rationally-plotted hard science fiction. Schwartz hedged his bet by sending Campbell *both* versions, but on September 2 he had to tell Bradbury that Campbell found it "a bit too far-fetched," more suitable to Campbell's "Probability Zero" liar's club column for stories that violate fundamental laws of physics. Neither Schwartz nor Bradbury, who had placed two earlier shorts in "Probability Zero," were surprised by Campbell's categorization, and Schwartz next sent "Defense Mech" on to Wilbur Peacock at *Planet Stories*. Unlike the monthly *Astounding, Planet* was a quarterly, and wartime paper rationing slowed down sales for many of the pulps. But on October 21, 1944, Bradbury received word from Schwartz that Peacock had accepted "Defense Mech." The backlog delayed actual publication until the spring 1946 issue, where it appeared with a facing page illustration by Doolin, who had illustrated two of Bradbury's earlier *Planet Stories* appearances.

The writing is unremarkable, but the central conceit of "Defense Mech" continued Bradbury's abiding interest in the human mind, psychology, and hypnotism; in fact, he would soon find that he was highly susceptible to the effects of hypnosis. Within two years of composing "Defense Mech," Bradbury would transfer the power of hypnotically-induced illusions to his Martians in his best-known tale of Martian contact, "Mars Is Heaven!" In a broader sense, his subsequent stories of space travel and alien landscapes often showed the effects of loneliness and alienation that he was sure would accompany the pioneers of space exploration.

Sources: Author's composition and submission log (1942–45); author's sales record (1941–49); author's agency listing (c. 1950); Schwartz to Bradbury, Aug. 5, Sep. 2, and Oct. 21, 1944; Bradbury-Eller interviews, Oct. 2, 2004.

—JE

## Textual Notes

*[title]* The S1 teaser represents a compressed editorial adaptation of Halloway's opening attempts to communicate his panicked thoughts to the captain; it reads: "Halloway stared down at Earth, and his brain tore loose and screamed, Man, how'd you get in a mess like this, in a rocket a million miles past the moon, shooting for Mars and danger and terror and maybe death."

78.7 Captain] Bradbury's intent seems to be to capitalize captain only in direct address, not in other references to him.

80.5–7 Yes, sir, . . . Yow!] This response to the Captain is doubled in S1; the error may have resulted from Bradbury's simultaneous submission of two versions, resulting in a doubling from one or more earlier drafts. It may also be a compositor's setting error. In either case, the doubling was missed by *Planet*'s editors. For the present edition, what appears to be the preliminary version of the paragraph is deleted and recorded in the Emendations list.

## Emendations

*[title]* Defense Mech] CE; DEFENSE MECH | By RAY BRADBURY S1

*78.7 Captain] CE; captain S1 *Also* 79.3, 79.17, 82.31, 84.17, 85.23, 85.30, 86.20

79.27 Earth] CE; earth S1 *Also* 79.28

*80.4–5 uniform." ¶ Yes, sir,] CE; uniform." ¶ Yes, sir. My baseball uniform. Where'd I put it? Over here. Head into, legs into, feet into it. There. Ha, this is great! Pitch her in here, old boy, old boy! *Smack!* Yow! ¶ Yes, sir, S1

80.27 block] CE; bloc S1

82.10 hard,] CE; ~^ S1

82.33 streetcar] CE; street-car S1 *Also* 83.5, 85.19

84.23 it's] CE; its S1 *Also* 86.33

84.26 Side] CE; side S1

86.36 ice-wagon] CE; ice ^ wagon S1

88.7 popcorn] CE; pop-corn S1

88.17 Your] CE; You're S1

## Line-End Hyphenation

81.27 ankle-/cuff] ankle-cuff

82.24 street-/car] streetcar

85.3 upper-/cut] uppercut

88.17 kow-/towing] kowtowing

88.18 earth-/man] earthman

## 10. Mr. Priory Meets Mr. Caldwell (Hell's Half-Hour)
## (Aug. 5, 1944)

Bradbury's third appearance in *New Detective* was as close as he would come to showcasing a conventional, logical crime solver in the detective pulps—Homicide Lieutenant Chris Priory. His composition and submission log confirms that he completed the 3,500-word "Mr. Priory Meets Mr. Caldwell" on August 5, 1944. His subsequent holograph note "SOLD!" appears just after the date. His author's sales record notes the sale to *New Detective,* with a post-commission payment of $45.00 received on September 12 (erroneously entered as July 12). Nolan's listing of sales by Julius Schwartz shows the actual sale date as September 6, 1944 and a pre-commission payment of $50.00. "Mr. Priory Meets Mr. Caldwell" was published under the editorially-imposed title "Hell's Half-Hour" in the March 1945 issue of *New Detective* (S1), with uncredited title art. Nearly four decades later, it joined many of his period detective pulp stories (once again under the imposed title "Hell's Half-Hour") in Dell's 1984 Bradbury collection, *A Memory of Murder* (*MeM*).

Julius Schwartz was greatly encouraged to receive a more or less conventionally plotted detective tale from Bradbury, and on August 20, 1944, he told Bradbury that "Priory promises to be an interesting character and I wonder if it wouldn't make a good series?" Schwartz's submission strategy was based on the editorial personalities at Popular Publications, home to most of the detective pulps during the war years. He sent the more off-trail murder mystery "I'm Not So Dumb!" to Mike Tilden, who had already placed some of Bradbury's peculiar plots in Popular's *Detective Tales* and *Dime Mystery*. Popular's editor-in-chief Alden Norton appreciated Bradbury's talent but stood firm for more orthodox genre tales in the magazines he handled for the syndicate; Schwartz realized the "Mr. Priory Meets Mr. Caldwell" was more in line with Norton's tastes, and immediately submitted the story to him. In spite of rising sales, *Flynn's Detective Fiction* had just been sacrificed to paper rationing so that Popular could continue the syndicate's love romance magazines; but Norton still ran *New Detective,* and on September 9, Schwartz relayed Norton's acceptance and payment for the story; the only casualty would be the title, which became the more pulpy "Hell's Half-Hour" to highlight the central mystery of the tale: Why did it take the murderer a very noisy half-hour to murder a blind man in his boarding house room?

Priory is a keen observer with the intuition to see that the only way the crime could have taken so long and created so much noise (overheard by the bed-ridden owner of the boarding-house) was if both the victim and the murderer were blind. The macabre nature of the solution was pure Bradbury, but his creation of a Holmes-like detective (complete with a narrator-companion detective sergeant) drew on his early love of Conan Doyle's master sleuth. He never wrote another Chris Priory detective tale, but in 1949 he included the story in a package of his better crime stories for anthology or reprint consideration by *Ellery Queen's* Fred Danay. Nothing came of this option, however, and Bradbury retired most of his early ventures into the detective pulps from active circulation.

But Julius Schwartz had not reserved any rights when he sold the crime stories, and four decades later Bradbury could not prevent the current rights holders from marketing *A Memory of Murder* (*MeM*), a 1984 collection of Bradbury's detective tales in a mass-market Dell paperback edition. Bradbury was able to provide a contextualizing introduction explaining that these stories predated his full maturity as a storyteller; although he could not restore his original titles, he was able to make some light revisions to some of the stories. None of the variants in *MeM*'s "Hell's Half-Hour" appear to be authorial. This collection was never reprinted or issued abroad, and remains an elusive Bradbury title.

S1, the sole serial version, stands as copy-text for the present edition. A handful of *MeM* editorial corrections to obvious spelling errors are emended into the present edition, but *MeM*'s editorial house stylings are rejected. Bradbury's intended title is restored by emendation, but the editorially-imposed title appears as a parenthetical subtitle to avoid bibliographical confusion.

Sources: Author's composition and submission log (1942–45); author's sales record (1941–49); author's agency listing (c. 1950); Schwartz to Bradbury, Aug. 20 and Sep. 9, 1944; Eller and Touponce, *Life of Fiction*, 317.

—JE

## Textual Notes

*[title]* The opening teaser in S1, just below title and by-line, is purely editorial: "Each man carries his own darkness with him—black as midnight, long as eternity—find this killer's private night, and you've probed the pit of hell!" The uncredited title art (a skeleton dressed like a blind street-corner beggar standing over the victim) is captioned by a line adapted from the bedridden boarding house matron's answers to Chis Priory's questioning at 91.19: "The little noises began . . . And me lying there not being able to do a thing. . . ." (ellipses editorial).

96.13 gouged his eyes out with merciless fingernails!] The story's closing line in *MeM* becomes "destroyed his eyes with merciless fingernails!" It's unclear whether the *MeM* reading is authorial or an editorial imposition to tone down the gruesomeness. The original reading was certainly more in line with the 1940s detective pulps, and given the different period audience for *MeM,* the possibility of editorial imposition is strong enough to justify retaining Bradbury's original reading.

Emendations

[title] Mr. Priory Meets Mr. Caldwell (Hell's Half-Hour)] CE; HELL'S HALF-
  HOUR | By Ray Bradbury S1

89.28 crescents] *MeM*; Crescents S1

90.39 It's] *MeM*; it's S1

91.25 Like] *MeM*; like S1

91.35 more,] *MeM*; more. S1

92.11 Digging] *MeM*; digging S1

93.26 young,] *MeM*; ~^ S1

93.32 assailant] *MeM*; assailent S1

## Historical Collation: Post-Copy-Text Substantives

[title] HELL'S HALF-HOUR | By Ray Bradbury] S1; Hell's Half Hour *MeM*

90.7 afterwards] S1; afterward *MeM*

91.23 towards] S1; toward *MeM*

◊91.25 like] S1; Like *MeM*

◊92.11 digging] S1; Digging *MeM*

92.25 a while] S1; awhile *MeM*

*96.13 gouged his eyes out with] S1; destroyed his eyes with *MeM*

## 11. "I'm Not So Dumb" (Aug. 8, 1944)

Bradbury occasionally developed somewhat gothic tales around hill people and small-town eccentrics who are not as feeble or limited as they appear to be. "I'm Not So Dumb" was an early attempt to bring such a character into his detective fiction. His composition and submission log shows that he completed a complete 2,500-word complete draft of the story on August 8, 1944, subsequently adding a holograph comment "SOLD!" His author's sales record reveals a sale to *Detective Tales* and a post-commission payment of $27.50 received on October 22, 1944. Both of these author's sources give the original title without the exclamation mark. Nolan's list of Schwartz's sales gives the actual sale date of October 17, 1944, and a pre-commission payment of $31.00. "I'm Not So Dumb!" appeared (with the exclamation added) in the February 1945 issue of *Detective Tales* (S1), with an uncredited, three-quarter page drawing inserted below the teaser and opening lines and above the by-line, which appears just below the corpse. There was no second serial, but the story was eventually collected in the Dell mass-market paperback 1984 anthology of Bradbury's detective tales, *A Memory of Murder* (*MeM*).

Bradbury sent Julius Schwartz "I'm Not So Dumb" (still without the closing exclamation) along with "Mr. Priory Meets Mr. Caldwell" (selection 10) in mid-August, 1944; a carbon of the first page, retained by Bradbury for his records, survives in the Albright Collection and confirms the submission title punctuation. Schwartz favored the originality of the former story, noting that "That 'Dumb' character was wonderful and the ending was not too difficult to guess, but entirely within the mood and purpose of the story." The first-person anecdotal narrator is regarded as the village idiot, but his shrewd deductions mesmerize the sheriff and most of the town worthies like a cobra, leading them to miss the cold-blooded intentions of the narrator himself. Bradbury had created, once again, a most unconventional criminal mind, but the story held together well enough as a gothic back-woods tale that Mike Tilden, who could be counted on to accept more Bradbury submissions than he rejected, bought "I'm Not So Dumb" in October 1944, adding only the suggestively haughty exclamation point to the title.

Bradbury thought enough of the story to include it in a 1949 package of his better detective tales that he prepared for *Ellery Queen*'s Fred Danay, probably for anthology or second serial consideration. Nothing came of this project, but it turned out that such subsidiary rights were not Bradbury's to control. Schwartz had not limited the pulp sales to first serial rights, and nearly four decades later, the rights had been purchased by the editors of the 1984 Dell mass-market paperback collection of Bradbury's detective fiction, *A Memory of Murder* (*MeM*). Bradbury felt that these tales should be left in the past, but he was able to provide a contextualizing introduction and lightly revised some of the stories. All of the *MeM* variants appear to be editorial stylings or corrected spellings.

The surviving opening page typescript carbon fragment of "I'm Not So Dumb" (designated TS) is dated August 9, 1944, the day after Bradbury logged completion of the story; the date is ribbon-struck, indicating that he added the date the following day to document when he sent the actual ribbon copy on to Julius Schwartz in New York. Collation of the TS carbon fragment against the same title and opening lines of S1 (97.1–24) reveals some variation in spelling and punctuation as well as several substantives. Studied as a group, these variants appear to result from styling and other impositions by the *Detective Tales* editors. The TS fragment represents a mature form of the story closer to the author's composing hand than S1, and stands as copy-text for the title and the first 322 words of the story. S1, the earliest known form for the subsequent portions, stands as copy-text for the rest of the story. In spite of the necessity of a split copy-text, very few emendations are required. S1 is a source of emendation for a few obvious spelling and punctuation errors in the TS fragment, and *MeM* is a source of emendation for two similar errors in S1. The resolution of a few problematic substantive variants are discussed in the textual notes below.

Peter, the chillingly clever narrator, is an early example of what Bradbury would sometimes present as "the fool who knows." The setting and protagonist are similar to those found in Bradbury's enduring horror tale "The Jar" (volume 2, selection 25); the big city equivalent would be the diminutive detective "Douser" Mulligan of "Enter—The Douser" (volume 2, selection 22) and this volume's "The Very Bewildered Corpses" (selection 5).

Sources: Author's composition and submission log (1942–45); author's sales record (1941–49); author's agency listing (c. 1950); Schwartz to Bradbury, Aug. 20, Oct. 12 and 24, 1944; Mogen, 150.

—JE

## Textual Notes

*[title]* The teaser, which also augments the large illustration, is anchored in the second section's opening paragraph (99.16–19), but is largely editorial in construction: "They made me stand on one foot with my arms in the air if I wanted to hang around while they examined the dead man . . . But this time I knew more than they did—not only who was dead, but who was going to be!" The actual caption, in small type, reads: "'Well,' I said, 'he's dead.'"

97.19 you should . . . you would] The referent "Peter" closes this sentence, indicating that the narrator is paraphrasing what the townsfolk told him, requiring a momentary shift to the second person in what is generally a first-person narrative; the original TS reading "I should ... I would" is therefore emended to complete Bradbury's intentions for the full passage.

97.24 shore line] The narrator's reference to an old Boy Scout fool's errand for Tenderfoot Scouts resolves, in context, as two words as emended here.

100.27 cold man] Context indicates that Bradbury intended cold man, referring to the cooling state of the corpse, rather than old man; the copy-text reading is retained.

100.29 phitted] The *MeM* reading "fightin'" attempts to retain dialect, but it changes the intended equivalent word; "phitted" equates more closely to the simple past tense "fought." The *MeM* reading would appear to be an editorial imposition rather than authorial revision, which in any case would reflect a far later intention for the story. The S1 copy-text reading is retained.

101.35 Irritate] *MeM*'s editorial styling of the parallel construction in this paragraph ("started" and "Irritated") degrades the dialect that Bradbury intended for the sheriff; the odd but apparently intentional S1 copy-text reading is retained.

## Emendations

97.2 Sherrif's] S1; sheriff's TS
97.7 Simmons's] *MeM*; Simmons TS
97.11 Sheriff] S1; sheriff TS *Also* 97.13, 97.22
97.14 it,] S1; it^ TS

*97.19 you should] CE; I would TS; *om.* S1
*97.19 you would] S1; I would TS
*97.24 shore line] S1; shoreline TS
100.11 damn] *MeM*; damn' S1
100.17–18 (1, 2) Simmons's] *MeM*; Simmons' S1 *Also* 101.19

## Historical Collation: Post-Copy-Text Substantives

◊97.7 Simmons'] S1; Simmons's *MeM Also* 100.17–18 (1, 2), 101.19
97.8 was larkspur,] S1; was a larkspur, *MeM*
97.11 Then, and *only then,*] TS; *Only then* S1
97.18 like an Italian labor crew] TS; like a labor crew S1
*◊97.19 I should go away, I] TS; go away, you S1
97.22 lied] TS; was lying S1
97.23 any more,] TS1; not any more S1
98.35 chuckling. ^ "Sure,] S1; ~. ¶ "~, *MeM*
98.37 Sheriff!"] S1; Sheriff!" said Jamie. *MeM*
100.8 Must of] S1; Must've *MeM*
*100.29 phitted] S1; fightin' *MeM*
101.34 you in] S1; you up *MeM*
*101.35 Irritate] S1; Irritated *MeM*

## 12. Invisible Boy (Aug. 11–Sept. 14, 1944)

"Invisible Boy," was the second of Bradbury's three breakthrough stories to sell to a major market magazine during late August and September 1945, and it was the first of this trio to reach print. But the trail from typewriter to the newsstands took fifteen months. Bradbury's composition and submission log shows that he completed a 3,000-word draft of what he initially titled "Old Lady's Invisible Boy" on August 11, 1944, and immediately sent it out to *The Rocky Mountain Review*. That entry is marked out (one of the ways that Bradbury short-handed a rejection), and a new line entered for September 14 giving his settled title ("Invisible Boy") and showing a rejection by *The Southwestern Review*. From the start, Bradbury was targeting this story for the academic creative journals and the major market magazines, and handling the submissions himself.

The Special Submissions list appended to his composition and submission log, as well as his author's notecard file box, reveals that "Invisible Boy" went to Whit Burnett's *Story Magazine* on June 13, 1945, then to *Mademoiselle* on August 2; the range of submissions reflects the recent advice of his friend Grant Beach, who recommended scattershot submissions regardless of readership. His author's sales record notes that he received a direct $300.00 payment from *Mademoiselle* on September 1, 1945. His income tax notes confirm both date and amount, and his author's notecard file shows a subsequent second serialization sale to *Story Digest* on March 5, 1946. "Invisible Boy" finally reached the public in the November 1945 issue of *Mademoiselle* (S1) with a two-page pen-and-ink drawing by Alston; a condensed version subsequently appeared in the November 1946 issue of *Story Digest* (S2), and a full reprint reached British readers in the April 1952 issue of *Argosy* (S3), as "The Invisible Boy."

In 1953 Bradbury's fourth book, Doubleday's *The Golden Apples of the Sun* (*GA*) included an extensively revised version of "Invisible Boy" along with several of his other breakout stories from the mid-1940s. He also selected *GA*'s revised version of this story for his first retrospective collection, the 1965 trade paperback *The Vintage Bradbury* (*VB*), and *Twice 22* (1966, *T22*). Bradbury also broadened the reach of Doubleday's *S Is for Space* (1966, *SS*) to include the Earthbound "Invisible Boy"; the *SS* stories were subsequently drawn into Bantam's *Classic Stories 2* (1990, *CS2*) and Avon/Morrow's *A Medicine for Melancholy and Other Stories* (1998, *MM&OS*). All of these derive from the *GA* revised version, varying, for the most part, only in editorial stylings.

"Invisible Boy" has had a robust history in multi-author anthologies, including *Invisible Man* (1960); *40 Best Stories From Mademoiselle* (1960, as "The Invisible Boy"); *Famous Tales of the Fantastic* (1965); *Some Things Fierce and Fatal* (1971); *Author's Choice 2* (1973); *A Chilling Collection* (1980); *Isaac Asimov's Magical Worlds of Fantasy 4: Spells* (1985, U.K. 1988); *Country Ways* (1988); *The Trick of the Tale* (U.K., 1991); and *The Wizard's Den* (2001). Although the story is essentially a realistic tale, Bradbury's enduring cachet as a light horror writer no doubt led to the inclusion of "Invisible Boy" in many of these fantasy and horror volumes. He was not involved in preparing the texts for these anthologies.

Late in life, Bradbury recalled the origin of this story in a private interview: "Once I got the idea of the witch who had no power, and a boy who has power, because he has imagination, then the story wrote itself." Improbably, Bradbury first saw the November 1945 issue of *Charm* with his story during his extensive auto trip through Mexico with Grant Beach, as they collected masks for the Los Angeles Museum; in fact, the payment for "Invisible Boy" and the other two major market sales of August and September 1945 financed that trip. Perhaps even more improbably, a forwarded letter praising "The Invisible Boy" finally caught up with Bradbury in Guadalajara. The wayward note was from Don Congdon, then an editor with Simon & Schuster in New York. Bradbury would soon begin to send stories and novel concepts to Congdon; by 1947, Congdon would become his agent for the rest of the twentieth century, and beyond.

Former colleagues of Congdon's at *Collier's* had tipped him off to the quality stories that Bradbury was now circulating (initially as "William Elliott," a coded homage, Bradbury would later say, to Modernist poets William Carlos Williams and T. S. Eliot). This sale began a long-standing editorial friendship with *Made-*

*moiselle*'s Rita Smith, a friend of Congdon's who would publish three Bradbury stories before the end of the 1940s. Bradbury was now a known quantity among publishers and editors beyond the pulp market, and "Invisible Boy" was in the vanguard of his major market success. In some ways "Invisible Boy" shared the adolescent tone and excitement of "becoming" found in "The Miracles of Jamie" (selection 3), also one of the three breakthrough sales of late summer 1945. Although "The Big Black and White Game" had preceded these three as his first major market sale, it was written much later than the other three. In preceding both "The Miracles of Jamie" and "One Timeless Spring" into the pages of a major market "slick" magazine, "Invisible Boy" stood as a sign of things to come.

S1, the original serial version of "Invisible Boy," serves as copy-text. It has not been available for readers since 1945, and captures Bradbury's seldom-seen early intention for this story. His extensive 1953 revisions for *GA* reached into almost every sentence, carefully reshaping the nuance and descriptions of every passage without changing the sequence or actions of the story at all. Compared to the readily accessible *GA* version available in various Bradbury collections today, the original S1 text shows a rapidly evolving fiction talent in the act of becoming a master storyteller. The S1 text requires almost no emendation; the hundreds of substantive variations introduced in *GA* are recorded below in the Historical Collation; significant *GA* variants are discussed in the textual notes.

Sources: Author's composition and submission log and 1945 appendix of special submissions (1942–45); author's sales record (1941–49); income tax notes (1945); author's expanded sales-by-publisher index (c. 1950); author's notecard story file (c. 1943–1975); Eller-Bradbury interviews, Oct. 8, 2004; Eller, *Becoming Ray Bradbury*, 127; Johnson, 19.

—JE

## Textual Notes

105.7 beating warm and shrieking] Bradbury retained this odd phrasing as he revised for *GA* in 1953. The captured bat's frantic movement centers on the beating action of its wings.

105.12–13 Gumming her excitement] This facial movement suggests that Old Lady is toothless. Bradbury retained this reading in *GA*, but Argosy's London editors altered the verb to "Suppressing."

108.2 He felt secret power, security, pleased with his invisibility.] In his *GA* revisions, Bradbury presented a more gradual and intuitive change in the invisible boy, rather than a pre-existing and hard sense of power: "Perhaps he felt the growing of a secret power, perhaps he felt secure from the world, certainly he was *pleased* with his invisibility."

## Emendations

*[title]* Invisible Boy] CE; invisible boy | A short story by Ray Bradbury S1

## Historical Collation: Post-Copy-Text Substantives

*[title]* invisible boy | A short story by Ray Bradbury] S1; INVISIBLE BOY |
    by RAY BRADBURY S3; ɪɴᴠɪsɪʙʟᴇ ʙᴏʏ GA; Invisible Boy VB, SS, SRB,
    MM&OS; INVISIBLE BOY T22, CS2; *Invisible Boy* SRB$^{1983}$, RBS1

103.1–4 Old Lady beat . . . thrown a stone.] S1; She took the great iron spoon and
    ♦the mummified [mummified SRB$^{1983}$] frog and gave it a bash and made dust
    of it, and talked to the dust while she ground it in her stony fists quickly. Her
    beady gray bird-eyes flickered at the cabin. Each time she looked, a head in
    the small thin window ducked as if she'd fired off a shotgun. GA, VB, T22, SS,
    SRB, SRB$^{1983}$, CS2, MM&OS, RBS1

103.5 "Charlie!"] S1; "~," S3

103.5 a magic] S1; a lizard magic GA$^{1953a}$, VB, T22, SS, SRB, SRB$^{1983}$, CS2,
    MM&OS, RBS1

103.6 that door; you] S1; that rusty door! You GA$^{1953a}$, VB, T22, SS, SRB, SRB$^{1983}$,
    CS2, MM&OS, RBS1

103.6 won't use it!"] S1; won't make the earth shake or the trees go up in fire or the
    sun set at high noon!" GA$^{1953a}$, VB, T22, SS, SRB, SRB$^{1983}$, CS2, MM&OS, RBS1

103.7–8 mountain sun on . . . trunk, the ants] S1; mountain light on the high
    turpentine trees, a tufted squirrel chittering around and around on a green-
    furred log, the ants GA$^{1953a}$, VB, T22, SS, SRB, SRB$^{1983}$, CS2, MM&OS, RBS1

103.10 been in] S1; been starving in GA$^{1953a}$, VB, T22, SS, SRB, SRB$^{1983}$, CS2,
    MM&OS, RBS1

103.10 ringing] S1; chiming GA$^{1953a}$, VB, T22, SS, SRB, SRB$^{1983}$, CS2, MM&OS, RBS1

103.11 at her waist to swing] S1; to swing at her waist GA$^{1953a}$, VB, T22, SS, SRB,
    SRB$^{1983}$, CS2, MM&OS, RBS1

103.11–12 Sweating sour,] S1; Sweating, S3

103.12 cabin, bearing the pulverized flesh. "Come] S1; cabin. "Come S3

103.16 other. ^ "Fling this door wide, o lord!" she intoned.] S1; other. ❡ "Fling
    this door wide, o lord!" she intoned! S3; other. "O Lord," she intoned, "fling
    this door wide!" GA$^{1953a}$, VB, T22, SS, SRB, SRB$^{1983}$, CS2, MM&OS, RBS1

103.17 another pinch and waited.] S1; another philter and held her breath.
    GA$^{1953a}$, VB, T22, SS, SRB, SRB$^{1983}$, CS2, MM&OS, RBS1

103.18 wonders] S1; darkness GA$^{1953a}$, VB, T22, SS, SRB, SRB$^{1983}$, CS2, MM&OS,
    RBS1

103.19 other charms] S1; scaly monsters GA$^{1953a}$, VB, T22, SS, SRB, SRB$^{1983}$, CS2,
    MM&OS, RBS1

103.19 like the frog which] S1; any charm finer than the frog GA$^{1953a}$, VB, T22,
    SS, SRB, SRB$^{1983}$, CS2, MM&OS, RBS1

103.21 gone] S1; pranced GA¹⁹⁵³ᵃ, VB, T22, SS, SRB, SRB¹⁹⁸³, CS2, MM&OS, RBS1

103.22 most] S1; almost S3

103.27 tromped] S1; ◆trampled [tramped SRB¹⁹⁸³] S3

103.28 crunch cricket] S1; cricket S3

103.30–31 heading home.] S1; heading for home. GA¹⁹⁵³ᵃ, VB, T22, SS, SRB, SRB¹⁹⁸³, CS2, MM&OS, RBS1

104.2 holed up] S1; hid himself away S3

104.3 whammed] S1; banged S3

104.6 there?"] S1; *there?"* GA¹⁹⁵³ᵃ, VB, T22, SS, SRB, SRB¹⁹⁸³, CS2, MM&OS, RBS1

104.8 finally] S1; firmly SRB¹⁹⁸³

104.9 wrestled the] S1; wrestled with the S3

104.10 wrong?] S1; ~. GA¹⁹⁵³ᵃ, VB, T22, SS, SRB, SRB¹⁹⁸³, CS2, MM&OS, RBS1

104.15 spunks] S1; blues S3

104.16 yourself,] S1; myself, GA¹⁹⁵³ᵃ, VB, T22, SS, SRB, SRB¹⁹⁸³, CS2, MM&OS, RBS1

104.16 company!"] S1; ~." GA¹⁹⁵³ᵃ, VB, T22, SS, SRB, SRB¹⁹⁸³, CS2, MM&OS, RBS1

104.16 smackered] S1; smacked S3, GA¹⁹⁵³ᵃ, VB, T22, SS, SRB, SRB¹⁹⁸³, CS2, MM&OS, RBS1

104.17 Charles] S1; Charlie SRB¹⁹⁸³

104.17 I] S1; I'll S3

104.18 suspicioned.] S1; countered suspiciously. S3

104.20 There."] S1; ~!" GA¹⁹⁵³ᵃ, VB, T22, SS, SRB, SRB¹⁹⁸³, CS2, MM&OS, RBS1

104.26 a white] S1; white S3

104.32–33 tambourine. ¶ The Knob] S1; ~. ^ ~~ S3

105.2 demanded.] S1; said. GA¹⁹⁵³ᵃ, VB, T22, SS, SRB, SRB¹⁹⁸³, CS2, MM&OS, RBS1

105.3 find] S1; catch GA¹⁹⁵³ᵃ, VB, T22, SS, SRB, SRB¹⁹⁸³, CS2, MM&OS, RBS1

105.3 "You find one!"] S1; "Start lookin'!" GA¹⁹⁵³ᵃ, VB, T22, SS, SRB, SRB¹⁹⁸³, CS2, MM&OS, RBS1

105.4–5 She watched him . . . and snail tracks.] S1; She gave him some jerky beef for his hunger and watched him climb a tree. He went high up and high up and it was nice seeing him there and it was nice having him here and all about after so many years alone with nothing to say good morning to but bird droppings and silvery snail tracks. GA¹⁹⁵³ᵃ, VB, T22, SS, SRB, SRB¹⁹⁸³, CS2, MM&OS, RBS1

105.6 wing came fluttering] S1; wing fluttered GA¹⁹⁵³ᵃ, VB, T22, SS, SRB, SRB¹⁹⁸³, CS2, MM&OS, RBS1

105.7 picked] S1; snatched GA¹⁹⁵³ᵃ, VB, T22, SS, SRB, SRB¹⁹⁸³, CS2, MM&OS, RBS1

105.7 sharp] S1; porcelain GA¹⁹⁵³ᵃ, VB, T22, SS, SRB, SRB¹⁹⁸³, CS2, MM&OS, RBS1

105.11 needles,] S1; cones, GA¹⁹⁵³ᵃ, VB, T22, SS, SRB, SRB¹⁹⁸³, CS2, MM&OS, RBS1

*105.12 Gumming] S1; Suppressing S3

105.13 sighted] S1; held S3

105.13 the needle] S1; the cold needle $GA^{1953a}$, *VB, T22, SS, SRB, SRB*$^{1983}$*, CS2, MM&OS, RBS1*

105.15 effort,] S1; perspirations and salts and sulphurs, $GA^{1953a}$, *VB, T22, SS, SRB, SRB*$^{1983}$*, CS2, MM&OS, RBS1*

105.15–16 She always hoped] S1; But she had always dreamt $GA^{1953a}$, *VB, T22, SS, SRB, SRB*$^{1983}$*, CS2, MM&OS, RBS1*

105.16–18 which would prove . . . except Old Lady.] S1; might spring up in crimson flowers and silver stars to prove that God had forgiven her for her pink body and her pink thoughts and her warm body and her warm thoughts as a young miss. But so far God had made no sign and said no word, but nobody knew this except Old Lady. $GA^{1953a}$, *VB, T22, SS, SRB, SRB*$^{1983}$*, CS2, MM&OS, RBS1*

105.19 asked of Charlie,] S1; asked Charlie, $GA^{1953a}$, *VB, T22, SS, SRB, SRB*$^{1983}$*, CS2, MM&OS, RBS1*

105.20 making] S1; showing his S3

105.20–21 "I'm ready," he said, shivering.] S1; "Ready," he whispered, shivering. $GA^{1953a}$, *VB, T22, SS, SRB, SRB*$^{1983}$*, CS2, MM&OS, RBS1*

105.22 "So! Like that!"] S1; "So!" $GA^{1953a}$, *VB, T22, SS, SRB, SRB*$^{1983}$*, CS2, MM&OS, RBS1*

105.23 cried] S1; screamed $GA^{1953a}$, *VB, T22, SS, SRB, SRB*$^{1983}$*, CS2, MM&OS, RBS1*

105.23 wadding up] S1; covering S3

105.24 you put] S1; put $GA^{1953a}$, *VB, T22, SS, SRB, SRB*$^{1983}$*, CS2, MM&OS, RBS1*

105.25 on."] S1; ~!" $GA^{1953a}$, *VB, T22, SS, SRB, SRB*$^{1983}$*, CS2, MM&OS, RBS1*

105.27–28 "Charlie! Charlie!" . . . see you, child!"] S1; "Charlie!" she shrieked fearfully. "Charlie, where are you? I can't see you, child!" $GA^{1953a}$, *VB, T22, SS, SRB, SRB*$^{1983}$*, CS2, MM&OS, RBS1*

105.29 so the] S1; so that the S3

105.31–32 watched many butterflies . . . others in flight.] S1; were watching a thousand fireflies crisscrossing each other in the wild night air. $GA^{1953a}$, *VB, T22, SS, SRB, SRB*$^{1983}$*, CS2, MM&OS, RBS1*

105.33 "You went *fast!* . . . Come back, Charlie!"] S1; "Charlie, oh, you sent *fast!* Quick as a hummingbird! Oh, Charlie, come *back* to me!" $GA^{1953a}$, *VB, T22, SS, SRB, SRB*$^{1983}$*, CS2, MM&OS, RBS1*

105.34 here!" He looked scared.] S1; *here!*" he wailed. $GA^{1953a}$, *VB, T22, SS, SRB, SRB*$^{1983}$*, CS2, MM&OS, RBS1*

105.36 "By the fire. . . . I'm *not* invisible!"] S1; "By the fire, the fire! ♦And—and I [And—I *SRB*$^{1983}$] can see myself. I'm not invisible at all!" $GA^{1953a}$, *VB, T22, SS, SRB, SRB*$^{1983}$*, CS2, MM&OS, RBS1*

105.37 yourself.] S1; *you!* $GA^{1953a}$, *VB, T22, SS, SRB, SRB*$^{1983}$*, CS2, MM&OS, RBS1*

105.38 go] S1; get $GA^{1953a}$, *VB, T22, SS, SRB, SRB*$^{1983}$*, CS2, MM&OS, RBS1*

105.39 me, so I know you."]S1; me. Touch me so I *know* you." $GA^{1953a}$, *VB, T22, SS, SRB, SRB*$^{1983}$*, CS2, MM&OS, RBS1*

105.41 jerk at his . . . as if startled.] S1; jerk, startled, at his touch. "Ah!" *GA*[1953a],
*VB*, *T22*, *SS*, *SRB*, *SRB*[1983], *CS2*, *MM&OS*, *RBS1*

106.1 find] S1; *find GA*[1953a], *VB*, *T22*, *SS*, *SRB*, *SRB*[1983], *CS2*, *MM&OS*, *RBS1*

106.2 least half rump] S1; least bit S3

106.3 look at and looked] S1; stare at, and stared *GA*[1953a], *VB*, *T22*, *SS*, *SRB*,
*SRB*[1983], *CS2*, *MM&OS*, *RBS1*

106.3 eyes shining,] S1; shining eyes, *GA*[1953a], *VB*, *T22*, *SS*, *SRB*, *SRB*[1983], *CS2*,
*MM&OS*, *RBS1*

106.4 did a trick that time," she] S1; *did* a trick *that* time!" She *GA*[1953a], *VB*, *T22*,
*SS*, *SRB*, *SRB*[1983], *CS2*, *MM&OS*, *RBS1*

106.5 ever did.] S1; *ever* made! *GA*[1953a], *VB*, *T22*, *SS*, *SRB*, *SRB*[1983], *CS2*,
*MM&OS*, *RBS1*

106.5 How you] S1; How d'you S3

106.5 How you feel, Charlie?"] S1; Charlie, Charlie, how do you *feel?*" *GA*, *VB*,
*T22*, *SS*, *SRB*, *SRB*[1983], *CS2*, *MM&OS*, *RBS1*

106.8 Then she added, after a pause,] S1; Then after a pause she added, *GA*[1953a],
*VB*, *T22*, *SS*, *SRB*, *SRB*[1983], *CS2*, *MM&OS*, *RBS1*

106.11 hell-fire] S1; fire *SS*, *CS2*, *MM&OS*

106.12 winds ∧ In] S1; ~ ⁊ ~ S3

106.21 fetch home] S1; go home S3; fetch yourself home *GA*[1953a], *VB*, *T22*, *SS*,
*SRB*, *SRB*[1983], *CS2*, *MM&OS*, *RBS1*

106.25 that.] S1; it. *GA*[1953a], *VB*, *T22*, *SS*, *SRB*, *SRB*[1983], *CS2*, *MM&OS*, *RBS1*

106.26 felt of his] S1; felt his S3

106.27 telescope,] S1; water glass, *GA*[1953a], *VB*, *T22*, *SS*, *SRB*, *SRB*[1983], *CS2*,
*MM&OS*, *RBS1*

106.29 women—"] S1; *women—*" *GA*[1953a], *VB*, *T22*, *SS*, *SRB*, *SRB*[1983], *CS2*,
*MM&OS*, *RBS1*

106.32 find."] S1; *find!*" *GA*[1953a], *VB*, *T22*, *SS*, *SRB*, *SRB*[1983], *CS2*, *MM&OS*, *RBS1*

106.33–35 "I'll stay invisible, . . . all. Stay out] S1; "Well, I'll stay invisible, anyway, for a spell. I'll have me some fun. I'll just be pretty careful, is all. I'll stay
out *GA*[1953a], *VB*, *T22*, *SS*, *SRB*, *SRB*[1983], *CS2*, *MM&OS*, *RBS1*

106.35 from front] S1; from in front S3, *GA*[1953a], *VB*, *T22*, *SS*, *SRB*, *SRB*[1983], *CS2*,
*MM&OS*, *RBS1*

106.35 least sound] S1; nariest sound *GA*[1953a], *VB*, *T22*, *SS*, *SRB*, *SRB*[1983], *CS2*,
*MM&OS*, *RBS1*

106.36 "Some day Pa'd fill me full of shot,] S1; "Why, with me invisible, some-
day Pa might just up and fill me with buckshot, *GA*[1953a], *VB*, *T22*, *SS*, *SRB*,
*SRB*[1983], *CS2*, *MM&OS*, *RBS1*

106.36 squirrel] S1; hill squirrel *GA*[1953a], *VB*, *T22*, *SS*, *SRB*, *SRB*[1983], *CS2*, *MM&OS*,
*RBS1*

106.38 She] S1; Old Lady *GA*[1953a], *VB*, *T22*, *SS*, *SRB*, *SRB*[1983], *CS2*, *MM&OS*,
*RBS1*

106.39–40 decided, "I'll be . . . tomorrow, Old Lady."] S1; decided slowly, "I'll stay invisible for tonight, and tomorrow you can fix me back whole again, Old Lady." *GA*^1953a, *VB*, *T22*, *SS*, *SRB*, *SRB*^1983, *CS2*, *MM&OS*, *RBS1*

107.1 "If] S1; "Now if *GA*^1953a, *VB*, *T22*, *SS*, *SRB*, *SRB*^1983, *CS2*, *MM&OS*, *RBS1*

107.1 boy,] S1; critter, *GA*^1953a, *VB*, *T22*, *SS*, *SRB*, *SRB*^1983, *CS2*, *MM&OS*, *RBS1*

107.3 asked] S1; said *GA*^1953a, *VB*, *T22*, *SS*, *SRB*, *SRB*^1983, *CS2*, *MM&OS*, *RBS1*

107.4 "Well, it was hard work," explained she, "fixing] S1; "Why," she explained, "it was real hard work, fixing *GA*^1953a, *VB*, *T22*, *SS*, *SRB*, *SRB*^1983, *CS2*, *MM&OS*, *RBS1*

107.4 time] S1; *time* *GA*^1953a, *VB*, *T22*, *SS*, *SRB*, *SRB*^1983, *CS2*, *MM&OS*, *RBS1*

107.6 demanded. "You make me see-able! You did this!"] S1; cried. "You did this to me! Now you make me back, you make me seeable!" *GA*^1953a, *VB*, *T22*, *SS*, *SRB*, *SRB*^1983, *CS2*, *MM&OS*, *RBS1*

107.8 showing?"] S1; ~." *GA*^1953a, *VB*, *T22*, *SS*, *SRB*, *SRB*^1983, *CS2*, *MM&OS*, *RBS1*

107.9 over] S1; on *GA*^1953a, *VB*, *T22*, *SS*, *SRB*, *SRB*^1983, *CS2*, *MM&OS*, *RBS1*

107.9 brambles."] S1; bramble." *GA*^1953a, *VB*, *T22*, *SS*, *SRB*, *SRB*^1983, *CS2*, *MM&OS*, *RBS1*

107.10 showing?] S1; ~! *GA*^1953a, *VB*, *T22*, *SS*, *SRB*, *SRB*^1983, *CS2*, *MM&OS*, *RBS1*

107.11 thicket!"] S1; ~." *GA*^1953a, *VB*, *T22*, *SS*, *SRB*, *SRB*^1983, *CS2*, *MM&OS*, *RBS1*

107.12 floating?"] S1; ~!" *GA*^1953a, *VB*, *T22*, *SS*, *SRB*, *SRB*^1983, *CS2*, *MM&OS*, *RBS1*

107.13 hairy balloon at the Chautauqua!"] S1; floating balloon with hair on!" S3; hairy balloon at the carnival!" *GA*^1953a, *VB*, *T22*, *SS*, *SRB*, *SRB*^1983, *CS2*, *MM&OS*, *RBS1*

107.14 all *whole?*"] S1; *whole?*" *GA*^1953a, *VB*, *T22*, *SS*, *SRB*, *SRB*^1983, *CS2*, *MM&OS*, *RBS1*

107.15 a year.] S1; an entire year. *GA*^1953a, *VB*, *T22*, *SS*, *SRB*, *SRB*^1983, *CS2*, *MM&OS*, *RBS1*

107.16–17 He groaned and . . . to go home."] S1; He groaned. He began to sob and bite his lips and make fists. "You magicked me, you did this, you did this thing to me. Now I won't be able to run home!" *GA*^1953a, *VB*, *T22*, *SS*, *SRB*, *SRB*^1983, *CS2*, *MM&OS*, *RBS1*

107.18 with me, I'll keep you fed well."] S1; stay on with me real comfort-like, and I'll keep you fat and saucy." *GA*^1953a, *VB*, *T22*, *SS*, *SRB*, *SRB*^1983, *CS2*, *MM&OS*, *RBS1*

107.19 at her.] S1; out: *GA*^1953a, *VB*, *T22*, *SS*, *SRB*, *SRB*^1983, *CS2*, *MM&OS*, *RBS1*

107.21 into] S1; through *GA*^1953a, *VB*, *T22*, *SS*, *SRB*, *SRB*^1983, *CS2*, *MM&OS*, *RBS1*

107.21 in an] S1; on the *GA*^1953a, *VB*, *T22*, *SS*, *SRB*, *SRB*^1983, *CS2*, *MM&OS*, *RBS1*

107.23–24 choking, passing swiftly off.] S1; choking cry which passed swiftly off and away. *GA*^1953a, *VB*, *T22*, *SS*, *SRB*, *SRB*^1983, *CS2*, *MM&OS*, *RBS1*

107.25 She kindled herself a] S1; She kindled a S3; She waited and then kindled herself a *GA*^1953a, *VB*, *T22*, *SS*, *SRB*, *SRB*^1983, *CS2*, *MM&OS*, *RBS1*

107.26 "I'll have company] S1; she said, "And now I'll have me my company GA$^{1953a}$, VB, T22, SS, SRB, SRB$^{1983}$, CS2, MM&OS, RBS1

107.26 spring into] S1; spring and into GA$^{1953a}$, VB, T22, SS, SRB, SRB$^{1983}$, CS2, MM&OS, RBS1

107.27 silence] S1; a silence GA$^{1953a}$, VB, T22, SS, SRB, SRB$^{1983}$, CS2, MM&OS, RBS1

107.30 rimed] S1; the rimed GA$^{1953a}$, VB, T22, SS, SRB, SRB$^{1983}$, CS2, MM&OS, RBS1

107.31 scattered] S1; the scattered GA$^{1953a}$, VB, T22, SS, SRB, SRB$^{1983}$, CS2, MM&OS, RBS1

107.32 on pebbles] S1; on some creek pebbles GA$^{1953a}$, VB, T22, SS, SRB, SRB$^{1983}$, CS2, MM&OS, RBS1

107.34 was about?] S1; was anywhere about? GA$^{1953a}$, VB, T22, SS, SRB, SRB$^{1983}$, CS2, MM&OS, RBS1

107.35 face.] S1; cheeks. GA$^{1953a}$, VB, T22, SS, SRB, SRB$^{1983}$, CS2, MM&OS, RBS1

107.36–37 all night, . . . to the dawn:] S1; from one end of the night to the other—Old Lady stood up, grunting and yawning, and turned in a circle to the dawn. GA$^{1953a}$, VB, T22, SS, SRB, SRB$^{1983}$, CS2, MM&OS, RBS1

107.39 to hills.] S1; to the far hills. GA$^{1953a}$, VB, T22, SS, SRB, SRB$^{1983}$, CS2, MM&OS, RBS1

107.39 She called over and over,] S1; She called out his name, over and over again, GA$^{1953a}$, VB, T22, SS, SRB, SRB$^{1983}$, CS2, MM&OS, RBS1

107.40 plumb] S1; straight S3; plumb straight GA$^{1953a}$, VB, T22, SS, SRB, SRB$^{1983}$, CS2, MM&OS, RBS1

107.40 restrained] S1; stopped GA$^{1953a}$, VB, T22, SS, SRB, SRB$^{1983}$, CS2, MM&OS, RBS1

107.40 "Oh Charles?"] S1; "Charlie? Oh, Charles!" she called, and heard the echoes say the very same. GA$^{1953a}$, VB, T22, SS, SRB, SRB$^{1983}$, CS2, MM&OS, RBS1

108.1 sat] S1; sat suddenly VB

108.1 bit, suddenly, knowing] S1; bit, knowing VB

*108.2 He felt secret . . . with his invisibility.] S1; Perhaps he felt the growing of a secret power, perhaps he felt secure from the world, certainly he was *pleased* with his invisibility. GA$^{1953a}$, VB, T22, SS, SRB, SRB$^{1983}$, CS2, MM&OS, RBS1

108.3–4 She said, . . . fix him breakfast."] S1; She said aloud, "Now where *can* that boy be? If he only made a noise so I could tell just where he is, maybe I'd fry him a breakfast." GA$^{1953a}$, VB, T22, SS, SRB, SRB$^{1983}$, CS2, MM&OS, RBS1

108.5 breakfast,] S1; the morning victuals, GA$^{1953a}$, VB, T22, SS, SRB, SRB$^{1983}$, CS2, MM&OS, RBS1

108.5–6 fried bacon on a stick.] S1; sizzled bacon on a hickory stick. GA$^{1953a}$, VB, T22, SS, SRB, SRB$^{1983}$, CS2, MM&OS, RBS1

108.6 nose."] S1; nose," she muttered. GA$^{1953a}$, VB, T22, SS, SRB, SRB$^{1983}$, CS2, MM&OS, RBS1

108.7 it.] S1; it ◆tastily [hastily *GA*¹⁹⁵³ᵇ, *VB*]. *GA*¹⁹⁵³ᵃ, ¹⁹⁵⁴⁻⁷⁹, *VB*, *T22*, *SS*, *SRB*, *SRB*¹⁹⁸³, *CS2*, *MM&OS*, *RBS1*

108.8 "Lord, Lord!"] S1; "Lord!" *GA*¹⁹⁵³ᵃ, *VB*, *T22*, *SS*, *SRB*, *SRB*¹⁹⁸³, *CS2*, *MM&OS*, *RBS1*

108.9 you?"] S1; *you?"* *GA*¹⁹⁵³ᵃ, *VB*, *T22*, *SS*, *SRB*, *SRB*¹⁹⁸³, *CS2*, *MM&OS*, *RBS1*

108.10 clean his mouth] S1; his mouth clean *GA*¹⁹⁵³ᵃ, *VB*, *T22*, *SS*, *SRB*, *SRB*¹⁹⁸³, *CS2*, *MM&OS*, *RBS1*

108.11 like] S1; as if S3

108.11–12 him and finally,] S1; him. Finally, *GA*¹⁹⁵³ᵃ, *VB*, *T22*, *SS*, *SRB*, *SRB*¹⁹⁸³, *CS2*, *MM&OS*, *RBS1*

108.13 are] S1; *are GA*¹⁹⁵³ᵃ, *VB*, *T22*, *SS*, *SRB*, *SRB*¹⁹⁸³, *CS2*, *MM&OS*, *RBS1*

108.15–16 an invisible boy,] S1; invisible boys, *GA*¹⁹⁵³ᵃ, *VB*, *T22*, *SS*, *SRB*, *SRB*¹⁹⁸³, *CS2*, *MM&OS*, *RBS1*

108.16 pouting,] S1; scowling, sputtering, *GA*¹⁹⁵³ᵃ, *VB*, *T22*, *SS*, *SRB*, *SRB*¹⁹⁸³, *CS2*, *MM&OS*, *RBS1*

108.17 hot] S1; bubbling *GA*¹⁹⁵³ᵃ, *VB*, *T22*, *SS*, *SRB*, *SRB*¹⁹⁸³, *CS2*, *MM&OS*, *RBS1*

108.18 over there!] S1; *there! GA*¹⁹⁵³ᵃ, *VB*, *T22*, *SS*, *SRB*, *SRB*¹⁹⁸³, *CS2*, *MM&OS*, *RBS1*

108.19 ran some more. "Now,] S1; ran again. "Now∧ *GA*¹⁹⁵³ᵃ, *VB*, *T22*, *SS*, *SRB*, *SRB*¹⁹⁸³, *CS2*, *MM&OS*, *RBS1*

108.20 said.] S1; shouted. *GA*¹⁹⁵³ᵃ, *VB*, *T22*, *SS*, *SRB*, *SRB*¹⁹⁸³, *CS2*, *MM&OS*, *RBS1*

108.21 snap a twig, press a grass blade.] S1; press a grass blade, knock a flower, snap a twig. *GA*¹⁹⁵³ᵃ, *VB*, *T22*, *SS*, *SRB*, *SRB*¹⁹⁸³, *CS2*, *MM&OS*, *RBS1*

108.21–22 rose flowers!"] S1; roses. They can hear the stars moving!" *GA*¹⁹⁵³ᵃ, *VB*, *T22*, *SS*, *SRB*, *SRB*¹⁹⁸³, *CS2*, *MM&OS*, *RBS1*

108.23 trees,] S1; pines, *GA*¹⁹⁵³ᵃ, *VB*, *T22*, *SS*, *SRB*, *SRB*¹⁹⁸³, *CS2*, *MM&OS*, *RBS1*

108.23 coming back.] S1; trailing back, *GA*¹⁹⁵³ᵃ, *VB*, *T22*, *SS*, *SRB*, *SRB*¹⁹⁸³, *CS2*, *MM&OS*, *RBS1*

108.24(1) set] S1; sitting S3

108.24 just set!"] S1; just ◆sit [*set GA*¹⁹⁵³ᵃ, *VB*, *T22*, *SS*, *SRB*, *SRB*¹⁹⁸³, *CS2*, *MM&OS*, *RBS1*]!" S3

108.25 an observatory] S1; a high S3

108.25 wind,] S1; clear wind, *GA*¹⁹⁵³ᵃ, *VB*, *T22*, *SS*, *SRB*, *SRB*¹⁹⁸³, *CS2*, *MM&OS*, *RBS1*

108.25–26 tongue-tied.] S1; sucking his tongue. *GA*¹⁹⁵³ᵃ, *VB*, *T22*, *SS*, *SRB*, *SRB*¹⁹⁸³, *CS2*, *MM&OS*, *RBS1*

108.27 the forest] S1; the deep forest *GA*¹⁹⁵³ᵃ, *VB*, *T22*, *SS*, *SRB*, *SRB*¹⁹⁸³, *CS2*, *MM&OS*, *RBS1*

108.27 eyes on] S1; eyes weaseling on *GA*¹⁹⁵³ᵃ, *VB*, *T22*, *SS*, *SRB*, *SRB*¹⁹⁸³, *CS2*, *MM&OS*, *RBS1*

108.29 but she didn't.] S1; But she swallowed her gall and gummed it tight. *GA*¹⁹⁵³ᵃ, *VB*, *T22*, *SS*, *SRB*, *SRB*¹⁹⁸³, *CS2*, *MM&OS*, *RBS1*

108.30–32 he began springing . . . could look in] S1; he did the ◆spiteful things [thing *GA*¹⁹⁵³ᵇ]. He began leaping from behind trees. He made toad-faces, frog-faces, spider-faces at her, clenching down his lips with his fingers, popping his raw eyes, pushing up his nostrils so you could peer in *GA*¹⁹⁵³ᵃ, ¹⁹⁵⁴⁻⁷⁹, *VB, T22, SS, SRB, SRB*¹⁹⁸³, *CS2, MM&OS, RBS1*

108.33–34 She made off as like it was a blue jay] S1; She ◆made off as if [pretended it was *GA*¹⁹⁵³ᵃ, *VB, T22, SS, SRB, SRB*¹⁹⁸³, *CS2, MM&OS, RBS1*] a blue jay S3, *GA*¹⁹⁵³ᵃ, *VB, T22, SS, SRB, SRB*¹⁹⁸³, *CS2, MM&OS, RBS1*

108.35–36 her. ¶ She] S1; ~. ^ ~ S3

108.37 He made another . . . spit on her cheek.] S1; He made another ◆motion [move *GA*¹⁹⁵³ᵃ, *VB, T22, SS, SRB, SRB*¹⁹⁸³, *CS2, MM&OS, RBS1*] as if ◆to [to bang her shins and *GA*¹⁹⁵³ᵃ, *VB, T22, SS, SRB, SRB*¹⁹⁸³, *CS2, MM&OS, RBS1*] spit on her cheek. S3, *GA*¹⁹⁵³ᵃ, *VB, T22, SS, SRB, SRB*¹⁹⁸³, *CS2, MM&OS, RBS1*

108.38 mouth-twitch] S1; a mouth-twitch *GA*¹⁹⁵³ᵃ, *VB, T22, SS, SRB, SRB*¹⁹⁸³, *CS2, MM&OS, RBS1*

108.39 strange bad noises] S1; strange noises S3

108.39 his ears] S1; his loose ears *GA*¹⁹⁵³ᵃ, *VB, T22, SS, SRB, SRB*¹⁹⁸³, *CS2, MM&OS, RBS1*

108.40 by saying,] S1; away quickly by saying, *GA*¹⁹⁵³ᵃ, *VB, T22, SS, SRB, SRB*¹⁹⁸³, *CS2, MM&OS, RBS1*

108.41 lizard.] S1; salamander! *GA*¹⁹⁵³ᵃ, *VB, T22, SS, SRB, SRB*¹⁹⁸³, *CS2, MM&OS, RBS1*

109.1 But at] S1; By *GA*¹⁹⁵³ᵃ, *VB, T22, SS, SRB, SRB*¹⁹⁸³, *CS2, MM&OS, RBS1*

109.1 whole affair reached its terrible climax.] S1; whole madness boiled to a terrible peak. *GA*¹⁹⁵³ᵃ, *VB, T22, SS, SRB, SRB*¹⁹⁸³, *CS2, MM&OS, RBS1*

109.2 It was at . . . valley stark naked!] S1; ◆It [For it *GA*¹⁹⁵³ᵃ, *VB, T22, SS, SRB, SRB*¹⁹⁸³, *CS2, MM&OS, RBS1*] was ◆then [at that exact hour *GA*¹⁹⁵³ᵃ, *VB, T22, SS, SRB, SRB*¹⁹⁸³, *CS2, MM&OS, RBS1*] that Charlie ◆raced [came racing *GA*¹⁹⁵³ᵃ, *VB, T22, SS, SRB, SRB*¹⁹⁸³, *CS2, MM&OS, RBS1*] down the valley stark ◆naked [boy-naked *GA*¹⁹⁵³ᵃ, *VB, T22, SS, SRB, SRB*¹⁹⁸³, *CS2, MM&OS, RBS1*]! S3, *GA*¹⁹⁵³ᵃ, *VB, T22, SS, SRB, SRB*¹⁹⁸³, *CS2, MM&OS, RBS1*

109.3 shock.] S1; ~! *GA*¹⁹⁵³ᵃ, *VB, T22, SS, SRB, SRB*¹⁹⁸³, *CS2, MM&OS, RBS1*

109.4 *not present*] S1; ¶ "Charlie!" she almost cried. *GA*¹⁹⁵³ᵃ, *VB, T22, SS, SRB, SRB*¹⁹⁸³, *CS2, MM&OS, RBS1*

109.4 the valley] S1; a hill *GA*¹⁹⁵³ᵃ, *VB, T22, SS, SRB, SRB*¹⁹⁸³, *CS2, MM&OS, RBS1*

109.4–5 other, his feet . . . of a humming-bird.] S1; other—naked as day, naked as the moon, raw as the sun and a newborn chick, his feet shimmering and rushing like the wings of a low-skimming hummingbird. *GA*¹⁹⁵³ᵃ, *VB, T22*, *SS, SRB, SRB*¹⁹⁸³, *CS2, MM&OS, RBS1*

109.6 locked her] S1; locked in her *GA*¹⁹⁵³ᵃ, *VB, T22, SS, SRB, SRB*¹⁹⁸³, *CS2, MM&OS, RBS1*

109.7 shame?] S1; *shame?* *GA*¹⁹⁵³ᵃ, *VB, T22, SS, SRB, SRB*¹⁹⁸³, *CS2, MM&OS, RBS1*

109.7 Stop] S1; *Stop GA*[1953a], *VB, T22, SS, SRB, SRB*[1983], *CS2, MM&OS, RBS1*

109.7 Oh, Charlie, God Almighty!] S1; Oh, Charlie, Charlie, God! *GA*[1953a], *VB, T22, SS, SRB, SRB*[1983], *CS2, MM&OS, RBS1*

109.8 now, *could* she?] S1; now? Well? *GA*[1953a], *VB, T22, SS, SRB, SRB*[1983], *CS2, MM&OS, RBS1*

109.9 Upon] S1; Up on *VB*

109.10 birth] S1; his birth *GA*[1953a], *VB, T22, SS, SRB, SRB*[1983], *CS2, MM&OS, RBS1*

109.10 stomping] S1; stamping S3, *SRB*[1983]

109.10 stark knees] S1; his knees *GA*[1953a], *VB, T22, SS, SRB, SRB*[1983], *CS2, MM&OS, RBS1*

109.13–14 here, I got . . . tell you!"] S1; here! I got something to *tell* you!" *GA*[1953a], *VB, T22, SS, SRB, SRB*[1983], *CS2, MM&OS, RBS1*

109.16 There] S1; *There GA*[1953a], *VB, T22, SS, SRB, SRB*[1983], *CS2, MM&OS, RBS1*

109.20 "I'm forming in, I'm forming in!"] S1; "I'm filling in, I'm filling in!" S3

109.22 both] S1; *both GA*[1953a], *VB, T22, SS, SRB, SRB*[1983], *CS2, MM&OS, RBS1*

109.32 all," she cried. She'd] S1; all." She'd S3

109.35–36 giving in.] S1; giving up. *GA*[1953a], *VB, T22, SS, SRB, SRB*[1983], *CS2, MM&OS, RBS1*

109.37 threw] S1; flung *GA*[1953a], *VB, T22, SS, SRB, SRB*[1983], *CS2, MM&OS, RBS1*

109.38 run toward home,] S1; run ◆off towards home, [toward home^ *GA*[1953a], *VB, T22, SS, SRB, SRB*[1983], *CS2, MM&OS, RBS1*] S3, *GA*[1953a], *VB, T22, SS, SRB, SRB*[1983], *CS2, MM&OS, RBS1*

109.40 toward] S1; towards S3, *SRB*[1983]

109.41 cone] S1; pine cone *GA*[1953a], *VB, T22, SS, SRB, SRB*[1983], *CS2, MM&OS, RBS1*

110.2 him invisible,] S1; him so invisible, *GA*[1953a], *VB, T22, SS, SRB, SRB*[1983], *CS2, MM&OS, RBS1*

110.2 and she fed him] S1; and her feeding him *GA*[1953a], *VB, T22, SS, SRB, SRB*[1983], *CS2, MM&OS, RBS1*

## Line-End Hyphenation
104.22 shot-/proof] shot-proof

## 13. Ylla (I'll Not Ask for Wine) (Fall 1944)

Bradbury's stories of Mars begin with his fanzine (1940) and prozine (1941) versions of "The Piper" (volume 1, selections 4 and 6), but his more mature variations of first contact and colonization begin with the two stories that, by 1950, would open and close his classic story cycle, *The Martian Chronicles:* "The Million Year Picnic" (volume 2, selection 11) and "Ylla." During the fall of 1945, more than two years after composing "The Million Year Picnic," Bradbury prepared what would be the first of seven or more drafts of a love story centering

on a Martian marriage grown cold on the eve of an impossibility—the arrival
of a spaceship from what Martian scientists considered the lifeless third planet
from the sun. The wife, Ylla, is telepathically drawn to the distant thoughts of
the captain of the approaching ship, who does not even know that she exists.

There are no notes for this tale in Bradbury's composition and submission
log, suggesting that "Ylla" was still a work-in-progress. During the fall and
winter of 1944–45 he was working on his closing half of his 10,000-word novella collaboration with Leigh Brackett, "Lorelei of the Red Mist" (selection
16); in finishing Brackett's vision of a sword and sorcery warrior civilization
on Venus, Bradbury was likely refining his own vision of a Martian civilization
at the other end of the spectrum—a highly advanced and jaded race that has
grown bored with life as their planet slowly dies. "The Million Year Picnic"
focused on an Earth family inheriting the legacy of a vanished Martian culture;
for "Ylla," Bradbury created his own kind of Martian, very distinct from those
of Burroughs and Brackett and other earlier creators who had shaped his own
creative imagination. Ylla and her husband Yll are surrounded by understated
technological wonders, living in a culture so old that there is no more curiosity
about their own world or the Cosmos.

Yet there are echoes of the Brackett-Bradbury Venus from "Lorelei of the
Red Mist" in the details of Bradbury's Mars, including the dark and golden-eyed
features of Ylla and Yll and the magical tones of Yll's harp. In later versions of
"Ylla," Bradbury also introduced a Martian version of Brackett's flame birds to
the story. These subtle elements of convergence between "Ylla" and "Lorelei"
also help anchor the early composition range of "Ylla" to the fall of 1944.

Bradbury was clearly determined to offer this science fiction tale in the
broader mainstream magazine market, but he was having enough trouble getting his more realistic tales published in the slicks until the end of 1945. During 1946 and into the spring of 1947, he sent Don Congdon (then at Simon &
Schuster) a half-dozen stories to review for major market submission. After
Congdon became a full-time agent, Bradbury engaged him to circulate a number of new stories, including "Ylla"; Bradbury's note card files show that "Ylla"
went to Congdon on September 9, 1947. Bradbury's seven drafts evolved as he
was writing other Martian tales, and for the next two years "Ylla" went out,
in various states of revision, to an amazing range of magazines. His "Report
on Stories with Don Congdon, prepared in June 1949," tells the tale: *Collier's*
(twice), *Cosmopolitan, Good Housekeeping, Harper's, Harper's Bazaar, Ladies'
Home Journal,* the Canadian weekly *Maclean's, Mademoiselle* (three times), the
*Saturday Evening Post, This Week, Today's Woman, Town & Country, Women's
Day, Woman's Home Companion,* and the British *Argosy.*

Along the way, various editors noticed that Bradbury's Martian love story
had too many Earth-like elements. After successive reviews, *Mademoiselle*'s Rita

Smith felt that Ylla's home seemed too similar to an Earth home; *Cosmopolitan's* Arthur Gordon balked at the Martians having guns. Bradbury soon added a boiling lava table to cook meats, magnetic dust (rather than magical cobwebs) to sweep away household dirt, and the eerie, lethal bee-like stinging weapon with which Ylla's husband will kill Earth's two astronauts when they arrive.

The seventh draft went back to the popular Canadian weekly *Maclean's* for a second time, and Bradbury's sales record shows an undated sale of both "Ylla" and a Martian fantasy, "The Exiles," to *Maclean's* for a combined payment of $540.00. *Maclean's* editors changed the titles of both stories, publishing "The Exiles" as "The Mad Wizards of Mars" on September 15, 1949, and "Ylla" on January 1, 1950 (designated S1), as "I'll Not Ask for Wine," an allusion to the Ben Jonson poem "To Ceclia" that Ylla telepathically perceives, in its popular verse form, within the stream-of-consciousness thoughts projected from Captain York as he approaches Mars. "Ylla" also went to Harry Junkin at *Radio City Playhouse,* where it was turned down for radio adaptation; Anthony Boucher, who reprinted "The Exiles" in the second issue of *The Magazine of Fantasy & Science Fiction,* declined a reprint option on "Ylla." The July, 1950 issue of the British *Argosy* (S2) reprinted "Ylla," setting type from the *Maclean's* version, as "I'll Not Ask for Wine."

But once it became the opening story-chapter of Doubleday's *The Martian Chronicles* (released May 1950, designated MC) as "February 1999: Ylla," it would have a long and continuous publication history through ten distinct typesettings (and many internal reprintings and reissues) of *MC.* The Hart-Davis 1951 first British edition of *MC* was published, with Bradbury's consent, as *The Silver Locusts* (SL), an allusion to the colonizing rockets on their launching pads, ready to leave Earth. The complicated history of the *MC* and *SL* texts (sometimes published with transposed titles) includes six variations in story content, but all begin with "February 1999: Ylla" and descend from either the Doubleday American first edition ($MC^{1950}$) or the Hart-Davis house-stylings of *The Silver Locusts* ($SL^{1951}$). The list of symbols includes all bibliographical distinctions, such as the Avon/Morrow 1997 title change to "February 2030: Ylla" in their hardbound edition of *MC.*

"Ylla" also appears, without the date prefix, in the *Vintage Bradbury* (1965; VB) and in the 100-story retrospective compilation, *Bradbury Stories* (2003, BS). These texts derive from the Doubleday *MC* typesetting. Multiple-author anthology appearances, which were not supervised by Bradbury at all, begin with *Avon Fantasy Reader* 14 (summer 1950), Donald Wollheim's hybrid magazine-anthology; other anthology appearances include *The Outer Reaches* (1951; U.K., 1963), *200 Years of Great American Short Stories* (1975), *Treasury of Great Short Stories* (U.K., 1984), *Space Movies II* (1996), and *Vintage Science Fiction* (U.K., 1999).

The *MC* and *SL* stems for "February 1999: Ylla" vary primarily in the trans-Atlantic editorial stylings; both descend from the complete October 1949 submitted typescript for this chapter (TS4, UCLA Special Collections), prepared for Doubleday from Bradbury's unlocated seventh draft by his wife, Marguerite McClure Bradbury. The *Maclean's* S1 version was prepared earlier, probably during the summer of 1949; it appears to descend from the sixth draft (TS2), the first eight pages of which survive in the Albright Collection (along with a carbon of the *MC* submitted TS4). The TS2 fragment was presented by Bradbury to his friend, the minor genre writer and fan E. Everett Evans, in June 1950, and marked by Bradbury as "6ᵗʰ draft." Another shorter partial fragment, designated TS3, falls between TS2 and S1; both contain the major revisions of magnetic dust, lava, and bee gun, as well as the other revisions that Bradbury entered in successive drafts during the two years that "Ylla" circulated.

But an even older sixteen-page typescript of "Ylla" survives, and it is complete (TS1). In 2015, the present editors reunited the middle pages (8 through 12) with the rest of the typescript pages; the complete TS1 resides in the Albright Collection. TS1 is the only known form that has the pre-revision elements of cobweb dusters, stove, and gun, as well as hundreds of variant readings that predate the TS2 and TS3 fragment precursors to all the published versions. TS1 is also as close as we will ever come to the long-lost work-in-progress stage of 1944–45, or the initial drafts leading up to Bradbury's September 1947 submission to Don Congdon for circulation. TS1 therefore stands as copy-text for the present edition, the first published glimpse at the earliest known complete draft of one of the best-known story chapters of *The Martian Chronicles*.

Substantive variants from the complex trail through the subsequent TS2 and TS3 typescript fragments open the Historical Collation, followed by the substantive variant record for all published versions of "Ylla," including "I'll Not Ask for Wine" and "February 1999: Ylla" in *MC* and *SL* editions. Significant points of comparison between the TS1 copy-text and subsequent versions are discussed in the textual notes below.

Sources: author's sales record (1941–49); author's sales-by-publisher indexes (c. 1950); "Report on Stories with Don Congdon, prepared in June 1949" (Albright Collection); Eller-Bradbury interviews, 2005; Johnson, 112–113; Mengeling, 89–90; Gallagher, 57–58, 60–61, 73–74, 79; Rabkin, 111–113; and Wolfe, 33, in Greenberg and Olander; Parnell, 17–18.

—JE

## Textual Notes

111.1–3 and every morning . . . fluffs of spider web.] Bradbury's change to fruits for food and magnetic dust for cleaning appears in great detail in TS2 (see

Historical Collation); he would severely cut back these remarkable descriptions as he made further revisions for S1 and *MC,* bringing these new elements of the story into the understated style found throughout the narrative.

111.5 stone town] In TS2 and all subsequent forms, the reading is "bone towns," suggesting the more fragile and attenuated structures that he envisioned for his Martians in the other *MC* stories he would soon write. The use of "bone" also prefigures the end of the Martian culture projected in the later *MC* stories, suggesting the etiolated nature of their corpses and crumbling structures. But none of this is present in TS1, which is preserved here to project his earliest vision of Martian civilization.

111.15 They were not happy now.] In subsequent forms, this statement is set off in a single-sentence paragraph that emphasizes its significance and accentuates the deliberately slow and understated pacing, almost Hemingway-esque, that Bradbury envisioned for the tale from the beginning.

114.6 the bubbling fire lava of the table.] This is the first alien characteristic introduced into descriptions of Ylla's home, indicating that TS1 benefitted from at least the first (1947) round of editorial critique from the New York magazines. More otherworldly features were added in TS2 and S1.

115.1–7 The sand ship . . . skimming sand.] In TS2 and, more extensively, in S1 and subsequent published versions, Bradbury replaces the sand-ship surface excursion with a flight of fire birds for Ylla's and Yll's journey to evening entertainment. Bradbury would eventually bring the sand ships back in such subsequent *MC* stories as "The Off-Season."

115.8 She watched the sky.] As his revisions progressed, Bradbury gradually created a more arid Mars, slowly dying beneath Ylla's airborne flame-birds, which have replaced the original TS1 surface journey of the sand-ship. In S1, Ylla explicitly avoids watching "the dead, ancient, bone-chess cities slide under, or the old canals filled with emptiness and dreams. Past dry rivers and dry lakes they flew like a shadow of the moon, like a torch burning."

116.4 Fog from off the long canals] By S1, Bradbury had transformed the canal fog into a bedroom feature: "All night she had hung above the floor, buoyed by the soft carpeting of mist which poured from the walls when she lay down to rest."

117.39 She did not answer,] Ylla's understated emotions became far more explicit as Bradbury revised toward S1, revealing her barely repressed desperation in her thoughts: "She wanted to break and run. She wanted to cry out. But she only sat in the chair, turning her fingers over, slowly, staring at them, expressionlessly, trapped."

118.8 drew out his hunting rifle.] The alien tube weapon firing the humming, insect-like percussion rounds replaced the rifle in TS2 and S1; Yll's silver mask, hiding all emotions, was introduced in *MC.*

118.38 a boll of smoke] Bradbury is describing a shape like the boll (or seed pod) of a plant; Ylla expects to see smoke from the landing Earth ship in such a shape, which may be elongated rather than a "ball" of smoke. The original reading is retained.

## Emendations

111.6 Mr. K] S1; Mr. K. TS1 *Also* 113.15, 116.10

112.29 pleasantly] S1; pleasently TS1

113.4 York—'"] S1; ~—^" TS1

113.5 all,"] TS2; ~." TS1

113.17 there] TS2; there' TS1

113.32 *know,*"] CE; ~." TS1

113.37 pledge] TS2; plege TS1

114.37 City."] S1; ~," TS1

114.39 She] S1; she TS1

116.9 pleasant] S1; pleasent TS1

116.17 dream."] TS2; ~," TS1

116.25 seen] S1; see TS1

116.25 half entertained] TS2; half-entertained TS1

118.32 time—'] S1; time.' TS1

## Historical Collation: Post-Copy-Text Substantives

*[title]* YLLA] TS1; I'll Not Ask for Wine | By RAY BRADBURY S1; I'LL NOT LOOK FOR WINE | by RAY BRADBURY S2; February 1999: YLLA *MC*[1950, 1951, 1954, 1979, 1990a]; February 1999 YLLA *SL*[1951, 1956, 1977], *MC*[1953]; *FEBRUARY 1999—YLLA MC*[1963]; Ylla *VB*; FEBRUARY 1999 *MC*[1974]; FEBRUARY 1999 *Ylla MC*[1990b]; February 2030 Ylla *MC*[1997, 2011]; FEBRUARY 1999: YLLA *MC*[2006], *BS*; February 1999 *Ylla MC*[2008]; February 1999: Ylla *MC*[2012]

111.1 crystal pillars by the] TS1; rain crystals by the TS2; crystal pillars on the planet Mars by the *MC*[1950-2012], *SL*[1951, 1956, 1977]

111.1 the quiet sea, and every] TS1; the empty sea. ¶ Every TS2, S1; the empty sea, and every S2; an empty sea, and every *MC*[1950-2012], *SL*[1951, 1956, 1977]

*111.2–3 Mrs. K in her . . . of spider web.] TS1; Mrs. ♦K [K in her viands room TS2] ♦eating [plucking TS2] the ♦golden [quick yellow TS2] fruits that grew from the ♦crystal walls, [moist walls every minute, the fruits that turned to a luscious steam in your mouth as you swallowed them. TS2] ♦ or cleaning the house with handfuls of [She could see the flinging clouds of golden TS2] magnetic ♦dust [dust through the corridors, TS2] which, ♦taking all dirt with it, [when the doors were tossed wide, TS2] blew away ♦on the hot wind. [in a glittering fury, taking all dirt, grease and clutter, magnetized, with it. TS2] S1, S2, *MC*[1950-2012], *SL*[1951, 1956, 1977]

111.3–4 In the afternoons, . . . and the trees] TS1; ◆¶ In the ◆afternoon, [^Afternoons $MC^{1950}$, $SL^{1951, 1956, 1977}$][afternoons TS2] when the fossil sea was ◆warm [hot TS2] and motionless, and the ◆universe [wine trees TS2, S2, $MC^{1950-2012}$, $SL^{1951, 1956, 1977}$] S1

111.4 were stiff and silent] TS1; stiff and silent S2; stood stiff $MC^{1950-2012}$, $SL^{1951, 1956, 1977}$

*111.5 stone town] TS1; bone town TS2, S1, S2, $MC^{1950-2012}$, $SL^{1951, 1956, 1977}$

111.5–6 moved out the doors] TS1; drifted through their doors TS2, S2; moved out their doors S1; drifted out their doors $MC^{1950-2012}$, $SL^{1951, 1956, 1977}$

111.6 sitting in] TS1; seated in TS2, S1, S2; in $MC^{1950-2012}$, $SL^{1951, 1956, 1977}$

111.7 heiroglyphs] TS1; hieroglyphics S2

111.7 fingers] TS1; hand $MC^{1950-2012}$, $SL^{1951, 1956, 1977}$

111.9–10 alive and fierce . . . shields and swords] TS1; red ◆steam [fire TS2] on the shore and ancient men had carried clouds of ◆metal insects [insects TS2] and electric spiders S1, S2, $MC^{1950-2012}$, $SL^{1951, 1956, 1977}$

111.11 the dead] TS1; this dead S1, S2

111.12 house] TS1; house, which turned and followed the ◆◆sun, [sun, like a flower, TS2] [sun, ◆[flowerlike S2] flower-like,] $MC^{1950-2012}$, $SL^{1951, 1956, 1977}$] S1

111.12 centuries. ^ They] TS1; ~. ¶ ~ TS2

111.12(1) ^ They] TS1; ¶ Mr. and Mrs. K S1, S2, $MC^{1950-2012}$, $SL^{1951, 1956, 1977}$

111.13 yellow eyes] TS1; yellow coin eyes S1, S2, $MC^{1950-2012}$, $SL^{1951, 1956, 1977}$

111.14–15 painting, swimming . . . blue phosphorous. They] TS1; painting pictures with chemical fire, swimming in the canals in the seasons when the wine trees filled them with green ◆liquors, [liquor. TS2, TS3] ◆and [Once they had liked TS2, TS3] talking ◆into [until TS2, TS3] ◆the dawn [dawn TS3] together [om. TS2, TS3] by ◆the [the flame of TS2, TS3] blue ◆phosphorous [phosphorous. TS2, TS3] ◆portraits in the speaking room. [om. TS2, TS3] S1, S2, $MC^{1950-2012}$, $SL^{1951, 1956, 1977}$

*111.15 ^ They were not happy now.] TS1; ¶ ◆They were not happy now. ["We are not happy now," thought Mrs. K. "We are lost." TS3] TS2, S1, S2, $MC^{1950-2012}$, $SL^{1951, 1956, 1977}$

111.16 This morning . . . wine room] TS1; om. TS3

111.16 pillars of her wine room,] TS1; ◆pillars [pillared walls TS2] of her ◆house [viand room TS2] S1, S2; pillars, $MC^{1950-2012}$, $SL^{1951, 1956, 1977}$

111.16 listening] TS1; She listened TS3

111.17 heat and melt] TS1; heat, melt TS3, S1, S2, $MC^{1950-2012}$, $SL^{1951, 1956, 1977}$

111.17–18 horizon. ^ Something was going to happen] TS1; horizon. ¶ Something was going to happen. TS3, $MC^{1950-2012}$, $SL^{1951}$; horizon. ¶ She wished that something would happen. S1, S2

111.19–20 She waited. ¶ She watched the blue sky] TS1; She waited watching the red sky of Mars S1, S2; She waited. ¶ She watched the blue sky of Mars $MC^{1950-2012}$, $SL^{1951, 1956, 1977}$

111.20 moment] TS1; instant TS2, TS3

111.21 down upon the sand.] TS1; upon the sands. TS3

111.22 Nothing happened.] TS1; *om.* S1, S2

111.23 misting pillars of the house.] TS1; misting pillars. S1, S2, $MC^{1950-2012}$, $SL^{1951, 1956, 1977}$

111.24 fluted tops of the pillars,] TS1; fluted pillar tops, TS2, TS3, S1, S2, $MC^{1950-2012}$, $SL^{1951, 1956, 1977}$

111.25 her as she moved.] TS1; ◆her. [her. The floor was skimmed with water. TS3] On hot days it was like ◆wading in a [splashing your fevered toes in a constant, flowing TS3] creek. ◆The [The whole TS3] ◆house ◆floors [floors of the house $MC^{1950-2012}$, $SL^{1951, 1956, 1977}$] glittered with cool streams. [whispered with water. TS3] S1, S2

111.26–27 tired, his ears never numb with the old songs.] TS1; tired of the old songs. TS3, S1, S2, $MC^{1950-2012}$, $SL^{1951, 1956, 1977}$

111.28 playing] TS1; ◆touching [caressing TS3] S1, S2; and touching $MC^{1950-2012}$, $SL^{1951, 1956, 1977}$

111.30 softly down upon] TS1; softly upon S2

111.30–32 familiar, even . . . were still young.] TS1; familiar, while still young. TS3, S1, S2, $MC^{1950-2012}$, $SL^{1951, 1956, 1977}$

112.1–2 moved to take . . . tightly and nervously.] TS1; clenched like a soft green hand to cradle her, even as she relaxed. She closed her eyes. ¶ "We are not old," she said to herself, at her cleaning. TS3

112.6 about swiftly] TS1; swiftly about TS2

112.7 the space] TS1; that the space TS2

112.7–8 empty. ¶ Her] TS1; ~. ^ ~ $MC^{1974}$

112.8 "Did you call?"] TS1; "Ylla, did you call?" S1, S2

112.10 she cried.] TS1; *om.* TS2, $MC^{1963}$

112.12 dream!"] TS1; dream." S1, S2

112.15 she said.] TS1; she murmured. TS2, S1, S2

112.17 man," said Mrs. K.] TS1; man." TS2, S1, S2, $MC^{1950-2012}$, $SL^{1951, 1956, 1977}$

112.19 feet] TS1; foot $MC^{2008}$

112.22 eyes."] TS1; eyes!" S1, S2

112.28 dressed] TS1; was dressed $MC^{1950-2012}$, $SL^{1951, 1956, 1977}$

112.33 into] TS1; in S1, S2

112.36 *worked* harder] TS1; worked harder S1, S2, $MC^{1950-2012}$, $SL^{1951, 1956, 1977}$

112.37 she said, laying back.] TS1; she lay back. TS2

112.38 skin; what] TS1; skin! What S1, S2, $MC^{1950-2012}$, $SL^{1951, 1956, 1977}$

113.3 from the third planet in my ship.] TS1; in my ship from the third planet S2

113.5 said] TS1; objected S1, S2, $MC^{1950-2012}$, $SL^{1951, 1956, 1977}$

113.8 John] TS1; Bert $MC^{1950-2012}$, $SL^{1951, 1956, 1977}$

113.9 Another] TS1; *Another* TS2, S1, S2, $MC^{1950-2012}$, $SL^{1951, 1956, 1977}$

113.10 *Earth*] TS1; Earth; TS2

113.11(1) said] TS1; continued S1, S2, $MC^{1950-2012}$, $SL^{1951, 1956, 1977}$

113.11–12 I remember . . . another language."] TS1; And he used another language. TS2, S1, S2, $MC^{1950-2012}$, $SL^{1951, 1956, 1977}$

113.13 ⸿ "And you *understood* him?" ⸿ "Somehow, I did.] TS1; ∧ Somehow I understood him. TS2, S1, S2, $MC^{1950-2012}$, $SL^{1951, 1956, 1977}$

◊113.15–17 called quietly. . . . if there' are] TS1; ◆called [asked TS2] quietly. "Do you ever wonder ◆if, [if— $MC^{1950-2012}$, $SL^{1951}$] well, if there ◆*are* [are TS2] S1, S2

113.20–21 One hundred times more oxygen than we have.] TS1; *om.* S1, S2, $MC^{1950-2012}$, $SL^{1951, 1956, 1977}$

113.22 interesting] TS1; fascinating TS2, S1, S2, $MC^{1950-2012}$, $SL^{1951, 1956, 1977}$

113.22 *were*] TS1; were $SL^{1951, 1956, 1977}$

113.22–24 people? ⸿ "I suppose." ⸿ "And they traveled] TS1; people? ∧And they ◆traveled [travelled TS2] S1, S2, $MC^{1950-2012}$, $SL^{1951, 1956, 1977}$

113.25 wailing."] TS1; ◆wailing. [*bef del* Lets go on with the *(illeg)* TSπ] Let's get on with our work." TS2, S1, S2, $MC^{1950-2012}$, $SL^{1951, 1956, 1977}$

113.30 song you're singing?"] TS1; song?" TS2, S1, S2, $MC^{1950-2012}$, $SL^{1951, 1956, 1977}$

113.30 the husband] TS1; her husband $MC^{1950-2012}$, $SL^{1951, 1956, 1977}$

113.30–31 coming to sit down at] TS1; walking in to sit at TS2, S1, S2, $MC^{1950-2012}$, $SL^{1951, 1956, 1977}$

◊113.32 *know.*" said . . . at herself even.] TS1; know." She looked up, surprised at herself. TS2, S1, S2, $MC^{1950-2012}$, $SL^{1951, 1956, 1977}$

113.33–34 unbelieving, as if . . . came out.] TS1; unbelieving. TS2, S1, S2, $MC^{1950-2012}$, $SL^{1951, 1956, 1977}$

113.34–35 A small wind . . . of silver lava.] TS1; The house was closing itself in, like a giant flower, with the passing of light. A wind blew among the ◆pillars, [pillars; $MC^{1950-2012}$, $SL^{1951, 1956, 1977}$] the fire table bubbled its fierce pool of silver lava. TS2, S1, S2, $MC^{1950-2012}$, $SL^{1951, 1956, 1977}$

113.35–36 blew her hair behind her ears, stirring it.] TS1; stirred her russet hair, crooning softly in her ears. TS2, S1, S2, $MC^{1950-2012}$, $SL^{1951, 1956, 1977}$

113.36 stood] TS1; stood silently TS2, S1, S2, $MC^{1950-2012}$, $SL^{1951, 1956, 1977}$

113.36 distance,] TS1; sallow distances of the sea-bottom TS2, S1, S2, $MC^{1950-2012}$, $SL^{1951, 1956, 1977}$

113.36 remembering] TS1; recalling TS2, S1, S2, $MC^{1950-2012}$, $SL^{1951, 1956, 1977}$

113.37(1) eyes] TS1; yellow eyes TS2, S1, S2, $MC^{1950-2012}$, $SL^{1951, 1956, 1977}$

113.37–38 "Drink . . . mine,"] TS1; *"Drink to me only with thine eyes, And I will pledge with mine,"* S2

113.38 she sang, softly, quietly, slowly.] TS1; her red lips moved, singing softly, singing quietly and slow. TS2

113.38–39 "Or leave . . . wine."] TS1; *"Or leave a kiss but in the cup And I'll not look for wine."* S2

113.39 ask] TS1; look $SL^{1951, 1956, 1977}$

113.39 hummed now,] TS1; hummed, S1, S2

113.39 moving her hand on the air] TS1; ◆moving her hands on [touching her hands into TS2] the wind S1, $MC^{1950-2012}$, $SL^{1951, 1956, 1977}$

114.2 you make it up?" he inquired,] TS1; you compose it?" he ◆◆enquired. [asked, TS2] [inquired $MC^{1950-2012}$, $SL^{1951, 1956, 1977}$] S1, S2

114.3 hesitated.] TS1; hesitated, wildly. TS2, S1, S2, $MC^{1950-2012}$, $SL^{1951, 1956, 1977}$

*114.6 a piece of meat . . . of the table.] TS1; ◆◆a piece [portions $MC^{1950-2012}$, $SL^{1951}$] of meat [meat TS2] numbly into the simmering lava. S1, S2

114.7–8 She took the . . . plate to him.] TS1; She drew the meat forth, a moment later, ◆cooked, [om. TS2] served on a plate for him. S1, S2, $MC^{1950-2012}$, $SL^{1951, 1956, 1977}$

114.8 crazy] TS1; silly S2

114.8 guess] TS1; suppose S2

114.9–10 He said nothing . . . and slowly slowly] TS1; He said nothing. He watched her drown meats in the hissing fire pool. The sun was gone. Slowly slowly TS2, S1, S2, $MC^{1950-2012}$, $SL^{1951, 1956, 1977}$

114.12 fire table's] TS1; silver lava's TS2, S1, S2, $MC^{1950-2012}$, $SL^{1951, 1956, 1977}$

114.12–14 faces. ∧ She . . . out of the room.] TS1; faces. ¶ She hummed the strange ◆tune [song TS2, $MC^{1950-2012}$, $SL^{1951, 1956, 1977}$] again. ¶ Instantly he leaped from his chair and stalked angrily from the room. S1, S2

114.17 He finished supper later, alone.] TS1; Later, in isolation, he finished supper. TS2, S1, S2, $MC^{1950-2012}$, $SL^{1951, 1956, 1977}$

114.17–18 ∧ When he arose, . . . ship in to] TS1; ¶ When he arose, he stretched, glanced at her and suggested, yawning, "Let's take the ◆flame birds [flamebirds TS2] to S1, S2, $MC^{1950-2012}$, $SL^{1951, 1956, 1977}$

114.20 she said. "Are you *feeling* all right?"] TS1; she said. ◆ "Are you feeling well?" [om. TS2] S1, S2, $MC^{1950-2012}$, $SL^{1951, 1956, 1977}$

114.22 gone for] TS1; gone to S2

114.22 in six] TS1; for at least six S2

114.25 "I wish you . . . he said, angrily.] TS1; "Don't talk ◆that way," [like that," S2] he said peevishly. TS2, S1, S2, $MC^{1950-2012}$, $SL^{1951, 1956, 1977}$

114.25 *not*] TS1; not TS2, $MC^{1950-2012}$, $SL^{1951, 1956, 1977}$

114.27 the desert] TS1; the pale desert S1, S2, $MC^{1950-2012}$, $SL^{1951, 1956, 1977}$

114.27 twin moons] TS1; twin white moons S1, S2, $MC^{1950-2012}$, $SL^{1951, 1956, 1977}$

114.27–39 ¶ She looked out . . .whispered to herself.] S1 om. TS2

114.27–28 The room was cool.] TS1; Cool water ran softly about her toes. S1, S2, $MC^{1950-2012}$, $SL^{1951, 1956, 1977}$

114.29–30 she had been expecting] TS1; expected S1, S2, $MC^{1950-2012}$, $SL^{1951, 1956, 1977}$

114.30 occur but *might*.] TS1; ◆happen, [occur $MC^{1950-2012}$, $SL^{1951, 1956, 1977}$] but might. S1, S2

114.30 went] TS1; brushed S1, S2, $MC^{1950-2012}$, $SL^{1951, 1956, 1977}$

114.31 "I—"] TS1; *om.* S2

114.33 along now.] TS1; along. S2

114.34 Tomorrow night or the next."] TS1; *om.* S1, S2, $MC^{1950-2012}$, $SL^{1951, 1956, 1977}$

114.35–36 "That's no way . . . stone sill.] TS1; "Here's your scarf." He handed her a ◆phial [vial *BS*]. S1, S2, $MC^{1950-2012}$, $SL^{1951, 1956, 1977}$

114.36 gone anywhere in months] TS1; gone out anywhere for months S2

114.37 Xi] TS1; XI *VB*

114.37 didn't] TS1; wouldn't S1, S2, $MC^{1950-2012}$, $SL^{1951, 1956, 1977}$

114.39 herself.] TS1; herself. ⁋ From the ◆phial [vial *BS*] a liquid poured, turned to blue mist, settled about her neck quivering. S1, S2, $MC^{1950-2012}$, $SL^{1951, 1956, 1977}$

*115.1–7 The sand ship . . . skimming sand.] TS1; The birds rose in a flurry of hot sparkles, like so many fireworks on the sky, tugging the silver ribbons. Like a flower petal the canopy raced, on traces of fire, the birds burning upon the wind. ⁋ She did not watch the dead ancient bone chess cities slide under, she saw the soul wells where old phantoms hung whining in the dawn cold, where eyes winked up like red coals, and souls, ten thousand years kept, mourned out their eternal days of keptness deep in the hard stone apertures. Past all of these went like a shadow of the moon, their fire birds casting down rivers of showery light. TS2; The flame birds waited, like a bed of ◆hot coals, [coals $MC^{1950-2012}$, $SL^{1951, 1956, 1977}$] glowing on the cool smooth sands. The white canopy ballooned on the night wind, flapping softly, tied by a thousand green ribbons to the birds. ⁋ Ylla laid herself back in the canopy and, at a word from her husband, the birds leaped up, burning, toward the dark sky. The ribbons tautened, the canopy lifted. The sand slid whining ◆under [beneath S2], the blue hills drifted by, drifted by, leaving their home behind, the raining pillars, the caged flowers, the singing books, the whispering floor creeks. ◆She [⁋ She, S2]did not look at her husband. She heard him crying out to the birds as they rose higher, like ten thousand hot sparkles, so many red-yellow fireworks in the heavens, tugging the canopy like a flower petal, burning through the wind. ⁋ She didn't watch the dead, ancient bone-chess cities ◆slide under, [slide past beneath them S2] or the old canals filled with emptiness and dreams. Past dry rivers and dry lakes they flew like ◆a shadow [the shadows *VB*] of the ◆moon, [moons, *VB*] like a torch burning. S1, S2, $MC^{1950-2012}$, $SL^{1951, 1956, 1977}$

*115.8 the sky.] TS1; only the sky. TS2, S1, S2, $MC^{1950-2012}$, $SL^{1951, 1956, 1977}$

115.10 The ship moved over the dry sea bottom.] TS1; The birds moved over the dry sea bottom. TS2; She watched the sky. S1, S2, $MC^{1950-2012}$, $SL^{1951, 1956, 1977}$

115.11 *said*?"] TS1; said?" TS2, S1, S2, $MC^{1950-2012}$, $SL^{1951, 1956, 1977}$

115.14 thinking. I'm sorry."] TS1; thinking." TS2, S1, S2, $MC^{1950-2012}$, $SL^{1951, 1956, 1977}$

115.16 sky] TS1; *sky* TS2

115.18 figuring] TS1; thinking S2

115.18 "I think I'll call Hulle tomorrow.] TS1; "I thought I'd ◆call ⌊get in touch with S2⌋ Hulle tonight. TS2, S1, S2, *MC*$^{1950-2012}$, *SL*$^{1951, 1956, 1977}$

115.19 us spending] TS1; our spending S2

115.21 held to the edge of the ship with] TS1; ◆◆gripped the canopy rim [held to the edge of the canopy TS2] [held to *MC*$^{1950-2012}$, *SL*$^{1951, 1956, 1977}$] with S1, S2

115.22 him. She stared back at him.] TS1; him. TS2, S1, S2, *MC*$^{1950-2012}$, *SL*$^{1951, 1956, 1977}$

115.24 asked.] TS1; asked, trembling. S1, S2, *MC*$^{1950-2012}$, *SL*$^{1951, 1956, 1977}$

115.26 that," he said, very casual about it.] TS1; ◆that," he said, very casually. [that." TS2] S1, S2, *MC*$^{1950-2012}$, *SL*$^{1951, 1956, 1977}$

115.27 *never*] TS1; never TS2

115.27 year!"] TS1; year." TS2

115.29 else] TS1; *else* TS2, S1, S2, *MC*$^{1950-2012}$, *SL*$^{1951, 1956, 1977}$

115.30 said,] TS1; replied. S1, S2, *MC*$^{1950-2012}$, *SL*$^{1951, 1956, 1977}$

115.31 "What?" . . . in surprise.] TS1; ◆ "What!" ["What?" TS2, *MC*$^{1950-2012}$, *SL*$^{1951, 1956, 1977}$] His cry startled the birds. The canopy jerked. S1, S2

115.33–34 She turned away . . . sands, whispering.] TS1; ◆She turned away. [*om.* TS2] ⁋ The birds flew on, ten thousand ◆fire-brands [torches TS2] down the wind. S1, S2, *MC*$^{1950-2012}$, *SL*$^{1951, 1956, 1977}$

115.37 She wakened at . . . of her bed.] TS1; In the dawn sun, through the ◆crystal pillars, [vast windows, TS2] melted the fog that supported Ylla as she slept. All night she had hung above the floor, buoyed by the soft carpeting of mist ◆which [that TS2, *MC*$^{1950-2012}$, *SL*$^{1951, 1956, 1977}$] poured from the walls when she lay down to rest. All night she had slept on this silent river, like a boat upon a soundless tide. Now the fog ◆dispursed, [burned away TS2, *MC*$^{1950-2012}$, *SL*$^{1951}$] the mist ◆withdrew [level lowered TS2, *MC*$^{1950-2012}$, *SL*$^{1951, 1956, 1977}$] until she was deposited ◆upon the ◆shores [shore *MC*$^{1950-2012}$, *SL*$^{1951, 1956, 1977}$] [from the shore TS2] of wakening. ⁋ She opened her eyes. ⁋ Her husband stood over her. S1, S2

115.38 watching her.] TS1; watching. S1, S2, *MC*$^{1950-2012}$, *SL*$^{1951, 1956, 1977}$

115.40 been dreaming again,"] TS1; dreamed again, TS2; been dreaming again! *MC*$^{1950-2012}$, *SL*$^{1951, 1956, 1977}$

115.40–41 "You moved . . . me awake.] TS1; "You spoke ◆out [aloud S2] and kept me awake." S1, S2, *MC*$^{1950-2012}$, *SL*$^{1951, 1956, 1977}$

115.41 I *really* think you should see a doctor."] TS1; *om.* S1, S2

116.2 sleep."] TS1; sleep." TS2, S1, S2; sleep!" *MC*$^{1950-2012}$, *SL*$^{1951, 1956, 1977}$

116.3 started up.] S1; started. S1, S2

*116.4–5 room. Fog from . . . she lay there.] TS1; room. A gray light filled her as she lay there. TS2, *MC*$^{1950-2012}$, *SL*$^{1951, 1956, 1977}$; room. S1, S2

116.6 dream?" he asked.] TS1; dream?" TS2, S1, S2, *MC*[1950-2012], *SL*[1951, 1956, 1977]

116.7 ship," she said. "It] TS1; ship," "It TS2; ship. It S1, S2, *MC*[1950-2012], *SL*[1951, 1956, 1977]

116.8 again, landed, and] TS1; again, and *MC*[1990b]

116.8-9 talked with me, . . . laughing] TS1; talked ◆with [to *MC*[1954]] me, laughing, S1, S2

116.10-12 crystal pillar. Clouds . . . warming, now.] TS1; crystal pillar. Fountains of warm water leaped up in them, steaming; the chill vanished from the room. TS2; pillar. Founts of warm water leaped up, steaming; the chill vanished from the room. S1, S2, *MC*[1950-2012], *SL*[1951, 1956, 1977]

116.13 then," she said,] TS1; then," TS2

116.14 told] TS1; tole TS2

116.15-16 cried the husband, . . . muscles working.] TS1; The husband turned violently away, his jaw muscles working. TS2; cried the husband, turning violently away. S1, S2; cried the husband, turning violently away, his jaw working. *MC*[1950-2012], *SL*[1951, 1956, 1977]

116.17 "You act so weirdly."] TS1; *om.* TS2, S1, S2, *MC*[1950-2012], *SL*[1951, 1956, 1977]

116.18 yourself!" he cried.] TS1; yourself!" TS2, S1, S2, *MC*[1950-2012], *SL*[1951, 1956, 1977]

116.19 into her pillows.] TS1; back upon the few remaining ◆bits [remnants TS2, *MC*[1950-2012], *SL*[1951, 1956, 1977]] of ◆◆chemical [a chemical *MC*[1953]] [*om.* TS2] mist. S1, S2

116.20 I thought] TS1; I've thought S2

116.20 *more*] TS1; more S1, S2

116.20 said.] TS1; confessed. S1, S2, *MC*[1950-2012], *SL*[1951, 1956, 1977]

116.22 *so*] TS1; so TS2, S1, S2, *MC*[1950-2012], *SL*[1951, 1956, 1977]

116.23 *can't*] TS1; can't TS2, S1, S2, *MC*[1950-2012], *SL*[1951, 1956, 1977]

◊116.25 see] TS1; seen TS2, S1, S2, *MC*[1950-2012], *SL*[1951, 1956, 1977]

116.25 this way!" she said,] TS1; this way," she ◆said, [replied, S1, *MC*[1950-2012], *SL*[1951, 1956, 1977]] TS2; like this," she replied, S2

◊116.25 half-entertained with him.] TS1; half entertained. TS2, S1, S2, *MC*[1950-2012], *SL*[1951, 1956, 1977]

116.30 him. O God,] TS1; him, oh ◆God, [gods, S1, S2, *MC*[1950-2012], *SL*[1951, 1956, 1977]] TS2

116.31 *heard*] TS1; heard TS2

116.33-34 damned ship?" he cried.] TS1; damnable ship!" TS2; ship! S1, S2; his damned ship? *MC*[1950-2012], *SL*[1951, 1956, 1977]

116.35 keep your voice down, please."] TS1; lower your voice." TS2, S1, S2, *MC*[1950-2012], *SL*[1951, 1956, 1977]

116.36 "Voice be damned!"] TS1; *om.* S1, S2

116.37 wrist in his fingers. "Didn't] TS1; wrist. ◆"Didn't ["—didn't S1, S2, *MC*[1950-2012], *SL*[1951, 1956, 1977]] TS2

116.40 *didn't*] TS1; didn't TS2, S1, S2, *MC*$^{1950-2012}$, *SL*$^{1951, 1956, 1977}$

116.41 *only*] TS1; only TS2, S1, S2, *MC*$^{1950-2012}$, *SL*$^{1951, 1956, 1977}$

117.1 "Well." He flung her hand from him, stiffly. "It's good you told the truth.] TS1; "Well." He flung her hand away, stiffly. "It's good you're truthful. TS2; "Well," he flung her hand away, rigidly. "It's good you're truthful! S1, S2; "Well"—he flung her hand away stiffly—"it's good you're truthful! *MC*$^{1950-2012}$, *SL*$^{1951, 1956, 1977}$

117.3 He was breathing hard now as he walked] TS1; Breathing ◆hard [hard, S1, S2, *MC*$^{1950-2012}$, *SL*$^{1951, 1956, 1977}$] he walked TS2

117.3 person] TS1; man TS2, S1, S2, *MC*$^{1950-2012}$, *SL*$^{1951, 1956, 1977}$

117.4 as if] TS1; as though S1, S2

117.5 him. ^ "Yll,"] TS1; ~. ¶ "~," MC$^{1974}$

117.6 right," he said, tiredly. "Let me alone."] TS1; right." TS2, S1, S2, *MC*$^{1950-2012}$, *SL*$^{1951, 1956, 1977}$

117.7 sick," she said.] TS1; sick." TS2, S1, S2, *MC*$^{1950-2012}$, *SL*$^{1951, 1956, 1977}$

117.8 a smile. "Just—. . . forgive me."] TS1; a tired smile. "Just childish. Forgive me, darling." S1, S2, *MC*$^{1950-2012}$, *SL*$^{1951, 1956, 1977}$

117.9 down awhile] TS1; down a whilc S1; down for a while S2

117.11 *excited.*] TS1; excited. TS2, S1, S2, *MC*$^{1950-2012}$, *SL*$^{1951, 1956, 1977}$

117.12 still breathed with difficulty.] TS1; exhaled. TS2, S1, S2, *MC*$^{1950-2012}$, *SL*$^{1951, 1956, 1977}$

117.12–14 it. Say, . . . talk about it.] TS1; it." S1, S2; it. Say, I heard a joke about Uel yesterday, I meant to tell you. What do you say you fix breakfast, I'll tell the joke, and let's not talk about all this." TS2, *MC*$^{1950-2012}$, *SL*$^{1951, 1956, 1977}$

117.15 dream," she said, holding his arm.] TS1; dream." TS2, S1, S2, *MC*$^{1950-2012}$, *SL*$^{1951, 1956, 1977}$

117.19–20 noon, the fog . . . into light.] TS1; noon the sun was ◆ hot [high and hot TS2, *MC*$^{1950-2012}$, *SL*$^{1951, 1956, 1977}$] and the hills shimmered in the light. S1, S2

117.21 Ylla of her husband.] TS1; Ylla TS2, S1, S2, *MC*$^{1950-2012}$, *SL*$^{1951, 1956, 1977}$

117.23 *always*] TS1; always TS2, S1, S2

117.23 adjusted] TS1; adjust TS2

117.23 cage of flowers] TS1; flower cage TS2, S1, S2, *MC*$^{1950-2012}$, *SL*$^{1951, 1956, 1977}$

117.24 moved within, . . . their small] TS1; stirred, opening their hungry TS2, S1, S2, *MC*$^{1950-2012}$, *SL*$^{1951, 1956, 1977}$

117.26 With the fog and all, it's too late."] TS1; It's too hot, and it's late." TS2, S1, S2, *MC*$^{1950-2012}$, *SL*$^{1951, 1956, 1977}$

117.27–29 and took off . . . *long* time.] TS1; and said gaily, "Well, I though I'd run over to Pao's this afternoon, she asked me to visit I haven't seen her in so long. TS2

117.27–35 took off the . . . wait, darling," he smiled.] TS1; moved toward the door. "Well, I'll be back soon." ¶ "Wait a minute! Where are you going?" ¶

She was in the door swiftly. "Over to Pao's. She invited me!" ꟻ "Today?" ꟻ "I haven't seen her in a long time. It's only a little way." ꟻ "Over in Green Valley, isn't it?" ꟻ "Yes, just a walk, not far, I thought I'd—" She hurried. ꟻ "I'm sorry, really sorry," he said, running to fetch her back, looking very concerned about his forgetfulness. "It slipped my mind. I invited Dr. Nlle out this afternoon." ꟻ "Dr. Nlle!" She edged toward the door. ꟻ He caught her elbow and drew her steadily in. "Yes." ꟻ "But Pao—" ꟻ "Pao can wait, Ylla. We must entertain Nlle." ꟻ "Just for a few minutes—" ꟻ "No, Ylla." ꟻ "No?" ꟻ He shook his head. "No. S1, S2, MC[1950-2012], SL[1951, 1956, 1977]

117.32 *would*] TS1; would TS2

117.33 were here to entertain him] TS1; entertained him TS2

117.36 way over through] TS1; way through S2

117.37 hot now the fog's gone. And] TS1; hot very hot, and TS2; ◆very [very, MC[1950-2012], SL[1951, 1956, 1977]] very hot, and S1, S2

117.37 *delighted*] TS1; delighted TS2, S1, S2, MC[1950-2012], SL[1951, 1956, 1977]

*117.39–40 answer, but . . . them, expressionlessly.] TS1; answer. She wanted to break and run. She wanted to cry out. But she only sat in the chair, turning her fingers over, slowly, staring at them, expressionlessly, trapped. S1, S2, MC[1950-2012], SL[1951, 1956, 1977]

117.41 inquired] TS1; said TS2; murmured S1, S2, MC[1950-2012], SL[1951, 1956, 1977]

118.3 "All afternoon." Her voice was dull.] TS1; Her voice was dull. "All afternoon." TS2, S1, S2, MC[1950-2012], SL[1951, 1956, 1977]

118.8 closet] TS1; cupboard S2

*118.8 in the wine room and drew out his hunting rifle.] TS1; and drew forth ◆an evil weapon, [*om.* S1, S2] a long yellowish tube, ending in a bellows and ◆a trigger [trigger MC[1990b]]. He ◆held [turned, and upon his face was a mask, hammered from silver metal, expressionless, the mask that he always wore when he wished to hide his feelings, the mask which curved and hollowed so exquisitely to his thin cheeks and chin and brow. The mask glinted, and he held MC[1950-2012], SL[1951, 1956, 1977]] ◆it [the evil weapon MC[1950-2012], SL[1951, 1956, 1977]] in his hands ◆and considered [considering MC[1950-2012], SL[1951, 1956, 1977]] it. It hummed constantly, an insect hum. From it hordes of golden bees could be flung out with a high shriek◆, like metal on the air [*om.* S1, S2, MC[1950-2012], SL[1951, 1956, 1977]]. Golden◆, horrid [*om.* S1, S2] bees that stung, poisoned, and fell lifeless like seeds on the sand. TS2

118.9 asked.] TS1; asked with interest she hadn't wanted to show.] S1

118.10 "What? Oh."] TS1; "What?" MC[1950-2012], SL[1951, 1956, 1977]

118.10 He checked the load quietly, inserting fresh shells.] TS1; He turned the bellows over, listening ◆carefully [*om.* S1] to its evil humming. TS1; He listened to the bellows, to the evil hum. MC[1950-2012], SL[1951, 1956, 1977]

118.11 insists on being late,] TS1; is late, MC[1950-2012], SL[1951, 1956, 1977]

118.11 I'll be damned if I'll wait for him.] TS1; I'm not waiting for him. S1; I'll be damned if I'll wait. $MC^{1950-2012}$, $SL^{1951, 1956, 1977}$

118.11–12 hunt for a bit] TS1; hunt a ◆bit [while S2] $MC^{1950-2012}$, $SL^{1951, 1956, 1977}$

118.12 You be sure to stay right here now,] TS1; You will stay at home, S2

118.12–13 He did not look at her.] TS1; The silver mask glimmered. $MC^{1950-2012}$, $SL^{1951, 1956, 1977}$

118.15 be back.] TS1; return TS2, S1; return shortly. S2

118.16 door] TS1; triangular door S1, S2, $MC^{1950-2012}$, $SL^{1951, 1956, 1977}$

118.18–20 returned to her . . . energetically,] TS1; resumed her tasks with the ◆golden [magnetic S1, S2, $MC^{1950-2012}$, $SL^{1951, 1956, 1977}$] dusts and the new fruits to be plucked from the ◆viands room [crystal S1, S2, $MC^{1950-2012}$, $SL^{1951, 1956, 1977}$] walls. She worked with energy and dispatch, TS2

118.21 came over her,] TS1; took hold of her^ TS2, S1, S2, $MC^{1950-2012}$, $SL^{1951, 1956, 1977}$

118.21 strange] TS1; ◆strange [odd $MC^{1950-2012}$, $SL^{1951, 1956, 1977}$] and memorable TS2, S1, S2

118.23 She stood] TS1; She held her breath and stood TS2, S1, S2, $MC^{1950-2012}$, $SL^{1951, 1956, 1977}$

118.24 nearer. It might happen any moment. It] TS1; nearer. At any moment it might happen. It TS2; nearer. ¶ At any moment it might happen. ¶ It S1, S2, $MC^{1950\ 2012}$, $SL^{1951, 1956, 1977}$

118.26 moved over] TS1; blew over S1, S2, $MC^{1950-2012}$, $SL^{1951, 1956, 1977}$

118.29 clouds thickened] TS1; clouds were thickened S1, $MC^{1950-2012}$, $SL^{1951, 1956, 1977}$

118.30 soft] TS1; faint S1, S2, $MC^{1950-2012}$, $SL^{1951, 1956, 1977}$

118.32 ever so faintly,] TS1; ever so gently; S1, $MC^{1950-2012}$, $SL^{1951, 1956, 1977}$; very gently S2

118.38 out of the] TS1; from the S1, S2, $MC^{1950-2012}$, $SL^{1951, 1956, 1977}$

118.39 walk,] TS1; path, S1, S2, $MC^{1950-2012}$, $SL^{1951, 1956, 1977}$

118.39 door and her *running* to answer!] TS1; door, and her *running* to ◆answer. [answer. . . . $MC^{1950-2012}$, $SL^{1951, 1956, 1977}$] S1, S2

118.41 these things] TS1; these wild things S1, S2, $MC^{1950-2012}$, $SL^{1951, 1956, 1977}$

119.3 sky.] TS1; sky, of metal S1, S2, $MC^{1950-2012}$, $SL^{1951, 1956, 1977}$

119.4 out. ^ Running] TS1; ~. ¶ ~ S1

119.4 house,] TS1; pillars, S1, S2, $MC^{1950-2012}$, $SL^{1951, 1956, 1977}$

119.4 the door] TS1; a door S1, S2, $MC^{1950-2012}$, $SL^{1951, 1956, 1977}$

119.6 run] TS1; race S1, S2, $MC^{1950-2012}$, $SL^{1951, 1956, 1977}$

119.9 hand out.] TS1; hand outstretched. S2

119.10 see but saw] TS1; see, over toward Green Valley, but saw S1, S2, $MC^{1950-2012}$, $SL^{1951, 1956, 1977}$

119.13 sat down.] TS1; sat S1, S2

119.15 the rifle.] TS1; the evil insect weapon. S1, S2, $MC^{1950-2012}$, $SL^{1951, 1956, 1977}$

119.17 shot. And then] TS1; shot. The swift humming distant bees. One shot. And then S1, S2, $MC^{1950-2012}$, $SL^{1951, 1956, 1977}$

119.18 distant.] TS1; far away. S1, S2, $MC^{1950-2012}$, $SL^{1951, 1956, 1977}$

119.21 again] TS1; more S1, S2, $MC^{1950-2012}$, $SL^{1951, 1956, 1977}$

119.24 yard two minutes, her face pale.] TS1; yard, her face pale. S1, S2; yard, her face pale, for five minutes. $MC^{1950-2012}$, $SL^{1951, 1956, 1977}$

119.25 house,] TS1; pillared rooms, S1, S2, $MC^{1950-2012}$, $SL^{1951, 1956, 1977}$

119.26 trembling,] TS1; quivering, S1, S2, $MC^{1950-2012}$, $SL^{1951, 1956, 1977}$

119.32 crashing] TS1; smashing S1, S2, $MC^{1950-2012}$, $SL^{1951, 1956, 1977}$

119.34 Should she speak, should] TS1; Should she speak? Should $MC^{1950-2012}$, $SL^{1951, 1956, 1977}$

119.34 in!"] TS1; in"? $MC^{1950-2012}$, $SL^{1951, 1956, 1977}$

119.36 steps.] TS1; ramp. S1, S2, $MC^{1950-2012}$, $SL^{1951, 1956, 1977}$

119.39 husband.] TS1; husband. His silver mask glowed dully. $MC^{1950-2012}$, $SL^{1951, 1956, 1977}$

119.40 and stopped and looked at her for only a minute.] TS1; and looked at her for only a moment. S1, S2, $MC^{1950-2012}$, $SL^{1951, 1956, 1977}$

119.41 his rifle] TS1; the weapon bellows S1, S2, $MC^{1950-2012}$, $SL^{1951, 1956, 1977}$

119.41 out two empty, odorous shells,] TS1; out two dead bees, S1, S2, $MC^{1950-2012}$, $SL^{1951, 1956, 1977}$

120.1–2 fell, and placed . . . as she bent] TS1; fell, stepped on them, and placed the empty bellows-gun in the corner of the room as Ylla bent S1, S2, $MC^{1950-2012}$, $SL^{1951, 1956, 1977}$

120.4 turned.] TS1; turned. He removed the mask. $MC^{1950-2012}$, $SL^{1951, 1956, 1977}$

120.6 you like] TS1; I like S2

120.6 Did Dr.] TS1; Has Dr. S2

120.8 now.] TS1; *now.* $MC^{1950-2012}$

120.9 visit *tomorrow*] TS1; visit us *tomorrow* S1, S2, $MC^{1950-2012}$, $SL^{1951, 1956, 1977}$

120.11 he asked,] TS1; he asked her $MC^{1990b}$

120.11 cutting his meat.] TS1; dipping his meat in the bubbling lava. S1, S2, $MC^{1950-2012}$, $SL^{1951, 1956, 1977}$

120.15 The wind was rising across the sky, the sun] TS1; The sun S1, S2

120.25 said.] TS1; asked. S1, S2, $MC^{1950-2012}$, $SL^{1951, 1956, 1977}$

120.31 dark] TS1; black S1, S2, $MC^{1950-2012}$, $SL^{1951, 1956, 1977}$

## 14. The Tombstone (Oct. 13, 1944)

Bradbury hadn't written a weird or horror tale since early July, but on October 13, 1944, he completed two. His composition and submission log has October 13 entries for the short 2,000-word story "The Tombstone" and his more terrifying 5,000-word tale, "The Watchers." Both entries indicate that these stories were intended for *Weird Tales,* and both are annotated "SOLD!" "The Tomb-stone" sold first; his final author's sales record entry for 1944 lists a post-com-mission payment of $18.00 received on November 7, and confirms the sale to *Weird Tales.* Nolan's listing of sales by Julius Schwartz shows an actual sale date of November 1, 1944, and a pre-commission payment of $20.00. Bradbury's sales-by-publisher listing shows a sale price of $30.00 that probably includes the $10 payment (noted in his author's sales records) for British reprint rights. "The Tombstone" was first published in the March 1945 issue of *Weird Tales* (S1), with a headpiece title drawing by Boris Dolgov and an uncredited house tail-piece cartouche of a witch in flight. It was reprinted (as usual, without further payment) in the Canadian *Weird Tales* issue of May 1945 (S2), without illustration or tailpiece; the British rights payment landed the story in the Feb-ruary 1946 inaugural issue of *Strange Tales #1* (S3), a two-issue experiment by Walter Gillings to produce a hybrid magazine-anthology under the magazine paper restriction that had carried over from World War II; in fact, S3 repre-sents the first of many Bradbury magazine appearances in Britain. The final serial printing, which derives from the *Dark Carnival* text, appeared in the January 1952 issue of *Argosy* (S4), as "Exit Mr. White."

Bradbury lightly revised "The Tombstone" for the 1947 publication of *Dark Carnival (DC)*, his first story collection; in spite of the continuing postwar pa-per shortages in Britain, the story also appeared in the abridged 1948 Hamish Hamilton English edition of *DC*. But "The Tombstone" did not make the cut when Bradbury carried fifteen of his *DC* stories into *The October Country;* in-stead, the story was published in Great Britain in the Ace mass market 1962 pa-perback *The Small Assassin (SA)*, a collection of thirteen stories revived from the British edition of *DC*. The *SA* paperback collection continued in various reissues and a 1976 Grafton new edition for many years; meanwhile, Bradbury finally pulled the *DC* version of "The Tombstone" into his 1988 Knopf story collection *The Toynbee Convector (TC)* and a subsequent mass-market paper-back edition of *TC* by Bantam (1989); the British *TC* edition by Grafton (1989) was used for both hardbound and mass-market paperback issues. Bradbury adapted "The Tombstone" for the final season of *The Ray Bradbury Theater,* broadcast on the USA cable television network on October 29, 1992. The 2001 Gauntlet limited press edition of *DC* includes "The Tombstone," but Bradbury did not take an active role in preparing this edition.

On October 12, 1944, Julius Schwartz sent Bradbury a postcard query, "Where's your next Weird Yarn?" Schwartz's postcard and Bradbury's dual sub-mission of "The Tombstone" and "The Watchers," sent out the next day, crossed in the mail. The inspiration for "The Tombstone" drew on a real-life experience; in an interview for the 2001 edition of *DC*, Bradbury reflected on the days and occasional nights he spent around the tenement owned by the mother of his friend Grant Beach. He worked on setting up Beach's ceramics studio, and spent a lot of time in the tenement itself. Bradbury discovered that someone had left a tombstone in one of the rooms: "I can't remember now if there was a name on it, or—it doesn't matter, it was a strange thing to leave there, and when you look at it you see your own name there anyway, automatically. So I'm sure that's how it started."

On October 21, 1944, Schwartz wrote back to say that he had received both stories, noting that "'The Tombstone has its moments, and maybe it's short enough to get by. Anyway, off they go to Buchanan." Monty Buchanan, assistant editor at *Weird Tales*, accepted the story for the March 1945 issue. Schwartz sent on the unusually early payment with his November 4 letter; *Weird* normally paid on publication, but Buchanan may have been showing his appreciation for "The Watchers," which was more in line with the kind of traditional terror tale that he and editor-in-chief Dorothy MacIlwraith had been pleading with Bradbury to produce for some time.

"The Tombstone" presents, in the form of dark humor, a lesser form of the neurotic terrors of "The Watchers." The couple, especially the wife's "Oklahoma man," are the kind of Midwest migrants that Bradbury would have known during his family's two cross-country attempts to find work during the worst years of the Great Depression. Similar characters would surface throughout his career in such tales as "The Inspired Chicken Bungalow Court" (1969, vt "The Inspired Chicken Motel") and "Sixty-Six" (2007). In "The Tombstone," Bradbury also shows a more significant movement into dark studies of husbands and wives. Leota uses superstition as a weapon against her husband, and he, in turn, takes wicked pleasure in plowing right through her admonitions and pronouncements as the story takes an otherworldly turn. He would soon learn to build real emotional tensions in such stories as "The Next in Line," "Interval in Sunlight," and "A Touch of Petulance," where the tensions explode into life-and-death struggles for dominance.

In the absence of any pre-publication typescripts or presswork for "The Tombstone," S1 stands as copy-text in the present edition. The very few and isolated revisions that Bradbury made for the 1947 DC text represent a later intention, and are relegated, along with editorial impositions and stylings from other serial and collected versions of the text, to the Historical Collations list below. The British S3 was heavily abridged, and is not included in the volume's collation record.

Sources: Author's composition and submission log (1942–45); author's sales record (1941–49); author's notecard story file (c. 1943–1975); author's sales-by-publisher record (c.1950); Agent's sales list (c.1950); Schwartz to Bradbury, Oct. 21 and Nov. 4, 1944; Albright-Bradbury interview, 2000; Moskowitz, 360; Parnell, 202; Tymn and Ashley, 625.

—JE

## Textual Notes

[*title*] The story was apparently too short to generate a true editorial teaser; beneath the first page of text is a single-line box enclosing: "There's some mighty peculiar things under a tombstone; some are dead, and some. . . ."

122.3–4 defense plant] In making his 1947 postwar revisions for *DC*, Bradbury changed the war plant reference to an "envelope factory." The *DC* reading represents a later intention, and is, like the other *DC* substantives, relegated to the Historical Collation.

122.32 truckers] The S4 (British *Argosy*), truckers is Anglicized to "carters."

123.15 whisked the colorful linoleum] Bradbury caught the omission of the rug reference in *DC*, adding "and the worn rug" first described at 122.36 as "that rug". The omission is not confusing to the reader, and the *DC* variant is relegated to the Historical Collation.

125.7 was dying] The *DC* revision "had just died" implicitly confirms that the male voice downstairs was Mr. Whetmore, rather than the dying husband. But the original reading is not an error, and is retained.

## Emendations

[*title*] The Tombstone] $DC^{1947}$; The Tombstone | By | *RAY BRADBURY* S1

122.35 ^Ain't] S2; "Ain't S1

## Historical Collation: Post-Copy-Text Substantives

[*title*] The Tombstone | By | *RAY BRADBURY*] S1; The Tombstone | By | RAY BRADBURY S1; The Tombstone | By RAY BRADBURY S2; EXIT MR. WHITE | by RAY BRADBURY S4; THE TOMBSTONE $DC^{1947}$, $SA^{1962, 1986}$; The Tombstone $DC^{1948}$, $SA^{1976}$, $TC^{1988, 1989US, 1989UK}$

121.8 head] S1; mind $DC^{1947, 1948}$, S4, $SA^{1962, 1976, 1986}$, $TC^{1988, 1989US, 1989UK}$

121.27 which] S1; that $TC^{1989US}$

122.3 quit] S1; stopped S4

*122.3–4 a defense plant] S1; an envelope factory $DC^{1947, 1948}$, S4, $SA^{1962, 1976, 1986}$, $TC^{1988, 1989US, 1989UK}$

122.6 Made] S1; He made S4, $DC^{1947, 1948}$, $SA^{1962, 1976, 1986}$, $TC^{1988, 1989US, 1989UK}$

122.17 cease] S1; quit S4, $DC^{1947, 1948}$, $SA^{1962, 1976, 1986}$, $TC^{1988, 1989US, 1989UK}$

122.22 commencing] S1; doing S4

122.27 which] S1; that $TC^{1988, 1989UK}$

*122.32 truckers] S1; carters S4

122.38 He wants his money, and] S1; You want your money. And $DC^{1947, 1948}$, S4, $SA^{1962, 1976, 1986}$, $TC^{1988, 1989US, 1989UK}$

122.40–41 chastising] S1; tongueing $DC^{1947}$, tonguing $DC^{1948}$, nagging S4; tonguing $SA^{1962, 1976, 1986}$, $TC^{1988, 1989US, 1989UK}$

123.2 in bed] S1; into bed $DC^{1948}$, S4, $SA^{1962, 1976, 1986}$

123.3 lights] S1; light $DC^{1947,\ 1948}$, $SA^{1962,\ 1976,\ 1986}$, $TC^{1988,\ 1989\text{US},\ 1989\text{UK}}$

123.5 us will get any sleep," she said.] S1; us," she said, nodding at the stone, "will get any sleep." $DC^{1947,\ 1948}$, S4, $SA^{1962,\ 1976,\ 1986}$, $TC^{1988,\ 1989\text{US},\ 1989\text{UK}}$

123.6 by various] S1; by the various $DC^{1947,\ 1948}$, $SA^{1962,1976,1986}$, $TC^{1988,\ 1989\text{US},\ 1989\text{UK}}$

123.8 up!] S1; ~? $DC^{1947,\ 1948}$, S4, $SA^{1962,\ 1976,\ 1986}$, $TC^{1988,\ 1989\text{US},\ 1989\text{UK}}$

123.9 come sleep] S1; come to sleep $TC^{1989\text{US},\ 1989\text{UK}}$

123.9 What you] S1; What are you S4

123.13 linoleum] S1; floor $DC^{1947,\ 1948}$, S4, $SA^{1962,\ 1976,\ 1986}$, $TC^{1988,\ 1989\text{US},\ 1989\text{UK}}$

*123.15 linoleum] S1; linoleum and the worn rug $DC^{1947,\ 1948}$, S4, $SA^{1962,\ 1976,\ 1986}$, $TC^{1988,\ 1989\text{US},\ 1989\text{UK}}$

123.19 spring] S1; springs $DC^{1947,\ 1948}$, S4, $SA^{1962,\ 1976,\ 1986}$, $TC^{1988,\ 1989\text{US},\ 1989\text{UK}}$

123.20 which] S1; that $TC^{1989\text{US},\ 1989\text{UK}}$

123.20 tune] S1; turn $TC^{1988,\ 1989\text{UK}}$

123.23 late] S1; later S2

123.32 beginning] S1; starting $DC^{1947,\ 1948}$, S4, $SA^{1962,\ 1976,\ 1986}$, $TC^{1988,\ 1989\text{US},\ 1989\text{UK}}$

124.1 said] S1; cried $DC^{1947,\ 1948}$, S4, $SA^{1962,\ 1976,\ 1986}$, $TC^{1988,\ 1989\text{US},\ 1989\text{UK}}$

124.11 Grandma] S1; Gran'ma $DC^{1947,\ 1948}$, S4, $SA^{1962,\ 1976,\ 1986}$, $TC^{1988,\ 1989\text{US},\ 1989\text{UK}}$

124.24–25 and was putting] S1; he put $DC^{1947,\ 1948}$, S4, $SA^{1962,\ 1976,\ 1986}$, $TC^{1988,\ 1989\text{US},\ 1989\text{UK}}$

124.25 boots. "This] S1; ~. ¶ "~ S4

124.25 stories] S1; floors $DC^{1947,\ 1948}$, S4, $SA^{1962,\ 1976,\ 1986}$, $TC^{1988,\ 1989\text{US},\ 1989\text{UK}}$

124.26 come] S1; came $TC^{1989\text{UK}}$

124.32 coffin] S1; tomb $DC^{1947,\ 1948}$, S4, $SA^{1962,\ 1976,\ 1986}$, $TC^{1988,\ 1989\text{US},\ 1989\text{UK}}$

124.41 take a moment] S1; take a minute S4

*125.7 was dying] S1; had just died $DC^{1947,\ 1948}$, S4, $SA^{1962,\ 1976,\ 1986}$, $TC^{1988,\ 1989\text{US},\ 1989\text{UK}}$

125.19 time left for] S1; time for $DC^{1947,\ 1948}$, $SA^{1962,\ 1976,\ 1986}$, $TC^{1988,\ 1989\text{US},\ 1989\text{UK}}$

125.24 explain.] S1; ~? $SA^{1976}$, $TC^{1989\text{UK}}$

125.24 woman!] S1; ~? S4, $SA^{1976}$

125.27 to the] S1; in the $DC^{1947,\ 1948}$, $SA^{1962,\ 1976,\ 1986}$, $TC^{1988,\ 1989\text{US},\ 1989\text{UK}}$

## Line-End Hyphenation

121.4 land-/lord] landlord

121.10 eye-/lids] eyelids

124.15 down-/stairs] downstairs *Also* 125.28

125.19 ten-/thirty] ten-thirty

## 15. The Watchers (Oct. 13, 1944)

Between July 1944 and July 1945, Bradbury only completed three original weird tales. As this volume's "Chronological Catalog" documents, much of this year he spent writing stories for his new-found market in the detective pulps, a couple of science fiction pieces, and a few months of work on his 10,000-word collaboration with Leigh Brackett, "Lorelei of the Red Mist" (selection 16). But on the same day in October 1944 he submitted two weird tales, and one of them, "The Watchers," was exactly the step *backwards* that his *Weird Tales* editors had been hoping for.

Bradbury's composition and submission log contains sequential entries for "The Tombstone" followed by "The Watchers," both dated October 13, 1944. "The Watchers" entry documents completion of a 5,000-word version intended for *Weird Tales,* with a subsequent typed note "SOLD!" His author's sales record shows a $47.00 post-commission payment received on January 6, 1945 and a subsequent April 1945 payment of $35.00 for a reprint of "The Watchers" in the Rex Stout and Louis Greenfield horror anthology *Rue Morgue No. 1.* Nolan's list of Schwartz sales gives the actual *Weird Tales* sale date of January 1, 1945, and a pre-commission payment of $55.00. Bradbury's sales-by-publisher listing shows a misremembered payment of $40.00 for first publication in the May 1945 issue of *Weird Tales* (S1). S1 included a headpiece illustration by veteran *Weird Tales* illustrator Boris Dolgov.

"The Watchers" was reset and published within a different group of stories for the July 1945 Canadian issue of *Weird Tales* (S2), without the title illustration. Since another Bradbury story was already scheduled for the Canadian issue under his byline, the editors replaced his name with the pseudonymous house-author by-line "Edward Banks" for "The Watchers" reprint. Bradbury intended to include "The Watchers" in his first book, the 1947 Arkham House collection *Dark Carnival* (*DC*), and made revisions even after the typescript went to Arkham House publisher August Derleth on June 2, 1946. He found "The Watchers" especially troublesome, and made revisions in the November 1946 galley sheets as well as the March 1947 page proofs. At the last minute, he pulled "The Watchers" out and had *DC* repaginated.

His problem with revising "The Watchers" was part of a broader problem with refashioning his *Dark Carnival* tales. Rather than simply chronicling his *Weird Tales* successes, Bradbury wanted to elevate the style and tone of certain stories to show where he was headed, not where he had been. "The Watchers" was a fairly mature horror tale in the tradition of Poe and Lovecraft, but it seemed more like a dead end for Bradbury, and he never took an active role in publishing the story again.

Don Congdon sold the original version for further serialization in the January–March 1973 issue of *Showpiece* (S3), and a reprise appearance in the new Summer 1973 revival of *Weird Tales* (S4). This version was collected in the elusive 1969 British two-author anthology, *Bloch and Bradbury* (*BB*), and again in the hundred-story 2003 retrospective *Bradbury Stories* (*BS*). An early sale to a Nero Wolfe anthology apparently fell through, but "The Watchers" did appear in two anthologies—the 1946 publication in *Rue Morgue No. 1* represented Bradbury's second appearance in a commercial anthology. The story was also collected in the 1966 anthology *I Can't Sleep at Night,* but Bradbury did not take an active role in preparing text for either volume.

"Where's your next WEIRD yarn—and don't forget *horror,* not arty or child stuff." Julius Schwartz's post-card admonition of October 12, 1944, characteristically blunt, relayed more than his own frustration with Bradbury's experiments with unconventional kinds of horror; he was also relaying the worries of *Weird Tales* editors Dorothy MacIlwraith and her assistant, Monty Buchanan. Bradbury had heard this message before, and his October 1944 submission of "The Tombstone" indicated that he would continue to resist his agent and editors. But along with "The Tombstone" he submitted "The Watchers," a much finer example of the Lovecraftian tales he wrote in high school and even published, like "Luana the Living," in the 1940 fanzine *Polaris* (volume 1, selection A5). On October 21, Schwartz wrote to congratulate Bradbury on his return to traditional genre subjects: "I think 'The Watchers' is the best weird story you've ever done; even better than 'The Crowd,' which has been my favorite up to now. See, you don't have to waste your time on that 'arty' stuff when you can turn out chiller-dillers like 'The Watchers.'" Schwartz had to make money for Bradbury (and his one-man agency) in the short term, and he may be forgiven for short-changing Bradbury's true talent for working beyond genre conventions at this point in time. His relationship with Bradbury was supportive on more than one level; when Bradbury needed holiday money for the story, Schwartz advanced payment from his own funds on December 9, 1944.

The tale is, in fact, fairly well-written, and represented more of a nod to Bradbury's early literary loves than a retrogression. The cautionary first-person narrative of "The Watchers" is intentionally hallucinatory, and the unreliability of the narrator accounts for the loose ends that remain; it's never clear how the malign colonial "mind" of Earth's microbes has managed to avoid detection, or how the actions of the protagonist can save Susan and other witnesses from the terrible knowledge that triggers deadly pursuit from the microscopic world. The sentience of microbes is similar in concept to Bradbury's "The Wind" (volume 1, selection 7), where an explorer-scientist is hunted down and killed by the Earth's sentient wind currents for discovering their hidden powers. The likely paranoia of Tinsley, and eventually of the narrator, reflects Bradbury's deep reading of Dr. Karen Horney's *The Neurotic Personality in Our Time* as well as more general observations on neuroses and psychoses from his Modern Library selected writings of Sigmund Freud; the invasion of the body by hostile microbes appears in Bradbury's early prose-poem anecdote "Wilber and His Germ" (*Script,* May 24, 1941) and his final *Weird Tales* story, "Fever

Dream" (*Weird Tales,* Sep. 1948). The extreme hypochondria that contributes to Tinsley's condition is reminiscent of Bradbury's early fanzine tale "How Am I Today, Doctor?" (*The Damn Thing,* Feb. 1941) and his more masterful November 1944 composition, "Skeleton" (selection 19). Hypochondria was also a chronic condition of his close friend Grant Beach, who read and critiqued Bradbury's stories all through the war years.

Copy-text for the present edition is S1. Substantive variants from subsequent serializations and collections are mostly editorial stylings or typesetting errors, and are recorded in the Historical Collation of substantives below the Emendations List. Bradbury prepared two typescripts from S1, possibly in preparation for the ill-fated attempt to bring "The Watchers" into *DC.* TS1 is a clean copy, but TS2, a carbon from a different ribbon copy, contains heavy holograph revisions by Bradbury through the first three pages. These revisions never reached print and reflect a subsequent intention; they are recorded below in the Historical Collation.

Sources: Author's composition and submission log (1942–45); author's sales record (1941–49); author's agency listing (c. 1950); Schwartz to Bradbury, Oct. 21, Nov. 4, and Dec. 9, 1944; Louis Greenfield to Julius Schwartz, Oct. 5, 1945; Eller and Touponce, 60–65.

—JE

## Textual Notes

*[title]* The teaser is purely editorial; the space required for the half-page title art may have limited it to a single line: *"When did you last kill a fly? Yes,* you! *Have a care . . . . and listen!"*

126.18 an instantaneous stroke] The TS2[AMS] holograph revisions introduce an interesting metaphor for the flyswatter, "a tennis stroke," possibly reflecting Bradbury's subsequent interaction with the game through his wife's playing routine.

127.37 have They!"] Bradbury is inconsistent in capitalizing "They," but it is clearly his intent to capitalize in Tinsley's words as well as the words of his companions when they refer to Tinsley's complex; these instances are capitalized and recorded in the Emendations List on the authority of the present editors, but noting TS2 as the first instance where Bradbury moved toward consistency.

131.10 them] Here Susan and Steve are referring to insects as insects, outside of Tinsley's neurotic contextalization. No capitalization is required at this point.

131.27 Elder] "Elder" is capitalized in the same way that "Lawyer Remington" is capitalized. This archaic usage is consistent with the gothic tone and narration, and is retained throughout. The TS styling to lower case reflects a later intention.

131.29 Susan, swerving the car] She's now driving, even though Steve picked her up in his car. They are old friends, so this degree of familiarity is plausible. The copy-text reading is retained.

137.4 them off, . . . them in] The narrator is describing microbes as microbes, and context suggests he has not yet transferred the upper-cased sense of fear to them.

137.21–138.22 But the . . . dddddddddddddddddddd] The entire Lovecraftian ending is deleted from S4 (1973).

137.40 neural] The error "neutral" was never corrected in any version, but context indicates a clear error. The present edition corrects the error by emendation, as Bradbury would have desired.

138.6 Or perhaps they are all.] This speculation represents a collective reference to animals and insects as such, not the microbial Overmind; the lower-case "they" is retained.

## Emendations

127.37 Neither] S4; Either S1

*127.37 They] CE; they S1 Also 132.40

129.33 fingers'] TS2; fingers S1

131.19 They'll] TS2; they'll S1

131.19 Them] TS2; them S1

131.24(2) They] TS2; they S1 Also 131.25

131.26 They're] S2; they're S1

131.39 gentle^] TS2; ~, S1

132.38 Them] CE; them S1 Also 132.39, 132.41, 133.18, 133.20

133.5 Their] CE; their S1

133.13 Their] TS2; their S1

133.19 wrong?] TS1; ~. S1

133.28 They'll] CE; they'll S1

133.36 intact.] TS1; ~? S1

136.34 Ones] TS2; ones S1

136.37(2) killing,] TS2; ~^ S1

137.20 His] TS2; his S1

*137.40 neural] CE; neutral S1

## Historical Collation: Post-Copy-Text Substantives

126.1 the tapping of the] S1; my TS2^AMS

126.1–2 keys is like knuckles on wood,] S1; is loud, TS2^AMS

126.2–3 the keys that . . . trembling fingers. And] S1; at trembling hands as I write, and TS2^AMS

126.3–4 writing comes the ironical melody of] S1; machine I hear the hum of TS2^AMS

126.4 over my bent head] S1; the room TS2^AMS

126.5 colliding with the wire screen.] S1; touching the window screen. TS2^AMS

126.5–6 naked filament-skeleton of the yellow] S1; naked yellow TS2^AMS

126.6–7 bit of torn . . . a moth flutters.] S1; moth flutters like a piece of torn white paper. TS2^AMS

126.7–8 it—I laugh . . . flies and the] S1; it—and laugh and cannot stop laughing. Oh, Lord, think on all the shining flies, the TS2^AMS

126.9 crickets.] S1; crickets of this world. TS2^AMS

126.10 do happen upon this,] S1; one day read this, TS2^AMS

126.12 upon] S1; on TS2^AMS

126.13 You remember] S1; You *do* remember TS2^AMS

126.14 certainly?] S1; Yes? TS2^AMS

126.14 threw away] S1; squandered TS2^AMS

126.14 fly-sprays and insecticides] S1; fly-sprays, insecticides TS2^AMS

*126.18 an instantaneous] S1; a tennis TS2^AMS

126.19 I shall never forget that instrument of death.] S1; *om.* TS2^AMS

126.19–20 Tinsley, a monarch, ruled his industry] S1; Tinsley, ruled his kingdom TS2^AMS

126.21 and right-hand man] S1; *om.* TS2^AMS

126.21–23 industry; sometimes . . . ¶ Tinsley carried] S1; industry on that day in July when he ^ first carried TS2^AMS

126.23 work with him] S1; ◆work and with him [work with him. TS2^AMS] TS2

126.23 under his arm in July, 1944.] S1; *om.* TS2^AMS

126.25 when Tinsley arrived] S1; *om.* TS2^AMS

126.25–26 swicking,] S1; ◆*om.* [whistling, *BB*^1969] TS2^AMS

126.26 the flyswatter through the air] S1; that device TS2^AMS

126.28–29 dictate to me, . . . north-south-east-west walls,] S1; dictate but his eyes would search the walls, TS2^AMS

126.29 north-south-east-west] S1; north-southeast-west *BS*^2003

126.30–127.2 clothing. Once I . . . as they please.] S1; clothes. TS2^AMS

127.3 "Hello, Steve."] S1; On a particular Friday TS2^AMS

127.3–4 one morning as I poised my pencil over my pad.] S1; at me and said: TS2^AMS

127.4 would you mind cleaning away the corpses."] S1; clean away the corpses!" TS2^AMS

127.5 were] S1; was S4

127.7 muttering.] S1; sighing. TS2^AMS

127.8 "To] S1; Tinsley began: "To TS2^AMS

127.8 Philadelphia.] S1; Philadelphis. BB[1969]

127.8–9 money in your . . . thousand dollars—"] S1; $5000 in your insect spray." TS2[AMS]

127.10 I complained.] S1; *om.* TS2[AMS]

127.11 "Five thousand dollars. Advise] S1; "Advise TS2[AMS]

127.12 war conditions] S1; conditions TS2[AMS]

127.12 twisted] S1; stared at TS2[AMS]

127.13 crazy," he said.] S1; crazy?" TS2[AMS]

127.14 p.s., or are you talking to me?"] S1; p.s.?" TS2[AMS]

127.15 rang and it] S1; Rang. It TS2[AMS]

127.15–16 Company, to whom Tinsley told me to write] S1; Company, asking for TS2[AMS]

127.16 his] S1; Tinsley's TS2[AMS]

127.20 THAT] S1; *that* TS1

127.37 Either] S1; Neither S4, BB[1969]

*◊127.37 they] S1; They TS2 *Also* 131.24(2), 131.25 BB[1969]

128.21 danced,] S1; dance^ BB[1969]

128.30(1) at] S1; a TS2

129.29 good glass of his sherry] S1; glass of his good sherry TS2

◊129.33 fingers] S1; fingers' TS2, BS[2003]

130.11 ashen] S1; ashed TS2

130.22 ants of every and all] S1; ants of all TS2

131.1 You've] S1; You have BS[2003]

131.11 flicked] S1; licked S4

◊131.19 they'll] S1; They'll TS2

◊131.19 them] S1; Them TS2

◊131.26 they're] S1; They're TS2

*131.27 Elder] S1; elder TS2 *Also* 137.36, 137.39, 138.3

132.3 he] S1; since he TS2

132.33 we] S1; us TS2

133.8 feed on your] S1; feed your TS1

◊133.13 their] S1; ◆these [Their BS[2003]] TS2

◊133.19 wrong.] S1; ~? TS1, TS2

133.20 told!] S1; fool! S2, BS[2003]

◊133.36 intact?] S1; ~. TS1, TS2

134.29 so] S1; and TS2

134.34 one another] S1; each other TS2

134.36 misty] S1; mistly TS2

136.10 help] S1; held TS1

136.30 in a slow] S1; in an amazingly slow S4

◊136.34 ones] S1; Ones TS2

137.16 wheel] S1; sheel TS1

137.19 flies, insects to] S1; flies to TS1

◊137.20 his] S1; His TS2

*137.21–138.22 But the Evil Ones . . . dddddddddddddddddddd. . . .] S1; *om.* S4

138.6 mandibled] S1; *om.* TS2

138.15 gripes] S1; grips TS1

138.21–22 until etaoin shrdlucmfwyp cmfwyp . . . cmfwaaaaa dddddddddddddddddddd. . . .] S1; until . . . TS2

138.21 shrdlucmfwyp] S1; ◆shrdlucm fwyp [shrdlucm-/fwyp S2] TS1

138.21 cmfwyp] S1; ◆cmfwym [*om.* BS²⁰⁰³] TS1

138.22 dddddddddddddddddddd] S1; ◆◆dddddddddddddddddd [dddddddddddddddd dddddd S2, BS²⁰⁰³] [ddddddddd ddd d-/dddd . . . BB¹⁹⁶⁹] TS1


## Line-End Hyphenation

126.15 ant-/pastes] ant-pastes

127.3 fly-/swatter] flyswatter *Also* 137.11(1)

136.7 night-/filled] night-filled


# 16. Lorelei of the Red Mist (Sept.–Oct. 1944)

During 1944 Bradbury had followed his good friend and mentor Leigh Brackett into the pages of *Planet Stories,* a reliable second-tier science fiction and fantasy quarterly. In September 1944, he agreed to finish the second half of a novella commitment she had made to *Planet* before signing on with Howard Hawks to collaborate on the script of Humphrey Bogart's next Warner Brother film, *The Big Sleep.* Bradbury's composition and submission log includes a special two-line entry for "RED SEA OF VENUS by Bracket and I," dated February 17, 1945; he subsequently typed "SOLD!" in the first line of the entry. His author's sales record notes a post-commission payment of $141.00 for his half of the novella (still listed under Brackett's working title, "Red Sea of Venus") and a payment received date of March 19, 1945. Bradbury's income tax notes confirm the date and amount under the shorthand title "Red Venus Sea." Nolan's list of sales by Schwartz establishes the actual sale date as March 16, 1945, and includes the pre-commission combined payment for both authors as $315.00. His sales-by-publisher listing for *Planet Stories* does not include the collaboration, nor does his notecard file.

The novella appeared under its final title, "Lorelei of the Red Mist," in the Summer (March–May) 1946 issue of *Planet Stories* (S1), with a large two-page title illustration and two interior pieces of line art by Rube Moore. Unfortunately, dozens of typesetting errors were introduced, and a few substantive errors (by both Bradbury and Brackett) remained uncorrected in S1. Nevertheless, "Lorelei of the Red Mist" dominated the issue; it was the opening major feature, running in two columns through the first 35 pages of the 120-page issue. The summer issue proved to be a double triumph; the final story was Bradbury's "The Million Year Picnic" (volume 2, selection 11), the first solo Bradbury story of quality in the pages of *Planet Stories;* it would eventually become the final story-chapter of *The Martian Chronicles,* and was the first of his *Chronicles* to reach print, well before he had the companion stories or the vision to consider building a Martian story-cycle.

Perhaps because of its length and the collaborative nature of the work, Bradbury never arranged to bring "Lorelei of the Red Mist" into his story collections, but the novella had a significant and often illustrated reprint history. It was reset and reprinted in the Fall 1953 issue of the digest-size *Tops In Science Fiction* (S2), abridged, with illustrations by Kelly Freas. "Lorelei of the Red Mist" was subsequently adapted to graphic form by R.A. Jones and Christy Marx and published in two issues (April and June 1992) by Conquest Press; the illustration team consisted of Dell Barras, Butch Burcham, and C. Manalac (covers by Marcus Boas).

In spite of its length, the novella was anthologized a number of times, including *Three Times Infinity* (abridged, 1958, with more variants introduced in the U.K. edition), William F. Nolan's *The Human Equation* (1971), *The Best of Planet Stories 1* (1975, with an introduction by Brackett), *Isaac Asimov Presents the Great Science Fiction Stories 8: 1946* (1982), *Isaac Asimov Presents the Golden Years of Science Fiction,* 4th series (1984), and *Echoes of Valor II* (1989). In 2007, the Haffner Press series of Brackett volumes published *Lorelei of the Red Mist: Planetary Romances* to include the novella and shorter works by Brackett alone.

Bradbury's close familiarity with Leigh Brackett's work, and the ease with which he transitioned into the daunting task of writing the final half of her 21,000-word novella, is apparent from the fact that he continued to compose his own stories unabated; during his October 1944 to February 1945 work on the novella, he also composed eleven stories of his own. "Lorelei of the Red Mist" is a rare example of seamless collaboration not unlike that of C. L. Moore and Henry Kuttner (undisguised by the many pseudonyms that the Kuttner-Moore team used throughout their married years). During the war Bradbury met with Brackett, often on a weekly basis, at Muscle Beach, near the Santa Monica Pier, but during the summer and fall of 1944 these meetings became more sporadic as Brackett moved into screenwriting.

The unexpected call from Hollywood producer Howard Hawks to join the William Faulkner and Jules Furthman team on the script of *The Big Sleep* put an end to work on her Venusian novella, which so far had evolved, from the preliminary title "Slaves of the Burning Sea," into "Red Sea of Venus," where a down-and-out interplanetary criminal finds himself reincarnated in the body of a barbaric Venusian hero caught between two rival civilizations on opposite shores of a surreal Venusian sea of mist. The previous spring Bradbury had in fact challenged her to write a novella for *Planet,* where she had been a mainstay author for years. She had seen his work evolve week by week for three or four years, and the fact that his earlier *Planet Story* tales had imitated her settings and characters actually worked to advantage in her present predicament. For his part Bradbury had the confidence, born of her unusual combination of friendship and mentorship, to pick up the thread in mid-story. Her hand-off note was characteristically brief and upbeat, a deliberate counterpoint to the significant challenges of the task: "All you have to do is get the sea-beasts on our side, get 'em back to Crom Dhu in time to save Beaudag & defeat—or I should say destroy—Rann's fleet—& of course Starke will have to take care of Rann."

Bradbury inherited Brackett's working title, "Red Sea of Venus," along with the first 10,000 words of the novella, and it still carried this designation at the time of his mid-February 1945 submission to Julius Schwartz, who at the time represented both authors in New York. Schwartz had seen Brackett's opening half in draft, and in his February 24 acknowledgement of receipt he complimented Bradbury on reworking the novella's opening description: "Leigh's beginning was too vague; something I've warned her against time and time again." It was never really clear if Bradbury contributed to Brackett's half, but in her 1975 introduction to *Best of Planet Stories 1,* she identified the exact point in mid-narrative where Bradbury picked up the story: "He saw the flock, herded by more of the golden hounds." From there he added sudden but consistent plot turns as well as two eerie armies of dead warriors from beneath the mystifying red sea of Venus. These living dead provide another marker in Bradbury's continuing fascination with life and death boundaries, beginning with "The Reincarnate" (selection 6) and continuing into the far more substantial novella "Pillar of Fire" (1947; published 1948).

The final published title, "Lorelei of the Red Mist," is almost certainly a Bradbury contribution as well. Brackett's hand-off note had left the fate of this commitment in his hands, and the final title echoes Bradbury's abiding fascination with this allusion; his unpublished novella of 1938, his first sustained work of fiction, had been titled "The Lorelei," and the luring enchantment he brought to his closing half of Brackett's tale is fully captured in the new title. At the same time, Bradbury was exploring a parallel trail of his own as he began to define his Martians, an equally exotic golden-eyed and masked civilization of great advancement. This was the opposite end of human progress from Brackett's semi-barbaric Venusians, but work on "Lorelei of the Red Mist" may have advanced his evolution of "Ylla" (selection 13) into full story form; it certainly paved the way for a larger group of Bradbury's "first contact" stories involving an advanced Martian culture capable of resisting our attempts at exploitation, but no longer willing to live. Bradbury did not fully abandon Venus after completing the novella, however; his subsequent "wet world" visions of Venus include "Death by Rain" (1950; collected in *The Illustrated Man* as "The Long Rain") and the often anthologized "All Summer in a Day" (1954).

Copy-text for "Lorelei of the Red Mist" is S1; dozens of typesetting errors in S1 are emended from S2 and, where undetected in S2, by the present edition (CE); other non-authorial substantive variants in S2, the resulting from styling and editorial impositions, appear in the Historical Collation below. The textual notes discuss problematic readings and previously undetected errors in the copy-text.

Sources: Author's composition and submission log (1942–45); author's sales record (1941–49); 1945 income tax notes; author's extended sales-by-publisher index (c. 1950); author's agency listing (c. 1950); Schwartz to Bradbury, Feb. 24 and Mar. 10, 1945; Brackett to Bradbury, undated [Sep. 1944]; Brackett, "Introduction," in *Best of Planet Stories No. 1* (New York: Ballantine, 1975), 7; Eller-Bradbury interviews, Oct. 2, 2004; Ashley, *History*, 58; Ashley, *Time Machines*, 193–194; Eller, *Becoming Ray Bradbury*, 110–111; Moskowitz, 31, 86; Tymn and Ashley, 477–478.

—JE

## Textual Notes

[title] The 1946 *Planet Stories* (S1) teaser is tucked between the title and the verso (left-hand) half of Rube Moore's two-page title illustration. It is a framing teaser, and is completely editorial in composition: "He died—and then awakened in a new body. He found himself on a world of bizarre loveliness, a powerful, rich man. He took pleasure in his turn of good luck . . . until he discovered that his new body was hated by all on this strange planet, that his soul was owned by Rann, devil-goddess of Falga, who was using him for her own gain." The 1953 *Tops in Science Fiction* (S2) teaser is editorial and brief: "Starke, space-rat and convict, lived again in great Conan's body. Lived for a little as a free-slave of the entwining Rann."

148.32 reived] The word is spelled 'rieved' in S1 and changed to 'theived' in S2. The context of the sentence is "to reive," that is, to rob and plunder, and the spelling is therefore emended for the present edition.

154.12 sleeping dun] Brackett's archaism is not easily resolved by the reader; it may seem, at first, to be a typesetting error for "sleeping den." She is actually referring to the fortress at the heart of Crom Dhu; a dun was a Celtic double-walled stronghold structure in ancient Britain. Her Venusians have harness and dress resembling the Celtic traditions of Earth. Bradbury follows suit, using "dun" again at 166.5.

156.14 Starke strained his in the gloom] It is possible, but unlikely, that the object referent is "Manhood" from the previous sentence, where it is used in reference to Faolan. It is far more likely that Bradbury omitted, or the *Planet Stories* compositor dropped, the word "eyes." That word is emended in the present edition to clarify the passage as Bradbury most likely intended.

166.34–35 over harp-threads] Context reveals that the S1 and S2 reading "hard threads" is an error originating in Bradbury's unlocated typescript or in the S1 typesetting.

169.6 sea shepherds] Here and at 170.28, the compound is rendered with a hyphen in S1 and S2, but all other instances in Bradbury's half of the novella are open. We emend these two instances to match the majority of the occurrences.

174.29 treads and convolutions] It is possible that this description of Starke's brain may be an error for "threads and cobwebs," which seems closer to the image that Bradbury intends. However, there's not enough contextual evidence to emend with a high degree of confidence, and the copy-text reading is therefore retained.

177.9 flame birds] At this point, "flame birds" is hyphenated and rendered as a compound in S1 and S2, but in all other instances they appear unhyphenated as two words. The present editors emend here to reflect both authors' clear preference through the novella.

179.41 Bron] Four dead Crom Dhu warriors lead Conan's victory over Rann in Bradbury's closing half of the novella. Three of them, Clev, Mannt, and Aesur, are consistently the same. Bron is corrupted here in S1 to "Bruce" and subsequently "Blucc" (184.34, 184.38), and finally "Brucc" (186.11). For the integrity of the story, the present editors emend these corruptions to the intended "Bron."

180.7 spider-silk] Although presented as two words here in S1 and S2, at all other times the word is rendered with a hyphen to form a compound noun in the copy-text. The present editors have emended in the hyphen here to complete Bradbury's clear preference for this compound.

180.17 longships] Rendered as two, non-hyphenated words in S1 and S2, all other instances of this word in the copy-text are closed together as one word. The editors have emended it in this instance as a single word for consistency and to follow Brackett and Bradbury's reference to vessels similar to the single-word Norse "longships" of Earth.

183.41 Crom Dhu] The original text has the city as Falga, but the context of the paragraph makes it very clear that Faolan is hearing the battle clashes just beyond the walls of Crom Dhu, where he is under siege. Although unchanged in S2, it is corrected in *The Best of Planet Stories* (Ballantine: New York, 1975), edited by Leigh Brackett, and emended in the present edition.

185.6 high seat] The text is hyphenated in S1 and S2 at this point, but at all other points in the novella it is an open compound. The editors have therefore emended this instance to meet Brackett's (and Bradbury's) intent.

187.6–7 thought he did.] The sentence is incomplete in S1 and S2, where it ends after the word 'thought'. Leigh Brackett corrected the mistake in *The Best of Planet Stories* (Ballantine: New York, 1975), and the current editors also emend the sentence to correct the error

## Emendations

*[title]* Lorelei of the Red Mist] CE; LORELEI OF THE RED MIST | By Leigh Brackett and Ray Bradbury S1; LORELEI of the RED MIST | By Ray Bradbury & Leigh Brackett S2

142.3 lips] S2; lipe S1

143.25 half-naked] CE; ~ ^ ~ S1

144.2 Faolan's] CE; Foalan's S1

144.3 Romna] S2; Roma S1

145.3 calculating] S2; calcudating S1

145.12 *time."*] CE; ~.^ S1

*148.32 reived] CE; rieved S1; thieved S2

149.5 sister] S2; sisted S1

149.18 and] S2; ad S1

149.34 for] CE; from S1

150.37 sea.] S2; ~^ S1

150.42 Come on,] CE; ~, ~, S1

151.38 asleep] S2; sleep S1

152.21 seeing."] S2; ~.^ S1

155.20 sandals] S2; sanadals S1

155.40 softly,] S2; ~^ S1

156.7 it] S2; its S1

156.13 manhood] S2; manhoods S1

*156.14 strained his eyes] CE; strained his S1

158.4 Cloud] CE; Clouds S1

158.18 others'] CE; others S1; other's S2

161.23 Hugh-] S2; High- S1

163.37 the] S2; he S1

164.36 that] S2; than S1

*166.34–35 harp-threads] CE; hard-threads S1

167.25 Called] CE; called S1

*169.6 sea shepherds] CE; sea-shepherds S1 *Also* 170.28

170.13 upward] S2; uward S1

170.27 people.] S2; ~? S1

170.29 at the circular] S2; at circular S1

172.8 against Falga?"] S2; aganst Falga?^ S1

172.19 man with a sword] S2; man a sword S1

176.35 warmth] CE; warth S1

*177.9 flame birds] CE; flame-birds S1; flame-/birds S2

177.13 rustling] S2; rusling S1

178.5–6 in a numbed] S2; in in a numbed S1

179.15 awaited] CE; waited S1 *Also* 187.11

179.15 to the garden] S2; to to the garden S1

*179.41 Bron] CE; Bruce S1

*180.7 spider-silk] CE; spider silk S1

*180.17 longships] CE; long ships S1

181.3 Linnl] S2; Linni S1

181.8 cheeks] S2; creeks S1

182.5 Mannt] S2; Mantt S1

182.11 Faolan,] CE; ~^ S1

182.34 Beudag] S2; Bendag S1

*183.41 Crom Dhu] CE; Falga S1

184.30 Faolan] S2; Faolen S1

*184.34 Bron] CE; Blucc S1 *Also* 184.38

*185.6 high seat] CE; high-seat S1

185.11 mouth of] CE; mout hof S1; mouth of S2

185.34(2) Rann,] CE; ~^ S1

186.9 Rann] S2; Ran S1

*186.11 Bron] CE; Brucc S1; Bruce S2

186.31 seeing] S2; seing S1

186.32 give] S2; gave S1

*187.6–7 thought he did.] CE; thought. S1

## Historical Collation: Post-Copy-Text Substantives

[title] By Leigh Brackett and Ray Bradbury] S1; By Ray Bradbury & Leigh Brack-
    ett S2

140.6–13 His head was tilted . . . a dropped stone.] S1; *om.* S2

141.3 I'll guide you] S1; and guide you S2

141.5–6 He drew back . . . his face.] S1; *om.* S2

141.16–22 He remembered his . . . steal his food.] S1; *om.* S2

141.30–32 He was . . . shaped to you . . .] S1; *om.* S2

◊142.3 pale lipe.] S1; pale lips. S2

142.5–8 He lay, the . . . away, empty.] S1; *om.* S2

◊145.3 calcudating] S1; calculating S2

145.8–10 Catspaw, huh? . . . leading up to.] S1; *om.* S2

146.5 breach] S1; reach S2

148.5–6 All he had . . . named Rann.] S1; *om.* S2

*◊148.32 raided and rieved] S1; raided and thieved S2

149.1–3 The bard's fingers . . . Romna went on:] S1; *om.* S2

◊149.5 sisted] S1; sister S2

◊149.18 ad from] S1; and from S2

150.8–10 And just where . . . him already.] S1; *om.* S2

150.35 don't] S1; won't S2

150.39 suggeston] S1; suggestion S2

151.30–32 He put his . . . She did not.] S1; *om.* S2

◊151.38 not sleep.] S1; not asleep. S2

153.28–30 Starke saw narrow . . . Rann's ships.] S1; *om.* S2

153.39 can] S1; ca S2

154.31 slip] S1; slipped S2

◊155.20 sanadals] S1; sandals S2

◊156.7 its] S1; it S2

◊156.13 manhoods] S1; manhood S2

156.14 gloom, measuring the ledge, measuring the place] S1; gloom, measuring
    the place S2

156.37 more tricks.] S1; more. S2

158.10–15 They were human . . . swarming masses.] S1; *om.* S2

158.21–24 They climbed, . . . the party through.] S1; *om.* S2

◊161.23 High-] S1; Hugh- S2

162.5–7 He held out . . . man's battles.] S1; *om.* S2

162.20–24 Tomorrow we go . . . Only a . . .] S1; *om.* S2

◊163.37 he] S1; the S2

163.40–164.2 They were like . . . and somehow deadly.] S1; *om.* S2

◊164.36 than] S1; that S2

165.16–17 Starke's eyes . . . believed that possible.] S1; *om.* S2

165.28–33 It wasn't like . . . shiver of ecstasy.] S1; *om.* S2

166.3–8 The thrumming . . . Starke's heart.] S1; *om.* S2

166.18–23 As he looked . . . Starke's attention.] S1; *om.* S2

166.37 screens] S1; screen S2

167.24–31 A hundred, two . . . blood-colored sea.] S1; *om.* S2

168.1–13 Long ago some . . . in its archway.] S1; *om.* S2

169.17 Clev!] S1; Cley! S2

170.1 words.] S1; words? S2

◊170.13 uward] S1; upward S2

◊170.27 people?] S1; ~. S2

◊170.29 at circular] S1; at the circular S2

171.19 pillagers.] S1; pillage S2

◊172.8 aganst] S1; against S2
◊172.19 man a sword] S1; man with a sword S2
172.37 He lay once . . . shepherds, struggling.] S1; *om.* S2
174.25–33 Starke gave him . . . couldn't believe it.] S1; *om.* S2
175.6–10 Occasional discharges . . . leaned forward.] S1; *om.* S2
176.5 harp-shepherd] S1; harp-shephear S2
176.13–18 Somebody yelled . . . was Starke.] S1; *om.* S2
176.35–38 Rann. Starke . . . silence now?] S1; *om.* S2
◊177.13 rusling] S1; rustling S2
177.37–40 A little laugh . . . with dead men.] S1; *om.* S2
179.1–8 An old man . . . were being finished.] S1; *om.* S2
◊179.15 to to] S1; to S2
180.17–20 The harbor held . . . of past dreams.] S1; *om.* S2
◊181.3 Linni] S1; Linnl S2
◊181.8 creeks] S1; cheeks S2
◊182.5 Mantt] S1; Mannt S2
182.9 One man,] S1; One, S2
◊182.34 Bendag] S1; Beudag S2
◊184.30 Faolcn] S1; Faolan S2
◊186.9 Ran] S1; Rann S2
◊186.11 Brucc] S1; Bruce S2
◊186.31 seing] S1; seeing S2
◊186.32 gave] S1; give S2

## Line-End Hyphenation

144.41 psycho-/neural] psycho-neural
146.30 long-/ships] longships *Also* 149.18
162.42 sword-/points] sword-points
180.11 long-/boats] longboats

## 17. One Minus One (Corpse-Carnival)
## (Oct. 27, 1944)

Bradbury occasionally mixed horror elements into his detective fiction; in "One Minus One," he also mixed in the kind of strangeness and "otherness" that he found so fascinating in genre fiction and film: the narrator, one half of a Siamese Twin circus act, awakens to find his brother dying from a knife wound to the chest. The inevitable trail through emergency surgical separation, the survivor's ever-increasing psychological trauma, and his relentless search for the murderer within the narrow confines of the circus world all contribute to this strange Bradburyian nightmare, but a more complicated biographical and textual history is buried between the lines. During October 1944, Bradbury completed two stories for submission to *Weird Tales* before mixing horror into his next crime story. His composition and submission log shows that he completed a 5,000-word draft of "One Minus One" on October 27, 1944, later changing the word count to 6,500 words. His typed shorthand note "(det)" (for detective genre) and a subsequent note "SOLD!" appear in the entry. His author's sales record includes a $72.00 post-commission payment (rounded down from the actual $72.90) received on March 14, 1945, noting the sale went to *Dime Mystery*. Bradbury's 1945 tax notes also record this information. Nolan's list of sales by Julius Schwartz confirms an actual sale date of March 7, 1945, and a pre-commission payment of $81.00.

Bradbury had completed both "One Minus One" and a more conventional mystery, "The Lady Up Ahead," on October 27, and he immediately sent them off to Julius Schwartz in New York. Schwartz was of two minds on the circus tale, which contained more than its share of Midway and Big Top oddities. On November 4, 1944, he responded to both submissions, starting with "One Minus One": "The first is an interesting yarn but frankly I couldn't warm up to it because of the freak theme. It's well-done though, and unless I receive some revision on it in a few days I'll ship it off to *Blue Book* as you ask." Bradbury had grown up reading his father's copies of *Blue Book,* a mainstream pulp with a nineteenth-century pedigree. He had wanted to place stories there for some time, but Schwartz reminded him on November 23 that it would be a long process: "*Blue Book* usually takes weeks and weeks, so don't expect anything on '1 – 1' for a while yet." But this was not the story that the magazine's editors could warm to, and on February 4, 1945, Schwartz reported that *Blue Book* bounced the story. He had already sent it on to Mike Tilden, who was fairly screaming for more Bradbury submissions to the Popular Publications stable of detective magazines. Tilden especially wanted stories for *Detective Tales,* but the horror elements of "One Minus One" made it a better fit for *Dime Mystery*. On March 3, 1944, Schwartz relayed the news that Tilden had taken the story, and a week later the $81.00 payment came in; Schwartz now had Popular's editors paying Bradbury one and a quarter cents per word (more than the long-standing *Weird Tales* rate of a penny a word), and on March 10 he sent on a post-commission check for $72.90.

"One Minus One" was first published in the July 1945 issue of *Dime Mystery* (S1), with the unfortunate editorially-imposed title of "Corpse-Carnival." But there were further complications; Popular Publications editor Mike Tilden had deferred publication of Bradbury's earlier noir "The Sea Cure" ("Dead Men Rise Up Never," selection 18) from the May to the July 1945 issue of *Dime Mystery,* thus necessitating removal of Bradbury's byline for "Corpse-Carnival" in the same issue. Instead of accepting a house pseudonym, Bradbury asked for "D. R. Banat," his own coded homage to one of his favorite poets of the day, Stephen Vincent Benet. The same solution was required when the story was reset for the August 1945 Canadian issue of *Strange Detective Mysteries* (S2), which also contained both Bradbury stories. Except for a few references by bibliographers, literary critics, and collectors, neither Bradbury's title nor his name would be associated with this story for the next forty years.

During the mid- and late-1940s Bradbury forwarded copies of some of his detective mysteries to CBS radio producer Bill Spier to consider for *Suspense,* and in 1949 he sent a similar selection to *Ellery's Queen's* Fred Danay for reprint and anthology consideration. But "One Minus One" was not part of either submission, and Bradbury eventually left this part of his career as a kind of fiction he no longer wrote. Julius Schwartz had not limited the rights he sold to the Popular Publications magazines, however, and in 1984 Bradbury had to acquiesce to the publication of a Dell mass-market paperback collection of his detective tales titled *A Memory of Murder* (*MeM*). He maintained a degree of control by writing the introduction and lightly revising some of the stories, but does not appear to have done so for this tale, which once again had to appear under the editorially-imposed title "Corpse-Carnival." The real textual mystery goes all the way back to the original S1 and S2 magazine printings, both of which appear to have been typeset independently from Bradbury's original submitted typescript.

S1 stands as copy-text for "One Minus One," but S2 contains a large number of short passages that do not appear in S1 at all. The story was slightly longer than his average short story sale to the detective pulps, and analysis of the variants indicates that the S1 *Dime Mystery* text was cut in ways that saved lines in the middle and final pages, most likely to make room for the full-page title art, two advertisement blocks (Doan's kidney pills, wartime paper drives), and two full columns of advertisements dropped into the final pages of the story. The Canadian S2 contains no title art and only one small advertisement, allowing the *Strange Detective Mysteries* typesetters to include the entire story as well as several points where the *Dime Detective* editors had bowdlerized references to God. The full text is restored by emendation from S2; corrections to obvious errors in S2 and *MeM* are also sources of emendation, but all editorial stylings and typesetting errors introduced in S2 and *MeM* are rejected. Bradbury's intended title is restored, but the editorially-imposed title is retained as a parenthetical subtitle to avoid bibliographical confusion.

His weekly readings of Leigh Brackett's story drafts on Santa Monica Beach almost certainly included her interplanetary solar circus murder tale "The Halfling" (*Astonishing Stories,* February 1943), and Bradbury's sojourn into an Earth-bound variation offers similar psychological weaknesses in his severed Siamese twin protagonist. He was still influenced by pursued or cornered Brackett archetypes, but the greater influence on "One Minus One" comes from his own family dynamic. By and large he had a supportive home life, stressed at times only by Depression-era poverty and the inability of his parents—and especially his older brother Skip—to understand his passion for reading and dreams of becoming a writer. But Skip's twin had died during the great influenza epidemic of 1918–19, two years before Ray Bradbury's birth. His mother had nearly succumbed as well, and as Bradbury entered childhood and adolescence he sometimes felt like a replacement twin. The dynamic was complicated by the fact that Skip was a great athlete with a temper that never allowed him to avoid a fight no matter how bad the odds were. They slept in the same bed until Bradbury was 27 and Skip was 31, tightly packed into the small rented houses and apartment rooms that the family shared after moving to Los Angeles. The narrator Raoul's near-death experience is reflected in the zero-sum title "One Minus One," but the complicated, combative nature of the lost twin also reflects Bradbury's early life with Skip. There is also a broader psychological identification with the buried twin in the story, and Raoul's phantom feelings of attachment that persist all through his search for the murderer—elements that reflect Bradbury's abiding fascination with the boundaries between the subconscious and the rational mind.

Sources: Author's composition and submission log (1942–45); author's sales record (1941–49); author's agency listing (c. 1950); author's notecard story file (c. 1943–1975); Schwartz to Bradbury, Nov. 4 and 23, 1944, Feb. 4 and Mar. 3, 1945; Eller and Touponce, 332–333; Mengeling, 35–37; Mogen, 150–151.

—JE

## Textual Notes

[*title*] S1's opening teaser is entirely editorial: "The surgeon's scalpel finally brought separation to Raoul and his murdered twin. . . . Then the one thing that strange survivor had to live for, was a future which offered only endless tomorrows of darkness. . . ."

188.6 gasping beside him,] S1's deletion of this phrase saved an "orphan" line from running to the top of the next page, which is not allowed in most layout styles. The phrase is restored by emendation from S2.

191.3 Lord!] S2 editors bowdlerized, presumably as a matter of policy, profanity and references to deity in both of the Bradbury stories published in this issue of the Canadian pulp, *Strange Detective Mysteries* (see also selection 18, "The Sea Cure" / "Dead Men Rise Up Never"). The copy-text reading is retained, and the S2 variant "Gosh!" is relegated to the Historical Collation (see also 195.2).

191.15 "Me? Thinking?"] The S1 omission of "Thinking?" did not save a line, but it may be the result of a compositor's eye-skip; the word and its root "think" occur three times in three consecutive sentences.

192.34 thundered] There's no way to be sure whether the S1 reading is correct or the S2 variant "blundered" is correct; since the collation record shows that both S1 and S2 were set from Bradbury's submitted typescript, either one could be a typesetting error. In the absence of any secondary evidence, the S1 copy-text reading stands.

194.33 clenching again.] Beginning at this point in the second half of the story, S1 editors cut single and multiple lines of text to conserve space; S2, lacking both title art and advertisements, restored these lines as the compositor worked from Bradbury's original submitted typescript. These S2 restorations (here and at 195.7, 195.9, 195.28–29, 195.36, 195.40, 196.5, 196.22–26, 196.29, 197.19) are emended into the S1 copy-text. Note that the S2 Bowdlerizers missed the profanity "Dammit" within this passage.

195.2 God's] Here (as at 191.3), S2's editors bowdlerize to eliminate reference to deity or suppress profanity. The copy-text reading is retained, and the S2 variant "goodness" is relegated to the Historical Collation.

198.3–4 "Pass the white . . . as he said:] The circus cant may have fallen victim to S2's bowdlerizing editors; the S1 reading is retained.

198.34 death-walking] Since the pattern of variations shows that both S1 and S2 were set independently from Bradbury's submitted (and unlocated) typescript, either the S1 or the S2 reading (death-stalking) could be a compositor's error. The lack of contextual or secondary evidence to the contrary, the S1 copy-text reading is retained.

199.29 I'd] The S2 variant "you'd" is an editorial misinterpretation of the context. S1 is retained, and the S2 reading is relegated to the Historical Collation.

200.13 *padme*] Bradbury's modification of a traditional meditation chant is spelled "*padne*" at this point in the copy-text. S2 and *MeM* altered the reading to "*padme*" to make it consistent with the earlier instance of the chant at 195.16. Since there is no right way to spell out the chant, the present edition emends from S2 for consistency.

## Emendations

[*title*] One Minus One (Corpse Carnival)] CE; By D. R. BANAT | Corpse-Carnival S1

*188.6 Roger gasping beside him, tugging] S2; Roger tugging S1

189.5 sequined] *MeM*; sequinned S1

189.8 "Almost,"] S2; "~." S1

190.27 anytime] *MeM*; any time

191.3 Deirdre's] S2; Deidre's S1

*191.15 "Me? Thinking?"] S2; "Me?" S1

191.27 Condiellas] CE; Condiella's S1

191.37 me,"] S2; ~." S1

192.38 foul-tongued] *MeM*; foul tongued S1

192.39 Hindu.] S2; ~.. S1

193.5 geeks'] *MeM*; ~^ S1

193.20 Venus] S2; enus S1

194.25 propeller-wise] *MeM*; propellor-wise S1

194.27 Ninety!"] S2; ~!^ S1

*194.33 clenching again.] S2; clenching. S1

*195.7 minutes, darling."] S2; minutes." S1

*195.9 Condiellas, as Papa Dan suggests."] S2; Condiellas." S1

195.15 its] CE; it's S1

*195.28–29 suicide, he was a Hindu."] S2; suicide." S1

*195.36 higher into the canvas firmament.] S2; higher. S1

195.40 grouped] CE; groped S1

*196.5 xylophone, all shaking!"] S2; xylophone!" S1

196.16 That] S2; that S1 *Also* 196.17

*196.22–26 mean?" ¶ Father Dann . . . "Look here,] S2; mean?" "Look here, S1

*196.29 Roger. That's the way it looks from here."] S2; Roger." S1

196.40 you,] S2; ~. S1

197.15 circuses] *MeM*; circuses S1

*197.19 she said, slowly,] S2; she said, S1

*200.13 *padme*] S2; *padne* S1

## Historical Collation: Post-Copy-Text Substantives

*[title]* By D. R. BANAT | Corpse-Carnival S1; CORPSE-CARNIVAL | By D. R.
   BANAT S2; Corpse Carnival *MeM*

188.1 face its reality] S1; face the reality of it, S2

*◊188.6 *not present*] S1; gasping beside him, S2

188.8 Raoul screamed.] S1; *om.* S2

188.17 lip] S1; lips S2

◊189.5 sequinned] S1; sequined *MeM*

190.15 Papa] S1; Father *MeM Also* 191.33, 197.11

190.17 *not*] S1; not S2

◊190.27 any time] S1; anytime *MeM*

190.28 canvasses] S1; canvases *MeM*

190.35 *that*] S1; that S2 *Also* 191.23

*191.3 Lord!] S1; Gosh! S2

◊191.3 Deidre's] S1; Deirdre's S2, *MeM*

191.10 West] S1; west *MeM*

*◊191.15 "Me?"] S1; "Me? Thinking?" S2

191.15 Father Dan] S1; F.D. S2

191.19 saxophone] S1; saxaphone S2

191.21 or shovel] S1; o shovel S2

192.3–4 Forget? ¶ Lal's] S1; ~? ^ ~ S2

192.9 TWINS!] S1; ~^ S2

*192.34 thundered] S1; blundered S2

◊193.5 geeks] S1; geeks' MeM

◊193.20 enus] S1; Venus S2, MeM

193.30 Stormclouds] S1; Storm clouds MeM

◊194.25 propellor-wise] S1; propeller-wise MeM

194.31 guywire] S1; guy wire MeM

*◊194.33 clenching.] S1; clenching again. S2

*195.2 God's] S1; goodness S2

*◊195.7 minutes."] S1; minutes, darling." S2

*◊195.9 Condiellas."] S1; Condiellas, as Papa Dan suggests." S2

195.25 look] S1; looking S2

*◊195.28–29 suicide."] S1; suicide, he was a Hindu." S2

*◊195.36 higher.] S1; higher into the canvas firmament. S2

*◊195.40 They've groped and gone] S1; They've gone MeM

*◊196.5 xylophone!"] S1; xylophone, all shaking!" S2

196.10 toot swcct] S1; tout de suite McM

◊196.16 that] S1; That S2, MeM

◊196.17 that] S1; That S2

*◊196.22–26 Mean?" "Look] S1; mean?" ¶ Father Dan pulled out his flask vi-
ciously and took a long vicious pull at it. "Dammit, I don't know what I mean.
All I know is I got half a Siamese twin act on my hands and I'm trying to be
decent, and the geeks are walking out unless I fire you." ¶ He sat down, his
voice softer, more logical. "Look S2

*◊196.29 Roger."] S1; Roger. That's the way it looks from here." S2

196.37–38 pieces!" ^ Father] S1; ~! ¶ ~ S2

196.38 Allright] S1; All right MeM

◊197.15 circusses] S1; circuses MeM

*◊197.19 said,] S1; said, slowly, S2

197.28 comment] S1; comments S2

197.30 me] S1; me S2

197.35 train and get] S1; train, get S2

197.38 had] S1; had S2

*198.3–4 "Pass the white . . . as he said:] S1; om. S2

198.9 in my own time] S1; om. MeM

198.32 nor guns] S1; or guns S2

*198.34 death-walking] S1; death-stalking S2

199.7 thing he'd] S1; thing he loved he'd S2

*199.29 I'd] S1; you'd S2

199.39 flittering] S1; glittering S2
200.10 Four—!"] S1; Four—^" S2
\*◊200.13 *padne*] S1; *padme* S2, *MeM*

## Line-End Hyphenation

189.32 un-/shelled] unshelled
190.23 tan-/bark] tanbark
195.26 cover-/up] cover-up
197.5 boot-/tip] boot-tip
197.30 un-/romantic] unromantic

## 18. The Sea Cure (Dead Men Rise Up Never) (Nov. 6, 1944)

Despite his new commitment to write the second half of Leigh Brackett's novella "Lorelei of the Red Mist" (selection 16), Bradbury was able to turn out three crime stories in quick succession from late October to early November 1944: "One Minus One" (selection 17), "The Lady Up Ahead," and "The Sea Cure." Bradbury's composition and submission log includes an entry for a 5,500-word story titled "The Sea Cure" dated November 6, 1944, subsequently annotated as "SOLD!" His author's sales record documents the sale to *Dime Mystery* and a post-commission payment of $63.00 received January 24, 1945, and his 1945 tax notes confirm this information. Nolan's list of sales by Julius Schwartz confirms an actual sale date of January 17, 1945, and a pre-commission payment of $70.00 from *Dime Mystery*. "The Sea Cure" appeared, under the editorially-imposed title "Dead Men Rise Up Never," in the July 1945 issue of *Dime Mystery* (S1), with uncredited three-quarter-page title art and a house tailpiece.

The story was reset and published in the Canadian August 1945 issue of *Strange Detective Mysteries* (S2), correcting some of S1's typesetting errors and introducing new ones. But S2 was unillustrated and free of advertisements, allowing the Canadian compositor (working, as often was the case with the Canadian pulp reprint process, directly from the author's typescript or *Dime Mystery*'s uncut galleys) to set the entire story, including a number of passages that the S1 editors, more constrained for space, had omitted.

In June 1949, Bradbury thought enough of this story to include it among a dozen of his detective stories sent on to *Ellery Queen* founder and editor Fred Danay for possible reprint or anthology consideration, but Bradbury had already moved on from this kind of story writing and did not intend to bring any of the pure detective and crime pieces into any of his future story collections. But Julius Schwartz had not limited the original sales for these stories, and in 1984 Bradbury was forced to allow a fifteen-story collection edited by subsequent owners of the rights. This 1984 Dell mass-market paperback, *A Memory of Murder* (*MeM*), included "The Sea Cure" under its imposed title "Dead Men Rise Up Never"; Bradbury was able to write a contextualizing introduction and lightly revised some of these stories, but collation does not indicate variation beyond a few editorial corrections and house stylings of spelling, punctuation, and grammar.

The early history of this tale is straightforward, but it nevertheless shows how Julius Schwartz often had to juggle multiple Bradbury submissions across the surprisingly wide range of pulps that survived the paper rationing of the war years. Schwartz had already sent Bradbury's circus murder mystery "One Minus One" to McCall Corporation's *Blue Book,* and "The Lady Up Ahead," with its commuter train femme fatale, to Mike Tilden for *Dime Mystery,* one of several detective pulps managed by Popular Publications. On November 24,1944, Schwartz wrote to report this strategy, and to indicate that he thought "The Sea Cure" fine enough to merit submission to the venerable *Black Mask,* a market that he had been trying to crack with Bradbury submissions for almost a year. On Christmas Day, 1944, Schwartz wrote with the disappointing news that *Black Mask* had rejected "The Sea Cure"; however, Tilden had coincidentally bounced "The Lady Up Ahead," so Schwartz filled the gap by sending Tilden "The Sea Cure" for *Dime Mystery.* On January 20, 1945, Schwartz confirmed that Tilden bought the story for the May 1945 issue of *Dime Mystery,* but it was subsequently moved to the July issue.

"The Sea Cure" evokes the mood of several Poe poems, and Bradbury would have known them all ("The City in the Sea," "Ulalume," and Poe's last poem, "Annabel Lee"). His own off-trail brand of such loss appeared in his earlier unpublished tale, "The Tar-pit Murders"; the S1 tailpiece (a lady's slender, grasping hand reaching out of a circle in water) is eerily reminiscent of that La Brea Tar-pit setting. Bradbury had also just made an actual auto excursion with his friend Grant Beach through the old Spanish coastal mission stations of northern Mexico and southern California; the sunken mission where the innocent girl and the rival criminals end their days may derive, in part, from his recent mission trip, and from the mysterious Venusian sea of his ongoing collaboration with Leigh Brackett, "Lorelei of the Red Mist."

Copy-text is S1, with S2 and *MeM* as sources of correction to punctuation and spelling. Some of the substantive variations in the later texts do not appear to be authorial, and only appear in the Historical Collation. These include four bowdlerized passages in S2 that may have fallen victim to Canadian editorial policies for *Strange Detective Mysteries.* But nine sentences or phrases in the looser layout of S2 restore readings cut (to save space) from the American S1, and these S2 restorations are emended into the copy-text. These readings, and others, are discussed in the textual notes below.

Sources: Author's composition and submission log (1942–45); author's sales record (1941–49); author's 1945 tax notes; author's extended sales-by-publisher index (c. 1950); author's agency listing (c. 1950); author's notecard story file (c. 1943–1975); Schwartz to Bradbury, Nov. 23 and Dec. 25, 1944, and Jan. 20, 1945.

—JE

## Textual Notes

*[title]* The S1 editorial teaser below the title art is adapted from the story text at 202.37–41, and reads as follows: "Mark figured we'd snatched the girl for the heavy ransom. . . . I figured that we were shielding her from Finlay's lugs, hot after dough, too. . . . But the boss had yet another idea, which none of us even guessed, until we'd heard the bells from that old Spanish mission, deep under the sea. . . ." (ellipses from S1).

203.38 said about it,] Context suggests a dropped word ("something"), but the S1 reading may reflect the character's idiosyncratic syntax. There is not enough evidence to emend, and the S1 reading stands.

204.27–31 I sat playing . . . as rushing.] The S2 omission of this passage is the first of four bowdlerized editorial cuts. The decision to cut may be based on the card game reference, but it is more likely the reference to "Dying is as good as living," which may have been cut for Canadian home front morale during World War II.

205.12 Look beyond that curve, Hank?] The Canadian S2 editorial styling "See" attempts to tailor the verb to the interrogative form of the sentence. Although "See?" is more acceptable than "Look?," the S1 reading may reflect Bradbury's intended speech pattern for this American crime gang character, and is therefore retained.

205.30–32 "That's from . . . wind dies."] Since there is no detectable bowdlerization here, it's not clear why S2 editors, who were not tight on space for this issue, omitted Hamphill's explanation of the imagined sound of submerged mission bells. The passage, which is crucial to Bradbury's haunting tone in this story, is retained.

207.14 hair—] The em-dash and paragraph break indicates a momentary pause in Finlay's cold-hearted bargain; the lack of closing quotation marks confirms there's no change in speaker, and there is no evidence in the historical collation of variants to indicate an intervening comment by Hamphill.

208.40 Hell] Here and at 209.9, S2 eliminates references to hell and God, suggesting that S2's Canadian editors may have censored profanities and swearing for Canadian crime pulp reprints of American originals.

210.18–20 It's too damn . . . chance to lam."] The two consecutive sentences deleted in S2 contain swearing in dialog; this cut, as well as similar cuts at 209.1 and 209.10, appear to result from S2's publishing policy.

210.37 "No."] Hank's contradictory "No" was probably cut from S1 to save space, but the omission creates reader confusion. The S2 restoration at this point is emended into the copy-text.

212.36 "But—"] Hank's interjection, creating a confusing paragraph break in the middle of Hamphill's speech, was almost certainly cut from S1 to save a line. It is restored by emendation from S2.

## Emendations

*[title]* The Sea Cure (Dead Men Rise Up Never)] CE; Dead Men Rise Up Never | By | RAY BRADBURY S1

203.10 pointed,] S2; ~^ S1

204.10 Why] S2; "~ S1

205.28 breathe] S2; breath S1

208.15 "It's] *MeM*; ^~ S1

209.21 while . . .] S2; ~ . . ." S1

210.26 Willie] S2; Wilile S1

*210.36–38 him. ¶ "No." ¶ "You] S2; him. ¶ "You S1

211.38 Mark, stepping back.] S2; Mark. S1

212.11 ¶ "Yes, boss."] S2; ^ "Yes," boss." S1

212.13 ¶ "Yes, boss."] S2; ^ "~, ~." S1

212.17–18 stopped, waiting for the big wave to collapse.] S2; stopped. S1

212.21 further] S2; futher S1

212.22–23 over, and the . . . I shivered.] S2; over. S1

212.26 broke. A long silence.] S2; broke. S1

212.30 off, happy to be ordered around.] S2 off. S1

*212.35–37 Willie." ¶ "But—" ¶ "I got] S2; Willie.^ ¶ "I got S1

212.37 late. Go on. *Now,*] S2; late. *Now,* S1

213.6 water all over the leather seat.] S2; water. S1

## Historical Collation: Post-Copy-Text Substantives

*[title]* Dead Men Rise Up Never | By RAY BRADBURY] S1; DEAD MEN RISE UP NEVER | By RAY BRADBURY S2; Dead Men Rise Up Never *MeM*

201.1 wheel and] S1; Wheen and and S2

201.18 back seat] S1; backseat *MeM*

204.23 sea gulls] S1; seagulls *MeM*

*204.27–31 I sat playing . . . as rushing.] S1; *om.* S2

*205.12 Look] S1; See S2

◊205.28 breath] S1; breathe S2, *MeM*

*205.30–32 "That's from the . . . the wind dies."] S1; *om.* S2

205.31 further] S1; farther *MeM*

◊208.15 It's] S1; "It's *MeM*

*208.40 Hell] S1; Gosh S2

*209.9 God, next] S1; Next S2

210.9 fussing] S1; futzing S2

*210.18–20 click. It's too damn . . . chance to lam."] S1; click." S2

◊210.26 Wilile] S1; Willie S2, *MeM*

*◊210.36–38 him. ¶ "You] S1; him. ¶ "No." ¶ "You S2

211.6 started] S1; lighted S2

◊211.38 Mark.] S1; Mark, stepping back. S2

◊212.17–18 stopped.] S1; stopped, waiting for the big wave to collapse. S2

◊212.21 futher] S1; further S2; farther *MeM*

◊212.22–23 over.] S1; over, and the waves smashed his voice into so many hysterical fragments. I shivered. S2

◊212.26 broke.] S1; broke. A long silence.

◊212.30 off.] S1; off, happy to be ordered around. S2

◊212.37 late. *Now,* Hank."] S1; late. Go on. Now, Hank." S2

*◊212.35–37 Willie. ¶ "I] S1; Willie." ¶ "But—" ¶ "I got S2

◊213.6 water.] S1; water all over the leather seat. S2

## Line-End Hyphenation

205.38 high-/way] highway

206.11 empty-/handed] empty-handed

208.33 double-/crossing] double-crossing

## 19. Skeleton (*Weird Tales*) (Nov. 30, 1944)

Bradbury's fascination with sensation and his readings of medical studies on the five senses often surfaced in his fiction, and it was only a matter of time before he would turn this fascination inward to the internal structures of the human body, mixing in an equal dose of paranoia to create "Skeleton," one of his most enduring horror stories. His composition and submission log sheets record the completion of a 5,000-word draft of "Skeleton" on November 30, 1944; a subsequent typed note reads "SOLD!" in the same entry line. His author's sales record contains an entry for the sale to *Weird Tales* and a $45.00 post-commission payment received March 6, 1945, and his 1945 tax notes show the same payment and date. Nolan's list of sales by Julius Schwartz confirms an actual sale date of March 1, 1945, and a pre-commission payment of $50.00.

Julius Schwartz acknowledged receipt on December 9, 1944, offering his reaction to the profound horrors personified by M. Munigant, the vaguely human-like creature that uses Mr. Harris's pathological fear of his own skeleton to relieve him of his symptoms—and his bones: "and quite a shocker it is too. Maybe too much for the pulps . . ." Schwartz decided to try it with Mary

Gnaedinger, editor of *Famous Fantastic Mysteries,* where his breakthrough science fiction story "King of the Gray Spaces" had reached print in the December 1943 issue. Bradbury had submitted the story with two slightly variant endings, and Schwartz offers a tantalizing comparison at the conclusion of his letter "I liked the first ending best, incidentally. The alternative, with the guy talking spoiled the effect. *Suggesting* the horror, seemed more effective to me" (emphasis Schwartz's). The first ending remains unlocated, possibly a casualty of the editor's hand; the story reached print with Mr. Harris's lovely wife recoiling in terror when the animate jelly-like creature on the floor calls her name.

Bradbury sent in a rewrite, and Schwartz's December 25 response again showed mixed emotions: "on rereading the new version I still think it's a good yarn but mighty, mighty gruesome." The rewrite finally went on to *Famous Fantastic Mysteries,* but *FFM's* editor Mary Gnaedinger brought in Alden Norton, editor-in-chief for all of the Popular Publications crime and fantasy pulps, for his opinion. Norton had admired Bradbury's talent from the beginning, but he was often frustrated by the off-trail plots and characters that came across his desk from Schwartz's office. Norton's rejection came back across Schwartz's desk with a clear sense of that frustration: "We found SKELETON imaginative and very original. But both Mary and I are of the reluctant opinion that he didn't quite succeed in holding the mood of outlandish horror that a story of this nature requires. It is with the deepest personal regret that I decided to send this one back, it came that close. This Bradbury kid certainly has an awful lot on the ball, and I do hope you can let me see some more stuff soon."

On January 20, 1945, Schwartz notified Bradbury that "Skeleton"—bones, paranoia, jelly, and all—was going on to *Weird Tales.* On March 3, he notified Bradbury that the editors had purchased "Skeleton," with payment coming within the week. The story appeared in the September 1945 issue (S1), with title art by Boris Dolgov and a skeleton tailpiece drawing signed Brosnatch. "Skeleton" was reset and reprinted in the November 1945 Canadian issue of *Weird Tales* (S2), without illustration. Bradbury sent the story, along with others, to CBS Radio producer William Spier for consideration, and subsequently probed interest with the *Nero Wolfe* mystery magazine and, at Henry Kuttner's suggestion, a possible British anthology deal with Walter Gillings. Nothing came of these overtures, but Schwartz was able to place another reprint (for $35.00) in the *Rex Stout's Mystery Magazine* issue of October 6, 1946 (S3). The S1 version was revived once more for the September 1960 issue of *Shock* (S4).

But by this time, "Skeleton" was already a Bradbury classic. He revised the S1 version significantly for his first book, the 1947 Arkham House collection *Dark Carnival* ($DC^{1947}$). This revised version was reset and published in the 1948 abridged edition of *Dark Carnival* published in Britain ($DC^{1948}$), and reset again for the 2001 limited press Gauntlet edition ($DC^{2001}$). Bradbury revised

"Skeleton" yet again and included it among the 15 *Dark Carnival* stories that he revised or rewrote for the 1955 publication of *The October Country* ($OC^{1955}$). This third version remains in print today, passing through nine distinct American and British typesettings to date. The Vintage Bradbury (*VB*, 1965), Bradbury's first fully retrospective collection, includes a resetting of the *OC* version, and his subsequent hundred-story retrospective compilation *The Stories of Ray Bradbury* ($SRB^{1980}$) also includes the *OC* version in four typesettings. Finally, "Skeleton" appeared, with the distinct but closely related *Script* story "Skeleton" (selection 21), in the 2008 limited Subterranean two-story collection *Skeletons* (*S*) which was set from the *OC* version. Neither *S* nor the $DC^{2001}$ limited press editions involved Bradbury in the preparation of the texts.

"Skeleton" was reprinted, without the direct involvement of Bradbury, in seven anthologies, including *Best Horror Stories* (U.K., 1957), *Spine Chillers* (U.K., 1961), *Famous Monster Tales* (1967), *Strange Beasts and Unnatural Monsters* (1968), *Christopher Lee: From the Archives of Evil Number 2* (1976), *The Best Horror Stories* (U.K., 1977; deleted from the U. S. edition), and *Venomous Tales of Villainy and Vengeance* (1984). The story was adapted for television by Bradbury for *Ray Bradbury Theater* (USA), first airing on February 6, 1988. It was adapted by other writers to comic-strip form for *Ray Bradbury's Tales of Terror Special #1* (May 1994).

Copy-text for the present edition is S1, which presents the rarely seen original intentions for "Skeleton." Bradbury's significant *DC* revisions and the even deeper sentence-by-sentence *OC* revisions represent subsequent intentions, and are not emended into the copy-text; however, all of the substantive variants appear in the Historical Collation below so that readers may trace the author's revising hand down through time. A handful of necessary corrections of spelling and punctuation are emended in from S2 and *DC* to correct the poor typesetting work of S1. Discussions of significant variants appear the textual notes below. The *Weird Tales* "Skeleton" presented here (Eller 45–11) is distinct from (but closely related to) the *Script* "Skeleton" (Eller 45–5); although published first, *Script*'s "Skeleton" was written later and appears in the present volume as selection 21. The rejected *S* reading "titbits" is probably a typographical error, but it is also an archaic word; this variant appears as a rejected substantive in the Historical Collation.

In "Skeleton," Bradbury's extension of hypochondria and psychosomatic manifestations from the clinical into the fantastic is both controlled and terrifying. The tragic power of suggestion that controls "Skeleton" is reminiscent of "The Watchers" (selection 15), and the indefinable, hybrid creature M. Munigant defies classification in much the same way that "The Man Upstairs" does (volume 2, selection 12). "Skeleton" also reflects Bradbury's careful readings in Dr. Karen Horney's early studies of neurosis and psychosis, his selective reading from his Modern Library Freud, and his more wide-ranging readings in sensation and awareness. Bradbury always maintained that the actual writing of "Skeleton" was the direct result of a visit to a physician for a general sense of malaise; the doctor's response—that many of the internal sensations he was feeling were normal movements and connections of his skeletal structure, related musculature, and soft-tissue organs—prompted his "what if" centering on Mr. Harris, as he is driven to his destruction by a pathological fear that his skeleton is a sentient creature waiting to destroy the mind it encases and the soft tissue it supports.

Sources: Author's composition and submission log (1942–45); author's sales record (1941–49); author's agency listing (c. 1950); author's notecard story file (c. 1943–1975); Schwartz to Bradbury, Dec. 9, 1944, Jan. 20 and Mar. 3, 1945, Apr. 13, 1946; Eller-Bradbury interviews; Mogen, 46, 53, 58; Pierce, in Greenberg and Olander, 169, 175–176.

—JE

## Textual Notes

214.14 Too much whiskey. . . . stop drinking] Drinking is not really in character with Harris's neurotic personality. In his 1955 *OC* revisions, Bradbury changed this diagnosis point from whiskey to protein.

215.13 He pointed at these.] The x-ray image is described in rich and mesmerizing detail in the 1955 *OC* expansion (see Historical Collation).

215.16 off-bound horror of a Dali painting.] The *OC* revisions add the Swiss painter Henry Fuseli, a more recent Bradbury Romantic Age favorite whose "The Nightmare" (1781) would be featured on the dust jacket of his 1976 story collection *Long After Midnight*.

215.22–38 Harris lay on a table . . . went home.] One of Bradbury's copies of the September 1945 issue of *Weird Tales* (preserved in the Center for Ray Bradbury Studies) has pencil strike-through markings in Bradbury's hand. These deletions focus on the more violent and supernatural aspects of M. Munigant's first examination of Harris (the jaw expander, Munigant's nose, "Skeletons were strange, unwieldy things," and the chewing of bread-sticks). These short passages all contain clues to Munigant's intentions, and Bradbury may have considered eliminating these passages as he revised for *DC*. None of these pencil deletions corresponds to actual revisions made in any of the *DC* or *OC* revisions, however, and appear to represent a momentary strategy that he quickly abandoned.

216.24–26 "Well, now, so . . . She demonstrated.] Clarisse's rational explanation of the apparent movement of the kneecap was deleted during Bradbury's 1955 *OC* revisions.

217.12–13 He saw his fingers . . . their quaking apprehension.] This simile of high speed "motion films" is not fully developed, and is difficult to visualize. Bradbury deleted the sentence in his 1955 revisions for *OC*.

218.3 Quite a drive. Over six hundred miles.] For his 1955 OC revisions, Bradbury moved Harris's home from San Francisco to Los Angeles, which is only 357 straight-line miles from Phoenix. He completed the change of setting by making the city-to-city distance less specific ("Hundreds of miles.").

218.18 shoving.] For the most part, Bradbury did not revise his tales for *SRB*. Context indicates that the variant "showing" introduced in the British *SRB*[1983] is an editorial imposition or a compositor's error.

218.19–20 slithered on the bed in animal cuddlesomeness,] Clarisse's animal-like liveliness was revised out by Bradbury for $OC^{1955}$, as was her motherly invitation to "tell mama" (218.26).

222.2 so titanic a reaction] S1's compositor may have dropped the indefinite article to keep "reaction" on the line-end and save a line in the page layout. It is restored by emendation from the $DC^{1947}$ typesetting.

223.22 Frisco to Phoenix] In his 1955 *OC* revisions, Bradbury moved Harris to Los Angeles and consequently shifted the mid-trip disaster from Death Valley to the Mojave Desert, about one hundred miles to the southeast. Bradbury's original version, including Harris's straight-line distance estimate of the San Francisco to Phoenix route through Death Valley of more than six hundred miles (218.3), is fairly accurate as originally narrated. The original geography and travel adventures are retained as an essential part of Bradbury's early settled intention for the story.

## Emendations

*[title]* Skeleton] CE; Skeleton | By RAY BRADBURY S1

214.27 druggist's] S2; druggists S1

215.21 M.] $OC^{1955}$; Mr. S1

217.14 granted?] $DC^{1947}$; ~. S1

217.33 it's] S2; its S1

218.25 hypochondriac] $OC^{1955}$; hypochrondriac S1

219.1 hypochondriac] CE; hypochrondriac S1

219.15 choking] $DC^{1947}$; chocking S1

219.18 bivalve] S2; bivavle S1

219.23 Clarisse] $DC^{1947}$; Clarrise S1 *Also* 226.31

219.24 meeting] $DC^{1948}$; meet S1

219.31 *cartilage*] S2; *cartilege* S1

220.9 carpals, metacarpals] CE; carpels, metacarpels S1

220.21 scale] $OC^{1955}$; scales S1

*222.2 titanic a reaction] $DC^{1947}$; titanic reaction S1

222.5 laid] $DC^{1947}$; layed S1

222.19 inquire] $DC^{1947}$; enquire S1

222.37 "It] $DC^{1947}$; ^~ S1

222.41 'most] $OC^{1955}$; ^~ S1

223.3 Perhaps.] $DC^{1947}$; ~? S1

223.14 possibly] S2; possible S1

223.23–24 Creldon,] S2; ~^ S1

223.24 money,] S2; ~^ S1

225.5 ever] $DC^{1947}$; every S1

225.35 breathe] S2; breath S1

226.32 jelly-fish] CE; jelly ^ fish S1

## Historical Collation: Post-Copy-Text Substantives

[title] Skeleton | *By RAY BRADBURY*] S1; Skeleton | By RAY BRADBURY S2;
THE SKELETON | *by RAY BRADBURY* S4; SKELETON $DC^{1947}$, $OC^{1961,}$
$^{1963, 1976, 1996}$, $SRB^{2010}$; *Skeleton* $DC^{1948}$, $OC^{1984}$, $SRB^{1983}$, $RBS1^{2008}$; Skeleton
$OC^{1970}$, $SRB^{1980}$; Skeleton $OC^{1999}$

214.3 After all,] S1; *om.* $OC^{1955-1999}$

214.5 got money] S1; was paid $DC^{1947}$, $DC^{1948}$, $OC^{1955-1999}$

214.6 him] S1; Mr. Harris $DC^{1947}$, $DC^{1948}$, $OC^{1955-1999}$

214.7 door and opened it to put] S1; door, opened it, and put $DC^{1947}$, $DC^{1948}$,
$OC^{1955-1999}$

214.8 Doctor?] S1; ~. $OC^{1955-1999}$

214.8 acid voice] S1; voice $OC^{1955-1999}$

214.10 snorted thinly.] S1; snorted. $OC^{1955-1999}$

214.11 at Harris] S1; *om.* $OC^{1955-1999}$

214.13 only] S1; just $OC^{1955-1999}$

214.13 Let me] S1; Let's $OC^{1955-1999}$

*214.14 whiskey] S1; protein $DC^{1947}$, $DC^{1948}$, $OC^{1955-1999}$

214.15 home to bed] S1; to bed $DC^{1947}$, $DC^{1948}$, $OC^{1955-1999}$

214.15 drinking] S1; the protein $DC^{1947}$, $DC^{1948}$, $OC^{1955-1999}$

214.15 stop smoking,] S1; no smoking, $DC^{1947}$, $DC^{1948}$, $OC^{1955-1999}$

214.16 stood there, sulking.] S1; stood sulking. $OC^{1955-1999}$

214.17 Dr. Burleigh looked] S1; The doctor glanced $DC^{1947}$, $DC^{1948}$, $OC^{1955-1999}$

214.17 You] S1; *You* $DC^{1947}$, $DC^{1948}$, $OC^{1955-1999}$

214.18 dollars, now] S1; dollars, please, now S2

214.20 addressed him like] S1; spoke as to $OC^{1955-1999}$

214.20 pained] S1; sore $DC^{1947}$, $DC^{1948}$, $OC^{1955-1999}$

214.21 keep at it] S1; ◆kept at it [kept $OC^{1955-1999}$] $DC^{1947}$, $DC^{1948}$

214.23 soreness.] S1; soreness, yourself. $DC^{1947}$, $DC^{1948}$, $OC^{1955-1999}$

214.24–25 now! Take that . . . you've been stewing] S1; and take that trip to
Phoenix you've stewed $DC^{1947}$, $DC^{1948}$, $OC^{1955-1999}$

214.25 get away] S1; travel $DC^{1947}$, $DC^{1948}$, $OC^{1955-1999}$

214.26 *not present*] S1; Five minutes later, $DC^{1947}$, $DC^{1948}$, $OC^{1955-1999}$

214.26 five minutes later,] S1; *om. DC*¹⁹⁴⁷, *DC*¹⁹⁴⁸, *OC*¹⁹⁵⁵⁻¹⁹⁹⁹

◊214.27 druggists] S1; druggist's S2, *DC*¹⁹⁴⁸, *OC*¹⁹⁵⁵, *OC*¹⁹⁵⁵⁻¹⁹⁹⁹

214.28 BONE SPECIALISTS] S1; Bone Specialists *SRB*¹⁹⁸⁰⁻²⁰¹⁰, *RBS1*

214.29 academical] S1; academic *OC*¹⁹⁵⁵⁻¹⁹⁹⁹

214.30 easily reached] S1; conveniently near *DC*¹⁹⁴⁷, *DC*¹⁹⁴⁸, *OC*¹⁹⁵⁵⁻¹⁹⁹⁹

215.3 shiny eyes,] S1; shiny moves of his eyes, *DC*¹⁹⁴⁷, *DC*¹⁹⁴⁸, *OC*¹⁹⁵⁵⁻¹⁹⁹⁹

215.3–4 he had an . . . every word,] S1; his accent was such that he softly whistled each word; *OC*¹⁹⁵⁵⁻¹⁹⁹⁹

215.4 due to] S1; because of *OC*¹⁹⁵⁵⁻¹⁹⁹⁹

215.9 flesh and bone] S1; flesh, and skeleton *OC*¹⁹⁵⁵⁻¹⁹⁹⁹

215.12 rattled] S1; slashed *OC*¹⁹⁵⁵⁻¹⁹⁹⁹

*215.12–18 X-rays and paintings . . . "That all depends,"] S1; X-rays to haunt the room with their look of things found floating in an ancient tide. Here, here! The skeleton surprised! Here luminous portraits of the long, the short, the large, the small bones. Mr. Harris must be aware of his position, his problem! M. Munigant's hand tapped, rattled, whispered, scratched at faint nebulae of flesh in which hung ghosts of cranium, spinal-cord, pelvis, lime, calcium, marrow, here, there, this, that, these, those, and others! Look! ¶ Harris shuddered. The X-rays and the paintings blew in a green and phosphorescent wind from a land peopled by the monsters of Dali and Fuseli. ¶ M. Munigant whistled quietly. Did Mr. Harris wish his bones—treated? ¶ "That depends," *OC*¹⁹⁵⁵⁻¹⁹⁹⁹

215.16 off-bound] S1; off -bounds *DC*¹⁹⁴⁷, *DC*¹⁹⁴⁸, *OC*¹⁹⁵⁵⁻¹⁹⁹⁹

215.17 of] S1; for *DC*¹⁹⁴⁷, *DC*¹⁹⁴⁸, *OC*¹⁹⁵⁵⁻¹⁹⁹⁹

215.19 *not present*] S1; Well *OC*¹⁹⁵⁵⁻¹⁹⁹⁹

215.20 NEED] S1; *need DC*¹⁹⁴⁷, *DC*¹⁹⁴⁸, *OC*¹⁹⁵⁵⁻¹⁹⁹⁹

215.20 of no use] S1; useless *OC*¹⁹⁵⁵⁻¹⁹⁹⁹

◊215.21 Mr.] S1; M. *OC*¹⁹⁵⁵ ¹⁹⁹⁹

215.22 off,] S1; switched off, *DC*¹⁹⁴⁷, *DC*¹⁹⁴⁸, *OC*¹⁹⁵⁵⁻¹⁹⁹⁹

215.23 ^ Something] S1; ¶ ~ *DC*¹⁹⁴⁷, *DC*¹⁹⁴⁸, *OC*¹⁹⁵⁵⁻¹⁹⁹⁹

215.24 ^ He] S1; ¶ ~ *DC*¹⁹⁴⁷, *DC*¹⁹⁴⁸, *OC*¹⁹⁵⁵⁻¹⁹⁹⁹

215.24 made noises.] S1; made faint cracking noises. *OC*¹⁹⁵⁵⁻¹⁹⁹⁹

215.25 pictures] S1; skeleton charts *OC*¹⁹⁵⁵⁻¹⁹⁹⁹

215.25–26 leap. A violent . . . and, involuntarily,] S1; quiver and jump. A violent shudder seized Harris. Involuntarily, *OC*¹⁹⁵⁵⁻¹⁹⁹⁹

215.27–28 cried out. He . . . was no use.] S1; shouted. His nose had almost been bitten off! No use, no use! *OC*¹⁹⁵⁵⁻¹⁹⁹⁹

215.28 time.] S1; ~! *OC*¹⁹⁵⁵⁻¹⁹⁹⁹

215.28–29 raised the shades. He looked dreadfully disappointed.] S1; whispered the shades up, dreadfully disappointed. *OC*¹⁹⁵⁵⁻¹⁹⁹⁹

215.30 *needed*] S1; *neded OC*¹⁹⁶¹

215.33 to study.] S1; to take home and study. $DC^{1947}$, $DC^{1948}$, $OC^{1955-1999}$

215.34 be aware] S1; be tremblingly aware $OC^{1955-1999}$

215.34 careful] S1; on guard $OC^{1955-1999}$

215.36 have] S1; care for $OC^{1955-1999}$

215.36 He] S1; M. Munigant $OC^{1955-1999}$

215.37 himself to chew on, and saying] S1; himself, saying $OC^{1955-1999}$

215.38 See you soon, Mr. Harris.] S1; Good day, good day, to Mr. Harris! $OC^{1955-1999}$

216.1–2 day was Sunday, . . . sorts of new] S1; ◆day was Sunday. [day, Sunday, $OC^{1955-1999}$] Mr. Harris ◆started the morning by feeling all sorts of new [discovered innumerable fresh $OC^{1955-1999}$] $DC^{1947}$, $DC^{1948}$, $OC^{1955-1999}$

216.2–4 some time glancing . . . anatomically perfect,] S1; the morning, his eyes fixed staring with new interest at the small, anatomically perfect painting $OC^{1955-1999}$

216.6–7 "Don't do that!"] S1; "Stop!" $OC^{1955-1999}$

216.8 remainder of the day] S1; rest of the afternoon $OC^{1955-1999}$

216.8–10 was seated at . . . fingering and weighing] S1; played bridge in the parlor laughing and chatting with three other ladies while Harris, hidden away, fingered and weighed $OC^{1955-1999}$

216.11 of this] S1; *om.* $OC^{1955-1999}$

216.11 stood up] S1; rose $OC^{1955-1999}$

216.11–12 called: ⁋ "Clarisse!"] S1; ~: ^ '~!' $OC^{1984}$

216.17 Are you] S1; Are you you $OC^{1961}$

216.17 darling] S1; sweet $OC^{1955-1999}$

*216.24–26 "Well, now, so . . . She demonstrated.] S1; ◆ "Well, now, so it does. Icky." She pondered. "No. On the other hand—it doesn't. It's only an optical illusion. I think. The skin moves over the bone; not vice-versa. See?" she demonstrated. [*om.* $OC^{1955-1999}$] $DC^{1947}$, $DC^{1948}$

216.34 just hope] S1; hope $OC^{1955-1999}$

216.34–37 he said, making . . . coming in, dear."] S1; The joke was most uneasy. Now, above all, he wished to be alone. Further discoveries, newer and stranger archaeological diggings, lay within reach of his trembling hands, and he did not wish to be laughed at. ⁋ "Thanks for coming in dear," he said. $OC^{1955-1999}$

216.36 him and poking fun.] S1; him. $DC^{1947}$, $DC^{1948}$, $OC^{1955-1999}$

216.38 time," she said, kissing him, rubbing her small pink nose warm against his.] S1; time." She rubbed her small nose softly against his. $OC^{1955-1999}$

216.39–41 "I'll be damned!" . . . from there on?"] S1; "Wait! Here, now . . ." He put his finger to touch his nose and hers. "Did you realize? The nose-bone grows down only *this* far. From there on a lot of gristly tissue fills out the rest!" $OC^{1955-1999}$

217.1 "So what?" And, dancing, she exited.] S1; "Of course, darling!" And she danced from the room. $OC^{1955-1999}$

217.2 He felt the sweat] S1; Now, sitting alone, he felt the perspiration $OC^{1955-1999}$

217.2–3 forming a salten tide to flow] S1; to flow in a thin tide $OC^{1955-1999}$

217.3–5 Next on the . . . messenger boys. But,] S1; He licked his lips and shut his eyes. Now . . . now . . . next on the agenda, what . . . ? The spinal cord, yes. Here. Slowly, he examined it, in the same way he operated the many push-buttons in his office, thrusting them to summon secretaries, messengers. But now, $OC^{1955-1999}$

217.7 Mr. Harris'] S1; his $OC^{1955-1999}$

217.7 him.] S1; ~! $OC^{1955-1999}$

217.7–8 felt awfully—bony. Like a fish, freshly eaten and skeletonized, on a china platter.] S1; felt horribly—unfamiliar. Like the brittle shards of a fish, freshly eaten, its bones left strewn on a cold china platter. $OC^{1955-1999}$

217.9 fingered] S1; seized $OC^{1955-1999}$

217.9 "My God."] S1; "Lord! Lord!" $OC^{1955-1999}$

217.11 years.] S1; ~? $DC^{1947}$, $DC^{1948}$, $OC^{1955-1999}$

217.11 around the world with] S1; around with $DC^{1947}$, $DC^{1948}$, $OC^{1955-1999}$

217.12 SKELETON] S1; *skeleton* $SRB^{1980-2010}$, *RBS1*

*217.12–13 He saw his fingers . . . their quaking apprehension.] S1; *om.* $OC^{1955-1999}$

217.13 that we] S1; we $OC^{1955-1999}$

217.14 so much] S1; *om.* $OC^{1955-1999}$

◊217.14 granted.] S1; ~? $DC^{1947}$, $DC^{1948}$, $OC^{1955-1999}$

217.22 a—skull] S1; a—a skull $SRB^{1983}$

217.32 BUT A SKELETON!] S1; ◆BUT A ◆*SKELETON!* [SKELETON! $OC^{1955-1999}$] [But a *skeleton!* $SRB^{1980-2010}$, *RBS1*] $DC^{1947}$, $DC^{1948}$

217.36 come in and meet] S1; come meet $OC^{1955-1999}$

217.36–37 called his wife's sweet, clear voice.] S1; His wife's clear, sweet voice called from far away. $OC^{1955-1999}$

217.38 stood upright.] S1; ◆stood up. [stood. $OC^{1955-1999}$] $DC^{1947}$, $DC^{1948}$

217.38 SKELETON] S1; ◆skeleton [*skeleton* $SRB^{1980-2010}$, *RBS1*] S2

217.38 was holding him upright.] S1; ◆was holding him up. [held him up! $OC^{1955-1999}$] $DC^{1947}$, $DC^{1948}$

217.39 inside him,] S1; inside, $OC^{1955-1999}$

217.39–40 legs and head.] S1; legs, and head! $OC^{1955-1999}$

217.41 step he took] S1; step, $OC^{1955-1999}$

217.41 upon] S1; on $OC^{1955-1999}$

218.2 "Come on, now, brace up.] S1; ^Come on, brace up! $OC^{1955-1999}$

218.2–3 And Friday you've got to] S1; Friday you must $OC^{1955-1999}$

*218.3 Quite a drive. Over six hundred miles.] S1; It's a long drive. Hundreds of miles. $DC^{1947}$, $DC^{1948}$, $OC^{1955-1999}$

218.4 Got to] S1; Must $OC^{1955-1999}$

218.4–5 put his money into] S1; invest in $OC^{1955-1999}$

218.5 now."] S1; ~!^ $OC^{1955-1999}$

218.6 Five minutes] S1; A moment $OC^{1955-1999}$

218.10 LORD!] S1; ◆~^ [*Lord!* $SRB^{1980-2010}$, *RBS1*] S2

218.12 ¶ "Excuse me," he said,] S1; ^ "Excuse me," he gasped, $OC^{1955-1999}$

*218.18 shoving] S1; showing $SRB^{1983}$

218.18–19 something concerning] S1; part of $OC^{1955-1999}$

*218.19–20 slithered on the bed in animal cuddlesomeness,] S1; was on the bed, her arms around his neck, $OC^{1955-1999}$

218.21 skin growths."] S1; epidermis!" $OC^{1955-1999}$

218.22 away with relief. "Glad to hear that. Feel] S1; down. "Are you certain? I hope so. I'd feel $OC^{1955-1999}$

218.23 ripe curves] S1; curve $OC^{1955-1999}$

◊218.25 hypochrondriac I ever saw," she said. She snuggled to him.] S1; hypochondriac!" She held him at arm's length. $OC^{1955-1999}$

218.26 on, what's wrong, tell] S1; on. What's wrong? Tell $DC^{1947}$, $DC^{1948}$, $OC^{1955-1999}$

218.28 the office downtown,] S1; his downtown office, $DC^{1947}$, $DC^{1948}$, $OC^{1955-1999}$

218.29 found that] S1; sorted out $OC^{1955-1999}$

218.29–30 displeased him.] S1; with displeasure. $OC^{1955-1999}$

218.31 obliged but gave forth a suspicious scowl.] S1; obliged, but scowled suspiciously. $DC^{1947}$, $DC^{1948}$, $OC^{1955-1999}$

218.33 him,] S1; him, purring like a kitten, $DC^{1947}$, $DC^{1948}$, $OC^{1955-1999}$

218.33–34 shutting her eyes . . . anatomical delicacies.] S1; and shutting her eyes. $OC^{1955-1999}$

218.35 war,] S1; war just over, $DC^{1947}$, $DC^{1948}$, $OC^{1955-1999}$

218.37 his own business, for himself.] S1; business for himself. $OC^{1955-1999}$

218.38 at artistic things, had dabbled in ceramics and pottery.] S1; ◆at artistic things, had dabbled in [for $OC^{1955}$, $OC^{1961}$] ceramics and sculpture. $DC^{1947}$, $DC^{1948}$, $OC^{1955-1999}$

218.39–40 possible, he'd go . . . his own shop.] S1; possible^ he'd ◆get over into Arizona and [head for Arizona, $OC^{1955-1999}$] borrow that money from Mr. ◆Creldon. It would build him his kiln and set up his own shop. [Creldon, build a kiln and set up shop. $OC^{1955-1999}$] $DC^{1947}$, $DC^{1948}$, $OC^{1955-1999}$

◊219.1 hypochrondriac] S1; case $DC^{1947}$, $DC^{1948}$, $OC^{1955-1999}$

219.1 it was a good thing] S1; luckily $OC^{1955-1999}$

219.2 had seemed] S1; seemed $OC^{1955-1999}$

219.2 understand and be eager to] S1; be eager to understand and $DC^{1947}$, $DC^{1948}$, $OC^{1955-1999}$

219.3 himself. He wouldn't] S1; himself, not go $DC^{1947}$, $DC^{1948}$, $OC^{1955-1999}$

219.4 nothing.] S1; space. $OC^{1955-1999}$

219.8 outer dermis,] S1; *om.* $OC^{1955-1999}$

219.9 while the] S1; while his $OC^{1955-1999}$

219.10–11 while his lips were drawn morosely downward,] S1; with his lips drawn morosely down, $OC^{1955-1999}$

219.12 him.] S1; him behind the flesh. $DC^{1947}$, $DC^{1948}$, $OC^{1955-1999}$

219.12 *It had its nerve, it did!*] S1; *om.* $OC^{1955-1999}$

219.13–14 "Let go of . . . Release them!"] S1; Let go! he cried. Let go of me! My lungs! Stop! $OC^{1955-1999}$

219.14 vise] S1; vice $DC^{1948}$

◊219.15 He experienced . . . pressing in, chocking] S1; He gasped convulsively, as if his ribs were crushing $OC^{1955-1999}$

219.17 squeezing] S1; ◆*squeezing* [squeezing $OC^{1955-1999}$] $DC^{1947}$, $DC^{1948}$

219.18–19 And terrible hot . . . of skull-bones.] S1; And terrifying headaches burnt his brain to a blind cinder. $OC^{1955-1999}$

219.20 "My vitals! All my organs,] S1; ^My insides, $OC^{1955-1999}$

219.21 His heart seemed . . . nearness of his ribs,] S1; His heart ◆seemed to cringe [cringed $OC^{1955-1999}$] from the fanning ◆nearness of his ribs. Ribs [motion of ribs $OC^{1955-1999}$] $DC^{1947}$, $DC^{1948}$, $OC^{1955-1999}$

◊219.24 meet] S1; meeting $DC^{1948}$, $OC^{1955-1999}$

219.24–26 again, and always . . . its exact symmetry] S1; but only grew more aware of the conflict between his dirty exterior and this beautiful cool clean calciumed thing inside. $OC^{1955-1999}$

219.26 symmetry continued.] S1; symmetry. $DC^{1947}$, $DC^{1948}$, $OC^{1955-1999}$

219.30 *small tiny*] S1; *tiny* $OC^{1955-1999}$

219.31 *Harris'*] S1; *the* $OC^{1955-1999}$

219.32 a bit plump?] plump? $OC^{1955-1999}$

219.33–34 *so slender, so . . . thin as a reed.*] S1; *slender, svelte, economical of line and contour. Exquisitely carved oriental ivory! Perfect, thin as a white praying mantis!* $OC^{1955-1999}$

219.35 protuberant and ordinary and numb looking?] protuberant, ordinary, numb-looking? $OC^{1955-1999}$

219.36 *skeleton's skull;*] S1; *skull;* $OC^{1955-1999}$

219.37 *sombre, quiet, dark pools, all knowing,*] S1; *somber, quiet pools, all-knowing,* $OC^{1955-1999}$

219.37 *deeply into skull sockets*] S1; *deep* $OC^{1955-1999}$

219.38 *understanding with any plumb line.*] S1; *understanding.* $OC^{1955-1999}$

219.39 *all sadism,*] S1; *om.* $OC^{1955-1999}$

220.1 hours, glib and explosive.] S1; hours. $OC^{1955-1999}$

220.2 quietly hung inside of Harris,] S1; hung quietly inside, $OC^{1955-1999}$

220.6 Then it came to Harris.] S1; Harris sat slowly up. $OC^{1955-1999}$

220.7 Hold on a minute,"] S1; Hold on!" $OC^{1955-1999}$

220.8 too!] S1; ~. $DC^{1947}$, $DC^{1948}$, $OC^{1955-1999}$

220.8 want you to, and] S1; ♦want you to! And [want! You $OC^{1955-1999}$] $DC^{1947}$, $DC^{1948}$

◊220.9 put up your carpels, metacarpels,] S1; move your carpales, metacarpa-les, $OC^{1955-1999}$

*220.9 swift!] S1; sswtt^ $DC^{1947}$, $DC^{1948}$, $OC^{1955-1999}$

220.10 giggled] S1; laughed $OC^{1955-1999}$

220.11 HUMM] S1; *Hunn* $DC^{1947}$, $DC^{1948}$, $OC^{1955-1999}$

220.11 Humm] S1; *Hunn* $DC^{1947}$, $DC^{1948}$, $OC^{1955-1999}$

220.12 There!"] S1; ♦~." [~!"$OC^{1955-1999}$] $DC^{1947}$, $DC^{1948}$

220.14 Even-steven] S1; ♦Even ^ steven [Even-Stephen $OC^{1955-1999}$] $DC^{1947}$, $DC^{1948}$

220.14 two, we shall.] S1; two! $OC^{1955-1999}$

220.15 thinks!"] S1; ♦*thinks!*" [thinks!^ $OC^{1955-1999}$] $DC^{1947}$, $DC^{1948}$

220.15–17 That was good, . . . could still think!"] S1; Yes, by God! yes. Even if I didn't have you, I could still think!" $OC^{1955-1999}$

220.18–19 he felt a pain . . . own treatment back.] S1; a tiger's jaw snapped shut, chewing his brain in half. Harris screamed. The bones of his skull grabbed hold and gave him nightmares. Then slowly, while he shrieked, nuzzled and ate the nightmares one by one, until the last one was gone and the light went out. . . . $OC^{1955-1999}$

220.19 right back.] S1; back. $DC^{1947}$, $DC^{1948}$, $OC^{1955-1999}$

220.20 had postponed] S1; postponed $OC^{1955-1999}$

220.21 He weighed] S1; Weighing $DC^{1947}$, $DC^{1948}$, $OC^{1955-1999}$

◊220.21 scales] S1; scale $OC^{1955-1999}$

220.21 and watched] S1; he saw $DC^{1947}$, $DC^{1948}$, $OC^{1955-1999}$

220.21–22 glide of the red arrow as it pointed to: "164."] S1; gliding red arrow point to: 165. $OC^{1955-1999}$

220.23 ten years] S1; years $OC^{1955-1999}$

220.25 "Hold on!] S1; You, you! $OC^{1955-1999}$

220.25 what're] S1; what $DC^{1947}$, $DC^{1948}$, $OC^{1955-1999}$

220.25 *you.*"] S1; you! $OC^{1955-1999}$

220.26 finger] S1; fist $OC^{1955-1999}$

220.28 ^ "You] S1; ¶ "~$DC^{1947}$, $DC^{1948}$, $OC^{1955-1999}$

220.28 rum thing, you.] S1; damn thing, you! $OC^{1955-1999}$

220.28 starve me off,] S1; starve me, $OC^{1955-1999}$

220.29 A victory for you, is it?] S1; ♦A victory for you, is that it? [*om.* $OC^{1955-1999}$] $DC^{1947}$, $DC^{1948}$

220.31 cafeteria immediately.] S1; cafeteria. $DC^{1947}$, $DC^{1948}$, $OC^{1955-1999}$

220.32 Ordering turkey] S1; Turkey $OC^{1955-1999}$

220.32 potatoes, cream, three desserts] S1; creamed potatoes, four vegetables, three desserts, $DC^{1947}$, $DC^{1948}$, $OC^{1955-1999}$

220.32–33 he soon found he could not eat it,] S1; he could eat none of it, $OC^{1955-1999}$

220.34 it?" he wanted to know,] S1; it?^ he thought^ $OC^{1955-1999}$

220.35 rotting] S1; rattling $DC^{1947}$, $DC^{1948}$, $OC^{1955-1999}$

220.36–37 ached, his breathing . . . but he had] S1; blazed, his breath jerked in and out of a constricted chest, his teeth raged with pain, but he knew one $OC^{1955-1999}$

220.39 will I eat foods again] S1; again shall I eat foods $DC^{1947}$, $DC^{1948}$, $OC^{1955-1999}$

220.40 minerals in them.] S1; minerals. $DC^{1947}$, $DC^{1948}$, $OC^{1955-1999}$

221.1 wailed] S1; said, $DC^{1947}$, $DC^{1948}$, $OC^{1955-1999}$

221.2 see] S1; *see* $OC^{1955-1999}$

221.7 he demanded indignantly.] S1; *om.* $OC^{1955-1999}$

221.8 him?"] S1; '*him*'?" $DC^{1947}$, $DC^{1948}$, $OC^{1955-1999}$

221.14 eat other foods] S1; keep other foods down $DC^{1947}$, $DC^{1948}$, $OC^{1955-1999}$

221.14–15 capsules] S1; pellets $DC^{1947}$, $DC^{1948}$, $OC^{1955-1999}$

221.15 ^ "But] S1; ¶ "~ $OC^{1955-1999}$

221.17 She came over . . . his head was] S1; ♦She came to him and sat down and made him lie so his head was [She made him lie with his head $OC^{1955-1999}$] $DC^{1947}$, $DC^{1948}$

221.21 dropped] S1; let escape you $DC^{1947}$, $DC^{1948}$, $OC^{1955-1999}$

221.24 *first,*] S1; first, $OC^{1955-1999}$

221.26 the more your bones stick out,] S1; *om.* $OC^{1955-1999}$

221.26 fret] S1; worry $DC^{1947}$, $DC^{1948}$, $OC^{1955-1999}$

221.26 now,] S1; *om.* $OC^{1955-1999}$

221.29(1) I] S1; ♦*I* [I $OC^{1955-1999}$] $DC^{1947}$, $DC^{1948}$

*221.29 Oh, my darling, I love you so."] S1; Go on Clarisse, keep talking." $OC^{1955-1999}$

221.31 sag again.] S1; sag $OC^{1955-1999}$

221.32 right] S1; very well $DC^{1947}$, $DC^{1948}$, $OC^{1955-1999}$

221.32 say everything was] S1; blame his $OC^{1955-1999}$

221.35 and then, at the] S1; he caught $DC^{1947}$, $DC^{1948}$, $OC^{1955-1999}$

221.35 M.] S1; ♦Mr. [M. $OC^{1955-1999}$] $DC^{1947}$, $DC^{1948}$

221.36 gold] S1; ancient, flaking gold $DC^{1947}$, $DC^{1948}$, $OC^{1955-1999}$

221.36 sign outside, Harris'] S1; plate outside the building. Then, his $DC^{1947}$, $DC^{1948}$, $OC^{1955-1999}$

221.37–38 He could hardly . . . the pains that] S1; Blinded, $OC^{1955-1999}$

221.38 Harris staggered away, and when] S1; he staggered away. When $DC^{1947}$, $DC^{1948}$, $OC^{1955-1999}$

221.39 corner, and M.] S1; corner. M. $DC^{1947}$, $DC^{1948}$, $OC^{1955-1999}$

221.40 ^ The] S1; ¶ ~ $DC^{1947}$, $DC^{1948}$, $OC^{1955-1999}$

222.1 M. Munigant, then, was] S1; M. Munigant was $DC^{1947}$, $DC^{1948}$, $OC^{1955-1999}$

222.1 must] S1; *must* $DC^{1947}$, $DC^{1948}$, $OC^{1955-1999}$

222.2 gilt-lettered name] S1; name $OC^{'1955-1999}$

*◊222.2 reaction] S1; a reaction $DC^{1947}$, $DC^{1948}$, $OC^{1955-1999}$

222.2–3 in the deepness of Harris' body, why,] S1; om. $OC^{1955-1999}$

222.3 *must*] S1; must $OC^{1984}$

◊222.5 layed him low.] S1; ◆laid him low. [took hold $OC^{1955-1999}$] $DC^{1947}$, $DC^{1948}$

222.5–6 stagger into a beer saloon for respite.] S1; ◆stagger into a cocktail bar for respite. [swayed into a cocktail bar. $OC^{1955-1999}$] $DC^{1947}$, $DC^{1948}$

222.7 floor of the beer palace,] S1; dim ◆room of the cocktail lounge, [lounge, $OC^{1955-1999}$] $DC^{1947}$, $DC^{1948}$, $OC^{1955-1999}$

222.9 his attention] S1; specific attention $DC^{1947}$, $DC^{1948}$, $OC^{1955-1999}$

222.9–10 brought home the entire psychological impact of it!] S1; let the psychological impact of it slam home! $OC^{1955-1999}$

222.11 even suspect] S1; suspect $OC^{1955-1999}$

222.16 beer parlor] S1; cocktail lounge $DC^{1947}$, $DC^{1948}$, $OC^{1955-1999}$

222.18 here] S1; *there* $DC^{1947}$, $DC^{1948}$, $OC^{1955-1999}$

222.18 fellow for you] S1; man $DC^{1947}$, $DC^{1948}$, $OC^{1955-1999}$

222.18 momentarily] S1; om. $DC^{1947}$, $DC^{1948}$, $OC^{1955-1999}$

◊222.19 him on his shoulder and enquire] S1; the fat man's shoulder, and inquire $DC^{1947}$, $DC^{1948}$, $OC^{1955-1999}$

222.23 that] S1; ◆*that* [that $OC^{1955-1999}$] $DC^{1947}$, $DC^{1948}$

222.23 but now,] S1; but not now, $OC^{1955-1999}$

222.26 *not present*] S1; Harris ordered a drink, drank it, and then dared to address the fat man: $DC^{1947}$, $DC^{1948}$, $OC^{1955-1999}$

222.27 inquired Harris.] S1; om. $DC^{1947}$, $DC^{1948}$, $OC^{1955-1999}$

222.30 down to the marrow. Adding weight seems an impossibility.] S1; down. Can't seem to put on any weight. $DC^{1947}$, $DC^{1948}$, $OC^{1955-1999}$

222.31 belly] S1; stomach $DC^{1947}$, $DC^{1948}$, $OC^{1955-1999}$

222.31 yours, it's tops.] S1; yours. $DC^{1947}$, $DC^{1948}$, $OC^{1955-1999}$

222.32 afraid?"] S1; afraid of something?" $DC^{1947}$, $DC^{1948}$, $OC^{1955-1999}$

222.34–35 you—" ¶ "Layer] S1; ~. ^^^ ~ $OC^{1955-1999}$

222.41 titbits] S1; tidbits S

◊222.41 most] S1; ◆almost ['most $OC^{1955-1999}$] $DC^{1948}$

◊223.3 Perhaps?"] S1; ~." $DC^{1947}$, $DC^{1948}$, $OC^{1955-1999}$

223.4 everybody] S1; everyone $OC^{1955-1999}$

223.13 *themselves,*] S1; themselves $OC^{1955-1999}$

◊223.14 possible know] S1; possibly meet $DC^{1947}$, $DC^{1948}$, $OC^{1955-1999}$

223.15 fat."] S1; ~!" $DC^{1947}$, $DC^{1948}$, $OC^{1955-1999}$

223.19 Phoenix] S1; Phoenix, now, $DC^{1947}$, $DC^{1948}$, $OC^{1955-1999}$

*223.22 Frisco] S1; Los Angeles $DC^{1947}$, $DC^{1948}$, $OC^{1955-1999}$

223.23 Death Valley] S1; Mojave desert $DC^{1947}$, $DC^{1948}$, $OC^{1955-1999}$

223.23–25 It was only . . . his ceramics business.] S1; Traffic was thin and inconstant, and for long stretches there would not be a car on the road for miles ahead or behind. Harris twitched his fingers on the steering wheel. Whether or not Creldon, in Phoenix, lent him the money he needed to start his business, it was still a good thing to get away, to put distance behind. $DC^{1947}$, $DC^{1948}$, $OC^{1955-1999}$

223.30 ran] S1; plunged $DC^{1947}$, $DC^{1948}$, $OC^{1955-1999}$

223.30 deepest sand. It] S1; boiling sand and $OC^{1955-1999}$

223.31 came on,] S1; came, $OC^{1955-1999}$

223.31 road] S1; roof $VB$

223.31–32 silent with no traffic, and] S1; ◆silent with little traffic. [silent. $OC^{1955-1999}$] ◆Those [The $OC^{1955-1999}$] few cars that passed went swiftly on their way, their view obstructed. $DC^{1947}$, $DC^{1948}$, $OC^{1955-1999}$

223.32–33 night roused a sandstorm out of the empty valleys.] S1; very late he heard a wind rising out of the desert, felt the sting of little sand needles on his cheeks, and opened his eyes. $DC^{1947}$, $DC^{1948}$, $OC^{1955-1999}$

223.34–35 awake and gritty-eyed . . . had layered it over.] S1; gritty-eyed and wandering in thoughtless, senseless circles, having, in his delirium, ◆gotten [got $OC^{1955-1999}$] away from the road. $DC^{1947}$, $DC^{1948}$, $OC^{1955-1999}$

223.36 bush, and the] S1; bush. The sun $DC^{1947}$, $DC^{1948}$, $OC^{1955-1999}$

223.36 struck at him] S1; ◆struck into him [struck him $OC^{1955-1999}$] $DC^{1947}$, $DC^{1948}$

223.37 seeping into his bones.] S1; cutting through to his—bones. $DC^{1947}$, $DC^{1948}$, $OC^{1955-1999}$

223.37 buzzard] S1; vulture $DC^{1947}$, $DC^{1948}$, $OC^{1955-1999}$

223.38 open weakly.] S1; open. $OC^{1955-1999}$

223.38 it,"] S1; ~?" $DC^{1947}$, $DC^{1948}$, $OC^{1955-1999}$

223.38 whimpered] S1; whispered $OC^{1955-1999}$

223.39 wreck me,] S1; *om.* $OC^{1955-1999}$

223.41 forth.] S1; out. $OC^{1955-1999}$

223.41 and breakfast from me, and then there] S1; off me, and there $OC^{1955-1999}$

224.2 that, eh?] S1; that. $DC^{1947}$, $DC^{1948}$, $OC^{1955-1999}$

224.3 on and on] S1; on $DC^{1947}$, $DC^{1948}$, $OC^{1955-1999}$

224.4 falling,] S1; falling flat, $DC^{1947}$, $DC^{1948}$, $OC^{1955-1999}$

224.5 flame] S1; fire $OC^{1955-1999}$

224.6 Safety. Water.] S1; Water. Safety. $DC^{1947}$, $DC^{1948}$, $OC^{1955-1999}$

224.9 "Hey!" somebody called again.] S1; ◆"Hey!" [*om.* $OC^{1963-1999}$] ⸿ The call was repeated. $DC^{1947}$, $DC^{1948}$, $OC^{1955-1999}$

224.10–11 a park ranger's arms.] S1; the arms of some one in a uniform with a badge. . . . $DC^{1947}$, $DC^{1948}$, $OC^{1955-1999}$

224.12 tediously repaired,] S1; tediously hauled, repaired, $DC^{1947}$, $DC^{1948}$, $OC^{1955-1999}$

224.13 any business] S1; the business $DC^{1947}$, $DC^{1948}$, $OC^{1955-1999}$

*224.13–14 would have to wait. This business of the] S1; was ◆more a numb pantomime than anything else. [a numb pantomime. $OC^{1955-1999}$] Even when he got the loan and held the money in his hand it meant nothing. This $DC^{1947}$, $DC^{1948}$, $OC^{1955-1999}$

224.14 its scabbard] S1; a scabbard $DC^{1947}$, $DC^{1948}$, $OC^{1955-1999}$

224.14–15 tainted his eating,] S1; tainted his business, his eating, $DC^{1947}$, $DC^{1948}$, $OC^{1955-1999}$

224.16–17 it must be . . . business or anything!] S1; this Thing had to be put in its ◆place before he could have love for business or anything. [place. $OC^{1955-1999}$] $DC^{1947}$, $DC^{1948}$, $OC^{1955-1999}$

224.17 That desert] S1; The desert $OC^{1955-1999}$

224.17 closely] S1; close $OC^{1955-1999}$

224.18–20 grimly phoned Mr. Creldon, . . . coast to Frisco.] S1; heard himself thanking Mr. Creldon, dimly, for the money. Then he turned his car and motored back across the long miles, this time cutting across to San Diego, ◆so that he [so he $OC^{1955-1999}$] would miss that desert stretch between El Centro and Beaumont. He drove north along the coast. $DC^{1947}$, $DC^{1948}$, $OC^{1955-1999}$

224.21 as he drove through Santa Barbara.] S1; outside Laguna. $DC^{1947}$, $DC^{1948}$, $OC^{1955-1999}$

224.24–25 If anything happened, . . . together, that way!] S1; *om.* $OC^{1955-1999}$

*224.24 desired casket burial] S1; wanted cremation. $DC^{1947}$, $DC^{1948}$, $OC^{1955-1999}$

224.24–25 rot together, that way!] S1; burn together that way. None of this graveyard burial stuff where little crawling things eat and leave nothing but unmantled bone! No, they'd burn. $DC^{1947}$, $DC^{1948}$, $OC^{1955-1999}$

224.25–26 Damn Him! And what about . . . one to turn?] S1; ◆Damn Him! He [Damn, he $OC^{1955-1999}$] was sick. ◆Where could he turn? Clarisse? Burleigh? ◆Munigant? Bone specialist. [Munigant, Bone specialist? $DC^{1948}$] Munigant. Well? [Where to turn? $OC^{1955-1999}$] $DC^{1947}$, $DC^{1948}$, $OC^{1955-1999}$

224.27–28 trilled Clarisse, kissing him so he winced at the solidness of her teeth] S1; Clarisse kissed him. He winced at the solidness of the teeth $OC^{1955-1999}$

224.30 deal—it didn't go through!"] S1; deal—?" $DC^{1947}$, $DC^{1948}$, $OC^{1955-1999}$

224.31 "I have to . . . That's it."] S1; "It went through. ◆Yeah, it went through. [*om.* $OC^{1955-1999}$] I guess. ◆Yeah, it did," he said. [Yes, it did." $OC^{1955-1999}$] $DC^{1947}$, $DC^{1948}$, $OC^{1955-1999}$

224.34 *not present*] S1; ◆She enthused. [*om.* $OC^{1955-1999}$] $DC^{1947}$, $DC^{1948}$

224.34–35 Lord, he couldn't . . . of this obsession.] S1; ◆Lord, he couldn't even enjoy kisses any more because of this obsession. [*om.* $OC^{1955-1999}$] $DC^{1947}$, $DC^{1948}$

224.35–36 unhappy dinner, with Clarisse trying to cheer him.] S1; falsely cheerful dinner, with Clarisse laughing and encouraging him. *DC*[1947], *DC*[1948], *OC*[1955–1999]

224.37 aside.] S1; down. *DC*[1947], *DC*[1948], *OC*[1955–1999]

224.37 ∧ His] S1; ¶ ~ *OC*[1955–1999]

224.37–39 "I'm sorry to . . . the Red Cross.] S1; "Well, sorry, but I have to ♦leave now," she laughed, and [leave." She *OC*[1955–1999]] pinched him lightly on the cheek. "Come on now, cheer up! I'll be back from the Red Cross in three hours. You lie around and snooze. *DC*[1947], *DC*[1948], *OC*[1955–1999]

◊225.5(2) every] S1; ever *DC*[1947], *DC*[1948], *OC*[1955–1999]

225.6 as many aspirin as] S1; all the aspirin *DC*[1947], *DC*[1948], *OC*[1955–1999]

225.8–9 cheeks, like a . . . answer the door?] S1; ♦cheeks, like a man on a torture rack. Would M. Munigant go away if the door was not answered? [cheeks. *OC*[1955–1999]] *DC*[1947], *DC*[1948]

225.10 in!" he tried to gasp it out. "Come] S1; in! Come *OC*[1955–1999]

225.11 door had been] S1; door was *OC*[1955–1999]

225.12 terrible.] S1; terrible. M. Munigant stood in the center of the living room, small and dark. *DC*[1947], *DC*[1948], *OC*[1955–1999]

225.12 nodded.] S1; ♦nodded at him. [nodded. *OC*[1955–1999]] *DC*[1947], *DC*[1948]

225.16 sobbing.] S1; sobbing. M. Munigant still whistled when he talked; something about his tongue and the whistling. No matter. *DC*[1947], *DC*[1948], *OC*[1955–1999]

225.16 he] S1; Harris *DC*[1947], *DC*[1948], *OC*[1955–1999]

225.17–18 trip to Phoenix] S1; Phoenix trip *DC*[1947], *DC*[1948], *OC*[1955–1999]

225.18 a—traitor!] S1; a—a traitor! *DC*[1947], *DC*[1948], *OC*[1955–1999]

225.19 FIX him once] S1; ♦*fix* [fix *OC*[1955]] him for once *DC*[1947], *DC*[1948], *OC*[1955–1999]

225.19 ∧ "Mister] S1; ¶ ∧Mr. *OC*[1955–1999]

225.19 I] S1; I—I *DC*[1947], *DC*[1948], *OC*[1955–1999]

225.20 before, you] S1; before. You *DC*[1947], *DC*[1948], *OC*[1955–1999]

225.20 you have such . . . I'm ready.] S1; ♦You have such an odd, odd tongue. Round. Tube-like. Hollow? Guess it's my eyes. Don't mind me. Delirious. I'm ready. [Your tongue. Round, tube-like. Hollow? My eyes. Delirious. *OC*[1955–1999]] *DC*[1947], *DC*[1948]

225.22–23 If Mr. Harris . . . appreciatively, coming closer.] S1; M. Munigant whistled softly, appreciatively, coming closer. If Mr. Harris would relax in his chair, and open his mouth? *DC*[1947], *DC*[1948], *OC*[1955–1999]

225.23–24 He switched off the lights, peering] S1; The lights were switched off. M. Munigant peered *DC*[1947], *DC*[1948], *OC*[1955–1999]

225.24 the first time,] S1; that first visit, *DC*[1947], *DC*[1948], *OC*[1955–1999]

225.25 rebellion.] S1; revolt. *OC*[1955–1999]

225.26 man anyway, . . . acting up somewhat.] S1; man, anyway, even if the skeleton protested. *OC*[1955–1999]

225.30–31 could not breathe.] S1; couldn't breathe! $DC^{1947}$, $DC^{1948}$, $OC^{1955-1999}$

225.31 He was corked.] S1; *om.* $OC^{1955-1999}$

◊225.35 breath again.] S1; breathe again, momentarily. $DC^{1947}$, $DC^{1948}$, $OC^{1955-1999}$

225.34 into his lungs, around.] S1; fire through his lungs. $OC^{1955-1999}$

225.37 rocking, rolling] S1; *om.* $OC^{1955-1999}$

225.38–39 unloosened swiftly, expertly.] S1; swiftly cast loose and ◆free, expertly. [free. $OC^{1955-1999}$] $DC^{1947}$, $DC^{1948}$, $OC^{1955-1999}$

225.39 ^ The] S1; ¶ ~ $DC^{1947}$, $DC^{1948}$, $OC^{1955-1999}$

225.40(1) Mr.] S1; M. $DC^{1947}$, $DC^{1948}$, $OC^{1955-1999}$

225.40 Where are you?] S1; *om.* $OC^{1955-1999}$

225.40–41 Mr. Munigant!] S1; M. Munigant? $DC^{1947}$, $DC^{1948}$, $OC^{1955-1999}$

226.1 gone!] S1; ~. $DC^{1947}$, $DC^{1948}$, $OC^{1955-1999}$

226.4 bodily well, he heard] S1; body, $OC^{1955-1999}$

226.5 twistings] S1; twistings and $DC^{1947}$, $DC^{1948}$, $OC^{1955-1999}$

226.12 Saint] S1; ◆St. [St^ $SRB^{1983}$, $RBS1$] $SRB^{1990, 2010}$

226.14 man standing there.] S1; dark man who smelled of iodine. $DC^{1947}$, $DC^{1948}$, $OC^{1955-1999}$

226.22 hall into] S1; hall and into $DC^{1947}$, $DC^{1948}$, $OC^{1955-1999}$

226.23 ¶ "Darling] S1; ^ "~ $DC^{1947}$, $DC^{1948}$, $OC^{1955-1999}$

226.25–26 That scream came . . . some ungodly fisherman.] S1; *om.* $DC^{1947}$, $DC^{1948}$, $OC^{1955-1999}$

226.28 lips puckered,] S1; his lips puckered, $OC^{1955-1999}$

## Line-End Hyphenation

214.12 tooth-/combs] tooth-combs

216.26 vice-/versa] vice-versa

217.16 shake-/fingered] shake-fingered

217.24–25 shot-/gun] shotgun

222.2 gilt-/lettered] gilt-lettered

223.34 gritty-/eyed] gritty-eyed

225.31 cork-/screwed] corkscrewed

## 20. Riabouchinska (And So Died Riabouchinska) (Jan. 19, 1945)

Bradbury had been fascinated by the shadow world of ventriloquism most of his life, and it was inevitable that his Muse would eventually channel this world into his fiction. He regarded the ventriloquist's dummy as a prime example of the approximations of reality found in everyday life, and the story he first titled "Riabouchinska" became a study of two murders: the ventriloquist has killed both the model for his beautiful manikin and, as the story opens, his would-be blackmailer. Does the simulacrum Riabouchinska have the power of speech, or is she the vessel through which the murderer betrays his own guilt?

Bradbury's composition and submission log shows completion of a 6,000-word typescript, titled "Riabouchinska!," on January 19, 1945. His author's sales record includes an undated (June 1946) direct payment of $350.00 for CBS radio adaptation (confirmed by his 1946 tax notes). The first publication sale (to *The Saint Detective Magazine*, 1953) is not documented in his sales records, which show a gap from 1950 through 1953, but Bradbury's 1954 sales record shows an undated reprint sale to *British Argosy* of $98.12 (after currency exchange). The 1955 sales record includes an undated $1,000.00 sale of "Riabouchinska" to *Alfred Hitchcock Presents* for CBS television adaptation during the show's first season.

In spite of its enduring popularity, the story's 6,000-word length and its multiple-genre characteristics made it problematic in the magazine market, and it took eight years to sell. Schwartz acknowledged receipt on February 4, 1945: "Despite the fact that I have a prejudice against dummy-talking stories I thought your yarn was nicely worked out." He felt that it was too long and unconventional for Bradbury to submit to the slick market, and wanted to run it through the genre magazines first. Schwartz tried all the major mystery pulps, including *Ellery Queen,* during February 1945, with no luck. Bradbury then made his own submissions directly to a wider range of magazines. His first offer to *The Saint's Choice* seemed to pay off; this was a new anthology magazine by Leslie Charteris, author of *The Saint* series of books and stories. A February 1946 letter from associate editor Roby Wentz gave an unofficial nod to the story, and the sale was final on March 20, 1946. But publication of the magazine was suspended after just one year, and "Riabouchinska" was back on the market. For the next year and a half, Bradbury directly shopped "Riabouchinska" to all the major market magazines that had shown an interest in his work: *Collier's* (June 17, 1946; rejected July 1); the *Saturday Evening Post* (July 4; rejected July 22); *Good Housekeeping* (July 22); *Cosmopolitan* (August 7); *American Magazine* (October 13); *Argosy* (Dec 17); *McCall's* (January 16, 1947); *Today's Woman* (February 15); *Liberty* (March 11); *Women's Home Companion* (April 26); *Ladies' Home Journal* (May 27); *Redbook* (July 5); and *This Week* (August 15). The story nearly sold to the slicks more than once; the editors of *Today's Woman* reluctantly turned it down, only because the story lacked a "live woman character to carry the story with our audience."

Along the way he submitted to pulp editors Donald Wollheim for his various hybrid magazine/anthologies (April 7, 1947) and Paul Payne at Fiction House (September 15). In March and April of 1949, Bradbury made a final effort at a pulp sale with three Popular Publications editors, Mary Gnaedinger

(*Famous Fantastic Mysteries*), Mike Tilden (*Detective Tales* and *Dime Mystery*), and Ejler Jakobsson (*Super Science Stories*). "Riabouchinska" finally came full circle, and was sold to a regenerated Leslie Charteris venture, now titled *The Saint Detective Magazine,* in May 1953 for publication in the June–July 1953 issue (S1) as "And So Died Riabouchinska."

At some point during its 1945 to 1953 circulation odyssey, Bradbury completely rewrote the story, and it was the complete rewrite that finally sold. Bradbury preferred that version, and S1 became the source for the July 1954 issue of *Argosy,* retitled "The Golden Box" (S2) and subsequently (with the S1 title) in the March 1957 British issue of *The Saint Detective Magazine* (S3). In 1964 Bradbury collected the story (again retaining the S1 title) in his 1964 Simon & Schuster story collection, *The Machineries of Joy* ($MJ^{1964}$) and the Bantam mass-market paperback resetting ($MJ^{1965}$). He subsequently included the story in his 1980 Knopf hundred-story retrospective *The Stories of Ray Bradbury* ($SRB^{1980}$) and two further editions in Britain, the second as *Ray Bradbury Stories Volume 1* ($SRB^{1983}$ and *RBS1*). "And Thus Died Riabouchinska" also appeared in two anthologies, *Hitchcock in Prime Time* (1985) and *Masterpieces of Mystery and Suspense* (1988).

The story has also had a rich four-decade history of media adaptation, beginning with an adaptation by Mel Dinelli for CBS radio's *Suspense* (first aired November 13, 1947). It was the first of ten CBS radio adaptations for the popular *Suspense* and *Escape* programs, and producer William Spier secured the distinguished British actor Claude Raines for the role of Fabian, Riabouchinska's doomed creator. Alfred Hitchcock read the story's first publication in *The Saint Detective Magazine* and purchased it for the first season of his CBS television half-hour series, *Alfred Hitchcock Presents.* Mel Dinelli was again brought in for the television script, and Claude Raines reprised his role as Fabian with Charles Bronson as Detective Krovitch. It was the first Bradbury story purchased for the series and the second one to be broadcast, airing on February 12, 1956. Bradbury subsequently adapted the story himself for *The Ray Bradbury Theater;* his adaptation aired on May 28, 1988 on the USA cable network, starring Alan Bates as Fabian.

The inspirational sources for this long-traveled story are fascinating, and reveal a great deal about Bradbury's fascination with the boundaries between illusion and reality. Bradbury's first fiction sketch for his Los Angeles High School newspaper was "The Death of Mr. McCarthy" (*Blue and White Daily,* April 21, 1938), a humorous "what if" involving the popular radio ventriloquist Edgar Bergen and his wooden sidekick, Charlie McCarthy. But Bradbury's teen-age extrapolation also probed the connection between the creation and the creator: In the world of prime time radio, if Edgar Bergen developed laryngitis, would Charlie McCarthy die? This was not really an idle question for Bradbury, who had been fascinated with fictional ventriloquists since childhood; he acknowledged the influence of Lon Chaney's two Hollywood versions of Mr. Echo in *The Unholy Three* (1925, 1930), Erich von Stroheim's film *The Great Gabbo* (1929), and John Kier Cross's chilling short story, "The Glass Eye," where the dummy is actually the creator (in 1953 he would include "The Glass Eye" in his first edited anthology, *Timeless Stories for Today and Tomorrow*).

The year after finishing his first version, "Riabouchinska," Bradbury saw the British Ealing Studio production *Dead of Night,* an unsettling story anthology film that had an abiding impact on his creativity. For Bradbury, the most important episode of the film was John Baines's "The Ventriloquist's Dummy," starring Michael Redgrave as an increasingly schizophrenic ventriloquist who is driven to murder by his own stage show creation. Bradbury's first version of the story predates the *Dead of Night* release by a year and a half, but the long typescript trail to publication may have been influenced by Redgrave's performance.

Finally, Riabouchinska herself was inspired by the prima ballerina Tatiana Riabouchinska, one of the so-called "Baby Ballerinas" who danced (beginning in her mid-teen years) with George Ballanchine's touring Ballet Russe until 1942. Bradbury attended many of the touring ballet performances in Los Angeles from the late 1930s and on through the war years, and followed the careers of Ballanchine's principal dancers well into the 1950s (he would name his youngest daughter after one of Riabouchinska's contemporaries).

Bradbury's unpublished first intention for the story survives in one fragment and four complete typescripts preserved in the Albright Collection. The preliminary and incomplete TSπ consists of an earlier unlocated draft (pages 1–2) and deeper carbon pages (5–8, 12–16) of TS1, which appears to contain a first carbon of these same pages. TSπ pages 3–4 and 9–11 are missing, and appear to have been pulled forward into TS1. The earliest complete 16-page draft is TS1; the first page bears the original "Riabouchinska" title, as does the cancelled underlayer of the title page coversheet. This title page was annotated by Bradbury, apparently some years later, with the comment "old version | never use."

The compositional distance between the 3,700-word TS1 ("Riabouchinska") and the complete rewrite ("And So Died Riabouchinska") is confirmed by the existence of three subsequent typescripts of the TS1 version. The 15-page TS2 has a cover sheet with the original title and word count of 4,000 words noted; the 15-page TS3 is also titled "Riabouchinska" and bears a title sheet annotated "original version, 1944, 1945, 1946 | 1947." It is paginated (in pencil) from 173 to 187, suggesting that TS3 was considered for (and withdrawn from) an anthology or an early Bradbury collection; more significantly, pages 183–187 contain many holograph revisions. TS4 is an amanuensis typescript of the unrevised TS3 underlayer, annotated (in William F. Nolan's hand) "copied from Bradbury's original *unprinted* story | Revised version appears in The Saint Mys

Mag." TS4 is not directly involved in the transmission of the text, but it does confirm that Bradbury's fellow writer and first bibliographer had access to the original version of "Riabouchinska."

TS5, titled "And So Died Riabouchinska," was probably prepared sometime after 1947 and no later than 1953. It is entirely rewritten with a new opening and many internal changes, and is the source of all the published versions of the story, all of which bear the revised title. TS5 is readily available in the various editions of *The Stories of Ray Bradbury* (*SRB*), and represents a later intention for the tale.

Copy-text for the present edition is TS1, the earliest complete version of Bradbury's unpublished original 1945 intention for "Riabouchinska." The Historical Collation for this selection is two-tiered: the first sequence of entries, keyed to the TS1 copy-text, records the pre-copy-text variants of TSπ and all of the substantive variants in TS2, TS3, and the TS4 Nolan transcription; the second sequence is also keyed to the TS1 copy-text, and records all substantive variants moving forward from the heavily revised TS5 version through S1–S4, *MJ*, *SRB*, and *RBS1*. In this way, the reader will be able to track the full range of variants through the original typescripts of "Riabouchinska," as well as the record of variants for Bradbury's canonical rewrite, "And So Dies Riabouchinska." Both the Historical Collation and the textual notes below are keyed to the present edition's text of "Riabouchinska," published here for the first time.

Sources: Author's composition and submission log (1942–45); author's sales record (1942–49 and 1953–58); author's 1945 tax notes; author's notecard file (1942–1978); Schwartz to Bradbury, Feb. 4, 1945 and June 20, 1946; The Saint Enterprises (Roby Wentz) to Bradbury, Feb. 27, 1946; Bradbury-Eller interviews; Eller, *Becoming Ray Bradbury*, 258; Eller, *Ray Bradbury Unbound*, 71–72; Johnson, 20, 45, 125.

—JE

## Textual Notes

[title] The TS1 coversheet is described in the headnote narrative above. The title line for the rewritten version first published in the June–July 1953 issue of *The Saint Detective Magazine* is followed by this brief editorial teaser: "The puppet was beautiful as a snowflake. Yet within her body lay locked her creator's fate."

227.5 theatre cellar] In his TS4 rewrite, Bradbury replaced the literal theatre cellar opening with an extended metaphor; the people surrounding Mr. Ockham's body stand as if they are in a solitary cave along a remote shoreline, pulled by an immense gravitational attraction to the crime scene. Riabouchinska's voice, calling from her box, is like the faint cry of a gull in the distance, sad and barely perceptible. In the final lines of TS4, after

Riabouchinska is silenced forever, Bradbury comes full circle back to that lonely cave where "A gull moved soundlessly, not beating its wings—a shadow."

227.6–7 thought John Fabian] The third person narrative in the TS1 copy-text often reflects Fabian's point of view. His thoughts are often in the forefront of the narrative, harshly punctuated by his headaches and vocal distress whenever Riabouchinska forces herself into the police investigation of Ockham's murder. The rewritten TS4 version also focuses on Fabian, but it is more fully omniscient.

228.13–23 There were . . . only a puppet . . .] This surreal description of Riabouchinska purposely avoids any literal elements; Bradbury's TS4 rewrite replaces the original with a much longer feature-specific description embedded in an even richer parade of metaphors.

230.12 He treated her as a real person] The TS4 rewrite adds extreme examples of indulgence by Fabian to Alyce's narrative: "He spent fifty thousand dollars a year on her wardrobes—one hundred thousand dollars for a doll house with gold and silver and platinum furniture."

230.16–17 She came out of him like a woman out of a dark god."] This chilling metaphor disappears from Alyce's statement in the TS4 rewrite, replaced with a longer description of the essential goodness found in Riabouchinska's "personality." These positive attributes are undeveloped in TS1, where she is simply "Everything that John wasn't."

230.32 Riabouchinska went on laughing for him,] In the TS4 rewrite, Fabian is shocked when he cannot transition his own laugh into Riabouchinska's voice: "there was no sound, save a little empty whisper of her lips moving and gasping." This revision foreshadows her loss of voice and "death" in the closing lines of the story.

231.9 Ilya Riamansk;] The TS1 name of Riabouchinska's inspiration lacks the Russian feminine ending; in his TS4 revisions, Bradbury changed the name of the missing woman to "Miss Ilyana Riamonova."

231.23 *Billboard* magazines] In his correspondence and his story typescripts, Bradbury often used all capitals to indicate title italics for book-length works. His TS1 all caps "BILLBOARD" is therefore rendered in italics by emendation.

232.4 He had given her the job] In his TS4 revisions, Bradbury significantly extended Fabian's reverie-like account of meeting, hiring, loving, hurting, and then losing his lovely assistant.

232.39–233.1 How could he fashion . . . her glowing life?] As he rewrote and expanded the story in TS4, Bradbury intensified the challenge Fabian faced in recreating his lost love: "There was no way even faintly to approximate that quality of rain and summer and the first powderings of snow upon a clear pane of glass in the middle of a December night. No way, no way at all to catch the snowflake without having it melt swiftly away in your clumsy fingers."

233.3 For twenty weeks he worked.] In the TS4 expansion, Bradbury added detail to the delicacy of his carving: "Another month and the skeleton, like a fossil imprint he was searching out, stamped and hidden in the wood, was revealed, all febrile and so infinitely delicate as to suggest the veins in the white flesh of an apple."

233.32 "That's not true, John Fabian. Don't lie."] Riabouchinska springs to life and "contradicts" Fabian's denial in the TS1 copy-text, but in the TS4 rewrite and expansion, Fabian continues to repress the truth. Lieutenant Krovitch has to pick up Riabouchinska, and physically place her in Fabian's lap, before he animates her to speak.

234.38–39 he could see it himself!] The macabre scene of Fabian, confessing to murder through the voice of Riabouchinska, her lips moving, his lips frozen, was originally framed from the perspective of Fabian, who sees himself, holding Riabouchinska, reflected in a large mirror. In his TS4 revisions, Bradbury eliminated the mirror and shifted the point of view over to the homicide detective: "Krovitch stepped back as if he were watching a motion picture that had suddenly grown monstrously tall."

## Emendations

[title] Riabouchinska (And So Died Riabouchinska)] CE; *AND SO DIED RI-ABOUCHINSKA | By | RAY BRADBURY* TS1

231.16 papier-mâché] *MJ*[1964]; papier-mache TS1

*231.23 *Billboard* magazines] *MJ*[1964]; BILLBOARD Magazines TS1

232.19 wherever] TS3; where ever TS1

## Historical Collation: Post-Copy-Text Substantives TSπ–TS4

[title] *AND SO DIED RIABOUCHINSKA | by | Ray Bradbury*] TS1; RI-ABOUCHINSKA TSπ; RIABOUCHINSKA | by | Ray | Bradbury TS2, TS3; RIABOUCHINSKA | by | Ray Bradbury TS4

227.1–22 Mr. Ockham . . . unnaturally.] TS1; *deleted* TS3[AMS]

227.1 Mr. Ockham had] TS1; John Fabian looked at the cold cellar floor and his head began to ache. ⁊ Mr. Ockham lay there upon the floor, quite dead. ⁊ Mr. Ockham had TSπ

227.4 *had*] TS1; had TSπ

*227.6–7 care, thought John Fabian.] TS1; care. TS3, TS4

227.7 but this] TS1; but TS3, TS4

227.9 John Fabian's hand twitched and struck] TS1; John Fabian's head gave a great agonized throb. His hand twitched. It struck TSπ

227.9–11 John Fabian's . . . words: "RIABOUCHINSKA] TS1; On a table he saw a small polished bronze box with certain words on the lid which read, 'Riabouchinska TS3, TS4

227.10 box lid were the words:] TS1; bronze box lid were certain words: TSπ

227.12–13 Fabian sensed . . . his press agent.] TS1; Krovitch looked from the box to the three figures standing stiffly before him. They were John Fabian, ventriloquist; Alyce, his wife; and Bernard Douglas, Fabian's press agent. TS3, TS4

227.12(2) to] TS1; and on to TSπ

227.18–20 The three others . . . raw, and he] TS1; The four people looked with startled eyes at the box on the table. Then Fabian, the ventriloquist, TS3, TS4

227.19 head beginning to ache,] TS1; brow hot, TSπ

227.20 stepped forward and spoke earnestly:] TS1; heard himself step forward swiftly and speak to the box: TSπ

227.22–23 unnaturally. ¶ There was a sharp stab of pain in his head.] TS1; unnaturally. TSπ

227.23–24 There was a sharp stab of pain in his head. ¶ From] TS1; ¶ From TS3, TS3^AMS, TS4

227.26 He swallowed the panic that rose swiftly in him.] TS1; His eyes were strangely grey and frightened. TS3, TS3^AMS, TS4

227.28 some other] TS1; at another TS3, TS3^AMS, TS4

227.28 this clear.] TS1; this matter clear. TS3, TS3^AMS, TS4

227.31 out."] TS1; ~!" TS3, TS3^AMS, TS4

228.4 "You mean *you*.] TS1; "    *you*. TS4

228.8 squeal] TS1; squealing TS2, TS3, TS3^AMS, TS4

228.9 box hinges.] TS1; hinges. TS3, TS3^AMS, TS4

228.12 not] TS1; now TS3, TS3^AMS, TS4

228.13 dreamed, thought John Fabian, and] TS1; dreamed, and TS3, TS3^AMS, TS4

228.24 Riabouchinska up.] TS1; up Riabouchinska. TS3, TS3^AMS, TS4

228.25 with pride.] TS1; proudly. TS3, TS3^AMS, TS4

228.30 him] TS1; her husband TS3, TS3^AMS, TS4

228.30 fine] TS1; pure TS3, TS3^AMS, TS4

228.34 you, Ria."] TS1; you." TS3, TS3^AMS, TS4

228.36 Fabian's] TS1; John Fabian's TS3, TS3^AMS, TS4

229.7 "Yes," he said, "I suppose] TS1; "Yes, I imagine TS3, TS3^AMS, TS4

229.18 live] TS1; love TSπ

229.22 a moment] TS1; a few moments TS3, TS3^AMS, TS4

229.25 ask even a] TS1; ask a TS2, TS3, TS3^AMS, TS4

229.28–30 John Fabian watched . . . moment. Krovitch puffed out smoke.] TS1; Krovitch unwrapped a ◆cigar, [fresh cigar, TS3, TS3^AMS, TS4] prepared it, lit it, and puffed out smoke. TS2, TS3, TS3^AMS, TS4

229.40 she] TS1; *she* TS3, TS3^AMS, TS4

230.1 a piece] TS1; a little piece TS3, TS3^AMS, TS4

230.6–7 Pain struck his . . . looking at her,] TS1; They all stared at the figurine. Even Fabian, TS2, TS3, TS3^AMS, TS4

230.9 while] TS1; time TS3, TS3<sup>AMS</sup>, TS4

230.15 doing] TS1; fault TS2, TS3, TS3<sup>AMS</sup>, TS4

230.19–20 silent. ¶ Fabian felt his throat shudder painfully.] TS1; silent. TS2, TS3, TS3<sup>AMS</sup>, TS4

230.21 Riabouchinska, moving her head.] TS1; Riabouchinska. TSπ, TS2, TS3, TS3<sup>AMS</sup>, TS4

230.29 man,"] TS1; man?" TS3, TS3<sup>AMS</sup>, TS4

230.30–31 laughed. ¶ His head ached with a sudden violence.] TS1; laughed. TS4

230.36–231.1 John Fabian sat . . . door. ¶ "Come in,"] TS1; Lieutenant Krovitch was back. He knocked on the upstairs dressing room door. ¶ "Yes. Come ◆in," [in." TS3, TS3<sup>AMS</sup>] TS2, TS3, TS3<sup>AMS</sup>, TS4

231.4 Krovitch] TS1; Lieutenant Krovitch TS3, TS3<sup>AMS</sup>, TS4

231.5 Fabian blinked, put out a startled hand, and then] TS1; The latter seemed surprised, startled for a moment, then he TS2, TS3, TS3<sup>AMS</sup>, TS4

231.6–7 and the knife cut . . . and the nausea.] TS1; as if with a great ache in his head. TS2, TS3, TS3<sup>AMS</sup>, TS4

231.8 carefully and began reading] TS1; over carefully and began to read TS2, TS3, TS3<sup>AMS</sup>, TS4

231.10–11 Of Russo-Slav . . . victim of amnesia.] TS1; Disappeared in 1934. Believed a victim of amnesia. Of Russo-Slav parentage. TS3, TS3<sup>AMS</sup>, TS4

231.12 Fabian shut his eyes tighter.] TS1; Fabian closed his eyes. TS3, TS3<sup>AMS</sup>, TS4

231.12 His skull was on fire.] TS1; His lips twitched. TS2, TS3, TS3<sup>AMS</sup>, TS4

231.14 search] TS1; go TS2, TS3, TS3<sup>AMS</sup>, TS4

231.17 glanced up] TS1; looked at the ventriloquist TS3, TS3<sup>AMS</sup>, TS4

231.19–20 it." Pain, . . . eyes. "I] TS1; it. I TS2, TS3, TS3<sup>AMS</sup>, TS4

231.22 read] TS1; went TS3, TS3<sup>AMS</sup>, TS4

231.24–25 *Fabian and Sweet William*] TS1; Fabian and Sweet William TS3, TS3<sup>AMS</sup>, TS4 *Also* 231.37

231.29–30 Riabouchinska on] TS1; Riabouchinska the puppet on TS3, TS3<sup>AMS</sup>, TS4

231.31 assistant, yes.] TS1; assistant. TS3, TS3<sup>AMS</sup>, TS4

232.23 "William, William,] TS1; "William, TS3, TS3<sup>AMS</sup>, TS4

232.23 on!"] TS1; on." TS3, TS3<sup>AMS</sup>, TS4

232.25 "No, no, I can't.] TS1; "No, I can't! TS3, TS3<sup>AMS</sup>, TS4

232.30 *slowly*] TS1; slowly TS3, TS3<sup>AMS</sup>, TS4

232.35–233.11 Blackness . . . gone!] TS1; *om.* TS3<sup>AMS</sup>

232.36 sighed] TS1; signed TS4

233.13 echoing and re-echoing] TS1; echoing, re-echoing TS3, TS3<sup>AMS</sup>, TS4

233.13 Ilya Riamansk] TS1; a certain special voice TS3<sup>AMS</sup>

233.13 By the year's ending] TS1; By end of the year TS3<sup>AMS</sup>

233.14 was thinned and without] TS1; had spent all of his TS3<sup>AMS</sup>

233.14–15 searched his stream of consciousness, experimented,] TS1; searched, experimented, TS3^AMS

233.15–16 gracious mannerisms and shy gestures of the real woman.] TS1; quiet manners and gestures that had once belonged to a creature summoned wholly out of memory. TS3^AMS

233.17 Ilya Riamansk in his arms again,] TS1; the Ilya Riamansk in his arms, TS3^AMS

233.18–20 she could reply. . . . you John Fabian."] TS1; very slowly the small mouth opened and the first words were spoken. And the words were good to hear. TS3^AMS

233.23 his chair, watching John Fabian.] TS1; ◆his [a TS3^AMS] chair, looking at ◆John Fabian [the ventriloquist TS3^AMS]. TS3, TS3^AMS, TS4

233.25 another] TS1; the 2^nd TS3^AMS

233.25 well and she] TS1; well. and God help her she TS3^AMS

233.26 I don't] TS1; Its hard to TS3^AMS

233.27 "I see. What] TS1; "What TS3^AMS

*233.30–32 The pain gripped . . . Don't lie."] TS1; Riabouchinska stirred in his lap. "That's not true. Don't lie, John Fabian." TS2, TS3, TS4; "That's not true." said a faint voice. "That's not true." TS3^AMS

233.33 Fabian's cheeks were . . . directly at Krovitch:] TS1; Fabian's waited for a long time, then reached over and opened the bronze box on the table, and took the small figurine out. The lips moved. At first there were no words then the voice came.TS3^AMS

233.34 "John received] TS1; om. TS3^AMS

233.34 letter a] TS1; letter came a TS3^AMS

233.34 said, simply:] TS1; said: TS3^AMS

233.36–41 Fabian's body froze. . . . He gave up.] TS1; Fabian ◆seemed paralyzed. He had a trapped, helpless, insane expression. [did not move. His eyes were fixed upon the figurine. TS3^AMS] His lips trembled. He searched the room as if seeking ◆some way out where a frustration or a truth did not wait to bar his way. He gave up. [for a door which did not exist. TS3^AMS] TS2, TS3, TS3^AMS, TS4

234.1 the world!"] TS1; everyone." TS3^AMS

234.3 love for Ilya kept] TS1; life TS3^AMS

234.4–5 "What sort of . . . really guessed] TS1; "What sort of future would I have if people guessed TS3^AMS

234.5 significance of] TS1; reason for TS3^AMS

234.6 be disgusted. . . . they'd shout!] TS1; turn away. TS3^AMS

234.7 revolting!] TS1; they'd say. TS3^AMS

234.7 scenes with] TS1; scenes on the stage with TS3^AMS

234.8–9 Not when with . . . else and whisper] TS1; Not ◆when someone [when someone TS4] in the audience ◆might [would nudge someone else and TS4] whisper, TS3^AMS, TS4

234.9–10 Disappeared. They . . . he killed her!'"] TS1; Disappeared. They say he killed her! They say he loved her! TS3, TS3^AMS, TS4

234.14 "No, I didn't! I paid him!"] TS1; "No, I didn't kill Ockham, Lieutenant. I paid him one thousand dollars." TS2, TS3, TS3^AMS, TS4

234.16 him!] TS1; ~. TS2, TS3, TS3^AMS, TS4

243.16 must've] TS1; must have TS2, TS3, TS3^AMS, TS4

234.18 eliminating me] TS1; ridding herself of me, TS2, TS3, TS3^AMS, TS4

234.19 "Just a moment,"] TS1; "Wait," TS3^AMS

234.19 wish to] TS1; must TS3^AMS

234.20 wailed helplessly,] TS1; cried, helplessly, TS3, TS4; whispered TS3^AMS

234.21–24 Krovitch backed away. . . . sank in and twisted.] TS1; Krovitch turned. He saw John Fabian's ◆eyes widen in his head, as if a terrible conflict were raging, fighting within. [eyes. TS3^AMS] ◆His throat convulsed again and again, [Saw his throat convulse again and again. TS3^AMS] ◆and lines cut deep in his cheeks, and the hollows of his face sank in. [The lines cut deep in his cheeks. TS3^AMS] TS2, TS3, TS3^AMS, TS4

234.25 came," Riabouchinska began] TS1; came," TS3^AMS

234.27 then controlled itself.] TS1; then went on. TS3^AMS

234.29 came] TS1; was TS3^AMS

234.29 sound," she cried.] TS1; ◆sound!" she cried. [sound!" TS3^AMS] TS3, TS3^AMS, TS4

234.30–31 swearing and sobbing, all in one.] TS1; swearing, I heard him crying. TS3^AMS

234.32 shouted.] TS1; ◆broke through. [said: TS3^AMS] TS2, TS3, TS3^AMS,TS4

234.32 deaf] TS1; dead TS4

234.32–33 blind and lifeless; you heard nothing! Your ears are carved!"] TS1; blind. You're nothing but wood!" TS3^AMS

234.34 they *hear*!"] TS1; ◆they [I TS3^AMS] hear!" TS3, TS3^AMS

234.34 difficulty.] TS1; difficulty now. TS3^AMS

234.34 the hissing, choking] TS1; the choking TS3^AMS

234.37 Down. . . .down. . down he took the body. . ."] TS1; Down. . .down. . ." TS3^AMS

234.38–235.6 Fabian was out . . . I do not know!] TS1; It was a scene so incongruous, so impossible, ◆so completely beyond the veil of sanity and reason that Krovitch recoiled even as he watched. If ever in the time of the world the forces that manipulate man struggled one side against another, this was the time! [that Krovitch stood up. TS3^AMS] The shocked, pallid face of John Fabian, wrenching, the ◆horrible protrusion [widening TS3^AMS] of the eyes, the clenching of ◆the [his TS3^AMS] teeth as a censor, then relaxing again; the subtle move of the throat, and the high, sad, and ◆accusative [far away TS3^AMS] voice of Riabouchinska ◆leaping from her ◆tiny, shining [tiny     TS4] lips! [moving from her mouth! TS3^AMS] Fabian ◆must have known what what was happening, and yet he did not know. [seemed unconscious. His body swayed, his eyes clamped shut suddenly. TS3^AMS] TS2, TS3, TS3^AMS, TS4

235.7 her] TS1; the TS3^AMS

235.8 There is] TS1; There's TS3^AMS

235.9 know of us.] TS1; know. TS3^AMS

235.9–10 in my bronze box] TS1; asleep TS3^AMS

235.14–15 him with her . . . in his eyes.] TS1; him. TS3^AMS

235.16 opened, silent, gaping and shutting, again] TS1; opened, again TS3^AMS

235.18 about] TS1; around TS3, TS3^AMS, TS4

235.19 glazed.] TS1; numbed. TS2, TS3, TS3^AMS, TS4

235.20 sounded, how to make it sound again,] TS1; sounded, how to make it sounded, how to make it sound again, TS4

235.22 gone," he whispered, frantically, clenching his throat.] TS1; gone," TS3^AMS

235.23 I try—but I can't] TS1; I can't TS3^AMS

235.24 down and far away in the night I'll] TS1; down. Far away, I'll TS3^AMS

235.25–26 again. She's gone." ⁋ His . . . throat was relaxed.] TS1; ◆again. She's gone." [again." TS3^AMS] TS2, TS3, TS4

235.28 the cold floor,] TS1; ◆the cold, dirty floor, [the floor, TS3^AMS] TS3, TS4

235.28–29 gently sealed.] TS1; shut. TS3^AMS

## Historical Collation: Post-Copy-Text Substantives, TS5–RBS1

*[title] AND SO DIED RIABOUCHINSKA | By | RAY BRADBURY]* TS1; *AND SO DIED RIABOUCHINSKA | by |* RAY BRADBURY TS5; and so died riabouchinska | *by . . . Ray Bradbury* S1; THE GOLDEN BOX | by RAY BRADBURY S2; and so died riabouchinska *MJ*^1964; AND SO DIED RIABOUCHISKA *MJ*^1965; And So Died Riabouchinska *SRB; And So Died Riabouchinska SRB*^1983, RBS1

227.1–16 Mr. Ockham had . . . soft and hidden away.] TS1; The cellar was cold cement and the dead man was cold stone and the air was filled with an invisible fall of rain, while the people gathered to look at the body ◆as if it had been washed in on an empty shore at morning. [*om.* S2] The gravity of the earth was drawn to a focus here in this single basement room – a gravity so immense that it pulled their faces down, bent their mouths at the corners and drained their cheeks. Their hands hung weighted and their feet were planted so they could not move without seeming to walk under water. ⁋ A voice was calling but nobody listened. ⁋ The voice called again and only after a long time did the people turn and look, momentarily, into the air. They were at the seashore ◆in November [*om.* S2] and this was a gull crying over their heads

in the grey ◆color [colour S2] of dawn. It was a sad crying, like the birds going south for the steel winter to come. It was an ocean sounding the shore
so far away that it was only a whisper of sand and wind in a seashell. ⁋ The
people in the basement room shifted their gaze to a table and a golden box
resting there, no more than twenty-four inches long, inscribed with the name
RIABOUCHINSKA. Under the lid of this small coffin the voice at last settled
with finality and the people stared at the box and the dead man lay on the
floor, not hearing the soft cry. TS5, S1, S2, *MJ*¹⁹⁶⁴, *MJ*¹⁹⁶⁵, *SRB*, *SRB*¹⁹⁸³, *RBS*1

227.17–20 "Please let me . . .and spoke earnestly:] TS1; "Let me out, let me out,
oh please please someone let me out." ⁋ And finally Mr. Fabian, the ventriloquist, bent and whispered to the golden box, TS5, S1, S2, *MJ*¹⁹⁶⁴, *MJ*¹⁹⁶⁵,
*SRB*, *SRB*¹⁹⁸³, *RBS*1

227.21–23 business, darling. Stay . . . pain in his head.] TS1; business. Later. Be
quiet now, that's a good girl." He shut his eyes and tried to laugh. TS5, S1, S2,
*MJ*¹⁹⁶⁴, *MJ*¹⁹⁶⁵, *SRB*, *SRB*¹⁹⁸³, *RBS*1

227.24 behind] TS1; under TS5, S1, S2, *MJ*¹⁹⁶⁴, *MJ*¹⁹⁶⁵, *SRB*, *SRB*¹⁹⁸³, *RBS*1

227.25 kind to me now,] TS1; much kinder now^ TS5, S1, S2, *MJ*¹⁹⁶⁴, *MJ*¹⁹⁶⁵,
*SRB*, *SRB*¹⁹⁸³, *RBS*1

227.26–27 Fabian's face . . . spoke, irritably.] TS1; Detective Lieutenant Krovitch
touched Fabian's arm. TS5, S1, S2, *MJ*¹⁹⁶⁴, *MJ*¹⁹⁶⁵, *SRB*, *SRB*¹⁹⁸³, *RBS*1

227.27–30 mind, Fabian, we'll . . . about something important—"] TS1; mind we'll
save your dummy act for later. Right now there is all *this* to clean up." He
glanced at the woman, who had now taken a folding chair. "Mrs. Fabian." He
nodded to the young man sitting next to her. "Mr. ◆Doughlas [Douglas S1,
S2, *MJ*¹⁹⁶⁴, *MJ*¹⁹⁶⁵, *SRB*, *SRB*¹⁹⁸³, *RBS*1], you're Mr. Fabian's press-agent and
manager?" ⁋ The young man said he was. Krovitch looked at the face of the
man on the floor. "Fabian, ◆Mr. [Mrs. S1, S2, *MJ*¹⁹⁶⁴, *MJ*¹⁹⁶⁵, *SRB*, *SRB*¹⁹⁸³,
*RBS*1] Fabian, Mr. Douglas – all of you say you don't know this man who was
murdered here last night, never heard the name Ockham before. Yet Ockham earlier told the stage manager he knew Fabian and had to see him about
something vitally important." TS5, S1, S2, *MJ*¹⁹⁶⁴, *MJ*¹⁹⁶⁵, *SRB*, *SRB*¹⁹⁸³, *RBS*1

227.31–228.2 The voice in . . . a silver bell.] TS1; The voice in the box began again
quietly. ⁋ Krovitch shouted. "*Damn* it, Fabian!" ⁋ Under the lid, the voice
laughed. It was like a muffled bell, ringing. TS5, S1, S2, *MJ*¹⁹⁶⁴, *MJ*¹⁹⁶⁵, *SRB*,
*SRB*¹⁹⁸³, *RBS*1

228.4 Her?" Krovitch glared. "You mean *you*.] TS1; Her? or *you*, damn it! TS5,
S1, S2, *MJ*¹⁹⁶⁴, *MJ*¹⁹⁶⁵, *SRB*, *SRB*¹⁹⁸³, *RBS*1

228.5–6 together again," murmured the small voice. "Never again after tonight. . ."]
TS1; together," said the quiet voice, "Never again after tonight." TS5, S1, S2,
*MJ*¹⁹⁶⁴, *MJ*¹⁹⁶⁵, *SRB*, *SRB*¹⁹⁸³, *RBS*1

228.7 held] TS1; put TS5, S1, S2, *MJ*¹⁹⁶⁴, *MJ*¹⁹⁶⁵, *SRB*, *SRB*¹⁹⁸³, *RBS*1

228.7 key to the box,] TS1; key, TS5, S1, S2, *MJ*¹⁹⁶⁴, *MJ*¹⁹⁶⁵, SRB, SRB¹⁹⁸³, RBS1

228.8 lock,] TS1; small lock, TS5, S1, S2, *MJ*¹⁹⁶⁴, *MJ*¹⁹⁶⁵, SRB, SRB¹⁹⁸³, RBS1

228.8–9 and the squeal of the tiny box hinges.] TS1; the squeal of the miniature hinges as the lid was opened and laid back against the table-top. TS5, S1, S2, *MJ*¹⁹⁶⁴, *MJ*¹⁹⁶⁵, SRB, SRB¹⁹⁸³, RBS1

228.11–12 Riabouchinska lying in] TS1; Riabouchinska in TS5, S1, S2, *MJ*¹⁹⁶⁴, *MJ*¹⁹⁶⁵, SRB, SRB¹⁹⁸³, RBS1

228.12 not believing] TS1; not quite believing TS5, S1, S2, *MJ*¹⁹⁶⁴, *MJ*¹⁹⁶⁵, SRB, SRB¹⁹⁸³, RBS1

*228.13–23 There were nights . . . only a puppet. . .] TS1; The face was white and it was cut from marble or from the whitest wood he had ever seen. It might have been cut from snow. And the neck that held the head which was as dainty as a porcelain cup with the sun shining through the thinness of it, the neck was also white. And the hands could have been ivory and they were thin small things with tiny fingernails and whorls on the pads of the fingers, little delicate spirals and lines. ¶ She was all white stone, with light pouring through the stone and light coming out of the dark eyes, with blue tones beneath like fresh mulberries. He was reminded of milk-glass ◆and cream [and of cream *MJ*¹⁹⁶⁴, *MJ*¹⁹⁶⁵, SRB, SRB¹⁹⁸³, RBS1] poured ◆in [into *MJ*¹⁹⁶⁴, *MJ*¹⁹⁶⁵, SRB, SRB¹⁹⁸³, RBS1] a crystal tumbler. The brows were arched and black and thin and the cheeks were hollowed and there was a faint pink vein in each temple and ◆a faint blue [a blue S2] vein barely visible above the slender bridge of the nose, between the shining dark eyes. ¶ Her lips were half-parted and it looked as if they might be slightly damp and the nostrils were arched and modeled perfectly as were the ears. The hair was black and it was parted in the middle and drawn ◆back of [behind SRB¹⁹⁸³] the ears and it was real—he could see every single strand of hair. Her gown was as black as her hair and draped in such a fashion as to show her shoulders, which were carved wood as white as a stone that ◆has [had S2] lain a long time in the sun. She was very beautiful. Krovitch felt his throat move and then he stopped and did not say anything. TS5, S1, S2, *MJ*¹⁹⁶⁴, *MJ*¹⁹⁶⁵, SRB, SRB¹⁹⁸³, RBS1

228.24–29 John Fabian tenderly . . . constructed of wood."] TS1; Fabian took Riabouchinska from her box. "My lovely lady," he said. "Carved from the rarest imported woods. She's appeared in Paris, Rome, Istanbul. Everyone in the world loves her and thinks she's really human, some sort of incredibly delicate midget-creature. They won't accept that she was once part of many forests growing far away from cities and idiotic people." TS5, S1, S2, *MJ*¹⁹⁶⁴, *MJ*¹⁹⁶⁵, SRB, SRB¹⁹⁸³, RBS1

228.30–32 John Fabian's wife, . . . him, it said:] TS1; Fabian's wife, Alyce, watched her husband, not taking her eyes from his mouth. Her eyes did not blink once in all the time he was ◆telling [speaking S2] of the doll he held in his arms. He in turn seemed aware of no one but the doll – the cellar and its people were lost in a mist that settled everywhere. ¶ But finally the small figure stirred and quivered. TS5, S1, S2, *MJ*¹⁹⁶⁴, *MJ*¹⁹⁶⁵, SRB, SRB¹⁹⁸³, RBS1

228.33 "Please don't go . . . doesn't like it."] TS1; "Please, don't talk about me! You know Alyce doesn't like it." TS5, S1, S2, *MJ*¹⁹⁶⁴, *MJ*¹⁹⁶⁵, SRB, SRB¹⁹⁸³, RBS1

228.34 "Alyce *never has* liked anything about you, Ria."] TS1; "Alyce never ◆*has* [has *MJ*¹⁹⁶⁴, *MJ*¹⁹⁶⁵, SRB, SRB¹⁹⁸³, RBS1] liked it." TS5, S1, S2, *MJ*¹⁹⁶⁴, *MJ*¹⁹⁶⁵, SRB, SRB¹⁹⁸³, RBS1

228.35–37 "Sh! Don't!" cried . . . poor Mr. Ockham?"] TS1; "Shh, don't!" cried Riabouchinska. "Not here, not now." And then, swiftly, she turned to Krovitch and her tiny lips moved. "How did it all happen? Mr. Ockham, I mean, Mr. Ockham." TS5, S1, S2, *MJ*¹⁹⁶⁴, *MJ*¹⁹⁶⁵, SRB, SRB¹⁹⁸³, RBS1

228.38–39 Krovitch stared at . . . to your box, Ria."] TS1; Fabian said, "You'd better go to sleep now, Ria. .." TS5, S1, S2, *MJ*¹⁹⁶⁴, *MJ*¹⁹⁶⁵, SRB, SRB¹⁹⁸³, RBS1

228.40 want] TS1; ◆*want* [want *MJ*¹⁹⁶⁴, *MJ*¹⁹⁶⁵, SRB, SRB¹⁹⁸³, RBS1] TS5, S1, S2

228.40 "I have] TS1; "I've TS5, S1, S2, *MJ*¹⁹⁶⁴, *MJ*¹⁹⁶⁵, SRB, SRB¹⁹⁸³, RBS1

228.41 or . . . or Mr. Douglas even—"] TS1; or—or Mr. Douglas even!" TS5, S1, S2, *MJ*¹⁹⁶⁴, *MJ*¹⁹⁶⁵, SRB, SRB¹⁹⁸³, RBS1

229.1–3 you little witch!" . . . a real person.] TS1; you –" And he looked at the doll as if it had suddenly become six feet tall and ◆was [were *MJ*¹⁹⁶⁴, *MJ*¹⁹⁶⁵, SRB, SRB¹⁹⁸³, RBS1] breathing there before him. TS5, S1, S2, *MJ*¹⁹⁶⁴, *MJ*¹⁹⁶⁵, SRB, SRB¹⁹⁸³, RBS1

229.4 said Riabouchinska.] TS1; Riabouchinska turned her head to see all of the room. TS5, S1, S2, *MJ*¹⁹⁶⁴, *MJ*¹⁹⁶⁵, SRB, SRB¹⁹⁸³, RBS1

229.5–6 bronze casket there . . . isn't it, John?"] TS1; coffin there'll be no truth for John's a consummate liar and I must watch after him, isn't that right, John?" TS5, S1, S2, *MJ*¹⁹⁶⁴, *MJ*¹⁹⁶⁵, SRB, SRB¹⁹⁸³, RBS1

229.7 said,] TS1; said, his eyes shut, TS5, S1, S2, *MJ*¹⁹⁶⁴, *MJ*¹⁹⁶⁵, SRB, SRB¹⁹⁸³, RBS1

229.10–12 Krovitch pounded the . . . I am helpless."] TS1; Krovitch hit the table with his fist. ◆ "God damn, oh God *damn* ["Damn, oh *damn* S2] ◆it! [it, *MJ*¹⁹⁶⁴, *MJ*¹⁹⁶⁵, SRB, SRB¹⁹⁸³, RBS1] Fabian! If you think you can —" ¶ "I'm helpless," said Fabian. TS5, S1, S2, *MJ*¹⁹⁶⁴, *MJ*¹⁹⁶⁵, SRB, SRB¹⁹⁸³, RBS1

229.13–15 "But she's in . . . I am powerless.] TS1; "But she's —" ¶ "I know, I know what you want to say." said Fabian quietly, looking at the detective. "She's in my throat, is that it? No, no. She's not in my throat. She's somewhere else. I don't know. Here, or here." He touched his chest, his head. ¶ "She's quick to hide. Sometimes there's nothing I can do. TS5, S1, S2, *MJ*¹⁹⁶⁴, *MJ*¹⁹⁶⁵, SRB, SRB¹⁹⁸³, RBS1

229.16–17 She watches over me, reprimands me,] TS1; She stands guard, she reprimands me, TS5, S1, S2, *MJ*¹⁹⁶⁴, *MJ*¹⁹⁶⁵, SRB, SRB¹⁹⁸³, RBS1

229.17–18 ethical where I . . . I live mine.] TS1; good when I am wicked as all the sins that ever were. She lives a life apart. TS5, S1, S2, *MJ*¹⁹⁶⁴, *MJ*¹⁹⁶⁵, SRB, SRB¹⁹⁸³, RBS1

229.18–19 She has raised . . . She lives there,] TS1; ¶ "She's raised a wall in my head and lives there, TS5, S1, S2, *MJ*¹⁹⁶⁴, *MJ*¹⁹⁶⁵, *SRB*, *SRB*¹⁹⁸³, *RBS*1

229.20 correct] TS1; right TS5, S1, S2, *MJ*¹⁹⁶⁴, *MJ*¹⁹⁶⁵, *SRB*, *SRB*¹⁹⁸³, *RBS*1

229.21 good."] TS1; good, no good at all." TS5, S1, S2, *MJ*¹⁹⁶⁴, *MJ*¹⁹⁶⁵, *SRB*, *SRB*¹⁹⁸³, *RBS*1

229.22–24 Lieutenant Krovitch sat . . . a decision. ¶ "All] TS1; Lieutenant Krovitch sat silently for the better part of a minute, then made his decision. ^ "All TS5, S1, S2, *MJ*¹⁹⁶⁴, *MJ*¹⁹⁶⁵, *SRB*, *SRB*¹⁹⁸³, *RBS*1

229.24 Maybe. . maybe] TS1; It just may be, by God, that TS5, S1, S2, *MJ*¹⁹⁶⁴, *MJ*¹⁹⁶⁵, *SRB*, *SRB*¹⁹⁸³, *RBS*1

229.28–31 John Fabian watched . . . the dead man?"] TS1; Krovitch unwrapped a fresh cigar, lit it, and puffed smoke. "So you don't recognize the dead man, Mr. Douglas?" TS5, S1, S2, *MJ*¹⁹⁶⁴, *MJ*¹⁹⁶⁵, *SRB*, *SRB*¹⁹⁸³, *RBS*1

229.32 Douglas looked at . . . actor-type, I believe."] TS1; "He looks vaguely familiar. Could be an actor." TS5, S1, S2, *MJ*¹⁹⁶⁴, *MJ*¹⁹⁶⁵, *SRB*, *SRB*¹⁹⁸³, *RBS*1

229.33–35 "One of you . . . with Mrs. Fabian?"] TS1; "Let's all stop lying, what do you say? Look at Ockham's shoes, his clothing. It's obvious he needed money and came here tonight to beg, borrow or steal some. Let me ask you this, Douglas – are you in love with Mrs. Fabian?" TS5, S1, S2, *MJ*¹⁹⁶⁴, *MJ*¹⁹⁶⁵, *SRB*, *SRB*¹⁹⁸³, *RBS*1

229.36–41 "Really, Lieutenant!" . . . stare at her."] TS1; "Now wait just a moment!" cried Alyce Fabian. ¶ Krovitch motioned her down. "You sit there, side by side, the two of you. I'm not exactly blind. When a press-agent sits where the husband should be sitting, consoling the wife, ◆*well*! [well! *MJ*¹⁹⁶⁴, *MJ*¹⁹⁶⁵, *SRB*, *SRB*¹⁹⁸³, *RBS*1] The way you look at the marionette's coffin, Mrs. Fabian, holding your breath when she appears. You ◆make fists [clench your fists S2] when she talks. Hell, you're obvious." TS5, S1, S2, *MJ*¹⁹⁶⁴, *MJ*¹⁹⁶⁵, *SRB*, *SRB*¹⁹⁸³, *RBS*1

230.1 piece] TS1; stick TS5, S1, S2, *MJ*¹⁹⁶⁴, *MJ*¹⁹⁶⁵, *SRB*, *SRB*¹⁹⁸³, *RBS*1

230.2 "Aren't you?" Krovitch softened his voice.] TS1; "◆*Aren't* [Aren't *MJ*¹⁹⁶⁴, *MJ*¹⁹⁶⁵, *SRB*, *SRB*¹⁹⁸³, *RBS*1] you?" TS5, S1, S2, *MJ*¹⁹⁶⁴, *MJ*¹⁹⁶⁵, *SRB*, *SRB*¹⁹⁸³, *RBS*1

230.3 "No!" She was . . . jealous of her!"] TS1; "No, no, I'm ◆*not* [not *MJ*¹⁹⁶⁴, *MJ*¹⁹⁶⁵, *SRB*, *SRB*¹⁹⁸³, *RBS*1]!" TS5, S1, S2, *MJ*¹⁹⁶⁴, *MJ*¹⁹⁶⁵, *SRB*, *SRB*¹⁹⁸³, *RBS*1

230.4 "You needn't tell him, Alyce," said John Fabian.] TS1; Fabian moved. "You needn't tell him anything, Alyce." TS5, S1, S2, *MJ*¹⁹⁶⁴, *MJ*¹⁹⁶⁵, *SRB*, *SRB*¹⁹⁸³, *RBS*1

230.5 "Let her!" cried Riabouchinska.] TS1; "◆*Let* [Let *MJ*¹⁹⁶⁴, *MJ*¹⁹⁶⁵, *SRB*, *SRB*¹⁹⁸³, *RBS*1] her!" TS5, S1, S2, *MJ*¹⁹⁶⁴, *MJ*¹⁹⁶⁵, *SRB*, *SRB*¹⁹⁸³, *RBS*1

230.6–8 Pain struck his . . . an alien throat.] TS1; They all jerked their heads and stared at the small figurine whose mouth was now slowly shutting. Even Fabian looked at the marionette as if it had struck him a blow. TS5, S1, S2, *MJ*¹⁹⁶⁴, *MJ*¹⁹⁶⁵, *SRB*, *SRB*¹⁹⁸³, *RBS*1

230.10–11 ago. He said . . . loved Riabouchinska, too.] TS1; ago because he said he loved me and because I loved him and I loved Riabouchinska. TS5, S1, S2, *MJ*¹⁹⁶⁴, *MJ*¹⁹⁶⁵, *SRB*, *SRB*¹⁹⁸³, *RBS*1

230.11–18 paid more attention . . . that John wasn't."] TS1; lived all of his life and paid most of his attentions to her and I was a shadow waiting in the wings every night. ¶ "He spent fifty thousand dollars a year on her ◆wardrobes[wardrobe *RBS*1]—◆one [a *MJ*¹⁹⁶⁴, *MJ*¹⁹⁶⁵, *SRB*, *SRB*¹⁹⁸³, *RBS*1] hundred thousand dollars for a ◆doll [doll's S2, *SRB*¹⁹⁸³] house with gold and silver and platinum furniture. He tucked her in a small satin bed each night and talked to her. I thought it was all an elaborate joke at first and I was wonderfully amused. ¶ "But when it finally came to me that I was indeed merely an assistant in his act I began to feel a vague sort of hatred and distrust, not for the marionette, because after all it wasn't her doing – but I felt a terrible growing dislike and hatred for John, because it *was* his fault. He, after all, was the control and all of his cleverness and natural sadism came out through his relationship with the wooden doll. ¶ "And when I finally became very jealous, how silly of me! It was the greatest tribute I could have paid him and the way he had ◆gone [set S2] about perfecting the art of throwing his voice. It was all so idiotic, it was all so strange. And yet I knew that something had hold of John, just as people who drink have a hungry animal somewhere in them, starving to death. ¶ "So I moved back and forth from anger to pity, from jealousy to understanding. There were long periods when I didn't hate him at all and I never hated the thing that Ria was in him, for she was the best half, the good part, the honest and the lovely part of him. She was everything that he never let himself try to be." TS5, S1, S2, *MJ*¹⁹⁶⁴, *MJ*¹⁹⁶⁵, *SRB*, *SRB*¹⁹⁸³, *RBS*1

230.19 She stopped talking, and] TS1; Alyce Fabian ◆stopped talking^ and [stopped and S2] TS5, S1, S2, *MJ*¹⁹⁶⁴, *MJ*¹⁹⁶⁵, *SRB*, *SRB*¹⁹⁸³, *RBS*1

230.19 room] TS1; basement room TS5, S1, S2, *MJ*¹⁹⁶⁴, *MJ*¹⁹⁶⁵, *SRB*, *SRB*¹⁹⁸³, *RBS*1

230.19–20 silent. ¶ Fabian felt his throat shudder painfully.] TS1; silent. TS5, S1, S2, *MJ*¹⁹⁶⁴, *MJ*¹⁹⁶⁵, *SRB*, *SRB*¹⁹⁸³, *RBS*1

230.21 "Tell] TS1; "Explain S2

230.21 murmured Riabouchinska, moving her head.] TS1; said a voice, whispering. TS5, S1, S2, *MJ*¹⁹⁶⁴, *MJ*¹⁹⁶⁵, *SRB*, *SRB*¹⁹⁸³, *RBS*1

230.22–23 With an effort, . . . to Mr. Douglas. . . ."] TS1; Mrs. Fabian did not look up at the marionette. With an effort she finished it out. "When the years passed and there was so little love and understanding from John I guess it was natural I turned to – Mr. Douglas." TS5, S1, S2, *MJ*¹⁹⁶⁴, *MJ*¹⁹⁶⁵, *SRB*, *SRB*¹⁹⁸³, *RBS*1

230.24–26 "So. And Mr. Ockham, . . . prevent that interview."] TS1; Krovitch nodded. "Everything begins to fall into place. Mr. Ockham was a very poor man, down on his luck, and he came to this theatre tonight because he knew something about you and Mr. Douglas. Perhaps he threatened to speak to Mr. Fabian if you didn't buy him off. That would give you the best of reasons to get rid of him." TS5, S1, S2, *MJ*¹⁹⁶⁴, *MJ*¹⁹⁶⁵, *SRB*, *SRB*¹⁹⁸³, *RBS*1

230.27 "I didn't kill him," said Alyce, tiredly.] TS1; "That's even sillier than all the rest," said Alyce Fabian, tiredly. "I didn't kill him." TS5, S1, S2, *MJ*¹⁹⁶⁴, *MJ*¹⁹⁶⁵, *SRB*, *SRB*¹⁹⁸³, *RBS*1

230.28 "Douglas might have, and not told you!"] TS1; "Mr. Douglas might have and not told you." TS5, S1, S2, *MJ*¹⁹⁶⁴, *MJ*¹⁹⁶⁵, *SRB*, *SRB*¹⁹⁸³, *RBS*1

230.29 man,"] TS1; ~?" TS5, S1, S2, *MJ*¹⁹⁶⁴, *MJ*¹⁹⁶⁵, *SRB*, *SRB*¹⁹⁸³, *RBS*1

230.29 it!"] TS1; us." TS5, S1, S2, *MJ*¹⁹⁶⁴, *MJ*¹⁹⁶⁵, *SRB*, *SRB*¹⁹⁸³, *RBS*1

230.30–31 Fabian, and laughed. ⁋ His head ached with a sudden violence.] TS1; Fabian^ and laughed. TS5, S1, S2, *MJ*¹⁹⁶⁴, *MJ*¹⁹⁶⁵, *SRB*, *SRB*¹⁹⁸³, *RBS*1

*230.32–33 Riabouchinska went on laughing for him, echoing in the dim concrete room.] TS1; his hand twitched, hidden in the snowflake interior of the tiny doll, and her mouth opened and shut, opened and shut – he was trying to make her carry the laughter on after he had stopped – but there was no sound, save the little empty whisper of her lips moving and gasping, while Fabian stared down at the little face and perspiration came out, shining, upon his cheeks. TS5, S1, S2, *MJ*¹⁹⁶⁴, *MJ*¹⁹⁶⁵, *SRB*, *SRB*¹⁹⁸³, *RBS*1

230.36–41 The next day, . . . knock at the door.] TS1; The next afternoon Lieutenant Krovitch moved through the theatre darkness backstage, found the iron stairs and climbed with great thought, taking as much time as he deemed necessary on each step, up to the second-level dressing room. He rapped on one of the thin-paneled doors. TS5, S1, S2, *MJ*¹⁹⁶⁴, *MJ*¹⁹⁶⁵, *SRB*, *SRB*¹⁹⁸³, *RBS*1

231.1 called Fabian, wearily.] TS1; said Fabian's voice from what seemed a great distance. TS5, S1, S2, *MJ*¹⁹⁶⁴, *MJ*¹⁹⁶⁵, *SRB*, *SRB*¹⁹⁸³, *RBS*1

231.2–8 door. "Fabian, I . . . data on the back:] TS1; door and stood looking at the man who was slumped before his dressing mirror. "I have something I'd like to show you," ◆he said at last. [Krovitch said. *MJ*¹⁹⁶⁴, *MJ*¹⁹⁶⁵, *SRB*, *SRB*¹⁹⁸³, *RBS*1] His face showing no emotion whatever ◆Krovitch [he *MJ*¹⁹⁶⁴, *MJ*¹⁹⁶⁵, *SRB*, *SRB*¹⁹⁸³, *RBS*1] opened a ◆manila folder [folder S2] and pulled out a glossy photograph which he placed on the dressing-table. ⁋ John Fabian raised his eyebrows, glanced quickly up at Krovitch and then settled slowly back in his chair. He put his fingers to the bridge of his nose and massaged his face carefully as if he had a headache. Krovitch turned the picture over and began to read from the typewritten data on the back. TS5, S1, S2, *MJ*¹⁹⁶⁴, *MJ*¹⁹⁶⁵, *MJ*¹⁹⁶⁵, *SRB*, *SRB*¹⁹⁸³, *RBS*1

*231.9–12 Ilya Riamansk; . . . was on fire.] TS1; Miss Ilyana Riamonova. One hundred pounds. Blue eyes. Black hair. Oval face. Born ◆nineteen hundred and fourteen, [1914, *MJ*¹⁹⁶⁴, *MJ*¹⁹⁶⁵, *SRB*, *SRB*¹⁹⁸³, *RBS*1] New York City. Disappeared ◆nineteen hundred and thirty-four. [1934. *MJ*¹⁹⁶⁴, *MJ*¹⁹⁶⁵, *SRB*, *SRB*¹⁹⁸³, *RBS*1] Believed a victim of amnesia. Of Russo-Slav ◆parentage. Et cetera. Et cetera." [parentage." S2] ¶ Fabian's lip twitched. TS5, S1, S2, *MJ*¹⁹⁶⁴, *MJ*¹⁹⁶⁵, *SRB*, *SRB*¹⁹⁸³, *RBS*1

231.13–14 "Fabian, it] TS1; "It TS5, S1, S2, *MJ*¹⁹⁶⁴, *MJ*¹⁹⁶⁵, *SRB*, *SRB*¹⁹⁸³, *RBS*1

231.14–16 search through the . . . not a puppet,] TS1; go through police files for a picture of a marionette. You should have heard the laughter at ◆headquarters. *God.* [Headquarters. S2] Still – here she ◆*is* [is *MJ*¹⁹⁶⁴, *MJ*¹⁹⁶⁵, *SRB*, *SRB*¹⁹⁸³, *RBS*1]– Ribouchinska. *Not* papier-mache, *not* wood, *not* a puppet, TS5, S1, S2, *MJ*¹⁹⁶⁴, *MJ*¹⁹⁶⁵, *SRB*, *SRB*¹⁹⁸³, *RBS*1

231.17 about] TS1; around TS5, S1, S2, *MJ*¹⁹⁶⁴, *MJ*¹⁹⁶⁵, *SRB*, *SRB*¹⁹⁸³, *RBS*1

231.17–18 glanced up. "Take it from there, Mr. Fabian."] TS1; looked steadily at Fabian. "Suppose you take it from there?" TS5, S1, S2, *MJ*¹⁹⁶⁴, *MJ*¹⁹⁶⁵, *SRB*, *SRB*¹⁹⁸³, *RBS*1

231.19–21 it." Pain, like . . . puppet after her."] TS1; it at all. I saw this woman's picture a long time ago, liked her looks and ◆copied [made S2] my marionette ◆after [like S2] her." TS5, S1, S2, *MJ*¹⁹⁶⁴, *MJ*¹⁹⁶⁵, *SRB*, *SRB*¹⁹⁸³, *RBS*1

231.22 it, eh?" drawled . . . morning I read] TS1; it at all." Krovitch took a deep breath and exhaled, wiping his face with a huge handkerchief. "Fabian, this very morning I shuffled TS5, S1, S2, *MJ*¹⁹⁶⁴, *MJ*¹⁹⁶⁵, *SRB*, *SRB*¹⁹⁸³, *RBS*1

*◊231.23 BILLBOARD Magazines] TS1; ◆magazines [*Billboard* magazines *MJ*¹⁹⁶⁴, *MJ*¹⁹⁶⁵, *SRB*, *SRB*¹⁹⁸³, *RBS*1] S2

231.23 *that*] TS1; that *MJ*¹⁹⁶⁴, *MJ*¹⁹⁶⁵, *SRB*, *SRB*¹⁹⁸³, *RBS*1

231.23 1934] TS1; nineteen hundred and thirty-four [1934 *MJ*¹⁹⁶⁴, *MJ*¹⁹⁶⁵, *SRB*, *SRB*¹⁹⁸³, *RBS*1] TS5, S1, S2

231.24–25 playing on a lesser circuit known as *Fabian and Sweet William.*] TS1; which played ◆on [in S2] a second-rate ◆circuit, [touring company, S2] known as Fabian and Sweet William. TS5, S1, S2, *MJ*¹⁹⁶⁴, *MJ*¹⁹⁶⁵, *SRB*, *SRB*¹⁹⁸³, *RBS*1

231.25 male] TS1; boy TS5, S1, S2, *MJ*¹⁹⁶⁴, *MJ*¹⁹⁶⁵, *SRB*, *SRB*¹⁹⁸³, *RBS*1

231.25–30 As usual in . . . all over again?"] TS1; ¶ "There was a girl assistant – Ilyana Riamonova. No picture of her in the article but I at least had a ◆*name*, [name *MJ*¹⁹⁶⁴, *MJ*¹⁹⁶⁵, *SRB*, *SRB*¹⁹⁸³, *RBS*1] the name of a ◆*real* [real *MJ*¹⁹⁶⁴, *MJ*¹⁹⁶⁵, *SRB*, *SRB*¹⁹⁸³, *RBS*1] person, to go on. It was simple to check police files then and dig up this picture. The ◆resemblance, needless [resemblance between S2] to say, between the live woman on one hand and the puppet on the other is nothing short of incredible. Suppose you go back and tell your story over again, Fabian?" [Fabian." *MJ*¹⁹⁶⁴, *MJ*¹⁹⁶⁵, *SRB*, *SRB*¹⁹⁸³, *RBS*1] TS5, S1, S2, *MJ*¹⁹⁶⁴, *MJ*¹⁹⁶⁵, *SRB*, *SRB*¹⁹⁸³, *RBS*1

231.31 yes. That was all.] TS1; that's all. TS5, S1, S2, *MJ*¹⁹⁶⁴, *MJ*¹⁹⁶⁵, *SRB*, *SRB*¹⁹⁸³, *RBS*1

231.31 simply used] TS1; used S2

231.32–35 Krovitch snorted. "Do . . . and you know it!"] TS1; "You're making me sweat," said the detective. "Do you think I'm a fool? Do you think I don't know love when I see it? I've watched you handle the marionette, I've seen you talk to it, I've seen how you make it react to you. You're in love with the puppet naturally, because you loved the original woman ♦very *very* [very, very *MJ*¹⁹⁶⁴, *MJ*¹⁹⁶⁵, *SRB*, *SRB*¹⁹⁸³, *RBS*1] much. I've lived too long not to sense that. Hell, Fabian, stop fencing around." TS5, S1, S2, *MJ*¹⁹⁶⁴, *MJ*¹⁹⁶⁵, *SRB*, *SRB*¹⁹⁸³, *RBS*1

231.36–41 Fabian lifted up . . . It was autumn. . ."] TS1; Fabian lifted his pale slender hands, turned them over, examined them and let them fall. ¶ "All right. In ♦nineteen hundred and thirty-four [1934 *MJ*¹⁹⁶⁴, *MJ*¹⁹⁶⁵, *SRB*, *SRB*¹⁹⁸³, *RBS*1] I was billed as Fabian and Sweet William. Sweet William was a small bulbnosed boy dummy I carved a long time ago. I was in Los Angeles when this girl appeared at the stage door one night. She'd followed my work for years. She was desperate for a job and she hoped to be my assistant. . ." TS5, S1, S2, *MJ*¹⁹⁶⁴, *MJ*¹⁹⁶⁵, *SRB*, *SRB*¹⁹⁸³, *RBS*1

232.1–2 stage alley. He remembered how startled he was at her fresh beauty, her] TS1; alley behind the theatre and how startled he was at her freshness and TS5, S1, S2, *MJ*¹⁹⁶⁴, *MJ*¹⁹⁶⁵, *SRB*, *SRB*¹⁹⁸³, *RBS*1

232.2–6 him. . . the way . . . lost to this woman.] TS1; him and the way the cool rain touched softly ♦down through the [down the S2] narrow alleyway and caught in small spangles through her hair, melting in dark warmness, and the rain beaded upon her white porcelain hand holding her coat together at her neck. ¶ He saw her ♦lips [lips' *MJ*¹⁹⁶⁴, *MJ*¹⁹⁶⁵, *SRB*, *SRB*¹⁹⁸³, *RBS*1] motion in the dark and her voice, separated off on another sound-track it seemed, speaking to him in the autumn wind, and he remembered that ♦without saying [without his saying *MJ*¹⁹⁶⁴, *MJ*¹⁹⁶⁵, *SRB*, *SRB*¹⁹⁸³, *RBS*1] yes or no or perhaps, she was suddenly on the stage with him, in the great pouring bright light, and in two months he, who had always prided himself on his cynicism and disbelief, had stepped off the rim of the world after her, plunging down a bottomless place of no limit and no light anywhere. TS5, S1, S2, *MJ*¹⁹⁶⁴, *MJ*¹⁹⁶⁵, *SRB*, *SRB*¹⁹⁸³, *RBS*1

232.7–12 Then there were . . . across the face!] TS1; Arguments followed and more than arguments – things said and done that lacked all sense and sanity and fairness. She had edged away from him at last, causing his rages and remarkable hysterias. Once he burned her entire wardrobe in a fit of jealousy. She had taken this quietly. But then one night he handed her a week's notice, accused her of monstrous disloyalty, shouted at her, seized her, slapped her again and ♦again across the face, bullied her about [again, bullied her about, S2] and thrust her ♦out the [out of the S2] door, slamming it! TS5, S1, *MJ*¹⁹⁶⁴, *MJ*¹⁹⁶⁵, *SRB*, *SRB*¹⁹⁸³, *RBS*1

232.13 Ilya Riamansk vanished that night.] TS1; She disappeared that night. TS5, S1, S2, *MJ*[1964], *MJ*[1965], *SRB*, *SRB*[1983], *RBS*1

232.14–19 He was desperate . . . he needed her.] TS1; When he found the next day that she was really gone and there was nowhere to find her, it was like standing in the center of a titanic explosion. All the world was smashed flat and all the echoes of the explosion came back to reverberate at midnight, at four in the morning, at dawn, and he was up early, stunned with the sound of coffee simmering and the sound of matches being struck and cigarettes lit and himself trying to shave and looking at mirrors that were sickening in their distortion. ¶ He clipped out all the advertisements that he ◆took [put S2] in the papers and pasted them in neat rows in a scrapbook – all the ads describing her and ◆telling [explaining S2] about her and asking for her back. He even put a private detective on the case. People talked. The police dropped ◆by [in S2] to question him. There was more talk. ¶ But she was gone like a piece of white incredibly fragile tissue-paper, blown over the sky and down. A record of her was sent to the largest cities, and that was the end of it for the police. But not for Fabian. She might be dead or just running away but wherever she was he knew that somehow and in some way he would have her back. TS5, S1, S2, *MJ*[1964], *MJ*[1965], *SRB*, *SRB*[1983], *RBS*1

232.20–21 One night he . . . upon a chair,] TS1; One night he came home, bringing his own darkness with ◆him, and collapsed upon a chair [him, S2] TS5, S1, S2, *MJ*[1964], *MJ*[1965], *SRB*, *SRB*[1983], *RBS*1

232.22 dark room:] TS1; black room. TS5, S1, S2, *MJ*[1964], *MJ*[1965], *SRB*, *SRB*[1983], *RBS*1

232.23 "William, William, this . . . can't go on!"] TS1; "William, it's all over and done. I ◆*can't* [can't *MJ*[1964], *MJ*[1965], *SRB*, *SRB*[1983], *RBS*1] keep it up!" TS5, S1, S2, *MJ*[1964], *MJ*[1965], *SRB*, *SRB*[1983], *RBS*1

232.24 "Coward! You] TS1; ◆ "Coward! Coward!" ["Coward!" S2] from the air above his head, out of the emptiness. "You TS5, S1, S2, *MJ*[1964], *MJ*[1965], *SRB*, *SRB*[1983], *RBS*1

232.24–25 want!" ¶ "No, no I can't. No, I can never get her back!" ¶ Sweet] TS1; ◆want!" [want!" ¶ "No I can't. No I can never get her back." S1, S2] ¶ Sweet TS5, S1, S2, *MJ*[1964], *MJ*[1965], *SRB*, *SRB*[1983], *RBS*1

232.26 him.] TS1; him in the night. TS5, S1, S2, *MJ*[1964], *MJ*[1965], *SRB*, *SRB*[1983], *RBS*1

232.27 away. Start all over. . ."] TS1; aside, lock me up. Start all ◆over." [over again." S2] TS5, S1, S2, *MJ*[1964], *MJ*[1965], *SRB*, *SRB*[1983], *RBS*1

232.28 over?"] TS1; over again?" S2

232.29–32 William. "Buy a . . . small, duplicate hollows. . ."] TS1; William and darkness moved within darkness. "Yes. Buy wood. Buy fine new wood. Buy hard-grained wood. Buy beautiful fresh new wood. And carve. Carve slowly ◆and carve carefully. [and carefully. S2] Whittle away. Cut delicately. Make the nostrils, so. ◆And cut [Cut S2] her thin black eyebrows, round and high,

◆*so,* [so, *MJ*¹⁹⁶⁴, *MJ*¹⁹⁶⁵, *SRB*, *SRB*¹⁹⁸³, *RBS*1] and make her cheeks in small hollows. Carve, carve. . ." TS5, S1, S2, *MJ*¹⁹⁶⁴, *MJ*¹⁹⁶⁵, *SRB*, *SRB*¹⁹⁸³, *RBS*1

232.33 "No!" shouted Fabian.] TS1; "No!" TS5, S1, S2, *MJ*¹⁹⁶⁴, *MJ*¹⁹⁶⁵, *SRB*, *SRB*¹⁹⁸³, *RBS*1

232.33 foolish!] TS1; ~. TS5, S1, S2, *MJ*¹⁹⁶⁴, *MJ*¹⁹⁶⁵, *SRB*, *SRB*¹⁹⁸³, *RBS*1

232.33 never] TS1; ◆*never* [never *MJ*¹⁹⁶⁴, *MJ*¹⁹⁶⁵, *SRB*, *SRB*¹⁹⁸³, *RBS*1] TS5, S1, S2

232.35–37 The voice faded . . . and solemnly unconscious.] TS1; The voice faded, a ripple of water in an underground stream. The stream rose up and swallowed him. His head fell forward. Sweet William sighed. And then the two of them lay like stones buried under a waterfall. TS5, S1, S2, *MJ*¹⁹⁶⁴, *MJ*¹⁹⁶⁵, *SRB*, *SRB*¹⁹⁸³, *RBS*1

232.38–233.2 The next morning, . . . "You can do it!"] TS1; The next morning, John Fabian bought the hardest finest-grained piece of wood that he could find and brought it home and laid it on the table but could not touch it. He sat for hours staring at it. It was impossible to think that out of this cold chunk of material he expected his hands and his memory to recreate something warm and pliable and familiar. There was no way even faintly to approximate that quality of rain and summer and the first powderings of snow upon a clear pane of glass in the middle of a December night. No way, no way at all to catch the ◆snowflake [snowflakes *SRB*¹⁹⁸³] without having it melt ◆swiftly away in [swiftly in *MJ*¹⁹⁶⁴, *MJ*¹⁹⁶⁵, *SRB*, *SRB*¹⁹⁸³, *RBS*1] your clumsy fingers. ¶ And yet, Sweet William spoke out, sighing and whispering, after midnight, "You can do it. Oh, yes, yes, you can do it!" TS5, S1, S2, *MJ*¹⁹⁶⁴, *MJ*¹⁹⁶⁵, *SRB*, *SRB*¹⁹⁸³, *RBS*1

*233.3 For twenty weeks he worked. He carved] TS1; And so he began. It took him an entire month to carve TS5, S1, S2, *MJ*¹⁹⁶⁴, *MJ*¹⁹⁶⁵, *SRB*, *SRB*¹⁹⁸³, *RBS*1

233.4 sun.] TS1; sun. Another month and the skeleton, like a fossil imprint he was searching out, stamped and hidden in the wood, was revealed, all febrile and so infinitely delicate as to suggest the veins in the white flesh of an apple. TS5, S1, S2, *MJ*¹⁹⁶⁴, *MJ*¹⁹⁶⁵, *SRB*, *SRB*¹⁹⁸³, *RBS*1

233.4–6 And Sweet William . . . untouched, inanimate wood.] TS1; And all the while Sweet William lay mantled in dust in his box that was fast becoming a very real coffin. Sweet William croaking and wheezing some feeble sarcasm, some sour criticism, some hint, some help – but dying all the time, fading, soon to be untouched, soon to be like a sheathe moulted in summer and left behind to blow in the wind. TS5, S1, S2, *MJ*¹⁹⁶⁴, *MJ*¹⁹⁶⁵, *SRB*, *SRB*¹⁹⁸³, *RBS*1

233.6 As weeks] TS1; As the weeks TS5, S1, S2, *MJ*¹⁹⁶⁴, *MJ*¹⁹⁶⁵, *SRB*, *SRB*¹⁹⁸³, *RBS*1

233.11 gone!] TS1; ~. TS5, S1, S2, *MJ*¹⁹⁶⁴, *MJ*¹⁹⁶⁵, *SRB*, *SRB*¹⁹⁸³, *RBS*1

233.12–20 Now, as Fabian . . . you, John Fabian."] TS1; Now as he worked a fluttering, a faint motion of speech began far back in his throat, echoing and re-echoing, speaking silently like a breeze among dry leaves. And then for the

first time he held the doll in a certain way in his hands and memory moved
down his arms and into his fingers and from his fingers into the hollowed
wood and the tiny hands flickered and the body became suddenly soft and
pliable and her eyes opened and looked up at him. ⸿ And the small mouth
opened the merest fraction of an inch and she was ready to speak and he
knew all of the ◆things that she [things she S2] must say to him, he knew
the first and the second and the third things he would have her say. There
was a whisper, a whisper, a whisper. ⸿ The tiny head turned this way gently,
that way gently. The mouth half-opened again and began to speak. And as it
spoke he bent his head and he could feel the warm breath – of *course* it was
there! – coming from her mouth and when he listened very carefully, holding her to his head, his eyes shut, wasn't *it* there, ◆◆too? [too— S2] [too,
*MJ*[1964], *MJ*[1965], *SRB*, *SRB*[1983], *RBS*1] softly, ◆*gently*? [*gently*— S2, *MJ*[1964],
*MJ*[1965], *SRB*, *SRB*[1983], *RBS*1] the beating of her ◆heart. [heart? S2, *MJ*[1964],
*MJ*[1965], *SRB*, *SRB*[1983], *RBS*1] TS5, S1, S2, *MJ*[1964], *MJ*[1965], *SRB*, *SRB*[1983], *RBS*1

233.23–24 Krovitch sat in . . . "And your wife?"] TS1; Krovitch sat in his chair for
a full minute after Fabian stopped talking. Finally he said, "I ◆*see*. [see. S1,
S2] And your wife?" TS5, S1, S2, *MJ*[1964], *MJ*[1965], *SRB*, *SRB*[1983], *RBS*1

233.25–26 "Alyce? She was . . . I married her."] TS1; "Alyce? She was my second
assistant, of course. She worked very hard and, God help her, she loved me.
It's hard now to know why I ever married her. It was unfair of me." TS5, S1,
S2, *MJ*[1964], *MJ*[1965], *SRB*, *SRB*[1983], *RBS*1

233.27 "I see. What] TS1; "What TS5, S1, S2, *MJ*[1964], *MJ*[1965], *SRB*, *SRB*[1983], *RBS*1

233.28 had never seen] TS1; never saw TS5, S1, S2, *MJ*[1964], *MJ*[1965], *SRB*, *SRB*[1983],
*RBS*1

233.28–29 downstairs in the cellar] TS1; in the theatre basement TS5, S1, S2,
*MJ*[1964], *MJ*[1965], *SRB*, *SRB*[1983], *RBS*1

233.30–33 The pain gripped . . . directly at Krovitch:] TS1; "Fabian," said the detective. ⸿ "It's the truth!" ⸿ "Fabian." ⸿ "The truth, the truth, damn it, I swear
it's the truth." ⸿ "The truth." There was a whisper like the sea coming in on
the grey shore at early ◆morning. The birds were flying south and always
south. The water [morning. The water *MJ*[1964], *MJ*[1965], *SRB*, *SRB*[1983], *RBS*1]
was ebbing in a fine lace on the sand. The sky was ◆cold and empty. [cold.
S2] There were no people on the shore. The sun was gone. ◆And the [The
S2] whisper said again, "The truth." ⸿ Fabian sat up straight and took hold
of his knees with his thin hands. His face was rigid. Krovitch found himself making the same motion he had made the day before – looking at the
grey ceiling as if it were a November sky and a lonely bird going over and
away, grey within the cold greyness. ⸿ "The truth." Fading. "The truth." ⸿
Krovitch lifted himself and moved as carefully as he could to the far side of
the dressing room where the golden box lay open and ◆inside of the [inside

the S2, *MJ*¹⁹⁶⁴, *MJ*¹⁹⁶⁵, *SRB*, *SRB*¹⁹⁸³, *RBS*1] box the thing that whispered and talked and could laugh sometimes and could sometimes sing. He carried the golden box over and set it down in front of Fabian and waited for him to put his living hand within the gloved delicate hollowness, waited for the fine small mouth to quiver and the eyes to focus. He did not have to wait long. TS5, S1, S2, *MJ*¹⁹⁶⁴, *MJ*¹⁹⁶⁵, *SRB*, *SRB*¹⁹⁸³, *RBS*1

233.24–41 "John received the first . . . up. He whispered:] TS1; "The first letter came a month ago." ⸿ "No." ⸿ "The first letter came a month ago." ⸿ "No, *no!*" "The letter said, '♦RIABOUCHINSKA, Born nineteen hundred and four-teen – Died nineteen hundred and thirty-four. [Riabouchinska, born 1914, died 1934. *MJ*¹⁹⁶⁴, *MJ*¹⁹⁶⁵, *SRB*, *SRB*¹⁹⁸³, *RBS*1] Born again in ♦nineteen hun-dred and thirty-five. [1935 *MJ*¹⁹⁶⁴, *MJ*¹⁹⁶⁵, *SRB*, *SRB*¹⁹⁸³, *RBS*1]' Mr. Ockham was a juggler. He'd been on the same bill with John and Sweet William years before. He remembered that once there had been a woman ♦*before* [before *MJ*¹⁹⁶⁴, *MJ*¹⁹⁶⁵, *SRB*, *SRB*¹⁹⁸³, *RBS*1] there was a puppet." ⸿ "No, that's not true!" ⸿ "Yes," said the voice. ⸿ Snow was falling in silences and even deeper silences through the dressing room. Fabian's mouth trembled. He stared at the blank walls as if seeking some new door by which to escape. He half rose from his chair. "Please. . ." TS5, S1, S2, *MJ*¹⁹⁶⁴, *MJ*¹⁹⁶⁵, *SRB*, *SRB*¹⁹⁸³, *RBS*1

234.1–2 "Ockham threatened to expose me to the world!" ⸿ "Go on."] TS1; "Ockham threatened to tell about us to everyone in the world." ⸿ "No, please. . ." The voice stopped. TS5, S1, S2, *MJ*¹⁹⁶⁴, *MJ*¹⁹⁶⁵, *SRB*, *SRB*¹⁹⁸³, *RBS*1

234.2–20 "Go on." . . . can't say it."] TS1; *om. MJ*¹⁹⁶⁴, *MJ*¹⁹⁶⁵, *SRB*, *SRB*¹⁹⁸³, *RBS*1

234.3–10 Fabian took time . . . he killed her!'"] TS1; Fabian looked down at the carved white face and nodded slowly. He swallowed and took a breath. He looked at the detective. "I wanted my life to myself. What sort of fu-ture would there be if everyone guessed the reason for my carving a doll that talked and moved and was so beautiful? ⸿ "People would laugh. People would turn away. 'Ugly,' they'd say. 'Horrible! *Look* at them on the stage!' they'd whisper. 'Listen to them quoting ♦Romeo and Juliet, oh God—*No!* Look, [*Romeo and Juliet*—Look S2] look at those terrible people on the stage! Hideous!' they'd whisper. 'She lived once, you know,' they'd whisper. 'She disappeared. They say he *killed* her. They say he *loved* her!'" TS5, S1, S2

234.11 "How] TS1; Krovitch spoke quietly. "How TS5, S1, S2

234.12 start with.] TS1; start. TS5, S1, S2

234.13 him?"] TS1; ~." TS5, S1, S2

234.14 didn't!] TS1; ~. TS5, S1, S2

234.14 him!"] TS1; him off!" TS5, S1, S2

234.16 "Nevertheless, I] TS1; "I TS5, S1, S2

234.16 must've] TS1; must have TS5, S1, S2

234.16–17 our conversation.] TS1; us talking. TS5, S1, S2

234.18 eliminating me] TS1; ridding herself of me, satisfying her jealousy TS5, S1, S2

234.18 She's nothing but a . . ."] TS1; It's all *very* clear!" TS5, S1, S2

234.19–20 "Just a moment," . . . "I can't say it."] TS1; "No." ¶ A single drop of clear water falling down into the cool surface of a well. ¶ "No . . ." ¶ A single harp-thread, touched, breathed upon. ¶ "There's something I must say. And yet," she whispered, "I can't say it. . ." TS5, S1, S2

234.21–24 Krovitch backed away. . . . in and twisted.] TS1; Krovitch saw the doll quiver, saw the fluttering of the lips, saw Fabian's eyes widen and fix and his throat convulse and tighten as if to stop the whispering. TS5, S1, S2, *MJ*[1964], *MJ*[1965], *SRB*, *SRB*[1983], *RBS*1

234.25–26 came," Riabouchinska began. Her voice was high and blurred now.] TS1; came. TS5, S1, S2, *MJ*[1964], *MJ*[1965], *SRB*, *SRB*[1983], *RBS*1

234.26 I heard,] TS1; ◆heard, [I heard S1] TS5, S1, S2, *MJ*[1964], *MJ*[1965], *SRB*, *SRB*[1983], *RBS*1

234.27 shook, then controlled itself.] TS1; blurred, then recovered and went on. TS5, S1, S2, *MJ*[1964], *MJ*[1965], *SRB*, *SRB*[1983], *RBS*1

234.28 destroy me, tear] TS1; tear TS5, S1, S2, *MJ*[1964], *MJ*[1965], *SRB*, *SRB*[1983], *RBS*1

234.29 came] TS1; was TS5, S1, S2, *MJ*[1964], *MJ*[1965], *SRB*, *SRB*[1983], *RBS*1

234.29 sound," she cried.] TS1; ◆sound! [sound. *MJ*[1964], *MJ*[1965], *SRB*, *SRB*[1983], *RBS*1] A ◆cry! [cry. *MJ*[1964], *MJ*[1965], *SRB*, *SRB*[1983], *RBS*1] TS5, S1, S2, *MJ*[1964], *MJ*[1965], *SRB*, *SRB*[1983], *RBS*1

234.30 floor!] TS1; floor. *MJ*[1964], *MJ*[1965], *SRB*, *SRB*[1983], *RBS*1

234.30 Mr. Fabian] TS1; John TS5, S1, S2, *MJ*[1964], *MJ*[1965], *SRB*, *SRB*[1983], *RBS*1

234.30–31 out, swearing and sobbing, . . . horrible sound!"] TS1; out and I heard him swearing, I heard him sobbing. I heard a gasping and a choking sound." TS5, S1, S2, *MJ*[1964], *MJ*[1965], *SRB*, *SRB*[1983], *RBS*1

234.32–33 Fabian shouted. "You . . . ears are carved!"] TS1; "You heard nothing! You're deaf, you're blind! You're ◆*wood!*" [wood!" *MJ*[1964], *MJ*[1965], *SRB*, *SRB*[1983], *RBS*1] cried Fabian. TS5, S1, S2, *MJ*[1964], *MJ*[1965], *SRB*, *SRB*[1983], *RBS*1

234.34–37 "But they *hear*!" . . . took the body. . ."] TS1; "But I *hear*!" she said, and stopped as if someone had put a hand to her mouth. ¶ Fabian had leapt to his feet now and stood with the doll in his hand. The mouth clapped twice, three times, then finally made words. "The choking sound stopped. I heard John drag Mr. Ockham down the stairs under the theatre to the old dressing rooms that haven't been used in years. Down, down, down I heard them going away and away – down. . ." TS5, S1, S2, *MJ*[1964], *MJ*[1965], *SRB*, *SRB*[1983], *RBS*1

234.38–235.6 Fabian was out . . . do not know!] TS1; Krovitch stepped back as if he were watching a motion picture that had suddenly grown monstrously tall. The figures terrified and frightened him, they were immense, they ◆*towered*! [towered! *MJ*[1964], *MJ*[1965], *SRB*, *SRB*[1983], *RBS*1] They threatened to inundate him with size. Someone had turned up the sound so that it ◆screamed. ⁋ Everything was white and bloodless, everything swayed and toppled, the avalanche trembled on the brink, ready to drop in thunders of shale and flint and marble and cutting ice. He [screamed. ⁋ He $MJ^{1964}$, $MJ^{1965}$, $SRB$, $SRB^{1983}$, $RBS1$] saw Fabian's teeth, a grimace, a whisper, a clenching. He saw the man's eyes squeeze shut. TS5, S1, S2, $MJ^{1964}$, $MJ^{1965}$, $SRB$, $SRB^{1983}$, $RBS1$

235.7 her] TS1; the soft TS5, S1, S2, $MJ^{1964}$, $MJ^{1965}$, $SRB$, $SRB^{1983}$, $RBS1$

235.7 was barely audible:] TS1; was like the last flake of snow moving ◆toward [towards S2] the warm ◆earth that in [earth, which in S2] a moment would melt it away to nothingness. TS5, S1, S2; trembled toward nothingness. $MJ^{1964}$, $MJ^{1965}$, $SRB$, $SRB^{1983}$, $RBS1$

235.8–9 way. There is . . . know of us.] TS1; way. This way. There's nothing for us now. Everyone will know, everyone will. TS5, S1, S2, $MJ^{1964}$, $MJ^{1965}$, $SRB$, $SRB^{1983}$, $RBS1$

235.9–12 in my bronze . . . with such knowledge. . ."] TS1; asleep last ◆night I dreamed. [night, I dreamt^ S2] I knew, I realized. Be both knew, we ◆both [both $MJ^{1964}$, $MJ^{1965}$, $SRB$, $SRB^{1983}$, $RBS1$] realized that these would be our last days, our last hours. ◆Because while I've lived with ◆your weakness [I've lived with weakness S2] [weakness S1] and I've lived with your lies, ◆I can't [but I can't S2] live with something that kills and hurts in killing. There's no way to on from here. How *can* I ◆live alongside [go on living with S2] such ◆knowledge. .." [knowledge . . .?" S2, $MJ^{1964}$, $MJ^{1965}$, $SRB$, $SRB^{1983}$, $RBS1$] TS5, S1, S2, $MJ^{1964}$, $MJ^{1965}$, $SRB$, $SRB^{1983}$, $RBS1$

235.13–17 Fabian took her . . . with no words.] TS1; Fabian held her into the sunlight which shone dimly through the small dressing-room window. She looked at him and there was nothing in her eyes. His hand shook and in shaking made the marionette tremble too. Her mouth closed and opened, closed and opened, closed and opened, again and again and again – ◆Silence. ⁋ The snowflakes touched the earth and melted. [Silence. $MJ^{1964}$, $MJ^{1965}$, $SRB$, $SRB^{1983}$, $RBS1$] TS5, S1, S2, $MJ^{1964}$, $MJ^{1965}$, $SRB$, $SRB^{1983}$, $RBS1$

235.18–21 Fabian began to . . . was the truth.] TS1; Fabian moved his fingers unbelievingly to his own mouth. Λ film slid across his eyes. He looked like a man lost in the street, trying to remember the number of a certain house, trying to find a certain window with a certain light. He swayed about, staring at the walls, at Krovitch, at the doll, at his free hand, turning the fingers over, touching his throat, opening his mouth. He listened. ⁋ Miles away in a cave, a single wave came in from the sea and whispered down in foam. A gull moved soundlessly, not beating its wings – a shadow. TS5, S1, S2, $MJ^{1964}$, $MJ^{1965}$, $SRB$, $SRB^{1983}$, $RBS1$

235.22–26 "She's gone," he . . . throat was relaxed.] TS1; "She's gone. She's gone. I can't find her. She's run off. I can't find her. I can't find her. I try, I try, but she's

run away ◆off ◆far. [far off. S2] Will you help me? Will you help me find her? Will you help me find her? Will you please help me find her? [far. Will you help me find her?' *SRB*¹⁹⁸³] TS5, S1, S2, *MJ*¹⁹⁶⁴, *MJ*¹⁹⁶⁵, *SRB*, *SRB*¹⁹⁸³, *RBS*1
235.28–29 gently sealed.] TS1; shut. TS5, S1, S2, *MJ*¹⁹⁶⁴, *MJ*¹⁹⁶⁵, *SRB*, *SRB*¹⁹⁸³, *RBS*1
235.30 not even look] TS1; not look TS5, S1, S2, *MJ*¹⁹⁶⁴, *MJ*¹⁹⁶⁵, *SRB*, *SRB*¹⁹⁸³, *RBS*1
235.30 away.] TS1; ◆◆◆toward [to S2] [out *MJ*¹⁹⁶⁴, *MJ*¹⁹⁶⁵, *SRB*, *RBS*1] [out of *SRB*¹⁹⁸³] the door. TS5, S1, S2, *MJ*¹⁹⁶⁴, *MJ*¹⁹⁶⁵, *SRB*, *SRB*¹⁹⁸³, *RBS*1

## 21. Skeleton (*Script*) (Feb. 20, 1945)

Early in 1945, Bradbury composed a "short-short" story (barely more than an extended anecdote) that was, both in title and content, an alternative version of his gruesome *Weird Tale* "Skeleton" (selection 19). It first surfaces as an entry in his composition and submission log for "Script 'Skeleton'" on February 20, 1945. The entry notes a 1,000-word tale and includes a subsequent typed notation "SOLD! SCRIPT!" *Script* did not pay, and there are no entries for this version of "Skeleton" in Bradbury's sales records or tax notes. His author's notecard file confirms the acceptance by *Script* on March 1, 1945. It appeared in the issue of April 28, 1945 (S1), a single-page three-column layout with a headpiece caricature of a jester (signed in a microscopic hand that may resolve as Kitty Farmer). The anecdotal tale was never collected by Bradbury, but very late in life he allowed a small-press limited edition to be bound with his far more famous *Weird Tales* "Skeleton" in *Skeletons* (S), with illustrations by Dave McKean (Subterranean, 2008). Bradbury was not involved with preparation of the S text.

*Script*'s "Skeleton" is a distinct tale with new characters, but it is a very positive and regenerative inversion of the *Weird Tales* "Skeleton." There is no shadowy M. Munigant waiting to extract anyone's skeleton; the new story offers a single domestic scene between Arnie, who has just "discovered" this hidden armature called a skeleton within his body, and his placid wife Lily, who calms his fears. There's no paranoia or hypochondria in this variation of the earlier tale, and Lily is able to guide her husband toward a more amorous kind of exploration.

Initially, Bradbury's history with Rob Wagner's *Script* was built on this kind of humorous anecdotal tale. *Script* was a regional, Beverly-Hills-based equivalent of a down-scaled *New Yorker*, with no pretensions for *New Yorker*-style standing; nevertheless, Wagner's film industry features and the liberal political counterpoint to establishment periodicals attracted established authors from time to time, including Bradbury favorites William Saroyan and Edgar Rice Burroughs. In 1940, Bradbury's first story appearance in a professional magazine was *Script*'s "It's Not the Heat, It's the Hu—" (volume 1, selection A7); this acceptance had been arranged by Robert A. Heinlein, but the aging Wagner and his wife liked Bradbury and published another story, two pieces of light verse, and two short articles during 1940 and 1941. Even though *Script* did not pay their authors, these insubstantial appearances were confidence builders at the very beginning of Bradbury's career. As an established author, he would send occasional light pieces to Wagner's widow Florence, whose lifetime of experience in journalism allowed her to continue *Script* after her husband's sudden death in 1942. "Skeleton" and "End of Summer" (September 1948) appeared in *Script* before the magazine quietly ended publication in 1949.

Copy-text is S1, which was carefully set by *Script*'s typesetter and requires only two emendations. Variants in *S* are not authorial, although the two emendations are given the *S* siglum to indicate first appearance in print.

Sources: Author's composition and submission log (1942–45); author's notecard files (1942–1978); UCLA interview, 81–82 (1961); Bradbury-Eller interviews (October 2002).

—JE

## Emendations
[*title*] SKELETON] CE; SKELETON *Ray Bradbury* S1; SKELETON | by Ray
    Bradbury | (First appeared in *Weird Tales*) S
237.30 cares?"] S; ~?^ S1
238.11 ¶ "Sure,] S; ^ "~, S1

## Historical Collation: Post-Copy-Text Substantives
◊238.11 ^ "Sure,] S1; ¶ "~, S

## 22. The Black Ferris (Mar. 1945)

This story seeded a long progression of expansion through a wordless graphic novel concept, a screen treatment, a much-traveled screenplay, and four drafts of the novel that became *Something Wicked This Way Comes* (*SW*, 1962). But it originates far earlier than its 1948 *Weird Tales* publication would suggest; in fact, the metaphor of a dark carnival shaped Bradbury's evolving concept for his first story collection early in 1945. On March 8, he wrote to Arkham House editor August Derleth with a picture-in-words of a dark carnival pitched in a woodland glade at twilight, with a young boy looking at a riderless carousel equipped with mystical creatures instead of wooden horses. He wanted the new collection to be titled *Dark Carnival,* adding that "I'm writing the *story* DARK CARNIVAL now and will submit it to Weird in a few weeks." His underlined "story" emphasized this tale as the thematic center of the new collection, but when Arkham House published his story collection *Dark Carnival* in May 1947, no such story was included. Bradbury had made the conscious decision to hold that story out, for it was beginning to grow in his mind into a much longer work of book-length fiction.

The genesis of "The Black Ferris" in the "Dark Carnival" story materials is confirmed by Bradbury's surviving yellow binder, dated "Summer 1945 and 1946," in the Albright Collection. The contents are titled "Original Materials 'Dark Carnival' which became 'Something Wicked T. W. C.'" More than thirty pages of fragmentary sketches and chapter openings include two evolving variations on the premise of "The Black Ferris": A man leaves his house for the strange carnival, but returns as a small boy who seems strangely familiar. Familiarity turns to terror when the boy is able to describe the woman's birthmark, which only her husband could know. The second variation shows the man returning, once again fully grown, after a series of unspecified adventures with the age-reversing Ferris ride. Bradbury's focus on the story had clearly radiated outward to shape an entire novel concept, leaving the original story a work-in-progress for the time being.

As a titled story, "The Black Ferris" finally surfaces two years later; his author's notecard file contains a card for a finished draft completed on September 19, 1947 and a sale to *Weird Tales* on January 12, 1948. Bradbury's composition and submission log ends in the spring of 1945 without a mention of the tale that was emerging as "Dark Carnival." There is a gap in Bradbury's files of letters from Julius Schwartz for this period, but Nolan's list of sales by Schwartz confirms an actual sale date to *Weird Tales* of January 2, 1945, and a pre-commission payment of $30.00. Bradbury's sales record for 1948 includes a payment received date of January 12, 1945, and a post-commission payment of $27.00 (inferred from a combined post-commission payment from Schwartz of $121.50 for "The Black Ferris," "Fever Dream," and "The Women"). "The Black Ferris" would be the last original Bradbury story sold to *Weird Tales,* and the next-to-last to reach print, before the demise of *Weird Tales* in 1955. It appeared in the May 1948 issue (S1), with a full-page title drawing by Lee Brown Coye.

Even in print, the story is a bit rough and unpolished as it presents the story of two small-town boys and their adventure with a predatory supernatural carnival. Hank Walterson has seen the carnival owner ride the Black Ferris backward and regress to the appearance of a small child. He retains his predatory adult mind, however, and has found lodging with the widow Foley. Hank shows his friend Pete the nightly ritual, and leads them both on a zany pursuit that ends with Hank's trapping the evil child-man on the Ferris as he tries to regain his adult form; Hank jams the Ferris machinery forward until the rapidly aging carnie disintegrates into a skeleton.

In this slightly ragged form, "The Black Ferris" would nevertheless have a long history. It was simultaneously reprinted from the same typesetting (and with the same Coye title art) in the Canadian May 1948 issue of *Weird Tales* (S2). Bradbury then prepared TS1, a new typescript made from (and not prior to) S1. Eye-skips in the typescript, accidentally omitting two sentences near the end of the story embedded in passages containing doubled words in close proximity on the S1 pages, confirm that TS1 post-dates S1 (see the Historical Collation at 244.25 and 245.3). These same lacunae carry through all subsequent book appearances, confirming that TS1 was the source of linear transmission. These include Knopf's hundred-story retrospective collection *The Stories of Ray Bradbury* (*SRB*[1980]), which in turn was the source for Granada's British trade paperback edition (*SRB*[1983]) and the 2008 British HarperCollins reissue as *Ray Bradbury Stories,* volume 1 (*RBS1*). A late serialization in the October 1997 issue of *Outré* (S5) appears to derive directly from S1.

"The Black Ferris" appeared in the 1967 textbook anthology *Scope Reading* (*SR*) as "The Ferris Wheel," set from TS2, an editorial typescript of that title prepared from Bradbury's TS1. *SR* has no authority in the transmission of the text, as Bradbury had no involvement in editing it. Media adaptations of "The Black Ferris" include the graphic adaptation by Al Feldstein (Jack Davis, illustrator) for EC Publications in *The Haunt of Fear* 18 (Mar.–Apr. 1953) and an uncredited graphic adaptation by Len Wein (Berni Wrightson, illustrator) for DC Publications in *The House of Mystery* 221 (Jan. 1974), as "He Who Laughs Last." Bradbury prepared his own teleplay adaptation for *The Ray Bradbury Theater,* first broadcast for the USA Network on August 10, 1990.

As a child's eye view of Bradbury's Depression Era hometown of Waukegan, Illinois, "The Black Ferris" would evolve into the catalyzing episode of a 1955 screenplay titled *The Dark Carnival.* In the process of transformation, the carnival's Black Ferris evolved into a carousel, coming full circle, as it were, to the original metaphor that Bradbury described for August Derleth in March 1945. Enthusiastic efforts by actor and director Gene Kelly failed to find backing for the film, and between 1958 and 1962 Bradbury prepared four drafts of the novel that would become, in 1962, *Something Wicked This Way Comes.* A rewritten version of "The Black Ferris" became the key chapters 17 and 18, from which all the subsequent action and suspense of the story flows. Pete and Hank are now older boys, the straight arrow Will Halloway and his more daring pal Jim Nightshade. And they are up against a far more worthy opponent, Mr. Dark, who has harvested generations of lonely people from countless towns, enslaving them to the carnival by transforming their souls into the tattoos that cover his body. Even in this completely transformed version, the original episode of "The Black Ferris" was extracted by Bradbury for two excerpt appearances just prior to publication of *Something Wicked This Way Comes* as "Nightmare Carousel," first in the January 1962 issue of *Mademoiselle* (S3) and again in the October 1962 issue of British *Argosy* (S4).

The transformed screenplay and novel chapter versions of "The Black Fer-ris" represent a later and far broader intention of the original story, and they are readily available in both film (Disney/Bryna, 1983) and novel form. Copy-text for the present edition is S1. With the exception of three necessary cor-rections of errors, the variants down through TS2 and the various editions of *The Stories of Ray Bradbury* result from either new errors or house styling; the substantive variants appear in the Historical Collation below.

Sources: Author's sales record (1941–49); author's agency listing (c. 1950); au-thor's notecard file (1942–1978); August Derleth (Arkham House) to Bradbury, Mar. 8, 1945; Eller and Touponce, *The Life of Fiction,* Ch. 5, 256–309; Weller, *Echoes,* 94.

—JE

## Textual Notes

239.7–8 Peter . . . Hank] Hank Walterson springs from the juvenile versions of Twain's Huck Finn in the Tom Sawyer books. Both Pete and Hank are younger here than Will Halloway and Jim Nightshade, the boys they will become as this story transforms into the key action chapter of *Something Wicked This Way Comes.* Bradbury's initial draft of the novel, titled "Jamie and Me," is a first-person experiment triggered by his first reading of *Huckleberry Finn,* where the Huck-narrator is more mature (and more complex) than we see in the Sawyer juveniles. The final novel drafts return to a third-person narrative.

240.4–5 Backwards instead of forwards!"] It's harder to visualize the backward and forward orientation for a Ferris wheel than a carousel, where the di-rection of the carousel horses clearly delineates direction. This practical consideration may have played into Bradbury's later transition from Fer-ris wheel back to the carousel he had first envisioned as the original story metaphor for life and death transitions through time.

241.3 Mrs. Foley's son] She becomes an unmarried school teacher in the *SW* rewrite, assuming a larger role and a more terrible supernatural fate as the story expanded.

243.16 you're naked!"] Hank's confiscated clothes are more of a confusing dis-traction than an advance of the narrative. Bradbury had effectively used a carnivalesque element of nudity for "Invisible Boy" to good effect, but the small degree of "Huck Finn" humor in Hank's lack of clothing holds no such value. This element completely disappears from the evolving screen-play and novel versions.

244.6–7 black painted bucket-seat] Evidence of earlier draft layers includes the description of Pike's Ferris wheel seat as both black (240.2, 240.10, 245.21, 245.22) and green (244.6, 244.14). The seat is black in the key opening trans-formation of Pike, and black in the closing scene. The two instances of green appear to be left over from an earlier draft, and are emended to "black" to match Bradbury's settled preference in composing this early form of the story. *SRB*'s replacement of "black" with "green" at three points is editorial rather than authorial in origin, and runs against the very title of "The Black Ferris."

## Emendations

[*title*] The Black Ferris] CE; The Black Ferris | *BY* | *RAY BRADBURY* S1
241.23–24 thirty-five-year-old man] *SRB*; thirty-five year man S1
243.27 house,] TS2; ~; S1
*244.6 black] *SRB*; green S1
244.14 there in] TS1; there is S1
*244.14 black] CE; green S1

## Historical Collation: Post-Copy-Text Substantives

[*title*] The Black Ferris | *BY* | *RAY BRADBURY*] S1; THE BLACK FERRIS TS1; THE FERRIS WHEEL | Ray Bradbury TS2; THE FERRIS WHEEL | RAY BRADBURY *SR*; The Black Ferris *SRB*; *The Black Ferris,* *SRB*¹⁹⁸³, *RBS*1
239.9–10 ¶ They left wads . . . the crashing shore.] S1; *om.* TS2, *SR*
*240.2 black] S1; green *SR Also* 240.10, 245.21, 245.22
241.17 that boy] S1; the boy TS2, *SR*
*◊241.23–24 thirty-five year man] S1; thirty-five-year ◆old [-old *SR*, *SRB*, *SRB*¹⁹⁸³, *RBS*1] man TS2, *SR*, *SRB*, *SRB*¹⁹⁸³, *RBS*1
241.27 backward] S1; backwards *SRB*¹⁹⁸³ *Also* 244.6
241.29 *forward,*] S1; *forwards,* *SRB*¹⁹⁸³
241.29–30 and he'll be . . . be gone forever!"] S1; and for ever!' *SRB*¹⁹⁸³
242.6 Soaked, you were, by God!] S1; You were soaked! TS2, *SR*
243.22 Pete] S1; Peter *SR*
244.6 forward and forward,] S1; forwards and forwards, *SRB*¹⁹⁸³
*◊244.6 green] S1; black *SRB*, *SRB*¹⁹⁸³, *RBS*1 *Also* 244.14
244.11 spaces. ^ And] S1; ~. ¶ ~ TS2, *SR*
◊244.14 there is] S1; there in TS1, TS2, *SR*, *RBS*1
244.20–21 He tried . . . the Ferris wheel.] S1; *om. SR*
244.25 Hank hit him on the other knee, hard.] S1; *om.* TS1, TS2, *SR*, *SRB*, *SRB*¹⁹⁸³, *RBS*1
244.38 hunks] S1; chunks TS1, *RBS*1
245.3 Terrible faces leered and gaped at him.] S1; *om.* TS1, TS2, *SR*, *SRB*, *SRB*¹⁹⁸³

## Line-End Hyphenation

240.2 hunch-/back] hunchback *Also* 240.9, 244.8, 244.18
240.8 twenty-/five] twenty-five
244.7 bucket-/seat] bucket-seat

# LINE-END HYPHENATIONS IN THE EDITION TEXT

The following listing identifies those compound words hyphenated at the ends of lines in the critical text of the present edition that, in being quoted or transcribed from the text, must retain their hyphens to preserve the copy-text reading. All other possible compounds hyphenated at the ends of lines in the present edition should be transcribed as single words.

4.13–14 short-circuited
4.14–15 light-trouble
5.6–7 dead-end
5.8–9 cut-out
10.4–5 snivel-nosed
28.36–37 five-thousand
32.6–7 boom-crash-bang
37.3–4 well-dressed
41.22–23 Drum-Tiddie-Um-Tum
63.8–9 half-pale
63.21–22 rain-rubbers
65.30–31 flute-lipped
68.2–3 poorly-paid
86.32–33 crazy-funny
87.36–37 boy-scout
108.25–26 tongue-tie
121.30–31 marble-cutter
127.35–36 high-flying

128.22–23 soft-voiced
133.12–13 insect-proofing
134.36–37 mind-culture
141.8–9 silver-green
156.31–32 green-eyed
159.12–13 shoal-water
160.22–23 Hugh-Starke-Called-Conan
164.32–33 up-turned
165.8–9 sword-wise
166.34–35 harp-threads
169.11–12 sand-specule
172.15–16 bone-sharp
189.21–22 twenty-seven
217.4–5 push-buttons
223.38–39 red-eyed
231.37–38 bulb-nosed
241.23–24 thirty-five-year-old